I'm
我識出版社
17buy.com.tw

I'm

我識出版社
17buy.com.tw

完全命中

TOEFL
托福單字

蔣志楡・馬亭奇 ◎編著

學科 (學術) 名稱總匯

01

15大主題式分類詞彙，有系統記憶單字：
涵括學科（學術）、文化、技術工
程、教育、政治與法律、財政與金
融、軍事、交通與通訊、生活、時
空、狀態與程度、運動與變化、肢體
動作、情感與心理、人際互動等領域
共7400多個單字，讓你準備考試面
面俱到，助你考前加強不熟悉的單字
群，完全命中托福必考單字

中文解釋扼要簡明，快速掌握詞彙用法：
搭配中英對照實用例句或慣用片語／諺
語，多面向閱讀讓你熟悉英語文化，融
入英語語言環境非夢事，許你一條快樂
的留學之路

---

angle [ˈæŋgl] ....★★★★
n. 角度，觀點：The roof is at an angle of 120° to the
walls. 屋頂和牆成120°。

arithmetic [əˈrɪθmətɪk] ....★★★
n. 算術：commercial arithmetic 商用數學

average [ˈævərɪdʒ] ....★★★★★
adj. ①平均的：The average temperature is higher this
year than last year. 今年的平均氣溫比去年高。②
通常的，一般的：His intelligence is average. 他的
智力普通。
v. ①求平均數：If you average 7, 14, and 6, you get 9.
你如果算7、14和6的平均數，就會得到9。②平均
達到（數目），平均分配：The rainfall averages 36
inches a year. 每年的平均雨量為36英寸。
n. 平均數【片語】on (an/the) average 平均而言

billionth [ˈbɪljənθ] ....★★★★
num. （美、法）十億分之一，（英、德）萬分之一

boundless [ˈbaundlɪs] ....★★★★★
adj. 無限的：The Chippewa people made their
home in the seemingly boundless forests of the
Canadian North. 齊佩瓦族人在加拿大北部看似無
邊的森林中蓋房子。

calculate [ˈkælkjəˌlet] ....★★★★
v. 計算，估計，計畫：The scientists are able to
calculate accurately when the spaceship will reach
the moon. 科學家能準確地計算出太空船什麼時候抵
達月球。

calculation [ˌkælkjəˈleʃən] ....★★★
n. 計算，計算結果，打算

calculus [ˈkælkjələs] ....★
n. 微積分，結石

circle [ˈsɝkl] ....★★★★★
n. 圓，圓周，週期，集團 v. 環繞，盤旋

circumference [səˈkʌmfərəns] ....★
n. 圓周

compute [kəmˈpjut] ....★★
v. 計算，求解，估計：①計算 compute the tax due 計
算稅款②估計：I compute my loss at 500 dollars.
我估計我的損失有五百元。

詞性標示條列分明，易讀好懂：
仿英漢字典模式將動詞、名詞、形容
詞、副詞、介系詞、連接詞、感歎詞等
詞性條列化分項編排，單字在句子或片
語中是什麼角色一目瞭然，讓你百分百
抓得住單字的心

★級標示出題機率，考前3個月衝刺必看：
以1～5顆★標示TOEFL出題機率，星級越高越常考，讓你即時掌握考題佈局，有效率提升準備成效

關鍵單字以不同顏色標示，視覺即時反應，強化記憶印象：
例句與片語／諺語中的關鍵單字皆以色彩標示，讓單字即時呈現在你眼前，閱讀一點都不吃力，不必費時費力找單字，讓你記憶效果加倍

近義詞組詳實辨析：
各單元穿插一至多組詞組解析比較異同，助你掌握近義詞有啥地方不同，讓你精準用字不出糗，TOEFL一路過關得高分

略語說明

v.	動詞	vt./vi.	及物／不及物動詞
n.	名詞	pron.	代名詞
adv.	副詞	adj	形容詞
conj.	連接詞	prep.	介系詞
（常單）	常用單數	int.	感歎詞
【美】	美式英語	（常複/pl.）	常用複數
【喻】	比喻用法	【英】	美式英語
【物】	物理術語	【喻】	諺語
【生物】	物理術語	【物】	化學術語
aux.	助動詞	【電】	電學術語

辨析 Analyze

fluid, liquid

1 fluid *n & a*「流體，液體，流體的，流動的」，指可自由流動的物質，包括液體和氣體：The glass tube of a thermometer contains a fluid, usually mercury. 溫度計的玻璃管內有流體，通常是水銀。

2 liquid *n & a*「液體，液體的，液態的，清澈的，晶瑩的，流暢的」，僅指液體，比fluid的意義狹窄，可用於比喻意義：Air is a fluid but not a liquid; water is both a fluid and a liquid. 空氣是流體，不是液體；水既是流體也是液體。

前言
Preface

托福測驗（TOEFL, Test of English as a Foreign Language）由美國教育測驗服務社（ETS, Educational Testing Service）在全世界舉辦，用以測試母語非英語者是否具備在英語系國家（尤其是美加）讀書甚至長期生活所需的英語應用能力。測驗的範圍涵蓋美國日常生活和學習中的常用詞彙，熟悉這些詞彙是通過測驗的基礎，是取得英美文化入場券的必經之途。

本書根據美國教育測驗服務社的考試大綱編寫，收錄7400餘條單字，以學科（學術）、文化、技術工程、教育、政治與法律、財政與金融、軍事、交通與通訊、生活、時空、狀態與程度、運動與變化、肢體動作、情感與心理、人際互動等15大單元分門別類介紹各項領域的單字，期能幫助考生有系統地學習和記憶單字，順利應試。

所有的單字皆以1～5星級標示重要性和出題機率，星級越高越重要、出題機率也越大。而為了方便考生快速掌握單字，也特別以條列式的說明幫助考生記憶單字的詞性和簡明中文解釋，達到一目瞭然之效。絕大多數的單字都搭配中英對照的實用例句、片語或諺語讓考生能熟悉單字的用法，其中有相當一部分的例句是源自托福測驗題庫，可以培養考生的詞彙敏感度，進而熟悉英語文化。也為了讓考生順利獲取高分，各單元皆穿插近義詞組辨析，讓考生得以掌握近義詞之間的異同處，精準用字不出糗。

《托福單字》係由我識出版社針對考生需求精心規劃的考試秘笈，希望能讓考生能得心應手地來準備測驗，通過考試。也期待《托福單字》能為考生上考場助一臂之力，與考生共創佳績。

目次
Contents

Contents

Unit 12 Exercise & Change
運動、變化名稱總匯 ▶332

▶420 Unit 13 Movement
肢體動作名稱總匯

Unit 14 Feeling
情感心理活動名稱總匯 ▶478

538 ◀ Unit 15 Relationship
人際互動名稱總匯

Unit 1
學科（學術）名稱總匯
Discipline

01

數學相關辭彙

Vocabulary of Mathematics

angle [ˋæŋɡḷ] .... ★★★★
n. 角度，觀點：The roof is at an angle of 120° to the walls. 屋頂和牆成120°。

arithmetic [əˋrɪθmətɪk] .... ★★★
n. 算術：commercial arithmetic 商用數學

average [ˋævərɪdʒ] .... ★★★★★
adj. ①平均的：The average temperature is higher this year than last year. 今年的平均氣溫比去年高。②通常的，一般的：His intelligence is average. 他的智力普通。
v. ①求平均數：If you average 7, 14, and 6, you get 9. 你如果算7、14和6的平均數，就會得到9。②平均達到（數目），平均分配：The rainfall averages 36 inches a year. 每年的平均雨量為36英寸。
n. 平均數【片語】on (an/the) average 平均而言

billionth [ˋbɪljənθ] .... ★★★★
n. （美、法）十億分之一，（英、德）萬分之一

boundless [ˋbaʊndlɪs] .... ★★★★★
adj. 無限的：The Chippewa people made their home in the seemingly boundless forests of the Canadian North. 齊佩瓦族人在加拿大北部看似無邊的森林中蓋房子。

calculate [ˋkælkjəˌlet] .... ★★★★
v. 計算，估計，計畫：The scientists are able to calculate accurately when the spaceship will reach the moon. 科學家能準確地計算出太空船什麼時候抵達月球。

calculation [ˌkælkjəˋleʃən] .... ★★★
n. 計算，計算結果，打算

calculus [ˋkælkjələs] .... ★
n. 微積分，結石

circle [ˋsɝkḷ] .... ★★★★★
n. 圓，圓周，週期，集團
v. 環繞，盤旋

circumference [səˋkʌmfərəns] .... ★
n. 圓周

compute [kəmˋpjut] .... ★★
v. 計算，求解，估計：①計算：compute the tax due 計算稅款②估計：I compute my losses at 500 dollars. 我估計我的損失有五百元。

computer [kəm`pjutə] .... ★★★★★
n. 電腦

computerize [kəm`pjutəˌraɪz] .... ★★★★★
v. 使電腦化，給…裝備電腦：The firm decided to computerize its wages department. 公司決定用電腦來管理發薪部門。

cone [kon] .... ★★★★★
n. 圓錐

cube [kjub] .... ★★★
n. 立方體，立方，三次冪

cubic [`kjubɪk] .... ★
adj. 立方體的，三次冪的：a cubic meter立方公尺

cylinder [`sɪlɪndə] .... ★
n. 汽缸，圓柱體

cylindrical [sɪ`lɪndrɪkḷ] .... ★
adj. 圓柱（形）的

decimal [`dɛsɪmḷ] .... ★
adj. 十進位的
n. 小數：decimal system 十進位法

diameter [daɪ`æmətə] .... ★★★
n. 直徑

digital [`dɪdʒɪtḷ] .... ★★★★★
adj. 數字的，數位的：A digital watch shows the time by electronically lit up numbers. 數位手錶是用電子式發光數字來顯示時間的。

dot [dɑt] .... ★★★
v. ①加點狀符號：Dot a "J". 在「J」字母加上點狀。②散佈於：a field dotted with sheep 到處是羊的田野

ellipse [ɪ`lɪps] .... ★
n. 橢圓：concentration ellipse 同心橢圓

encircle [ɪn`sɝkḷ] .... ★★★★★
v. 圍住，關閉住，圈起，封入，附上：encircle the globe 環繞全球（特指外交戰略）

enumerate [ɪ`njuməˌret] .... ★
v. 枚舉，計數：A spokesperson enumerated the strikers' demands. 發言人列舉出罷工者的要求。

equation [ɪ`kweʃən] .... ★★★
n. 等式

even [`ivən] .... ★★★★★
adj. 平的，偶數的：If we each take half, then we'll be even. 如果我們雙方各拿一半，我們就互不虧欠了。

exponential [ˌɛkspo`nɛnʃəl] .... ★
adj. 指數的：exponential curve 指數曲線

formulate [`fɔrmjəˌlet] .... ★
v. 用公式表示，系統地闡述（提出）：formulate strategy 制定策略

geometry [dʒɪ`ɑmətrɪ] .... ★★★
n. 幾何學

infinitesimal [ˌɪnfɪnə`tɛsəml] .... ★
adj. 無窮小的：Cobalt in infinitesimal amounts is one of the metals essential to life. 微量的鈷是生命必需的一項基本金屬元素。

mathematical [ˌmæθə`mætɪkḷ] .... ★★★
adj. 數學的：He's some kind of mathematical genius. 他有些數學天賦。

mathematics [ˌmæθə`mætɪks] .... ★★★★
n. 數學

minus [`maɪnəs] .... ★★★★★
adj. 負的，減去的：a minus quantity/sign 負數／負號
prep. 減（去）：Four minus two is two. 4-2=2

nil [nɪl] .... ★
n. 無，零：Our profits were nil. 我們無利可圖。

planar [`plenə] .... ★
n. 平面的，平面型的

plumb [plʌm] .... ★
adv. 垂直地，精確地：to fall plumb in the middle of the puddle 恰好落在水坑裡。

plus [plʌs] .... ★★★★
adj. 表示加的，正的：a plus growth rate 正增
　長率
prep. 加，加上：Three plus six is nine. 3+6=9

proportion [prə`porʃən] .... ★★
n. 比例，部分

quantitative [`kwɑntə͵tetɪv] .... ★
adj. 定量的：a quantitative change 量變；
　quantitative analysis 定量分析

quantity [`kwɑntətɪ] .... ★★★★★
n. 數量，量，大量

radius [`redɪəs] .... ★
n. 半徑：every family within a radius of 25
　miles of the city center 住在市中心半徑25英
　里範圍內的家庭

ratio [`reʃo] .... ★★★★
n. 比，比率：The ratio of 10 to 5 is 2 to 1.
　10:5=2:1

reckon [`rɛkən] .... ★★★★
vt. ①計算：My pay is reckoned from the first
　day of the month. 我的薪水是從每月的第一
　天算起。②估計，推斷：How much do you
　reckon that she earns? 你估計她賺多少
　錢？③認為
vi. ①數，算帳②估計，推斷③指望，依賴
　【片語】①reckon sth. in 把…計算／考慮在
　內②reckon on/upon 依賴，指望③reckon
　up 計算出④reckon with 將…加以考慮，處
　理，解決

rectangle [rɛk`tæŋgl̩] .... ★
n. 長方形，矩形

statistical [stə`tɪstɪkl̩] .... ★★★★
adj. 統計的，統計學的

statistics [stə`tɪstɪks] .... ★★★
n. 統計學

symmetry [`sɪmɪtrɪ] .... ★
n. 對稱(性)，勻稱

triangle [`traɪ͵æŋgl̩] .... ★★★
n. 三角形

辨析
Analyze

percent, percentage, proportion, rate, ratio

1 **percent** *n.* 「百分之一」，與數字連用：
Prices have risen 3 percent / per cent in
the past year. 去年的價格漲了3%。

2 **percentage** *n.* 「百分比，百分率」，一
般不與數字連用：What percentage of his
income is paid in income tax? 他的收入
有多少比例是用來繳納所得稅？

3 **proportion** *n.* 「比例：部分，一份：均
衡，相稱」，主要指比例、成比例、（…
與…）之比：The proportion of imports to
exports is worrying the government. 進、
出口的比例讓政府感到擔憂。

4 **rate** *n.* 「比率，率；速度，進度；價格，
費用」：birth/death/unemployment/crime
rate 出生率／死亡率／失業率／犯罪率；
the rate of interest 利率；What's the rate
between dollars and pounds today? 今天
美元與英鎊的兌換率是多少？

5 **ratio** *n.* 「比，比率」，數學用語，強調
兩個數的量之比：The ratios of 1 to 5 and
20 to 100 are the same. 1比5和20比100
是相同的。

學科（學術）名稱總匯

學科（學術）名稱總匯

02

物理相關辭彙

Vocabulary of Physics

aerial [ˋɛrɪəl] .... ★
n. 空氣的，航空的：aerial current 氣流；aerial reconnaissance 空中偵察

amalgamate [əˋmælgəmet] .... ★
v. 混合，合併：The unions will attempt to amalgamate their groups into one national body. 工會想把他們的小組合併成全國性的團體。

ampere [æmˋpɪr] .... ★★★
n. 安培

anticlockwise [͵æntɪˋklɑkwaɪz] .... ★
adv. 逆時針方向地

antiparticle [ˋæntɪ͵pɑrtɪk!] .... ★
n. 反粒子

atomic [əˋtɑmɪk] .... ★★★
adj. 原子的：atomic weapons 原子武器

attrition [əˋtrɪʃən] .... ★
n. 磨損

blackmail [ˋblæk͵mel] .... ★★★★★
v. 勒索：The strange man tried to blackmail the clerk into helping him draw the money, but he failed. 陌生人想威脅職員，迫使他幫他取出錢，但未能得逞。

blueprint [ˋblu͵prɪnt] .... ★★★★★
n. 藍圖

brunt [brʌnt] .... ★
n. 正面的衝擊，主要的壓力

bulge [bʌldʒ] .... ★
n. 膨脹部分，凸出部分

chelate [ˋki͵let] .... ★
v. 與（金屬）結合成絡合物：To chelate something is to combine (a metal ion) with a chemical compound to form a ring. 與（金屬）結合成絡合物就是把（一個金屬離子）與化學複合物結合成環。

chemical [ˋkɛmɪk!] ....★★★★
adj. 化學的：A chemical change takes place in any substance when it burns. 物質燃燒時會發生化學變化。
n. 化學藥品

chemically [ˈkɛmɪklɪ] .... ★★★★
adv. 在化學（性質）上，用化學方法，從化學上分析

chemistry [ˈkɛmɪstrɪ] .... ★★★★
n. 化學，融洽，相互吸引或意氣相投

circuit [ˈsɝkɪt] .... ★★★★
n. 電路，環行，巡迴

circuitry [ˈsɝkɪtrɪ] .... ★★★★
n. 電路（學）

conduct [kənˈdʌkt] .... ★★★★★
n. 行為：Most religions are concerned with the worship of one or several deities as well as ethical rules of conduct. 大多數宗教都以崇敬一個或多個神為宗旨，同時以道德戒律來約束行為。

conductivity [ˌkɑndʌkˈtɪvətɪ] ..... ★★★★★
n. 導電率，傳電率

conductor [kənˈdʌktɚ] .... ★★★
n. ①（公共汽車）售票員，列車員②（樂隊）指揮，領隊③導體，導線

decibel [ˈdɛsɪbɛl] .... ★
n. 分貝

dilute [daɪˈlut] .... ★
v. 稀釋，沖淡：The nurse diluted the drug with saline water. 護士用生理食鹽水來稀釋藥物。

dimension [dɪˈmɛnʃən] .... ★★★
n. 尺度，維（數）

diode [ˈdaɪod] .... ★
n. 二極體

distance [ˈdɪstəns] .... ★★★★★
n. 距離，間距：a distance of five miles 五英里的距離
【片語】in the distance 在遠處

distillation [ˌdɪstʃˈeʃən] .... ★
n. 蒸餾：the distillation of water 水的蒸餾淨化

dynamics [daɪˈnæmɪks] .... ★★★
n. 力學，動力學，動態

dynamite [ˈdaɪnəˌmaɪt] .... ★
n. 甘油炸藥

dynamo [ˈdaɪnəˌmo] .... ★
n. （直流）發電機；精力特別充沛和強而有力的人：a vice president who was the real dynamo of the corporation 副總裁是公司真正強而有力的人物。

echo [ˈɛko] .... ★★★★
n. 回聲，反響
v. 發出回聲，共鳴，（聲音）被傳回：Our voices echoed in the empty room. 我們的聲音在空房間裡迴盪。

elastic [ɪˈlæstɪk] .... ★★★
n. 鬆緊帶，橡皮圈
adj. 彈性的，有彈力的，靈活的：The Earth is not an absolutely rigid body but is elastic under conditions of stress. 地球不是一個絕對堅硬的球體，而是在多種壓力條件下有彈性的球體。

elasticity [ɪˌlæsˈtɪsətɪ] .... ★★★
n. 彈性：His mind has lost elasticity. 他的頭腦不再靈活。

electric [ɪˈlɛktrɪk] .... ★★★★
adj. 電的，導電的，帶電的，電動的，驚人的，令人興奮的：The president's speech had an electric effect on the crowd, and the students all cheered at him. 校長的演說震撼人心，學生們都向他歡呼。

electrical [ɪˈlɛktrɪkl] .... ★★★
adj. 電的，電氣科學的，電力的：The cooker isn't working because of an electrical fault. 這副炊具因為電力故障不能用了。

electricity [ɪˌlɛkˈtrɪsətɪ] .... ★★★
n. 電，電流，電學：electricity bills 電費單；electricity costs 電費

electrify [ɪˈlɛktrəˌfaɪ] .... ★★★
v. （使）電（氣）化，使激動，使震驚：The national orchestra gave an electrifying performance of classical music. 國家交響樂團舉行了一場震撼的古典音樂演出。

electrode [ɪˋlɛktrod] .... ★
n. 電極

electrolysis [ɪlɛkˋtrɑləsɪs] .... ★
n. 電解

electrolytic [ɪˋlɛktrəˋlɪtɪk] .... ★
adj. 電解的，電解質的

electromagnetic [ɪlɛktromægˋnɛtɪk] ★★★
n. 電磁體，電磁鐵

electromagnetism
[ɪˋlɛktroˋmægnətɪzəm] .... ★
n. 電磁，電磁學

electron [ɪˋlɛktrɑn] .... ★★★
n. 電子

electronic [ɪlɛkˋtrɑnɪk] .... ★★★★★
adj. 電子的

electronics [ɪlɛkˋtrɑnɪks] .... ★
n. 電子學，電子裝置和元件：The electronics aboard the new aircraft are very sophisticated. 安裝在新飛行器上的電子零件非常複雜。

electroplate [ɪˋlɛktrəˌplet] .... ★
v. 電鍍

electrostatics [ɪlɛktrəˋstætɪks] .... ★
n. 靜電學

equilibrium [ˌikwəˋlɪbrɪəm] .... ★
n. 平衡狀態：the equilibrium of demand and supply 供需平衡

ferromagnetic [ˌfɛromægˋnɛtɪk] .... ★
adj. 鐵磁（體）的

filament [ˋfɪləmənt] .... ★
n. （電燈泡、電子管）燈絲，細絲

flake [flek] .... ★
n. 片，薄片
v. （常與 away、off 連用）剝落：The paint's beginning to flake off. 油漆開始剝落。

flame [flem] .... ★★★★★
n. 火焰，火苗，火，熱情，激情
v. 發火焰，燃燒：In old times, the message was flamed by signal fires from one village to another. 古代用烽火將消息從一個村子傳送到另一個村子。

flash [flæʃ] .... ★★★★★
n. 閃爍，閃光：a flash of lighting 閃電
v. ①（使）閃光，閃爍：The lighting flashed across the sky. 閃電自天空閃過。②飛馳，掠過：The express train flashed past. 火車飛馳而過。③閃現，閃耀：The idea flashed into his mind. 他的頭腦中閃過一個念頭。

fray [fre] .... ★
v. （織物的邊緣）磨損：Her nerves were frayed by the noisy children. 〔喻〕吵吵嚷嚷的孩子讓她神經衰弱。

freeze [friz] .... ★★★★
v. （使）結冰，（使）凍結：The lake froze over. 湖面全結了冰。

frequency [ˋfrikwənsɪ] .... ★★★
n. 頻率，頻繁

frequent [ˋfrikwənt] .... ★★★★
adj. 時常發生的，頻繁的：He is a frequent visitor. 他是常客。

frequently [ˋfrikwəntlɪ] .... ★★★★★
adv. 常常，往往，頻繁地，屢次

frozen [ˋfrozn̩] .... ★★★★
adj. 結冰的，凝結的：frozen in their tracks with fear 在他們的軌道上凍住且心存恐懼

fuse [fjuz] .... ★
n. 保險絲，導火線，引信
v. 熔化，熔合：There was no separation between joy and sorrow；they fused into one. 痛苦與歡樂之間沒有界限：它們融為一體了。

fusion [ˋfjuʒən] .... ★★★★★
n. 核聚變，熔合，聯合

gallon [ˋgælən] .... ★★★
n. 加侖

gild [gɪld] .... ★
v. 鍍金，虛飾：The morning sun gilds the sky.
朝陽把天空染成金色。

glow [glo] .... ★★★
v. 發熱，發光，燃燒
n. 白熱，光輝

glowing [ˋgloɪŋ] .... ★★★
adj. 生動的，熱情的，有利的：a glowing
  description 生動的描述

golden [ˋgoldn̩] .... ★★★★
adj. ①金（黃）色的：golden hair 金色的頭髮
  ②金的，金製的：a golden crown 金皇冠
  ③極好的，興盛的：a golden opportunity
  絕佳的機會

gram(me) [græm] .... ★★★
n. 公克

granular [ˋgrænjələ] .... ★
adj. 顆粒狀的：granular cells 顆粒細胞；
  coarsely granular 粗粒狀的。

gravity [ˋgrævətɪ] .... ★★★
n. 引力，重大的後果，嚴重或重大

green [grin] .... ★★★★★
n. 綠色
adj. 綠的，生澀的，未成熟的：at the green
  age of 18 正值年輕的十八歲。

grey/gray [gre] .... ★★★★★
adj. 灰色（的），灰白色（的）

heater [ˋhitɚ] .... ★
n. 加熱器，暖氣設備：electric heater 電熱器

hologram [ˋhɑləˌgræm] .... ★
n. 全息圖

holography [həˋlɑgrəfɪ] .... ★
n. 全像攝影

hydrodynamic [ˌhaɪdrodaɪˋnæmɪk] .. ★
adj. 流體動力的

iceberg [ˋaɪsˌbɝg] .... ★★★★★
n. 冰山：ice island iceberg 島狀冰山；
  pinnacled iceberg 峰形冰山

impetus [ˋɪmpətəs] .... ★★★★★
n. 推動力

inelastic [ˌɪnɪˋlæstɪk] .... ★
adj. 無彈性的：inelastic collision【物】非彈性
  碰撞

inertia [ɪnˋɝʃə] .... ★
n. 慣性，惰性：the inertia of an entrenched
  bureaucracy 根深蒂固的官僚體制的惰性

insulate [ˋɪnsəˌlet] .... ★
v. 隔音，絕緣，保溫：Many houses in the
  north are warm in winter because they are
  insulated so that the heat is not lost. 北方
  的許多房子都作了隔熱處理，讓熱量不致散
  失，在冬天很暖和。

insulation [ˌɪnsəˋleʃən] .... ★
n. 絕緣：soundproof cork insulation 隔音的軟
  木材料

insulator [ˋɪnsəˌletɚ] .... ★
n. 絕緣體

intermediary [ˌɪntɚˋmidɪˌɛrɪ] .... ★★★
n. 媒介物，居間者

invent [ɪnˋvɛnt] .... ★★★★
v. ①發明，創造：Edison invented the electric
  light. 愛迪生發明了電燈。②捏造，虛構：
  He invented an excuse for being late. 他為
  自己遲到編造了一個藉口。

invention [ɪnˋvɛnʃən] .... ★★★★
n. ①發明，創造②捏造，虛構

inventive [ɪnˋvɛntɪv] .... ★★★★
adj. 發明創造的，有創造能力的，富於創造
  的：an inventive person 有發明才智的人

kinetic [kɪˋnɛtɪk] .... ★
adj. 動力（學）的，（運）動的

laser [ˋlezɚ] .... ★★★
n. 鐳射，雷射器：a laser space-to-ground
  voice link 鐳射式空對陸通話

liquefy [ˋlɪkwəˌfaɪ] .... ★
adj. 液體的，液態的
v. （使）液化

liquid [ˋlɪkwɪd] .... ★★★
n. 液體：Mechanics is the study of the effects of forces on bodies or liquids at rest or in motion. 力學是一門研究力在靜止或運動的物體或液體上作用的效果的科學。

maglev [ˋmæglɛv] .... ★
n. 磁懸浮

magnesium [mægˋniʃɪəm] .... ★
n. 鎂：powdered magnesium 鎂粉，粉狀鎂；refined magnesium 精煉鎂

magnet [ˋmægnɪt] .... ★★★
n. 磁鐵，磁體，磁石，有吸引力的人（或物）：Guilin is a magnet for tourists. 桂林是吸引遊客的地方。

magnetic [mægˋnɛtɪk] .... ★★★
adj. 磁性的，有吸引力的：magnetic eyes 迷人的眼睛；a magnetic personality 有魅力的人。

magnetism [ˋmægnəˌtɪzəm] .... ★
n. 磁性，磁力，磁學：the magnetism of money 錢的吸引力；animal magnetism 動物（對異性）的吸引力。

magnetite [ˋmægnəˌtɪzəm] .... ★
n. 磁鐵礦

magnetize [ˋmægnəˌtaɪz] .... ★
v. 使磁化：You can magnetize a needle by rubbing it with a magnet. 用磁鐵磨擦針可使之磁化。

malleable [ˋmælɪəbḷ] .... ★★★
adj. 有延展性的，可鍛造的：Materials such as clay, wax, glass, and rubber are widely used in industry today because they are malleable. 黏土、石蠟和橡膠這些材料因為具有可延展性，在現今產業中廣泛應用。

megawatt [ˋmɛgəˌwɑt] .... ★★★
n. 兆瓦

meson [ˋmɛzɑn] .... ★
n. 介子：meson field 介子場

metalworking [ˋmɛtḷˌwɝkɪŋ] .... ★★
n. 金屬製造

microminiature [ˌmaɪkroˋmɪnɪətʃə] ...... ★★
adj. 超小型的，微型的

microwave [ˋmaɪkroˌwev] .... ★
n. 微波

molecular [məˋlɛkjələ] .... ★
adj. 分子的：molecular attraction 分子引力；molecular conductivity 分子電導率

molecule [ˋmɑləˌkjul] .... ★★★
n. 分子

辨析
Analyze

fluid, liquid

1 **fluid** *n. & a.*「流體，液體，流體的，流動的」，指可自由流動的物質，包括液體和氣體：The glass tube of a thermometer contains a fluid, usually mercury. 溫度計的玻璃管內有流體，通常是水銀。

2 **liquid** *n. & a.*「液體，液體的，液態的，清澈的，晶瑩的，流暢的」，僅指液體，比fluid的意義狹窄，可用於比喻意義：Air is a fluid but not a liquid; water is both a fluid and a liquid. 空氣是流體，不是液體；水既是流體也是液體。

molten [ˈmoltən] .... ★
adj. 熔融的，熔化的：Molten iron is transported to the factory immediately. 熔化的鋼立即被送往工廠。

nanosecond [ˈnænəˌsɛkənd] .... ★
n. 毫微秒

neutron [ˈnjutrɑn] .... ★
n. 中子

nuclear [ˈnjuklɪə] .... ★★★★
adj. 原子的：nuclear physics 核子物理學

nucleus [ˈnjuklɪəs] .... ★★★
n. 原子核，核子，核，核心

optical [ˈɑptɪkl̩] .... ★★★
adj. 光學的，光的：an optical defect 視覺缺陷；optical instruments 光學儀器

optics [ˈɑptɪks] .... ★★★
n. 光學

orbit [ˈɔrbɪt] .... ★★★
n. （天體等的）運行軌道
v. 環繞（天體）作軌道運行，（衛星等）沿軌道運行，環行：Satellites that orbit the globe transmit detailed pictures of cloud cover. 圍繞地球的人造衛星傳送詳細的雲層覆蓋圖片。

particle [ˈpɑrtɪkl̩] .... ★★★
n. 顆粒，微粒：not a particle of doubt 沒有一絲懷疑

particulate [pəˈtɪkjəˌlet] .... ★★★
n. 粒子：particulate inheritance 單獨遺傳，顆粒遺傳

physicist [ˈfɪzɪsɪst] .... ★★★
n. 物理學家

physics [ˈfɪzɪks] .... ★★★★
n. 物理學，物理

pink [pɪŋk] .... ★★★★
adj. 粉紅色的，桃紅色的：Pink is my favorite color. 粉紅色是我最喜歡的顏色。

pneumatic [njuˈmætɪk] .... ★
adj. 氣動的，風動的：a pneumatic tire 充氣輪胎

poise [pɔɪz] .... ★
v. 平衡，穩定：The gymnast poised herself on the balance beam. 體操運動員在平衡木上保持平衡。

polarity [poˈlærətɪ] .... ★
n. 極

polarize [ˈpoləˌraɪz] .... ★
v. （使）極化，（使）兩極分化：a society polarized towards gaining money 有拜金傾向的社會

press [prɛs] .... ★★★★★
v. ①壓，掀，按：He pressed the door bell. 他按了門鈴。②壓榨，壓迫：press the juice out of the watermelon 榨西瓜汁③催促：Don't press me on this point. 別在這問題上逼我。
n. ①壓，掀，按：a press of a button 按電鈕②報刊，出版社，通訊社：members of the Press 新聞界人士③壓榨機，壓力機

pressure [ˈprɛʃə] .... ★★★★
n. 壓力，壓迫

purple [ˈpɝpl̩] .... ★★★★★
adj. 紫（紅）的
n. 紫（紅）色：He has a taste for purple prose. 他喜歡風格華麗的散文。

quark [kwɔrk] .... ★
n. （容量單位）夸脫（＝2品脫，1/4加侖）

radiological [ˌredɪoˈlɑdʒɪkəl] .... ★
adj. 輻射學的，放射學的

reactor [rɪˈæktə] .... ★★★★★
n. 核反應堆

reflection [rɪˈflɛkʃən] .... ★★★★
n. 反映

refrigeration [rɪˌfrɪdʒəˈreʃən] .... ★★★
n. 冷凍，製冷，冷藏

semiconductor [ˌsɛmɪkənˈdʌktɚ] ..... ★★★
n. 半導體

solid [ˈsɑlɪd] .... ★★★★
adj. ①固體的：What they're more interested in is physics of the solid state. 他們更感興趣的是固態物理。②實心的：The box is heavy because it is solid. 這個盒子是實心的，所以很重，③結實的，穩固的，可靠的：a huge solid mass of rock 一塊堅硬的巨石
n. 固體

solidarity [sɑləˈdærətɪ] .... ★
n. 團結

speedy [ˈspidɪ] .... ★★★★★
adj. 快的，迅速的：speedy calculation 速算

sphere [sfɪr] .... ★★★★
n. 球體，領域，範圍，界：a sphere of influence 勢力範圍

spherical [ˈsfɛrəkl̩] .... ★
adj. 球形的，球面的：spherical geometry 球面幾何學

strength [strɛnθ] .... ★★★★★
n. 實力，力量：a man of great strength 力量強大的人

strengthen [ˈstrɛnθən] .... ★★★★
v. 加強，鞏固：The front army troops were strengthened by a large contingent of students from the military academy. 前線部隊得到了一大批軍事學院學員的增援。

stress [strɛs] .... ★★★★
n. 壓力，緊迫，應力
v. 強調，著重，重讀，用重音讀：Some theorists suggest that modern society produces more stress than earlier periods of human life. 一些理論家提出現代社會比早期社會給人帶來了更多的壓力。

subatomic [ˌsʌbəˈtɑmɪk] .... ★★
adj. 亞原子的，原子內的，比原子更小的：subatomic decompostion 亞原子分解

sublimate [ˈsʌbləˌmet] .... ★
v. 使昇華

substantial [səbˈstænʃəl] .... ★★★
adj. 物質的，堅固的，多的，有重大價值的，富裕的：The Chickasaw Indians of the Southeast lived in substantial wooden houses grouped in towns of up to 2,000 people. 東南部的契卡索印第安人居住在結實的木屋中，並組成了多達2,000人的城鎮。

superconducting [ˌsupɚkənˈdʌktɪŋ] .... ★★★★★
adj. 超導（電）的

superconductivity [ˌsupɚˌkɑndʌkˈtɪvətɪ] .... ★★★★★
n. 超導（電）性

supersonic [ˌsupɚˈsɑnɪk] .... ★
adj. 超音波的，超音速的：a supersonic plane 超音速飛機

tepid [ˈtɛpɪd] .... ★
adj. 微溫的：the tepid conservatism of the fifties 五○年代的那種溫和保守主義

thaw [θɔ] .... ★★
v. 使溶化，使溶解：When the glaciers thawed after the last ice age, the five Great Lakes of North America were formed. 最後一次冰河時期解凍形成了北美洲的五大湖。

vapor [ˈvepɚ] .... ★★★
n.（水）蒸汽，汽化：water vapor 水蒸氣

volt [volt] .... ★★★
n. 伏特

voltage [ˈvoltɪdʒ] .... ★★★
n. 電壓，伏特數

03

化學相關辭彙

Vocabulary of Chemic

acid [ˈæsɪd] .... ★★★
adj. ①酸的：an acid solution 酸性溶液②尖刻的：
　　Dorothy Parker's book reviews for *Vanity Fair*
　　were deemed to be too acid. 帕克對於《浮華世
　　界》的書評被認為過於尖刻。

alcohol [ˈælkəˌhɔl] .... ★
n. 酒精

alcoholic [ˌælkəˈhɔlɪk] .... ★★★
adj. 酒精的，酒精中毒的：The airlines serve alcoholic
　　drinks to keep its planes full of passengers. 航空
　　公司向乘客提供含酒精的飲料，以使航班滿座。

anhydrous [ænˈhaɪdrəs] .... ★
adj. 【化】無水的

aromatic [ˌærəˈmætɪk] .... ★
n. 芬芳的，芳香的

aura [ˈɔrə] .... ★
n. 氣味，氣氛：be enveloped in an aura of grandeur.
　　被一種壯麗的氣氛所籠罩。

biochemistry [ˌbaɪoˈkɛmɪstrɪ] .... ★
n. 生物化學

brew [bru] .... ★
v. 釀造，圖謀：As you brew, so you must drink. 【諺】
　　自作自受；自食其果。

bronze [brɑnz] .... ★★
n. 青銅（製品），青銅色

bubble [ˈbʌbl̩] .... ★★★
n. 泡，水泡，氣泡：to blow soap bubbles 吹肥皂泡
v. 吹泡，起泡：The water was bubbling gently in the
　　pan. 水在鍋裡輕輕地冒著氣泡。

buoy [bɔɪ] .... ★
n. 浮標，救生圈
v. 使浮起：We were buoyed up by good news. 我們為
　　好消息所鼓舞。

carbohydrate [ˈkɑrbəˈhaɪdret] .... ★
n. 【化】碳水化合物，醣類

carbon [ˈkɑrbən] .... ★★★
n. 碳，副本

carbonize [ˈkɑrbənˌaɪz] .... ★★
v. 使…碳化

catalyst [ˈkætəlɪst] .... ★
n. 催化劑

caustic [ˈkɔstɪk] .... ★
adj. 腐蝕性的，刻薄的：First of all, there is caustic shame for my own stupidity. 最嚴重的是因為我自身的愚蠢而產生深深的羞辱。

celluloid [ˈsɛljəˌlɔɪd] .... ★
adj. 人造的，人工合成的：a novel with flat, celluloid characters 一部人物平淡無味、做作的小說。

coagulate [koˈægjəˌlet] .... ★★
v. 凝結：Blood coagulates when it meets air. 血液接觸空氣就會凝結。
adj. 凝結的

compound [ˈkɑmpaʊnd] .... ★★★
n. 混合物，化合物：Water is a compound of hydrogen and oxygen. 水是氫和氧的化合物。
adj. 複合的：compound substance 合成物質；compound interest 複利

corrode [kəˈrod] .... ★
v. 損害：Platinum is neither corroded by moisture nor affected by oxygen or ordinary acids. 鉑既不會因潮濕而腐蝕，也不會被氧氣或酸所氧化破壞。

corrosion [kəˈroʒən] .... ★
n. 腐蝕：corrosion remover 防腐劑；corrosion by gases 氣體腐蝕

corrosive [kəˈrosɪv] .... ★
adj. 腐蝕的：Acid is corrosive. 酸是有腐蝕性的。

dioxide [daɪˈɑksaɪd] .... ★
n. 二氧化物：carbon dioxide 二氧化碳

distillery [dɪˈstɪlərɪ] .... ★
n. 蒸餾室

dye [daɪ] .... ★★★
n. 顏料
v. 染色：She dyed her hair black. 她把頭髮染黑了。

element [ˈɛləmənt] .... ★★★★★
n. 元素，天氣，壞天氣

factor [ˈfæktə] .... ★★★★
n. 因素，要素

fermentation [ˌfɝmɛnˈteʃən] .... ★
n. 發酵

foam [fom] .... ★★
n. 泡沫

formula [ˈfɔrmjələ] .... ★★★★
n. 公式，程式

foul [faʊl] .... ★★
adj. 違規的，邪惡的：to use foul means to gain power 用卑鄙的手段來得到權力

fragrant [ˈfregrənt] .... ★
adj. 香的，芬芳的：This perfume is made in several fragrant spices. 這種香水是由幾種香料所製成的。

gaseous [ˈfregrənt] .... ★
adj. 氣體的：a gaseous condition 氣體狀態；a gaseous mixture 氣體混合物

germanium [dʒɝˈmenɪəm] .... ★
n. 鍺：germanium transistor 鍺電晶體

glue [glu] .... ★★★
adj. 膠水，黏聚力，具有黏合凝聚的因素：Idealism was the glue that held our group together. 理想主義是把我們這個團體結合起來的凝聚力。

hydrochloric [ˌhaɪdrəˈklɔrɪk] .... ★
adj. 鹽酸的：hydrochloric acid 鹽酸，氫氯酸

hydrogen [ˈhaɪdrədʒən] .... ★★★
n. 氫：hydrogen bomb 氫彈；hydrogen bond 氫鍵

lead [lɛd] .... ★★★★★
n. 鉛

023

n. 鉛

v. 用鉛包，在…中襯鉛：leaded gasoline 含鉛汽油；leaded paint 含鉛塗料

melt [mɛlt] .... ★★★★
n. 融化的金屬
v. 溶化，融化，熔化，軟化：The snow on top of the mountains melted away under the sun. 山頂上的雪在陽光下融化了。

neon [ˋniˌɑn] .... ★
n. 氖：a neon lamp 霓虹燈

neutral [ˋnjutrəl] .... ★★★
adj. 中性的，中立的

neutralize [ˋnjutrəˌaɪz] .... ★
v. 中和，壓制：Acids neutralize alkalis and vice versa. 酸能中和鹼，鹼也能中和酸。

nicotine [ˋnɪkəˌtin] .... ★
n. 尼古丁

nitric [ˋnaɪtrɪk] .... ★
adj. （含）氮的：nitric oxide 氧化氮

nitrogen [ˋnaɪtrədʒən] .... ★★★
n. 氮：nitrogen monoxide 一氧化二氮

odor [ˋodɚ] .... ★★
n. 臭氣，名聲

oxygen [ˋɑksədʒən] .... ★★★
n. 氧氣：oxygen blast 氧氣煉鋼

perfume [ˋpɝfjum] .... ★
n. 香水，香料

petrify [ˋpɛtrəˌfaɪ] .... ★
v. 變為化石，使發呆：be petrified with terror /amazement 因恐懼／驚異而呆掉

petrochemical [ˌpɛtroˋkɛmɪkl̩] .... ★
n. 石油化學產品：the petrochemical industry 石油化學工業

poison [ˋpɔɪzn̩] .... ★★★★
n. 毒物，毒藥：It was a deadly poison. 那是致命的毒藥。
v. 使…中毒，下毒於，毒害：He tried to poison my cat. 他想毒死我的貓。

poisonous [ˋpɔɪznəs] .... ★★★
adj. 有毒的，有害的：This medicine is poisonous if taken in large quantities. 這種藥若服用過量是有害的。

rust [rʌst] .... ★★★
v. 生鏽，氧化：If you leave your metal tools outside in the rain, they will rust. 如果你在雨天把金屬工具放在外面，它們會生鏽的。

辨析
Analyze

dissolve, melt, resolve

1 **dissolve** *vt. & vi.* 「溶解，融化，消失」，指由於化學反應（使）溶解，也指由於溫度升高（使）融化，還指消失、減弱：Salt dissolves in water. 鹽溶於水。

2 **melt** *vt. & vi.* 「融化，熔化」，指由於溫度升高（使）融化、（使）熔化，還指（使）消散、（使）逐漸消失：Lead has a lower melting point than iron. 鉛的熔點比鐵低。

3 **resolve** *vi.* 「解決，解答，決定，分解」，指分解（與into連用），還指決心、決議等：Water may be resolved into hydrogen and oxygen. 水可分解為氫和氧。

rusty [ˋrʌstɪ] .... ★★★
adj. （生）鏽的：a bit rusty on history 對歷史
　　有點生疏

scarlet [ˋskɑrlɪt] .... ★★
n. 猩紅色，鮮紅色
adj. 猩紅色，鮮紅色：In anatomical diagrams,
　　the aorta is frequently depicted in scarlet.
　　在解剖圖譜中，主動脈通常用鮮紅色來表
　　示。

scent [sɛnt] .... ★★★
n. 氣味，香氣，香水：the scent of flowers 花
　　香

sediment [ˋsɛdəmənt] .... ★
n. 沉積物，沉澱物：sediment bowel 沉澱池

silver [ˋsɪlvɚ] .... ★★★★★
n. 銀，銀器，銀幣

smell [smɛl] .... ★★★★
n. 氣味，臭味
v. ①嗅，聞到：The dog smelled at the meat.
　　那隻狗聞了這塊肉。②散發（…的）氣味：
　　The meat is beginning to smell. 肉開始發臭
　　了。

smog [smɑg] .... ★
n. 煙霧

sodium [ˋsodɪəm] .... ★
n. 鈉

solution [səˋluʃən] .... ★★★★★
n. 解決（辦法），解答，溶解，溶液

sticky [ˋstɪkɪ] .... ★★★
adj. 黏連的：This sticky liquid empties slowly.
　　這種黏液很慢才會流光。

sulfur [ˋsʌlfɚ] .... ★
n. 硫：sulfur dyes硫化染料；sulfur spring 硫
　　磺溫泉

tan [tæn] .... ★
v. 曬黑，鞭打
adj. 黝黑的：to tan a person's hide 鞭打某人

toxic [ˋtɑksɪk] .... ★
adj. 有毒的，有毒性的：food preservatives
　　that are toxic in concentrated amounts 濃
　　縮後有毒的食物防腐劑

wax [wæks] .... ★★★★
n. 蠟，蜂蠟：Candles are made from wax. 蠟
　　燭是蠟做的。
v. 打蠟：wax the floor 把地板打蠟

04

文學相關辭彙

Vocabulary of Literature

adverb [ˈædvɚb] .... ★★★
n. 副詞：a relative adverb 關係副詞

article [ˈɑrtɪkḷ] .... ★★★★★
n. 論文，物品：an article of furniture 一件傢俱；
　　articles of clothing 衣著用品

author [ˈɔθɚ] .... ★★★★★
n. 作者

autobiography [ˌɔtəbaɪˈɑgrəfɪ] .... ★
n. 自傳

chapter [ˈtʃæptɚ] .... ★★★★★
n. （書籍中的）章，回，篇

essay [ˈɛse] .... ★★★★★
n. 散文，短文，隨筆，短論

fable [ˈfebḷ] .... ★
n. 寓言，傳說

fiction [ˈfɪkʃən] .... ★★★★★
n. 小說：science fiction 科學小說、科學幻想故事

fictional [ˈfɪkʃənḷ] .... ★★★★★
adj. 虛構的，想像的：fictional characters 虛構的人物

fictitious [fɪkˈtɪʃəs] .... ★★★★★
adj. 虛構的：Fictitious creatures like centaurs
　　and mermaids are frequently given animal
　　characteristics. 半人馬、美人魚之類的虛構生物，
　　經常被賦予動物的特徵。

genre [ˈʒɑnrə] .... ★
n. 體裁，風格

gist [dʒɪst] .... ★
n. 要旨

grammar [ˈgræmɚ] .... ★★★
n. 文法（書）

grammatical [grəˈmætɪkḷ] .... ★★★
adj. 文法的：That is not a grammatical sentence. 那個
　　句子不符合文法規則。

idiom [ˈɪdɪəm] .... ★
n. 習語，成語，風格

index [ˈɪndɛks] .... ★★★★★
n. 索引，指數，食指，指標：
The trade of a nation is an index of its economic well-being. 一國的貿易是反映其經濟發展的一項指標。
v. 附以索引，編入索引

literacy [ˈlɪtərəsɪ] .... ★★★★★
n. 識字能力，有閱讀和寫作的能力

literal [ˈlɪtərəl] .... ★
adj. 文字的，字面的：a literal description 平實的描述；a literal mind 死腦筋

literature [ˈlɪtərətʃɚ] .... ★★★★★
n. 文學（作品），（有關某學科或專題的）文獻

logical [ˈlɑdʒɪkl̩] .... ★★★
adj. 邏輯的：Rain was a logical expectation, given the time of year. 按時節來看，下雨是必然的。

logician [loˈdʒɪʃən] .... ★★★
n. 邏輯學家

masterpiece [ˈmæstɚˌpis] .... ★
n. 傑作，名著

metaphorical [ˌmɛtəˈfɔrɪkl̩] .... ★
adj. 隱喻的

noun [naʊn] .... ★★★
n. 名詞

outline [ˈaʊtˌlaɪn] .... ★★★★
n. 輪廓，外形，大綱，概要，圖略：
He drew the outline of a house on the paper. 他把房子的輪廓畫在紙上。
v. 概述，列提綱

paragraph [ˈpærəˌgræf] .... ★★★★
n. 段，節，段落，小新聞，短評

paraphrase [ˈpærəˌfrez] .... ★
v. 意譯，改寫：paraphrase an obscure passage in modern English 用現代英語改寫一段晦澀的文字

phrase [frez] .... ★★★★
n. 短語，片語，用語

playwright [ˈpleˌraɪt] .... ★
n. 劇作家

poetry [ˈpoɪtrɪ] .... ★★★★★
n. 詩，詩歌：the poetry of the dance movements 舞蹈動作中的詩意

preposition [ˌprɛpəˈzɪʃən] .... ★★★
n. 介詞

prose [proz] .... ★★
n. 散文

punctuation [ˌpʌŋktʃʊˈeʃən] .... ★
n. 標點符號

satire [ˈsætaɪr] .... ★
n. 諷刺文學：Some of Aesop's Fables are satires.《伊索寓言》中有一些是諷刺作品。

sentence [ˈsɛntəns] .... ★★★★★
n. 句子

sign [saɪn] .... ★★★★★
n. 標記，符號，招牌，徵兆，跡象
v. 簽名，簽署：There are four letters here for you to sign. 這裡有4封信需要您簽名。

signal [ˈsɪgn̩l] .... ★★★★
v. 發信號，打信號
n. 信號，暗號

signature [ˈsɪgnətʃɚ] .... ★★★
n. 簽名：to witness a signature 簽名作證

signify [ˈsɪgnəˌfaɪ] .... ★★
v. 表示，意味著：He signified his content with a nod. 他以點頭表示同意。

stor(e)y [ˈstorɪ] .... ★★★
n. 故事，傳說，小說

synopsis [sɪˈnɑpsɪs] .... ★
n. 大綱，梗概：synopsis of the week's news 一週新聞概要

tale [tel] .... ★★★★★
n. 故事，傳說

verb [vɝb] .... ★★★
n. 動詞

verbal [ˈvɝbl̩] .... ★★★
n. 動詞的非謂語形式（指不定式、分詞和動名詞）

adj. 語句的，口頭的：a verbal description 口頭描述

verbalize [ˈvɝbəˌlaɪz] .... ★★★★★
v. 把⋯變成動詞

verbally [ˈvɝbl̩ɪ] .... ★★★★★
adv. 口頭上，逐字地

verdict [ˈvɝdɪkt] .... ★★★★★
n. 判決：After listening to the testimony, the members of the jury delivered their verdict. 陪審團的成員聽完了證詞後，宣布了裁決。

辨析 Analyze

fiction, legend, myth, novel, story, tale

1 fiction *n.* 「小說」，不可數名詞，指虛構的、不是真實發生的故事，包括 short story 和 novel：She has read much detective/science fiction. 她看過許多偵探／科幻小說。

2 legend *n.* 「傳說，傳奇故事；傳奇人物」，指古代人的偉大功績的故事，有一定的真實性：There are many legends about the exploits of Robin Hood. 有許多關於羅賓漢英勇事蹟的傳說。

3 myth *n.* 「神話；杜撰出來的人（或事物）」，指古代的神話故事：She enjoys reading the Greek myths. 她喜歡讀希臘神話故事。

4 novel *n. & a.* 「（長篇）小說」，尤指篇幅較長、講述虛構人物和事件的故事，當形容詞意為「新穎的，新奇的」：The Dreams of Red Mansion is a great Chinese novel. 《紅樓夢》是一部中國的巨著。

5 story *n.* 「故事，傳說，小說；情況，事情，經歷；新聞報導」，用法較廣，可指民間流傳的故事，也可指短篇小說：I am writing a short story; it goes on fairly well. 我正在寫一篇短篇小說，進展很順利。

6 tale *n.* 「故事，傳說」，尤指虛構的故事、神話或傳說：When I was a boy, I read a lot of oriental folk tales. 我小時候讀了很多東方民間傳說。

05

學科（學術）名稱總匯

歷史相關辭彙

Vocabulary of History

ancestor [ˈænsɛstɚ] .... ★★★★
n. 祖先，祖宗

antique [ænˈtik] .... ★★★
adj. 古代的：The cart was made in 1800, it is now regarded as an antique one. 這輛馬車是1800年製造的，現在被看成是古董。

document [ˈdɑkjəmənt] .... ★★★★★
n. 文獻，檔，資料，記錄：a historical document 歷史文獻

documentary [ˌdɑkjəˈmɛntərɪ] .... ★★
adj. 文獻的
n. 記錄片：a full length documentary 大型紀錄片

extant [ɪkˈstænt] .... ★★★★★
adj. 現存的：extant manuscripts 尚存的手稿

historic [hɪsˈtɔrɪk] .... ★★★
adj. 歷史性的：a historic meeting between the two leaders 兩位領導人具有歷史意義的會面

historical [hɪsˈtɔrɪkl] .... ★★★★★
adj. 歷史的，有關歷史的，歷史上的：Mr. Thompson gave all the historical papers of his grandfather to the public library according to his grandfather's will. 湯普森先生按照他祖父的遺囑，將他祖父所有關於歷史學的論文都贈送給公共圖書館。

naturalist [ˈnætʃərəlɪst] .... ★★★★★
n. 博物學家

辨析 Analyze

historic, historical

1 **historic** *a.* 「歷史上著名的，具有重大歷史意義的」，帶有主觀色彩：Waterloo is a historic battle field. 滑鐵盧是歷史上有名的戰場。

2 **historical** *a.* 「歷史（上）的，史學的」，指客觀存在的東西：He gave all the historical papers to the library. 他把所有的歷史文件都交給了圖書館。

06

宗教、哲學相關辭彙

學科（學術）名稱總匯

Vocabulary of Religion & Phylosophy

Discipline

aboriginal [æbəˈrɪdʒənḷ] .... ★
n. 土著
adj. 土著的：Her studies of the primitive art forms of the aboriginal Indians were widely reported in the scientific journal. 一些科學雜誌廣泛報導了她對印第安土著原始藝術形式的研究工作。

atheism [ˈeθɹɪzəm] .... ★
n. 無神論

believer [bɪˈlivə] .... ★★★★★
n. 信徒

bishop [ˈbɪʃəp] .... ★★
n. 主教：bishop's stool 主教的職權或座位

bless [blɛs] .... ★★
v. 祝福，保佑：The priest blesses the people. 牧師為人們祝福。

blessed [ˈblɛsɪd] .... ★★
adj. 愉快的，神聖的：a few moments of blessed silence 令人愉快的片刻寧靜。

blessing [ˈblɛsɪŋ] .... ★★
n. 祝福

Buddhism [ˈbudɪzəm] .... ★
n. 佛教

bum [bʌm] .... ★
n. 遊民，笨蛋：go on the bum 過流浪生活

bury [ˈbɛrɪ] .... ★★★★★
v. ①埋葬，安葬：They buried the dead. 他們埋葬了死者。②掩埋，埋藏：They buried their treasure under the ground. 他們把財寶埋在地下。

cadre [ˈkædrɪ] .... ★
n. 幹部

cathedral [kəˈθidrəl] .... ★★
n. 天主教教堂

catholic [ˈkæθəlɪk] .... ★★
adj. 普遍的，寬大的：The 100-odd pages of formulas and constants are surely the most catholic to be found. 這一百多頁的公式和常數無疑是目前所見最廣博的。

celestial [sɪˈlɛstʃəl] .... ★
adj. 天的，神聖的：The sun, the stars, and the moon are celestial bodies. 太陽、星星、月亮都是天體。

chaste [tʃest] .... ★
adj. 貞潔的，純正的：He wrote in a chaste style. 他文筆樸實。

Christ [kraɪst] .... ★★★★★
n. 救世主（特指耶穌基督）：Jesus Christ 基督

Christian [ˈkrɪstʃən] .... ★★★★★
n. 基督教徒
adj. 基督教的

church [tʃɜtʃ] .... ★★★★★
n. 教堂，教會：When he graduated from the university, he joined the church and two years later became a priest. 他大學畢業後開始任神職，兩年後成為一名牧師。
adj. 教堂的，教會的

clergy [ˈklɜdʒɪ] .... ★
n. 牧師，教士

clerical [ˈklɛrɪkl̩] .... ★
adj. 文書的，事務性的：clerical work 文書工作，雜務

creed [krid] .... ★
n. 信仰，信條

cult [kʌlt] .... ★
n. 崇拜，崇拜者：the cult of leadership 對領袖的崇拜

deification [ˌdiəfəˈkeʃən] .... ★
n. 祭祀為神，神格化，奉若神明

devout [dɪˈvaut] .... ★★
adj. 虔誠的：Please extend my devout thanks to them for their help. 請轉達我對他們幫助的誠摯謝意。

disciple [dɪˈsaɪpl̩] .... ★
n. 門徒

divine [dəˈvaɪn] .... ★★
adj. 神的，神聖的：The moon, the sun, and the visible planets were considered by earliest observers to be divine objects. 月亮、太陽和其他可見行星，被早期的觀察者看作是神聖的物體。

doctrine [ˈdɑktrɪn] .... ★★
n. 教義，主義，學說：the doctrine of evolution 進化論

dogma [ˈdɔgmə] .... ★
n. 教義，教條

dogmatic(al) [dɔgˈmætɪk(l̩)] .... ★
adj. 教條的，武斷的：a dogmatic(al) statement 武斷的說法

dogmatism [ˈdɔgmətɪzəm] .... ★
n. 教條主義

ego [ˈigo] .... ★
n. 自我：The greatest of them are the least ego-pushing. 他們當中最偉大的人物是最不愛出風頭的。

egoist [ˈigoɪst] .... ★
n. 自我主義者

factional [ˈfækʃənl̩] .... ★★★★
〔記〕{faction（小集團，宗派）+al（的）}
adj. 派系的，小派別的

faith [feθ] .... ★★★★★
n. 信任，信心，信仰，信條

faithful [ˈfeθfəl] .... ★★★★
n. 信徒
adj. 忠實的：Feudal society depended on the existence of faithful vassals. 封建社會建立在忠誠的諸侯上。

feudal [ˈfjudl̩] .... ★
adj. 封建主義：the feudal age/days/times 封建時代

feudalism [ˈfjudl̩ɪzəm] .... ★
n. 封建主義

hermit [ˈhɜmɪt] .... ★
n. 隱居者

holy [ˈholɪ] .... ★★★★★
adj. 神聖的，聖潔的：The pursuit of peace is our holiest quest. 追求和平是最值得敬仰的。

hono(u)r [ˈɑnɚ] .... ★★★★★
n. 光榮，榮譽
【片語】①in honour of 為向…表示敬意，為慶祝②on one's honour 以名譽擔保
v. ①給…以榮譽：We are deeply honoured that you should come. 你願意前來，我們深感榮幸。②向…表示敬意，尊敬：an honoured guest 貴賓

humanitarian [hjuˌmænəˈtɛrɪən] .... ★★
adj. 人道主義的
n. 人道主義者：humanitarian aid 人道主義援助

idealism [aɪˈdiəˌlɪzəm] .... ★
n. 唯心主義，理想主義

idealist [aɪˈdɪəlɪst] .... ★★★★★
n. 理想主義者

idealize [aɪˈdiəˌlaɪz] .... ★★★★★
v. 使理想化：He tends to idealize his life in the college. 他往往把他在大學的生活理想化。

ideology [ˌaɪdɪˈɑlədʒɪ] .... ★★★★★
n. 意識形態

impracticable [ɪmˈpræktɪkəbl̩] .... ★
adj. 不現實的，行不通的：Refloating the sunken ship intact proved impracticable because of its fragility. 由於沉船易碎，所以讓整艘沉船再次浮起被證實行不通。

impressionism [ɪmˈprɛʃənˌɪzəm] ★★★★★
n. 印象派

lord [lɔrd] .... ★★★★★
n. 上帝，主，主人，長官，君主，貴族：the Lord Mayor of London 倫敦市長閣下

Marxist [ˈmɑrksɪst] .... ★★★
adj. 馬克思主義的
n. 馬克思主義者

materialism [məˈtɪrɪəlˌɪzəm] .... ★
n. 唯物主義：communist materialism 共產主義的唯物主義

materialist [məˈtɪrɪəlɪst] .... ★★★★★
n. 唯物主義者，唯物論者：materialist dialectics 唯物辯證法

missionary [ˈmɪʃənˌɛrɪ] .... ★★
n. 傳教士：missionary fervor 宣傳的狂熱

monastic [məˈnæstɪk] .... ★
adj. 寺院的，修士的，僧侶的

monk [mʌŋk] .... ★★
n. 和尚，修士：a Carthusian monk 卡爾特會僧侶；a Buddhist monk 佛教和尚

native [ˈnetɪv] .... ★★★★★
n. 土著，當地人，土人：a native of Scotland now living in the United States 現居於美國的蘇格蘭人
adj. 本國的，本地的，土生的，土著的，非歐美（人）的

nun [nʌn] .... ★
n. 修女，尼姑

optimism [ˈɑptəmɪzəm] .... ★
n. 樂觀主義

optimistic [ˌɑptəˈmɪstɪk] .... ★★★
adj. 樂觀（主義）的

oracle [ˈɔrəkl̩] .... ★
n. 神諭

pagan [ˈpegən] .... ★
n. 異教徒

paradise [ˈpærəˌdaɪs] .... ★★
n. 天堂

pessimistic [ˌpɛsəˈmɪstɪk] .... ★★★
adj. 悲觀的，悲觀主義的：take a pessimistic view of... 對…抱悲觀見解

philosopher [fəˈlɑsəfɚ] .... ★★★★
n. 哲學家，哲人：a moral philosopher 道德哲學家

philosophical [ˌfɪləˈsɑfɪk!] .... ★★★★★
adj. 哲學的

philosophically [ˌfɪləˈsɑfɪk!ɪ] .... ★★★★★
adv. 達觀的，具有哲人態度的

philosophy [fəˈlɑsəfɪ] .... ★★★★★
n. 哲學：the philosophy of a culture 文化的價值體系

pilgrim [ˈpɪlɡrɪm] .... ★★
n. 香客，朝聖者：pilgrim('s) signs 朝聖紀念品。

pious [ˈpaɪəs] .... ★★
adj. 虔誠的：a pious fraud 借宗教名義進行的詐欺

pope [pop] .... ★★
n. 教皇

preach [pritʃ] .... ★★
v. 說教，佈道，鼓吹：A former state senator who preached judicial restraint, Sandra Day O'Connor was conservatives when she was appointed to the United States Supreme Court. 鼓吹限制司法權力的前參議員桑德·戴伊·奧康納，被指派到美國最高法院工作時是一名保守黨員。

priest [prist] .... ★★★★★
n. 教士，牧師，神父

recluse [rɪˈklus] .... ★
n. 隱士：live a life of a recluse 過隱居生活

religion [rɪˈlɪdʒən] .... ★★★★★
n. 宗教

religious [ɪˈlɪdʒəs] .... ★★★★★
adj. 宗教（上）的，虔誠的：The cathedral at Charters is an expression of the religious fervor of the Middle Ages. 查特斯的大教堂是中世紀時期宗教熱情的表現之一。

sacred [ˈsekrɪd] .... ★★
adj. 上帝的，神聖的：Temples, mosques, churches and synagogues are all sacred buildings. 寺廟、清真寺、基督教堂及猶太教堂都是奉獻給神的建築物。

saint [sent] .... ★★★★★
n. 聖人，聖徒

sermon [ˈsɝmən] .... ★★
n. 說教

shrine [ʃraɪn] .... ★
n. 神殿，神龕

skeptical [ˈskɛptɪk!] .... ★
adj. 懷疑論的，懷疑的：be skeptical about something 對某事懷疑

skepticism [ˈskɛptəsɪzəm] .... ★
n. 懷疑態度，懷疑主義

socialism [ˈsoʃəˌlɪzəm] .... ★★★
n. 社會主義

socialist [ˈsoʃəlɪst] .... ★★★
n. 社會主義者，社會黨人
adj. 社會主義的

sociological [ˌsoʃɪəˈlɑdʒɪk!] .... ★★
adj. 針對社會問題的，社會學的

sociologist [ˌsoʃɪˈɑlədʒɪst] .... ★★
n. 社會學家

sociology [ˌsoʃɪˈɑlədʒɪ] .... ★★
n. 社會學

temple [ˈtɛmp!] .... ★★★★★
n. 神殿，廟宇

vandalism [ˈvændəlɪzəm] .... ★
n. 汪達爾主義，藝術破壞

07

社會相關辭彙

Vocabulary of Sociology

affair [ə`fɛr] .... ★★★★★
n. 事情，事件

alien [`elɪən] .... ★★
n. 外國人
adj. 外國的，陌生的：adjust to an alien culture 適應外國文化

alumnus [ə`lʌmnəs] .... ★
n. 男校友

ambition [æm`bɪʃən] .... ★★★★★
n. 野心，企圖心

ambitious [æm`bɪʃəs] .... ★★★★★
adj. 有野心的，企圖心的：Jack London was an ambitious man who wrote many books, not all of which are good. 傑克·倫敦是一個很有抱負的人，一生寫了許多書，但並非每本都寫得很好。

amenable [ə`minəbl] .... ★
adj. 有責任的，肯接受的：We are all amenable to the law. 我們都有遵守法律的義務。

anthropologist [ˌænθrə`palədʒɪst] .... ★★★★★
n. 人類學者

anthropology [ˌænθrə`palədʒɪ] .... ★★★★★
n. 人類學

aptitude [`æptətjud] .... ★★★★★
n. 才能，自然傾向

aunt [ænt] .... ★★★★★
n. 姑母，姨母，舅母，嬸母

authoritative [ə`θɔrəˌtetɪv] .... ★★★★★
adj. 權威性的，官方的：an authoritative dictionary 具有權威性的辭典

authority [ə`θɔrətɪ] .... ★★★★★
n. 官方，當局，當權者，權威。

bachelor [`bætʃələ] .... ★★
n. 單身漢，學士

baron [`bærən] .... ★★
n. 男爵

benefactor [`bɛnəˌfæktə] .... ★★★
n. 恩人

brotherhood [ˈbrʌðə‚hud] .... ★★★★★
n. 兄弟般的關係

burden [ˈbɝdn̩] .... ★★★
n. 負擔，重擔

category [ˈkætə‚gorɪ] .... ★★★★
n. 種類，目錄，範疇

character [ˈkærɪktə] .... ★★★★★
n. 性格，角色，文字

characteristic [‚kærəktəˈrɪstɪk] ..... ★★★★
adj. 特有的，獨特的：Since crystals have characteristic surfaces and shapes, crystallography can be a valuable tool in mineral identification. 由於水晶擁有獨特的表面和形狀，晶體學在礦物鑒定方面可說是一種有用的工具。
n. 特徵，特性

circumstance [ˈsɝkəm‚stæns] ... ★★★★★
n. 情況，環境，情形，狀況，形勢

citizenship [ˈsɪtəzn̩‚ʃɪp] .... ★★★★★
n. 公民身份；公民權

colleague [ˈkɑlig] .... ★★★★
n. 同僚，同事

concept [ˈkɑnsɛpt] .... ★★★★
n. 概念，觀念，（基本）原理

conception [kənˈsɛpʃən] .... ★★
n. 概念

conscience [ˈkɑnʃəns] .... ★★★★★
n. 良心，良知

conscientiously [‚kɑnʃɪˈɛnʃəslɪ] .... ★
adv. 盡職地，正直地：Stockbrokers are expected to work conscientiously to increase the profits of their clients. 人們希望股票經紀人能夠盡心地工作，為他們的客戶獲取利潤。

cosmopolitan [‚kɑzməˈpɑlətn̩] .... ★
adj. 全世界的：a cosmopolitan city 國際都市

cousin [ˈkʌzn̩] .... ★★★★★
n. 堂／表兄弟，堂／表姊妹

daughter [ˈdɔtə] .... ★★★★★
n. 女兒

demographic [‚dimə‚ɡræfɪk] ...... ★★★★★
n. 人口統計的

descendant [dɪˈsɛndənt] .... ★★
n. 子孫，後代

desegregation [di‚sɛɡrəˈɡeʃən] .... ★
n. 取消種族隔離

disreputable [dɪsˈrɛpjətəbl̩] .... ★
adj. 聲名狼藉的：a disreputable-looking fellow 樣子難看的人

drudgery [ˈdrʌdʒərɪ] .... ★
n. 苦工

elation [ɪˈleʃən] .... ★
n. 得意洋洋

eminent [ˈɛmənənt] .... ★
adj. 傑出的：The students are expecting the arrival of an eminent scientist. 同學們正期待一位著名科學家的來訪。

enslave [ɪnˈslev] .... ★★★★★
v. 奴役：He was enslaved to drinking. 他耽溺於飲酒。

ethics [ˈɛθɪks] .... ★★★★★
n. 倫理學

ethnic [ˈɛθnɪk] .... ★★★★★
adj. 種族的：ethnic restaurants 民族風味的飯館；ethnic art 民族藝術

exemplary [ɪɡˈzɛmplərɪ] .... ★★★★★
adj. 模範的，典範的：He was an exemplary prisoner despite of his past experience. 他儘管過去有過不光彩的經歷，但現在是個模範囚犯。

fame [fem] .... ★★★★
n. 名聲，聲望：He was not anxious for fame. 他不急於成名。

family [ˈfæməlɪ] .... ★★★★★
n. 家，家庭成員，氏族，家族

famine [ˈfæmɪn] .... ★★★
n. 饑荒，饑饉

famous [ˈfeməs] .... ★★★★★
adj. 著名的：The place is famous for its green
tea. 此地因綠茶而出名。
【片語】be famous for 因⋯而著名

fatuous [ˈfætʃʊəs] .... ★
adj. 愚昧的：What a fatuous remark! 多麼愚
蠢的話呀！

feat [fit] .... ★★
n. 功績，壯舉

fellow [ˈfɛlo] .... ★★★★★
n. 人，傢伙，小夥子：What a fellow! 這傢
伙！
adj. 同伴的，同類的：a fellow worker 同事

fellowship [ˈfɛloʃɪp] .... ★★
n. 夥伴關係，交情，聯誼會，團體：be
admitted to fellowship 獲准入會；bear
somebody fellowship 與某人有交誼；give/
offer the right hand of fellowship 與人結交

female [ˈfimel] .... ★★★★★
n. 雌性的動物
adj. 雌性的，女性的：female dog 母狗

figurehead [ˈfɪgjɚˌhɛd] .... ★★★★★
n. 名義領袖

folk [fok] .... ★★★★★
n. 人們

folklore [ˈfokˌlor] .... ★
n. 民俗學，民間傳說

forerunner [ˈforˌrʌnɚ] .... ★★★★★
n. 先驅，祖先

fraternal [frəˈtɝnl] .... ★
adj. 兄弟的，兄弟般的，友愛的：a close
fraternal tie 親密的兄弟情誼；a fraternal
association 兄弟會的社團

friend [frɛnd] .... ★★★★★
n. 朋友

friendship [ˈfrɛndʃɪp] .... ★★★★★
n. 友誼，友好

genteel [dʒɛnˈtil] .... ★
adj. 上流社會的：He is a genteel young man.
他是個彬彬有禮的年輕人。

ghetto [ˈgɛto] .... ★
n. 少數民族集中居住區

glory [ˈglorɪ] .... ★★★★★
n. 光榮，榮譽

gratuitous [grəˈtjuətəs] .... ★
adj. 無理由的，不需要的：gratuitous criticism
沒有根據的批評

gregarious [grɪˈgɛrɪəs] .... ★
adj. 群居的，合群的：The walrus, a
gregarious aquatic mammal related to the
seal, is found in arctic waters. 海象是一種
在水中群居的哺乳動物，與海豹有親緣關
係，人們通常可以在北極的水域中見到它
們。

gypsy [ˈdʒɪpsɪ] .... ★
n. 吉普賽人：gypsy music 吉普賽音樂

herald [ˈhɛrəld] .... ★★
n. 傳令官，使者
v. 預示，預報：The fragrant scent of the lilac
is said to herald the beginning of spring. 丁
香花的香味據說預示著春天的來臨。

hero [ˈhɪro] .... ★★★★★
n. ①男主角，男主人：the hero of the movie
電影的男主角②英雄：He was no hero. 他
算不上英雄。

hideous [ˈhɪdɪəs] .... ★★★★★
adj. 駭人聽聞的，醜惡的：a hideous face 醜
惡的面孔

hobby [ˈhɑbɪ] .... ★★★
n. 業餘愛好，嗜好，興趣

host [host] .... ★★★★★
n. 主人，東道主，節目主持人

humanity [hjuˈmænətɪ] .... ★★
n. 人類，人性，人情，人文科學

humanize [ˈhjumənˌaɪz] .... ★★★★★
v. 使具有人的屬性，賦予人性：The acts of
courtesy humanize life in a big city. 禮貌的
行為讓大城市裡的生活充滿了人情味。

husband [ˈhʌzbənd] .... ★★★★★
n. 丈夫

ideal [aɪˈdiəl] .... ★★★★
adj. 理想的，稱心如意的，理想主義的，唯心
論的：This dictionary is ideal—it's exactly
what I needed. 這本辭典很棒，正是我所
需要的。
n. 理想

ignorance [ˈɪgnərəns] .... ★★★★
n. 無知

illiterate [ɪˈlɪtərɪt] .... ★
n. 文盲

illustrious [ɪˈlʌstrɪəs] .... ★
adj. 輝煌的，著名的：Dr. Elizabeth Blackwell,
an illustrious leader in the field of
medicine, founded the Women's Medical
College of the New York Infirmary. 在醫
學界卓有聲望的領導人物伊利莎白‧布拉
克威博士，創建了紐約醫院的女子醫學學
院。

immorality [ˌɪməˈrælətɪ] .... ★★★★★
n. 不道德

immortal [ɪˈmɔrtl̩] .... ★★
adj. 不朽的：The heroes of the people are
immortal. 人民英雄永垂不朽。

innocence [ˈɪnəsn̩s] .... ★★★★
n. 天真，無知

intellectual [ˌɪntl̩ˈɛktʃʊəl] .... ★★★★★
adj. 智力的：intellectual education 智育；
intellectual faculties 智力，智慧；
intellectual work 腦力工作

intelligence [ɪnˈtɛlədʒəns] .... ★★★★★
n. 智力

junior [ˈdʒunjɚ] .... ★★★★
adj. ①年少的，較年幼的：He is junior to me
by three years. 他比我小3歲。②資歷較
淺的，等級較低的：He is junior to me
though he's older. 他雖然比我年長，但級
別比我低。
n. 年少者，等級較低者，晚輩

juvenile [ˈdʒuvənl̩] .... ★
adj. 青少年的：The problem of juvenile
delinquency presented itself for the
attention from the whole society. 少年犯罪
的問題引起了全社會的注意。

layman [ˈlemən] .... ★★★★★
n. 門外漢

male [mel] .... ★★★★★
adj. 男性的，雄性的
n. 男性，雄性

mankind [mænˈkaɪnd] .... ★★★★
n. 人類

masculine [ˈmæskjəlɪn] .... ★
adj. 男性的，具男子氣概的，強壯的：The
opera singer has a deep, booming,
masculine voice. 這位歌劇演唱家有一副
深沉又渾厚有力的嗓音。

master [ˈmæstɚ] .... ★★★★★
n. （男）主人，雇主，大師，(M-)碩士
v. 精通，掌握：It makes many years to
master a new language. 要精通一門新語言
要花多年時間。

mate [met] .... ★★★★
n. 夥伴，配偶

matter [ˈmætɚ] .... ★★★★★
n. 事情，問題
【片語】What's the matter with...? 怎麼了？
出什麼事了？
v. 有關係，要緊：It doesn't matter whether
you come or not. 你來不來都無所謂。

modernization [ˌmɑdɚnəˈzeʃən] ★★★★★
n. 現代化

moral [ˋmɔrəl] .... ★★★★★
adj. 道德（上）的，有道德的：a man of high moral principles 一個有高道德原則的人
n. 寓意

morale [məˋræl] .... ★★★★★
n. 民心，士氣

morality [məˋrælətɪ] .... ★★★★★
n. 道德，美德

morally [ˋmɔrəlɪ] .... ★★★★★
adv. 道德上：What you did wasn't actually against the law, but it was morally wrong. 你所做的事並未真正觸犯法律，但在道義上是錯誤的。

mother [ˋmʌðɚ] .... ★★★★★
n. 母親

name [nem] .... ★★★★★
n. 名字，名稱，名聲，名譽

neighbo(u)r [ˋnebɚ] .... ★★★★
n. 鄰居，鄰接的東西

nephew [ˋnɛfju] .... ★★★★
n. 侄子，外甥

niece [nis] .... ★★★
n. 侄女，外甥女

nominate [ˋnɑməˌnet] .... ★★
v. 任命，具有特定名字的：He was nominated (as) Minister of Finance. 他被任命為財政部長。

noted [ˋnotɪd] .... ★★
adj. 著名的，知名的：The ring-necked pheasant is noted for its brilliant plumage. 頸部有色環的雉雞因其羽毛鮮豔而聞名。

notion [ˋnoʃən] .... ★★★★
n. 概念，意念，看法，觀點

notorious [noˋtorɪəs] .... ★
adj. 惡名昭彰的，聲名狼藉的：In those days everyone in the town was talking about the notorious murderer and his gang. 那些日子裡，鎮上所有的人都在談論那個惡名昭彰的兇手及其匪幫。

novice [ˋnɑvɪs] .... ★
n. 新信徒，生手：a novice at swimming 游泳初學者

oath [oθ] .... ★★
n. 誓言，誓約，宣誓

offspring [ˋɔfˌsprɪŋ] .... ★★
n. 子孫，後代

辨析
Analyze

affair, business, matter

1 **affair** *n.*「事情」，強調行為或過程，其複數形式含有重要事情之意：I'm not interested in other people's private affairs. 我對別人的私事不感興趣。

2 **business** *n.*「事情，生意」，指有責任、義務該做的事情，常表示生意、商務等意思：Keeping the school clean is every student's business. 保持學校清潔是每個學生的職責。

3 **matter** *n.*「事情」，指客觀存在的事物或事情，有時指需考慮或需處理的事物，matter 常用於以下搭配：a matter of opinion（看法不同的問題），in matter of sth（在…問題上），a matter of life and death（生死攸關）。另如：I have several matters on hand to deal with. 我手上有幾件事情要處理。

orphan [ˈɔrfən] .... ★★
n. 孤兒

overbearing [ˈovəˈbɛrɪŋ] .... ★
adj. 傲慢的：an overbearing manner 傲慢的
　　態度

pacific [pəˈsɪfɪk] .... ★★
adj. 太平洋的，和平的，太平的：the pacific
　　relation of the two countries 兩國和平友好
　　關係

parent [ˈpɛrənt] .... ★★★★
n. 父親或母親

patriot [ˈpɛtrɪət] .... ★★
n. 愛國者

patriotic [ˌpɛtrɪˈɑtɪk] .... ★
adj. 愛國的：patriotic oversea Chinese 愛國華
　　僑

pattern [ˈpætən] .... ★★★★
n. 型式，模型，樣式，花樣，圖案

pauper [ˈpɔpə] .... ★
n. 貧民，乞丐：a pauper school 貧民學校

person [ˈpɜsn] .... ★★★★★
n. 人，人身

personnel [ˌpɜsnˈɛl] .... ★★★★
n. 人員，職員：personnel department 人事
　　處／科；personnel director 人事主任；
　　personnel manager 人事經理

phenomenally [fɪˈnɑmənəlɪ] .... ★★★
adv. 顯著地，難以置信地，非凡地：American
　　steel production increased phenomenally
　　right after 1900, from 10 to 25 million
　　tons. 美國的鋼產量在1900年以後顯著地增
　　長，從1,000萬噸增加到2,500萬噸。

phenomenon [fəˈnɑmənɑn] .... ★★★
n. 現象：a social phenomenon 社會現象；the
　　phenomenon of nature 自然現象

populace [ˈpɑpjələs] .... ★★★★★
n. 人口，平民

posterity [pɑsˈtɛrətɪ] .... ★
n. 後代：Everything he writes is consigned to
　　posterity. 他所寫的一切都是為了後代。

prestige [prɛsˈtiʒ] .... ★
n. 威望，聲望

pride [praɪd] .... ★★★★★
n. 自豪，引以自豪的東西，驕傲，傲慢
v. 使自豪，使自誇：Mrs. Jones prided herself
　　on her looking. 瓊斯太太為她自己的容貌感
　　到自豪。

privacy [ˈpraɪvəsɪ] .... ★★★★★
n. 獨處，秘密，隱私

private [ˈpraɪvɪt] .... ★★★★★
adj. ①私人的，個人的：The fields were
　　private property. 那些田地都是私人財產。
　　②秘密的，私下的：a private interview 一
　　次秘密面談

privilege [ˈprɪvlɪdʒ] .... ★★★★
n. 特權

problem [ˈprɑbləm] .... ★★★★★
n. 問題，疑難問題

prophet [ˈprɑfɪt] .... ★★
n. 預言家，先知

prototype [ˈprotəˌtaɪp] .... ★
n. 原型，典型

qualitative [ˈkwɑləˌtetɪv] .... ★
adj. 質的，定性的：qualitative change 質變；
　　qualitative analysis 定性分析；qualitative
　　relation 種別關係

quality [ˈkwɑlətɪ] .... ★★★★★
n. 品質

queen [ˈkwin] .... ★★★
n. 女王，王后

question [ˈkwɛstʃən] .... ★★★★★
n. 問題
【片語】①out of question 毫無疑問②out of
the question 不可能的，辦不到的

condition [kənˈdɪʃən] .... ★★★★★
n. 條件，狀況，健康情形

race [res] .... ★★★★★
n. 種族，人種，種類；比賽，賽跑，競賽，疾行
v. 比賽，賽跑，競賽，疾行：We were racing the sick woman to hospital. 我們急忙把生病的婦人送到醫院。

racial [ˈreʃəl] .... ★★★
adj. 種族的，人種的：racial conflict 種族衝突；racial discrimination 種族歧視

rational [ˈræʃənl] .... ★★★
adj. 合理的：the stage of rational knowledge 理性認知階段

relative [ˈrɛlətɪv] .... ★★★★★
adj. ①關於，與…有關的，有關係的：The facts relative to this problem have been clarified. 與此問題有關的事實已經被澄清了。②(to) 比較的，相對的：They are living in relative comfort. 他們現在過得比較舒適了。
n. 親戚，親屬

reputation [ˌrɛpjəˈteʃən] .... ★★★★
n. 名聲，聲望，名譽：a person of reputation 有信譽的人，體面的人

repute [rɪˈpjut] .... ★
n. 名聲，聲譽
v. 稱為，認為：He is reputed as a good man. 他被公認是個好人。
【片語】be reputed for 以…而著稱；be well/bad reputed 有好／壞名聲

rite [raɪt] .... ★★★★★
n. 宗教儀式：the burial/funeral rites 喪禮

ritual [ˈrɪtʃuəl] .... ★★★★★
n. 儀式，典禮

role [rol] .... ★★★★★
n. 角色，作用，任務

routine [ruˈtin] .... ★★★★
adj. 例行的，常規的：a routine medical treatment 常規療法
n. 例行公事，慣例，慣常的程式：Do it according to routine. 按常規辦事。

scandal [ˈskændl] .... ★★★
n. 醜聞

辨析
Analyze

issue, matter, problem, question

1 **issue** n.「問題，爭論點；發行，（報刊的）一期；分發，流出」，一般指討論到或涉及到的問題：They are debating an issue raised by the workers. 他們正在討論工人們提出的問題。

2 **matter** n.「事情，問題，情況；物質，物品」，泛指各種問題、事情：They talked of other matters for a while. 他們談論了一會兒其他事情／問題。

3 **problem** n.「問題，疑難問題；思考題，討論題」，多指需要解決的問題或困難：Tom told me how to tackle the problem. 湯姆告訴我如何處理這個問題。

4 **question** n.「問題；疑問，不確定；難題，需討論或考慮的問題」，用法較廣，多指需要回答的問題：May I ask you a question? 我可以問你一個問題嗎？

Discipline 學科（學術）名詞總匯

secretarial [ˌsɛkrəˈtɛrɪəl] .... ★★★★★
adj. 秘書的，書記的：the secretarial staff 秘書處

sensible [ˈsɛnsəbl] .... ★★★★
adj. 理智的，明顯的，感覺得到的：If you are sensible, you will study for another year. 如果你明智的話，你就再學習一年。

significant [sɪgˈnɪfəkənt] .... ★★★★★
adj. 有意義的，重要的：a significant speech 意味深長的演講

situation [ˌsɪtʃuˈeʃən] .... ★★★★★
n. ①形勢，局面，環境，狀況：the economic situation 經濟形勢②位置，地點：the situation of the city 城市的位置

slave [slev] .... ★★★★★
n. 奴隸，苦工

slavery [ˈslevərɪ] .... ★★
n. 奴役，奴隸制

slogan [ˈslogən] .... ★
n. 口號，標語：chant slogans 喊口號

sociable [ˈsoʃəbl] .... ★★★★★
adj. 友善的，好交際的：The Smiths are a sociable family. 史密斯一家人善於交際。

social [ˈsoʃəl] .... ★★★★★
adj. ①社會的：a particular culture and social structure 一種獨特的文化及社會結構②交際的，社交的：social occasion 社交場合

society [səˈsaɪətɪ] .... ★★★★★
n. 社會，社會團體，協會，社

soul [sol] .... ★★★★★
n. 靈魂，心靈

spouse [spauz] .... ★★★★★
n. 配偶

status [ˈstetəs] .... ★★★★
n. 狀況，地位

stereotyped [ˈstɛrɪəˌtaɪpt] .... ★
adj. 已成陳規的，對…有成見的

subject [ˈsʌbdʒɪkt] .... ★★★★★
n. 學科，科目，主語

subsist [səbˈsɪst] .... ★★★★★
v. 生存：He subsisted on one meal a day. 他每天只吃一頓飯。

supreme [səˈprim] .... ★★★★
adj. 至高的：The most important law court is called the Supreme Court. 最重要的法院叫做最高法院。

supremely [suˈprimlɪ] .... ★★★★
adv. 最高地，天上地，極度地，最重要地

symbol [ˈsɪmbl] .... ★★★★
n. 符號：phonetic symbols 注音符號

system [ˈsɪstəm] .... ★★★★★
n. 系統，體制，體系，制度

systematic [ˌsɪstəˈmætɪk] .... ★★★
adj. （有）系統的，（有）體系的

systematize [ˈsɪstəmətaɪz] .... ★★★
v. 使系統化，使成體系：The aim of science is surely to amass and systematize knowledge. 科學的目的當然是為了積累科學並使之系統化。

state [stet] .... ★★★★★
n. 狀態，情況，國家（側重政治方面），州

taboo [təˈbu] .... ★★★★★
n. 禁忌，禁止

theorem [ˈθiərəm] .... ★
n. 定理，原理

theoretical [ˌθiəˈrɛtɪkl] .... ★★★
adj. 理論的：theoretical linguistics 理論語言學

theory [ˈθiərɪ] .... ★★★★★
n. 理論，原理，學說，理論

thesis [ˈθisɪs] .... ★★
n. 學位論文

thing [θɪŋ] .... ★★★★★
n. 事，東西，（個人的）物品，用品

token [ˋtokən] .... ★★
n. 象徵，標誌，代用貨幣

trait [tret] .... ★★
n. 特性，特點

trappings [ˋtræpɪŋz] .... ★★★★
n. 外部標誌

tribal [traɪbl] .... ★★★★★
adj. 部落的，宗族的

tribe [traɪb] .... ★★★★★
n. 部落，宗族

tribute [ˋtrɪbjut] .... ★★
n. 頌詞，貢獻，貢物

truth [truθ] .... ★★★★★
n. 真相，實情，真實性，忠實性，真理
【片語】in truth 其實，實際，的確

truthfully [ˋtruθfəlɪ] .... ★★★★★
adv. 真實地，如實地

unit [ˋjunɪt] .... ★★★★★
n. ①單元，單位：The family is the smallest
social unit. 家庭是最小的社會單位。②部
件，零件，裝置

venerate [ˋvɛnəˌret] .... ★
v. 敬仰，崇拜：In China, people venerate
their ancestors. 在中國，人們敬拜他們的祖
先。

virgin [ˋvɝdʒɪn] .... ★★
adj. 處女的，未開墾的
n. 處女

virtually [ˋvɝtʃʊəlɪ] .... ★★★
adv. 幾乎：Deserts, arid areas with virtually
no vegetation, cover more than one third
of the Earth's land surface. 沙漠，那幾乎
沒有植被的貧瘠土地，覆蓋了超過三分之
一的地球陸地表面。

辨析 Analyze

case, circumstance, condition, situation, state

1 **case** n. 「事例，實例；情況，事實；病
例；案件」：If that's the case, we will
have to work another five days. 如果真是
那樣，我們得再工作五天才行。

2 **circumstance** n. 「環境，條件，形勢；
(pl.)境況，經濟狀況」，多用複數：under
such circumstances 在這種情況下；
Circumstances forced the enemy to sign
the ceasefire agreement. 形勢迫使敵人
簽署停火協議。

3 **condition** n. 「狀態，狀況；(pl.)環境，
形勢；條件，前提」，常指工作條件或生
活條件：The astronauts must get used to
the condition of weightlessness in space.
太空人必須適應太空中的無重力狀態。

4 **situation** n. 「形勢，環境，狀況」，尤
其指一段時期的事態：I found myself in
a financially difficult situation which was
worse than ever before. 我發覺自己陷入
了人生中最糟糕的經濟困境。

5 **state** n. 「狀態，情況」，強調某一時
刻正處於某一狀況或正經歷某事：The
American government proclaimed a state
of emergency. 美國政府宣佈了緊急狀
態。

virtue [ˈvɝtʃu] .... ★★★★★
n. 美德

virtuous [ˈvɝtʃʊəs] .... ★★★★★
adj. 貞潔的：a virtuous woman 貞潔的女子。

vital [ˈvaɪtl̩] .... ★★★★
adj. 極重要的，生命的，充滿活力的，致命
　　的：a vital examination 至關重要的考試。

vitally [ˈvaɪtl̩ɪ] .... ★★★★
adv. 極度，非常，致命地：vitally important 極
　　為重要

vocation [voˈkeʃən] .... ★
n. 職業，行業：agricultural vocations 農務

welfare [ˈwɛlˌfɛr] .... ★★★★
n. 福利：a welfare hotel 福利旅館；welfare
　　families 福利家庭

whim [hwɪm] .... ★
n. 奇想：governed by whim 由衝動支配

widow [ˈwɪdo] .... ★★★★
n. 遺孀，寡婦

widower [ˈwɪdoɚ] .... ★★★★
n. 鰥夫

worldly [ˈwɝldlɪ] .... ★★★★
adj. 現世的，世俗的：You must leave your
　　worldly goods behind you when you go to
　　meet your Maker. 當你去見上帝時，必須
　　捨棄世俗的財產。

young [jʌŋ] .... ★★★★★
adj. 年輕的，年幼的：Listen to me, young
　　lady. 小姐，聽我說。

youngster [ˈjʌŋstɚ] .... ★★★
n. 兒童，少年

08

醫學相關辭彙

Discipline

Vocabulary of Medicine

abortive [əˋbɔrtɪv] .... ★★
adj. 失敗的：We had to abandon our abortive attempts. 我們不得不放棄流產的打算。

ambulance [ˋæmbjələns] .... ★★★
n. 救護車

ankle [ˋæŋkl] .... ★★★
n. 踝，踝節部

antiseptic [͵æntəˋsɛptɪk] .... ★
adj. 防腐的，殺菌的：It is advisable to apply an antiseptic to any wound, no matter how slight or insignificant. 不管傷口是多麼的微不足道，最好還是在上面擦消毒藥品。

arm [ɑrm] .... ★★★★★
n. 手臂，胳膊，臂狀物：She was carrying her son in her arms. 她懷中正抱著兒子。
【片語】①in one's arms 抱著②on one's arm 掛在手臂上③under one's arm 手臂夾著

artery [ˋɑrtərɪ] .... ★
n. ①動脈：central artery 中央動脈 ②幹線，要道：main artery 主要幹線

backbone [ˋbækͺbon] .... ★★★★★
n. （人等的）脊骨，脊柱，（團體等的）支柱，中堅

bandage [ˋbændɪdʒ] .... ★
n. 繃帶
v. 包紮：The surgeon bandaged up his injured head. 外科醫生把他受傷的頭部包紮起來。

beard [bɪrd] .... ★★★★
n. 鬍鬚

birth [bɝθ] .... ★★★★★
n. 出生，分娩，出身，血統

bladder [ˋblædɚ] .... ★
n. 膀胱

blind [blaɪnd] .... ★★
adj. ①瞎的，失明的：He is blind in his left eye. 他左眼失明。②盲目的：Love is blind. 愛是盲目的。
【片語】go blind 失明

v. ①使失明：He was blinded in the war. 他在戰爭中失明了。②矇蔽：His admiration for her beauty blinded him to her faults. 他對她的傾慕使他看不見她有缺點。

blood [blʌd] .... ★★★★
n. ①血，血液②血統，宗族，門第：He is of Indian blood. 他有印第安血統。③血氣，氣質

bloodshot [ˋblʌdˏʃɑt] .... ★★★★
adj. （眼睛）充血的

body [ˋbɑdɪ] .... ★★
n. 身體，軀體

bone [bon] .... ★★★★★
n. 骨，骨骼

born [bɔrn] .... ★★★★★
adj. ①出生的，產生的：a Chinese-born American scientist 美籍華裔科學家②天生的：a born poet 天生的詩人

brain [bren] .... ★★★★★
n. ①腦，腦髓：an electronic brain 電腦②腦袋，智力：Use your brain and you will have a method. 動動腦筋，你會有辦法的。

breast [brɛst] .... ★★★★★
n. 乳房，胸部

bruise [bruz] .... ★
n. 瘀傷
v. 打傷，擦傷（水果、植物等），碰損：She bruised her knee. 她的膝蓋擦傷了。

capillary [ˋkæplˏɛrɪ] .... ★
n. 毛細管：capillary attraction 毛細管引力

capsule [ˋkæpsl̩] .... ★
n. 膠囊，密封艙

carnal [ˋkɑrnl̩] .... ★
adj. 肉體的：Gluttony and drunkenness have been called carnal vices. 貪食嗜酒已被稱為肉體上的罪惡。

chamber [ˋtʃembɚ] .... ★★★★★
n. 房間，室

cheek [tʃik] .... ★★★★★
n. 面頰，臉蛋

chest [tʃɛst] .... ★★★★
n. 櫃子，櫥，胸腔，胸脯：a tool chest 一個工具箱

choke [tʃok] .... ★★★
v. 使窒息：The smoke from the stove almost choked me. 爐子裡冒出的煙嗆得我幾乎透不過氣來。

chronic [ˋkrɑnɪk] .... ★★★★★
adj. 長期的，慢性的：a chronic complainer 常抱怨的人

clinic [ˋklɪnɪk] ....★
n. 門診所

clinical [ˋklɪnɪkl̩] ....★
adj. ①臨床的，臨診的②（感情、態度等）冷靜的，不偏不倚的；分析的

clot [klɑt] ....★
n. 凝塊：a clot of automobiles blocking the tunnel's entrance 密集的車輛堵塞了隧道的入口。
v. 凝塊：Perspiration clotted his hair. 汗水使他的頭髮黏在一起。

contagious [kənˋtedʒəs] .... ★★★★★
adj. 傳染的： Stayed at home, until he was no longer contagious. 待在家裡，直到他不再帶傳染原。

corpse [kɔrps] .... ★★
n. 屍體：corpse candle (light) 點在屍體旁邊的蠟燭，預兆死亡的鬼火

corpulent [ˋkɔrpjələnt] .... ★
adj. 肥胖的

cough [kɔf] .... ★★★
n. 咳嗽：have a bad cough 咳得很厲害
v. 咳嗽：He coughed very hard. 他咳得很厲害。

cripple [ˋkrɪpl̩] .... ★★★
n. 跛子，殘疾者：cannot race a horse that is a cripple 不能用一匹跛足的馬進行賽馬

v. 使殘疾，使跛：She was crippled in the car accident. 她在車禍時把腿傷成了殘廢。

cure [kjʊr] .... ★★★★
v. 矯正，糾正，治癒
n. 治癒，醫治，療法，良藥，措施

cyborg [ˈsaɪbɔrg] .... ★
n. 靠機器裝置維持生命的人（如太空人）：military cyborg 軍用生控體

deafen [ˈdɛfn̩] .... ★
v. 震聾：This noise will deafen us all! 這種噪音將使我們什麼也聽不見！

deafness [ˈdɛfnɪs] .... ★★★
n. 耳聾，聾度

dental [ˈdɛntl̩] .... ★★★
adj. 牙科的，牙醫的：The interns spent the first month in the dental ward. 實習醫生第一個月在牙科病房實習。

dentist [ˈdɛntɪst] .... ★
n. 牙醫

diagnose [ˈdaɪəgnoz] .... ★
v. 診斷，分析：Before social inequality can be alleviated, its principal causes must be diagnosed. 在社會不平等得到解決之前，其主要起因需要被分析。

diagnosis [ˌdaɪəgˈnosɪs] .... ★
n. 診斷

digest [daɪˈdʒɛst] .... ★★★★
v. 消化，領會：Cheese is believed to digest everything except itself. 乾酪據說有助於消化除它本身之外的其他食物。
n. 摘要

digestive [dəˈdʒɛstɪv] .... ★★★★
adj. 消化的：digestive power 消化力；digestive juice 消化液

disease [dɪˈziz] .... ★★★★★
n. 病，疾病

dispense [dɪˈspɛns] .... ★★★★★
v. 分配，發放，廢除：a country that has dispensed with tariff barriers 已廢除關稅壁壘的國家。

dissect [dɪˈsɛkt] .... ★
v. 解剖，詳細研究：They dissected the plan afterward to learn why it failed 他們事後仔細分析那項計畫，以便了解它為何失敗。

dizzy [ˈdɪzɪ] .... ★
adj. 眩暈，頭暈眼花：a dizzy height 令人眩暈的高度；be/feel dizzy 感到頭暈目眩；dizzy and exuberant rhetoric 令人昏亂、華而不實的言辭

dose [dos] .... ★★★
n. 劑量，一服，一劑

drug [drʌg] .... ★★★★★
n. 藥品，藥，麻醉品，毒品
v. 摻麻藥，下麻藥：His wine had been drugged, and they stole his money while he was sleeping heavily. 他的酒被人下了麻醉藥，他們趁他沉睡時偷走了他的錢。

dumb [dʌm] .... ★★★
adj. 啞的，無言的：I was dumb with unbelief. 我難以置信，一時說不上話來。

ear [ɪr] .... ★★★★★
n. 耳朵：Walls have ears. 隔牆有耳。

enzyme [ˈɛnzaɪm] .... ★
n. 酶

epidemic [ˌɛpɪˈdɛmɪk] .... ★
n. 流行病

eye [aɪ] .... ★★★★★
n. 眼睛，眼光，眼力

eyesight [ˈaɪˌsaɪt] .... ★★★
n. 視力

face [fes] .... ★★★★★
n. 臉，面貌
【片語】①make a face 做鬼臉②face to face 面對面地

v. 面對著：He faced her and made a face. 他對著她，做了一個鬼臉。

facial [ˈfeʃəl] .... ★★★★★
adj. 面部的：facial expressions 面部表情

fat [fæt] .... ★★★★★
adj. 肥胖的：a fat baby 胖胖的嬰孩
n. 脂肪，肥肉：Give me lean meat please, I don't like fat. 請給我瘦肉，我不喜歡肥肉。

fester [ˈfɛstə] .... ★
v. 化膿：A dirty wound will probably fester. 一個弄髒了的傷口，可能會化膿。

feverish [ˈfivərɪʃ] .... ★★★★
adj. 發燒的：feverish activities 瘋狂的活動

fidget [ˈfɪdʒɪt] .... ★
v. 坐立不安，動個不停：He fidgeted with his notes while lecturing. 他在教課時不停地擺弄稿子。

fist [fɪst] .... ★★★
n. 拳頭

flank [flæŋk] .... ★★
n. 脅，側面

flush [flʌʃ] .... ★★
v. 沖洗
n. 臉紅

foot [fʊt] .... ★★★★★
n. 腳，足，英尺
【片語】on foot 步行，著手進行

football [ˈfʊtˌbɔl] .... ★★★★★
n. 足球：football season 足球賽季

footprint [ˈfʊtˌprɪnt] .... ★★★★★
n. 腳印，足跡

gash [gæʃ] .... ★
n. 深的切口

hair [hɛr] .... ★★★★★
n. 頭髮，毛髮，汗毛

haircut [ˈhɛrˌkʌt] .... ★
n. 理髮

hairy [ˈhɛrɪ] .... ★★★★★
adj. （多）毛的：a hairy caterpillar. 一條毛茸茸的毛毛蟲。

hand [hænd] .... ★★★★★
n. 手，指針
【片語】hand in 交出，遞交

hand-crank [ˈhændˌkræŋk] .... ★
n. 手搖曲柄

handful [ˈhændfəl] .... ★★★
n. ①一把，一撮：a handful of beans 一把豆子 ②少數

handicraft [ˈhændɪˌkræft] .... ★★★★★
n. 手工藝（品）：artistic handicrafts 工藝品

handily [ˈhændɪlɪ] .... ★★★
adv. 便利地，靈巧地

handkerchief [ˈhæŋkətʃɪf] .... ★★
n. 手帕

handle [ˈhændl̩] .... ★★★★★
n. 把手，拉手
v. 處理，操縱：Clerks handle most routine office jobs. 辦事員處理辦公室主要的日常工作。

handler [ˈhændlə] .... ★★★★★
n. 管理者：the candidate's campaign handlers 候選人的競選操盤者

handy [ˈhændɪ] .... ★★★
adj. 方便的，靈巧的：a handy reference book 一本簡易參考書

head [hɛd] .... ★★★★★
n. 頭
v. 向某處去：Like most migratory birds, warblers head south in the fall. 鳴鳥就像絕大多數的候鳥一樣，在秋天會向南方飛。

headache [ˈhɛdˌek] .... ★★★
n. 頭痛

heal [hil] .... ★★★★
v. 治癒，使和解
n. 痊癒

health [hɛlθ] .... ★★★★★
n. ①健康，健康狀況：Fresh air and enough exercises are good for the health. 新鮮的空氣和足夠的運動有益於健康。②衛生：the World Health Organization 世界衛生組織

healthful [ˈhɛlθfəl] .... ★★★★★
adj. 有益健康的：a healthful diet 保健飲食

healthy [ˈhɛlθɪ] .... ★★★★
adj. 健康的，健壯的：You must look after yourself and keep healthy. 你要照顧好自己，保持健康。

heart [hɑrt] .... ★★★★★
n. 心，心臟：She hugged the child to her heart. 她把孩子摟到懷裡。
【片語】get/learn sth. by heart 記住，背誦

heartily [ˈhɑrtɪlɪ] .... ★★
adv. 衷心地，熱心地：She greeted us heartily. 她親熱地和我們打招呼。

hearty [ˈhɑrtɪ] .... ★★
adj. 衷心的，熱誠的，豐盛的：a hearty welcome 熱誠的歡迎

heel [hil] .... ★★★★
n. 腳跟，鞋跟

hip [hɪp] .... ★★★
n. 臀部，胯部

hoarse [hors] .... ★
adj. 嘶啞的：His voice was hoarse after talking for an hour. 他講了一個小時的話後，聲音啞了。

hospitable [ˈhɑspɪtəbl] .... ★★★★★
adj. 好客的：The hospitable host had his spare room emptied very quickly for the honored guest. 好客的主人很快為貴賓騰空了閒置著的房間。

hospital [ˈhɑspɪtl] .... ★★★★★
n. 醫院：be in hospital 在住院

idiocy [ˈɪdɪəsɪ] .... ★
n. 白癡：amaurotic idiocy 黑矇性白癡

ill [ɪl] .... ★★★★★
adj. 有病的，不健康的：She is ill and keeps his bed. 她生了病，佔用他的床。

illness [ˈɪlnɪs] .... ★★★★★
n. 病，疾病：a serious illness 重病；She is recovering after a long illness. 她久病之後正逐漸康復。

immunity [ɪˈmjunətɪ] .... ★★★★★
n. 免疫系統

inborn [ɪnˈbɔrn] .... ★★★★★
adj. 天生的：Psychologists still wonder if some personality traits are inborn. 心理學家對「某些個人特質是天生的」這種說法表示懷疑。

infancy [ˈɪnfənsɪ] .... ★★★★★
n. 初期，嬰兒期

infant [ˈɪnfənt] .... ★★★★
n. 嬰兒，幼兒

辨析
Analyze

disease, illness

1 **disease** n. 「病，疾病」，指從醫學角度看具體的某一種疾病：He suffered from several diseases. 他身患多種疾病。

2 **illness** n. 「病，疾病」，指生病，強調人患病的狀態、某人的病：His illness was caused by several diseases. 他的病是由多種疾病引起的。

infect [ɪnˈfɛkt] .... ★★★
v. 傳染，感染：She infected the whole class with her laughter. 她的笑聲感染了全班同學。

infectious [ɪnˈfɛkʃəs] .... ★
adj. 傳染的，感染性的：Infectious diseases may be spread by viruses and bacteria. 傳染性疾病可以通過病毒及細菌傳播。

inject [ɪnˈdʒɛkt] .... ★
v. 注射，注入：inject penicillin 注射青黴素；inject a remark into the conversation 在談話中插入一句話，插嘴。

injection [ɪnˈdʒɛkʃən] .... ★★★
n. 注射，注入，噴射：hypodermic injection 皮下注射

innate [ˈɪnˈet] .... ★★★★★
adj. 天生的：Correct ideas are not innate in the mind, but come from social practice. 正確的思想不是頭腦中固有的，而是來自於社會實踐。

jaw [dʒɔ] .... ★★★★
n. 頜，顎

kidney [ˈkɪdnɪ] .... ★
n. 腎，腎臟：kidney basin 腰盤

knee [ni] .... ★★★★★
n. 膝，膝蓋

lame [lem] .... ★
adj. ①跛的，殘廢的：That illness left her permanently lame. 那場大病給她留下了永久性的殘疾。②站不住腳的，差勁的，蹩腳的：I don't believe his story, it sound a bit lame. 我不相信他的話，聽起來靠不住。

lap [læp] .... ★★★★
n. 膝部，（跑道的）一圈

leg [lɛg] .... ★★★★★
n. 腿：front legs 前腿

limb [lɪm] .... ★★★★
n. 肢，手足，翼，大樹枝

limp [lɪmp] .... ★★★
v. 蹣跚，瘸著走：He limped off the football field. 他一瘸一拐地走出足球場。

lip [lɪp] .... ★★★★★
n. 嘴唇

lipstick [ˈlɪpˌstɪk] .... ★
n. 口紅，唇膏

lung [lʌŋ] .... ★★★
n. 肺：an iron lung 鐵肺，人工呼吸器

辨析 Analyze

cripple, lame, limp

1 **cripple** *n. & vt.* 「跛子，傷殘人(或動物)；使跛；使受傷殘；使陷於癱瘓」：The accident crippled him for life. 這次事故使他終身殘疾。

2 **lame** *a.* 「跛的，瘸的」，還指「蹩腳的」：The lame man needs a stick when he walks. 這位腿瘸的人走路時需要拐杖。

3 **limp** *vi.* 「一瘸一拐地走，蹣跚」；當形容詞意為「軟弱的，無生氣的，無精神的」：The injured player limped off the pitch. 這個受傷的球員一瘸一拐地走出了球場。

mad [mæd] .... ★★★★★

adj. ①發瘋的，瘋狂的：She was almost mad with grief. 她傷心得幾乎發瘋了。②惱火的，狂怒的：The boss got mad at me because I was late again. 我又遲到了，老闆對我很惱火。③狂熱的，著迷的：These boys are mad about football. 這些孩子對足球很著迷。

malady [ˈmælədɪ] ....★

n. 疾病：an incurable malady 不治之病；a social malady 社會上的歪風

medical [ˈmɛdɪkl] .... ★★★★★

adj. 醫學的，醫療的，內科的：The soldiers at the front were in great need of medical care. 前線的士兵特別需要醫療照顧。

medicate [ˈmɛdɪˌket] ....★

vt. ①用藥治療②用藥（劑）浸③加藥物於

medicine [ˈmɛdəsn̩] .... ★★★★★

n. 內服藥，醫藥

mental [ˈmɛntl̩] .... ★★★★

adj. 思想的，精神的，腦力的，智力的，精神病的：a mental test智力測驗；mental deficiency 智力不足

mentality [mɛnˈtælətɪ] .... ★★★★

n. 心理，精神

morbid [ˈmɔrbɪd] ....★

adj. 病態的，不健康的：a morbid state 病態；morbid anatomy 病理解剖學

mouth [maʊθ] .... ★★★★★

n. 口，口狀物：The mouth of a cave 山洞入口處

mouthful [ˈmaʊθfəl] .... ★★★

n. 一口，少量：There was only a mouthful of food left in the house. 家裡剩下的糧食不多了。

mummy [ˈmʌmɪ] .... ★★★★★

n. 〔美口〕媽媽

muscular [ˈmʌskjələ] ....★

adj. 肌肉的，肌肉發達的，強健的：a muscular body肌肉發達的身體；The player's big and muscular. 這個運動員長得魁梧強壯。

mute [mjut] .... ★★

adj. 深默的，無聲的：keep mute 保持沈默；mute thanks 無言的感謝

辨析
Analyze

crazy, insane, mad

1　**crazy** *a.* 「荒唐的，古怪的，發瘋的」，口頭用語；「be crazy about」則指「狂熱愛好的，著迷的」：After his wife deserted him, he went crazy. 他在被被妻子拋棄之後，就瘋了。

2　**insane** *a.* 「（患）神經病的，精神失常的，瘋狂的」，醫學用語；日常口語中也可以表示「蠢極的，荒唐的」：When people are insane, they are put away in mental hospitals to be cured. 人們患了精神病後，就被送進精神病院治療。

3　**mad** *a.* 「瘋的，神經錯亂的；惱火的，狂怒的；狂熱的，著迷的；愚蠢的，瘋狂的」，指失去自控、失去理智，常用語，用法較廣；指狂熱行為時mad與crazy可以互換：I am afraid of mad people. 我害怕瘋子。

nail [nel] .... ★ ★ ★
n. 釘，指甲，爪
v. 釘，釘住：He hammered a nail into the wall and hung a picture on it. 他把釘子釘進牆，然後把畫掛在上面。

neck [nɛk] .... ★ ★ ★ ★
n. 頸，脖子

nervous [ˈnɝvəs] .... ★ ★ ★ ★
adj. 神經的，易激動的：When she came to see the interviewer, Jone was nervous at first but soon composed herself. 瓊會見面試官時起初很緊張，但很快就鎮定下來了。

nose [noz] .... ★ ★ ★ ★ ★
n. 鼻子

numb [nʌm] .... ★
adj. 麻木的：How can you be so numb, don't you see he is bleeding? 你怎麼會這麼麻木？難道看不見他在流血嗎？

nurse [nɝs] .... ★ ★ ★ ★ ★
n. 護士，保育員：a hospital nurse 醫院的護士；a wet nurse 奶媽

nursery [ˈnɝsərɪ] .... ★ ★ ★
n. 托兒所，保育室，苗圃，繁殖場

opium [ˈopjəm] .... ★
n. 鴉片：opium den 鴉片窯，鴉片煙館；opium eating/smoking 吸鴉片；Opium War 鴉片戰爭(1839-1842)

organ [ˈɔrgən] .... ★ ★ ★ ★
n. 器官，風琴，發音器官

organic [ɔrˈgænɪk] .... ★ ★ ★
adj. 器官的，有機的，有機物的：an organic whole 有機的整體

pain [pen] .... ★ ★ ★ ★ ★
n. ①疼痛，痛苦：I have a pain in my leg. 我的腿很痛。②努力，勞苦：She has taken great pains to do this. 她為此煞費苦心。

painstaking [ˈpenzˌtekɪŋ] .... ★
n. 辛勞

adj. 勞苦的：be painstaking with one's work 辛勤地工作

pale [pel] .... ★ ★ ★ ★ ★
adj. ①蒼白的，灰白的：You're looking pale today. 你今天臉色不好。②淺色的，淡的：pale blue 淺藍色

palm [pɑm] .... ★ ★ ★ ★
n. 手掌，棕櫚樹：He put the insect on the palm of his hand. 他把昆蟲放在他的手掌上。

paw [pɔ] .... ★ ★ ★
n. 爪：in the lions paws 在致命的危險中；under the cat's paw〔口〕怕老婆，懼內

penicillin [ˌpɛnɪˈsɪlɪn] .... ★
n. 青黴素

perspiration [ˌpɝspəˈreʃən] .... ★
n. 出汗，汗

physical [ˈfɪzɪkl] .... ★ ★ ★ ★ ★
adj. ①身體的，肉體的：He never used physical punishment in me. 他從不對我進行體罰。②物理的，物理學的：This is one of basic physical laws. 這是一項物理學的基本定律。③物質的，有形的：Please give an opportunity for children to look at the physical world around them. 請給孩子們觀察周圍物理世界的機會。

physician [fɪˈzɪʃən] .... ★ ★ ★ ★
n. 內科醫生

physiology [ˌfɪzɪˈɑlədʒɪ] .... ★ ★ ★ ★ ★
n. 生理學：human physiology 人體生理學

pill [pɪl] .... ★ ★ ★
n. 藥丸

plague [pleg] .... ★ ★
n. 疫病，災禍
v. 使苦惱：We are plagued by a gnawing question. 我們被這個棘手的問題所困擾。

pore [por] .... ★
n. 毛孔

pregnant [ˈprɛɡnənt] .... ★★★
adj. 懷孕的，孕育的：A woman is pregnant for nine months before a child is born. 在小孩出生前，婦女要懷胎九個月。

premature [ˌpriməˈtjʊr] .... ★★★
adj. ①比預期（或正常）時間早：a premature baby 早產兒 ②（做法等）不成熟的，倉促的：a premature opinion 未成熟的意見

prescribe [priˈskraɪb] .... ★★★
v. 處方，開（藥），規定，指示：Weight lifting is the gymnastic sport of lifting weights in a prescribed manner. 舉重是一項以規定的動作把啞鈴舉起來的體育運動。

prescription [priˈskrɪpʃən] .... ★
n. 指示，藥方

psychiatry [saɪˈkaɪətrɪ] .... ★
n. 精神病學：psychiatry phenomena 心理現象

psychological [ˌsaɪkəˈlɑdʒɪkl̩] .... ★★
adj. 心理（上）的，心理學的

psychologist [saɪˈkɑlədʒɪst] .... ★★
n. 心理學者

psychology [saɪˈkɑlədʒɪ] .... ★★
n. 心理學，心理

psychosomatic [ˌsaɪkosoˈmætɪk] .... ★
adj. 身心相關的：psychosomatic medicine 身心醫學

pulse [pʌls] .... ★★★
n. 脈搏，脈衝
v. 搏動，跳動：He could feel the blood pulsing through his body. 他能感覺到渾身的血液在奔騰。

remedy [ˈrɛmədɪ] .... ★★★★
n. 治療法，藥物
v. 治療：Hundreds of years ago cloves were used to remedy headaches. 幾百年前，人們用丁香來治療頭痛。

retina [ˈrɛtɪnə] .... ★
n. 視網膜

辨析
Analyze

cure, heal, remedy, treat

1　**cure** vt. 「治癒，治好；消除，矯正」，指治癒疾病，強調治療的結果，固定句型有 cure sb. of sth.（治好的…病／根除…的…）：This medicine will cure (you of) your cold. 這種藥將會治好你的感冒。

2　**heal** vt. vi. 「使癒合，治癒，使康復；癒合，痊癒，恢復健康」，尤指治好外傷，也可指治癒精神創傷，還指「調停（爭吵等），消除（分歧等）」：It is an everlasting pain in you, a wound that does not heal. 它是你內心永遠的痛，是無法治癒的創傷。

3　**remedy** vt. 「醫治，治療」，指補救或矯正：Those pills will do nothing to remedy your poor eyesight. 這些藥對於你矯正視力沒有什麼作用。

4　**treat** vt. 「對待，處理；醫療，治療；款待，招待」，指治療的過程或動作，而不是結果：The dentist is treating (me for) my tooth. 牙醫在為我治療牙齒。

Discipline 學科（學術）名稱總匯

rib [rɪb] .... ★★★
n. 肋骨，肋狀物：the rib of an umbrella 傘骨

sanity [ˋsænətɪ] .... ★
n. 神智清楚

shoulder [ˋʃoldɚ] .... ★★★★
n. 肩部
v. 肩負，承擔：Many of us would rather someone else shouldered the responsibility. 我們許多人都寧可由別人來承擔責任。

sick [sɪk] .... ★★★★★
adj. ①有病的，患病的：She is taking care of her sick father. 她在照料生病的父親。② 噁心的，想吐的：I always feel sick when I travel by ship. 我坐船旅行時總感到噁心。
【片語】be sick of 厭惡…

sicken [ˋsɪkən] .... ★★★★
v. 使厭倦，使作嘔：sicken at the sight of blood 看見血就要嘔吐

skeleton [ˋskɛlətn].......................... ★★
n. 骨骼，骨架：a skeleton crew 基本成員

skin [skɪn] .... ★★★★★
n. 皮（膚），獸皮，毛皮

smother [ˋsmʌðɚ] .... ★
v. 使窒息，悶死：Don't put that cloth over the baby's face, you'll smother him! 不要把那塊布蓋在嬰兒的臉上，你會把他悶死的！

sneeze [sniz] .... ★
vi. 打噴嚏：The dust made him sneeze. 灰塵使他打了個噴嚏。

spew [spju] .... ★
v. 嘔吐：a volcano that spewed molten lava 噴出大量熔岩的火山

spine [spaɪn] .... ★
n. 脊骨

sterile [ˋstɛrəl] .... ★
adj. 貧瘠的，不育的，消毒的：sterile land 貧瘠的土地；a sterile operating area 無菌手術區；sterile instruments 無菌器材

stodgy [ˋstɑdʒɪ] .... ★
adj. 難消化的，軀體笨重的：stodgy food 不易消化的食物

stomach [ˋstʌmək] .... ★★★★
n. 胃，胃口

stout [staut] .... ★★
adj. 矮胖的，堅固的：He has a stout makeup. 他體格強壯。

辨析 Analyze

ill, sick

1 **ill** *a.*「有病的」，此意只能做表語而不能做定語；還指「壞的，不好的，惡劣的，惡意的」，此意只能做定語而不能做表語：ill temper/luck/consequences/name/comments 壞脾氣／壞運氣／不好的後果／壞名聲／惡毒評論；He looked worried and ill. 他看上去焦慮而且身體不好。

2 **sick** *a.*「有病的」，做表語或定語皆可，也指「噁心的、想吐的」，還指「厭煩的、厭惡的」：Robert's wife was sick with a cold. 羅伯特的妻子因感冒生病了。

succumb [sə`kʌm] ....★

v. 屈服：In Nathaniel Hawthorne's *The Scarlet Letter*, Reverend Dimmesdale succumbed to Hester's charms. 在霍桑的《紅字》中，丁梅斯戴爾被赫斯特所迷住。

surgeon [`sɝdʒən] ....★★★

n. 外科醫生

surgery [`sɝdʒərɪ] ....★★★

n. 外科，外科手術

susceptible [sə`sɛptəbl] ....★

adj. 易受感染的：be susceptible to cold 容易感冒

swell [swɛl] ....★★★★

v. 膨脹：A bee has stung my hand and it is swelling up. 一隻蜜蜂螫了我的手，手腫了起來。

symptom [`sɪmptəm] ....★★★

n. 症狀，徵候，徵兆

syndrome [`sɪn‚drom] ....★★★

n. ①綜合病徵，綜合症狀②在某條件下有共同特徵的一系列言論、事件、行動等

tablet [`tæblɪt] ....★

n. 片，藥片，碑，匾：a sleeping tablet 一片安眠藥

tail [tel] ....★★★★

n. 尾巴，後部，尾部

thermometer [θɚ`mɑmətɚ] ....★

n. 溫度計

throat [θrot] ....★★★★

n. 咽喉，噪音

thumb [θʌm] ....★★★

n. (大) 拇指：Jack pressed his thumb on the book. 傑克把姆指按在書上。

tiptoe [`tɪp‚to] ....★★★★★

n. 腳趾尖

v. 踮著腳走：I tiptoed past the sleeping child. 我踮著腳從睡著的孩子旁邊走過。

toe [to] .... ★★★

n. 腳趾，足尖：I stumped my toe against a stone. 我的腳趾在石頭上絆了一下。

tongue [tʌŋ] ....★★★★★

n. 舌，舌頭，語言

tooth [tuθ] ....★★★★★

n. 牙齒

tremble [`trɛmbl] ....★★★★★

v. ①顫抖，抖動：Her voice trembled with emotion. 她的聲音因激動而顫抖。②搖晃，搖動：The whole world trembled on the brink of war. 瀕臨戰爭邊緣，舉世為之震動。

tremor [`trɛmɚ] ....★

n. 顫抖，戰慄：a tremor of aspen leaves 山楊樹葉的顫動

vaccinate [`væksn‚et] ....★

v. 種牛痘，接種疫苗：Has your child been vaccinated against smallpox? 你的小孩接種牛痘疫苗了嗎？

vein [ven] ....★★

n. 靜脈，血管，礦脈：A fly's wings are so thin that the veins show through. 蒼蠅的翅膀非常薄，以至於血管都是透明的。

waist [west] ....★★★

n. 腰，腰部：wear a sash round the waist 在腰際圍飾帶

wholesome [`holsəm] ....★

adj. 有益健康的：wholesome food 有益健康的食物

wound [wund] ....★★★★★

n. 創傷，傷口：a knife wound 刀傷

v. 使受傷，傷害：Many people were killed or wounded in that accident. 在那次事故中有很多人傷亡。

wrinkle [`rɪŋkl] ....★★

v. 起皺紋：The wind wrinkles the water with waves. 風刮得水面泛起波紋。

n. 皺紋

學科（學術）名稱總匯

09

地理相關辭彙
Vocabulary of Geography

abroad [ə`brɔd] .... ★★★★★
adv. ①到國外，在國外：I think I'll take a trip abroad.
我想要出國旅行。②傳開：The bad news soon
got abroad. 壞消息很快傳了開來。

Africa [`æfrɪkə] .... ★★★★★
n. 非洲

African [`æfrɪkən] .... ★★★★★
adj. 非洲（人）的，非洲人

aftershock [`æftəˌʃɑk] .... ★★★★★
n. 餘震

altitude [`æltəˌtjud] .... ★★★
n. 高空，高度（尤指海拔）

antarctic [æn`tɑrktɪk] .... ★★★
adj. 南極的：a typical Antarctic plant 典型的南極植
物；They started on Antarctic expedition. 他們動
身去南極探險。

apex [`epɛks] .... ★
n. 頂點，最高點

Arabian [ə`rebɪən] .... ★
adj. 阿拉伯（人）的：The Arabian architectural
method is of special interest. 阿拉伯的建築方法令
人十分感興趣。
n. 阿拉伯人

Arabic [`ærəbɪk] .... ★★★★★
n. 阿拉伯語
adj. 阿拉伯（人）的

Arctic [`ɑrktɪk] .... ★★★
adj. 北極（區）的
n. the Arctic 北極（圈）

area [`ɛrɪə] .... ★★★★★
n. 面積，地區，地域

arid [`ærɪd] .... ★
adj. 乾旱的：Most members of the camel family are
found on arid habitats. 駱駝物種的大部分成員被發
現棲息於乾旱地區。

astronomer [ə`strɑnəmə] .... ★
n. 天文學家

astronomical [ˌæstrəˈnɑmɪkl̩] .... ★

adj. 天文學的，天體的：an astronomical
    telescope 天文望遠鏡

astronomy [əsˈtrɑnəmɪ] .... ★

n. 天文學

Atlantic [ətˈlæntɪk] .... ★★★

adj. 大西洋的

n. (the-) 大西洋

atmosphere [ˈætməsˌfɪr] .... ★★★

n. 大氣，大氣層

atmospheric [ˌætməsˈfɛrɪk] .... ★★★

adj. 大氣（層）的，空氣的：atmospheric
    pollution 大氣污染；an atmospheric
    nuclear test 大氣層核子試驗

avalanche [ˈævl̩ˌæntʃ] .... ★

n. 雪崩

balmy [ˈbɑmɪ] .... ★

adj. 溫和的，芳香的：Florida, the
    southernmost state of the eastern
    United States, has a balmy climate and
    extraordinary beaches that make it a
    playground for vacationers. 美國東部最南
    邊的佛羅里達州擁有溫和的氣候、美妙的
    沙灘，因而成為度假者的聖地。

bay [be] .... ★★★★

n. 飛機的機艙，（海）灣

beach [bitʃ] .... ★★★★

n. 海灘，河灘，湖灘

bedrock [ˈbɛdˌrɑk] .... ★★★★★

n. 基石，基本事實或原則

Belgian [ˈbɛldʒən] .... ★

n. 比利時人

adj. 比利時的

Belgium [ˈbɛldʒɪəm] .... ★

n. 比利時

belt [bɛlt] .... ★★★

n. 腰帶或皮帶，地帶

blizzard [ˈblɪzəd] .... ★

n. 暴風雪

bonanza [boˈnænzə] .... ★

n. 富礦帶，幸運：a bonanza business 興旺的
    事業；a bonanza farm 興旺的大農場

border [ˈbɔrdə] .... ★★★★★

n. 邊緣，邊界，邊境

v. 交界，與…毗鄰：France borders Spain. 法
    國與西班牙接壤。

boundary [ˈbaʊndrɪ] .... ★★★

n. 邊界

breeze [briz] .... ★★★★

n. 微風，輕易通過：Those cute boys breezed
    through the examination with no trouble at
    all! 那些聰明的男孩子輕而易舉地通過了考
    試。

British [ˈbrɪtɪʃ] .... ★★★★★

adj. 大不列顛（人）的，英國（人）的：
    British English 英式英語

brook [brʊk] .... ★★★★

n. 小河，溪

vt. 容忍：He would brook no interruptions. 他
    不容許別人打岔。

Bulgaria [bʌlˈgɛrɪə] .... ★

n. 保加利亞

calamity [kəˈlæmətɪ] .... ★

n. 不幸之事，災難

canal [kəˈnæl] .... ★★★

n. 運河，渠

cataclysm [ˈkætəˌklɪzəm] .... ★

n. （洪水、地震等）大災難，猝變：atomic
    cataclysm 原子激變

cave [kev] .... ★★★★

adj. 山洞，洞穴

cavern [ˈkævən] .... ★★★★

adj. 大山洞，大洞穴

v. 將…挖出來，挖空(out)；使成洞，使凹：
    The rock was caverned out to make a
    tunnel. 挖出岩石，造一條隧道。

Chicago [ʃəˋkɑgo] .... ★★★★★
n. 芝加哥（美國城市）

chill [tʃɪl] .... ★★★★
v. 使變冷：The freezing weather chilled me to the bone. 寒冷的天氣使我感到冰冷刺骨。
n. 寒冷

chilly [ˋtʃɪlɪ] .... ★★★
adj. 寒冷的，冷淡的：The President was given a chilly welcome when he arrived in the country for a visit. 總統來到這個國家訪問時受到冷淡的歡迎。

cleft [klɛft] .... ★
n. 裂縫：cleft lip 兔唇；cleft palate 裂齶

cliff [klɪf] .... ★★★★
n. 懸崖，崖

climate [ˋklaɪmɪt] .... ★★★★
n. 氣候

climatological [ˌklaɪmətəˋlɑdʒɪkl] .. ★★★★
adj. 氣候學的，氣象學的

climax [ˋklaɪmæks] .... ★
n. 高峰，頂點

cloud [klaud] .... ★★★★★
n. 雲（狀物）

cloudy [ˋklaudɪ] .... ★
adj. ①多雲的，陰天的：What's the weather like today? It's cloudy. 今天天氣如何？多雲。②混濁的，模糊的

coast [kost] .... ★★★★★
n. 海岸，海濱：a town on the coast 海濱城鎮

coastal [ˋkostl] .... ★★★★★
adj. 海岸的：coastal defense 海岸防禦

coastline [ˋkostˌlaɪn] .... ★★★★★
n. 海岸線

comet [ˋkɑmɪt] .... ★★★★★
n. 彗星

compass [ˋkʌmpəs] .... ★★★
n. 羅盤，指南針：the points of the compass 羅盤上的方位

constellation [ˌkɑnstəˋleʃən] .... ★
n. 星座

continent [ˋkɑntənənt] .... ★
n. 大陸

continental [ˌkɑntəˋnɛntl] .... ★★★★
adj. 大陸的：continental climate 大陸性氣候

cosmic [ˋkɑzmɪk] .... ★
adj. 宇宙的：a coming together of heads of governments to take up the cosmic business of nations 各國首腦集會以處理各國的各方面事務

cosmogenic [ˌkɑzməˋdʒɛnɪk] .... ★
adj. 產生於宇宙的，來自宇宙的

cosmos [ˋkɑzməs] .... ★
n. 宇宙：microscopic cosmos 微觀宇宙

creek [krik] .... ★★★★★
n. 小溪，小灣

crest [krɛst] .... ★
n. （山）頂，頂峰：the crest of a hill 一座小山的山頂

crevice [ˋkrɛvɪs] .... ★
n. 裂縫，破口

desert [dɪˋzɝt] .... ★★★★★
v. 遺棄：During the Industrial Revolution, lots of farmers deserted the farm for the city. 在工業革命的時候，很多農民離開農場，遷往城市。

desert [ˋdɛzɝt] .... ★★★★★
adj. 荒蕪的
n. 沙漠

dew [dju] .... ★★
n. 露，露水

disaster [dɪˋzæstɚ] .... ★★★★
n. 災難

disastrous [dɪzˋæstrəs] .... ★

adj. 災難性的，悲慘的：After the disastrous collapse accident the bodies were too badly mangled to be recognized. 災難性的倒塌事故發生後，屍體被壓得血肉模糊，難以辨認。

drizzle [ˋdrɪzl] .... ★

v. 下細雨：It drizzled off and on all day. 整日在時停時續地下著毛毛雨。

drought [draʊt] .... ★

n. 乾旱

dry [draɪ] .... ★★★★★

adj. 乾燥的，乾旱的：The dry weather has brought a great loss to the farmers. 乾旱的氣候使農民蒙受了很大的損失。

v. 使乾燥，曬乾：Dry the clothes in time after wash. 洗後及時曬乾衣服。

earth [ɝθ] .... ★★★★★

n. 地球：If we don't grow more food and have smaller families, there will be noenough space even to stand on the earth. 如果我們不種植更多的糧食，不使家庭規模變小，我們將在地球上無立足之地。

【片語】on earth 在人間，在世界上，究竟

earthmover [ˋɝθ͵muvɚ] .... ★

n. 大型挖／推土機

earthquake [ˋɝθ͵kwek] .... ★★★★★

n. 地震

east [ist] .... ★★★★★

n. 東，東方，東部

　【片語】①in the east 在東方，在東部②on the east 在東方，在東部③to the east 在…以東

adj. 東部的，東方的：East China has more advantages than North China. 華東比華北有更多的優勢。

eastern [ˋistɚn] .... ★★★★

adj. 東方／部的，朝東的

eclipse [ɪˋklɪps] .... ★

n. （日、月）食，蝕

v. 使…黯然失色，超過：She is quite eclipsed by her clever younger sister. 她那聰明的妹妹讓她變得黯然失色。

eddy [ˋɛdɪ] .... ★

adj. 旋渦的，渦流的

n. 渦流，旋渦：The motor car disappeared in eddy of dust. 汽車在一片瞞天飛塵中不見了。

edge [ɛdʒ] .... ★★★★★

n. 邊

v. 沿邊慢慢移動：Children edged themselves / their way to the front of the crowd to see the actors and actresses more clearly. 孩子們側身擠到人群的前面，想更清楚地看看演員們。

environment [ɪnˋvaɪrəmənt] .... ★★★★★

n. 周圍，環境，四周，外界

equator [ɪˋkwetɚ] .... ★

n. 赤道：the celestial equator 天球赤道

exotic [ɛgˋzɑtɪk] .... ★

adj. 奇異的，外國產的：exotic tropical plants in a greenhouse 溫室裡的外來熱帶植物

flat [flæt] .... ★★★★

adj. 平坦的，扁平的，平淡的，漏氣的

n. 一套房間，公寓套房：The sky was bright but flat, the color of oyster shells. 萬里晴空，牡蠣殼般的色彩。

flatcar [ˋflæt͵kɑr] .... ★★★★

n. 平板車

floe [flo] .... ★

n. 浮冰塊：ice floe（海洋的）浮冰塊，冰盤

fog [fɑg] .... ★★★

n. 霧：The fog is the sailor's worst enemy. 霧是船員最大的敵人。

foggy [ˋfɑgɪ] .... ★★★

adj. 有霧的：The foggy weather has made driving very dangerous. 霧天開車很危險。

學科（學術）名稱總匯

fossil [ˈfɑsl̩] .... ★
n. 化石
adj. 化石似的：Coal is a fossil fuel. 煤是一種
　　礦物燃料。

frontier [frʌnˈtɪr] .... ★★★★
n. 邊境，國境，尖端新領域

galaxy [ˈgæləksɪ] .... ★
n. ①星系，銀河②一群：a galaxy of
　　entertainers 一群演員

gale [gel] .... ★
n. 大風：Many trees were blown down in the
　　gale. 很多樹在大風中被刮倒了。

geochronological [dʒɪoˌkrɑnəˈlɑdʒɪkl̩] .... ★
adj. 地質年代的：According to some
　　archaeologists, geochronological changes
　　were the main reason for the distinction of
　　dinosaurs. 據某些考古學家解釋，恐龍的
　　滅絕主要是由於地質年代的變化引起的。

geochronologist [dʒɪoˌkrɑnəˈlɑdʒɪst] .... ★
n. 地質年代學家

geographical [dʒɪəˈgræfɪkl̩] .... ★★★★
adj. 地理的，地理學上的：The northwest
　　part of China accounts for one third of
　　this country in the geographical sense;
　　however its GDP attribution is just a
　　fractional part to the country. 中國的西北
　　地方面積占該國的三分之一，而國內生產
　　總值卻只占該國的零頭。

geography [ˈdʒɪɑgrəfɪ] .... ★★★★
n. 地理，地理學：In our geography class, we
　　are learning about rivers. 我們正在地理課上
　　學習有關河流的知識。

geological [dʒɪəˈlɑdʒɪkl̩] .... ★
n. 地質（學）的

geologist [dʒɪˈɑlədʒɪst] .... ★
n. 地質學家

geology [dʒɪˈɑlədʒɪ] .... ★
n. 地質學

Georgia [ˈdʒɔrdʒɪə] .... ★★★★★
n. 喬治亞州

geothermal [ˌdʒɪoˈθɝml̩] .... ★
adj. 地熱的：Geothermal is something relating
　　to the internal heat of the earth. 與地球內
　　部的熱相關的稱為地熱。

辨析 Analyze

border, boundary, frontier

1　**border** *n.* 「邊界線，邊境地區」，指
　緊臨分界線的區域：Border incidents
　occurred from time to time between the
　two countries five years ago. 五年前，這
　兩個國家間不時發生邊境衝突。

2　**boundary** *n.* 「分界線，邊界」，指兩
　地或兩國之間的分界線：The river forms
　the boundary between the two countries.
　這條河是這兩個國家的分界線。

3　**frontier** *n.* 「邊界，邊疆」，指兩個國家
　之間的官方分界線，是正式用語：frontier
　guards 邊防戰士

German [ˈdʒɝmən] .... ★★★★★
adj. ①德國的②德國人的③德語的
n. 德國人；德語

geyser [ˈgaɪzɚ] .... ★
n. 間歇噴泉

glacier [ˈgleʃɚ] .... ★★★★★
n. 冰河，冰川：glacier plain 冰川平原

global [ˈglobl̩] .... ★★★★★
adj. 全球的，球狀的：global war 世界戰爭；
　　 global monetary policies 全球金融政策

globe [glob] .... ★★★★
n. 地球，地球儀，天體：a terrestrial globe 地
　　 球儀

ground [graʊnd] .... ★★★★★
n. 土地，地面，場所

gulf [gʌlf] .... ★★★★
n. ①海灣②深淵，深溝：A great gulf opened
　　 before us. 我們面前裂開了一道深溝。

hail [hel] .... ★★
n. 冰雹
v. 歡呼，歡迎：Philip Roth was hailed as a
　　 major new author in 1960. 菲力普・羅斯被
　　 讚譽為1960年主要的新作家。

hemisphere [ˈhɛməsˌfɪr] .... ★★
n. 半球

hill [hɪl] .... ★★★★★
n. 小山，山崗，高地

hillside [ˈhɪlˌsaɪd] .... ★★★
n. （小山的）山腰，山坡

horizon [həˈraɪzn̩] .... ★★
n. 地平線，眼界，見識

horizontal [ˌhɑrəˈzɑntl̩] .... ★★★
adj. 水平的：On a map there are horizontal
　　 lines and vertical lines. 在地圖上有水平的
　　 線和垂直的線。

humid [ˈhjumɪd] .... ★★★
adj. 潮濕的：Metals rust most rapidly in humid
　　 regions. 金屬在潮濕的地區鏽蝕得很快。

humidity [hjuˈmɪdətɪ] ....★
n. 潮濕

hurricane [ˈhɝɪˌken]...............................★
n. 颶風

indigenous [ɪnˈdɪdʒɪnəs] .... ★
adj. 土產的，固有的：Nearly half of the
　　 town's inhabitants are descendants of
　　 indigenous civilizations. 這個小鎮幾乎一
　　 半的居民是當地文明社會的後裔。

inland [ˈɪnlənd] .... ★
adj. 內地的，內陸的：There exists an uneven
　　 development of economy between inland
　　 and coastal cities. 內陸和沿海城市之間，
　　 存在著不平衡的經濟發展。

insular [ˈɪnsələ] .... ★
adj. 海島的，狹隘的：an insular climate 海島
　　 性氣候

interface [ˈɪntɚˌfes] .... ★★
n. 兩個獨立體系的相交處：atmosphere
　　 interface 大氣介面

interscience [ɪntɚˈsaɪəns] .... ★
n. 邊緣科學

island [ˈaɪlənd] .... ★★★★★
n. 島，島嶼

journey [ˈdʒɝnɪ] .... ★★★★★
n. 旅行，旅程

Jupiter [ˈdʒupətɚ] .... ★
n. 木星

lake [lek] .... ★★★★★
n. 湖：the Ness Lake = Loch Ness 尼斯湖

land [lænd] .... ★★★★★
v. 著陸，降落：land an airplane smoothly 使
　　 飛機平穩著陸；land a seaplane on a lake
　　 將水上飛機降落於湖面上

landmark [ˈlændˌmark] .... ★★★★
n. 里程碑：a landmark court ruling 具有深遠
　　 意義的法庭裁定

landmass [ˈlændˌmæs] .... ★★★★
n. 大片陸地

landscape [ˈlændˌskep] .... ★★★
n. 景色，風景

latitude [ˈlætəˌtjud] .... ★
n. 緯度：Our position is latitude 40 degrees north. 我們的位置是北緯40度。

level [ˈlɛvl̩] .... ★★★★
n. ①水平面，水平線：six kilometers above sea level 海拔6,000公尺 ②水平，等級：students of different levels 等級不同的學生
adj. 平的，水平的：A football field needs to be level. 足球場地需要是平的。

lion [ˈlaɪən] .... ★★★★
n. 獅子

locate [loˈket] .... ★★★★
v. 找出，設置：The spleen is a small organ located beneath the left side of the rib cage. 脾是位於胸腔左側下部的一個小器官。

longitude [ˈlɑndʒəˌtjud] .... ★
n. 經度

lunar [ˈlunɚ] .... ★
adj. 月的，月亮的：lunar naut 登月太空人

maritime [ˈmærəˌtaɪm] .... ★★★★
adj. 沿海的：maritime provinces 沿海省份

meander [mɪˈændɚ] .... ★★★★
v. 蜿蜒而流：A brook meanders through the meadow. 一條小溪從草地中蜿蜒流過。

Mediterranean [ˌmɛdətəˈrenɪən] .... ★
n. 地中海：Mediterranean climate 地中海氣候

meteorite [ˈmitɪɚˌaɪt] .... ★
n. 隕星（石）：iron-stony meteorite 鐵隕石

meteorologist [ˌmitɪəˈrɑlədʒɪst] .... ★
n. 氣象學家

meteorology [ˌmitɪəˈrɑlədʒɪ] .... ★
n. 氣象（學）

microclimate [ˈmaɪkroˌklaɪmɪt] .. ★★★★★
n. 小氣候

mine [maɪn] .... ★★★★★
v. 採礦
n. 礦

moist [mɔɪst] .... ★★★
adj. 濕潤的，多雨的：Food must be moist in order to have taste. 食物必須保持濕潤才會有味道。

moisten [ˈmɔɪsn̩] .... ★★★
v. 使濕潤：Her eyes moistened as she listened to the sad story. 她聽著這個悲哀的故事，兩眼含淚。

moisture [ˈmɔɪstʃɚ] .... ★★★
n. 濕氣，潮濕，濕度

moon [mun] .... ★★★★★
n. 月亮

mound [maʊnd] .... ★★★★★
n. 小山，小丘：There's a mound of business letters on my desk for me to deal with. 〔喻〕我的辦公桌上放了一大堆商務信函要我處理。

mountain [ˈmaʊntn̩] .... ★★★★★
n. 高山，山狀物：The waves ran mountains high. 波濤洶湧高如山。

mountainous [ˈmaʊntənəs] .... ★
adj. 多山的，山一般的：A mountainous country is one in which there are many mountains. 山國是多山的國家。

natural [ˈnætʃərəl] .... ★★★★★
adj. 自然的：Milk is the natural food for young babies. 牛奶是嬰兒的天然食物。

nature [ˈnetʃɚ] .... ★★★★★
n. ①大自然，自然界：the balance of nature 自然界的平衡 ②性質，天性：It's only human nature to like money. 愛財乃人之天性。
【片語】in nature 本質上

negro [ˈnigro] .... ★★★★
adj. 黑人的

n. 黑人：Discrimination is a hellhound that gnaws at Negroes in every waking moment of their lives to remind them that the lie of their inferiority is accepted as truth in the society dominating them. 歧視是地獄之犬，在黑人們醒來後的每時每刻向他們狂吠，提醒他們在這個統治著他們的社會裡，他們地位卑下的謊言是被當作真理受到公認的。

north [nɔrθ] .... ★★★★★
n. 北，北方
adj. 北方的：A cold north wind has begun to blow. 開始刮寒冷的北風了。

northeastern [ˌnɔrθ'istən] .... ★★★★★
adj. 東北的

Norwegian [nɔr'widʒən] .... ★★★★★
adj. 挪威（人）的，挪威語的
n. 挪威人，挪威語

oasis [o'esɪs] .... ★
n. （沙漠中的）綠洲：an oasis of serenity amid chaos 鬧中取靜的避風港

ocean ['oʃən] .... ★★★★★
n. 海洋，大洋：the Pacific Ocean 太平洋

oriental [ˌorɪ'ɛntl̩] .... ★★
adj. 東方的：oriental countries 東方國家

orientation [ˌorɪɛn'teʃən] .... ★★
n. 定位，方向：orientation for incoming students 向新同學進行介紹

oversea(s) ['ovə'si(z)] .... ★★★★
adv. 在（或向）海外，在（或向）國外：travel overseas 去國外旅行
adj. （在）海外的，（在）國外的：overseas students 外國留學生

Pakistan [ˌpækɪ'stæn] .... ★★★★★
n. 巴基斯坦

Pakistani [ˌpækɪ'stæni] .... ★★★★★
adj. 巴基斯坦的

Palestine ['pæləstaɪn] .... ★★★★★
n. 巴勒斯坦

peak [pik] .... ★★★★
n. 高峰，尖端

peninsula [pə'nɪnsələ] .... ★
n. 半島：Italy is a peninsula. 義大利是個半島。

pit [pɪt] .... ★★★★
n. 坑，窯

planet ['plænɪt] .... ★★★★
n. 行星

planetarium [ˌplænə'tɛrɪəm] .... ★★★★
n. 天文館

planetary ['plænəˌtɛrɪ] .... ★★★★
adj. 行星的，有軌道的

plateau [plæ'to] .... ★
n. 高原：Qinghai and Tibet Plateau 青藏高原

辨析
Analyze

abroad, overseas

1 **abroad** *ad. & a.* 「國外，海外」，指在國外或在海外，一般用作副詞，也可用作形容詞放在名詞後：On our trip abroad we visited relatives in France. 我們在國外旅遊時，探望了在法國的親戚。

2 **overseas** *ad. & a.* 「國外，海外」，作副詞用時與abroad 基本相同，作形容詞用時放在名詞前：My brother has gone to live overseas. 我的兄弟已去國外居住。

Discipline 學科（學術）名詞總匯

prairie [ˈprɛrɪ] .... ★★
n. 大草原

puddle [ˈpʌdl̩] .... ★★★
n. 小水窪

quagmire [ˈkwæɡˌmaɪr] .... ★
n. 泥潭，沼澤地

rainfall [ˈrenˌfɔl] .... ★★★★
n. 降雨量：Heavy rainfalls flooded the lowlands. 大雨淹沒了低窪地。

reef [rif] .... ★★
n. 礁石

remnant [ˈrɛmnənt] .... ★
v. 殘餘，遺跡：A fossil is a remnant of an onceliving organism. 化石是由生物的殘骸生成的。

ridge [rɪdʒ] .... ★★★★
n. 嶺，山脈，（山）脊，屋脊，鼻樑，隆起

river [ˈrɪvɚ] .... ★★★★★
n. 河流

road [rod] .... ★★★★★
n. 路，道路，途徑

Saturn [ˈsætən] .... ★
n. 土星

scene [sin] .... ★★★★★
n. （戲劇的）一場，（電影等的）一個鏡頭：All we saw was about three scenes from a much bigger play. 我們所看到的只是一齣大型劇中的 3 場戲。②（戲劇，事件等發生的）地點，背景，現場：Our reporter was the first person on the scene. 我們的記者是第一個趕到現場的。③背景，景象：a peaceful country scene 寧靜的鄉村景色④舞臺：That professor had ever been very active on the world scene. 那位教授曾在國際舞臺上非常活躍。

scenery [ˈsinərɪ] .... ★★★
n. ①風景，景致：The mountain scenery is impressive. 山上的風景令人神往。②舞臺，佈景：The scenery for the opera was designed by a famous artist. 這個歌劇的舞臺佈景是一位著名藝術家設計的。

scenic [ˈsinɪk] .... ★★★
adj. 景色優美的：I would like to visit some scenic spots. 我想看些風景優美的地方。

seaside [ˈsiˌsaɪd] .... ★
v. 海濱，海邊

shore [ʃor] .... ★★★★★
n. 海濱，湖濱，岸

shower [ˈʃaʊɚ] .... ★★★
n. 陣雨，暴雨，（一）陣，（一）大批，沐浴，淋浴間：The shower laid the dust. 陣雨洗清了空中飛揚的灰塵。
v. 下陣雨，傾注，大量地給予：They showered honors upon the hero. 他們紛紛向英雄致敬。

sky [skaɪ] .... ★★★★★
n. 天空，天

skyrocket [ˈskaɪˌrakɪt] .... ★
n. 焰火，高空探測火箭
v. 上升，猛漲：The cost of living in nearly every country in the world has skyrocketed in the past ten years. 在過去的 10 年裡，生活花費幾乎在每個國家都大幅攀升。

skyscraper [ˈskaɪˌskrepɚ] .... ★
n. 摩天大樓

sloppy [ˈslapɪ] .... ★
adj. 稀薄的，泥濘的：sloppy ground 泥濘的地面

snow [sno] .... ★★★★★
n. 雪：After a while we will take a walk in the snow. 等會我們要去雪地散步。
v. 下雪：It is snowing thick and fast. 大雪紛飛。

solar [ˋsolɚ] .... ★★★
adj. 太陽的：solar heat 太陽熱力；solar cell 太陽能電池

Spanish [ˋspænɪʃ] .... ★★★★★
adj. 西班牙的，西班牙人的，西班牙語的
n. 西班牙語

star [stɑr] .... ★★★★★
n. 星，恒星

steam [stim] .... ★★★
n. （蒸）汽
v. ①用蒸汽力行駛：A ship was steaming into Valetta Harbor. 一艘輪船正駛入瓦萊塔港。②蒸煮：to steam puddings 蒸布丁

strait [stret] .... ★★
n. 海峽，困難：in desperate straits 處於幾近絕望的境地

stratosphere [ˋstrætəˏsfɪr] .... ★
n. 同溫層：oceanic stratosphere 海洋同溫層；海洋恒溫層

stream [strim] .... ★★★★★
n. ①小河，溪流：underground streams 地下水流②一股，一串；a stream of smoke 一縷煙
v. 流湧：Tears streamed down her face. 眼淚從她臉上流了下來。

streamline [ˋstrimˏlaɪn] .... ★
v. 使成流線型，使合理化：A whale shark's body is stout but streamlined, like that of a whale. 鯨鯊的體型粗壯且呈流線型，就像鯨魚的體型一樣。

sun [sʌn] .... ★★★★★
n. ①太陽：The sun was shining. 陽光普照。②陽光：The sun was in her eyes. 太陽光照著她的眼睛。

辨析
Analyze

landscape, scene, scenery, sight, view

1 landscape *n.*「風景，景色，風景畫，全景」，指範圍比較廣的陸上風光：From the hill we looked down on the peaceful landscape. 我們從山上俯視山下一片恬靜的風光。

2 scene *n.*「景色，景象；舞臺」，指具體某一地的風景或景色，也指戲劇或事件等發生的地點、現場，還指戲劇的一場，可數名詞：The boats in the harbor made a beautiful scene. 港口的小船構成了一道美麗的風景線。

3 scenery *n.*「風景，景色」，指較大範圍風景或某一類風景的總稱，還指舞臺佈景，不可數名詞：Why? Don't you like English scenery? 什麼？你不喜歡英格蘭的風光嗎？

4 view *n.*「風景，景色」，指具體某一地的風景或景色，強調從人的視覺角度出發可以看得見的風景，還指看法、觀點、眼界等，可數名詞：One splendid mountain view followed another during the journey. 旅途中，一幅幅壯麗的山景映入我們的眼簾。

5 sight *n.*「視力，視覺，看見，瞥見，視域，眼界，情景，景象，(pl.) 風景，名勝」，指風景、名勝時為常用語，常用複數：The sunset is a beautiful sight/scene/view. 日落風景很美。

sunrise [ˋsʌnˏraɪz] .... ★★★
n. 日出

sunset [ˋsʌnˏsɛt] .... ★★★
n. 日落

sunspot [ˋsʌnˏspɑt] .... ★★★★
n. 太陽黑子

supernatural [ˏsupɚˋnætʃərəl] .... ★★★★★
adj. 超自然的，神秘的，異常的

surge [sɝdʒ] .... ★★★★★
v. 洶湧，澎湃，激動
n. 巨浪，波濤

swamp [swɑmp] .... ★★
n. 沼澤，沼地

teem [tim] .... ★
v. 充滿：Typically, ocean reefs teem with fishes. 海洋珊瑚中通常會有大量的魚。

temperature [ˋtɛmprətʃɚ] .... ★★★
n. 溫度，氣溫，體溫，冷熱

tidal [ˋtaɪdḷ] .... ★★★★
adj. 潮汐的：the tidal maximum 漲潮

tide [taɪd] .... ★★★★
n. 潮水

torrent [ˋtɔrənt] .... ★★
n. 激流，山洪：The river was a torrent after the storm. 暴風雨過後，河水成了激流。
v. 用魚雷襲擊或擊沉

tourist [ˋturɪst] .... ★★★
n. 旅行者，觀光客，遊人

travel [ˋtrævḷ] .... ★★★★★
n. 旅行
v. 旅行：Have you ever travelled on a train? 你坐火車旅行過嗎？

trip [trɪp] .... ★★★★★
n. 旅行，遠足

tropic [ˋtrɑpɪk] .... ★
n. 熱帶地區，回歸線

tunnel [ˋtʌnḷ] .... ★★★
n. 隧道，地道，山洞
v. 挖隧道，把…鑿成隧道：They tunneled for weeks before they reached the other side of the hill. 他們挖了幾個星期的隧道，才通到小山的另一邊。

辨析 Analyze

journey, tour, travel, trip, voyage

1 **journey** *n.* 「旅行，行程」，尤指長途旅行：His journeys took him all over the world. 他的旅行讓他走遍了全世界。

2 **tour** *n.* 「旅行，遊歷」，尤指周遊各地、巡迴演出或訪問：The neighbors are taking a three-week tour of France and Italy. 鄰居們正在法國和義大利進行一趟三週的旅行。

3 **travel** *n.* 「旅行，遊歷」，指各種旅行、旅遊，用法很廣，而且可用作定語：He is fond of travel. 他喜歡旅遊。

4 **trip** *n.* 「旅行，旅遊」，強調往返旅行：The astronauts are interested in a trip to the moon. 這些太空人對月球旅行很感興趣。

5 **voyage** *n.* 「航海，航行，旅行」，指水上旅行、航行：When I retire I will make/take a long sea voyage. 退休後我要來一次海上長途旅行。

twilight [ˈtwaɪˌlaɪt] .... ★★
n. 黎明，黃昏，曙光，暮色

typhoon [taɪˈfun] .... ★★★
n. 颱風

universe [ˈjunəˌvɝs] .... ★★★★
n. 宇宙，萬物，世界

valley [ˈvælɪ] .... ★★★★★
n. 溪谷，流域

veer [vɪr] .... ★★★★★
v.（風）改變方向：After what seemed an
   eternity, the wind veered to the east and the
   storm abated. 在過了很久以後，風才轉向東
   方，暴風雨也減緩了。

Venus [ˈvinəs] .... ★
n. ①金星②維納斯（愛和美的女神）

verge [vɝdʒ] .... ★★
n. 邊緣，界限：a grass verge beside the road
   草地邊緣靠近馬路。

vestige [ˈvɛstɪdʒ] .... ★
n. 痕跡，遺跡

volcanic [vɑlˈkænɪk] .... ★★★
adj. 火山的

warm [wɔrm] .... ★★★★★
adj. ①暖和的，溫暖的：The weather is
   getting warmer day by day. 天氣一天比一
   天暖和。②熱情的，熱烈的，熱心的：We
   received a warm welcome. 我們受到了熱
   情的歡迎。

wasteland [ˈwestˌlænd] .... ★
n. 荒野，荒地：a cultural wasteland 文化荒漠

water [ˈwɔtɚ] .... ★★★★★
n. 水
v. 向（某物）灑水，澆水：Please remember
   to water the flower in the morning. 早上請記
   得為花澆水。

waterproof [ˈwɔtɚˌpruf] .... ★★★
adj. 耐水的，防水的：a waterproof coat 雨衣

watertight [ˈwɔtɚˈtaɪt] .... ★
adj. 不漏水的，密封的，無隙可乘的：a
   watertight alibi 無懈可擊的藉口

weather [ˈwɛðɚ] .... ★★★★★
v. 風化，侵蝕：The walls of the barn had
   weathered. 穀倉的牆壁已經褪色了。

west [wɛst] .... ★★★★★
n. 西，西方，西部，西邊
adj.（指風等）來自西方的，從西面來的，西方
   的，西部的：The west wind brought a lot
   of sand. 西風帶來了許多沙子。

western [ˈwɛstɚn] .... ★★★★★
adj. 西部的，西方的：Western nations 西方國
   家

westernize [ˈwɛstɚˌnaɪz] .... ★★★★★
v. 使西洋化，歐化

wet [wɛt] .... ★★★★
adj. ①濕的，潮濕的：Your coat is wet
   through. 你的上衣濕透了。②有雨的，多
   雨的：We can't go out. It's too wet. 我們
   不能出去，雨太大了。

wind [wɪnd] .... ★★★★★
n. 風

windmill [ˈwɪndˌmɪl] .... ★
n. 風車，風力發動機

windy [ˈwɪndɪ] .... ★
adj. 有風的，多風的

zone [zon] .... ★★★★
n.（氣候）帶：the frigid zone 寒帶；a danger
   zone 危險地帶

辨析
Analyze

area, belt, district, region, zone

1 **area** *n.* 「面積；地區，地域，地方；領域，範圍」，普通用語，詞義較廣：The school covers an area of forty acres. 這所學校占地 40 英畝。

2 **belt** *n.* 「腰帶，皮帶；地區，地帶」，指具有自身特點、區別於其他地區的地帶，如cotton belt（棉花種植帶），the belt of rain（降雨帶），尤指長條地帶、林帶：They also planted shelter belts with a total length of 64 kilometers. 他們還種植了 64 公里長的防護林帶。

3 **district** *n.* 「區，地區，行政區」，指劃分的行政區域：The city is divided into nine districts. 這座城市劃分成 9 個行政區。

4 **region** *n.* 「地區，地帶，區域，範圍幅度」，指地理上的自然分界區域：The north of our country is the forest region. 我們國家北部是森林地區。

5 **zone** *n.* 「地區」，指具有某種明顯特點的地區，如軍事區、商業區、經濟區等：special economic zone 經濟特區

10

生物相關辭彙

Vocabulary of Biology

animal [ˈænəm!] .... ★★★★★
n. 動物，牲畜

ant [ænt] .... ★★★
n. 螞蟻

ass [æs] .... ★★
n. 驢，傻瓜

bacterium [bækˈtɪrɪəm] .... ★
n. 細菌：All bacteria are larger than viruses. 所有的細
　 菌都比病毒大。

bamboo [bæmˈbu] .... ★
n. 竹子

barley [ˈbɑrlɪ] .... ★
n. 大麥

bear [bɛr] .... ★★★★★
v. 具有，帶有，支撐：The cost of elections in the
　 United States is borne by both the government and
　 the private sector. 在美國，選舉的費用是由政府和私
　 人企業共同承擔的。
n. 熊：polar bear 北極熊

beast [bist] .... ★★★★★
n. 獸，牲畜，兇殘的人：They hate that beast-like
　 foreman. 他們恨那像野獸般的工頭。

beaver [ˈbivɚ] .... ★
n. 河狸，海狸：a coat trimmed with beaver 有海狸毛
　 皮裝飾的外衣

bee [bi] .... ★★★★
n. 蜜蜂

beetle [ˈbit!] .... ★
n. 甲蟲

being [ˈbiɪŋ] .... ★★★★★
n. ①存在，生存：Those sciences owe their being to
　 the achievement of the geniuses. 那些科學的存在
　 歸功於天才的成就。②生物，人：He is no common
　 being. 他絕非泛泛之輩。

biological [ˌbaɪəˈlɑdʒɪkl̩] .... ★★★
adj. 生物學的：Physical anthropology is the study of the evolution, variation and classification of humans as biological organisms. 自然人類學把人類當作一種生物有機體，研究其演化、變異和分類。

biology [baɪˈɑlədʒɪ] .... ★★★
n. 生物學，生態學

bionicist [ˌbaɪˈɑnɪsɪst] .... ★★★
n. 仿生學家

bionics [baɪˈɑnɪks] .... ★★★
n. 仿生學

bloom [blum] .... ★★★★
v. 開花：These flowers bloom in the spring. 這些花春天開放。
n. 花，開花：What beautiful blooms! 多麼美麗的花啊！

blossom [ˈblɑsəm] .... ★★
v. 繁盛，開花：New industries can blossom over night if we find an outlet for their products. 如果我們為他們的產品找到出路，新的工業一夜間就能出現。

botany [ˈbɑtənɪ] .... ★★★★★
n. 植物學

bough [baʊ] .... ★★
n. 大樹枝，主枝

branch [bræntʃ] .... ★★★★★
n. ①樹枝，分支：the branches of the tree 樹枝；a branch road 岔路②家族的關係，學術的部門，機構的分支機構：We have branches all over the country. 我們在全國各地均有分支。③支流，支脈，支線

breed [brid] .... ★★★★★
v. 養育，繁殖：It is observed that many animals do not breed when in captivity. 人們注意到許多動物被關入籠中就不生育了。
n. 品種：a new breed of aeroplane 一種新型飛機

bristle [ˈbrɪsl̩] .... ★
n. 硬毛，鬃：a face covered with bristle 滿臉粗鬍鬚

brute [brut] .... ★★
n. 禽獸，畜生

buck [bʌk] .... ★★
n. 雄鹿，雄兔

bud [bʌd] .... ★★★★
n. 發芽：branches in full bud 長滿芽的枝條
v. 發芽：Some flowers bud very early in spring. 有些花在春季很早就發出芽來。

bug [bʌg] .... ★★
n. 蟲，臭蟲
v. 竊聽：The police have bugged my office. 警方在我辦公室裡裝了竊聽器。

bulb [bʌlb] .... ★★★
n. 燈泡，球狀物：the bulb of an electric lamp 電燈泡；the bulb of a hair 毛／髮根

bush [bʊʃ] .... ★★★★★
n. 灌木（叢）：a clump of bushes 一片灌木林；a bush of hair 濃密的頭髮

bushel [ˈbʊʃəl] .... ★
n. （穀物、水果等容量單位）蒲式耳：measure other people's corn by one's won bushel 以己度人

butter [ˈbʌtɚ] .... ★★★★
n. 奶油：apple butter 蘋果醬

camel [ˈkæml̩] .... ★★★
n. 駱駝

cat [kæt] .... ★★★★★
n. 貓：Does a cat eat apples? 貓吃蘋果嗎？

cattle [ˈkætl̩] .... ★★★★
n. （單複同）牲畜，（總稱）牛

cell [sɛl] .... ★★★★
n. 細胞，電池，元件，單人牢房

chestnut [ˈtʃɛsˌnʌt] .... ★
n. 栗子，栗樹：water chestnut 菱

chrysanthemum [krɪˋsænθəməm] ....★

n. 菊，菊花：a cluster of chrysanthemum 一束菊花

claw [klɔ] .... ★★★

n. 爪，腳爪

v. 抓：Their favorite cat clawed a hole in my stocking. 他們疼愛的貓在我的襪子上抓了個洞。

cluster [ˋklʌstə･] .... ★★

v. 叢生

n. 束

cock [kɑk] .... ★★★

n. ①公雞②（水管等的）龍頭，旋塞

cocoon [kəˋkun] .... ★

n. 繭

coral [ˋkɔrəl] .... ★

n. 珊瑚，珊瑚玩具，海蝦卵，珊瑚色（尤指紅色），珊瑚蟲

adj. 珊瑚的，珊瑚色的，珊瑚製的

core [kor] .... ★★★★

n. 核（心），中心部分

cow [kaʊ] .... ★★★★

n. 母牛，奶牛

v. 威脅，嚇唬：The natives were cowed by the army. 本地人受到軍隊的恐嚇。

cowherd [ˋkaʊˏhɝd] .... ★★★★★

n. 牧牛者

cranberry [ˋkrænˏbɛrɪ] .... ★

n. 小紅莓的果實：European cranberry 小紅莓

crane [kren] .... ★★★

n. 鶴，起重機

v. 伸（頸），躊躇(at)：The audience craned forward as their conjuror came to the crucial part of his trick. 當魔術師的魔術變到關鍵時刻，觀眾們都伸著脖子向前看。

crow [kro] .... ★★★★

n. 烏鴉

crow [kro] .... ★

v. 雞啼，（嬰兒）歡叫：Roosters crowed the sleeping barnyard up. 公雞的啼聲把沉睡的穀倉喚醒了。

cuckoo [ˋkuku] .... ★

n. 杜鵑，布穀鳥

deer [dɪr] .... ★★★

n. 鹿：a herd of deer 一群鹿

descend [dɪˋsɛnd] .... ★★★★★

v. 下來，下降，傳下：A rough path descended like a steepstair into the plain. 一條坎坷的小路像陡峭的樓梯一樣，向下延伸入平原。

digit [ˋdɪdʒɪt] .... ★★★★★

n. 手指，足趾，數字，位元（數）

dog [dɔg] .... ★★★★★

n. 狗：Love me, love my dog. 愛屋及烏。

dolphin [ˋdɑlfɪn] .... ★

n. 海豚

donkey [ˋdɑŋkɪ] .... ★★★

n. 驢：ride a donkey 騎驢；drive a donkey 趕驢

dove [dʌv] .... ★★

n. 鴿子

duck [dʌk] .... ★★★

n. 鴨子

eagle [ˋigl̩] .... ★★★★

n. 鷹：eagle-eyed 目光銳利的

ecology [ɪˋkɑlədʒɪ] .... ★

n. 生態學

eel [il] .... ★

n. 鰻魚

elephant [ˋɛləfənt] .... ★★★

n. 象，大象

evergreen [ˋɛvəˏgrin] .... ★

adj. 常綠的：Some trees are evergreen; they are called evergreen. 有的樹是常青的，叫做常青樹。

feather [ˈfɛðɚ] .... ★★★★
n. 羽毛

feature [ˈfitʃɚ] .... ★★★★★
n. 特徵，面貌，容貌，（電影）正片
v. 以⋯為特色：Painting in her spare time features largely her life. 業餘時間内畫畫成為她生活中的一大特色。

fin [fɪn] .... ★
n. 鴨腳板，鰭
v. 在⋯上裝翅片／鰭板：The cylinder head is heavily finned for strength. 汽缸頭裝上了許多突片以增加強度。

finch [fɪntʃ] .... ★
n. 雀科鳴禽

fish [fɪʃ] .... ★★★★★
n. 魚
v. 捕魚，釣魚：They fished in the lake all day. 他們在湖裡捕了一天魚。

flora [ˈflorə] .... ★
n. 植物界：the flora and fauna of Africa 非洲的動植物

fluffy [ˈflʌfɪ] .... ★
adj. 絨毛的：fluffy curls 柔軟的捲髮

forest [ˈfɔrɪst] .... ★★★★★
n. 森林，山林，森林地帶

fowl [faʊl] .... ★★
n. 雞，家禽

frogman [ˈfrɑgmən] .... ★
n. 蛙人

fungi [ˈfʌngaɪ] .... ★
n. 真菌

gene [dʒin] .... ★★★
n. 遺傳因數，基因：gene type 基因型，遺傳型

genetic [dʒəˈnɛtɪk] .... ★★★
adj. 遺傳學的：Biochemical scientists have traced many diseases to the genetic causes. 生化科學家已經發現許多疾病是遺傳性的。

germ [dʒɝm] .... ★★★
n. 細菌，病原菌

germinate [ˈdʒɝməˌnet] .... ★
v. 發芽：Seeds will not germinate without water. 種子沒有水是不會發芽的。

gill [gɪl] .... ★
n.（魚）鰓

goat [got] .... ★★★★
n. 山羊

goose [gus] .... ★★★
n. 鵝

gorilla [gəˈrɪlə] .... ★
n. 大猩猩

grass [græs] .... ★★★★★
n. 草，草地：Keep off the grass! 禁入草坪！

grasshopper [ˈgræsˌhɑpɚ] .... ★
n. 蝗蟲，螞蚱

grove [grov] .... ★★
n. 林子，樹叢：an orange grove 橘子叢

harness [ˈhɑrnɪs] .... ★★★
n. 馬具，輓具
v. 利用：People have harnessed the Sun's energy since ancient times. 人類在遠古時代就會利用太陽能。

hatch [hætʃ] .... ★★
v. 孵出：Ostriches hatch from the largest of all eggs. 鴕鳥是從最大的蛋中孵化出來的。

hawk [hɔk] .... ★★
n. 鷹，隼：doves and hawks 鴿派和鷹派；war hawk 好戰分子；戰爭叫囂者

hay [he] .... ★★★
n. 乾草

hedgehog [ˈhɛdʒˌhɑg] .... ★★★
n. 豪豬

herb [hɝb] .... ★★
n. 草，藥草

071

heredity [həˋrɛdətɪ] .... ★
n. 遺傳

holly [ˋhɑlɪ] .... ★★★★
n. 冬青屬植物

horn [hɔrn] .... ★★★★
n. ①（觸）角②角狀物，角製品③岬，海角④號，喇叭：All automobiles have horns. 汽車都有喇叭。

horse [hɔrs] .... ★★★★★
n. 馬

hound [haʊnd] .... ★★
n. 狗，獵狗
vt. 追逐，不斷騷擾，糾纏：The police are always hounding him. 警方一直在追捕他。

human [ˋhjumən] .... ★★★★★
adj. 人類的，人性的：He seems quite human when you know him. 你如果瞭解他，就會覺得他是很有人情味的。

hump [hʌmp] .... ★
n. 駝峰：A camel has a hump on its back. （單峰）駱駝背上有一個駝峰。
v. 隆起

hybrid [ˋhaɪbrɪd] .... ★
n. 雜種，混血兒

inanimate [ɪnˋænəmɪt] .... ★
adj. 無生命的：an inanimate object 無生物；an inanimate conversation 沉悶的對話

inorganic [ˌɪnɔrˋgænɪk] .... ★
adj. 無生物的，無機的：inorganic chemistry 無機化學；inorganic nature 無生物界；inorganic matter 無機物

insect [ˋɪnsɛkt] .... ★★★★
n. 昆蟲，蟲

insecticide [ɪnˋsɛktəˌsaɪd] .... ★★★★
n. 殺蟲劑

ivory [ˋaɪvərɪ] .... ★★
n. 象牙：ivory paper （藝術上用的）帶象牙光澤的厚光紙

jellyfish [ˋdʒɛlɪˌfɪʃ] .... ★
n. 水母

jungle [ˋdʒʌŋgl̩] .... ★★★★
n. 叢林，密林：a jungle of wrecked automobiles 一堆破汽車

kangaroo [ˌkæŋgəˋru] .... ★
n. 大袋鼠：tree kangaroo 樹袋鼠

kernel [ˋkɝnl̩] .... ★
n. 核，仁：the kernel of a walnut 核桃仁；a kernel of wheat 一粒麥

knot [nɑt] .... ★★★
n. （繩等的）結，節疤，節，海裡：to tie a knot in a piece of string 在一根繩子上打結

lamb [læm] .... ★★★★
n. 羔羊，小羊，羔羊肉

lark [lɑrk] .... ★
n. 嬉耍，玩樂，百靈鳥，雲雀：What a lark! 真有趣！

laurel [ˋlɔrəl] .... ★
n. 月桂樹：gain laurels 贏得聲望，獲得榮譽，獲得冠軍

lawn [lɔn] .... ★★★
n. 草地，草坪，草場

leopard [ˋlɛpəd] .... ★
n. 豹

lifespan [ˋlaɪfˌspæn] .... ★★★★★
n. 壽命，平均生命期

lily [ˋlɪlɪ] .... ★★
n. 百合，睡蓮：white pond lily 白睡蓮

livestock [ˋlaɪvˌstɑk] .... ★
n. （總稱）家畜：livestock prices 家畜價格

locust [ˋlokəst] .... ★
n. 蝗蟲

lyrebird [ˋlaɪrˌbɝd] .... ★
n. 琴鳥

magpie [ˋmæɡˏpaɪ] .... ★
n. 鵲：chatter like a magpie 像喜鵲一樣饒舌，喋喋不休

mammals [ˋmæmlz] .... ★
n. 哺乳動物

mammoth [ˋmæməθ] .... ★
adj. 巨大的：The construction of mammoth shopping malls has contributed to the decline of small stores in neighboring towns. 巨型購物商場的建立促使臨近城鎮小商店的數量減少。

maple [ˋmepl] .... ★
n. 楓樹：white maple 糖槭，銀槭，白楓

mature [məˋtjʊr] .... ★★★
adj. 成熟的，考慮周到的：You are a mature man now; you are no longer a boy. 你現在是成人了，不再是孩子了。

meadow [ˋmɛdo] .... ★★
n. 草地，牧場：meadow ore 沼鐵礦

metabolism [mɛˋtæblˏɪzəm] .... ★
n. 新陳代謝：water metabolism 水的代謝

monkey [ˋmʌnkɪ] .... ★★★
n. 猴子

mosquito [məsˋkito] .... ★★★
n. 蚊子：mosquito net 蚊帳，〔英〕蚊式轟炸機

moss [mɔs] .... ★★
n. 苔蘚，地衣

moth [mɔθ] .... ★
n. 蛾

mouse [maʊs] .... ★★★★
n. 老鼠：a field mouse 田鼠

mule [mjul] .... ★
n. 騾子：as stubborn as a mule 頑固之人

mushroom [ˋmʌʃrʊm] .... ★★★
n. 蘑菇
v. 迅速發展：In the 1820's cities in the United States mushroomed as a result of the Industrial Revolution. 在 1820 年代，城市因工業革命而在美國迅速發展了起來。

nest [nɛst] .... ★★★★
n. 巢，窩：an ant's nest 螞蟻窩

oak [ok] .... ★★
n. 櫟樹，橡樹，橡木
adj. 橡木製的：a heart of oak 櫟樹內層最堅實的心材，〔喻〕堅強勇敢的人，果斷的人

辨析
Analyze

grassland, lawn, meadow, pasture

1 **grassland** *n.*「草地，草原」，指大片野生草地、草原：Have you ever been to the grassland in the Inner Mongolia? 你去過內蒙古的大草原嗎？

2 **lawn** *n.*「草地，草坪」，指花園、公園裡或建築物前人工維護的草坪：The lawn needs mowing. 這片草坪需要修剪。

3 *meadow* *n.*「草地」，指野生的草地，上面有野生的草和花。There are some wild horses on the meadow. 草地上有幾匹野馬。

4 **pasture** *n.*「牧草地，牧場」，指放牧牲畜的草場：The sheep needed fresh pasture, so we had to move them to other fields. 羊群需要新鮮的牧草場，所以我們把它們趕到別的地方去。

olive [ˋɑlɪv] .... ★★
n. 橄欖，橄欖樹

orange [ˋɔrɪndʒ] .... ★★★★
n. 橘子，桔子，橙子
adj. 橙色的：Our desks are orange. 我們的桌子是橙色的。

organism [ˋɔrgən͵ɪzəm] .... ★★★
n. 生物，生物體，有機體：the social organism 社會有機體

owl [aʊl] .... ★★
n. 貓頭鷹：as grave as an owl 擺出一副嚴肅的神情，板起臉孔

ox [ɑks] .... ★★★
n. 牛，公牛：You cannot flay the same ox twice.〔諺〕一頭牛不能剝兩次皮。

oyster [ˋɔɪstɚ] .... ★
n. 蠔，牡蠣

panacea [͵pænəˋsɪə] .... ★
n. 萬靈藥

panda [ˋpændə] .... ★★★
n. 熊貓

panther [ˋpænθɚ] .... ★★
n. 豹，美洲豹

parasite [ˋpærə͵saɪt] .... ★
n. 寄生蟲，寄生植物

parasitic [͵pærəˋsɪtɪk] .... ★
adj. 寄生的：parasitic diseases 寄生性疾病

parrot [ˋpærət] .... ★
n. 鸚鵡：the parrot of other men's thinking 人云亦云而不知所云者

peacock [ˋpikɑk] .... ★
n. 孔雀：vain as a peacock 孔雀般地炫耀自己

pet [pɛt] .... ★★★
n. 愛畜，寵兒
adj. 寵愛的，表示親暱的：She has two cats as pets. 她養了兩隻貓。

petal [ˋpɛtl] .... ★★
n. （通常有顏色的）花瓣

plant [plænt] .... ★★★★★
n. 植物，作物
v. 種植，栽培：Trees are planted in spring every year while trees becomes fewer and fewer. 每年春天都種樹，樹卻變得越來越少。

pony [ˋponɪ] .... ★
n. 小馬

poultry [ˋpoltrɪ] .... ★
n. 家禽：poultry farm 家禽飼養場

prey [pre] .... ★★
v. 捕獲，捕食
n. 獵物，犧牲品：Jumping spiders have excellent eyesight and can see their prey from a distance twenty times of their own length. 跳躍蜘蛛的眼力極好，能夠看到自己身長 20 倍距離之遠的獵物。

proliferate [prəˋlɪfə͵ret] .... ★
v. 繁衍：Some cells, such as epithelia, proliferate more rapidly when the body is asleep than when it is awake. 有些細胞，比如上皮細胞，在身體睡著的時候繁殖得更快。

prolific [prəˋlɪfɪk] .... ★
adj. 多產的：The most surprising feature is that she was such a prolific writer even at an early age. 她最令人吃驚的特點是：她在年輕時就是一個多產的作家。

propagate [ˋprɑpə͵get] .... ★
v. 繁殖，宣傳：Water easily propagates sound. 水容易傳導聲音。

propagation [͵prɑpəˋgeʃən] .... ★
n. 宣傳，繁殖，遺傳

protein [ˋprotiɪn] .... ★★★
n. 蛋白質：protein diets 富含蛋白質的食物

protoplasm [ˋprotə͵plæzəm] .... ★★★
n. 原生質，細胞質

puppy [ˋpʌpɪ] .... ★
n. 小狗

rabbit [ˋræbɪt] .... ★★★
n. 兔

ramification [ˌræməfəˋkeʃən] .... ★
n. 分支，結果：the ramifications of a court decision 法庭判決的結果

ramify [ˋræməˌfaɪ] .... ★
v.（使）分支：The problem merely ramified after the unsuccessful meeting. 那次不成功的會議後，問題變得更加複雜了。

rat [ræt] .... ★★★★
n. ①鼠：I hate rat. 我不喜歡鼠。②見風轉舵的人
v. 去捕鼠：Let's go ratting. 我們去捕鼠吧。

reproduction [ˌriprəˋdʌkʃən] .... ★★
n. 繁殖，複製品

ripe [raɪp] .... ★★★
adj. 成熟的：The most important crop in Alberta Canada is winter wheat and is ripe for harvesting by late spring. 加拿大的亞伯達地區最主要的作物是冬小麥，它會在隔年春末成熟供採收。

ripen [ˋraɪpən] .... ★★★
v. 熟，成熟

rod [rɑd] .... ★★★★
n. 棍，桿，棒（狀物），條，線材

rooster [ˋrustɚ] .... ★
n. 公雞

root [rut] .... ★★★★★
n. 根，根本，根源

rose [roz] .... ★★★★
n. 玫瑰：Rose indicates love. 玫瑰表示愛情。

辨析 Analyze

breed, feed, grow, plant, raise

1. **breed** vt. & vi.「飼養，繁殖；養育，培育」，指飼養動物，也指培育種子和植物，還指教養、餵養小孩：Farmers usually breed pigs and cows. 農民一般都飼養豬和奶牛。

2. **feed** vt. & vi.「餵(養)，為…提供食物」，主要指餵食物這一具體動作，另有片語 feed on（以…為生）和 be fed up（膩了，厭煩）：Do not feed the animals in the zoo. 不要餵動物園裡的動物。

3. **grow** vt. & vi.「生長，種植」，指種養或栽培植物，表延續性動作，強調長期餵養、培育：We have grown a lot of flowers in the garden this summer. 今年夏天，我們在花園裡種了很多花。

4. **plant** vt.「種植，播種」，指種植時瞬間的動作：People plant trees on a large scale in the spring. 在春天，人們大規模種樹。

5. **raise** vt.「養育，養殖」，主要指栽培或種植植物，也可指飼養動物或撫養小孩：We raise/grow rice in our hometown. 我們在家鄉種水稻。

sample [ˈsæmpl̩] .... ★★★
n. 範例，樣品

sardine [sɑrˈdin] .... ★
n. 沙丁魚
v. 緊緊地裹起來，塞滿：The bars are
 sardined with hungry hopefuls. 酒吧裡擠滿
 了餓著肚皮卻滿懷希望之人。

secretion [sɪˈkriʃən] .... ★★★★★
n. 分泌（物）：secretion of hormones 荷爾蒙
 的分泌

seed [sid] .... ★★★★
n. 種子
v. ①播種②結實，結籽

sequoia [sɪˈkwɔɪə] .... ★
n. 紅杉

serpent [ˈsɝpənt] .... ★★
n. 毒蛇：The serpent fascinated its prey. 蛇嚇
 倒了它要捕食的動物。

sex [sɛks] .... ★★★★★
n. ①性別②性關係／行為
vi. 區別…的性別：His job is sexing day-old
 chickens. 他的工作是鑒別出生一天的小雞
 的性別。

shark [ˈʃɑrk] .... ★
n. 鯊魚

shrub [ʃrʌb] .... ★
n. 灌木

snail [snel] .... ★
n. 蝸牛：Snails and octopuses are mollusks.
 蝸牛和章魚是軟體動物。

snake [snek] .... ★★★★★
n. 蛇：poisonous snake 毒蛇

sort [sɔrt] .... ★★★★★
n. 種類，類別：All sorts of wonderful things
 are laid out during Christmas season. 各種
 各樣的好東西在聖誕季都擺了出來。
v. 分類，整理：Sort out colors! 請按顏色分
 類。

sparrow [ˈspæro] .... ★
n. 麻雀

spawn [spɔn] .... ★
n. 產卵
v. 產卵，醞釀，引起：Meteorologists issue
 tornado watches when they become aware
 of conditions leading to the unusually severe
 thunderstorms that spawn tornadoes. 當氣
 象學家發現異常強烈且會引起龍捲風的暴風
 雨時，就會發佈龍捲風警報。

辨析
Analyze

mature, ripe

1 **mature** *a.* 「熟的，成熟的；成年人的；
 深思熟慮的，慎重的」，指人在生理或心
 理上成熟的，也指農產品等植物成熟，
 還指計畫或技術等成熟：He is a mature
 man who can make his own decisions.
 他是成年人，可以自己做出決定。

2 **ripe** *a.* 「成熟的」，指農作物等植物成
 熟，還指時機、條件成熟：The apples
 are ripe/mature. 蘋果熟了。

species [ˈspiʃiz] .... ★★★★★

n. （物）種，種類，品種，族：Some species of animals have become extinct because they could not adapt to a changing environment. 有一些動物因不能適應環境的變化，已經滅種了。

sprout [spraʊt] .... ★

v. 萌芽，長出：Buds sprout in the spring. 芽在春天萌發。

squirrel [ˈskwɝəl] .... ★

n. 松鼠

stalk [stɔk] .... ★★

v. 跟蹤（獵物），闊步

n. 莖：Jonquils bear from three to six flowers on a stalk about a foot high. 長壽花在約一英尺長的莖上結 3 至 6 朵花。

stem [stɛm] .... ★★★

n. 莖，幹，詞幹

v. 起源，導源：Today's success in weather forecasting stems from applied rather than pure science. 今天天氣預報能成功是由於應用科學而不是純科學。

swan [swɑn] .... ★

n. 天鵝、

swarm [swɔrm] .... ★★

n. （蜜蜂、螞蟻等的）群

v. 群集，湧入：During hard times, rural people tend to swarm into cities. 在經濟蕭條的時候，農村人口會湧入城市。

sweat [swɛt] .... ★★★

n. 汗：wipe the sweat from one's forehead 擦掉額頭上的汗水

v. （使）出汗：The doctor sweated his patient. 該醫生讓病人發汗了。

tear [tɪr] .... ★★★★★

n. 眼淚【片語】in tears 流著淚，哭泣

v. 撕，撕裂：I watched John tear open the envelope. 我看見約翰撕開信封。

tentacled [ˈtɛntəkḷd] .... ★

adj. 有觸角的，有觸手的

thorn [θɔrn] .... ★★

n. 刺，荊棘

tiger [ˈtaɪgɚ] .... ★★★

n. 虎

tortoise [ˈtɔrtəs] .... ★

n. 龜

transplant [trænsˈplænt] .... ★

v. 移植：undergo a heart transplant 做心臟移植手術

tree [tri] .... ★★★★★

n. 樹：The tree is known by its fruit. 〔諺〕樹以其實，為人所知（人以其言行，為人所識）。

trunk [trʌŋk] .... ★★★★

n. 樹幹，軀幹，大衣箱，（車後部）行李箱

tulip [ˈtjuləp] .... ★

n. 鬱金香

tuna [ˈtunə] .... ★

n. 金槍魚

turkey [ˈtɝkɪ] .... ★★

n. 火雞，火雞肉

tusk [tʌsk] .... ★

n. 長牙，象牙

twig [twɪg] .... ★

n. 小樹枝

vegetarian [ˌvɛdʒəˈtɛrɪən] .... ★★★★

adj. 吃素的：a vegetarian diet 素食餐

vegetation [ˌvɛdʒəˈteʃən] .... ★★★★

n. （植物）生長，草木

vine [vaɪn] .... ★★

n. 葡萄藤，藤本植物

violet [ˈvaɪəlɪt] .... ★★★

n. 紫羅蘭

vitamin [ˈvaɪtəmɪn] .... ★★★

n. 維生素

walnut [ˈwɔlnət] .... ★★

n. 核桃，核桃樹

wasp [wɑsp] .... ★
n. 黃蜂，馬蜂

weed [wid] .... ★★★
n. 雜草，野草
v. 除草：weed the garden 除去園子裡的雜草

whale [hwel] .... ★★★★
n. 鯨魚

whisker [ˋhwɪskɚ] .... ★
n. 連鬢鬍子，落腮鬍

wild [waɪld] .... ★★★★★
adj. 野生的，狂熱的：We must protect the
　　　wild plants and animals. 我們必須保護野
　　　生動植物。

wildlife [ˋwaɪldˏlaɪf] .... ★★★★★
n. 野生動物

willow [ˋwɪlo] .... ★★
n. 柳樹

wing [wɪŋ] .... ★★★★★
n. 翼，翅膀

wither [ˋwɪðɚ] .... ★★
v. 枯萎，使凋謝，使枯萎：The flowers
　　　withered in the cold. 花在寒冷的天氣裡凋謝
　　　了。

wolf [wʊlf] .... ★★★★
n. 狼

wood [wʊd] .... ★★★★★
n. 木材，小樹林

wooden [ˋwʊdn̩] .... ★★★★
adj. ①木製的②呆板的，笨拙的：The actress
　　　gave a rather wooden performance. 那女
　　　演員的表演相當呆板。

woodpecker [ˋwʊdˏpɛkɚ] .... ★
n. 啄木鳥

worm [wɝm] .... ★★★
n. 蟲，蠕蟲

yeast [jist] .... ★
n. 酵母

zebra [ˋzibrə] .... ★
n. 斑馬

zoo [zu] .... ★★★
n. 動物園

zyme [zaɪm] .... ★
n. 酶

zymo [ˋzaɪmɔ] .... ★
n. 酶，酵母，發酵

Discipline　學科（學術）名稱總匯

學科（學術）名稱總匯

11

體育相關辭彙
Vocabulary of Gymnastics

athlete [ˈæθlit] .... ★★★
n. 運動員

badminton [ˈbædmɪntən] .... ★
n. 羽毛球

ball [bɔl] .... ★★★★★
n. ①球，球狀物：The Earth is a ball. 地球是一個球
體。②（盛大，正式的）舞會：a birthday ball 生日
舞會

balloon [bəˈlun] .... ★★★
n. 氣球

basket [ˈbæskɪt] .... ★★★★
n. 籃子，簍：waste-paper basket 廢紙簍

basketball [ˈbæskɪtˌbɔl] .... ★★★
n. 籃球：Can you play basketball? 你會打籃球嗎？
【片語】play basketball 打籃球

bat [bæt] .... ★★★
n. 球拍，蝙蝠

champion [ˈtʃæmpɪən] .... ★★★★
v. 支持：He championed the cause of civil rights for
the whole life. 他畢生為人權理想奮鬥。
n. 冠軍，提倡者

coach [kotʃ] .... ★★★★★
n. ①客車，長途汽車，四輪大馬車②私人教師，教練：
Our football coach trains the team. 我們的足球教練
訓練這個隊。
v. 輔導，當教練：He coached her for the English
examination. 他輔導她準備英語考試。

compete [kəmˈpit] .... ★★★★
v. 競爭：The children compete against each other to
reach the other end of the pool. 孩子們互相比賽要抵
達池子的另一端。

competitor [kəmˈpɛtətə] .... ★★
n. 競爭者，比賽者

contest [ˈkɑntɛst] .... ★★★★
n. 競賽，競爭，爭奪，比賽
vt. ①爭奪，與…競爭：to contest every inch of the
ground 爭奪每一寸土地②對…提出質疑，辯駁：to
contest a statement 對一項聲明提出質疑

cricket [ˋkrɪkɪt] .... ★★
n. 板球，蟋蟀

game [gem] .... ★★★★★
n. 遊戲，娛樂，比賽，(pl.)運動會

gymnasium [dʒɪmˋneʒɪəm] .... ★★★
n. 體育館，健身房

hoop [hup] .... ★
n. 籃圈

hunt [hʌnt] .... ★★★★★
v. ①打獵：to hunt a lion 獵獅②搜尋，尋找：The hunt for the escaped criminal still continues. 搜捕逃犯仍在進行中。

hunter [ˋhʌntɚ] .... ★★★★★
n. 獵人，搜索者

match [mætʃ] .... ★★★★★
n. 火柴，比賽，競賽
【片語】have a match 舉行一場比賽
v. 匹配，相配，相稱：The picture matches the story. 這張圖很適合這個故事。

mounted [ˋmauntɪd] .... ★★★★★
adj. 騎在馬上的：a mounted point 騎兵尖兵

opponent [əˋponənt] .... ★★★★
n. 敵人，對手

pace [pes] .... ★★★★★
n. 步子，步速，步調，速度：
A policeman with plain clothes stood a dozen paces behind me. 一個便衣警察站在我後面十幾步遠的地方。
v. 踱步

pest [pɛst] .... ★
n. 害蟲

play [ple] .... ★★★★★
v. 玩，遊戲：They are playing hide-and-see. 他們在玩捉迷藏。
【片語】play with 與／拿…玩
n. 遊戲，比賽，劇本，戲劇

player [ˋpleɚ] .... ★★★★★
n. ①遊戲／玩耍的人②選手③演員，演奏者

playground [ˋpleˏgraund] .... ★★★
n. (學校的) 操場，(兒童) 遊樂場

racket [ˋrækɪt] .... ★★★
n. 球拍：tennis racket 網球拍；badminton racket 羽毛球拍

relay [rɪˋle] .... ★
n. 接力賽，中繼轉播
【片語】in/by relays 輪流地
v. 中繼轉播：The Sunday football game will be relayed live. 這個星期天的球賽將實況轉播。

辨析
Analyze

compete, contest

1 **compete** *vi.*「競爭，比賽」，指為達到最優而與人一試高低，只作不及物動詞用，常用句型有：compete with/against sb. for sth.（與某人競爭以得到某物）：Western banks compete over interest rates. 西方銀行在利率問題上展開競爭。

2 **contest** *vt.*「競賽，比賽；爭奪，競爭」，強調爭奪和佔有，及物動詞：We must contest every inch of land. 我們必須寸土必爭。

Discipline

學科（學術）名稱總匯

rival [ˈraɪvl̩] .... ★★★★
v. 競爭，匹敵
n. 對手

rowboat [ˈroˌbot] .... ★★★★★
n. 划艇

run [rʌn] .... ★★★★★
v. (使) 跑，(使) 奔跑：If you run after two
　 hares, you will catch neither. 你如果三心二
　 意將一無所得。
【片語】run across 偶然碰到

skate [sket] .... ★★★
v. 滑冰：Then we go skating. 我們接下來去溜
　 冰。
【片語】go skating 去溜冰

soccer [ˈsɑkɚ] .... ★★★
n. 英式足球

sport [sport] .... ★★★★★
n. 運動，運動會
【片語】do sports (進行) 體育運動

sportsman [ˈsportsmən] .... ★★★
n. 運動員

step [stɛp] .... ★★★★★
n. 步，腳步，步驟，措施
【片語】①in step 齊步②step by step 逐步地

strife [straɪf] .... ★★
n. 衝突，競爭：internal strife 內訌；at strife
　 不和，相爭

swim [swɪm] .... ★★★★
v. 游泳：Have you ever swum in sea? 你曾在
　 海裡游過泳嗎？
n. 游泳：Let's go out for a swim. 我們去游泳
　 吧。
　 【片語】have a swim 游泳

team [tim] .... ★★★★★
n. 隊，團體：Is he on that team? 他是那個隊
　 的嗎？

track [træk] .... ★★★★★
n. 跑道，小路，軌道，足跡，蹤跡
v. 跟蹤：track the terrorists 追蹤恐怖分子

tractor [ˈtræktɚ] .... ★★★
n. 拖拉機，牽引車

training [ˈtrenɪŋ] .... ★★★★★
n. 訓練，培養

volleyball [ˈvɑlɪbɔl] .... ★★★
n. 排球，排球運動

wrestle [ˈrɛsl̩] .... ★
n. 摔角，搏鬥，鬥爭

辨析 Analyze

pace, step

1 pace n. (一)「步；步速，速度，節
　 奏」，指步，還指速度、進度：I cannot
　 walk at that pace. 我無法以那種速度走
　 路。

2 step n.「步，腳步；步驟，措施；臺
　 階，梯級」，指步、腳步聲、腳印、臺
　 階、樓梯的一級：Take one step/pace
　 forward. 向前走一步。

辨析 Analyze

opponent, rival

1 opponent n.「敵手，對手；反對者」，
　 指競爭或比賽中的對手、敵手（多指個
　 人），還指政治或經濟等領域的反對者：
　 Tyson knocked his opponent out in the
　 first round. 泰森在第一輪就把對手擊敗
　 了。

2 rival n.「競爭對手，敵手；可與匹敵的
　 人或物」，指競爭或比賽中的對手、敵
　 手，可指個人、團體、組織，可做定語：
　 John and Tom are rivals for the first place
　 in the class. 約翰和湯姆在班上互相競爭
　 第一名。

Unit 2
文化名稱總匯
Civilization

01

語言相關辭彙

Vocabulary of Language

civilization 文化名稱總匯

abstraction [æbˋstrækʃən] ....★★★★
n. 抽象概念，摘要

abstractness [æbˋstræknɪs] ....★★★★
n. 抽象性

adage [ˋædɪdʒ] .... ★
n. 格言，諺語

alphabet [ˋælfəˌbɛt] .... ★★★
n. 字母表

Americanism [əˋmɛrəkənˌɪzəm] .... ★★★★★
n. 美國用語，美國發音

biography [baɪˋɑgrəfɪ] .... ★★★★★
n. 傳記

civilize [ˋsɪvəˌlaɪz] .... ★★★
v. （使）文明，開化：The African countries hoped to civilize all the primitive tribes on the land. 非洲國家希望把非洲所有的原始部落都變成文明社會。

colloquial [kəˋlokwɪəl] .... ★
adj. 會話的，口語的：Colloquial speech may contain many metaphors and idiomatic expressions. 口語中可能會包含許多比喻和習慣用語。

comma [ˋkɑmə] .... ★★★★★
n. 逗號：comma free code 無逗點密碼

concrete [ˋkɑnkrit] .... ★★★
n. 水泥
adj. 具體的：Do you have any concrete suggestions on how to deal with these difficulties? 你對於解決這些難題有沒有什麼具體建議？

connotation [ˌkɑnəˋteʃən] .... ★
n. 涵義

construe [kˋɑnstru] .... ★
v. 解釋，翻譯：You may construe the statement of the government spokesman in a number of different ways. 你可以對政府發言人的聲明有很多種詮釋。

content [ˋkɑntɛnt] ....★★★★★
n. 內容

context [ˋkɑntɛkst] ....★★★★
n. 上下文，前後關係

cultural [ˈkʌltʃərəl] .... ★★★★★

adj. 文化上的：Cultural communication between two countries built a bridge of understanding. 兩國間的文化交流架起了理解的橋樑。

culture [ˈkʌltʃə] .... ★★★★★

n. ①文化，文明：Universities should be centres of culture. 大學應該是文化的中心。②教養，修養：a man of culture 有教養的人

define [dɪˈfaɪn] .... ★★★★★

v. 下定義，解釋，規定，限定：The mountain was clearly defined against the light of the eastern sky. 東方天空的光芒，使那座山清晰地顯露出來。

dialogue [ˈdaɪəˌlɔg] .... ★★★

n. 對話

expound [ɪkˈspaʊnd] .... ★★★★★

v. 解釋：The speaker expounded the approach of positive thinking. 演講者闡述了正面思潮的出現。

express [ɪkˈsprɛs] .... ★★★★★

v. 表示，表達：I find it difficult for me to express myself in English. 我發現我難以用英語表達自己的想法。

adj. 特快的，快速的

n. ①快車：the 10 a.m. express 上午十點的快車②快遞：an express company 快遞公司

expression [ɪkˈsprɛʃən] .... ★★★★★

n. ①詞句，措辭②表達，表示，表現：give expression to one's gratitude 表示感激 ③表情：read with expression 生動地朗誦 ④形式，符號：mathematical expression 數學符號

intonation [ˌɪntoˈneʃən] ....★

n. 語調：the intonation of a psalm 聖歌的語調

language [ˈlæŋgwɪdʒ] .... ★★★★★

n. 語言：Which language is most widely spoken in the world? 世界上哪種語言使用最廣？

Latin [ˈlætɪn] .... ★★★★★

n. 拉丁語

adj. 拉丁語的：a Latin scholar 拉丁語學者；Latin verse 拉丁語詩句

Latinate [ˈlætɪnet] .... ★★★★★

adj. 拉丁語的，從拉丁語演化或衍生出的：a Latinate word 由拉丁語衍生的詞；a formal Latinate prose style 正規的拉丁散文風格

linguistics [lɪŋˈgwɪstɪks] ....★

n. 語言學；theoretical linguistics 理論語言學

literate [ˈlɪtərɪt] .... ★★★★★

adj. 有文化的，能讀寫的：a literate essay 一篇優美的散文

maxim [ˈmæksɪm] .... ★★★

n. 格言，箴言

monogram [ˈmɑnəˌgræm] ....★

v. 把花押字印／刻於：monogram one's handkerchief 在手帕上綴上（某人姓名起首字母組成的）花押字

nonverbal [ˌnɑnˈvɝbl] .... ★★★★★

adj. 非語言的：Gestures are a nonverbal means of expression. 打手勢是一種非言語的表達方式。

omit [oˈmɪt] .... ★★★

v. 省略，省去，遺漏：You have omitted my name from the list. 你在名單上漏掉我的名字了。

phonetics [foˈnɛtɪks] .... ★★★★★

n. 語音學

poem [poɪm] .... ★★★★★

n. 詩

poet [ˈpoɪt] .... ★★★★★

n. 詩人

pronoun [ˈpronaʊn] .... ★★★

n. 代詞

pronunciation [prəˌnʌnsɪˈeʃən] .... ★★★

n. 發音

query [ˈkwɪrɪ] .... ★★★★
n. 質問，問題
v. 詢問：I have several queries about the
work you gave me. 我對於你給我的工作有
一些問題。

quotation [kwoˈteʃən] .... ★★★
n. 引語，引文，語錄

quote [kwot] .... ★★★★★
v. 引用，援引，引證：The saxophonist
quoted a Duke Ellington melody in his solo.
薩克斯風手在他的獨奏中引用了一段艾靈頓
公爵的曲子。

represent [ˌrɛprɪˈzɛnt] .... ★★★★★
v. ①作為…代表（或代理）：The girl was
singled out to represent of the school. 那女
孩被挑選為學校代表。②表示，象徵：The
red lines on the map represent railways. 地
圖上的紅線表示鐵路。③表現，描繪：This
painting represents a storm at sea. 這幅畫
畫的是大海上的暴風雨。

representative [rɛprɪˈzɛntətɪv] .. ★★★★★
n. 代表，代理人
adj. 代表性的：The representatives were all
amazed by what had happened in the
factory. 代表們聽了這間工廠裡發生的事都
感到驚愕。

rhyme [raɪm] .... ★★★
n. 韻，押韻：Gay broad leaves swung in
rhyme. 輕盈的寬葉子有節奏地搖擺。

spell [spɛl] .... ★★★★
v. （用字母）拼寫：How do you spell it? 這個
字怎麼拼？

spelling [ˈspɛlɪŋ] .... ★★★
n. 拼法，拼寫法

theme [θim] .... ★★★★
n. 主題，題目

verse [vɝs] .... ★★
n. 詩，韻文

version [ˈvɝʒən] .... ★★★★★
n. 說法，版本：I have heard two versions of
the accident. 我已經聽到關於這個事故的兩
種說法了。

vocabulary [vəˈkæbjəˌlɛrɪ] .... ★★★
n. 辭彙（量），辭彙表

vowel [ˈvauəl] ....★
n. 母音，母音字母

word [wɝd] .... ★★★★★
n. ①詞，單詞，話，話語，字：Please leave
a word for me. 請給我留言。②（常用pl.）
所說的話，談話，言辭：He is a man with
few words. 他是個少言寡語的人。
【片語】①have a word with sb. 和某人說句話
②have words with sb. 和某人吵架③in a word
總而言之

文化名稱總匯

02

藝術相關辭彙
Vocabulary of Art

aesthetic [εs`θεtɪk] .... ★

adj. 審美的，美學的：Because of his aesthetic nature, he was frequently disturbed by ugly things. 由於他天性愛美，因此一些醜惡的東西常使他心情煩亂。

album [`ælbəm] .... ★★

n. 相冊，集郵冊，唱片

allegory [`ælə‚gorɪ] .... ★

n. 諷喻，寓言

amateur [`æmə‚tʃur] .... ★★★

adj. 業餘的：an amateur orchestra 業餘管弦樂隊

n. 業餘愛好者

artist [`ɑrtɪst] .... ★★★★★

n. 藝術家

artistic [ɑr`tɪstɪk] .... ★★★

adj. 藝術的：artistic works 藝術品

axiomatic [‚æksɪə`mætɪk] .... ★

adj. 公理的，格言的：an axiomatic truth 自明的真理

cartoon [kɑr`tun] .... ★★★

n. 漫畫，動畫片：Many children's movies are cartoons. 許多兒童電影都是卡通。

carve [kɑrv] .... ★★★

v. 刻，雕刻：The talented artist carved an interesting decoration from this piece of tree root. 有才華的藝術家把這塊樹根雕成一件有趣的裝飾品。

cello [`tʃεlo] .... ★

n. 大提琴

ceramic [sə`ræmɪk] .... ★

adj. 陶瓷的：ceramic manufactures 陶器，瓷器

chorus [`korəs] .... ★★

n. 合唱團

classic [`klæsɪk] .... ★★★★

n. 名著，傑作

adj. 第一流的，不朽的，古典的：That joke is a classic, and it is really funny. 那個笑話真是經典，非常有趣。

classical [ˋklæsɪkl̩] ★★★
adj. 經典的，古典的：Both Bach and Beethoven wrote classical music. 巴哈與貝多芬譜寫的都是古典音樂。

comedy [ˋkɑmədɪ] ★★★★★
n. 喜劇，喜劇場面

comic [ˋkɑmɪk] ★★
n. 喜劇演員，連環畫

concert [ˋkɑnsɚt] ★★★★
n. 音樂會

concerted [kənˋsɝtɪd] ★★★★
adj. 協定的，協調的：to take concerted action 採取一致行動

craft [kræft] ★★★★
n. 手藝，（單複同）船

craftsman [ˋkræftsmən] ★★★★
n. 工匠

dance [dæns] ★★★★★
n. 跳舞，舞會
v. 跳舞：She is dancing with a handsome boy. 她正與一位帥哥跳著舞。

drama [ˋdrɑmə] ★★★★
n. 劇本，戲劇，戲劇性事件，戲劇性場面

dramatic [drəˋmætɪk] ★★★★
adj. 引人注目的，戲劇性的，緊張的：to make a dramatic entrance in a swirling cape 戲劇性地披上旋動的斗篷

drum [drʌm] ★★★★
n. 鼓狀物，鼓，圓筒
v. 敲擊：He nervously drummed on the table. 他緊張地在桌上嗒嗒敲著。

enamel [ɪˋnæml̩] ★
n. 琺瑯，瓷釉，指甲油

euphonious [juˋfonɪəs] ★
adj. 悅耳的

farce [fɑrs] ★
n. 鬧劇

gallery [ˋgælərɪ] ★★★★
n. 畫廊：a picture gallery 圖片陳列室

guitar [gɪˋtɑr] ★★★
n. 吉他，六弦琴：electrical guitar 電吉他

handwriting [ˋhændˏraɪtɪŋ] ★★★
n. 筆跡，筆法，書法

image [ˋɪmɪdʒ] ★★★★★
n. 形象，映射，圖像，肖像

impromptu [ɪmˋprɑmptju] ★
adj. 臨時的，即興的：a speech made impromptu 即席演說

improvise [ˋɪmprəvaɪz] ★★★★★
v. 即興創作，臨時做：A number of his remarks were obviously improvised. 他的一些評論，很明顯是臨場發表的。

jazz [dʒæz] ★★★
n. 爵士樂

lyric [ˋlɪrɪk] ★
n. 抒情詩，歌詞：lyric poet 抒情詩人

melody [ˋmɛlədɪ] ★★
n. 旋律，曲調，歌曲

mode [mod] ★★★★★
n. 作風，方式，樣式

monotonous [məˋnɑtənəs] ★★
adj. 單調的：The monotonous routine of an assembly line can result in boredom and frustration for workers. 裝配線的單調例行工作，會讓工人覺得厭煩。

music [ˋmjuzɪk] ★★★★★
n. 音樂：popular music 流行音樂

musical [ˋmjuzɪkl̩] ★★★★
adj. 音樂的，悅耳的，喜歡音樂的，有音樂才能的：She's not at all musical. 她對音樂一竅不通。

musician [mjuˋzɪʃən] ★★★★
n. 音樂家，樂師

opera [ˈɑpərə] .... ★★★
n. 歌劇：opera stars 歌劇明星； an opera libretto 歌劇的歌詞

orchestra [ˈɔrkɪstrə] .... ★★★
n. 管弦樂隊

piano [pɪˈæno] .... ★★★★
n. 鋼琴

pictorial [pɪkˈtorɪəl] .... ★★
adj. 圖示的
n. 畫報

portrait [ˈportret] .... ★★★★
n. 肖像，畫像，描寫：The majority of United States coins today are stamped with the portrait of a President. 大多數的美國硬幣上都有總統的肖像。

portray [porˈtre] .... ★★★★★
v. 繪製：Who portrayed King Lear? 誰扮演李爾王？

pottery [ˈpɑtəɪ] .... ★
n. 陶器（製造術）

profile [ˈprofaɪl] .... ★★★★
adj. 外形，輪廓：a profile of the new prime minister 新首相的簡介

Renaissance [rəˈnesṇs] .... ★
n. 文藝復興

renowned [rɪˈnaʊnd] .... ★★★★★
adj. 知名的：Handy, the renowned composer and musician, was known as the "father of the blues." 漢迪是一位著名的音樂家和作曲家，以「藍調之父」聞名。

rhythm [ˈrɪðəm] .... ★★★
n. 節奏，韻律

sculpture [ˈskʌlptʃɚ] .... ★
n. 雕塑品
vt. 雕刻，用雕刻裝飾：sculpture a statue out of ivory 雕刻象牙雕像

singer [ˈsɪŋɚ] .... ★★★★
n. 歌唱家

song [sɔŋ] .... ★★★★★
n. 歌曲，歌聲：a fork song 民歌

statue [ˈstætʃʊ] .... ★★★★
n. 雕像：The Statue of Liberty was presented to the United States of America in the nineteenth century by the people of France. 自由女神雕像是法國人民在19世紀送給美國的。

studio [ˈstjudɪo] .... ★★
n. 工作室，播音室，畫室：a painter's studio 畫家的工作室

stunt [stʌnt] .... ★
n. 驚人的技藝：partner stunt 雙人技巧

style [staɪl] .... ★★★★★
n. ①風格，文體：style of painting 畫風②式樣，類型：She always keeps up with the latest styles in hair dressing. 她總是跟得上最新的髮型。

syllable [ˈsɪləbḷ] .... ★
n. 音節

symphony [ˈsɪmfənɪ] .... ★
n. 交響樂：symphony orchestra 交響樂團

versatile [ˈvɝsətḷ] .... ★
adj. 多才多藝的：He was a versatile athlete; at college he had earned varsity letters in baseball, football, and track. 他先前是個多才多藝的運動員，在大學時，早已獲得了籃球、橄欖球及田徑等代表隊優秀隊員的榮譽。

violin [ˌvaɪəˈlɪn] .... ★★★
n. 小提琴

03

新聞、出版、宣傳相關辭彙

Vocabulary of Word-relatedness

advertisement [ˌædvɚˋtaɪzmənt] .... ★★★
n. 廣告

bulletin [ˋbʊlətɪn] .... ★★
n. 告示，公告：the latest bulletin about the President's health 總統健康狀況的最新報告

caption [ˋkæpʃən] .... ★★★★★
n. （章、節、文章、檔等的）標題：under the caption of 在⋯標題下，以⋯為標題
vt. 在⋯上加標題

edit [ˋɛdɪt] .... ★★★★★
v. 編輯，校訂，編纂：The author has edited out all references to his own family. 作者已將涉及自己家庭之處刪掉了。

edition [ɪˋdɪʃən] .... ★★★★★
n. 版，版本，版次：The new edition of encyclopedia will appear in the bookstores next week. 新版的百科全書下週就會在書店上架。

editor [ˋɛdɪtɚ] .... ★★★★★
n. 編輯，編者：chief editor = editor in chief 主編

editorial [ˌɛdəˋtorɪəl] .... ★★
n. 社論
a. 編輯的，社論的：an editorial position with a publishing company 出版公司中的編輯職位

excerpt [ˋɛksɝpt] .... ★★★★★
n. 摘錄

heading [ˋhɛdɪŋ] .... ★★★★
n. 標題，信頭，題目

headline [ˋhɛdˏlaɪn] .... ★★★★
n. 大字標題，新聞提要

hearsay [ˋhɪrˏse] .... ★★★★★
n. 謠傳，風聞

hookup [ˋhʊkˏʌp] .... ★
n. 實驗線路，聯播電臺

informant [ɪnˋfɔrmənt] .... ★★★★★
n. 提供消息的人

information [ˌɪnfɚˋmeʃən] .... ★★★★★
n. 資訊：We need some information on computer industry. 我們需要一些電腦行業的資訊。

interview [ˈɪntɚˌvju] .... ★★★★★
n. 接見，會見，面試：I thank you very much indeed for this interview. 真的非常感謝您這次的接見。
v. 接見，會見，會晤

issue [ˈɪʃju] .... ★★★★★
n. 問題，出版，發行，（報刊的）期
v. 發行：When high voltage is applied to the electrodes of a vacuum tube, a stream of electrons issues from the negative electrode. 當高壓電加在電極真空管上時，真空管的負極上就會發射出電子流。

journal [ˈdʒɝnl] .... ★★★★★
n. 雜誌，定期刊物，日報，期刊，日誌，日記：The doctor reads the *Journal of Medical Science.* 這位醫生在閱讀《醫學科學》雜誌。

journalism [ˈdʒɝnlˌɪzm] .... ★★★★
n. 新聞寫作

journalist [ˈdʒɝnəlɪst] .... ★★★★
n. 記者，新聞工作者：accredited journalist 特派新聞記者

magazine [ˌmæɡəˈzin] .... ★★★★★
n. 雜誌，期刊

mouthpiece [ˈmaʊθˌpis] .... ★★★
n. （樂器的）吹口，代言人：The newspaper is the mouthpiece of the government. 這家報紙是政府的機關報。

news [njuz] .... ★★★★★
n. 新聞，消息：Please write soon and tell me all your news. 請儘快回信，把你的近況都告訴我。

newsman [ˈnjuzmən] .... ★★★★★
n. 新聞記者

newspaper [ˈnjuzˌpepɚ] .... ★★★★★
n. 報紙：I saw your name in a newspaper. 我在報紙上看見你的名字了。

pirate [ˈpaɪrət] .... ★★
n. 海盜

preface [ˈprɛfɪs] .... ★★★
n. 序言，前言

prelude [ˈprɛljud] .... ★
n. 序幕：a prelude to a piece of great work 一件偉大作品的序言

premise [ˈprɛmɪs] .... ★★★★★
v. 提出前提
n. 前提

printer [ˈprɪntɚ] .... ★★
n. 印刷機，印表機

辨析 Analyze

journal, magazine

1 **journal** *n.* 「雜誌，期刊，日報，日誌，日記」，指嚴肅或學術性的期刊、雜誌，作為具有文學意味的用法也指日報、日記、日誌：The study appeared in a leading medical journal. 該研究發表在一家著名的醫療期刊上。

2 **magazine** *n.* 「雜誌，期刊」，指一般或娛樂性的雜誌、期刊，還指彈藥庫、彈夾：Children like magazines full of illustrations. 兒童喜歡插圖多的雜誌。

public [ˈpʌblɪk] .... ★★★★★
adj. ①公共的，公用的：public telephones 公用電話②公眾的：The politicians have to respond to public opinion. 政治人物必須回應輿論。③公開的，公然的：We hold weekly public meetings. 我們每週都召開公開會議。
【片語】in public 公開地，當眾
n. 公眾，民眾：The gardens are open to the public. 所有公園都對大眾開放。

publication [ˌpʌblɪˈkeʃən] .... ★★★★★
n. 出版物，出版，公佈：the list of new publications 新書目錄；a monthly/weekly publication 月／週刊

publicity [pʌbˈlɪsətɪ] .... ★★★★★
n.（公眾的）注意，名聲，宣傳

publish [ˈpʌblɪʃ] .... ★★★★★
v. ①出版，刊印：That dictionary was published in 1990. 那本字典是在1990年出版的。②公佈，發表：He received a long prison term for publishing his views. 他因為發表了自己的觀點，受到長期監禁。

report [rɪˈport] .... ★★
n. 報告，彙報，報導
v. 報告，彙報：I'll report this question to the officer. 我會把這個問題向長官報告。

speech [spitʃ] .... ★★★★★
n. 演講，演說，言語，語言

spokesman [ˈspoksmən] .... ★★★
n. 發言人

subscribe [səbˈskraɪb] ....★
v. 訂閱，訂購：He subscribed his name to the contract. 他在合同上簽名。

summarize [ˈsʌməˌraɪz] .... ★★★
v. 概括，總結，摘要，概述

summary [ˈsʌməˌraɪz] .... ★★★★
n. 摘要，概要，概略
adj. 概括的，大略的：summary justice 簡明的審判

telecast [ˈtɛləˌkæst] .... ★★★★★
v. 用電視播送：live telecast 電視實況轉播

title [ˈtaɪtl] .... ★★★★★
n. ①題目，標題：He wrote a book with the title The Castle. 他寫了一本名為《城堡》的書。②標號，頭銜：There were a lot of gentlemen in tweed suits, some with title and some really rich. 那裡有許多穿著花呢西服的紳士，一些是有頭銜的，一些是非常富有的。

transcribe [trænsˈkraɪb] .... ★★★★★
v. 抄寫，把（速記符號）譯成文字

transcript [ˈtrænˌskrɪpt] .... ★★★★★
n. 成績單：an academic transcript 學生成績單

transcription [ˌtrænˈskrɪpʃən] ... ★★★★★
n. 抄寫，（速寫符號記錄等的）翻譯，抄本

translate [trænsˈlet] .... ★★★★
v. 翻譯：Can someone translate this legal jargon into plain English for me? 誰能把這個法律術語用簡單易懂的英語說給我聽？
【片語】①translate sth. into sth. 把…翻譯／轉化轉…②translate sth. as sth. 斷定或猜想某事物的意義或意圖，（用另外的詞語）解釋某事物

translation [trænsˈleʃən] .... ★★★★★
n. 翻譯，譯文

underline [ˌʌndəˈlaɪn] .... ★★★
vt. ①在…下面劃線：The example sentences were underlined. 例句下面都劃了線。②強調：He wrote an article to underline the same problem. 他寫了篇文章強調相同的問題。

writer [ˈraɪtə] .... ★★★★★
n. 作者，作家

文化名稱總匯

04

影視、娛樂相關辭彙

Vocabulary of Amusements

actress [ˈæktrɪs] ....★★★★
n. 女演員

cassette [kəˈsɛt] ....★★★★
n. 卡式錄音帶

channel [ˈtʃænl] ....★★★★
n. ①（電視等的）頻道，波段：a commercial on channel 5. 5頻道的一則商業廣告②管道：They dug a channel to bring water to the field. 他們挖一道溝渠引水灌田。③海峽，水道，航道：the English Channel 英吉利海峽④（常用複數）路線途徑：He has secret channels of information. 他有秘密的消息來源。

cinema [ˈsɪnəmə] ....★★★★
n. 電影院，電影，影片
【片語】go to the cinema 看電影

circus [ˈsɝkəs] ....★
n. 馬戲，馬戲團，馬戲場，雜技場

club [klʌb] ....★★★★★
n. ①俱樂部，夜總會，社團：She's just joined our chess club. 她剛剛加入我們的棋藝社。②球棒③（撲克牌中的）梅花

compile [kəmˈpaɪl] ....★★
v. 收集，編纂：He is going to compile the data requested by the tax collector. 他按照收稅人的要求，將彙整出所需的資料。

coverage [ˈkʌnərɪdʒ] ....★★★★★
n. 涉及範圍

fanatic [fəˈnætɪk] ....★
n. 盲從者
adj. 狂熱的：My friend, Crawley, has always been a fanatical opponent of Mr. Lane's Radical Progressive Party. 我的朋友克勞萊，一向是萊恩先生的激進進步黨的狂熱反對者。

fanaticism [fəˈnætəˌsɪzəm] ....★
n. 狂熱，盲從

film [fɪlm] ....★★★★★
n. 影片，電影，膠捲
【片語】go to a film 去看電影

idol [ˈaɪdḷ] .... ★
n. 偶像

joke [dʒok] .... ★★★★
n. 笑話，玩笑
v. 說笑話，開玩笑：You mustn't joke with him.
你千萬不能跟他開玩笑。

labyrinth [ˈlæbərɪnθ] .... ★
n. 迷宮，錯綜複雜之事件：a labyrinth of rules
and regulations 錯綜複雜的規章和制度

magic [ˈmædʒɪk] .... ★★★★
n. 魔法，魔術：Do you believe in magic? 你
相信魔術嗎？
adj. 有魔力的，魔術的：a magic weapon 法寶

magician [məˈdʒɪʃən] .... ★
n. 魔術家，術士：a magician with words 說話
有魔力的人

microfilm [ˈmaɪkrəˌfɪlm] .... ★★★★★
n. 微縮膠捲，微縮照片

movie [ˈmuvɪ] .... ★★★★★
n. 電影：go to the movies 去看電影

percussion [pəˈkʌʃən] .... ★
n. 打擊樂器，震盪：percussion hammer
〔醫〕叩診槌，擊診槌

photograph [ˈfotəˌgræf] .... ★★★★★
n. 攝影，相片，照片

photographic [ˌfotəˈgræfɪk] .... ★★★
adj. 照相的，攝影的，攝影用的，攝影術的：a
photographic memory 過目不忘的能力

plot [plɑt] .... ★★★
v. 策劃，繪製，測定位置：Amateur
archaeologists start out by learning how to
plot records of their finds in a given area. 業
餘考古愛好者開始在某一指定地點學習如何
去記錄其發現。

recite [rɪˈsaɪt] .... ★★★
v. 朗讀，背誦：He recited the passage
accurately with slow, impressive emphasis.
他準確地背誦了一段文章，背得舒緩有致、
有聲有色。

recreation [ˌrɛkrɪˈeʃən] .... ★★★
n. 消遣

rehearsal [rɪˈhɝsḷ] .... ★
n. 排練，彩排：a long rehearsal of his woes
關於他的痛苦的詳細敘述

rehearse [rɪˈhɝs] .... ★
v. 預演，排練：He rehearsed his speech last
night. 他昨晚排練了演講。

screen [skrin] .... ★★★★★
v. 遮蔽
n. 螢幕：On the television screen we see the
announcer holding up a cereal box with the
name WAKE—UPS in big letters. 我們在電
視螢幕上看到主持人舉著一個上有大寫字母
「WAKE-UPS（清醒）」字樣的麥片盒。

scripture [ˈskrɪptʃɚ] .... ★★
n. 手稿，聖書，聖經：Holy Scripture 聖經

spectator [spɛkˈtetɚ] .... ★★
n. 旁觀者，觀眾

theatre / theater [ˈθɪətɚ] .... ★★★★★
n. 戲院，劇場，劇院：There are many
theatres in Italy. 義大利有許多戲院。

toy [tɔɪ] .... ★★★★
n. 玩具

tragedy [ˈtrædʒədɪ] .... ★★★★
n. ①慘事，災難：the principal cause of the
tragedy 這場災難的主要起因②悲劇：I write
both tragedies and comedies. 我寫悲劇也
寫喜劇。

tragic [ˈtrædʒɪk] .... ★★
adj. 悲劇的，悲慘的：a tragic accident 不幸的
事故

文化名稱總匯

05

民間習俗相關辭彙

Vocabulary of Convention

bride [braɪd] .... ★★★★
n. 新娘

bridegroom [ˈbraɪdˌgrʊm] .... ★
n. 新郎

byword [ˈbaɪˌwɝd] .... ★
n. 諺語，綽號

carol [ˈkærəl] .... ★
n. 歡樂之歌：Christmas carols 聖誕頌歌

cemetery [ˈsɛməˌtrɪ] .... ★
n. 公墓，墓地：public cemetery 公墓

Christmas [ˈkrɪsməs] ....★★★★
n. 聖誕節

convention [kənˈvɛnʃən] .... ★★★★★
n. 會議，協定，傳統

custom [ˈkʌstəm] .... ★★★★★
n. 習慣，進口稅

customary [ˈkʌstəmˌɛrɪ] .... ★★★★★
adj. 習慣的，慣常的：It is customary to give people gifts on their birthday. 送生日禮物是一種社會風俗。

deity [ˈdiətɪ] .... ★
n. 神
v. 神化：For centuries before the first astronomers' probings, the Sun had been viewed only as a deity and was therefore not often the subject of scientific study. 太陽在天文學先驅們進行探索之前的幾百年裡，一直被認為是神而不是科學研究的對象。

dialect [ˈdaɪəlɛkt] .... ★★★
n. 方言，土語，地方話：English is a West Germanic dialect. 英語是西日耳曼語的一支。

Easter [ˈistə] .... ★
n. 復活節：Easter egg（復活節用的）彩蛋

embroider [ɪmˈbrɔɪdə] .... ★
v. 繡花，裝飾：embroider a design on a bedspread 在床單上繡出一個圖案

embroidery [ɪmˈbrɔɪdərɪ] .... ★
n. 刺繡

enigma [ɪˈnɪgmə] .... ★
n. 謎

enigmatic [ˌɛnɪgˈmætɪk] .... ★
adj. 像謎般的，難解的：a professor's
　　enigmatic grading system 某位教授令人
　　迷惑的評分標準

eve [iv] .... ★★★★
n. 前夜，前夕：on the eve of the great event
　　大事件前夕

fairy [ˈfɛrɪ] .... ★★★★
n. 仙女，妖精：a fairy tale 神話故事，童話

feast [fist] .... ★★★★
n. 盛宴，筵席：a book that is a veritable feast
for the mind 一本心靈饗宴的書
v. 盛宴款待

festival [ˈfɛstəvl̩] .... ★★★★
n. 節日，喜慶：A happy festival atmosphere
　　pervaded the whole town. 整個鎮上充滿了
　　歡樂的節慶氣氛。

forbear [fɔrˈbɛr] .... ★★★★★
n.（常用複數形）祖先
v. 容忍，忍住：He forbore claiming the
　　reward. 他放棄報酬。

funeral [ˈfjunərəl] .... ★★★★
n. 葬禮，喪禮：a funeral procession 送葬的行
　　列

ghost [gost] .... ★★★★
n. 鬼魂，幽靈
v. 代筆：He was hired to ghost the
　　autobiography of a famous executive. 他受
　　雇替一有名的官員代筆寫自傳。

holiday [ˈhɑlə‚de] .... ★★★★
n. 假日，假期，休假
【片語】on holiday 度假

kite [kaɪt] .... ★★★
n. ①鳶②風箏

legend [ˈlɛdʒənd] .... ★★
n. 傳說，傳奇

legendary [ˈlɛdʒən‚dɛrɪ] .... ★★
adj. 傳奇的

monster [ˈmɑnstɚ] .... ★★
n. 怪物，巨獸

mosque [mɑsk] .... ★
n. 清真寺

mysterious [mɪsˈtɪrɪəs] .... ★★★★
adj. 神秘的，難以理解的：They're being very
　　mysterious about their holiday plans. 他們
　　對於度假計畫顯得很神秘。

mystery [ˈmɪstərɪ] .... ★★★★★
n. 神秘，神秘的事，玄妙（之物），秘密，神
　　秘小說，偵探小說：The murder remained
　　an unsolved mystery. 那起謀殺案仍然是個
　　未解之謎。

mystical [ˈmɪstɪkl̩] .... ★★★★★
adj. 神秘的，不可理解的，虛構的：The story
　　is mythical. 這個故事很神秘。

myth [mɪθ] .... ★★★
n. 神話：The history of the United States flag
　　is embroidered with myth and tradition. 美
　　國國旗的歷史，是神話和傳統交織而成的。

Apollo [əˈpɑlo] .... ★★★★★
n. 阿波羅（太陽神）

parabolic [ˌpærəˈbɑlɪk] .... ★
adj. 寓言的，拋物線的

proverb [ˈprɑvɝb] .... ★
n. 諺語，格言："Don't put all your eggs in one
　　basket." is a proverb.「不要把所有的雞蛋放
　　在一個藍子裡」是一句諺語。

puppet [ˈpʌpɪt] .... ★
n. 木偶，傀儡：puppet government 傀儡政府

pyramid [ˈpɪrəmɪd] .... ★
n. 金字塔

riddle [ˈrɪdl̩] .... ★
n. 謎

salamander [ˋsæləˌmændɚ] .... ★
n. （傳說中的）火蛇，火怪

slang [slæŋ] .... ★
n. 俚語，行話，黑話：army slang 軍隊俚語

souvenir [ˋsuvəˌnɪr] .... ★
n. 紀念品

superstition [ˌsupɚˋstɪʃən] .... ★★
n. 迷信

tomb [tum] .... ★★★★
n. 墳，墓

witch [wɪtʃ] .... ★
n. 女巫

Zeus [zjus] .... ★
n. （希臘神）宙斯

辨析
Analyze

mystery, myth, secret

1 **mystery** *n.* 「神秘（性），神秘的人（或事物）」，指基本上無人知道或理解的神秘之人或物，可能會使人感到茫然、迷惑或感興趣：An air of mystery surrounded the events leading up to his resignation. 導致他辭職的事件籠罩著一股神秘的氣氛。

2 **myth** *n.* 「神話，杜撰出來的人或事物」，指杜撰或瞎傳出來的人或物，很多人相信但卻不是真的，還指神話：The strange thing reminds us of classical myth. 這件奇怪的事情讓我們想起古代的神話。

3 **secret** *n.* 「秘密」，指僅有一個或少數幾個人知道而又不讓別人知道的秘密：The process is a secret. 這個過程是個秘密。

Unit 3
技術工程名稱總匯
Technique

01

科技相關辭彙

Technique

技術工程名稱總匯

Vocabulary of Technology

aeronautical [ˌɛrəˋnɔtɪkl̩] .... ★
adj. 航空的，航空術的：aeronautical charts 航空地圖

alchemist [ˋælkəmɪst] .... ★
n. 煉金術士

astronaut [ˋæstrənɔt] .... ★★★
n. 太空人

automated [ˋɔtometɪd] .... ★
adj. 自動化的：automated business equipment 自動化的商業設備

automatic [ˌɔtəˋmætɪk] .... ★★★
adj. 自動的：an automatic dishwasher 自動洗碗機

automation [ˌɔtəˋmeʃən] .... ★
n. 自動化

coaxial [koˋæksɪəl] .... ★
adj. 共軸的，同軸的：coaxial cable 同軸電纜

expert [ˋɛkspɚt] .... ★★★★★
n. 專家，能手

expertise [ˌɛkspɚˋtiz] .... ★★★★★
n. 專門知識：technical expertise 技術專長

function [ˋfʌŋkʃən] .... ★★★★★
n. 機能，官能，功能，職責，作用，函數
v. 活動，運轉，起作用：The old machine won't function properly if you don't oil it regularly. 那臺舊機器如果不經常加油，就不能正常運轉。

functional [ˋfʌŋkʃənl̩] .... ★★★★
adj. 有用的：functional organization 職能機構

functionally [ˋfʌŋkʃənl̩ɪ] .... ★★★★
adv. 機能上的，功能作用方面的

hydraulics [haɪˋdrɔlɪks] .... ★
n. 水力學，液動裝置

idiosyncrasy [ˌɪdɪəˋsɪŋkrəsɪ] .... ★
n. 個人特性

ken [kɛn] .... ★★★★★
n. 視野，知識：complex issues well beyond our ken 複雜的問題超出我們的理解範圍

mechanics [məˋkænɪks] .... ★
n. 力學：atomic quantum mechanics 原子的量子力學

microelectronics [ˌmaɪkroɪˌlɛk'trɑnɪks] ... ★
n. 微電子學

patent ['pætṇt] .... ★★
adj. 專利的，特許的
n. 專利，專利權，專利品
v. 批准專利，獲得專利：The government patented the device to its inventor. 政府給予發明者專利權。

rocket ['rɑkɪt] .... ★★★
n. 火箭

science ['saɪəns] .... ★★★★★
n. 科學，科學研究

scientific [ˌsaɪən'tɪfɪk] .... ★★★★★
adj. ①科學的，科學上的②合乎科學的③有技術的

scientist ['saɪəntɪst] .... ★★★★
n. 科學家

solder ['sɑdə] .... ★
v. （低溫）焊接
n. （低溫）焊料，焊錫

spacecraft ['spes'kræft] .... ★★★
n. （單複同）太空船

spacelab ['spesˌlæb] .... ★★★
n. 太空實驗室

spaceship ['spesˌʃɪp] .... ★★★
n. 太空船

special ['spɛʃəl] .... ★★★★★
adj. 特別的，特殊的：This is a way of thinking special to woman. 這是女性特有的想法。
【詞性變化】specially 特殊地

specialist ['spɛʃəlɪst] .... ★★★★★
n. 專家

specialize ['spɛʃəˌlaɪz] .... ★★★★★
v. 專攻，專門研究，專業化

specialty ['spɛʃəltɪ] .... ★★★★★
n. 專業：His specialty is biology, mine is physiology. 他的專業是生物學，我的專業是生理學。

specimen ['spɛsəmən] .... ★★★
n. 標本，樣本

technical ['tɛknɪkḷ] .... ★★★
adj. 技術的，工藝的：scientific and technical knowledge 科學技術知識

technician [tɛk'nɪʃən] .... ★★★
n. 技術員，技術專家，技師，技工

technique [tɛk'nik] .... ★★★★
n. ①技術，技能：Because of modern technique we have a much higher standard of living. 我們由於有現代技術，所以有了高水準的生活。②工藝，技巧：He is not very fast but he's got marvelous technique. 他的速度不是很快，卻有高超的技藝。

technological [tɛknə'lɑdʒɪkḷ] .... ★★★★★
adj. 工藝的，技術的，工藝學的

technologist [tɛk'nɑlədʒɪst] ...... ★★★★★
n. 工藝師

technology [tɛk'nɑlədʒɪ] .... ★★★★★
n. 工藝，技術：Modern civilization depends greatly on technology. 現代文明很依賴科技。

thermodynamics [ˌθɝmodaɪ'næmɪks] ...... ★
n. 熱力學

tip [tɪp] .... ★★★★★
n. 竅門
v. 接觸：Who tipped you off? 誰告了你的狀？

transistor [træn'zɪstə] .... ★
n. 〔電〕電晶體，晶體管收音機

UFO ['jufo] .... ★★★★★
n. 不明飛行物，飛碟

xerography [zɪ'rɑgrəfɪ] .... ★
n. 靜電印刷術

xerox ['zɪrɑks] .... ★
v. 用靜電複印

02

工程相關辭彙

Vocabulary of Engineering

applied [əˋplaɪd] .... ★★★★★
adj. 應用的，實用的，外加的：an applied technologist
應用技術人員

arch [ɑrtʃ] .... ★★
n. 拱門，橋洞：an arch bridge 拱橋
v. 拱起，成為弓形：The meteor arched across the
sky. 流星呈弧形劃過天空。

architect [ˋɑrkəˏtɛkt] .... ★★
n. 建築師，締造者：He was one of the principal
architects of the revolution. 他是那次革命的主要發
起人之一。

architecture [ˋɑrkəˏtɛktʃə] .... ★★★★
n. ①建築學，建築書②建築式樣／風格：I like the
architecture of the 19th century very much. 我非常
喜歡 19 世紀的建築風格。

build [bɪld] .... ★★★★★
vt. 造，建築，建設，建立：The school is built of
wood. 該校舍是用木頭造的。

building [ˋbɪldɪŋ] .... ★★★★★
n. 建築，房屋，大樓：There are a lot of tall buildings
in this city. 這座城市裡有許多大樓。

carpenter [ˋkɑrpəntə] .... ★
n. 木工，木匠：carpenter's bench 木工檯

column [ˋkɑləm] .... ★★★★★
n. 柱，柱狀物，專欄：Can you add up this column of
figures? 你能把這行數字加起來嗎？

component [kəmˋponənt] ....★★★★
n. 組成部分

configuration [kənˏfɪgjəˋreʃən] .... ★
n. 構造：compound configuration 混合式構造

dome [dom] .... ★★
n. 岩穹，圓蓋，圓頂，圓頂屋，拱頂：the dome of a
church 教堂的圓頂

drain [dren] .... ★★★
n. 排水管，水溝，下水道，排出之物
v. 排（水），放（水），使徐徐流出：The day's
events completely drained me of all strength. 這天的
事情讓我是精疲力竭。

embankment [ɪmˈbæŋkmənt] .... ★
n. 路堤，堤岸

gutter [ˈgʌtɚ] .... ★
n. 溝，槽

malfunction [mælˈfʌŋʃən] .... ★
n. 失靈，故障：system malfunction 系統故障

mechanic [məˈkænɪk] .... ★★★
n. 技工，機械工

mechanical [məˈkænɪkl̩] .... ★★★
adj. 機械的：He was asked the same question so many times that the answer became mechanical. 同一個問題他被詢問了好幾遍，所以他的回答變得很制式化。

pedestal [ˈpɛdɪstl̩] .... ★
n. 底座，臺座：Poet Emma Lazarus is perhaps best known for having written the sonnet inscribed on the pedestal of the Statue of Liberty. 伊瑪‧拉扎羅斯或許是因為其刻在自由女神底座上的十四行詩，成為了最著名的詩人。

pivotal [ˈpɪvətl̩] .... ★
adj. 樞紐的，關鍵的：Its pivotal location has also exposed it to periodic invasions. 其地點的重要性也使得它每隔一段時間就遭受侵略。

plumber [ˈplʌmɚ] .... ★
n. 水管工

reservoir [ˈrɛzɚˌvɔr] .... ★★★★★
n. 水庫，貯存器，蓄水池

scheme [skim] .... ★★★★
v. 計畫，預謀
n. 計畫，方案，預謀，詭計：Alexander Hamilton was accused of being involved in a scheme to establish a separate nation in the western part of the United States. 亞歷山大‧漢米爾頓被指責涉入美國西部建國的陰謀。

structure [ˈstrʌktʃɚ] .... ★★★★★
n. 結構，構造，組織，建築物，裝置：The builders had put up a tall structure between the shops. 建築工人已經在商店之間建起一座很高的建築。

tower [ˈtauɚ] .... ★★
n. 塔
v. ①高聳，屹立：The skyscrapers towered into the sky. 摩天大樓高聳入雲。②高出，超出：He towers over his mother by one foot. 他比他母親高出一英尺。

unearth [ʌnˈɝθ] .... ★★★★★
v. 發掘，發現：unearth a plot 破獲一起陰謀

03

測量、計算相關辭彙 Vocabulary of Measure

centigrade [ˈsɛntəˌgred] .... ★★★
adj. 攝氏度的：In the summer, the temperature is sometimes forty degrees centigrade. 在夏天，溫度有時達攝氏 40 度。

centimeter [ˈsɛntəˌmitɚ] .... ★★★
n. 公分

contemplate [ˈkɑntɛmˌplet] .... ★★★★★
v. 凝視，沉思：The young surgeon contemplated the difficult operation of kidney transplant. 年輕的外科醫生苦思著棘手的腎臟移植手術。

count [kaʊnt] .... ★★★★★
v. ①數，點數：Can you count the stars in the sky? 你能數清天上的星星嗎？②包括，計算：There are thirty people, not counting the children. 不包括孩子，共 30 人。

exploit [ˈɛksplɔɪt] .... ★★★
n. 功績，功勳：Their heroic exploits will go down in history. 他們的英雄功績將會名留青史。
v. 開拓，開發，開採，利用，剝削：a country that exploited peasant labor 壓榨農民的國家

exploration [ˌɛkspləˈreʃən] .... ★★
n. 探索，探險，考察，勘探，調查：pressure exploration 壓力分佈測定；space exploration 太空探索；extensive exploration 廣泛調查

exploratory [ɪkˈsplorəˌtorɪ] .... ★★
adj. 探險的，考察的：an exploratory report 考察報告

explore [ɪkˈsplor] .... ★★★★★
v. 探險，探索：Lewis and Clark's expedition was organized to explore the land beyond to the Pacific Ocean. 路易士和克拉克經過規劃，探索太平洋的另一邊土地。

explorer [ɪkˈsplorɚ] .... ★★★★★
n. 探索者，考察者：an Arctic explorer 北極探險家

gauge [gedʒ] .... ★★★
v. 精確計量：Calipers are instruments that can be used to gauge the distance between two surfaces. 卡尺是用來測量兩個表面之間距離的儀器。

inch [ɪntʃ] .... ★★★★
n. 英寸

liter（美），litre（英）[ˋlitɚ] .... ★★★
n.（容量單位）升，公升

measurable [ˋmɛʒərəbl] .... ★★★
adj. 可測量的：a measurable figure in
　　literature 文學界的一個值得注意的人物；
　　come within a measurable distance of 臨
　　近，逼近，接近

measure [ˋmɛʒɚ] .... ★★★★★
v. ①量，測量：The dress designer measured
　　her. 服裝設計師量了她的尺寸。②有…
　　（寬、高等）：That building must measure
　　at least 30 metres. 那座建築物必須至少有
　　30 公尺高。
n. 分量，分寸，措施，辦法

measurement [ˋmɛʒəmənt] .... ★★★
n. 測量，測定，尺寸，量度，大小

mile [maɪl] .... ★★★★
n. 英里

mileage [ˋmaɪlɪdʒ] .... ★★★★★
n. 汽車消耗一加侖汽油所行的平均英里數

millimeter [ˋmɪləˌmitɚ] .... ★★★★★
n. 公釐

ounce [aʊns] .... ★★★
n. 盎司，英兩

outflow [ˋaʊtˌflo] .... ★★★★★
n. 流出，外流

pint [paɪnt] .... ★★★
n. 品脫

pound [paʊnd] .... ★★★★★
n. 英鎊，磅
v. 搗爛，舂爛：penny-wise and pound-foolish
　　省小錢卻吃大虧，因小失大

specification [ˌspɛsəfəˋkeʃən] .... ★
n. 規格

standard [ˋstændɚd] .... ★★★★★
adj. 標準的，合規格的：a standard sample 標
　　準樣品

survey [ˋsɚve] .... ★★★★★
v. 俯瞰，審察，測繪，環視，測量，勘察：
　　According to a recent survey, in Shanghai
　　alone there are more than 25 million migrant
　　workers. 根據最近的一項調查，光上海就有
　　2,500 多萬外地工人。

weight [wet] .... ★★★★
n. ①重量，分量：Can you guess the weight
　　of this sack? 你猜得出這個袋子有多重嗎？
　　②砝碼，稱砣③重／負擔④影響，力量，重
　　要／大

辨析
Analyze

criterion, standard

1　criterion n.「（批評、判斷等的）標準、
　　準則」，指評判事物好壞的要素或條件，
　　複數形式為criteria：What criteria do you
　　use when judging the quality of a school?
　　你用什麼標準判斷一所學校的素質？

2　standard n.「標準，規格」，指達到一
　　定質量或數量的目標、要努力達到的標
　　準：The service in the hotel is up to the
　　standard. 這家旅館的服務是符合標準
　　的。

04

帳、冊、圖表相關辭彙

Vocabulary of Accounts

chart [tʃɑrt] .... ★★★★
n. 圖表，圖，曲線圖：a sales chart 銷售圖

copy [ˈkɑpɪ] .... ★★★★★
v. 複製，模仿：Please send a copy of this letter to Mr. Grey. 請把這封信的副本送給格雷先生。

diagram [ˈdaɪəˌɡræm] .... ★★★
n. 圖表

draft [dræft] .... ★★★★
n. 草稿，草案，草圖
v. 起草，草擬，製圖：John Hanson helped draft instructions for Maryland's delegates to the *Stamp Act Congress*. 約翰·漢森幫助馬里蘭州的代表起草了《國會郵票法》的說帖。

draw [drɔ] .... ★★★★★
v. 拉，拖，拔出，引出，繪製：Immigrants were drawn to the United States by the growing cities and industries. 移民受到城市和工業增加的吸引而來到美國。

drawback [ˈdrɔˌbæk] .... ★
n. 弊端，退款：They met to consider the drawbacks in the proposal. 他們聚在一起討論這項提案的弊端。

drawing [ˈdrɔɪŋ] .... ★★★★★
n. 圖畫，素描（畫）：a drawing of a cat 一幅貓的素描畫

figure [ˈfɪɡjɚ] .... ★★★★★
n. 輪廓，體形，身影，圖形，圖表，數位，數值，形象，人物
v. 想，認為：I never figured that this would happen. 我從沒想到會發生這樣的事。

form [fɔrm] .... ★★★★★
n. ①形狀，形式：Any form of cheat is not allowed. 不允許任何的作弊形式。②種類：She doesn't like any form of exercise. 各類練習她都不喜歡。
v. ①組成，構成：The flying cloud forms some strange shapes constantly. 飛雲不斷地組成一些奇怪的形狀。②形成：These ideas have been formed in my mind. 這些想法已在我腦海中形成。

formal [ˈfɔrml̩] .... ★★★★
adj. 正式的，禮儀上的：Business letters are usually formal, but we write in an informal way to family members or friends. 商業信件通常都是正式的，但我們寫給家人或朋友的信就比較隨便了。

formation [fɔrˈmeʃən] .... ★★★★
n. （岩）層，形成

graphic [ˈgræfɪk] .... ★★
adj. 圖的，圖解的，生動的：Alice Walker's graphic depiction of the lives of Black people in the South has established her as one of the most promising contemporary writers in the United Sates. 愛麗絲．華克對（美國）南部黑人生活的生動描述，讓她成為美國當代最有前途的作家之一。

graphically [ˈgræfɪkl̩ɪ] .... ★★
adv. 用圖表表示

list [lɪst] .... ★★★★★
n. 表，目錄，名單：Here is a shopping list so you won't forget anything. 這裡有張購物單，這樣你就不會忘記東西了。
【片語】on the list 在表格上

pamphlet [ˈpæmflɪt] .... ★★
n. 小冊子：a single-article pamphlet 單行本

schedule [ˈskɛdʒʊl] .... ★★★★★
n. 時間表，計畫表

sketch [skɛtʃ] .... ★★★★
n. 草圖
v. 勾畫：This sketch can be easily drawn. 這個草圖很好畫。

辨析 Analyze

draft, illustration, picture, sketch

1 **draft** *n.* 「草稿，草圖」，指文字或繪畫的草稿，還指文件的草案：He's now revising the draft of the essay/the machine. 他正在修訂文章的草稿／機器的草圖。

2 **illustration** *n.* 「圖解，插圖，說明，例證」，指有助於理解文字的插圖，還指例證或用實物、實例解釋：Children like books with lots of illustrations. 兒童喜歡有很多插圖的書。

3 **picture** *n.* 「圖片，照片，描繪」，指圖片、圖畫或照片，常用語，用法很廣：You can't draw a picture without inspiration. 你沒有靈感無法作畫。

4 **sketch** *n.* 「略圖，梗概，速寫」，指繪畫中的素描、速寫，也指文章、計畫或其他事物的要點：They made sketches of the dancing children. 他們畫了一些跳舞的兒童的速描。

05

機械、工具相關辭彙

Vocabulary of Machinery

ammeter [ˈæmˌmitɚ] .... ★
n. 電流計，安培計

annex [əˈnɛks] .... ★
v. 附加：Happiness is not always annexed to wealth.
財富未必能增添幸福。

antenna [ænˈtɛnə] .... ★
n. 天線，觸角，感覺，直覺：have the antenna for...
對⋯有敏感性

apparatus [ˌæpəˈretəs] .... ★★
n. 器具，裝置，器，機構：electric scoring apparatus
電子記分器

appliance [əˈplaɪəns] .... ★★★
n. 器械，裝置，用具，器具：Vacuum cleaners,
washing machines and refrigerators are household's
appliances. 吸塵器、洗衣機和冰箱都是家電用品。

arc-lamp [ˈɑrkˌlæmp] .... ★
n. 弧光燈

autopilot [ˈɔtoˌpaɪlət] .... ★
n. 自動駕駛儀

axis [ˈæksɪs] .... ★
n. 軸，（植物的）主莖：The axis of the skeleton is the
spinal column. 骨骼的主幹是脊椎。

barrel [ˈbærəl] .... ★★★
n. 炮管，槍管，桶：a gun barrel 槍管，炮管

battery [ˈbætərɪ] .... ★★★
n. 電池（組），炮兵連，炮組：Our bus won't start
because the battery is flat. 我們的大客車發動不了，
因為電池用完了。

beaker [ˈbikɚ] .... ★★★★★
n. 燒杯

bell [bɛl] .... ★★★★★
n. 鐘，鈴

blade [bled] .... ★★★★
n. 刀刃：the blade of a knife 小刀的刀刃

bolt [bolt] .... ★★★
n. 螺栓，插梢
v. 閂門，關窗，拴住：This door bolts on the inside. 這
扇門是從裡面栓上的。

bottle [ˈbɑtl̩] .... ★★★★
n. 瓶子

bottleneck [ˈbɑtl̩nɛk] .... ★★★★
n. 瓶頸，狹道，影響生產流程的因素：At five o'clock in the afternoon, the city streets are a series of bottlenecks. 下午五點，市區街道就成了擁擠不堪的窄路。

box [bɑks] .... ★★★★★
n. 箱子，盒子，包廂
v. 擊拳，打耳光：Nobody can box as well as Jack. 沒有人擊拳贏得了傑克。

bucket [ˈbʌkɪt] .... ★★★
n. 吊桶，水桶

carburetor [ˈkɑrbəˌretə] .... ★
n. 汽化器

casket [ˈkæskɪt] .... ★★★★★
n. 小匣子

chisel [ˈtʃɪzl̩] .... ★★
n. 鑿子

connector [kəˈnɛktə] .... ★★★★★
n. 連接物，連接器，連接插頭

copier [ˈkɑpɪə] .... ★★★★★
n. 印刷器，複製器：a copier of ancient manuscripts 謄抄古代手稿者

crucible [ˈkrusəbl̩] .... ★
n. 坩堝，熔爐

detector [dɪˈtɛktə] .... ★
n. 探測器

device [dɪˈvaɪs] .... ★★★★
n. 器械，裝置，設計：Be careful! That is a dangerous device. 小心！那是個危險設備。

drill [drɪl] .... ★★★
v. 鑽，鑽孔，操練，練習：They drilled boulders for inserting dynamite. 他們在大石頭上鑽孔以便裝炸藥。
n. 鑽，鑽頭，操練

effector [əˈfɛktə] .... ★★★★★
n. 操縱裝置，實驗器

engine [ˈɛndʒən] .... ★★★★★
n. 發動機，引擎，火車頭，機車

engineer [ˌɛndʒəˈnɪr] .... ★★★★
v. 設計，建造，操縱，管理
n. 工程師，技師

engineering [ˌɛndʒəˈnɪrɪŋ] .... ★★★★★
n. 工程，工程學：engineering college 工學院

equipment [ɪˈkwɪpmənt] .... ★★★★★
n. 設備

flashlight [ˈflæʃˌlaɪt] .... ★★★★★
n. 手電筒

flask [flæsk] .... ★
n. 細頸瓶，燒瓶

frame [frem] .... ★★★★★
n. 框架，框子，骨架，體格，結構

辨析 Analyze

engineering, project

1 **engineering** *n.*「工程（學）」，指一門學科：My brother is studying mechanical engineering. 我的哥哥在研究機械工程（學）。

2 **project** *n.*「工程」，指建築工程、土建工程，還指計畫、項目等，可用於引申義：Hope Project 希望工程

v. 裝框子：This old bed has a copper frame. 這張舊床的床架是銅的。

v. 框住：I'll have this picture framed. 我要把這張照片裝入鏡框。

framework [ˈfremˌwɝk] .... ★★★★

n. 構架，框架，結構，機構，組織，體制：The theory of plate tectonics provided scientists with a framework for understanding how and why the various features of the Earth constantly change. 地殼構造學說的理論框架，讓科學家們得以了解地球各部分何以不斷變化、如何不斷變化。

furnace [ˈfɝnɪs] .... ★★★

n. 爐子，熔爐

gadget [ˈgædʒɪt] .... ★

n. 小配件，小玩意：a useful gadget for loosening bottle lids 一件開瓶蓋用的小工具

gadgetry [ˈgædʒətrɪ] .... ★

n. （總稱）小玩意，小玩意的發明

gear [gɪr] .... ★★★

n. 齒輪；（汽車的）排擋

v. 為…準備好為一將要發生的行動或事件做好準備：The truck driver changed gear to go up the hill. 卡車司機換擋上山坡。

generator [ˈdʒɛnəˌretə] .... ★★★

n. 發電機，（信號等）發射器

gyroscope [ˈdʒaɪrəˌskop] .... ★

n. 陀螺儀

hammer [ˈhæmə] .... ★★★★

n. 榔頭

v. 錘：Teacher hammered the information into the students' heads 老師反覆向學生們強調這條資訊。

harp [hɑrp] .... ★

n. 豎琴

v. 不停地說 (on/upon)：harp on the same string 老調重彈；harp on one's troubles 嘮嘮叨叨地訴苦

hatchet [ˈhætʃɪt] .... ★

n. 短柄斧：hatchet job 惡毒的誹謗

hinge [hɪndʒ] .... ★

n. 鉸鏈

v. 依…而定：The lid of the suitcase had a broken hinge, so it wouldn't open easily. 小提箱箱蓋的鉸鏈壞了，因此不容易打開。

hoe [ho] .... ★

v. 鋤地

n. 鋤頭：This hoe is his, not mine. 這把鋤頭是他的，不是我的。

hook [hʊk] .... ★★★★

n. 鉤

v. 鉤住：a novel that hooked me on the very first page 從第一頁起就牢牢吸引我的小說

implement [ˈɪmpləmənt] .... ★★

n. 工具

injector [ɪnˈdʒɛktə] .... ★★★

n. 噴嘴：close oil injector 閉式噴油器

jack [dʒæk] .... ★★

n. 插座

jackhammer [ˈdʒækˌhæmə] .... ★

n. 風鎬，氣錘，手持風鑽

jigsaw [ˈdʒɪgˌsɔ] .... ★

n. 鋸齒線機，線鋸：a jigsaw pattern 鋼絲鋸鋸成的圖案

keg [kɛg] .... ★

n. 小桶：wooden keg 小木桶

kit [kɪt] .... ★★

n. 用具包，旅行行裝：The soldiers packed their kit for the journey. 士兵們整理他們的裝備，準備行軍。

lantern [ˈlæntən] .... ★★

n. 燈，燈籠

lens [lɛnz] .... ★★★

n. 透鏡，鏡頭：the power of a lens 透鏡的放大率

loudspeaker [ˈlaʊdˌspikɚ] .... ★★★
n. 擴音器，揚聲器，喇叭：There is a loudspeaker in a radio. 收音機裡有個喇叭。

machine [məˈʃin] .... ★★★★★
n. 機器，機械

machinery [məˈʃinərɪ] .... ★★★★
n. （總稱）機器，機械：How much machinery has been installed? 已經安裝多少部機器了？

mainframe [ˈmenˌfrem] .... ★★★★★
n. 主機架

mechanism [ˈmɛkəˌnɪzəm] .... ★★★★
n. 機構，結構，機理

mechanize [ˈmɛkəˌnaɪz] .... ★★★★
v. 使機械化，用機械裝備：A good deal of housework can be mechanized. 大量家事可以用機械操作。

mesh [mɛʃ] .... ★
n. 網眼，網狀物：We put some wire mesh over the chimney so that the birds wouldn't fall in. 我們在煙囪上掛了一些鐵絲網，鳥就不會掉進來了。

microprocessor [ˌmaɪkroˈprɑsɛsɚ] .... ★
n. 微處理器

microscopic [ˌmaɪkroˈskɑpɪk] .... ★
adj. 微觀的，顯微鏡的：It's impossible to read his microscopic handwriting. 要看清他那極小的筆跡是不可能的。

module [ˈmɑdʒul] .... ★★
n. （太空船上各個獨立的）艙，模數：the lunar excursion module of a spacecraft 太空船（一部分）的月球登陸艇／艙

noisemaker [ˈnɔɪzˌmekɚ] .... ★★★★
n. 發出噪音的東西

noisemeter [ˈnɔɪzˌmitɚ] .... ★★★★★
n. 噪音表

padlock [ˈpædˌlɑk] .... ★★★
n. 掛鎖

pail [pel] .... ★★★
n. 提桶：a pail of milk 一桶牛奶

pallet [ˈpælɪt] .... ★
n. 平板架

panel [ˈpænl] .... ★★★★
n. ①專門小組：The date for the panel discussion is fixed now. 座談會的日期現已確定。②畫，板：an instrument panel 儀表板

pendulum [ˈpɛndʒələm] .... ★
n. 擺，鐘擺：a simple/compound pendulum 單／複擺

photodetector [ˈfotoˌdɪˈtɛktɚ] .... ★
n. 光電探測器

piledriver [ˈpaɪldraɪvɚ] .... ★
n. 打樁機

pin [pɪn] .... ★★★★
n. 針，別針，飾針，大頭針，徽章，銷，栓
v. 釘住，別住：She wore her school pin. 她戴著校徽。

piston [ˈpɪstn̩] .... ★
n. 活塞：air piston 氣動汽缸的活塞

pitchfork [ˈpɪtʃˌfɔrk] .... ★★★★
n. 乾草叉，草耙

pivot [ˈpɪvət] .... ★
n. 軸，關鍵，轉捩點：The mother is often the pivot of family life. 母親往往是家庭生活的中心人物。

plug [plʌg] .... ★★★
v. 插，接，堵，塞
n. 插頭，塞子：The local system is plugged into the national telephone network. 這個地區性電話系統已與全國的電話網連接。

probe [prob] .... ★
v. 探察：probe a wound to find its extent 探查傷口以確定其大小

projector [prəˈdʒɛktɚ] .... ★
n. 規劃者，企劃者，（電影）放映機，投影儀，幻燈機

pump [pʌmp] .... ★★★
v. 抽（水），打（氣），盤問，追問
n. 泵，抽水機：The octopus has three hearts that pump blood through its body. 章魚有三個心臟，可以將血輸遍全身。

pushbutton [ˌpʊʃˈbʌtn̩] .... ★★★★★
n. 按鈕

rake [rek] ....★
n. 搜索，探索，耙
v. 搜索，探索，耙：He raked through the files for the misplaced letter. 他在那些檔案中找一封放錯的信。

reflector [rɪˈflɛktə] .... ★★★★★
n. 反射器，反射鏡

refrigerator [rɪˈfrɪdʒəˌretə] .... ★★★
n. 冰箱，冷凍機，冷藏庫

regulator [ˈrɛgjəˌletə] .... ★★★★
n. 調節器

robot [ˈrobət] .... ★★★
n. 機器人，自動機

saw [sɔ] .... ★★★★★
n. 鋸子，鋸床
v. 鋸，鋸開：He sawed the wood into three pieces. 他把木頭鋸成三塊。

scanner [ˈskænə] .... ★★★
n. 掃描裝置，掃描器，多點測量儀

scoop [skup] ....★
n. 勺子
v. 汲取，挖取：She scooped flour out of the bag. 她從袋子裡舀出麵粉。

sensor [ˈsɛnsə] ....★
n. 感測器，探測器，靈敏元件

shovel [ˈʃʌvl̩] ....★
n. 鏟，鐵鍬
v. 鏟起：They shovels out the hall closet once a year. 他們每年清掃一次大廳的櫃子。

spectrometer [spɛkˈtrɑmətə] ....★
n. 分光計，分光儀

speedometer [spiˈdɑmətə] .... ★★★★★
n. 測速計，轉速計

synthesizer [ˈsɪnθəˌsaɪzə] .... ★★★
n. 合成器

tank [tæŋk] .... ★★★
n. ①箱，罐，槽：The tank will only hold three gallons. 這油箱只能裝 3 加侖。②坦克

tool [tul] .... ★★★★★
n. 工具，用具，受人利用的人：A screwdriver and a hammer are the only tools you need. 你需要的工具只是螺絲起子和錘子。

tracer [ˈtresə] .... ★★★★★
n. 追蹤物，追蹤器，（貨運中的）失物追查人，追查單

transducer [trænsˈdjusə] ....★
n. 換能器，變換器，感測器

transformer [trænsˈfɔrmə] ....★
n. 變壓器

transmitter [trænsˈmɪtə] .... ★★★
n. 發射機

turbine [ˈtɝbɪn] .... ★★★
n. 渦輪機，氣輪機

utility [juˈtɪlətɪ] .... ★★★
n. 效用：utility service 公用事業

wrench [rɛntʃ] ....★
n. 擰，扭傷，扳手
v. 擰，扭傷：He wrenched the door open. 他用力扭開了門。

辨析 Analyze

apparatus, appliance, device, equipment, facility, installation, instrument, tool, utility

1 **apparatus** *n.* 「器械，器具，儀器」，多指各種用於機械設備或裝置，包括機器、儀錶、工具，用法很廣，其複數形式可以是apparatus或apparatuses：His firm supplies heating and water-purifying apparatuses. 他的公司提供加熱和淨水裝置。

2 **appliance** *n.* 「器具，器械，裝置」，多指家用器具，尤指家用電器：A can-opener is an appliance for opening cans of food. 開罐器是用來開啟罐頭的器具。

3 **device** *n.* 「裝置，設備，器械」，指有特定用處的器具或裝置，大到核電廠，小到開關：This is a device for catching flies and mosquitoes. 這是一種捕捉蒼蠅和蚊子的裝置。

4 **equipment** *n.* 「設備，器械，裝置」，不可數名詞，指用於某種特定活動或目的的一整套物品，但不包含建築物：His firm supplies kitchen/fire-fighting/camping/experiment/metal-cutting equipment. 他的公司提供廚房／滅火／野營／實驗／金屬切割設備。

5 **facility** *n.* 「設備，設施」，多用作複數形式，指用於某一特定活動或目的的各種設施，可包含建築物：Our teaching facilities include teaching buildings, libraries and laboratories. 我們的教學設施包括教學大樓、圖書館和實驗室。

6 **installation** *n.* 「裝置，設備，設施」，指大型設備/設施或大型設備/設施所在地，可包含建築物：The delegation visited the military installations / the North Sea oil and gas installations. 代表團參觀了該軍事設施／北海油氣設施。

7 **instrument** *n.* 「工具，器械，儀器」，指科學儀器或樂器：We have many first-class instruments in our laboratories. 我們實驗室裡有許多一流的儀器。

8 **tool** *n.* 「工具，器具，用具」，指簡單的操作、勞動工具，可用於引申用法，指人時有貶意：Man has hands, with which he can make tools for himself. 人類有兩隻手，可以用來為自己製造工具。

9 **utility** *n.* 「公用設施」，指水、電、路、煤氣、交通、通訊等公用設施：Railroads, buses, and gas and electric companies are public utilities. 鐵路、公共汽車、煤氣公司和電力公司都屬於公用設施。

06

聲、光、電、磁、水利相關辭彙

Vocabulary of Electricity

ablaze [əˋblez] .... ★

adj. 閃耀的：In the autumn, the northern mountains are ablaze with shades of red, yellow, and orange. 在秋天，北方的山上閃耀著深淺不同的紅色、黃色和橙色。

beam [bim] .... ★★★★

n. （光）束，射線

v. 微笑，發光：He beamed on his visitors. 他對著客人們微笑。

brighten [ˋbraɪtn̩] .... ★★

v. 使發光，使快活：His face brightened up when he was told to have won the first prize. 當他得知他得了第一名時，臉上露出了喜色。

chime [tʃaɪm] .... ★

n. 鐘聲：The chime of the clock woke me up. 時鐘的聲響把我吵醒了。

consonant [ˋkɑnsənənt] ....★★

adj. （和⋯）一致的，調和的

dam [dæm] .... ★★★

v. 築壩攔（水）：Beavers usually begin their construction work with the damming of a small stream. 海狸經常截斷一條小溪來開始修築工事。

n. 水壩，水閘

flare [flɛr] .... ★★★

v. 閃耀：The rockets flared a warning. 火箭發出閃光警告。

flicker [ˋflɪkɚ] .... ★

v. 閃爍：The candle flickered in the wind. 蠟燭在風中閃爍不定。

flood [flʌd] .... ★★★★

n. 洪水，水災：The rainstorms caused floods in the low-lying parts of the town. 暴風雨在該城的低窪地區釀成水災。

v. 淹沒，發大水，氾濫

glare [glɛr] .... ★★

v. ①怒視：They glared defiantly at me. 他們以輕蔑的目光瞪著我。②閃耀：The tropic sun glares down on us all the day. 熱帶的太陽整日照著我們。

n. 瞪眼，閃光

glaring [ˈglɛrɪŋ] .... ★★
adj. 耀眼的，瞪眼的：This glaring light hurts eyes. 這耀眼的燈光傷眼睛。

gleam [glim] .... ★★
v. 閃光，閃爍：A gleam of interest in the matter came into her eye. 她的眼睛裡顯露出一絲對此事感興趣的神情。

glimmer [ˈglɪmɚ] .... ★★★★★
v. 發出微光：A faint light glimmered at the end of the corridor. 走廊的盡頭閃著一絲微光。

glitter [ˈglɪtɚ] .... ★★
n. 光輝，燦爛
v. 閃耀，閃爍：eyes that glittered because of revenge 閃動著復仇光芒的雙眼

glossy [ˈglɔsɪ] .... ★★
adj. 有光澤的：glossy satin 光滑的緞；glossy trendsetters 富麗堂皇的時髦者

hydraulic [haɪˈdrɔlɪk] .... ★
adj. 水力的，液壓的：hydraulic power plant 水力發電廠

illuminate [ɪˈlumɚˌnet] .... ★★
v. 照明，照亮，說明：The river was illuminated by the setting sun. 落日照亮了這條河。

lighthouse [ˈlaɪtˌhaus] .... ★★★★★
n. 燈塔

lightning [ˈlaɪtnɪŋ] .... ★★★★
n. 閃電：The tree was struck by lightning. 這棵樹曾遭雷擊過。

lightwave [ˈlaɪtˌwev] .... ★★★★★
n. 光波

luminous [ˈlumənəs] .... ★
adj. 發光的，光亮的：Are you sure that you have seen a luminous body? 你確定你看到了一個發光體？

multispectual [ˈmʌltɪˌspɛktʃuəl] .... ★
adj. 多光譜的，多頻譜的

radiation [ˌrediˈeʃən] .... ★★★
n. ①放射物，輻射能：This apparatus produces harmful radiation. 這個裝置產生了有害放射物。②輻射：heat radiation 熱輻射

radiator [ˈrediˌetɚ] .... ★
n. 散熱器，暖氣片

radioactive [ˌredioˈæktɪv] .... ★
adj. 發射性的，發射引起的：radioactive waste 放射性廢物

radioactivity [ˌredioækˈtɪvətɪ] .... ★
n. 放射體：We have to learn to control radioactivity. 我們必須學會控制放射能。

radiogenic [ˌredioˈdʒɛnɪk] .... ★
adj. 放射產生的

rattle [ˈrætl] .... ★★
n. ①咯咯聲②喋喋不休
vt. ①使發出咯咯聲：The windows rattled in the wind. 窗子在風中作響。②喋喋不休
vi. ①發出咯咯聲②急促地講

辨析
Analyze

light, ray

1 **light** *n.*「光，光線，光亮；光源，燈」，指可見光：The light in his room is poor. 他房間的光線很差。

2 **ray** *n.*「光線，射線」，指各種光，尤指不可見光：What are the properties of X-rays? X 光有什麼特性？

【片語】① rattle off 急促背誦② rattle on/away 喋喋不休③ rattle through 迅速做好

ray [re] .... ★★★★★
n. 光線：A ray of light pierced the darkness. 一道亮光劃破黑暗。

resonant [ˋrɛzənənt] .... ★
adj. 洪亮的，共鳴的：Because it is tuned a fifth lower, the viola produces a sound that is more resonant than that of the violin. 中提琴由於音調低 5 度，所以發出的聲音比小提琴洪亮。

resound [rɪˋzaʊnd] .... ★
v. 迴響，回蕩，鳴響，馳名：The hall resounded with cries of dissent. 大廳裡充滿反對的叫聲。

rumble [ˋrʌmbl̩] .... ★
v. 隆隆行駛，低沉地說：The truck rumbled through the street. 卡車沿著大街隆隆地駛過。

shine [ʃaɪn] .... ★★★★★
v. ①照耀，發光：The sun is shining. 太陽照耀。②擦亮：Go and shine your shoes. 去把你的皮鞋擦亮。

sonar [ˋsonɑr] .... ★★★★★
n. 聲納，聲波導航和測距系統：sonar pinger system 聲納脈衝測距系統

sparkle [ˋspɑrkl̩] .... ★★★★
vi. ①發光，閃耀，閃爍：The snowmantled peaks sparkled in the sun. 白雪覆蓋的山峰在陽光下閃耀。②活躍，(才智等)煥發：She always sparkles at parties. 她在宴會上總是容光煥發。
n. ①閃光，閃耀，閃爍 ②活力，生氣

spectral [ˋspɛktrəl] .... ★
adj. 光譜的，頻譜的：spectral analysis 光譜分析

辨析
Analyze

flash, glare, gleam, glitter, shine, sparkle

1 **flash** *vi.*「閃光，閃爍，閃耀，閃現」，指發出短暫的、閃爍的光，與 gleam 詞義相近，還指「飛馳，掠過」：The light on top of the police car was flashing. 警車頂上的警燈閃爍著。

2 **glare** *vi.*「發射強光，發出刺眼的光線」，還指「怒目而視」：The sunlight glared on the ice. 太陽光照耀在冰上，發出眩目的光。

3 **gleam** *vi.*「閃亮，閃爍」，指發出微弱的、閃爍的或短暫的光：A light gleamed in the fog. 有一盞燈在霧中閃爍。

4 **glitter** *vi.*「閃閃發光，閃耀」，指固體表面閃光，如金屬或服飾發光：All that glitters is not gold. 閃光的未必都是金子（金玉其表，敗絮其中）。

5 **shine** *vt. & vi.*「閃閃發光，閃耀，把…光投向」，常用詞，既可指自身發光，也可指反射其他物體發出的光：The lights of the harbor shine across the bay. 港口的燈光照亮了整個海灣。

6 **sparkle** *vi.*「發光，閃耀，閃爍」，指明亮、短暫而數不清的小亮光在閃爍，還指「(活躍，才智等)煥發」：The jewels sparkled/shone/glittered in the lamplight. 珠寶在燈光的照耀下閃閃發光。

Technique 技術工程名稱總匯

spectrum [ˈspɛktrəm] .... ★★
n. 頻譜，光譜，範圍：the whole spectrum of industry 整個工業領域

sunshine [ˈsʌnˌʃaɪn] .... ★★★★
n. 日光，日照

thunder [ˈθʌndɚ] .... ★★★★
n. 雷，轟隆聲
v. 打雷，轟隆響，大聲說，吼叫：The reformers thundered against drinking and gambling. 改革者大聲疾呼，反對酗酒和賭博。

tick [tɪk] .... ★
n. 滴答聲，打勾符號：All the correct answers had ticks beside them. 所有正確答案的旁邊都打了勾。
v. 滴答響，打勾於：The watch ticked the minutes. 手錶滴答滴答地報時。

twinkle [ˈtwɪŋkl̩] .... ★★
v. 閃爍，閃亮：The stars twinkled in the sky. 繁星在天空閃爍。

ultrasonic [ˌʌltrəˈsɑnɪk] .... ★
n. 超音波
adj. 超音波的，超音速的：ultrasonic vibrations 超音波震動

vocal [ˈvokl̩] .... ★★★★
adj. ①喜歡暢所欲言的，直言不諱的：vocal criticism 坦率的批評②嗓音的，發聲的：the vocal organs 發音器官
n. 聲樂節目

voice [vɔɪs] .... ★★★★★
n. ①說話聲，聲音，嗓音：The operator has a sweet voice. 這位接線生的聲音甜美。②發言權，表達的意見：You have no voice in the matter. 你對此事無發言權。③語態：I am writing this sentence in the active voice. 我用主動語態寫這個句子。
v. 說（話），（用言語）表達：The spokesman voiced the feeling of the crowd. 這位發言人表達了群眾的感受。

X-ray [ˈɛksˌre] .... ★★★★★
n. X射線，X光

07

材料相關辭彙

Vocabulary of Materials

alkali [ˈælkəˌlaɪ] .... ★
n. 鹼

aluminum [əˈlumɪnəm] .... ★★★
n. 鋁：wrap something with aluminum foil 以鋁箔包裝某物

ammonia [əˈmonjə] .... ★
n. 氨，氨水

ash [æʃ] .... ★★★★
n. （有時用複數形式）灰，灰燼：Clean the ash/ashes from the fire place. 把壁爐裡的灰燼清除掉。

bakelite [ˈbekəˌlaɪt] .... ★
n. 酚醛塑料，電木

bauxite [ˈbɔksaɪt] .... ★
n. 鋁土礦，礬土

block [blɑk] .... ★★
n. 一塊（木或石等），堵塞，妨礙：Recently the professor often has a memory block. 近來教授常常出現記憶障礙。

board [bord] .... ★★★★★
n. 木板，委員會：The board of the directors unanimously agreed that Mr. White was the best candidate for the job. 董事會一致同意懷特先生是擔任這項工作的最佳候選人。

brass [bræs] .... ★★★★
n. 黃銅，銅，厚顏無恥：How did she have the brass? 她怎麼會如此厚顏無恥？

brick [brɪk] .... ★★★★
n. 磚（狀物）

bung [bʌŋ] .... ★
n. （桶等的）塞子
v. (up) 阻塞，堵住：My nose is bunged up with a cold. 我的鼻子因為感冒塞住了。

cable [ˈkebl̩] .... ★★★★
n. 纜，索，電纜，海底電纜，電報：We have already advised you by cable. 我們已去電通知您。
v. 拍電報：Father cabled the poor villager's son some money for his further study. 神父把錢電匯給這個貧苦村民的兒子，供他繼續學習。

cement [sɪˋmɛnt] .... ★★★
n. 水泥
v. 黏結，膠黏：Barnacles use secretions to cement their shells to underwater objects. 藤壺用分泌物將它們的殼黏結在水底的物體。

charcoal [ˋtʃɑrˌkol] .... ★
n. 炭，木炭

chip [tʃɪp] .... ★★★
n. 積體電路塊，薄片，（金屬）切屑，(pl.)薯條：a cup with a chip 一個有缺口的杯子
v. 切成小片：The mason was chipping away the rock with a hammer. 石匠用錘子一點一點地把那塊石頭敲碎。

clay [kle] .... ★★★★
n. 黏土，泥土：fire clay 耐火黏土

coal [kol] .... ★★★★
n. 煤，煤塊：raw coal 原煤

copper [ˋkɑpɚ] .... ★★★
n. 銅：He had only a few coppers in his pocket when he came to Detroit. 他到底特律時，口袋裡只有幾枚銅幣。

cork [kɔrk] .... ★
n. 軟木塞：The cork flew off with a pop. 瓶塞砰地一聲飛出去了。

crystal [ˋkrɪstl̩] .... ★★★
n. 水晶，晶體：salt crystals 鹽的結晶體
adj. 清澈的：a crystal lake 清澈見底的湖

datum [ˋdetəm] .... ★★
n. 資料，材料，資料

diamond [ˋdaɪəmənd] .... ★★★★
n. 鑽石，金剛石

dust [dʌst] .... ★★★★★
n. 塵土，灰塵
v. 撣掉…上的塵土：dust a table 擦亮桌子

fabric [ˋfæbrɪk] .... ★★★
n. ①織物，紡織品，布②結構：The fabric of our society has been broken by crime and a bad economy. 我們的社會結構已受犯罪和不好的經濟狀況所破壞。

fiber [ˋfaɪbɚ] .... ★★★★★
n. 纖維，纖維製品，纖維質，性格：to stir the deeper fibers of my nature 觸動到我深層的本性

filter [ˋfɪltɚ] .... ★★★
n. 篩檢程式
v. 過濾，濾清：Baleen whales swim with their mouths open and obtain food by filtering the crustaceans and the smallest fishes from the water. 鬚鯨游泳時張著嘴，過濾水中的甲殼類動物和最小的魚來獲取食物。

fuel [ˋfjuəl] .... ★★★★
n. 燃料，刺激因素：Money is the fuel of a volunteer organization. 錢是促成志願組織的動機。
v. 給…加燃料

gasoline [ˋgæsəˌlin] .... ★★★
n. 汽油

gem [dʒɛm] .... ★
n. 寶石

granite [ˋgrænɪt] .... ★
n. 花崗岩，花崗石

graphite [ˋgræfaɪt] .... ★
n. 石墨

hose [hoz] .... ★
n. 軟管，水龍帶
v. 用軟管澆、淋或洗：hose down the deck 用軟管沖洗甲板；hose off the dog 用軟管噴水把狗趕走

inlay [ˋɪnˌle] .... ★★★★★
n. 鑲嵌物

inventory [ˋɪnvənˌtorɪ] .... ★★★
n. 物品清單，庫存品

v. 編詳細目錄，開清單，清點存貨：Some stores inventory their stock once a month. 有些商店每月盤點一次。

iron [ˈaɪən] .... ★★★★★
n. ①鐵：Strike while the iron is hot. 打鐵趁熱。②烙鐵，熨斗：an electric iron 電熨斗

jewel [ˈdʒuəl] .... ★★★★
n. 寶石，石頭飾物：She has many jewels. 她有許多珠寶。

kerosene [ˈkɛrəˌsin] .... ★
n. 煤油

limestone [ˈlaɪmˌston] .... ★
n. 石灰石：limestone cliffs 石灰岩峭壁

lodestone [ˈlodˌston] .... ★
n. 磁石，天然磁鐵

log [lɔg] .... ★★★★★
n. 圓木，日誌：The captain described the wreck accident in details in the ship's log. 船長在航海日誌裡詳細描述了這次的沉船事故。

lubricant [ˈlubrɪkənt] .... ★
n. 潤滑劑，潤滑油
v. 潤滑，加潤滑油：abrasive belt grinding lubricant 磨帶潤磨油

lubricate [ˈlubrɪˌket] .... ★★★
vt. 使潤滑：This oil lubricates the machine. 這油潤滑了機器。

lumber [ˈlʌmbɚ] .... ★
n. 木材，木料

marble [ˈmɑrbl̩] .... ★★★★
n. 大理石，彈子：a marble hearth 大理石壁爐

material [məˈtɪrɪəl] .... ★★★★★
n. 材料，原料

mercury [ˈmɝkjərɪ] .... ★
n. 水銀，汞：The mercury in thermometer mounted up/rose to 35℃. 溫度計的水銀柱升到攝氏 35 度。

metal [ˈmɛtl̩] .... ★★★★
n. 金屬，金屬製品

metallic [məˈtælɪk] .... ★
adj. 金屬的：The strange metallic note of the meadow lark, suggests the clash of vibrant blades. 野雲雀刺耳的怪異叫聲，令人聯想到刀劍震動時的鏗鏘聲。

metallurgy [ˈmɛtəˌlɝdʒɪ] .... ★
n. 冶金學

mineral [ˈmɪnərəl] .... ★★★
n. 礦物，礦石：rich in minerals 礦產豐富

mud [mʌd] .... ★★★★
n. 泥，泥漿：stick in the mud 陷入泥淖，墨守成規

muddy [ˈmʌdɪ] .... ★★★
adj. 多泥的，泥濘的：When it rains the ground becomes very muddy. 下雨時，地面變得很泥濘。

nylon [ˈnaɪlɑn] .... ★
n. 尼龍：nylon coating 尼龍塗層

oil [ɔɪl] .... ★★★★★
n. ①油：olive oil 橄欖油②石油，燃料，油：drilling oil 鑽探石油
v. 給…加潤滑油，使塗滿油：Oil one's bicycle 替自行車上油

ore [or] .... ★★★
n. 礦，礦石，礦砂：magnetic iron ore = magnetite 磁鐵礦

oxhide [ˈɑksˌhaɪd] .... ★
n. 牛皮

paint [pent] .... ★★★★★
n. 油漆，顏料：Where are those tins of green paint? 那些綠漆的罐子呢？
v. ①油漆：He painted the door blue. 他把門漆成了藍色。②繪畫：Who painted this picture? 這幅畫是誰畫的？

painter [ˈpentɚ] .... ★★★★
n. 油漆；畫家：She is a painter. 她是一名畫家。

painting [ˈpentɪŋ] .... ★★★★
n. 上油漆，繪畫，油畫，水彩畫

pebble [ˈpɛbḷ] .... ★
n. 卵石：Scotch pebbles 瑪瑙

pesticide [ˈpɛstɪˌsaɪd] .... ★★★★★
n. 殺蟲劑，農藥：contact pesticide（接）觸
　殺（蟲）農藥

petrol [ˈpɛtrəl] .... ★★★
n. 石油，汽油：motor petrol 車用汽油

petroleum [pəˈtrolɪəm] .... ★★★
n. 石油：crude/raw petroleum 原油，重油

pigment [ˈpɪgmənt] .... ★
n. 色素，顏料：pigment granule 色素粒

pillar [ˈpɪlə] .... ★★★
n. 支柱，柱

pipe [paɪp] .... ★★★★
n. ①管子，導管：hot water pipes 熱水管②煙
v. 用管道輸送：Hot water is piped to all the
　rooms. 熱水經管道輸送到所有的房間。

pitch [pɪtʃ] .... ★★★★
n. 瀝青

plastic [ˈplæstɪk] .... ★★★
n. 塑膠，塑膠製品
adj. 塑膠（製）的，可塑的：Clay, wax and
　plaster are plastic substances. 黏土、蠟
　和灰泥都是塑膠材料。

pole [pol] .... ★★★★
n. ①柱，桿：telegraph poles 電線桿②地極，
　磁極，電極：the North Pole 北極

porous [ˈporəs] .... ★
adj. 多孔的：porous soil 可滲透的土壤

powdery [ˈpaʊdərɪ] .... ★★★★
adj. 粉狀的，粉的：powdery mildew 白粉菌，
　白粉病

quartz [kwɔrts] .... ★
n. 石英：quartz clock 石英鐘

rack [ræk] .... ★★★
n. 擱板，行李架：a trophy rack 獎品架

辨析
Analyze

rack, shelf

1　**rack** *n.*「掛架，擱架」，指用金屬桿／
　條或塑膠桿／條等連在一起裝物品的架
　子，如火車上的行李架、自行車後部的
　夾物架：Put the luggage on the luggage
　rack. 把行李放在行李架上。

2　**shelf** *n.*「架子，擱板」，指用板子搭成
　的架子，如書架、貨架：Put the book on
　the book shelf. 把書放在書架上。

v. 使痛苦，折磨

radiocarbon [ˌredɪoˈkɑrbən] .... ★
n. 放射性碳

refractory [rɪˈfræktɔrɪ] .... ★
n. 耐火材料
adj. 耐熔的，難以控制的：a refractory
　material 耐熱材料

resistor [rɪˈzɪstə] .... ★★★★
n. 電阻器，電阻

ruby [ˈrubɪ] .... ★
n. 紅寶石：ruby wedding 紅寶石婚（結婚後第
　45 年）

scrap [skræp] .... ★★
v. 敲碎，拆毀，廢棄，報廢
n. 碎片，廢金屬，廢料：scraps of broken
　porcelain 碎瓷片

screw [skru] .... ★★★
v. 旋緊，擰，擰緊：He screwed the mirror
　onto the wall. 他把鏡子用螺絲固定在牆上。
n. 螺絲釘，螺絲：male screw 陽螺旋

screwdriver [ˈskruˌdraɪvə] .... ★
n.（螺絲）起子：You turn the screws round
　and round with a screwdriver. 你用螺絲起子
　把螺絲轉幾圈。

shelf [ʃɛlf] .... ★★★★
n. 架子，擱板，暗礁：He took the cup off the shelf. 他把杯子從架子上拿走。

silica [ˈsɪlɪkə] .... ★
n. 矽土

silicon [ˈsɪlɪkən] .... ★
n. 矽：Silicon Valley 矽谷

splint [splɪnt] .... ★
n. 夾板

sponge [spʌndʒ] .... ★
n. 海綿，多孔塑膠

stake [stek] .... ★★★★
n. 椿，標椿，賭注，利害關係

steel [stil] .... ★★★★
n. 鋼

stock [stɑk] .... ★★★★★
n. 備料，庫存，庫存品，現貨，股票，公債

stone [ston] .... ★★★★★
n. 小石頭，石料：The boy threw a stone at me. 這男孩向我扔石頭。

straw [strɔ] .... ★★★★
n. 稻草，麥稈，吸管：He drank the milk through a straw. 他用吸管喝牛奶。

string [strɪŋ] .... ★★★★★
v. 掛，拉（電線等），縛，捆
n. 一串，一行，一列，弦線，細繩：a string of pearls 一串珍珠

stuff [stʌf] .... ★★★★
n. 材料，原料，東西：There's some white stuff on this plate. 這個盤子上有些白色的東西。
v. 填滿，塞滿，把…裝滿：The bed was stuffed with cotton, so it was very soft. 這張床以棉花填充，因此很柔軟。

stuffy [ˈstʌfɪ] .... ★★★★★
adj. 悶熱的，不通風的：This room seems stuffy. Open a window. 這間房子好像不通風，開扇窗吧。

tar [tɑr] .... ★
n. 焦油，瀝青，柏油：We use tar to make roads. 我們用瀝青鋪路。

thatch [θætʃ] .... ★
n. 蓋屋頂用的茅草，稻草等材料

timber [ˈtɪmbɚ] .... ★★★
n. 木材，木料：It is made of timber. 這是木製的。

辨析 Analyze

material, matter, stuff, substance

1 **material** n.「材料，原料，素材，資料」，指各種材料，尤指原材料，可數名詞，用法很廣：The price of building materials has gone up. 建築材料價格已經上揚。

2 **matter** n.「物質，物品，材料，事情，情況，問題」，不可數名詞，意為「物質」時指物質的總稱：World is made up of matter. 世界是由物質組成的。

3 **stuff** n.「原料，材料，東西」，非正式用語，指各種材料，尤指填充材料，不可數名詞，有時含貶義，指質量低劣或不值錢的東西：What is the stuff in the doll? 這個玩具娃娃裡是裝什麼？

4 **substance** n.「物質，實質」，指某一種物質，可數名詞：Carbon is a substance found in many forms. 碳是以多種形式存在的物質。

tube [tjub] .... ★★★

n. ①管：These amplifiers have long been made with tiny election tubes. 這些放大器長久以來是用微型電子管製成的。②（倫敦）地下鐵：Underneath Piccadilly Circus, there is an important tube station with escalators leading down to two different lines. 在皮卡迪利廣場的下面，有個重要的地鐵站，裡面的電梯將乘客分別往下送到兩條不同的路線。

valve [vælv] .... ★

n. 真空管，電子管，閥，閥門

varnish [ˈvɑrnɪʃ] .... ★★★★★

n. 油漆，光澤（面）：The varnish protected the table from being damaged. 光澤面保護桌子不受損壞。

wafer [ˈwefɚ] .... ★

n. 薄片，晶片

wedge [wɛdʒ] .... ★

n. 嵌，楔狀

v. 嵌牢，嵌入，擠進：The nuthatch gets food by wedging a nut into a crevice in a tree trunk and then opening the nut with its sharp beak. 五子雀把堅果楔入樹幹的裂縫中，然後用尖銳的喙將堅果啄開來得到食物。

wire [waɪr] .... ★★★★

n. ①金屬絲，電線：telephone wires 電話線②電報，電信：send sb. a wire 給某人拍電報

v. ①為…安裝電線：Has the house been wired for electricity? 這房子已裝好電線了嗎？②向…發電報：He wired me that he would be delayed. 他發電報給我，說會延期到達。③發電報：He wired to his brother to buy oil shares. 他拍電報給他兄弟要購買石油股票。

辨析 Analyze

log, timber, wood

1 **log** *n.* 「原木，木材」，指被砍伐下來但未經加工的樹木，即原木、圓木，可數名詞，還指航海或飛行日誌：The cabin was made of logs. 這座小屋是用原木建的。

2 **timber** *n.* 「木材，原木」，指各種木材，包括原木、條木等，不可數名詞，但作「橫樑，棟木」解時是可數名詞：Stack the timber near the tool shed. 把木材堆在工具棚附近。

3 **wood** *n.* 「木材，木頭，木料，木柴」，不可數名詞，強調「木頭」這種物質，和其他物質區別；但指「樹林，林地」時多用作複數：This table is made of wood. 這張桌子是用木頭做的。

辨析 Analyze

hose, pipe, tube

1 **hose** *n.* 「（橡皮、帆布、軟塑膠等製作的）軟管，水龍帶」：A powerful engine forces the water through firemen's hoses. 強大的引擎把水從消防隊員的水管裡噴出。

2 **pipe** *n.* 「管子，導管」，指金屬、硬塑膠等做成的硬管，如自來水管、輸油管等，還指「煙斗；管樂器」：Water comes to the tap through a pipe. 水通過水管流到水龍頭。

3 **tube** *n.* 「管子」，指硬管、軟管皆可，尤指玻璃試管，還指「地鐵」以及電子儀器中的各種「電子管、顯像管」等：Have you cleaned the test tubes? 你把試管洗乾淨了嗎？

Unit **4**
教育名稱總匯
Education

01

院校相關辭彙

Education

教育名稱總匯

academic [ˌækəˈdɛmɪk] .... ★★★★★
adj. 學院的，理論的：Academic exchanges between China and America have been carried out for years. 中美之間的學術交流已經開展多年了。

Borstal [ˈbɔrstl̩] .... ★
n. (英國的) 青少年犯教育感化院

college [ˈkɑlɪdʒ] .... ★★★★★
n. ①學院，高等專科學校：We were good friends at college. 我們在大學時是好朋友。②學會，社團
【片語】go to college 上大學

dean [din] .... ★★
n. 院長，教務長，訓導長

department [dɪˈpɑrtmənt] .... ★★★★★
n. 部，部門，系，學部：the Department of Education 教育系

headmaster [ˈhɛdˈmæstɚ] .... ★★★
n. 首長

institute [ˈɪnstətjut] .... ★★★★★
v. 建立 *n.* (研究) 所

institution [ˌɪnstəˈtjuʃən] .... ★★★★★
n. 公共機關，協會，機構，學校，制度，慣例：Marriage became an institution in ancient societies. 婚姻在古代社會就已成為一種制度。

museum [mjuˈzɪəm] .... ★★★★★
n. 博物館，展覽館，陳列館：the National Palace Museum 故宮博物院

pupil [ˈpjupl̩] .... ★★★★
n. 學生，小學生

scholarship [ˈskɑlɚʃɪp] .... ★★★★
n. 獎學金

school [skul] .... ★★★★★
n. 學校

student [ˈstjudn̩t] .... ★★★★★
n. 學生，學者，大學生

teacher [ˈtitʃɚ] .... ★★★★★
n. 老師

university [ˌjunəˈvɝsətɪ] .... ★★★★★
n. (綜合性) 大學

02

書籍、文具相關辭彙

Vocabulary of Books

bookplate [ˋbʊkˏplet] .... ★
n. 藏書票

bookshop [ˋbʊkˏʃɑp] .... ★★★★★
n. 書店

catalog [ˋkætəlɔg] .... ★★★★★
v. 按目錄分類：Can you catalogue the VCD sets you sell and send me a copy? 你能不能把你們出售的 VCD編成目錄送我一份？

chalk [tʃɔk] .... ★★★
n. 白堊，粉筆：The teacher wrote on the blackboard with a piece of chalk. 老師用一支粉筆在黑板上寫字。
v. 用粉筆寫

conservatory [kənˋsɝvəˏtorɪ] .... ★
n. 溫室，音樂學校

desk [dɛsk] .... ★★★★
n. 書桌，辦公桌，服務台

desktop [ˋdɛsktɑp] .... ★★★★★
n. 桌上型電腦：a desktop computer 桌上型電腦

duplicate .... ★
n. [ˋdjupləkɪt] 複製品，副本，抄件
v. [ˋdjupləˏket] 複製，複寫：Academic records from other institutions often become part of a university's official file and can neither be returned to a student nor duplicated. 由其他學院提供的學業成績常變成大學官方的部分檔案，既不能退給學生，也不能複製。

encyclopedia [ɪnˏsaɪkləˋpidɪə] .... ★
n. 百科全書：A dictionary explains words and an encyclopedia explains facts. 字典解釋字義，百科全書則解釋事物。

Fahrenheit [ˋfærənˏhaɪt] .... ★
adj. 華氏的：Water freezes at 32 degrees Fahrenheit (32°F). 水在華氏32度結冰。

glossary [ˋglɑsərɪ] .... ★★
n. 辭彙表：monolingual glossary 單語詞彙

homework [ˋhomˏwɝk] .... ★★★★★
n. 家庭作業
【片語】do one's homework 寫作業

Education

ink [ɪŋk] .... ★★★★
n. 墨水，油墨：a pen and ink drawing 鋼筆畫

instrument [ˋɪnstrəmənt] .... ★★★★★
n. 儀器，工具，樂器：a percussion
　　instrument 打擊樂器

instrumental [ˏɪnstrəˋmɛntl̩] .... ★
adj. 有幫助的，儀器的，器械的：Technical
　　innovation is instrumental in improving the
　　qualities of products. 技術革新有助於提升
　　產品的品質。

keyboard [ˋkiˏbord] .... ★★★
n. 鍵盤

lamp [læmp] .... ★★★★
n. 燈

learned [ˋlɜnɪd] .... ★★★★★
adj. 博學的，有學問的：The learned
　　professor helped her on her papers. 這位
　　博學的教授幫助她寫論文。

librarian [laɪˋbrɛrɪən] .... ★★★★★
n. 圖書館管理員：assistant librarian 圖書館館
　　長助理

microcomputer [ˏmaɪkrokəmˋpjutɚ] . ★★★
n. 微電腦

nib [nɪb] .... ★★★★★
n. 筆尖

note [not] .... ★★★★★
n. ①注釋：Please read the notes to the text.
　　請看一下這篇課文的注釋。②記錄，筆
　　記：She makes notes carefully when the
　　teacher speaks. 老師講課時她認真做筆記。
　　③鈔票，紙票：a ￡5 note 一張5英鎊的紙
　　幣。④音符，音調：a quarter note 四分音
　　符
【片語】make notes 做筆記

page [pedʒ] .... ★★★★★
n. （書，報等的）頁，版

pen [pɛn] .... ★★★★
n. （鋼）筆：a ball point pen 圓珠筆

pencil [ˋpɛnsl̩] .... ★★★★
n. 鉛筆：a hair pencil 畫筆

ruler [ˋrulɚ] .... ★★★★
n. 尺

stationery [ˋsteʃənˏɛrɪ] .... ★
n. 文具

telescope [ˋtɛləˏskop] .... ★★★
n. 望遠鏡

text [tɛkst] .... ★★★★★
n. 課文，課本，文本

textbook [ˋtɛkstˏbuk] .... ★★★
n. 教科書，課本

type [taɪp] .... ★★★★★
n. ①類型，種類，品種：They tested your
　　blood type during pregnancy. 他們在你懷孕
　　時驗了你的血型。②〔印〕鉛字：The title
　　should be in bold type. 標題應該用黑體字。
v. 打字：Please type the letter within ten
　　minutes. 請在10分鐘內將此信件打完。

typewriter [ˋtaɪpˏraɪtɚ] .... ★★★
n. 打字機

typical [ˋtɪpɪkl̩] .... ★★★
adj. 典型的，代表性的：It is a typical Gothic
　　church. 這是座典型的哥德式教堂。

typically [ˋtɪpɪklɪ] .... ★★★ad
v. 典型地，獨特地

typist [ˋtaɪpɪst] .... ★★★
n. 打字員

03

教學相關辭彙
Vocabulary of Teaching

curriculum [kə`rɪkjələm] ....★★★★
n. （一門）課程：curriculum enhancements 課程的改進

definition [ˌdɛfə`nɪʃən] ....★★★★★
n. 定義，解釋：With the drizzle, the trees in the little clearing had lost their definition. 綿綿細雨中，那片小空地上的樹木都分辨不出輪廓了。

digress [daɪ`grɛs] ....★
v. 離開本題：The old professor used to digress from his subject for a moment to tell his students a funny story. 老教授過去常常偏離主題，花個片刻為學生們講一個有趣的故事。

edify [`ɛdəˌfaɪ] ....★
v. 陶冶，教化：Young students are advised to read edifying books to improve their mind. 青年學子們被建議讀一些陶冶性情的書籍以提升心智。

educate [`ɛdʒəˌket] ....★★★★
v. 教育，培養，訓練：educate the new generation 教育下一代

education [ˌɛdʒə`keʃən] ....★★★★★
n. 教育：Every father wants his child to have a good education. 每位父親都想讓孩子受良好的教育。

educator [`ɛdʒuˌketə] ....★★★★★
n. 教育工作者：Mildred Helen Mcafee, an educator, was president of Wellesley College from 1936 to 1949. 教育家米蘭德・海倫・麥考非在1936到1949年期間是韋爾茲利學院的院長。

elective [ɪ`lɛktɪv] ....★★★★★
n. 選修課程：elective courses 選修課程

enroll [ɪn`rol] ....★★
v. 入學，登記，招收，編入：enrolled the children in kindergarten 孩子們註冊入幼稚園；enroll the minutes of the meeting 作會議記錄

experience [ɪk`spɪrɪəns] ....★★★★★
n. ①經驗，感受，體驗：Does he have experience in work of this kind? 他有做過這種工作的經驗嗎？ ②經歷：an unpleasant experience 一次不愉快的經歷
v. 經歷，體驗：Our country has experienced great changes in the past thirty years. 我國在過去三十年經歷了巨大變化。

experienced [ɪkˋspɪrɪənst] .... ★★★★★
adj. 有經驗的：be well experienced in the
　　ways of the world 閱世頗深

experiment [ɪkˋspɛrəmənt] .... ★★★★
n. 實驗，試驗

forum [ˋforəm] .... ★★
n. 討論會，座談會

foster [ˋfɔstɚ] .... ★★
v. 養育，撫養：Frequent cultural exchange
　　will certainly help foster friendly relations
　　between our two universities. 經常性的文化
　　交流肯定有助於發展我們兩間大學之間的友
　　好關係。

infuse [ɪnˋfjuz] .... ★★★★★
v. 灌輸，浸漬：infuse herbs 泡製草藥；infuse
　　somebody with courage 鼓起某人的勇氣

instance [ˋɪnstəns] .... ★★★★★
n. 例子，實例，事例：I'll give you some
　　instances. 我給你舉些例子。
【片語】for instance 例如，比如

instruct [ɪnˋstrʌkt] .... ★★★★
v. 教導，命令：After having been instructed
　　to drive out of town, I began to acquire
　　confidence. 我在接到把車開出城的指令後，
　　開始信心十足了。

instruction [ɪnˋstrʌkʃən] .... ★★★★★
n. 講授，指令，說明（書），指導，教導

instructional [ɪnˋstrʌkʃənl] .... ★★★★★
adj. 教學的：for instructional purpose 用於教
　　育目的； instructional film 教學影片

instructor [ɪnˋstrʌktɚ] .... ★★
n. 講師，指導者：He is a sports instructor. 他
　　是個體育教師。

know [no] .... ★★★★★
v. ①知道，瞭解：He knows nothing except
　　eating. 他只知道吃。②認識，熟悉：I knew
　　him when I first came to this school. 我第一
　　次來這間學校的時候認識了他。

knowledge [ˋnɑlɪdʒ] .... ★★★★★
n. ①知識，學問：My knowledge of French is
　　poor. 我知道的法語很少。②知道，瞭解：
　　He did it without my knowledge. 我不知道他
　　做那件事。③通曉，消息

knowledgeable [ˋnɑlɪdʒəbl] ...... ★★★★★
adj. 有見識的：He made some knowledgeable
　　remarks at the meeting. 他在會上的發言
　　頗有見地。

laboratory [ˋlæbrəˌtorɪ] .... ★★★★
n. 實驗室，研究室：a hygienic laboratory 衛
　　生實驗室

learn [lɝn] .... ★★★★★
v. ①學習，學會：He studied hard and finally
　　learned the new words. 他努力學習，終
　　於把這些生字學會了。②聽說，獲悉：I
　　learned this from someone else. 我是從別人
　　那兒知道這事的。

lecture [ˋlɛktʃɚ] .... ★★★★★
n. 講課，演講，講座

lecturer [ˋlɛktʃərɚ] .... ★★★★★
n. 講演者，講師

lesson [ˋlɛsn] .... ★★★★★
n. ①課：We are going to learn Lesson Ten
　　tomorrow. 我們明天學第十課。②功課，學
　　業：You know your lessons well enough. 你
　　把課文記得相當熟。
【片語】①have lessons 上課②do one's
lessons 做功課

matriculate [məˋtrɪkjəˌlet] ....★
vt. 錄取，准許入學

platform [ˋplætˌfɔrm] .... ★★★★
n. 臺，講臺，月臺，政綱，黨綱：The
　　headmaster stood on a platform at one end
　　of the hall. 校長站在大廳一端的講臺上。

practice [ˋpræktɪs] .... ★★★★★

n. ①實踐，實際：Correct ideas come from social practice. 正確的思想來自社會實踐。②練習，實習：The students were very pleased to do practice with their English teacher in speaking English. 學生們非常高興地和英語老師練習講英語。

practice [ˋpræktɪs] .... ★★★★

v. ①練習，實習，訓練：You mustn't practice the drums while the baby is sleeping. 孩子睡覺時，你不能練鼓。②從事（職業）：One of my brothers practices medicine. 我的一個兄弟在行醫。③執行：Torture was certainly practiced in these countries. 這些國家還在執行酷刑。④開業：He's passed his law examinations and is now practicing. 他已經通過法律考試，現在在當律師。

quiz [kwɪz] .... ★★★

n. 小型考試，測驗，問答比賽：quiz bee/ game〔美〕（廣播、電視中的）問答比賽

semester [səˋmɛstɚ] .... ★★★★

n. 學期：There are two semesters in a year. 一年中有兩個學期。

seminar [ˋsɛmə͵nɑr] .... ★★★

n. （大學）研究班，研究班討論會／課程，〔美〕專家討論會，講習會：a seminar course 討論式的課程

squad [skwɑd] .... ★

n. 小隊，班：squad drill 班級訓練

symposium [sɪmˋpozɪəm] .... ★

n. 座談會，研討會

term [tɝm] .... ★★★★★

n. 術語，學期

tuition [tjuˋɪʃən] .... ★

n. 學費：tuition payments 繳納學費

tutor [ˋtjutɚ] .... ★★★

n. 負責管理學生的教師，導師：Her tutor teaches her at home. 她的家教在家裡教她。

04

考試、證書相關辭彙

Vocabulary of Test

certification [ˌsɝtɪfəˈkeʃən] .... ★★★
n. 證明，證明書

doctor [ˈdɑktɚ] .... ★★★★★
n. 博士，醫生：a doctor of traditional Chinese medicine 中醫
【片語】see a/the doctor 看病，就診

exam [ɪgˈzæm] .... ★★★★★
n. 考試，測驗：I must pass the exam. 我必須考及格。

examination [ɪgˌzæməˈneʃən] .... ★★★★
n. ①考試：an examination on mathematics數學考試②
檢查：The prisoner was still under examination. 那
個犯人還在受審訊。

examine [ɪgˈzæmɪn] .... ★★★★★
v. ①檢查，仔細觀察：examine old records 檢查舊記
錄②對…進行考查：examine sb. in German 對某人
的德語進行考查

example [ɪgˈzæmpl̩] .... ★★★★★
n. 例子，實例：Parents should set a good example for
their child. 父母應當為孩子樹立好的榜樣。
【片語】for example 例如

grade [gred] .... ★★★★★
n. 年級，等級，級別

gradual [ˈgrædʒʊəl] .... ★★★★★
adj. 逐漸的，逐步的：a gradual increase in the cost of
living 生活費用的逐漸增高

graduate [ˈgrædʒʊɪt] .... ★★★★★
n. （大學）畢業生
adj. 研究生的，畢業的：graduate courses 研究生課程

postgraduate [postˈgrædʒʊɪt] .... ★★★★★
n. 研究生

professor [prəˈfɛsɚ] .... ★★★★★
n. 教授：He is a professor. 他是一位教授。

qualification [ˌkwɑləfəˈkeʃən] .... ★★★
n. 資格，合格，合格，條件：He fulfilled the
qualifications for registering to vote in the
presidential election. 他符合在總統大選中登記投票
的條件。

score [skor] .... ★★★★★

n. 刻痕，傷痕，成績，記分：The score in the
football game was 4:1. 這場足球賽的比較
是四比一。

Unit 5

政治法律 名稱總匯

Politics & Law

國家、政體相關辭彙

Vocabulary of Government

affiliate [əˈfɪlɪˌet] .... ★

v. 加盟，入會：He refused to affiliate into any political party. 他拒絕參加任何政黨。

America [əˈmɛrɪkə] .... ★★★★★

n. ①美洲：South America 南美洲②美國：the United States of America 美利堅合眾國（美國）

aristocrat [æˈrɪstəˌkræt] .... ★

n. 貴族：come the aristocrat over somebody 對某人裝出貴族的派頭

Asia [ˈeʃə] .... ★★★★★

n. 亞洲

Asian [ˈeʃən] .... ★★★★★

adj. 亞洲的，亞洲人的

n. 亞洲人

Australia [ɔˈstreljə] .... ★★★

n. 澳大利亞，澳洲

Australian [ɔˈstreljən] .... ★★★

adj. 澳大利亞的，澳洲的，澳大利亞人的

n. 澳大利亞人

Canada [ˈkænədə] .... ★★★★★

n. 加拿大

Canadian [kəˈnedɪən] .... ★★★★

adj. 加拿大的，加拿大人的

n. 加拿大人

capital [ˈkæpətl] .... ★★★★★

adj. 主要的，基本的

n. 首都，資本，資金，大寫：Only after the Civil War did the United States have the capital to create the modern factories and transportation necessary for a machine-age society. 美國直到南北戰爭之後，才有資金為一個機器時代的社會建立現代工廠，生產必要的運輸工具。

charter [ˈtʃɑrtə] .... ★★★

v. ①租船，租車②給予…特權，特許設立：a chartered plane 一架包租的飛機

n. 租賃，特許狀，許可證，憲章：A royal charter exempted the Massachusetts colony from direct interference by the Crown. 一張皇家的特許狀，使麻塞諸塞州殖民地免受英國王室直接干涉。

China [`tʃaɪnə] .... ★★★★★
n. 中國

citizen [`sɪtəzn̩] .... ★★★★★
n. 公民，市民，平民：As a citizen, you must obey the law, or you will be punished. 你是一個公民，就必須遵守法律，否則將會受到懲罰。

city [`sɪtɪ] .... ★★★★★
n. 城市，都市

communism [`kɑmjʊˏnɪzm̩] .... ★★★
n. 共產主義

communist [`kɑmjʊˏnɪst] .... ★★★
n. 共產主義者
adj. 共產主義的：the international communist movement 國際共產主義運動；C-Party 共產黨；*Manifesto of the C-Party*《共產黨宣言》

confer [kən`fɝ] .... ★★★★★
v. 協商，頒給，賦予：The research team needs to confer with the director before it begins its final report. 研究小組在作最後的報告之前，要和召集人協商一下。

conference [`kɑnfərəns] .... ★★★★★
n.（尤指以討論或交換意見為目的，具有協商性的）會議：the peace conference 和平會談

country [`kʌntrɪ] .... ★★★★★
n. ①國家，國土②鄉下，農村：My uncle lives in the country. 我叔叔住在鄉下。
【片語】in the country 在鄉下

county [`kaʊntɪ] .... ★★★★★
n.〔英〕州或郡，〔美〕郡或縣：county alderman〔美〕郡／縣議員

district [`dɪstrɪkt] .... ★★★★★
n. 轄區，行政區，區域

domain [do`men] .... ★★★★★
n. 領域：the domain of history 歷史領域

domestic [də`mɛstɪk] .... ★★★★★
adj. 家内的，國内的：domestic issues such as tax rates and highway construction 稅率和公路建設之類的國内問題

Egyptian [ɪ`dʒɪpʃən] .... ★★
adj. 埃及（人）的
n. 埃及人

embassy [`ɛmbəsɪ] .... ★★★
n. 大使館：American Embassy in Japan 美國駐日本大使館

empire [`ɛmpaɪr] .... ★★★★★
n. 帝國：the Roman Empire 羅馬帝國

England [`ɪŋglənd] .... ★★★★★
n. 英格蘭，英國

English [`ɪŋglɪʃ] .... ★★★★★
n. 英語：How do you say the word in English? 這個字的英語怎麼說？
【片語】in English 用英語
adj. ①英國的②英語的，用英語寫的，用英語說的

Europe [`jʊrəp] .... ★★★★★
n. 歐洲

European [ˏjʊrə`piən] .... ★★★★★
adj. 歐洲的，歐洲人的

Finn [fɪn] .... ★★★★★
n. 芬蘭人

flag [flæg] .... ★★★★
v. 衰退，枯萎：My interest in this business has flagged. 我對這筆生意已沒什麼興趣。

foreign [`fɔrɪn] .... ★★★★★
adj. 外國的，外來的，陌生的：He is able to speak several foreign languages. 他能講好幾種外語。

French [frɛntʃ] .... ★★★★★
adj. 法國的，法語的
n. 法國人，法語

Frenchman [`frɛntʃmən] .... ★★★★★
n. 法蘭西人，法國人

Germany [ˋdʒɝmənɪ] .... ★★★★★
n. 德國

Greek [grik] .... ★★★★★
n. 希臘人，希臘語
adj. 希臘（人）的，晦澀難懂的事物：
　　Quantum mechanics is Greek to me. 我對
　　量子力學一竅不通。

Hawaii [həˋwaɪjɪ] .... ★★★★★
n. 夏威夷

India [ˋɪndɪə] .... ★★★★★
n. 印度
n. 印度：The capital of India is New Delhi. 印
　　度的首都是新德里。

Indian [ˋɪndɪən] .... ★★★★★
adj. ①印度的②印度人的，印第安人的③印第
　　安語的
n. ①印度人，印第安人②印第安語

international [͵ɪntɚˋnæʃənḷ] .... ★★★★★
adj. 國際的，世界的：an international
　　commission 國際委員會

Italian [ɪˋtæljən] .... ★★★★★
adj. 義大利的，義大利人的，義大利語的
n. 義大利人，義大利語

Japan [dʒəˋpæn] .... ★★★★★
n. 日本

Japanese [͵dʒæpəˋniz] .... ★★★★
adj. 日本的，日本人的，日語的
n. 日本人，日語

Jewish [ˋdʒuɪʃ] .... ★★★★
adj. 猶太人的：Jewish customs 猶太習俗；
　　the Jewish calendar 猶太曆（希伯來人用
　　的陰陽合曆）

local [ˋlokḷ] .... ★★★★★
adj. ①地方性的，當地的：local radio station
　　地方電臺②局部的：a local inflection 局部
　　感染

metropolitan [͵mɛtrəˋpɑlətṇ] .... ★★
adj. 大都會的，大城市的：Vermont has
　　the lowest percentage of metropolitan
　　residents of any state in the United
　　States. 佛蒙特州的大城市居民比例是美國
　　各州最低的。

monarch [ˋmɑnɚk] .... ★★
n. 君主：Mont Blanc is the monarch of the
　　mountains. 白朗峰是山岳之王。

nation [ˋneʃən] .... ★★★★★
n. 國家，民族：The whole nation is/are
　　excited. 全國上下都非常振奮。

national [ˋnæʃənḷ] .... ★★★★★
adj. 國家的，全國的：a national flag 國旗
n. （某國的）公民：Foreign nationals are
　　protected by the law. 外國僑民是受法律保
　　護的。

nationality [͵næʃəˋnælətɪ] .... ★★★
n. 國籍：Richard is an American, John is a
　　British—they have different nationalities. 理
　　查是美國人，約翰是英國人，他們的國籍不
　　同。

Oceania [͵oʃɪˋænɪə] .... ★★
n. 大洋洲

outskirts [ˋaʊt͵skɝts] .... ★★★
n. 郊區

premier [ˋprimɪɚ] .... ★★
n. 總理，首相

province [ˋprɑvɪns] .... ★★★★★
n. 省，領域，範圍

provincial [prəˋvɪnʃəl] .... ★★★★★
adj. 省的，外省的，鄉下的：Well-educated
　　professional women made me feel
　　uncomfortably provincial. 受過良好教育的
　　職業婦女讓我覺得自己像個鄉下人，很不
　　舒服。

realm [rɛlm] .... ★★★
n. 王國，領域：the realm of science 科學領域

regime [rɪˋʒim] .... ★★
n. 政體，統治（方式），制度：people
suffered under the new regime 在新政權下
受苦的人民

regimen [ˋrɛdʒəˏmɛn] .... ★★
n. 政權，養生法：Under such a regimen you'll
certainly live long. 你這樣養生一定可以長
壽。

region [ˋridʒən] .... ★★★★★
n. 地區，領域，區域，範圍：The Polar
Regions are generally covered with ice and
snow. 極地地區通常被冰雪覆蓋著。

republic [rɪˋpʌblɪk] .... ★★★★★
n. 共和國，共和政體：the Republic of Korea
大韓民國

Roman [ˋromən] .... ★★★★★
adj. 羅馬的
n. 羅馬人

Russian [ˋrʌʃən] .... ★★★★★
adj. 俄羅斯的，俄國的，俄國人的，俄語的
n. 俄羅斯人，俄國人，俄語

sovereign [ˋsɑvrɪn] .... ★★
n. 統治者，君主
adj. 統治的，有主權的：Only sovereign states
are able to make treaties. 只有主權國家才
能簽署條約。

sovereignty [ˋsɑvrɪntɪ] .... ★★
n. 主權：The neighboring country demanded
its complete sovereignty and territorial
integrity. 鄰國要求其主權和領土的完整。

territory [ˋtɛrəˏtorɪ] .... ★★★★
n. 領土，領域，地區，範圍：Wild animals
will not allow other animals to enter their
territory. 野生動物不許其他動物進入牠們的
地盤。

throne [θron] .... ★★
n. 王位，君權：They must obey the throne.
他們必須服從王權。

town [taʊn] .... ★★★★★
n. 城，城鎮：Would you rather live in a town
or in the country? 你喜歡住在城裡還是鄉
下？
【片語】①home town 家鄉②go to town 進城

urban [ˋɝbən] .... ★★★★
adj. 城市的：The world urban population is
increasing. 世界城市人口正在增長。

world [wɝld] .... ★★★★★
n. 世界，地球：They have all changed the
world. 他們都曾改變了世界。

worldwide [ˋwɝldˏwaɪd] .... ★★★★
adj. 世界範圍的，全世界的

政治法律名稱總匯

02

機構、組織相關辭彙 Vocabulary of Institutions

alliance [əˋlaɪəns] ....★★★★
n. 聯盟，同盟

ambassador [æmˋbæsədə] ....★★
n. 大使：the British ambassador to France 英國駐法大使

autonomous [ɔˋtɑnəməs] ....★
adj. 自治的，自主的：This island is a colony; however, in most matters, it is autonomous and receives no orders from the motherland. 這塊島是個殖民地，然而在大部分事務上，它保持自主權，不受其宗主國的命令。

autonomy [ɔˋtɑnəmɪ] ....★
n. 自治權

bourgeois [burˋʒwɑ] ....★
adj. 資產階級的，中產階級的

bureau [ˋbjuro] ....★★★★
n. 署，局：a travel bureau 旅遊局

bureaucracy [bjuˋrɑkrəsɪ] ....★
n. 官僚主義，官僚機構：promised to reorganize the federal bureaucracy 發誓整頓聯邦官僚作風

cabin [ˋkæbɪn] ....★★★★
n. 機艙，船艙，小木屋：a four-cabin 四個鋪位的船艙

cabinet [ˋkæbənɪt] ....★★★★
n. 櫥櫃，內閣：a Cabinet Minister 內閣部長

chair [tʃɛr] ....★★★★★
n. 椅子：Sit on the chair, please. 請坐到椅子上。

chairman [ˋtʃɛrmən] ....★★★★★
n. 主席，議長：Chairman of the committee 委員會主席

civil [ˋsɪvḷ] ....★★★★★
adj. 民用的，土木的，國內的，公民的，國民間的：The lecturer continued that civil law was different to criminal law. 授課者繼續解釋說民法與刑法是不同的。

civilian [sɪˋvɪljən] ....★★★★
n. 平民
adj. 平民的：civilian life 平民的生活

commission [kə'mɪʃən] .... ★★★★★
n. 委員會，傭金：The Federal Trade Commission investigated false advertising. 聯邦貿易委員會調查不實廣告。

committee [kə'mɪtɪ] .... ★★★★★
n. 委員會，委員：The football club committee arranges all the matches. 足球俱樂部委員會安排所有的比賽。

commonwealth ['kɑmənˌwɛlθ] .... ★★
n. 共和國，聯邦，共同體：The Commonwealth of Puerto Rico 波多黎各聯邦

commune [kə'mjun] .... ★★★★
n. 公社
v. 親密地交談，（與周圍的事物）處於親密、加深的情感和感受的狀態：hikers communing with nature 徒步旅行者與自然界親密無間

community [kə'mjunətɪ] .... ★★★★★
n. 社區，社會，公社：The whole community was astir when the news came that the enemy bombing would be restored. 敵人將恢復轟炸的消息傳來，整個社區都騷動著。

confederate [kən'fɛdərɪt] .... ★
adj. 同盟：the confederate states of America 美國南部聯邦

consul ['kɑnsl̩] .... ★★
n. 領事執政：an acting consul 代理領事

consultant [kən'sʌltənt] .... ★★★
n. 顧問：The consultant committee met at the call of the chairman. 顧問委員會應主席的召集而開會。

council ['kaʊnsl̩] .... ★★★★★
n. 理事會，委員會，議事機構：a council chamber 議事廳

countryside ['kʌntrɪˌsaɪd] .... ★★★
n. 鄉下，農村：The English countryside looks its best in May and June. 英國的鄉村在五、六月間景色最美。

delegate ['dɛləgɪt] .... ★★★
n. 代表

delegation [ˌdɛlə'geʃən] .... ★★★
n. 代表團

faction ['fækʃən] .... ★★
n. 宗派，派系，小集團

factious ['fækʃəs] .... ★
adj. 黨派的：factious quarrels 派別之爭

federal ['fɛdərəl] .... ★★★★★
adj. 聯邦的，聯盟的，聯合的：The senator's federal leanings were well known. 該參議員的聯邦制傾向是眾所周知的。

government ['gʌvənmənt] .... ★★★★★
n. 政府，內閣，管理，支配，政治，政體：The Government is/are planning new tax increases. 政府正打算提高徵稅額。

governor ['gʌvənə] .... ★★★★★
n. 總督，地方長官：the Governor of the Bank of England 英格蘭銀行行長

hierarchy ['haɪəˌrɑrkɪ] .... ★
n. 統治集團，等級制度：put honesty first in her hierarchy of values 把誠實擺在她自己價值觀裡的第一位

league [lig] .... ★★★★★
n. 同盟，聯盟，聯合會：Our team plays in the football league. 我們球隊在足球聯賽中比賽。

legislature ['lɛdʒɪsˌletʃə] .... ★★★★
n. 立法機關，議會

magistrate ['mædʒɪsˌtret] .... ★
n. 行政長官，地方法官：the first/chief magistrate （美國的）最高行政長官

mayor ['meə] .... ★★★★
n. 市長

member ['mɛmbə] .... ★★★★★
n. 成員，會員：You are a League member. 你是團員之一。

minister ['mɪnɪstə] .... ★★★★★
n. 部長，大臣，牧師：the Minister for/of Foreign Affairs 外交部長

ministry [ˈmɪnɪstrɪ] .... ★★★★
n. （政府的）部：the Ministry of National
Defense 國防部

mission [ˈmɪʃən] .... ★★★★★
n. 使節，代表團，使命，任務，天職

Nazi [ˈnɑtsɪ] .... ★
adj. 納粹的
n. 納粹分子

office [ˈɔfɪs] .... ★★★★★
n. 辦公室，辦公處

officer [ˈɔfəsɚ] .... ★★★★★
n. ①軍官，警官：Some commissioned and
noncommissioned officers attended the
meeting. 部分軍官和士官出席了會議。②官
員，高級職員：officers and crew 全體工作
人員

official [əˈfɪʃəl] .... ★★★★★
n. 官員，行政人員
adj. 官方的，正式的，公務的：Although
the retired architects of the party do not
occupy any official positions, they have a
lot of authority. 雖然退休的創黨元老現在
沒有任何正式職位，但他們還是有很大的
權威性。

parliament [ˈpɑrləmənt] .... ★★★★★
n. 議會，國會：Parliament makes laws. 議會
制訂法律。

parliamentary [ˌpɑrləˈmɛntərɪ] .. ★★★★★
adj. 議會的，國會的：parliamentary
government 議會政府

partisan [ˈpɑrtəzn] .... ★★★★★
adj. 黨派的，派系感強的：partisan politics 政
黨政治

prefecture [ˈprifɛktʃɚ] .... ★
n. 專區，府

preside [prɪˈzaɪd] .... ★★
v. 主持：The special workshop was presided
over by a famous scientist. 那次專題研討會
是由一位著名的科學家主持的。

president [ˈprɛzədənt] .... ★★★★★
n. 總統，校長，會長，主席：the
assassination of President Lincoln 暗殺林
肯總統

propaganda [ˌprɑpəˈgændə] .... ★
n. 宣傳：the selected truths, exaggerations,
and lies of wartime propaganda 經選擇出來
的事實、誇張的話語以及戰時宣傳的謊言

sheriff [ˈʃɛrɪf] .... ★★
n. （某些城市的）行政司法長官，〔英〕郡長

senator [ˈsɛnətɚ] .... ★★
n. 參議員

union [ˈjunjən] .... ★★★★★
n. ①工會，協會，同盟：Mr. White is the
leader of the union. 懷特先生是工會的會
長。②結合，聯合，合併：We are working
for the union of the two countries. 我們正
在為兩國的合併而努力。③團結，一致，融
洽：They lived in perfect union. 他們和睦相
處。

warlord [ˈwɔrˌlɔrd] .... ★
n. 軍閥

政治法律名稱總匯

03

政治活動相關辭彙
Vocabulary of Politics

anarchy [ˈænəkɪ] .... ★

n. 無政府狀態：The assassination of the leaders led to a period of anarchy. 領導群被暗殺造成了一段混亂時期。

ballot [ˈbælət] .... ★

n. 選票：The club members held a secret ballot to choose the chairperson. 俱樂部成員用無記名投票選舉負責人。

boycott [ˈbɔɪkɑt] .... ★

v. 聯合抵制，杯葛：The people who work there are on strike to boycott a meeting. 在那裡工作的人為了抵制一場會議而罷工。

candidate [ˈkændədet] .... ★★★★

n. 候選人：young actors who are candidates for stardom 註定要成為大明星的年輕演員

colonial [kəˈlonjəl] .... ★★

adj. 殖民地的，殖民的：The Latin American and African people have successfully fought against colonial rule. 拉丁美洲和非洲人民成功地反抗殖民統治。

colonist [ˈkɑlənɪst] .... ★

n. 殖民地開拓者，殖民地居民：A colonist is an original settler or founder of a colony or an inhabitant of a colony. 殖民者是指殖民地的最初定居者或創建者，或指殖民地居民。

condone [kənˈdon] .... ★

v. 寬恕，赦免：People cannot condone the use of fierce violence. 人們無法寬恕使用凶殘的暴力。

congress [ˈkɑŋgrəs] .... ★★★★★

n. 國會，（代表）大會：Congress has approved the new publication laws. 國會已通過新的出版法規。

democracy [dɪˈmɑkrəsɪ] .... ★★★★

n. 民主：The teacher's democracy made her popular among her pupils. 這位教師的民主作風使她受到學生的歡迎。

democratic [ˌdɛməˈkrætɪk] .... ★★★★

adj. 民主的：A proper democratic system scorn for bloated dukes and lords. 真正的民主制譴責傲慢的貴族和地主。

dominant [ˈdɑmənənt] .... ★★★
adj. 佔優勢的，主導的：The dominant theme in the music is of tranquility and peacefulness. 音樂的主題是寧靜和和平。

dominion [dəˈmɪnjən] .... ★★★
n. 領土，主權：the government's claim of dominion over the resources of the marginal sea 政府對於領海資源的管轄權

dominate [ˈdɑməˌnet] .... ★★★
v. 統治，支配，控制：Successful leaders dominate events rather than react to them. 成功的領導者是事先控制事件，而不是事後才反應。

empower [ɪmˈpauɚ] .... ★★★★★
v. 授權，使能夠：Modern science and technology empower human beings to control natural forces more effectively. 現代科學技術使人類能更有效地控制自然力量。

enact [ɪnˈækt] .... ★
v. 制定（法律），扮演：The United States Congress and the state legislatures enact thousands of laws each year. 美國國會和各州議會每年都制定幾千條法律。

fascism [ˈfæʃˌɪzəm] .... ★★★
n. 法西斯主義

fascist [ˈfæʃɪst] .... ★★★
n. 法西斯主義者

govern [ˈgʌvɚn] .... ★★★★
v. 決定，支配，控制：to govern yourselves like civilized human beings 注意你們的言行，要像有教養的人

independence [ˌɪndɪˈpɛndəns] .... ★★★★
n. 獨立，自主：They declared independence in 1962. 他們在1962年宣佈獨立。

independent [ˌɪndɪˈpɛndənt] ...... ★★★★★
adj. (of) 獨立的，自主的：He is very far from being independent. 他現在還談不上獨立自主。

intrigue [ɪnˈtrig] .... ★
v. 引起…興趣：Because of its old mannerisms, the praying mantis has always intrigued human beings. 合掌螳螂因其老邁怪異的舉止，總能引起人們的興趣。

organize [ˈɔrgəˌnaɪz] .... ★★★★
v. 組織，把…編組：organize a political party 組織政黨

parade [pəˈred] .... ★★★
v. 遊行，檢閱
n. 遊行：The circus performers and animals paraded down the Main Street. 馬戲團的演員們和那些動物沿著主街遊行。

party [ˈpɑrtɪ] .... ★★★★★
n. ①團體，黨派：the Liberal Party（英國）自由黨②集會，聚會：We'll have an English party next Saturday. 下個星期六我們將有一場英文派對。

political [pəˈlɪtɪkl] .... ★★★★★
adj. 政治（上）的：Calling a meeting is a political act in itself. 召開會議本身就是一種政治性行為。

politician [ˌpɑləˈtɪʃən] .... ★★★
n. 政客，政治家：Mothers may still want their favorite sons to grow up to be President, but they do not want them to become politicians in the process. 母親們也許仍然希望她們寵愛的兒子長大後成為總統，但並不想讓他們在當上總統這一過程中成為政客。

politics [ˈpɑlətɪks] .... ★★★★★
n. ①政治，政治學②政綱，政見③政治活動：Politics has never interested me. 我從未對政治感興趣。

poll [pol] .... ★★★
n. 投票記錄，民意測驗，投票（數）

v. 投票：In a 1983 newspaper poll, Ann Landers, an advice columnist, was listed among the twenty-five most influential women in the United States. 在1983年的一次報紙民調中，一位專欄評論家安娜‧蘭德斯被列為美國前25位最有影響力的婦女。

powerful [ˈpaʊəfəl] .... ★★★★★
adj. ①強大的，有力的，有權的：Powerful nations should not try to control the weaker ones. 強國不應企圖控制弱國。② 強壯的，強健的：He is a powerful, well-built man. 他體魄強健。

quell [kwɛl] .... ★
v. 壓制：He finally quelled the children's fears. 他最終讓孩子們不再恐懼。

reign [ren] .... ★★
v. 統治：The Queen reigns but does not rule. 女王在位，但不當政。

session [ˈsɛʃən] .... ★★★★★
n. 會議，一段時間，一次：The general session approved the report of the investigation committee. 全體會議認可了調查委員會的報告。

statement [ˈstetmənt] .... ★★★★★
n. 陳述，聲明 ：The punishment for making false statements to the tax authorities can be severe. 向稅務機關不實申報會受到很重的懲罰。

statesman [ˈstetsmən] .... ★★★★
n. 國務活動家，政治家

subvert [səbˈvɝt] .... ★★★★★
v. 顛覆，推翻：Economic assistance must subvert the existing feudal or tribal order. 經濟援助必會推翻現存的封建或部族秩序。

supervise [ˈsupəvaɪz] .... ★
v. 管理，監視，指導：The teacher supervised our drawing class. 該老師上我們的畫畫課。

supervision [ˌsupəˈvɪʒən] .... ★
n. 監督，管理，指導：The house was built under the careful supervision of an architect. 這房子是在一位建築師的細心監督下建造的。

supervisor [ˌsupəˈvaɪzə] .... ★
n. 管理人，監督（人），導師

supervisory [ˌsupəˈvaɪzərɪ] .... ★
adj. 監督的，管理的

suppress [səˈprɛs] .... ★★
v. 鎮壓，壓制，抑制，隱瞞，查禁：Although poisonous, many alkaloids are valuable as medicines, and some can suppress coughing. 許多生物鹼儘管有毒，還是像藥物一樣貴，有些也可以用來治療咳嗽。

辨析 Analyze

politician, statesman

1 **politician** *n.*「政治家，政客」，指政治家時是中性詞，指政客時是貶義詞：The mayor is an experienced politician. 這位市長是個有經驗的政治家。

2 **statesman** *n.*「國務活動家，政治家」，指政治家時是褒義詞：Lincoln was a famous American statesman. 林肯是著名的美國政治家。

04

政策、條例相關辭彙

Vocabulary of Policy

Politics & Law

clause [klɔz] .... ★★★★★
n. 分句，條款：The clause in the contract is unsusceptible of another interpretation. 合約中的這項條款不能有其他解釋。

criterion [kraɪˋtɪrɪən] .... ★★
n. （批評、判斷的）標準：admission criterion 招生條件，錄取標準

decree [dɪˋkri] .... ★★
n. 法令，規定
v. 頒佈：In 394 A.D., Emperor Theodosius I of Rome decreed that the Olympic Games should be ceased. 西元394年，羅馬皇帝狄奧多西一世下令禁止奧運會舉行。

dictator [ˋdɪk͵tetɚ] .... ★
n. 獨裁者，專制者：Hitler is a typical dictator. 希特勒是典型的獨裁者。

dictatorial [͵dɪktəˋtorɪəl] .... ★
adj. 獨裁的，專斷的

diplomacy [dɪˋploməsɪ] .... ★
n. 外交，策略：The union leader used all his diplomacy to settle the quarrel between the employer and the employees. 工會領導人使盡所有交際手段才平息了勞資雙方間的爭論。

diplomatic [͵dɪpləˋmætɪk] .... ★★
adj. 外交的，有策略的：Julia joined the diplomatic service after her graduation from the university. 茱莉亞大學畢業後就到外交部門工作了。

duty [ˋdjutɪ] .... ★★★★★
n. ①職責，責任：the student on duty 值日生 ②義務：Rights and duties can't be divided. 權利和義務不可分。
【片語】do one's duty 盡本分，盡義務，盡職責

execute [ˋɛksɪ͵kjut] .... ★★★★
v. 實行，執行，實施，處死，處決：The manager assistant came here to execute a few small commissions for the manager. 經理的助理到這裡來是代經理辦幾件小事的。

executive [ɪgˋzɛkjutɪv] .... ★★★★★
adj. 執行的，實施的

n. 執行者，行政官：the executive director of a drama troupe 戲劇團的執行導演；executive experience and skills 管理的經驗和技能

guidance [ˋgaɪdṇs] .... ★★★★
n. 指導，引導：He did the work with his teacher's guidance. 他在老師的指導下做了這件工作。

guide [gaɪd] .... ★★★★★
n. ①導遊，嚮導：We need a guide to show us the way. 我們需要一個嚮導帶路。②指南，手冊：a guide to a museum 博物館指南
v. ①為⋯導引：She guided us to the station. 她帶我們去車站。②指導：guide sb.'s studies 指導某人學習

item [ˋaɪtəm] .... ★★★★★
n. 專案，條目，條款，一則（新聞）：There was an interesting item in the newspaper today. 今天的報紙上有一條有趣的新聞。

policy [ˋpɑləsɪ] .... ★★★★★
n. 政策，方針：It is the policy of the government to improve education. 教改是政府的政策。

precept [ˋprisɛpt] ....★
n. 規則，戒律

presumptuous [prɪˋzʌmptʃʊəs] ....★
adj. 專橫的：It is too presumptuous of him to do so. 他這樣做太放肆了。

regular [ˋrɛgjələ] .... ★★★★★
adj. ①有規律的，規則的：There are regular lines of holes between the windows. 窗戶間有一排排規則的小洞。②整齊的，勻稱的：His nose is very regular. 他的鼻子長得很勻稱。③定期的，固定的：regular working hours 固定的工作時間④常規的，經常的：our regular customs 我們的老顧客

regularity [ˌrɛgjəˋlærətɪ] ....★
n. ①規則性②整齊，勻稱③正規④經常，定期

regulation [ˌrɛgjəˋleʃən] .... ★★★★
n. 規定，規則，調節，調整：laws and regulations 法令

rule [rul] .... ★★★★★
v. 統治，控制，支配：The military government ruled the country. 軍政府統治了這個國家。
n. ①規章，條例：It's against the rules to pick up the ball. 用手撿球是犯規的。②習慣，慣例：Her rule is to lunch at 1 p.m. 她通常在下午1:00吃午餐。③統治，管轄：under the rule of the country 在國家的統治下

treaty [ˋtritɪ] .... ★★★★
n. 條約：a peace treaty 和平條約

tyranny [ˋtɪrənɪ] .... ★★
n. 暴政，暴虐，殘暴，暴行，專橫：I have sworn eternal hostility against every form of tyranny over the mind of man. 我已發誓將永遠反抗以任何形式對人類思想施行的暴政。

tyrant [ˋtaɪrənt] .... ★★
n. 暴君，專制君主：a local tyrant 惡霸

warrant [ˋwɔrənt] .... ★★
n. 保證，許可權：He almost gives his failings as a warrant for his greatness. 他幾乎把他的缺點當成是對自己偉大之處的保證。

absolve [əbˋsɑlv] .... ★★★★★

v. 赦免，解除（責任等）：The officers would be given a certificate absolving them of/from any blame. 官員們會拿到一張免予追究的證明。

accusation [ˌækjəˋzeʃən] .... ★★

n. 控告：The accusation of falsehood against him was untenable. 指控他說謊的罪名不能成立。

accuse [əˋkjuz] .... ★★★★

v. 控告，歸咎：They accused her publicly of stealing their books. 他們公開指責她偷他們的書。

acquit [əˋkwɪt] .... ★★★★★

v. 宣告無罪：That man was acquitted on two of the charges. 那個男子被宣告的罪行中，有兩樣是無罪的。

admonish [ədˋmɑnɪʃ] .... ★

v. 警告，勸告：He admonished his listeners to change their wicked ways. 他勸聽眾改變他們不好的方式。

appeal [əˋpil] .... ★★★★★

v. 呼籲，申述：The woman appealed to the government for assistance in resisting forced marriage. 那婦女請求政府幫助她對抗強迫的婚姻。

n. 呼籲，申述

appealing [əˋpilɪŋ] .... ★★★★★

adj. 吸引人的，懇求的，求助的：San Francisco, one of the most appealing cities in the United States, is built on many hills. 美國最有吸引力的城市之一——舊金山，是在許多山丘上建立的。

applicant [ˋæpləkənt] .... ★★★

n. 申請人：a job applicant 求職者

application [ˌæpləˋkeʃən] .... ★★★★★

n. 請求，申請，施用：an application for financial aid 申請經濟援助

apply [əˋplaɪ] .... ★★★★★

v. 適用，適應，應用，施加，申請：You may apply in person or by letter. 你可以親自到場或去信提出申請。

arbitration [ˌɑrbəˋtreʃən] .... ★

n. 調停，仲裁：submit the points in a dispute to arbitration 把爭議點提請裁決

arrest [əˋrɛst] .... ★★★★
v. 逮捕：A man was arrested on suspicion of having murdered the girl. 那個男人因涉嫌謀害那少女被捕。

attorney [əˋtɝnɪ] .... ★★★★
n. 代理人，辯護律師

avow [əˋvaʊ] .... ★
v. 公開，承認：He avowed that he would never cooperate with them again. 他聲明他永不再與他們合作。

belong [bəˋlɔŋ] .... ★★★★★
v. ①（所有權，關係等方面）屬於（後接to）：These books belong to me. 這些書是我的。②屬，應歸入（類別，範疇等）：She belongs to the Labor Party. 她是工黨黨員。

case [kes] .... ★★★★★
n. ①情況，事實：That isn't the case with her. 她的情況並非如此。②病例：three cases of fever 三個發燒病例③案件：He took the case to court. 他把這個案子交給法庭。【片語】①in any case 無論如何，不管怎樣②in case 假使，以防萬一③in case of 假如，如果發生④in no case 無論如何不，絕不

casualty [ˋkæʒjʊəltɪ] .... ★★★
n. 意外，受害人，事故中受傷或死亡的人：The corner grocery was a casualty of the expanding supermarkets. 位在角落的雜貨店，是不斷擴張的超級市場的受害者。

client [ˋklaɪənt] .... ★★★★
n. 顧客，訴訟委託人：clients of the hotel 飯店的客人

clue [klu] .... ★★★
n. 思路，暗示，線索

commit [kəˋmɪt] .... ★★★★★
v. 使承擔義務，做（錯事），把…託交給：Booker T. Washington started the National Negro Business League, a group that was committed to the goal of black economic independence. 布克‧華盛頓創立了全國黑人商業聯盟，是一個致力於黑人經濟獨立的團體。

confess [kənˋfɛs] .... ★★★★★
v. 懺悔，坦白：Mr. Foster confessed that he'd broken the speed limit. 福斯特先生坦承自己超速了。

confiscate [ˋkɑnfɪsˏket] .... ★
v. 沒收，充公：The customs officials confiscated the contraband. 海關官員沒收了走私物品。

convict [kənˋvɪkt] .... ★★★★
v. 判罪，證明：We need jurors who will not convict them guilty merely because they are suspicious. 我們需要不會僅僅因為他們有嫌疑就判定他們有罪的陪審員。

conviction [kənˋvɪkʃən] .... ★★★★
n. 確信，信服，定罪：This was her third conviction for cheating. 這是她第三次被判詐欺罪。

court [kort] .... ★★★★★
n. 法庭：a civil court 民事法庭
v. 追求，說服：a salesperson courting a potential customer 一位正在說服有可能成交的顧客的推銷員。

covenant [ˋkʌvɪnənt] .... ★
n. 契約：The rival nations signed a covenant to reduce their armaments. 敵對國家簽署了裁減軍備條約。
v. 立保證書：I covenanted to pay $10 a week to the church. 我立約每週捐10美元給教會。

crime [kraɪm] .... ★★★★★
n. 罪，罪行，犯罪：commit a high crime 犯重大罪行

criminal [ˋkrɪmənl̩] .... ★★★★★
n. 罪犯，犯人：a wanted criminal 通緝犯
adj. 犯罪刑事的（只作定語）：a criminal act 犯罪行為

culprit [ˋkʌlprɪt] .... ★
n. 犯人

delinquency [dɪˋlɪŋkwənsɪ] .... ★
n. 少年犯罪，過失：delinquency problems 青少年犯罪問題

despoil [dɪˋspɔɪl] .... ★

v. 奪取，搶劫：The region has been despoiled of its scenic beauty by unchecked development. 這個地區由於不加限制的發展，喪失了其美麗的景色。

detain [dɪˋten] .... ★★

v. 使延遲，拘留：The disruptive students were detained after school until their parents had been notified. 搗亂的學生在放學後被留了下來，直到他們的家長已收到通知。

discipline [ˋdɪsəplɪn] .... ★★★★

n. 紀律，風紀，思想，性格的訓練，學科

v. 懲罰，懲戒：She, under no circumstances, disciplines her children and they are uncontrollable. 她無論在什麼情況下都不會管自己的孩子，孩子們因而變得無法無天。

divorce [dəˋvors] .... ★★★

v. 離婚，離異，脫離，分離：Did Mr. Hill divorce his wife or did she divorce him? 是希爾先生和他太太離婚，還是他太太和他離婚？

episode [ˋɛpəˏsod] .... ★★

n. 插曲

equitable [ˋɛkwɪtəbl] .... ★★★★★

adj. 公平的，公正的：a more equitable distribution of available resources 更公正的分配現有可用的資源

evidence [ˋɛvədəns] .... ★★★★★

n. 證據，證人

v. 顯示，證明：The McCaslin family evidences the guilt of slaveholding more than Faulkner's other characters do. McCaslin家與福克納筆下的其他角色相比，對擁有奴隸的罪惡感表露得更徹底。

eyewitness [ˋaɪˏwɪtnɪs] .... ★★★

n. 目擊者：Were there any eyewitnesses to the murder crime? 這樁謀殺案有沒有目擊者？

heirship [ˋɛrˏʃɪp] .... ★★★★★

n. 繼承權

homicide [ˋhɑməˏsaɪd] .... ★

n. 殺人：justifiable homicide 正當防衛殺人

hostage [ˋhɑstɪdʒ] .... ★

n. 人質，制約：Superpowers held hostage to each other by their nuclear arsenals 超級大國因各自擁有核能廠而互相抗衡。

identification [aɪˏdɛntəfəˋkeʃən] .... ★★

n. 認出，識別，鑒定，身份：His only means of identification was his passport. 他惟一能證明身份的證件就是他的護照。

identify [aɪˋdɛntəˏfaɪ] .... ★★★★★

v. 認出：That politician is too closely identified with the former government to become a minister in ours. 那位政治人物與上屆政府的關係過於密切，所以無法成為本屆政府裡的首長。

illegal [ɪˋligl] .... ★★★

adj. 不合法的，非法的，違法的：It is illegal to steal things. 偷東西是違法的。

illegitimate [ˏɪliˋdʒɪtəmɪt] .... ★★★

adj. 非法的，私生的

impartial [ɪmˋpɑrʃəl] .... ★

adj. 公正的，無偏見的：I don't think it is impartial for the professor to flunk my Chemistry test. 我認為教授給我化學考試不及格是不公正的。

impeach [ɪmˋpitʃ] .... ★

v. 控告，彈劾：impeach somebody's motives 懷疑某人的動機

imprisonment [ɪmˋprɪznmənt] .... ★★★

n. 監禁

incriminate [ɪnˋkrɪməˏnet] .... ★

v. 控告，使負罪：In his confession, the thief incriminated two others who helped him steal. 這個小偷在供詞中供出了另外兩個協助他偷竊的人。

indictment [ɪnˋdaɪtmənt] .... ★

n. 起訴：bring in an indictment against somebody 控告某人的訴狀

inherit [ɪnˋhɛrɪt] .... ★★★
v. 繼承：Children inherit half of their 23 pairs of chromosomes from each parent. 子女從父母身上各遺傳到一半的23對染色體。

judge [dʒʌdʒ] .... ★★★★★
n. 法官，審判員，裁判員
v. ①裁決，評判：judge a talent contest 評判智力比賽②判定，斷定：Judging by his accent, he must be an American 從他的口音判斷，他一定是美國人。③審判，判決：Who will judge the case? 誰將審判這起案子？④評判，下判斷：Without the facts, I can't judge. 沒有真憑實據，我無法判斷。

judgment [ˋdʒʌdʒmənt] .... ★★★★★
n. 判決：In her judgment, we shouldn't change our plans. 照她看來，我們不應改變計畫。

jurisdiction [ˏdʒurɪsˋdɪkʃən] .... ★
n. 司法權

justice [ˋdʒʌstɪs] .... ★★★★★
n. ①正義，公正：We thanked them for upholding justice. 我們感激他們對正義的支持。②司法，法律制裁：the minister of justice 司法部長

justify [ˋdʒʌstəˏfaɪ] .... ★★★★
v. 證明⋯是正當的：He justified each budgetary expense as necessary. 他證明每一項預算費用都是必要的。

justly [ˋdʒʌstlɪ] .... ★★★★★
ad. 公正地：Maine is justly famous for its beautiful lakes and ponds. 緬因州的美麗湖泊的確是名不虛傳。

kill [kɪl] .... ★★★★★
v. ①殺死：He was killed in the war. 他在戰爭中犧牲了。②槍殺，毀滅：That mistake killed his chances. 那個錯誤葬送了他的機會。

law [lɔ] .... ★★★★★
n. ①法律，法制：Parliament makes laws. 國會制定法律。②規律，法規，定律：the laws of nature 自然規律

lawsuit [ˋlɔˏsut] .... ★★★★★
n. 訴訟

lawyer [ˋlɔjə] .... ★★★★
n. 律師

辨析
Analyze

lawful, legal, legitimate

1. **lawful** *a.*「合法的」，就是純粹指合法的，沒有引申義：Charles is the lawful heir of the property. 查理是這項財產的合法繼承人。

2. **legal** *a.*「法律（上）的，合法的，法定的」，指合法的，還指法律上的、與法律有關的：We'd better have a legal document / adviser. 我們最好有一項法律文件／一位法律顧問。

3. **legitimate** *a.*「合法的，法律認可的，合情合理的」：He has a legitimate excuse for being absent from school. 他有合理的藉口不去上學。

政治法律名稱總彙

legacy [ˈlɛgəsɪ] .... ★★★★★
n. 遺產，遺物：inherit a legacy 繼承遺產；a
  legacy of hatred/ill-will 宿怨，世仇；a rotten
  legacy 爛攤子

legal [ˈligl̩] .... ★★★★★
adj. ①法律上的：He took legal action. 他採
  取了法律行動。②合法的，法定的：Is it
  legal to do so? 這樣做合法嗎？

legalize [ˈligl̩ˌaɪz] .... ★★★★★
v. 合法化，法律認可

legally [ˈligl̩ɪ] .... ★★★★★ad
v. 合法地：A corporation is a business
  organization that is formed to act as a
  single person and is legally endowed with
  particular rights and duties. 企業是一個以獨
  立法人運作並合法享有特定權利和履行特定
  義務的商業組織。

legislate [ˈlɛdʒɪsˌlet] .... ★★★★
v. 立法：legislate somebody out of an office
  依法免某人的職

legislation [ˌlɛdʒɪsˈleʃən] .... ★★★★
n. 立法，法規：air pollution legislation 關於空
  氣污染的法規

legislative [ˈlɛdʒɪsˌletɪv] .... ★★★★
adj. 立法的：a legislative body 立法機構

liability [ˌlaɪəˈbɪlətɪ] .... ★★
n. 責任，義務，負債

marital [ˈmærətl̩] .... ★★★★★
adj. 婚姻的：marital status 婚姻狀況

marriage [ˈmærɪdʒ] .... ★★★★★
n. ①結婚，婚姻②婚禮，結婚儀式

married [ˈmærɪd] .... ★★★★★
adj. ①已婚的：Are you married or single? 你
  結婚了還是單身？②married (to) 與…結
  婚的：She was married to a handsome
  man. 她與一位英俊的男士結婚。

marry [ˈmærɪ] .... ★★★★★
v. 結婚，嫁娶：She married a foreigner. 她嫁
  給了一個外國人。

matrimony [ˈmætrəˌmonɪ] .... ★★★
n. 婚姻，結婚，婚姻生活：How to unite a
  couple in holy matrimony? 怎麼使男女雙方
  結合並進入神聖的婚姻關係？

monitor [ˈmɑnətɚ] .... ★★★★
n. 監視器，班長
v. 監控：The pulse is most easily monitored
  where an artery is close to the skin. 在動脈
  距離皮膚最近的地方，最容易覺察到脈搏的
  跳動。

murder [ˈmɝdɚ] .... ★★★★★
n. 謀殺，兇殺
v. 謀殺，兇殺：An actor was murdered last
  night. 昨天晚上一位演員被謀殺了。

obligation [ˌɑbləˈgeʃən] .... ★★★★
n. 義務，責任：We are under an obligation to
  help. 我們有義務幫忙。

obligatory [əˈblɪgəˌtorɪ] .... ★★★★
adj. 義務的，必須的：Attendance is
  obligatory. 必須要出席的。

offensive [əˈfɛnsɪv] .... ★★★
adj. 無理的，攻擊性的：The offensive troops
  gained ground quickly. 這支進攻的軍隊很
  快地贏得了陣地。

outlaw [ˈaʊtˌlɔ] .... ★★
n. 逃犯，歹徒
v. 宣佈…非法：outlaw the sale of drink 宣佈出
  售酒類為非法

outspoken [ˈaʊtˈspokən] .... ★★★★★
adj. 坦率直言的：It has been said that the
  essayist Henry David Thoreau was
  outspoken and usually put forth little effort
  to please others. 據說評論家亨利‧大衛‧
  梭羅是一個坦率直言的人，幾乎不會特別
  去討別人的歡心。

owner [ˈonɚ] .... ★★★★★
n. 物主，所有人：I'm the owner of the shop.
  我是這家商店的老闆。

ownership [ˈonɚʃɪp] .... ★★★
n. 所有權：feudal land ownership 封建土地所有制

own [on] .... ★★★★★
adj. 自己的
【片語】of one's own 屬於某人自己的：
You must have a mind of your own. 你一定要有主見。
vt. 擁有：Many peasants now own cars. 許多農民現在都有汽車了。

penal [ˈpinl] .... ★★★★
adj. 受刑罰的，刑事的：penal laws 刑法

penalize [ˈpinḷaɪz] .... ★★★★
v. 處罰，罰款，懲罰：The baseball player was penalized for unnecessary roughness. 那個棒球隊員因不需要的暴力而受到懲罰。

penalty [ˈpɛnḷtɪ] .... ★★★★
n. 處罰，懲罰，罰金：The death penalty has been abolished in this country. 這個國家已廢除死刑。

plaintiff [ˈplentɪf] .... ★
n. 原告（defendant 被告）

police [pəˈlis] .... ★★★★★
n. ①警察部門，警方：The police were called. 有人打電話報警。②警察（相當於 policeman）

policeman [pəˈlismən] .... ★★★
n. 警察

premeditated [priˈmɛdɚtetɪd] .... ★
adj. 預謀的：a premeditated murder 謀殺

prison [ˈprɪzn̩] .... ★★★★★
n. 監獄

prisoner [ˈprɪznɚ] .... ★★★★★
n. 囚徒

probation [proˈbeʃən] .... ★
n. 緩刑，察看（以觀後效）：place (an offender) on/under probation 對（犯人）判緩刑；probation officer 監督緩刑犯的官員；be placed on probation within the school 留校察看

proof [pruf] .... ★★★★★
n. ①證據，證明：Do you have any proof of that allegation? 你有什麼證據可支持這種說法嗎？②校樣，樣張：proofs of new novel 新小說的校稿

prosecute [ˈprɑsɪkjut] .... ★
v. 起訴，檢舉：He was prosecuted for robbery. 他因搶劫而被起訴。

punish [ˈpʌnɪʃ] .... ★★★★
v. 懲罰，處罰：They discovered his crime and punished him for it. 他們發現了他的罪行並懲罰了他。

punishment [ˈpʌnɪʃmənt] .... ★★★★
n. ①（不可數）懲罰：We are determined that the terrorists will not escape punishment. 我們決心不讓那些恐怖分子逍遙法外。②（可數）一種懲辦方式

receipt [rɪˈsit] .... ★★★
n. 收到，收據：When you have paid for something, a receipt is given to you. 當你付了某樣東西的錢時，就會拿到收據。

register [ˈrɛdʒɪstɚ] .... ★★★★★
v. 登記：He registered the birth of his child. 他登記了孩子的出生日。

registration [ˌrɛdʒɪˈstreʃən] .... ★★★★★
n. 登記，掛號：a registration fee 掛號費，登記費

responsibility [rɪˌspɑnsəˈbɪlətɪ] . ★★★★★
n. 責任，職務，任務：Included in the responsibilities of public schools in the United States is the socialization of school-age population. 美國公立學校的責任之一是讓到學齡人口進行社會化。

responsible [rɪ'spɑnsəbl] .... ★★★★
adj. 有責任的：The cabinet is responsible to the parliament. 內閣是對國會負責的。

rob [rɑb] .... ★★★★
v. ①搶劫，盜取：They knocked the old man down and robbed him of his watch. 他們把那老人打倒在地並搶走了他的手錶。②非法剝奪，使喪生：You've robbed me of my happiness. 你奪走了我的幸福。③搶劫，盜竊：He said he would not rob again. 他說他不會再搶劫了。

robbery ['rɑbərɪ] .... ★
n. 搶劫，盜取：The news of the robbery of the bank was quickly bandied about. 銀行遭到搶劫的消息很快傳開了。

sin [sɪn] .... ★★★★★
n. 罪過，過失：It's a sin to tell lies. 說謊是一種罪惡。

steal [stil] .... ★★★★★
v. 盜，偷竊：She stole a book from the library. 她從圖書館偷了一本書。

sue [su] .... ★★★
vt. ①控告，控訴，對…提起訴訟：He sued the railroad, because his cow was killed by the engine. 火車頭輾死了他的牛，所以他告了鐵路公司。②請求，祈求：The thief sued the police for mercy. 小偷向警方求饒。
vi. 控告，起訴，提起訴訟：He threatened to sue. 他威脅要進行控告。

suicide ['suə‚saɪd] .... ★★★
v. 自殺：It is professional suicide to involve oneself In Illegal practices. 從事非法活動即是職業性的自殺行為。

surveillance [sɚ'veləns] ....★
n. 監視：electronic surveillance 電子監視；surveillance radar equipment （略作 S.R.E.）監視雷達，警戒雷達

test [tɛst] .... ★★★★★
n. 測驗，測試，檢驗：a blood test 抽血檢測
v. 測驗，測試，檢驗：I will test your knowledge of French. 我將考一下你學的法語。

testify ['tɛstə‚faɪ] .... ★★
v. 證明，證實，作證：Her tears testified her grief. 她的眼淚說明了她很悲傷。

辨析
Analyze

accuse, charge, appeal, sue

1. **accuse** *vt.* 與charge 一樣意為「指控，控告，指責」，所不同的是句型不同：①accuse sb. of (doing) sth②charge sb. with (doing) sth.和charge that...：They accused him of murder / charged him with murder. 他們控告他謀殺。They accused Jack of reckless driving / charged Jack with reckless driving. 他們指責傑克飆車。

2. **appeal** *vt. & vi.* 「上訴，申訴，將…上訴」，後接物或事做賓語，其句型為 appeal against sth.，一般不接人做賓語：I'll appeal to the law against your crime. 我將把你的罪行訴諸法律。

3. **sue** *vt. & vi.* 「控告，起訴」，一般接人做賓語：Are you going to sue (him)? 你要起訴（他）嗎？

testimony [ˈtɛstəˌmonɪ] .... ★★
n. 證言

trial [ˈtraɪl] .... ★★★★
n. 審判：The trial ended with a hung jury. 此審判最後懸而未決。

unbiased [ʌnˈbaɪəst] .... ★★★★★
adj. 公正的

unfair [ʌnˈfɛr] .... ★★★
adj. 不公平的：It's unfair to devalue anyone's work unjustly. 不公正地貶低任何人的工作都是不公平的。

unruly [ʌnˈrulɪ] .... ★★★★★
adj. 難控制的，不守法的：an unruly child 任性的小孩

violate [ˈvaɪəˌlet] .... ★★★
v. 違犯，違背，侵犯：violated our privacy 侵犯我們的隱私

violence [ˈvaɪələns] .... ★★★★★
n. 強暴，暴力，暴行，激烈，猛烈，強烈：He slammed the door with violence. 他砰的一聲用力把門關上。

violent [ˈvaɪələnt] .... ★★★★
adj. 激烈的：Not a few violent scenes were cut from the film before it came to show. 這部影片在放映前，剪去了不少暴力鏡頭。

vote [vot] .... ★★★★★
v. 投票：Older citizens in the United States vote more regularly than younger ones, particularly when local and state issues are being considered. 在美國，年長的公民比年輕的公民更常參與投票，尤其是針對地方或州的問題的時候。

voter [ˈvotɚ] .... ★★★★★
n. 投票人，選舉人

warranty [ˈwɔrəntɪ] .... ★★
n. 擔保，保證：The purchaser of this automobile is protected by the manufacturer's warranty. 這輛汽車的買主可享製造商的保固期限。

wedding [ˈwɛdɪŋ] .... ★★★★
n. 婚禮：invite one's friends to one's wedding 邀請朋友參加婚禮

witness [ˈwɪtnɪs] .... ★★★★★
n. 證人
v. 目擊：In 1905 he was sent to Paris as art apprentice to an art dealer, and in the years that followed he witnessed the birth of Cubism, discovered primitive art, and learned the techniques of woodcarving from a frame maker. 他於1905年被派往巴黎到一位藝術品商人那裡當學徒，在接下來的幾年中目睹了立體派的誕生，發現了原始的藝術，並且從一位骨架製造者學會了木雕的技能。

辨析
Analyze

marriage, wedding

1 **marriage** *n.* 「結婚，婚姻，婚禮」，多指長時間的婚姻狀況，也指婚禮 (=wedding)：Marriage is a very serious thing. 婚姻是一件非常嚴肅的事情。

2 **wedding** *n.* 「婚禮」，指短時間的婚禮，可用作定語，如：wedding ring/day/march 結婚戒指／結婚日／婚禮進行曲；The wedding will take place on Saturday. 婚禮將於星期六舉行。

Unit 6
財政金融名稱總匯
Finance

acting [ˈæktɪŋ] .... ★★★★★

adj. 代理的：The acting chairman was in charge of the company when the chairman himself was in absence. 董事長不在公司的時候，由代理董事長管理公司。

administer [ədˈmɪnəstɚ] .... ★★★★★

v. 管理：In many Japanese homes, the funds are administered by the wife. 在許多日本家庭裡，錢財是由妻子掌管的。

administration [ədˌmɪnəˈstreʃən] .... ★★★★★

n. 行政：The two countries run parallel administration on the island. 這兩個國家在那座島上行使平行的行政權。

agent [ˈedʒənt] .... ★★★★★

n. 劑量，介質，代理人：an oxidizing agent 氧化劑；a sole agent in Japan for an American company 美國公司在日本的獨家代理商

appraise [əˈprez] .... ★

v. 鑑定：It is difficult to appraise the value of old paintings; it is easier to call them priceless. 要鑑定古畫的價值很困難，把它們稱為無價之寶就容易多了。

apprentice [əˈprɛntɪs] .... ★

n. 學徒：an apprentice to a blacksmith 鐵匠的學徒

apprentice [əˈprɛntɪs] .... ★

n. 藝徒，學徒，初學者，生手
vt. 使…當學徒

assess [əˈsɛs] .... ★★★

v. 估計：assess the present state of the economy 評估現今的經濟狀況

asset [ˈæsɛt] .... ★★★★★

n. 財產，財富，長處，優點：He has invested five percent of his assets in gold. 他把自己百分之五的資產投資於黃金。

authorize [ˈɔθəˌraɪz] .... ★★

v. 授權：The *Morill Act* 1862 authorized the states to use federal lands for the establishment of colleges that would offer programs in agriculture and the mechanical arts. 1862 年的《莫里耳法》授權各州使用聯邦土地，建立可提供農業和機械課程的學院。

avocational [ˌəvoˈkeʃən!] .... ★
adj.（個人）副業的，業餘愛好者

behalf [bɪˈhæf] .... ★★★★
n. 利益，方面，代表：On behalf of everyone here, may I wish you a happy retirement. 我代表在座的各位，祝你退休生活愉快。
【片語】on behalf of 代表，為了

bid [bɪd] .... ★★
v. 命令，吩咐，報價：He bade the soldiers to shoot. 他命令士兵開槍。
n. 報價，投標，企圖：Bids for building the bridge were invited. 我們受邀參加建造橋樑的投標。

bidding [ˈbɪdɪŋ] .... ★★
n. 邀請，投標，命令，要求：The bidding began furiously. 出價一開始就很高。

bond [bɑnd] .... ★★★★
n. 聯結，聯繫，公債：Communication is one of the most important bonds that hold cultural systems together. 「交流」是維繫各個文化體系最重要的紐帶之一。

bonus [ˈbonəs] .... ★
n. 紅利，獎金：The workers got a Christmas bonus. 員工獲發聖誕節獎金。

boss [bɔs] .... ★★★
n. 老闆，上司：Who's the boss in the house? 誰是這間房子的主人？
v. 指揮，對…發號施令：Does he want to boss the job? 他想主導這件麻煩事嗎？

brand [brænd] .... ★★★★
n. 商標，標記：What brand of soap do you like? 你喜歡什麼牌子的肥皂？
v. 打火印，打烙印：Prison has branded him for life. 坐牢使他留下了終生的烙印。

bribe [braɪb] .... ★
n. 賄賂
v. 賄賂：The murderer tried to bribe the judge into convicting him of being unguilty. 那個殺人犯試圖賄賂法官宣判他無罪。

bribery [ˈbraɪbəri] .... ★
n. 賄賂：commit bribery 行／受賄；bribery case 受賄／行賄案件

buy [baɪ] .... ★★★★★
v. 買：I want to buy some flowers on my mother's birthday. 母親過生日那天，我想買些鮮花。

career [kəˈrɪr] .... ★★★★★
n. 生涯，職業

charge [tʃɑrdʒ] .... ★★★★★
v. ①要價：He charged me five dollars for the cup. 這個杯子他賣我 5 塊錢。②控告，指控：He was charged with murder. 他被控犯下謀殺罪。③充電：charge the battery 給電池充電

cheap [tʃip] .... ★★★★
adj. ①便宜的：cheap article 便宜貨②低劣的，不值錢的：Tom is always holding Alice cheap. 湯姆一直瞧不起愛麗絲。

clerk [klɝk] .... ★★★★
n. 店員，辦事員，職員

commercialize [kəˈmɝʃəˌlaɪz] ... ★★★★★
v. 商業化：Even in a highly commercialized society, law of value still holds good. 即使是在高度商業化的社會裡，價值規律仍然有效。

corrupt [kəˈrʌpt] .... ★★
v. 賄賂，收買：The businessman was sent to prison for trying to corrupt a tax official with money. 那名商人因企圖向稅務官員行賄而被判入獄。
adj. 腐化的，貪污的：a corrupt judge 貪污的法官

customer [ˈkʌstəmɚ] .... ★★★★★
n. 顧客，主顧，用戶：Market surveys have made retailers more conscious of the needs of their customers. 市場調查使零售商對顧客的需求更加瞭解。

cybernetics [ˌsaɪbɚˈnɛtɪks] .... ★
n. 控制論：economic cybernetics 經濟控制論

deputy [ˈdɛpjətɪ] .... ★★
n. 代理人：When the mayor was away, the deputy mayor did his job. 當市長不在時，代市長代理他的工作。

earn [ɝn] .... ★★★★★
v. 撐得，賺得，獲得：earn one's living 謀生

earnings [ˈɝnɪŋz] .... ★★
n. 工資，收入：Our total earnings were, clear of all expenses, about forty dollars. 除去各種開銷，我們全部的收入是 40 美元。

economic [ˌikəˈnɑmɪk] .... ★★★★★
adj. 經濟的

economical [ˌikəˈnɑmɪkl̩] .... ★★★
adj. 節約的，經濟的：Mrs. Macclain is always economical. 麥可林夫人是一位節儉的人。For most working people in the city, it is more economical to go to work by subway. 對大多數城市裡的上班族來說，搭地鐵上班倒省錢些。

economics [ˌikəˈnɑmɪks] .... ★★
n. 經濟（學）：Economics are slowly killing the family farm. 目前的經濟體系正在使家庭農場慢慢解體。

economist [iˈkɑnəmɪst] .... ★★★★★
n. 經濟學家：Some economists strongly believe in private enterprise. 有些經濟學家非常相信私人企業有好處。

economy [iˈkɑnəmɪ] .... ★★★★★
n. ①經濟：feudal economy 封建經濟②節約，節省：practice economy 厲行節約

embezzle [ɪmˈbɛzl̩] .... ★
v. 盜用（公款、公物）：The head of the branch bank embezzled ten thousand dollars from the bank where he worked. 該銀行分行行長在他工作的銀行裡盜用了一百萬美元。

employ [ɪmˈplɔɪ] .... ★★★★★
vt. ①雇傭：They employed five new servants. 他們雇用了五名新僕人。②用，使用：How do you employ your spare time? 你如何利用閒暇時間呢？
n. 雇用

employee [ˌɛmplɔɪˈi] .... ★★★★★
n. 員工：employee benefits 員工利益；employee unions 員工工會；employee relations 員工關係

employer [ɪmˈplɔɪɚ] .... ★★★★
n. 雇傭者，雇主：The car industry is one of our biggest employers. 汽車工業是我們最大的雇主之一。

employment [ɪmˈplɔɪmənt] .... ★★★★★
n. 使用，雇用，職業，就業，工作：a vicious spiral of rising prices under full employment 價格在就業飽和的情況下上漲的惡性循環

辨析
Analyze

economic, economical

1 **economic** *a.* 「經濟的」，指與經濟有關的、經濟學上的：economic system/crises/reasons 經濟體制／經濟危機／經濟上的原因

2 **economical** *a.* 「經濟的，節約的」，指節約的、節儉的：One must be economical of one's time. 大家一定要節約時間。

entity [ˈɛntətɪ] .... ★★★★★
n. 實體：Persons and corporations are equivalent entities under the law. 個人和企業在法律下是對等的獨立實體。

entrepreneur [ˌɑntrəprəˈnɝ] .... ★
n. 企業家，主辦人：marginal entrepreneur 邊際企業家

entrust [ɪnˈtrʌst] .... ★★★★★
v. 委託：He still has the aura of the priest to whom you would entrust your darkest secrets. 他仍散發出牧師的魅力，使你願將自己內心最深處的秘密交付予他。

estate [ɪsˈtet] .... ★★★★★
n. 房地產，地皮

estimable [ˈɛstəməbl] .... ★★★★★
adj. 可估計的：estimable assets 可估計的財產；an estimable distance 可估算的距離

estimate [ˈɛstəˌmet] .... ★★★★★
v. 估計：While an author is yet living we estimate his powers by his worst performance. 當一個作家還活著時，我們是以他最差的作品來評斷他的影響力。

evaluate [ɪˈvæljuˌet] .... ★★★
v. 評價，估價：The research project has only been under way for three months, so it's too early to evaluate its success. 這項研究方案進行了不過三個月，所以要評價它的成績為時尚早。

fee [fi] .... ★★★
n. 酬金，手續費，學費，費用：Postal fees are determined primarily by the class and weight of the parcel mailed. 郵政費用主要是由所寄包裹的等級和重量決定的。

fortune [ˈfɔrtʃən] .... ★★★★★
n. 財富：She pursued her fortune in another country. 她到他鄉尋求她的財富。

goods [gʊdz] .... ★★★★★
n. 貨物，商品：Half of his goods were stolen. 他一半的貨物被偷走了。

guarantee [ˌgærənˈti] .... ★★★★
n. 確保：Lack of interest is a guarantee of failure. 缺乏興趣肯定會失敗。

husbandry [ˈhʌzbəndrɪ] .... ★★★★★
n. 耕種，管理：To let the roof leak would be bad husbandry. 屋漏不修，不是個好管家。

income [ˈɪnˌkʌm] .... ★★★★★
n. 收入，所得，收益：He has an income of $20,000 a year. 他的年收入是兩萬美元。

incorruptible [ˌɪnkəˈrʌptəbl] .... ★
adj. 廉潔的：a man of incorruptible integrity 廉潔正直的人

inflation [ɪnˈfleʃən] .... ★
n. 通貨膨脹：Inflation erodes the purchasing power of the families with lower income. 通貨膨脹使低收入家庭的購買力不斷下降。

invest [ɪnˈvɛst] .... ★★★★
v. 投資：The state has planned to invest two millions in the dam. 該州已計畫投資兩百萬元修建這個大壩。

investment [ɪnˈvɛstmənt] .... ★★★★★
n. 投資，投資額：investment analysis 投資分析；investment dollars 投資美金

job [dʒɑb] .... ★★★★★
n. ①職業，職位：a part-time job 兼職工作②（一件）工作：He has done a good job. 他幹得好！

labo(u)r [ˈlebɚ] .... ★★★★★
n. ①勞動：physical/manual labour 體力勞動②勞工，工人：skilled labours 技巧熟練的工人③分娩，陣痛
v. ①幹苦活，辛勤地工作，費力地做某事②費力地行走，艱難的前行

landlady [ˈlændˌledɪ] .... ★★★
n. 女房東，女地主

landlord [ˈlændˌlɔrd] .... ★★★★
n. 地主

lease [lis] .... ★★
v. 出租 (out)，租得 (from)：Rockefeller Center has leased part of its land from Columbia University. 洛克斐勒中心部份的土地是從哥倫比亞大學租來的。

lend [lɛnd] .... ★★★★
v. 借給，貸款：Thank you very much for lending the gun to me. 謝謝你借給我槍。

manage [ˋmænɪdʒ] .... ★★★★★
v. ①管理，經營，處理：He managed the company instead of his father. 他代替父親管理公司。②設法，對付：She knows how to manage him when he's angry. 她知道當他發怒時如何處理。③處理，設法對付："Do you need any help?" "No thanks, I can manage."「你需要幫忙嗎？」「不用，謝謝，我可以處理。」

manager [ˋmænɪdʒɚ] .... ★★★★★
n. 經理，管理人：The young lady is the manager of the restaurant. 這位年輕的女士是餐廳經理。

merchandise [ˋmɝtʃənˌdaɪz] .... ★
v. 經營
n. 商品：Colorful parades were commonly organized on the frontier to display newly arrived merchandise. 人們通常會在國境地帶舉辦色彩斑斕的遊行來展示新到的商品。

merchant [ˋmɝtʃənt] .... ★★★★
n. 商人，零售商：merchant bank〔英〕證券銀行；merchant fleet 商船隊

millionaire [ˌmɪljənˋɛr] .... ★
n. 百萬富翁：mega millionaire 億萬富翁

monopoly [məˋnɑplɪ] .... ★★
n. 壟斷，獨佔：A university education shouldn't be the monopoly of the minority whose parents are rich. 大學教育不應是少數富家子弟的專利。

mortgage [ˋmɔrgɪdʒ] .... ★
v. 抵押，抵押借款：repay one's mortgage in monthly installment 每月分期付款償還抵押借款

negotiate [nɪˋgoʃɪˌet] .... ★★★
v. 談判，交涉，議定：It is difficult to negotiate where neither will trust. 雙方彼此不信任便很難進行協商。

partner [ˋpɑrtnɚ] .... ★★★★★
n. ①配偶，搭檔：dancing partner 舞伴②夥伴，合夥人：profits shared equally among all the partners 合夥人之間均分的利潤

pawn [pɔn] .... ★
v. 典當，抵押：an underdeveloped nation that was a pawn in international politics 在國際政治中被利用的不發達國家

payoff [ˋpeˌɔf] .... ★★★★★
n. 發薪，報酬：expected payoff 期望的報酬

pension [ˋpɛnʃən] .... ★★★
n. 撫恤金，養老金，年金：live on pension 靠退休金生活

possession [pəˋzɛʃən] .... ★★★★★
n. ①所有，佔有：The possession of a degree does not guarantee you a job. 有了學位不保證你能找到工作。②所有物：Check your possessions on arrival. 到達時檢查一下你所帶的物品。

price [praɪs] .... ★★★★★
n. ①價格，價錢：The price expresses the value. 價格體現價值。②代價：He went to college finally at the price of his eyesight. 他以視力為代價終於上了大學。

prize [praɪz] .... ★★★★
n. 獎賞，獎金，獎品：a prize for the best novel 最佳小說獎
v. 珍視，珍惜：The boy's motorcycle was his most prized possession. 那男孩的摩托車是他最珍貴的東西。

profit [ˋprɑfɪt] .... ★★★★★
n. 利益，益處，利潤：profiting from the other team's mistakes 因另一隊的失誤而得分

profitable [ˋprɑfɪtəbl] .... ★★
adj. 有利可圖的，有益的

property [ˋprɑpɚtɪ] .... ★★★★★
n. 性能，性質，特性，財產，地產，所有
物：properties such as copyrights and
trademarks 像版權和商標這類的所有物

proxy [ˋprɑksɪ] ....★
n. 代理人：a proxy vote 委託人投票

purchase [ˋpɝtʃəs] .... ★★★★★
v. & n. 購買：The new couple spent some
money for the purchase of the furniture
necessary for their new house. 這對新
婚夫婦花了一些錢購買新房子裡必需的
傢俱。

quota [ˋkwotə] ....★★★
n. 限額，定額：No boat is allowed to catch
more than its quota of fish. 任何船都不允許
捕獲超過限量的魚。

redeem [rɪˋdim] ....★
v. 取回，贖回：You botched the last job but
can redeem yourself on this one. 你把上次
的工作搞砸了，但可藉這次工作挽回聲譽。

redress [rɪˋdrɛs] ....★
n. 救濟，補償：Any man deserves redress if
he has been injured unfairly. 任何人若蒙受
不公平的損害，都應獲得賠償。

refund [rɪˋfʌnd] .... ★★★★★
v. 退還，償還：They refunded the purchase
money. 他們退還了購買的金額。

reimburse [͵riɪmˋbɝs] ....★
v. 償還：Companies in the United States
usually reimburse employee's travel
expenses incurred on business trips. 美國的
公司通常會核銷員工在商務旅行的花費。

rent [rɛnt] .... ★★★★★
v. ①租借，租用：He rented a colour TV soon
after moving in. 他搬進去後不久，就租了臺
新的彩色電視。②出租，出借：They had to
rent out the upstairs room for years. 他們幾
年來不得不出租樓上的房間。
n. 租金：He made enough money to pay the
monthly rent punctually. 他賺到了足夠的
錢，每月可以準時付房租。

辨析 Analyze

hire, lease, let, rent

1 **hire** *vt.*「租用，雇傭」，指向別人臨
時租用物品，也指雇人，還指出租：He
hired a car and a man to drive it. 他租了
一輛汽車，並請了一個司機開車。

2 **lease** *vt.*「出租，租得，租有」，指根據
合約、協定長期租借或出租房屋、土地、
貴重物品，正式用語：Instead of buying
computers, we lease some to cut our
cost. 我們不買電腦，而是租借一些電腦
以降低我們的花費。

3 **let** *vi.*「出租」，僅限於指出租房屋、土
地：This house is to (be) let. 這間房子可
供出租。

4 **rent** *vt.*「租借，租用，出租，出借」，
指向別人臨時或長期租用物品（主要指
房屋、土地），還可指出租：We rented
a house from him. 我們向他租了一棟房
子。

repay [rɪˈpe] .... ★★
vt. ①歸還（款項）：He repaid Mrs. Black the money he owed her. 他償還欠布萊克太太的錢。②報答：The company repaid its employees for their hard work in the summer. 員工們在夏天工作很努力，公司發了獎金給他們。

retail [ˈritel] .... ★★★
n. 零售
adj. 零售的：a small retail business 小額零售生意

salary [ˈsælərɪ] .... ★★★★
n. 薪金，薪水：He earns a high salary as an accountant. 他當會計的薪水很高。

sale [sel] .... ★★★★★
n. ①賣，出售：new laws to control the sale of guns 控制槍隻出售的新法規 ②廉價出售：The department store is having a clearance sale. 這家百貨店正舉行清倉出售。③銷售額：Sales of cocoa have gone up. 可可的銷售額增加了。
【片語】on sale 出售，廉價出售

salesman [ˈselzmən] .... ★★★
n. 售貨員，推銷員

sell [sɛl] .... ★★★★★
v. 賣，出售：This dictionary sells well. 這本字典很暢銷。
【片語】sell out 賣完

staff [stæf] .... ★★★★★
n. 全體人員或職員

supply [səˈplaɪ] .... ★★★★★
v. 供給，供應：Germany is supplying much of the steel for the new pipeline. 德國正為新管道供應大量鋼材。
n. 供應（量）

surcharge [ˈsɝtʃɑrdʒ] .... ★★★★
n. 額外費用
vt. 向⋯收取附加稅：He was surcharged on the parcel. 他被收取了包裹的額外費用。

tax [tæks] .... ★★★★★
v. 徵稅，加負擔，使勞累
n. 稅，負擔：These two shopkeepers are in prison for tax evasion. 這兩個店主因逃稅而坐牢。

taxation [tæksˈeʃən] .... ★★★★★
n. 徵稅，納稅：be subject to taxation 應納稅；be exempt from taxation 免稅；taxation bureau 稅務局

tenant [ˈtɛnənt] .... ★★
n. 租戶，房客

trade [tred] .... ★★
n. ①貿易，商業：foreign trade 對外貿易 ②行業，職業：The school offers courses in a variety of trades. 這所學校提供多種的職業課程。
v. 相互交換，用⋯進行交換：trade his knife for her pen 用他的刀子換她的鋼筆

treasure [ˈtrɛʒɚ] .... ★★★★★
n. ①金銀財寶，財富：dig for buried treasure 挖掘埋藏的財寶 ②珍品，珍藏品：The museum has many art treasures. 這家博物館有許多藝術珍藏品。
v. 珍愛，珍視：She treasured those memories. 她珍惜那些回憶。

unemployed [ˌʌnɪmˈplɔɪd] .... ★★★★★
adj. 失業的，未受雇傭的：Much of the legislation passed during Franklin Roosevelt's New Deal was designed to benefit the unemployed. 在羅斯福新政期間通過的許多法規，都是規劃使失業者受惠的。

wage [wedʒ] .... ★★★★★
n. （常複）薪水，報酬：The railroad workers have asked for a wage increase. 鐵路工人已要求增加薪水。

02

財政、金融類相關辭彙 Vocabulary of Finance

account [əˈkaʊnt] .... ★★★★★
n. 原因，解釋，戶頭，帳目：In calculating the daily calorie requirements for an individual, variations in body size, physical activity, and age should be taken into account. 在計算每個人每天所需的熱量時，應當把個人體重、活動量以及年齡都考慮進去。

accountant [əˈkaʊntənt] .... ★★★★★
n. 會計人員：chartered accountant 執業會計師

bail [bel] .... ★
n. 保釋金：She was released on bail of $5,000. 她交了五千美元的保釋金後，就被釋放了。
v. 保釋：Clarke's family paid $400 to bail him out. 克拉克的家人用四百美元保釋他。

bank [bæŋk] .... ★★★★★
n. ①銀行，庫：He has much money in bank. 他在銀行有很多錢。②（多指河的）岸，堤：The river burst over its bank. 河流潰堤了。

banker [ˈbæŋkɚ] .... ★★
n. 銀行家

bankrupt [ˈbæŋkrʌpt] .... ★★★
n. 破產者
v. 使破產：War had bankrupted the nation's natural resources. 戰爭已耗盡了那個國家的自然資源。
adj. 無力還債的，破產的：The company went bankrupt because of its poor management. 那家公司因經營不善破產了。

bankruptcy [ˈbæŋkrʌptsɪ] .... ★★★
n. 破產：There were bankruptcies in the business world last year. 去年商界發生了許多破產事件。

beneficial [ˌbɛnəˈfɪʃəl] .... ★★★
adj. 有益的：At many companies, flexible work schedules have proven beneficial for both employers and employees in terms of decreasing absenteeism and increasing productivity. 在許多公司裡，靈活的工作行程在減少曠工和提高生產力方面，被證明對雇主和員工都有益。

beneficiary [ˌbɛnəˈfɪʃərɪ] .... ★★★
n. 受益者：You may change your beneficiary as often as you wish. 你可以隨心所欲地隨時更換你的受益人。

benefit [ˈbɛnəfɪt] .... ★★★★

n. 利益：The outcome is benefit from her good example. 可以從她樹立的好榜樣中受益。

bill [bɪl] .... ★★★★

n. 鈔票，帳單，法案：If you don't pay the bill for months running, the telephone service may disconnect your telephone. 如果你連續幾個月不付電話費，電話公司就會切斷你的電話線路。

billfold [ˈbɪlˌfold] .... ★★★★★

n. 鈔票夾

broker [ˈbrokɚ] .... ★★★★★

n. 掮客，經紀人

cash [kæʃ] .... ★★★★

n. 錢，現款：pay in cash 用現金支付

cheque [tʃɛk] .... ★★★

n. 支票：a cheque for two hundred pounds 一張兩百鎊的支票

coin [kɔɪn] .... ★★★★

n. 鑄幣：a pizza topped with coins of pepperoni 上有錢幣狀義大利香腸的披薩餅

v. 造字：The term "automation" was coined in the 1940's. 「自動化」一詞是於 1940 年代新創的字。

contract .... ★★★★★

n. [ˈkɑntrækt] 契約

v. [kənˈtrækt] 簽約：Their firm has contracted to build a double-purpose bridge across the river. 他們公司已簽約承建一座跨河的兩用大橋。

credential [krɪˈdɛnʃəl] .... ★

n. 憑證

credit [ˈkrɛdɪt] .... ★★★★★

n. 信譽，學分：Do you give credit to what the man said? 你相信那人講的話嗎？

creditor [ˈkrɛdɪtɚ] .... ★★★★★

n. 債權人：creditor nation 債權國

currency [ˈkɝ ənsɪ] .... ★★★★

n. 通貨，通用，市價：Many slang words have short currency, soon go out of use. 許多俚語流行不久就不再使用了。

debt [dɛt] .... ★★★★★

n. 債務，欠債：If I pay all my debts, I shall have no money left. 如果我償清了所有的債，我就一毛錢不剩了。

debtor [ˈdɛtɚ] .... ★★★★★

n. 債務人：debtor and creditor 貸方和借方

deficit [ˈdɛfɪsɪt] .... ★★★★★

n. 赤字：They rallied from a three-game deficit to win the playoff. 他們三場比賽失利後重整旗鼓，贏得了延長賽。

deposit [dɪˈpɑzɪt] .... ★★★★

v. 放置，存款：The old lady deposited her money in the bank. 老太太把錢存在銀行裡。

n. 押金：They put a deposit on the goods. 他們付了貨物的押金。

depreciate [dɪˈpriʃɪet] .... ★

v. 貶值，跌價：The purchasing power of money has depreciated since she bought her savings certificates. 她自從買了儲蓄證券以後，購買力已降低了。

disburse [dɪsˈbɝs] .... ★★★★

v. 支付，支出，分配：The State Government decided to disburse a large amount of money for education. 州政府決定投入大筆資金於教育上。

dollar [ˈdɑlɚ] .... ★★★★★

n. 美元

finance [faɪˈnæns] .... ★★★★★

n. 財政

v. 資助：The government will finance the building of the new roads with the taxes it collects. 政府將以所徵得的稅收用於修建這條新公路。

financial [faɪˈnænʃəl] .... ★★★★★
adj. 財政（上）的，會計的，金融的：Many computer software corporations are experiencing financial reverses. 許多電腦軟體公司在財務上面臨了窘境。

fund [fʌnd] .... ★★★★★
n. 資金，基金
v. 投資：Funds from the Tennessee Valley Authority in the 1930's paid for the introduction of hydroelectric power to the Tennessee River Basin. 在 1930 年代，由田納西峽谷管理當局提供的資金，為田納西河盆地引入了水力發電設備。

fundamental [ˌfʌndəˈmɛntl] .... ★★★★
n. （複）基本原則：If the young boys and girls are going to camp for two weeks by themselves, they'll need to know the fundamentals of taking of themselves. 孩子們如果要靠自己出去露營兩個星期，便須懂得照顧自己的基本能力。

garner [ˈɡɑrnɚ] .... ★
v. 存儲，取得，獲得：Mr. Smith gradually garnered a national reputation as a financial expert. 史密斯先生逐漸贏得金融專家的全國性聲譽。

impose [ɪmˈpoz] .... ★★★★
v. 把…強加給，採用，利用：Don't impose yourself on people who don't want you. 不要勉強和不需要你的人在一起。

installment [ɪnˈstɔlmənt] .... ★
n. 分期付款：We decided to pay for the furniture on the installment plan. 我們計畫以分期付款的方式來購買傢俱。

insurance [ɪnˈʃʊrəns] .... ★★★★
n. 保險，保險費

insure [ɪnˈʃʊr] .... ★★★
v. 保險，替…保險，保證：It is advisable to insure your life against accident. 最好參加人壽保險，以防意外。

invoice [ˈɪnvɔɪs] .... ★
n. 發票，清單：A signed invoice presumes receipt of the shipment. 經過簽收的發貨單表示運去的貨物已收到。

levy [ˈlɛvɪ] .... ★
n. 課稅
v. 徵收：levy a fine/tax on somebody 向某人徵收罰金／稅款

loan [lon] .... ★★★★★
v. 借
n. 貸款：an efficiency expert on loan from the main office 從總公司借調的貸款效率專家

lottery [ˈlɑtərɪ] .... ★
n. 獎券，抽獎，碰巧之事：The state uses a lottery to assign spaces in the campground. 政府用抽籤來指定營地內的地點。

money [ˈmʌnɪ] .... ★★★★★
n. 貨幣，錢：Money talks.〔美口〕金錢萬能。

passbook [ˈpæsˌbʊk] .... ★★★★★
n. 銀行存摺：bank passbook 銀行存摺

penny [ˈpɛnɪ] .... ★★★★
n. 便士，分：A hundred pennies make a pound. 100便士合1英鎊。

revenue [ˈrɛvəˌnju] .... ★★★★★
n. 收入：a revenue officer 稅務員

toll [tol] .... ★★
n. 費：toll on long-distance telephone calls 長途電話費用
v. 鳴（鐘）：The clock tolls the hour. 時鐘報時。

treasurer [ˈtrɛʒərɚ] .... ★★
n. 司庫，財務主管

yen [jɛn] .... ★
n. 日元
v. 渴望，熱望

03

工農、商貿相關辭彙 Vocabulary of Business

agrarian [əˈgrɛrɪən] .... ★★

adj. 土地的，農業的：Between 1870 and 1914，the United States changed from an agrarian economy to an industrial economy. 在 1870 至 1914 年間，美國由農業經濟體轉變為工業經濟體。

agricultural [͵ægrɪˈkʌltʃərəl] .... ★★★★★

adj. 農業的，農學的：agricultural products 農產品

agriculture [ˈægrɪ͵kʌltʃə] .... ★★★★★

n. 農業

agronomy [əˈgrɑnəmɪ] .... ★★★★★

n. 農藝學，農學

arable [ˈærəbl̩] .... ★

adj. 適於耕種的：There is not much arable land on the side of a rocky mountain. 在多岩石的山坡上沒有多少可耕之地。

bargain [ˈbɑrgɪn] ....★★★★

v. 討價還價：She bargained with the trader till he sold her the fruit cheaply. 她和賣水果的人討價還價，直到他把水果便宜賣給了她。

n. 契約，合同，交易：He finally reached a bargain with the antique dealer over the lamp. 他最後和這古董商簽訂了關於這個燈的買賣合約。

barter [ˈbɑrtə] .... ★

n. 易貨：barter trade 以物易物交易

v. 易貨：By producing an excess amount of some household articles, a New England colonial family could barter with other families. 新英格蘭殖民時期的家庭藉生產過剩的某些家庭用品，可以和其他家庭進行以物易物的交易。

business [ˈbɪznɪs] .... ★★★★★

n. ①商業，生意：Business has been bad this year. 今年的生意不景氣。②業務，職責，（用作單數）事務：It's parents' business to help their children. 幫助孩子是父母的天職。

【片語】on business 因公，因事

butcher [ˈbʊtʃə] .... ★★★

n. 屠夫，肉商：He is a butcher. 他是一個屠夫。

byproduct [ˈbaɪ͵prɑdʌkt] .... ★★★

n. 副產品

commerce [ˋkɑmɝs] .... ★★★★

n. 商業：Our country has been trying to broaden its commerce with other nations. 我國一直在努力擴大與其他國家的貿易往來。

commercial [kəˋmɝʃəl] .... ★★★★

adj. 貿易的，商業的：We saw a lot of commercial buildings in Chicago. 我們在芝加哥看到了許多商業大樓。

commodity [kəˋmɑdətɪ] .... ★★

n. 商品，日用品：Salt has been a respected commodity for much of recorded time. 在有記載的歷史中，鹽一直是極為重要的商品。

cotton [ˋkɑtn] .... ★★★★

n. 棉花，棉線，棉紗

crop [krɑp] .... ★★★★

n. ①（常複）作物，莊稼：a variety of crops 各種莊稼②（穀物等的）一熟，收成：a big/good/rich crop 豐收③（同時出現的）一批，一群：There is a large crop of new graduates. 有一批新的畢業生。

crude [krud] .... ★★★

adj. 未提煉的，生的：The wheels of the first road vehicles were fashioned from crude stone disks. 第一批陸上交通工具的輪子是用天然的碟狀石製成的。

cultivate [ˋkʌltəˏvet] .... ★★★★

v. 耕種，培養：Parsley is cultivated throughout much of the world. 芹菜是世界上大部分地區都種植的蔬菜。

cultivation [ˏkʌltəˋveʃən] .... ★★★★

n. 耕種，培養：intensive/extensive cultivation 集約／粗放耕作

dairy [ˋdɛrɪ] .... ★★★

n. 乳製品

ditch [dɪtʃ] .... ★★★

n. 溝，渠，水溝

field [fild] .... ★★★★

n. ①田，田野：How many cotton fields have his father got? 他父親有多少棉花田了？② 運動場：They are playing football on the football field. 他們在足球場上踢球。③領域，方面：In some special fields, he shows great interest. 他在某些特殊領域表現出極大的興趣。

garden [ˋgɑrdn] .... ★★★★

n. （菜，花）園

graze [grez] .... ★

v. 餵草，吃草，放牧：Cattle graze on the dry uplands of the island of Hawaii. 牛群在夏威夷島乾燥的丘陵上吃草。

harvest [ˋhɑrvɪst] .... ★★★★

v. 收穫：The best olive oil is obtained from olives that are harvested just after they ripen and before they turn black. 從收成的橄欖中萃取橄欖油的最好時機，是在橄欖剛剛成熟且沒有變黑以前。

herd [hɝd] .... ★★★★

n. 群，獸群，牛群

v. 放牧，群集：Explorers in the 1800's encountered herds of mustangs throughout North America. 1800 年代的探險家在北美遇到成群的野馬。

industrial [ɪnˋdʌstrɪəl] .... ★★★★

adj. 工業的：Many European countries are developed industrial nations. 許多歐洲國家都是發達的工業國。

industrialist [ɪnˋdʌstrɪəlɪst] .... ★★★

n. 實業家，工業主義者

industrialization [ɪnˏdʌstrɪələˋzeʃən] ★★★

n. 工業化：bring about industrialization 實現工業化

industrialize [ɪnˋdʌstrɪəˏlaɪz] .... ★★★
v. 工業化：Today, because of industrialization, a typical family will be required to move even more often than before, so families will be even smaller. 今天由於工業化，一般的家庭將會比以往遷徙得更加頻繁，所以家庭規模會更小。

industry [ˋɪndəstrɪ] .... ★★★★★
n. ①工業，產業：America is the leading country whose output of industry is much more than any other country. 美國是個工業產值比任何其他國家都多的大國。②努力，勤奮工作：His success is due to industry and thrift. 他的成功歸因於勤勉和節儉。

irrigate [ˋɪrəˏget] .... ★★
v. 灌溉：The Yangtze River irrigates vast stretches of farmland along its course. 長江灌溉著沿岸的大片農田。

leather [ˋlɛðɚ] .... ★★★★
n. 皮革，皮革製品
adj. 皮革的，皮革製的

manure [məˋnjʊr] .... ★
n. 糞肥，肥料

output [ˋaʊtˏpʊt] .... ★★★★
n. 產量，輸出量

peasant [ˋpɛznt] .... ★★★★
n. 農民：the Alliance of the Workers and Peasants 工農聯盟

plough [plaʊ] .... ★★★
n. 犁
v. 犁，耕：The ship ploughed through waves. 那艘船破浪前進。

raise [rez] .... ★★★★★
v. 養殖，募捐：Conifers are generally raised from seed. 針葉樹一般是從種子開始種植的。

rural [ˋrʊrəl] .... ★★★★
adj. 農村的，田園的：Grandma Moses based her simple but realistic paintings of rural life on memories of her own youth in the late 1800's. 摩西奶奶憑她在 1800 年代末期的青年時期回憶，畫出了簡單卻真實反映田園生活的繪畫。

salesclerk [ˋselzˏklɝk] .... ★★★★★
n. 售貨員

shepherd [ˋʃɛpəd] .... ★★
n. 牧民，牧羊人
v. 看管，帶領：The passengers were shepherd across the tarmac to the airliner. 旅客們被引導走過柏油碎石跑道登上飛機。

sow [so] .... ★★★★
v. 播種：In Canada the cereal grain is often sown as a winter crop because it prevents erosion and supplies pasture grass in the spring. 在加拿大，穀類作物燕麥常常是在冬天播種，因為它能防止水土流失，並且在春天提供草料。

staple [ˋstepl] .... ★
n. 大宗產品，主要特產，重要商品：Rice is the staple food in many Asian countries. 稻米是許多亞洲國家的主食。

substantiate [səbˋstænʃɪˏet] .... ★★★
v. 證實，加強：substantiate an accusation 證實一樁控告

thresh [θrɛʃ] .... ★
v. 打穀，脫粒

verification [ˏvɛrɪfɪˋkeʃən] .... ★★★★★
n. 證實，核實：adequate verification 充分的核查

04

經營場所相關辭彙 Vocabulary of Industry

bar [bɑr] .... ★★★★★
n. ①酒吧間，售酒的櫃檯：Put your glass back to the bar, please. 請把杯子放回櫃檯上。②條，桿：a bar of soap 一條肥皂③棚，欄
v. 阻止，阻攔 ：Soldiers barred the way and we couldn't go any further. 士兵們擋住了道路，我們無法再向前了。

barrier [ˈbærɪr] .... ★★★★
n. 柵欄，屏障，障礙

company [ˈkʌmpənɪ] .... ★★★★★
n. 夥伴，公司：Two's company, three's none. 兩人成伴，三人不歡。

enterprise [ˈɛntɚˌpraɪz] .... ★★★★★
n. 事業，企業：Lack of enterprise and faith, men are where they are, buying and selling, and spending their lives like serfs. 人類由於缺乏進取心和信仰，始終駐足不前，或買或賣，過著農奴般的生活。

enterprising [ˈɛntɚˌpraɪzɪŋ] .... ★★★★★
adj. 有事業心的：The enterprising children opened a lemonade stand. 一些有事業心的孩子擺攤賣檸檬汽水。

factory [ˈfæktərɪ] .... ★★★★
n. 工廠：How large the factory is! 這間工廠真大！

farm [fɑrm] .... ★★★★★
n. 農場，飼養場：working on the farm 在農場工作
v. 耕作，經營農牧業：He farms 200 acres. 他耕作200英畝田地。

farmer [ˈfɑrmɚ] .... ★★★★★
n. 農夫，農場主

freight [fret] .... ★★★
n. 貨物，客貨，運費：This aircraft company deals with freight only; it has no passenger service. 這家航空公司只辦理貨運業務，沒有客運服務。

furrier [ˈfɝɪɚ] .... ★★★★★
n. 皮貨商

grocer [ˈɡrosɚ] .... ★★★
n. 食品商，雜貨商

grocery [ˈgrosərɪ] .... ★★★
n. 雜貨店，雜貨：corner grocery 食品店，酒店

guest [gɛst] .... ★★★★★
n. 客人，賓客，旅客

hall [hɔl] .... ★★★★★
n. ①門廳，過道：The hall was crowded with children. 走道裡也擠滿了孩子。②禮堂，大廳：Lincoln Hall 林肯紀念館③辦公大樓

label [ˈlebl] .... ★★★★
n. 標籤，標記
v. 貼標籤，加標籤，把…稱為，標明，標示：Professor Baker told me this bottle was labeled as being poison. 貝克教授告訴我這個瓶子被標示為有毒物。

mark [mɑrk] .... ★★★★★
n. ①痕跡，斑點：marks of ink 墨水污點②記號，標記：Every garment in the shop has a price mark. 商店的每件衣服都有標價。③（考試等的）分數：She got the highest mark in the test. 她考試得了最高分。
v. ①作記號於，標明：Mark the parcel "Handle with care." 給包裹標上「小心輕放」。②給（試卷等）打分：I have 50 papers to mark. 我有 50 份試卷要改。
【片語】mark time 原地踏步，停止不前

marked [mɑrkt] .... ★★★★★
adj. 顯著的，清楚的：This writer's plays are marked by a gentle humor. 這位作家寫的戲劇有諧而不謔的幽默感。

market [ˈmɑrkɪt] .... ★★★★★
n. 集市，市場

mill [mɪl] .... ★★★★
n. 磨房，磨粉機，製造廠，工廠

outlet [ˈautlɛt] .... ★★★
n. 出口，出路，電源插座，發洩方法，排遣：In a slmple clrcult, one end of a conducting light, and the other end to an electric outlet. 一個簡單的電流迴路的一端接燈，另一端接電源插座。

plantation [plænˈteʃən] .... ★★★
n. 植物園

purify [ˈpjurəˌfaɪ] .... ★★★★★
v. 使淨化，精鍊，淨化：Shellac varnish is purified laic that is secreted by scale insects. 蟲漆是由介殼蟲分泌的紫膠焠鍊而成的。

refine [rɪˈfaɪn] .... ★★★★
vt. ①精煉，精製： Gasoline is refined from crude oil. 汽油是從原油提煉的。②使優美，使完善：My professor refined his lectures and used them to write a textbook. 我的教授對他的講稿加以潤色，並用它們編寫了一本教材。

辨析 Analyze

purify, refine

1 **purify** *vt.* 「使純淨，使純潔」，即把雜質或不想要的東西去掉：They purified the water. 他們將水淨化。

2 **refine** *vt.* 指「精煉，精製」，即用一定的工藝把需要的物質萃取出來，尤指煉製石油；還指「使優美，使完善」：They refined the oil/gold/salt/sugar. 他們提煉石油／金子／鹽／糖。

refined [rɪ'faɪnd] .... ★★★
adj. 精緻的，文雅的：highly refined 高度洗鍊的

restaurant ['rɛstərənt] .... ★★★★
n. 餐廳；飯店

shop [ʃɑp] .... ★★★★★
n. 商店，店鋪：a flower shop 花店
v. 尋東西，購貨：You can't shop for a coat in a grocery store. 你去雜貨店是買不到大衣的。

shopkeeper ['ʃɑp͵kipə] .... ★★★
n. 店主

shopping ['ʃɑpɪŋ] .... ★★★★
n. ①買東西，購物：I normally do all my shopping on Saturdays. 我一般都是在星期六把所有要買的東西都買好。②（機器等）大檢修

steelworks ['stil͵wɜks] .... ★★★★
n.（單複同）煉鋼廠

storage ['storɪdʒ] .... ★★★
n. 貯藏，保管，庫房：place the goods in storage 把貨物貯藏起來

store [stor] .... ★★★★★
v. 儲藏，儲備：When winter comes, the farmers have stored enough foods. 冬天到來時，農夫們已儲備了足夠的食物。
n. 商店，店鋪

supermarket ['supə͵mɑrkɪt] .... ★★★
n. 超級市場

tag [tæg] .... ★★★
n. 附加語，標籤：a price tag 價格標籤

辨析 Analyze

enormous, giant, gigantic, huge, immense, tremendous, vast

1. **label** *n.*「標籤，記號，稱號」，指繫或貼在行李、貨物等物品上的標籤：Can you read the label on the box? 你看得懂盒子標籤上寫的是什麼嗎？

2. **mark** *n.*「痕跡，斑點，污點，記號，標誌」，含義很廣，還指考試分數：The tires left marks on the road. 輪胎在路上留下了痕跡。

3. **notation** *n.*「記號，標記法」，指用於音樂或數學等領域的標記法：Music has a special system of notation, and so does chemistry. 音樂有一套特殊的標記法，化學也一樣。

4. **sign** *n.*「標記，符號，招牌，徵兆，跡象」，指數學或地圖等所用的符號、交通或商店等用的標牌或招牌，還指隱含的跡象、徵兆：For some reason the computer can't display the dollar sign. 這部電腦由於某種原因，不能顯示美元符號。

5. **signal** *n.*「信號，暗號，標誌，表示」：Traffic signals tell drivers when to stop and when to go. 交通號誌指示駕駛何時停、何時走。

6. **tag** *n.*「標籤，標牌」，指繫或貼在行李、貨物等物品上的標籤，基本上可與 label 互換使用：Each item in the store carries a printed price tag. 商店的每件商品上都有印好的價格標籤。

Unit 7
軍事類名稱總匯
Military
Affairs

01

軍隊設制類相關辭彙 Vocabulary of Army

Military Affairs

軍事類名稱總匯

armada [ɑr`mɑdə] .... ★
n. 艦隊，軍用機機群，軍用車車隊：an air armada 大批飛機群

armament [`ɑrməmənt] .... ★
n. 兵力，軍力：reduce nuclear armaments 裁減核武

armorer [`ɑrmərɚ] .... ★★
n. 武器製造者

army [`ɑrmɪ] .... ★★★★★
n. ①軍隊 ：Most armies are controlled by government. 大多數（國家）的軍隊由政府控制。②大群，大批：an army of students 一大批學生

barrack [`bærək] .... ★
n. 兵營，臨時工房

bugler [`bjuglɚ] .... ★
n. 號兵

capsize [kæp`saɪz] .... ★★
v. （船等）傾覆

colonel [`kɝnl] .... ★★★★★
n. （陸軍）上校：colonel commandant〔英〕旅長

command [kə`mænd] .... ★★★★★
v. 命令，指揮：The officer commanded his men to fire. 軍官命令士兵們開火。
n. ①命令，指揮：The soldiers must obey their officer's command. 士兵們必須服從軍官的命令。②控制，指揮：lose command of the sea 失去對海洋的控制③（常單）掌握，運用能力：He has (a) good command of English. 他精通英語。

commander [kə`mændɚ] .... ★★★★
n. 司令官，指揮員

corps [kɔr] .... ★★
n. 軍團，兵團：diplomatic corps 外交使團

force [fors] .... ★★★★★
v. 強迫，迫使：force sb. to work hard 強迫某人努力工作
n. ①暴力，武力：The enemy attacked in great force. 敵人猛烈攻擊。②力（量），力氣：the force of a blow 一擊之力③軍隊，部隊：join the forces 入伍【片語】come/go into force 生效

forcibly [ˋforsəblɪ] .... ★★★★★

adv. 強制地，用力地：The foreign traveler complained that he's been forcibly held by the local police without good reason. 這位外國遊客抱怨說，他曾經被當地警方毫無道理地強行關押。

frontline [ˋfrʌntˋlaɪn] .... ★★★

n. 前線

grenadier [ˏgrɛnəˋdɪr] .... ★

n. 英國近衛軍步兵

headquarters [ˋhɛdˋkwɔrtɚz] .... ★★★★

n. (單複同) 司令部，總部

knight [naɪt] .... ★★

n. 騎士，武士，爵士：knight of the Rueful/ Woeful Countenance 愁顏騎士 (指唐·吉訶德)

lieutenant [luˋtɛnənt] .... ★★

n. 陸軍中尉，海軍上尉，副職官員，代理官員

marshal [ˋmɑrʃəl] .... ★

n. 元帥

military [ˋmɪləˏtɛrɪ] .... ★★★★★

n. 軍隊

adj. 軍事的，軍用的，軍隊的：a military bearing 軍人的氣度

militia [mɪˋlɪʃə] .... ★

n. 民兵，民兵組織

naval [ˋnevl̩] .... ★★★

a. 海軍的：a great naval power 強大的海軍力量

navy [ˋnevɪ] .... ★★★★

n. 海軍

procession [prəˋsɛʃən] .... ★★★

n. 列隊行進，隊伍，行列：They watched the procession go past. 他們觀看遊行隊伍經過。

queue [kju] .... ★★★

n. 行列，長隊：stand in a queue 排成人龍

v. 排長隊

rank [ræŋk] .... ★★★★★

n. ①軍銜：hold the rank of colonel 掛上校軍銜②地位，社會階層：people from the upper and middle ranks of society (來自) 上層及中層社會地位的人們③排橫列：Jim examined the ranks of boys. 吉姆檢視男孩子的行列。

v. ①把…分等，給…平定等級：Where do you rank him? 你怎麼評價他？②列入：This town ranks the highest among the England beauty spots. 這個鎮被列為英國景點之首。

regiment [ˋrɛdʒəmənt] .... ★★

n. 團，軍團：regiment commander 團長

scout [skaʊt] .... ★★★

n. 偵察員，童子軍

v. 巡邏，〔美〕物色人才：She scouts for a professional basketball team. 她在物色一支職業籃球隊。

sentry [ˋsɛntrɪ] .... ★

n. 步兵

serviceman [ˋsɝvɪsmən] .... ★★★★★

n. 維修人員，軍人

snorkel [ˋsnɔrkl̩] .... ★

n. (潛水艇或潛遊者的) 換氣裝置

soldier [ˋsoldʒɚ] .... ★★★★★

n. 士兵，軍士

spy [spaɪ] .... ★★★★

n. 間諜，密探

troop [trup] .... ★★★★★

n. ①軍隊，部隊：They have more than 11,000 troops in Northern Ireland. 他們在北愛爾蘭有11,000多人的駐軍。②一隊，一群，(一) 大批：Did you see a troop of children passby? 你有沒有看到一群孩子走過？

trumpet [ˋtrʌmpɪt] .... ★★★

n. 喇叭，小號

vanguard [ˋvænˏgɑrd] .... ★

n. 尖兵，先鋒

02

軍用器物相關辭彙 Vocabulary of Military Equipment

ammunition [ˌæmjəˈnɪʃən] .... ★

n. 彈藥，證據：to have powerful ammunition for one's arguments 擁有強有力的證據可支持自己的觀點；How much ammunition did they shoot in training? 他們在打靶訓練中打了幾發子彈？

armor [ˈɑrmɚ] .... ★★

n. 盔甲，裝甲，武器，保護物：a knight in full armor 全副武裝的騎士；a chink in somebody's political armor 某人政治防線上的缺口

arrow [ˈæro] ....★★★★

n. 箭，箭狀物，箭頭記號

bomb [bɑm] ....★★★★

n. 炸彈：an atomic bomb 原子彈

v. 轟炸，投彈於：The airforce bombed two towns. 空軍轟炸了兩座城鎮。

bombard [bɑmˈbɑrd] .... ★★★★★

v. 轟擊，轟炸：The spokesman was bombarded with questions on the press conference. 發言人在新聞記者會上遭到了連珠炮般的發問。

bugle [ˈbjugl̩] .... ★

n. 軍號，喇叭：a bugle call 進軍號，集合號

bullet [ˈbʊlɪt] .... ★★★

n. 子彈：Bullet-proof glass stops bullets from passing through it. 防彈玻璃使子彈射不穿。

cannon [ˈkænən] .... ★★

n. 大炮，火炮

castle [ˈkæsl̩] .... ★★★★★

n. 城堡：Sir Roger Young was murdered last night in his castle. 羅傑‧揚男爵昨夜在他的城堡裡被謀殺。

dagger [ˈdægɚ] .... ★

n. 短劍：at daggers drawn with somebody 劍拔弩張，勢不兩立

fort [fort] .... ★★

n. 要塞，堡壘：Fort Knox 諾克斯堡（美國聯邦政府的黃金貯存地）

fortress [ˈfortrɪs] .... ★

n. 堡壘，要塞：The easiest way to capture a fortress is from within. 最容易攻下堡壘的方式是從內部開始。

gun [gʌn] .... ★★★★

n. 槍炮：machine gun 機關槍

helmet [ˈhɛlmɪt] .... ★★

n. 頭盔，鋼盔

landmine [ˈlændmaɪn] .... ★★★★

n. 地雷

missile [ˈmɪsl̩] .... ★★★★

n. 導彈，飛彈，發射物：missile technology 導彈技術；a missile silo 導彈倉庫

munitions [mjuˈnɪʃənz] .... ★

n. 軍火，軍需品

outfit [ˈaʊtˌfɪt] .... ★

n. 服裝，裝備，用具

parachute [ˈpærəˌʃut] .... ★

v. 用降落傘降落，用降落傘投送：The man parachuted safely to the ground. 這人跳傘安全著陸。

n. 降落傘

periscope [ˈpɛrəˌskop] .... ★★

n. 潛望鏡

pistol [ˈpɪstl̩] .... ★★

n. 手槍：pistol carbine 駁殼槍

shell [ʃɛl] .... ★★★★

v. 炮轟，射擊，剝…的殼：shell peas 剝豌豆

n. 殼，外殼，貝殼，炮彈

shelter [ˈʃɛltɚ] .... ★★★★

n. 掩蔽處，躲避處，庇護所，藏身（處）

v. （使）遮蔽：shelter under a tree 躲在樹下；shelter from the rain 避雨

squadron [ˈskwɑdrən] .... ★

n. 士兵寢室

submarine [ˈsʌbməˌrin] .... ★★★

n. 潛水艇

adj. 水底的，海底的：A guyot is a submarine mountain that does not reach the surface of the sea. 海底平頂山是存在於海下而不露出水面的山。

sword [sord] .... ★★★★

n. 劍，刀：All who draw the sword will die by the sword. 凡動刀的必死在刀下。

torpedo [tɔrˈpido] .... ★

n. 魚雷

trench [trɛntʃ] .... ★

n. 溝，壕，戰壕：open the trenches 掘戰壕，開溝

trigger [ˈtrɪgɚ] .... ★

n. 扳機，觸發器

v. 觸發，導致：The flower bud of a water lily opens at sunset since its opening is triggered by the decreased light. 水蓮是在日落時分開花，因為光照減弱才能讓水蓮開花。

weapon [ˈwɛpən] .... ★★★★★

n. 武器，兵器，兇器

03

軍事行動相關辭彙
Vocabulary of Military Actions

aggressive [əˈgrɛsɪv] .... ★★★
adj. 好鬥的：Some animals become aggressive to protect themselves and their territory from predators. 有些動物在保護自己和領域不受侵害時會變得好鬥。

aim [em] .... ★★★★★
v. 打算，意欲，瞄準：The questionnaire aims to highlight some of the major issues raised during the debate. 該問卷著重在辯論中提出的若干重要問題。

air-raid [ˈɛrˌred] .... ★★★★★
a. 空襲的：an air-raid alarm 空襲警報

annihilate [əˈnaɪəˌlet] .... ★
v. 削減：The enemy in its revenge tried to annihilate the entire population. 敵人企圖消滅全部人口進行報復。

assail [əˈsel] .... ★
v. 猛擊，決然面對：He was assailed with questions after his lecture. 他在演講之後，遭到如同攻擊般的質問。

assault [əˈsɔlt] .... ★★
v. 襲擊：a passerby assaulted by the hooligans 受到流氓襲擊的過路人
n. 攻擊

attack [əˈtæk] .... ★★★★★
v. 攻擊，進取，抨擊，非難：The government was attacked for the steps taken. 政府由於採取了這些措施而遭到抨擊。
n. ①攻擊，進攻（後接on sb. or sth.）：make an attack on the enemy 向敵人進攻②（病）發作：an attack of asthma 哮喘發作

batter [ˈbætɚ] .... ★★
v. 擊破，搗壞，炮擊：While the battered car was moving away, Roy stopped his bus and telephoned the police. 羅伊在那輛被撞壞的車移開的時候，把他的車停了下來報警。

battle [ˈbætl] .... ★★★★★
n. 戰役，戰鬥，鬥爭
v. 作戰，鬥爭（後接against/for/with）：They battled with winds and waves. 他們與風浪搏鬥。

battlefield [ˈbætl̩fild] .... ★★★★★

n. 戰場：He delivered a short speech at the battlefield. 他在戰場上作了簡短演說。

belligerent [bəˈlɪdʒərənt] .... ★

adj. 好戰的，交戰的：The boys found it hard to get along with Tom, because he always said some very belligerent things. 孩子們覺得湯姆很難相處，因為他老是說些挑釁的話。

beset [bɪˈsɛt] .... ★★★★★

v. 包圍：The project was beset with difficulties. 這項計畫困難重重。

besiege [bɪˈsidʒ] .... ★★★★★

v. 包圍，圍攻：doubts that besieged him 困擾著他的種種疑問

brace [bres] .... ★★

n. 支撐物

v. 支援，使固定：He braced his foot against the wall. 他把腳頂著牆站穩。

camp [kæmp] .... ★★★★★

n. 野營

vi. 宿營，陣營：The council members disagreed, falling into liberal and conservative camps. 理事會的成員們意見不和，分成自由和保守兩個陣營。

campaign [kæmˈpen] .... ★★★★★

v. 出征，運動

n. 戰役，運動：Grant's Vicksburg campaign secured the entire Mississippi for the Union. 格蘭特的維克斯堡戰役為聯邦挽救了整個密西西比。

carnage [ˈkɑrnɪdʒ] .... ★

n. 大屠殺，殘殺

combat [ˈkɑmbæt] .... ★★

n. 戰鬥，格鬥，鬥爭：In the United States, there are numerous federal, states, and local programs aimed at combating air pollution. 在美國，有許多聯邦、州和地方的目標都鎖定在防止空氣污染。

combative [kəmˈbætɪv] .... ★★

adj. 好鬥的：A combative person is usually eager or disposed to fight. 好鬥的人往往渴望或傾向戰鬥。

conquest [ˈkɑŋkwɛst] .... ★★★★

n. 征服：The pianist made a conquest of every audience for whom she played. 這位鋼琴家以她的演奏征服了每一位聽眾。

convoy [kənˈvɔɪ] .... ★

v. 護送：He convoyed her home. 他護送她回家。

cruise [kruz] .... ★★★

v. 巡航：A lot of babies cruised imperiously in their strollers, propelled by their mothers or by pairs of grandmothers. 許多嬰兒悠閒自在地躺在嬰兒車裡，由母親或祖母推著走來走去。

defeat [dɪˈfit] .... ★★★★

v. ①失敗，戰勝：They were defeated in their attempt to reach the top of the mountain 他們試圖登上山頂，可是沒有成功。②挫敗，使落空：Our hopes were defeated. 我們的希望落空了。

n. ①擊敗，戰勝：our defeat of the enemy 我們戰勝了敵人②戰敗，失敗：a volleyball team that has never suffered defeat 從沒輸過的排球隊

defence/defense [dɪˈfɛns] .... ★★★★★

n. ①防禦，保衛：money needed for national defence 國防所需的費用②防禦物：A thick overcoat is a good defence against the cold. 一件厚大衣足以禦寒。③辯護，答辯：The accused man made no defence. 被告不作答辯。④（常用複數）防務，防禦工程：coastal defence 沿海防禦工程

defend [dɪˈfɛnd] .... ★★★★

v. 防護，辯護：He's better at defending than attacking. 他的防守優於進攻。

demobilize [diˈmobl̩aɪz] .... ★

v. 使復員：a demobilized soldier 復員軍人

軍事類名稱總匯

disarm [dɪs'ɑrm] .... ★

v. 繳械，消除（敵意）：Have the courage to appear poor, and you disarm poverty. 有勇氣顯出貧窮，那麼你就消除了貧窮。

disarming [dɪs'ɑrmɪŋ] .... ★★★★★

adj. 消除敵意的：a disarming smile 使人消除敵意的微笑

encroach [ɪn'krotʃ] .... ★

v. 蠶食，侵佔：We will never allow anybody to encroach upon our territorial integrity and sovereignty. 我們的領土和主權絕不允許任何人侵犯。

enemy ['ɛnəmɪ] .... ★★★★★

n. 敵人，仇敵，敵軍：A successful man often has many enemies. 成功的人常會有許多敵人。

extricate ['ɛkstrɪˌket] .... ★

v. 救出，使解脫：The farmer extricated the dog from the barbed wire fence. 農夫把狗從帶刺的鐵柵欄中救了出來。

fire [faɪr] .... ★★★★★

n. ①火：A burnt child dreads the fire. 一朝被火燒，見火就害怕。②火爐：There is a fire in the next room. 隔壁有個火爐。③火災：A fire broke out last night. 昨晚發生火災。

v. 開火，射擊：He ran into the bank and fired his gun in the air. 他跑進了銀行並朝天鳴槍。

fireman ['faɪrmən] .... ★★★

n. 消防隊員

foe [fo] .... ★

n. 敵人

foil [fɔɪl] .... ★

v. 阻止：The police foiled the murderer's attempt to escape. 警方粉碎了殺人犯逃跑的企圖。

holocaust ['hɑləˌkɔst] .... ★

n. 大屠殺

invade [ɪn'ved] .... ★★★

v. 侵入，侵略，侵犯：to invade another person's rights 侵害他人的權益

invasion [ɪn'veʒən] .... ★★★

n. 入侵，侵略：an invasion of disease 疾病的侵害

loot [lut] .... ★

v. 掠奪：Widespread looting often occurs during wartime. 戰爭期間，大面積的掠奪十分普遍。

mandate ['mændet] .... ★★★★★

n. 命令，要求：mandate desegregation of public school 命令廢除公立學校中的種族隔離

mandatory ['mændəˌtorɪ] .... ★★★★★

adj. 命令的，強制的：mandatory administration/rule 委託管理

march [mɑrtʃ] .... ★★★★★

v. ①行軍，前進：The soldiers marched north. 士兵們向北行軍。②遊行示威：Thousands of workers marched along the street. 數千名勞工沿著街道遊行示威。

n. ①遊行示威：a peace march 和平遊行②進行，進展：The science is on the march. 科學在發展。③行進，行軍：a long march 長征

massacre ['mæsəkɚ] .... ★

n. 大屠殺，殘殺：the massacre of Jews by Nazi in World War II 二次世界大戰中德國納粹對猶太人的殺戮

meddle ['mɛdl̩] .... ★

v. 干預：Do not meddle in things that do not concern you. 別干涉和自己無關的事。

missing ['mɪsɪŋ] .... ★★★★

adj. 失去的，漏掉的：You can find the names of the dead, wounded and missing in the newspaper. 你可以報紙上找到死傷和失蹤者的名字。

onset [ˈɑnˌsɛt] .... ★★★★

n. 攻擊，開始：The onset of sleep is determined by many factors. 睡眠的開始是由許多因素決定的。

onslaught [ˈɑnˌslɔt] .... ★

n. 猛攻：When the governor said he was raising taxes, there was an onslaught of criticism. 該州長說要加稅時，馬上受到輿論痛批。

oust [aʊst] .... ★

v. 驅逐：the American Revolution, which ousted the English 將英國人驅逐出境的美國獨立戰爭

overcome [ˌovəˈkʌm] .... ★★★★

v. 戰勝，克服：overcome temptation 克服誘惑

patrol [pəˈtrol] .... ★

n. 巡邏，偵察：The patrol police on duty are on the alert against any possible disturbances. 值班巡警處於戒備狀態，隨時準備應付任何可能發生的騷亂。

plunder [ˈplʌndə] .... ★★

v. 掠奪，搶劫：The Normandy coast was plundered repeatedly by seafaring marauders during the twelfth century. 諾曼第海岸在十二世紀屢次遭到海盜的掠奪。

raid [red] .... ★★★

n. 襲擊：Fear of pirate raids caused the Spaniards to fortify their coastline. 西班牙人由於害怕海盜的襲擊，把自己的海岸線修築得很堅固。

reconnaissance [rɪˈkɑnəsəns] .... ★

n. 偵查，勘察：high reconnaissance 高空偵察

recruit [rɪˈkrut] .... ★★★★

v. 徵兵，徵募：colleges recruiting minority students 招收弱勢族群學生的大學

resist [rɪˈzɪst] .... ★★★★

v. 抵抗，堅持：Fibrous silicate minerals such as asbestos are able to resist fire and acid better than other materials. 像石棉這樣含纖維的矽酸鹽礦物質比其他材料更能防火耐酸。

resistance [rɪˈzɪstəns] .... ★★★★

n. 抵抗運動, 抵抗，抵制，阻力，電阻，抵抗力：wind resistance to an aircraft 風對飛機的阻力

resistant [rɪˈzɪstənt] .... ★★★

adj. 抵抗的，反抗的，耐…的：These are the insects that have become resistant to DDT. 這些是對 DDT 已有抵抗力的昆蟲。

revolt [rɪˈvolt] .... ★★

v. 反抗，起義：Students revolt against the administrative policies. 學生們抗議管理政策。

riot [ˈraɪət] .... ★★★

n. 暴亂，騷動：There was a riot when the workers were told they had lost their jobs. 當工人們聽說自己失業時，發生了暴動。

snag [snæg] .... ★

n. 障礙，斷枝

v. 加以阻撓：His sweater snagged on a tree branch. 他的毛衣掛在樹枝上。

shoot [ʃut] .... ★★★★★

v. ①射擊：We suddenly realized we were being shot at. 我們猛然意識到我們正是被射擊的目標。②疾馳，飛快地移動：The boat shot forward. 小船疾速前馳。③射門，投門：He missed a great opportunity to shoot at goal. 他錯失了一次極佳的射門機會。④射中，射死：The judge was shot and critically wounded as he left the court. 法官在離開法庭時遭到槍擊，傷勢很重。⑤發射：shoot the rocket up into the sky 向天空發射火箭

n. ①嫩枝，苗：bamboo shoots 竹筍②射擊，發射：He is studying shoot. 他正在學習射擊。

shot [ʃɑt] .... ★★★★★
n. ①開槍，射擊：How many shots did you hear? 你聽到幾聲槍響？②射擊，投籃：Good shot! 好球！／射得好！③彈藥，炮彈，子彈

siege [sidʒ] .... ★★
v. 圍困，圍攻
n. 包圍，圍困，圍攻

slaughter [ˈslɔtɚ] .... ★★
v. & n. 屠殺，屠宰：Hoof-and-mouth disease was eliminated in the United States by slaughtering affected herds of cattle. 美國把感染口蹄疫的牛群全部銷毀，疫病因而滅絕。

strategy [ˈstrætədʒɪ] .... ★★★★★
n. 戰略，策略

strike [straɪk] .... ★★★★★
v. ①打，襲擊：A stone struck me on the head. 一塊石頭打中了我的頭。②使突然想到：It struck him how foolish her behavior was. 他突然想到她的行為是多麼愚蠢。③給…深刻的印象：She was struck by his handsome appearance. 他英俊的外表讓她留下了極深的印象。④發現，找到：They struck oil in the North Sea. 他們在北海發現了石油。⑤罷工：They are striking for more money. 他們罷工要求加薪。⑥襲擊：We'll strike at the invaders at night. 我們將夜襲入侵者。⑦（鐘等）敲響：The clock was striking. 鐘敲響了。
n. 罷工
【片語】sell out 賣完

strikingly [ˈstraɪkɪŋlɪ] .... ★★★★
adv. 顯著地，引人注目地：The wind-chill factor, the combination of low temperature and wind speed, strikingly increases the degree of cold felt by a person who is outdoors. 冷風是由低溫和風速結合而成的，能夠讓戶外的人明顯地感到寒冷。

surmount [sɚˈmaʊnt] .... ★
v. 克服，登上，越過：to surmount a hill 登上一座山

surrender [səˈrɛndɚ] .... ★★★★
n. 投降
v. 使投降，交出，放棄：surrender to the enemy 向敵人投降

surround [səˈraʊnd] .... ★★★★★
v. 包圍，環繞：The house is surrounded on three sides by a wide veranda. 房子的三面環繞著寬闊的走廊。

surrounding [səˈraʊndɪŋ] .... ★★★
n. 周圍的事物，環境：The house is situated in very pleasant surroundings. 那間房子所處的環境非常優美。
adj. 周圍的，附近的

tactics [ˈtæktɪks] .... ★
n. 戰術

trample [ˈtræmpl] .... ★★
v. 踐踏，蹂躪：Don't trample on the flowers when you play in the garden. 你在花園裡玩耍時，不要踩到花朵。

tread [trɛd] .... ★★
v. 踩，踐踏：They get the juice out of the fruit by treading it. 他們踩踏水果從中榨汁。

unrest [ʌnˈrɛst] .... ★
n. 不安，動亂，騷亂

uproar [ˈʌpˌror] .... ★★★★★
n. 騷動，擾亂，喧囂

vanquish [ˈvænkwɪʃ] .... ★
v. 征服，克服：Success vanquished their fears. 成功讓他們克服了恐懼。

vengeance [ˈvɛndʒəns] .... ★★
n. 報復，復仇

versus [ˈvɝsəs] .... ★
prep. 以…為對手：Brazil versus Italy 巴西隊對義大利隊

victim [ˈvɪktɪm] .... ★★★★★
n. 犧牲品，受害者

war [wɔr] .... ★★★★★
n. 戰爭：The modern war doesn't have the
front. 現代戰爭沒有前線。

Unit 8

交通、通訊名稱總匯
Communications

01

交通運輸相關辭彙 Vocabulary of Transportation

access [ˈæksɛs] .... ★★★★★
n. 通路，入門
v. 接近：Branch officials can access the central data bank. 分部的官員可以利用中央資料庫。

aground [əˈgraʊnd] .... ★
adj. 擱淺，觸礁：The ship went aground after a hard shock on the shoals. 船隻猛烈地撞上暗礁後就擱淺了。

airborne [ˈɛrˌbɔrn] .... ★
adj. 空中的，飛行的，空運的：airborne troops 空降部隊

aircraft [ˈɛrˌkræft] .... ★★★
n. (單複同) 航空器，飛機：an assortment of fighter aircraft 各種戰鬥機

aircrew [ˈɛrˌkru] .... ★★★
n. 空勤人員

airline [ˈɛrˌlaɪn] .... ★★★
n. ①航線②(pl.) 航空公司：There are two airlines offering flights from A to B. 提供 A 地到 B 地航班的航空公司有兩家。

airman [ˈɛrmæn] .... ★★★
n. 飛行員，航空兵

airplane [ˈɛrˌplen] .... ★★★
n. 飛機

airport [ˈɛrˌport] .... ★★★
n. 機場，航空站

anchor [ˈæŋkɚ] .... ★★★
n. 錨
v. 拋錨，停泊：Most plants depend upon their roots to anchor themselves in the soil and to absorb water and inorganic chemicals. 大多數植物依靠根部固定於泥土之中來吸收水和無機化學物質。

auto [ˈɔto] .... ★
n. 汽車

automobile [ˈɔtəməˌbɪl] .... ★★★
n. 汽車，機動車

aviation [ˌevɪˈeʃən] .... ★★
n. 航空，飛行：artillery reconnaissance aviation 炮兵偵察機

aviator [ˈevɪˌetə] .... ★★
n. 飛行家

badge [bædʒ] .... ★
n. 徽章

beacon [ˈbikn̩] .... ★
n. 燈塔，信標

bicycle [ˈbaɪsɪkl̩] .... ★★★
n. 自行車：ride a bicycle 騎自行車

boat [bot] .... ★★★★★
n. 小船，艇

brake [brek] .... ★★★
v. 制動器，剎車：to brake a car 剎車
n. 閘，剎車：The town government put
  brakes on all these projects by giving them
  less money. 鎮公所刪減所有這些工程的款
  項，使它們都停工了。

bridge [brɪdʒ] .... ★★★
n. 橋樑

bus [bʌs] .... ★★★
n. 公共汽車

canoe [kəˈnu] .... ★★
n. 獨木舟，小遊艇

cargo [ˈkɑrgo] .... ★★★
n. 貨物，載貨

carriage [ˈkærɪdʒ] .... ★★★★★
n. 馬車，客車，車廂

carrier [ˈkærɪə] .... ★★★★
n. 運送人，搬運人：baggage carriers 行李搬
  運工：a message carrier 傳信人

cart [kɑrt] .... ★★★★
n. 大車，手推車
v. 用車運：The police carted the criminals
  away to the lockup for prisoners. 警方把罪
  犯用車押送到看守所。

convey [kənˈve] .... ★★★★
v. 運輸，表達：Oil can be conveyed by
  pipeline from an oil region to a refinery. 石油
  可以從產油區通過管道運輸到煉油廠。

crew [kru] .... ★★★★
n. 一組工作人員：a stage crew 舞臺工作人員

cycle [ˈsaɪkl̩] .... ★★★
n. ①自行車，摩托車②循環，週期：the cycle
  of the seasons 季節的循環
v. ①騎自行車，騎摩托車：He cycles to
  school every day. 他每天騎自行車上學。
  ②循環，作循環運動：The machine cycles
  automatically. 這部機器會自動循環運轉。

cyclist [ˈsaɪklɪst] .... ★★★★★
n. 騎自行車的人

deck [dɛk] .... ★★★★
n. 甲板，橋面，層面：the upper/lower deck
  上／下甲板；the top deck of a double-deck
  bus/train 雙層巴士／火車的上層

deport [dɪˈport] .... ★
v. 驅逐出境，放逐，舉止：This country began
  to deport dangerous aliens after suffering
  the terrorists' attack. 這個國家在遭受恐怖分
  子襲擊後，開始把危險的外國人驅逐出境。

detour [ˈditur] .... ★
n. 迂迴：Vehicles have to make a detour
  because of the traffic jam. 由於交通堵塞，
  車輛不得不繞道而行。

dock [dɑk] .... ★
n. 船塢，碼頭
v. 入塢，靠碼頭，扣錢：The company docks
  its employees for unauthorized absences.
  該公司因其職員無端曠職而扣薪。

embark [ɪmˈbɑrk] .... ★★★★★
v. 從事，開始做，上船，上飛機：
  We embarked at Southampton, and
  disembarked in New York a week later. 我們
  在南安普敦上船，一星期後到紐約下船。

entrance [ˈɛntrəns] .... ★★★★
n. ①入口，大門：the front entrance 正門，前
  門②進入，入場：No entrance! 不准進入！

entry [ˈɛntrɪ] .... ★★★★★
n. 進入，入口，登記：Their entry into the war changed the whole situation. 他們的參戰改變了整個局勢。

excursion [ɪkˈskɜʒən] .... ★★★
n. 短途旅行，集體遊覽：On hunting excursions, which are usually solitary and lengthy, river otters often travel many miles from their burrows. 河水獺在通常是孤獨和漫長的獵食過程中，常要游到離其洞穴好幾英里之外的地方。

exit [ˈɛksɪt] .... ★★★★
n. 出口
v. 退出：Make your exit through the door at the back of the stage. 請你從舞臺後面的門退場。

expedition [ˌɛkspɪˈdɪʃən] .... ★★
n. 遠征：an expedition to find the beginning of the Hudson River 一次尋找哈德遜河源頭的探險

ferry [ˈfɛrɪ] .... ★
n. 渡船，渡口
v. 運送，空運：People used to cross the river by ferry, but now here is built a new concrete bridge. 從前人們在這裡常乘渡船過河，然而現在這裡已經建起了一座新的混凝土大橋。

flight [flaɪt] .... ★★★★★
n. ①飛翔，飛行：I hope I can have a round-the-world flight. 我希望我能來一趟環球航行。②航班：What is the flight number of their plane leaving San Francisco? 他們離開舊金山的航班編號是多少？③樓梯的一段：He fell down a flight of stairs and died. 他跌下樓梯死了。

flotilla [floˈtɪlə] .... ★
n. 小艦隊，船隊：a destroyer flotilla 驅逐艦隊

garage [gəˈrɑʒ] .... ★★★
n. 車庫，飛機庫，汽車間，汽車修理

gate [get] .... ★★★★★
n. 大門

glider [ˈglaɪdə] .... ★
n. 滑翔機，滑翔者／物：The boat glided over the river. 船在河上滑行。

harbo(u)r [ˈhɑrbə] .... ★★
n. 港口，海港，避難所，藏身處
v. 隱匿，窩藏，包庇：Medieval cities grew rapidly when they had harbors nearby. 中世紀的城市若附近有港口會發展得很快。

haven [ˈhevən] .... ★
n. 港口，避難所

helicopter [ˈhɛlɪkɑptə] .... ★★★
n. 直升機
v. 乘直升機：The president helicoptered to California yesterday. 總統昨天乘直升機飛赴加州。

hovercraft [ˈhʌvəˌkræft] .... ★★
n. 氣墊船

hull [hʌl] .... ★
n. 船體，外殼
v. 去殼，去皮：Rice is gathered, cleaned and hulled before being sold. 米經過收割，篩清和去殼以後才出售。

hydrofoil [ˈhaɪdrəˌfɔɪl] .... ★
n. 水翼艇

jet [dʒɛt] .... ★★★
n. ①噴氣式飛機，噴氣式發動機：travelling by jet 乘噴射機旅行②噴嘴，噴射口：Put a match to the gas jet to light the gas. 把火柴放在噴氣噴口，點燃瓦斯。③噴射，噴流：The firemen directed jets of water at the burning building. 消防隊員們朝失火的大樓噴水。

lane [len] .... ★★★★
n. 規定的單向車道，通道，小路，小巷，行車道：The St. Lawrence Seaway links the Great Lakes with the shipping lanes of the world. 聖勞倫斯海上航道把北美五大湖與世界上的海上航道連接了起來。

load [lod] .... ★★★★★
n. 重載，負載，負荷，負擔，重物
v. 裝，裝載，裝貨，裝填：That is a big load.
那（輛車）裝得真滿。

locomotive [ˌlokə`motɪv] ....★
adj. 運動的，移動的，機車的
n. 機車，火車頭：The U.S. could no longer
serve as the locomotive for the world
economy. 美國再也無力承擔世界經濟推動
力的重任了。

lorry [`lɔrɪ] .... ★★★
n. 卡車，貨車

marine [mə`rin] .... ★★★★
adj. 海的，海上的：The adult polar bear is
almost totally a marine animal. 成年的北
極熊幾乎完全是海洋動物。

motor [`motɚ] .... ★★★★
n. 發動機，電動機：a small electric motor 小
型電動機

motorcycle [`motɚˌsaɪkl] .... ★★★★★
n. 摩托車：chain-drive motorcycle 鏈動摩托車

motorist [`motərɪst] .... ★★★★★
n. 駕駛汽車的人，乘汽車旅行的人

motorway [`motəˌwe] .... ★
n. 快車道

nautical [`nɔtɪkl] ....★
a. 航海的，海上的：nautical receiving set 航
海接收器；nautical scale 海圖比例尺；
nautical terms 航海用語

navigable [`nævəgəbl] .... ★★★
adj. 可航行的，可通航的：a navigable river 可
通航的河流

navigate [`nævəˌget] .... ★★★
v. 駕駛（船、飛機）：He navigated the plane
through the low cloud. 他駕駛飛機穿過低空
的雲層。

navigation [ˌnævə`geʃən] .... ★★★
n. 航海：navigation canal 通航運河

oar [or] .... ★★
n. 槳，櫓：This boat pulls six oars. 這條船用
六根槳划。

outing [`autɪŋ] .... ★★★★★
n. 郊遊，遠足

辨析
Analyze

cargo, freight, goods, load

1 **cargo** *n.*「貨物」，指船或飛機等交通工
具所運載的貨物：The cargo has been put
in the train to be transported to Boston.
貨物已裝入火車準備運往波士頓。

2 **freight** *n.*「貨物，貨運」，與 cargo 是
同義詞，指車、船等運輸工具上的貨物，
還指「運送」，與客運形成對比，可做
定語：A freight train carries all kinds of
things, but no passengers. 貨運列車裝載
各種物資，但不載人。

3 **goods** *n.*「貨物，商品」，指買賣的商
品或貨物，普通用語：This shopkeeper
kept a large stock of goods in war times.
這家店主在戰爭時期囤積了一大批貨物。

4 **load** *n.*「負擔，載荷」，指人、畜或運
輸工具等所負荷的東西，比喻用法可指人
精神上的負擔：The old woman carried a
heavy load of wood on her shoulder. 那
個老婦人肩上扛著沉重的木柴。

交通、通訊名稱總匯

paddle [ˋpædl̩] .... ★★★★★
n. 槳
vt. 用槳划：The merry girl paddled her boat
along the river. 快樂的女孩沿河划著小船。

pass [pæs] .... ★★★★★
v. ①經過：The ship passed the channel. 船
通過海峽。②傳遞：Please pass this book
to her. 請把這本書遞給她。③通過（考試
等）：He passed the examination. 他考試及
格了。
【片語】pass...on to 傳…下去給

passage [ˋpæsɪdʒ] .... ★★★★★
n. ①通道：Do you know there is a passage
through the forest? 你知道有一條穿過森林
的小路嗎？②一段，一節：There are eight
passages in this poem. 這首詩共八段。

passenger [ˋpæsn̩dʒɚ] .... ★★★★
n. 乘客，旅客

passkey [ˋpæsˏki] .... ★
n. 總鑰匙，萬能鑰匙

passport [ˋpæsˏport] .... ★★★
n. 護照

path [pæθ] .... ★★★★★
n. 小徑，路線，〔喻〕道路

pave [pev] .... ★
v. 鋪道：The garden path is paved with slabs
of stone. 這條花園小路是用石板砌成的。

pavement [ˋpevmənt] .... ★★
n. 人行道：pavement artist〔英〕（在人行道
上繪圖賺錢的）馬路畫家，街頭展畫出售者

pilot [ˋpaɪlət] .... ★★★★
n. 飛行員

plane [plen] .... ★★★★
n.〔口〕飛機(=〔英〕aeroplane)

port [port] .... ★★★★★
n. 港口

portable [ˋportəbl̩] .... ★★★
adj. 可攜帶的：a portable TV 手提式電視

porter [ˋportɚ] .... ★★★★
n. 搬運工人，清潔工：porter's knot 搬運工用
的墊肩

rail [rel] .... ★★★★
n. ①欄杆，橫杆：Keep your hand on the rail
as you climb the steps. 你在爬樓梯時手握
住欄杆。②鐵軌，軌道：The accident was
caused by some of the rails becoming bent
in the heat. 該事故是由高溫造成部分鐵軌扭
曲引起的。③鐵路：rail travel 乘火車旅行

ride [raɪd] .... ★★★★★
v. 騎，乘：Can you ride a horse? 你會騎馬
嗎？

road [rod] .... ★★★★★
n. 路，道路：It is not really a road, only a
path. 這不是一條真正的路，只是一條小
徑。
【片語】on the road 在旅途中；在…過程中

sail [sel] .... ★★★★★
n. ①帆：a ship in full sail 一艘揚帆的船②航
行：Is it two week's sail from London to
New York? 從倫敦航行至紐約要兩週嗎？
v. ①航行：Churchill asked Luce to sail back
to England with him. 邱吉爾要求露斯與他一
塊兒乘船返回英國。②駕駛（船隻）：She
sailed the cockboat out to the island. 她駕著
那艘小艇前往該島。

sailor [ˋselɚ] .... ★★★★
n. 海員，水手

ship [ʃɪp] .... ★★★★★
n. 船艦，船舶

shipment [ˋʃɪpmənt] .... ★
n. 裝船，出貨

shipwreck [ˋʃɪpˏrɛk] .... ★
n. 船舶失事

shuttle [ˋʃʌtl̩] .... ★
n. 梭子，短程穿梭運輸工具，太空梭

siren [ˋsaɪrən] .... ★
n. 警報器，汽笛，(S-)(希神)塞壬（半鳥半女
人的海妖）：a police car siren 警車汽笛

station [ˈsteʃən] .... ★★★★

n. ①所，站，局：The tall building near our school is the broadcasting station. 我們學校附近的大樓是廣播電臺。②車站：There is a big modern station under construction. 有座大型的現代化車站正在蓋。

steer [stɪr] .... ★★★

v. 駕駛，掌舵：He steered the ship carefully between the rocks. 他小心地在礁石間駕著船。

steward [ˈstjuwəd] .... ★★

n. 男服務員，招待員，管家

stewardess [ˈstjuwədɪs] .... ★

n. 空中小姐，女服務員

streetcar [ˈstritˌkɑr] .... ★★★★

n. 街車

tanker [ˈtæŋkə] .... ★

n. 油船，空中加油機

taxi [ˈtæksɪ] .... ★★★

n. 計程車：I took taxis only twice. 我只搭過兩次計程車。

ticket [ˈtɪkɪt] .... ★★★★

n. ①（車）票，入場券：May I see your ticket please, madam? 小姐，請出示您的車票。②標籤，標牌

traffic [ˈtræfɪk] .... ★★★★

n. 交通，運輸，貿易，交通量，運輸量：Traffic police are sometimes very polite. 交通警察有時很有禮貌。

vi. （常與in連用）非法買賣：trafficking in stolen goods 非法買賣贓物

trailer [ˈtrelə] .... ★★★★★

n. 拖車，掛車

train [tren] .... ★★★★★

n. 列車，火車

tram [træm] .... ★

n. （有軌）電車

transport [trænsˈpɔrt] .... ★★★★★

v. 運輸，輸送，搬運：Before it could be transported to the United States, a site had to be found for it and a pedestal had to be built. 雕像在可以運往美國之前，必須為它選個地點，還要建造一個雕像底座。

truck [trʌk] .... ★★★

n. （載重）卡車

tyre [taɪr] .... ★★★

n. 車胎

van [væn] .... ★★★★★

n. 有篷貨車，搬運車

vehicle [ˈviɪkl̩] .... ★★★★

n. 運載工具，車輛，飛行器：The *Fountainhead* by Ayn Rand is a lengthy novel that serves as a vehicle for her philosophy of objectivism. 安．蘭德所寫的《泉源》，是作為她客觀主義哲學載體的一部長篇小說。

vessel [ˈvɛsl̩] .... ★★★★★

n. 船舶，艦，飛機，容器，導管，血管：What the monitor is watching is an ironclad vessel. 這監視器監測的是一般裝甲船。

voyage [ˈvɔɪɪdʒ] .... ★★★★

n. 航海，航空，航程，航行：The voyage is a recurrent metaphor in Romantic literature. 航行是浪漫主義文學中反覆出現的比喻。

wagon [ˈwægən] .... ★★★★

n. 運貨馬車，運貨車，敞篷車廂

wharf [hwɔrf] .... ★

n. 碼頭，停泊所

wheel [hwil] .... ★★★★★

n. 輪，車輪

yacht [jɑt] .... ★

n. 遊艇，快艇

02

郵政相關辭彙

Vocabulary of Mail

Communications

accept [ək'sɛpt] .... ★★★★★

v. ①接受，領受：Thank you all the same, but I can't accept your gift. 還是謝謝你，我不能收下你的禮物。 ②認可：I accept your reasons for being late. 我可接受你這次遲到的原因。

bearer ['bɛrɚ] .... ★★★★★

n. 持信人：The note says "payable to the bearer". 票據上寫著「見票即付」。

card [kɑrd] .... ★★★★★

n. 卡片，名片：make a Teachers' Day card in the art lesson 在美術課上做一張教師節賀卡

deliver [dɪ'lɪvɚ] .... ★★★★★

v. ①投遞，送交：Did you deliver my message to your father? 你把我的訊息轉達給你父親了嗎？ ②發表，表達：deliver a series of lecture 舉行一系列講座 ③使…分娩，接生：The doctor delivered her of twins. 醫生為她接生，生下一對雙胞胎。 ④釋放：May God deliver us from all evil. 願上帝使我們脫離一切邪惡。

mail [mel] .... ★★★★★

n. 郵件：e-mail 電子郵件

【片語】by mail 郵寄

post [post] .... ★★★★★

v. 投寄，郵寄：Do you mind posting this letter for me? 可以幫我寄這封信嗎？

n. ①郵政，郵寄：Post is not the best way to pass an immediate message to your friend. 傳送緊急消息給朋友時，郵寄不是最好的辦法。 ②職位，崗位，哨所工作：She has a post in an office. 她在辦公室裡工作。

【片語】post office 郵局

postage ['postɪdʒ] .... ★★★

n. 郵費，郵資：Stamps show how much postage has been paid. 郵票表明已付了多少郵資。

receive [rɪ'siv] .... ★★★★★

v. ①接到，收到，遭受：I received his invitation but did not accept. 我接到了他的請帖，但沒有接受邀請。 ②接受，接納：He would not receive her. 他不願接納她。

receiver [rɪˈsivɚ] .... ★★★
n. 話筒，受話器，接受機，接待者，接受者，收件人：The part of a telephone you speak into and listen at is called a receiver. 電話上你用來對著聽和說的地方叫話筒。

seal [sil] .... ★★★★
n. 封口，封蠟，封條，印記，圖章，海豹
v. 封，密封：An unused wing of the hospital was sealed off. 醫院一處未啓用的側廳被封起來了。

stamp [stæmp] .... ★★★★
n. 郵票，印花

code [kod] .... ★★★★★
n. 法典，法規，準則，代碼，電碼，密碼：civil code 民法；criminal code 刑法；moral code 道德準則；code of the school 校規

dial [ˈdaɪəl] .... ★★★
v. 撥（電話號碼），打電話
n. 刻度盤，鐘面，撥號盤：Put in the money before dialing. 先投錢幣再撥號。

message [ˈmɛsɪdʒ] .... ★★★★★
n. ①訊息，電文，便條，口信：Would you please give him a message? 你能向他傳個口信嗎？②啓示，要旨：What's the message of his speech? 他演講的主題是什麼？

net [nɛt] .... ★★★★★
n. 網，網狀系統：a fishing net 魚網
adj. 淨的，純淨的：net weight 淨重

network [ˈnɛtwɝk] .... ★★★★★
n. 網路，網狀系統，廣播網，電視網；a network of railway 鐵路網

ring [rɪŋ] .... ★★★★★
n. ①戒指：She wears a wedding ring. 她戴著結婚戒指。②圓圈，環：Some Africans have nose rings. 一些非洲人有鼻環。③（打）電話：I'll give you a ring this evening. 我傍晚會打電話給你。
v. 按（鈴）：How long has that telephone been ringing? 那電話響了多久啦？
【片語】ring (sb.) up 打電話給某人

telephone [ˈtɛləˌfon] .... ★★★★★
n. 電話
v. 打電話：He telephoned to say that he would come the next month. 他打電話說下個月會來。

transmit [trænsˈmɪt] .... ★★★
v. 傳播，播送，傳遞，傳導：Parents transmit some of their characteristics to their children. 父母把一些自己的特質遺傳給兒女。

辨析
Analyze

accept, receive

1 **accept** *vt.* 「接受」，指經過思考後願意接受某事物：I sent her my invitation, but she didn't accept it. 我向她發了請帖，但她沒有接受我的邀請。

2 **receive** *vt.* 「收到」，指客觀上收到某物，不表示接受與否。在表示接受或接納時，要有搭配的副詞或介系詞片語表示接受方式：They did receive my invitation, but they didn't want to come. 他們的確收到了我的邀請函，但不願意來。

Unit 9
生活類名稱總匯
Life

01

飲食類相關辭彙

Vocabulary of Food

apple [ˈæpl̩] .... ★★★★
n. 蘋果（樹）：apple pie 蘋果派

bacon [ˈbekən] .... ★★★
n. 鹹肉，燻肉：bring home the bacon 獲得成功，維持家庭生計

banana [bəˈnænə] .... ★★★
n. 香蕉

banquet [ˈbæŋkwɪt] .... ★★
n. 宴會，盛會

bean [bin] .... ★★★
n. 豆子：soybean 大豆

beef [bif] .... ★★★
n. 牛肉：He likes eating beef. 他喜歡吃牛肉。

beer [bɪr] .... ★★★★
n. 啤酒

berry [ˈbɛrɪ] .... ★★
n. 漿果（如草莓、葡萄、番茄等）：the berries of the coffee plant 咖啡豆

beverage [ˈbɛvərɪdʒ] .... ★
n. 飲料

biscuit [ˈbɪskɪt] .... ★★★
n. 餅乾

bitter [ˈbɪtɚ] .... ★★★★
adj. 苦的，痛苦的：a bitter disappointment 痛苦的失望

bowl [bol] .... ★★★★★
n. 滾球運動，木球，碗，鉢：She dropped the bowl of water. 她灑了一碗水。

bowler [ˈbolɚ] .... ★
n. 圓頂帽，投球手

bread [brɛd] .... ★★★★★
n. 麵包

cabbage [ˈkæbɪdʒ] .... ★★★
n. 白菜，捲心菜：Chinese cabbage 大白菜

cake [kek] .... ★★★★
n. 餅，糕，蛋糕

carrot [`kærət] .... ★★★
n. ①胡蘿蔔②（用以引誘的）報酬，許諾，誘
　騙：a policy of (the) stick and (the) carrot
　胡蘿蔔與棍棒策略（獎懲並行的策略）

cereal [`sɪrɪəl] .... ★
n. 五穀，禾穀：cereal-leguminous crops 豆類
　作物

cheese [tʃiz] .... ★★★
n. 乾酪，乳酪

chicken [`tʃɪkɪn] .... ★★★★
n. 雞，雞肉

chocolate [`tʃɑkəlɪt] .... ★★★
n. 巧克力

cigar [sɪ`gɑr] .... ★★★
n. 雪茄煙：Have a cigar? = How do you do?
　〔美俚〕你好！

cigarette/cigaret [ˌsɪgə`rɛt] .... ★★★
n. 香煙：a pack/tin of cigarettes 一包香煙

coffee [`kɔfɪ] .... ★★★★
n. 咖啡（色）

condiment [`kɑndəmənt] .... ★
n. 調味品：Pepper and salt are condiments.
　辣椒和鹽都是調味品。

cook [kʊk] .... ★★★★★
n. 廚師，炊事員
vt. 烹調，煮，燒：I'm cooking supper. 我正在
　做晚飯。
　【片語】cook the dinner 做晚飯

corn [kɔrn] .... ★★★★★
n. 莊稼，玉米

cream [krim] .... ★★★
n. ①奶油，奶油食品，奶油狀物②奶油色

crumble [`krʌmbl̩] .... ★
v. 粉碎，崩潰：Her hopes crumbled. 她的希
　望落空了。

crumple [`krʌmpl̩] .... ★
v. 壓皺，崩潰：The enemy crumpled under
　our attacks. 敵軍在我軍攻擊下全盤崩潰

crust [krʌst] .... ★★★
n. 地殼，硬外皮：snow with a firm crust 有一
　層堅硬冰面的雪

cucumber [`kjukəmbə] .... ★
n. 黃瓜

cuisine [kwɪ`zin] .... ★
n. 烹調，菜餚

delicious [dɪ`lɪʃəs] .... ★★★
adj. 美味的，怡人的：The soup is delicious.
　湯美味極了。

dessert [dɪ`zɜt] .... ★
n. 甜點

diet [`daɪət] .... ★★★
v. 節食
n. 飲食，食物：When preparing a diet, a
　person should be aware that vitamin D acts
　to increase the amount of calcium absorbed
　by the body. 準備飲食時，應該注意維生素D
　有幫助人體吸收鈣的功能。

dinner [`dɪnə] .... ★★★★★
n. 晚餐，宴會：Let's go and have dinner
　together. 我們一起去吃晚飯吧。

dish [dɪʃ] .... ★★★★★
n. ①碟子，盤子②（一道）菜餚：The table is
　full of dilicious dishes. 桌上滿是美味佳餚。

drink [drɪŋk] .... ★★★★★
v. 飲，喝，飲酒：Many people don't drink and
　smoke. 許多人不喝酒也不抽煙。
n. 飲料

edible [`ɛdəbl̩] .... ★
adj. 可食的：Are these berries edible, or are
　they poisonous? 這些草莓可以吃嗎？還是
　有毒？

egg [ɛg] .... ★★★★★
n. 蛋，卵，雞蛋：fried eggs 煎蛋

flavor [`flevə] .... ★★★
n. 味道，風味

flesh [flɛʃ] .... ★★★★★
n. 肉，果肉，肉體，肌膚

fleshy [ˈflɛʃɪ] .... ★★★★★
adj. 肉的，似肉的：the fleshy fringes of show business 娛樂界的輕浮之人

flour [flaʊr] .... ★★★
n. 麵粉，粉狀物

food [fʊd] .... ★★★★★
n. 食品，食物

foodstuff [ˈfʊd͵stʌf] .... ★
n. 食品，食料

fruit [frut] .... ★★★★★
n. 水果，果實

fruiterer [ˈfrutərɚ] .... ★★★★★
n. 水果商

fruitful [ˈfrutfəl] .... ★★★
adj. 果實累累的，多產的，富有成效的：It proved to be a fruitful meeting. 這次會議被證實很有成效。

fry [fraɪ] .... ★★★
v. 油煎／炸，炒：The eggs were frying in the pan. 雞蛋在平底鍋裏煎著。

garlic [ˈgɑrlɪk] .... ★★★
n. 大蒜：a clove of garlic 一瓣大蒜

ginger [ˈdʒɪndʒɚ] .... ★
n. 生薑
v. (與up連用) 使更有活力，使更有生氣：to ginger up a performance 使表演更加生動活潑

grain [gren] .... ★★★★
n. ①穀粒，穀物：a grain of wheat 麥粒；coarse grain 粗糧②顆粒，細粒：grains of sand 沙粒

grape [grep] .... ★★★
n. 葡萄

grapevine [ˈgrep͵vaɪn] .... ★★★
n. ①葡萄酒②傳播小道消息，傳播謠言：I heard it on the grapevine. 我是從小道消息聽到的。

grease [gris] .... ★
n. (動物) 脂肪

greasy [ˈgrizɪ] .... ★
adj. 多脂的，油脂的：a greasy hamburger 油膩的漢堡；a greasy character 滑頭的角色

ham [hæm] .... ★★★
n. 火腿

hamburger [ˈhæmbɝgɚ] .... ★★★
n. 漢堡，牛肉餅

hunger [ˈhʌngɚ] .... ★★★
v. 使挨餓，渴望
n. 饑餓，渴望：a hunger for affection 對愛的渴望

hungry [ˈhʌngrɪ] .... ★★★★
adj. 饑餓的：Lucy, are you hungry? 露西，你餓了嗎？

ice cream [ˈaɪs͵krim] .... ★★★
n. 冰淇淋：I like chocolate ice cream best. 我最愛吃巧克力冰淇淋。

jam [dʒæm] .... ★★★
n. ①阻塞：We were held for an hour in a traffic jam. 我們因為塞車耽擱了一個小時。②果醬
v. (使) 阻塞：The accident jammed the main road for two hours. 該起事故使主要道路塞了兩個小時。

jelly [ˈdʒɛlɪ] .... ★
n. 凍，果凍

juice [dʒus] .... ★★★
n. (水果) 汁，液：orange juice 柳橙汁

loaf [lof] .... ★★★
n. 一塊 (麵包)：two loaves of bread 兩條麵包

lunch [lʌntʃ] .... ★★★★
n. 午飯

luncheon [ˈlʌntʃən] .... ★
n. 午餐，午餐約會

maize [mez] .... ★★★
n. 玉米

marmalade [ˈmɑrml̩ed] .... ★
n. 橘子醬，果醬：marmalade toast 塗了橘子
　醬的土司

meal [mil] .... ★★★★
n. 膳食，一餐

meat [mit] .... ★★★★
n. （食用）肉類

melon [ˈmɛlən] .... ★★★★★
n. 甜瓜：melon cutting〔俚〕瓜分，分贓

menu [ˈmɛnju] .... ★★★
n. 菜單

milk [mɪlk] .... ★★★★
n. 乳，牛奶

mint [mɪnt] .... ★
n. 薄荷，薄荷糖，造幣廠：royal mint 英國的
　皇家造幣廠

mustard [ˈmʌstəd] .... ★
n. 芥子，芥末

mutton [ˈmʌtn̩] .... ★★★
n. 羊肉：braised mutton 紅燒羊肉

noodle [ˈnudl̩] .... ★★★
n. （常pl.）麵條，麵點

nut [nʌt] .... ★★★
n. 堅果（如胡桃等），螺帽：nut meat 堅果
　仁，核仁

onion [ˈʌnjən] .... ★★★
n. 洋蔥（頭）

palatable [ˈpælətəbl̩] .... ★
adj. 美味的

peach [pitʃ] .... ★★★
n. 桃，桃樹

pear [pɛr] .... ★★★
n. 梨子，梨樹，梨木

picnic [ˈpɪknɪk] .... ★★★
n. 野餐

pie [paɪ] .... ★★★
n. 餡餅

pig [pɪg] .... ★★★★
n. 豬

pineapple [ˈpaɪnæpl̩] .... ★★★★★
n. 鳳梨

plum [plʌm] .... ★★★★★
n. 李子，梅子

pork [pork] .... ★★★
n. 豬肉

porridge [ˈpɔrɪdʒ] .... ★★★
n. （麥片）粥

potato [pəˈteto] .... ★★★
n. 馬鈴薯

pumpkin [ˈpʌmpkɪn] .... ★
n. 南瓜

radish [ˈrædɪʃ] .... ★
n. 小蘿蔔：a bunch of radishes 一捆小蘿蔔

radium [ˈredɪəm] .... ★
n. 鐳：radium therapy 鐳放射療法

raisin [ˈrezn̩] .... ★
n. 葡萄乾

rice [raɪs] .... ★★★
n. 米，米飯

salad [ˈsæləd] .... ★★★
n. 沙拉，涼拌

salt [sɔlt] .... ★★★★
n. 鹽（類）：common salt 食鹽
v. 醃，加鹽於：Have you salted the potatoes?
　你在馬鈴薯裡放了鹽嗎？

sandwich [ˈsændwɪtʃ] .... ★
n. 三明治
v. 夾入，擠進：The kid was sandwiched in
　between two other men. 這孩子擠進了另外
　兩個男人中間。

sauce [sɔs] .... ★★★
n. 調味汁，醬料

sausage [ˋsɔsɪdʒ] .... ★★★
n. 香腸，臘腸：sausage meat 香腸用肉餡

savor [ˋsevɚ] .... ★
n. 味道：enjoying the savor of victory 享受勝
利的滋味

seasoning [ˋsizn̩ɪŋ] .... ★
n. 調味品，佐料

snack [snæk] .... ★
n. 速食，小吃

soup [sup] .... ★★★
n. 湯

spice [spaɪs] .... ★★
n. 香料，調料：Pepper is a spice. 胡椒是一種
調味料。

steak [stek] .... ★★★
n. 肉片，牛排

stew [stju] .... ★
n. 燉菜，燉肉
v. 燉，煮：You can stew fruit in water and
sugar. 你可以用水和糖燉煮水果。

sugar [ˋʃʊgɚ] .... ★★★★
n. 糖，糖塊

supper [ˋsʌpɚ] .... ★★★★
n. 晚飯
【片語】have supper 吃晚飯

sustenance [ˋsʌstənəns] .... ★★★★★
n. 生計，營養物：Inuits depend mainly on
fishing and hunting for their sustenance. 因
紐特人主要以漁獵為生。

taste [test] .... ★★★★★
n. 品味，味道，審美觀：She has good taste
in clothes. 她的服裝品味不錯。

tea [ti] .... ★★★★★
n. ①茶葉：black tea 紅茶②茶：Have a cup
of tea, please. 請用茶。

tin [tɪn] .... ★★★★
n. 錫，罐頭（尤指食品等）

tobacco [təˋbæko] .... ★★★★
n. 煙草，煙葉

tomato [təˋmeto] .... ★★★
n. 番茄

vegetable [ˋvɛdʒətəbl̩] .... ★★★★
n. 蔬菜，植物

vinegar [ˋvɪnɪgɚ] .... ★★★
n. 醋

vodka [ˋvɑdkə] .... ★
n. 伏特加

wheat [hwit] .... ★★★★
n. 小麥

wine [waɪn] .... ★★★★★
n.（葡萄）酒

zest [zɛst] .... ★
n. 濃烈的興趣，熱心：She joined in the
games with zest. 她興緻盎然地參加了比
賽。

02

衣著類相關辭彙 Vocabulary of Clothes

array [əˋre] .... ★★
n. 排列，隊形，一批，大量，裝扮：The troops were formed in battle array. 軍隊按戰鬥隊形一字排開。
v. 排列，（整）隊，裝扮：The soldiers were arrayed on the opposite hill. 士兵們被部署在對面的山頭上。

baggage [ˋbægɪdʒ] .... ★★★
n. 行李

baggy [ˋbægɪ] .... ★
adj. 寬鬆下垂的：a clown's baggy trousers 小丑穿的燈籠褲

blanket [ˋblæŋkɪt] .... ★★★
n. 毯子，覆蓋層，羊毛毯：a blanket of mist 一層霧

blouse [blauz] .... ★★★
n. 女用襯衫，童衫

boot [but] .... ★★★★
n. （長統）靴子

bracelet [ˋbreslɪt] .... ★★
n. 手鐲

brim [brɪm] .... ★
n. （杯、碗的）邊：full to the brim 滿到邊緣

button [ˋbʌtn] .... ★★★★
n. 鈕扣，按鈕：press the button 按（電）鈕
v. 扣上，扣緊：It is cold today, so button your coat. 今天很冷，扣上大衣鈕扣吧。

cap [kæp] .... ★★★★★
n. ①帽子，便帽：a service cap 軍帽②帽狀物，蓋：the cap of a pen 筆帽
v. 覆蓋於…頂端

cloak [klok] .... ★★
n. 外套，斗篷
v. 掩蓋，掩飾：The history of the family is cloaked in mystery. 這個家族的歷史被披上了一層神秘的色彩。

cloth [klɔθ] .... ★★★★
n. ①布織物，衣料：a piece of cotton cloth 一塊棉布②（一塊）抹布：Pass the cloth please; I want to clean the table. 請把抹布遞過來，我要擦桌子。

clothes [kloz] .... ★★★★★
n. 衣服

clothing [ˈkloðɪŋ] .... ★★★★

n. (總稱) 衣服，衣著：People wear clothing in cold weather. 天冷時，人們穿很多的衣服。

coat [kot] .... ★★★★★

n. ①衣，外套②表皮③層，覆蓋物：a coat of paint 一層漆

costume [ˈkɑstjum] .... ★

n. 服裝

dress [drɛs] .... ★★★★★

n. 服裝，女裝：a pretty dress 漂亮的洋裝

v. 穿衣，打扮：Dress yourself neatly. 穿整齊點！

【片語】dress up 打扮

flannel [ˈflænl̩] .... ★

n. 法蘭絨：opera flannel 淺色全毛法蘭絨

garment [ˈgɑrmənt] .... ★★

n. 衣服，服裝

girdle [ˈgɝdl̩] .... ★

n. 腰帶，帶狀物

v. 環繞：a ring of hills that girdled the city 環繞城市的群山

glove [glʌv] .... ★★★★

n. 手套

gorgeous [ˈgɔrdʒəs] .... ★

adj. 絢麗的，極好的：Tennessee possesses many caverns with gorgeous rock formations. 田納西州有許多由美麗的石頭形成的山洞。

gown [gaʊn] .... ★★

n. 長袍，禮服

guise [gaɪz] .... ★

n. 外觀，裝束

hat [hæt] .... ★★★★★

n. 帽子

jacket [ˈdʒækɪt] .... ★★★

n. 短上衣，夾克

lace [les] .... ★★

n. 花邊，帶子，鞋帶

v. 絲帶，紮帶：That area of the country is laced with large and often dangerous rivers. 該國的那地區常年被危險的大河流包圍著。

line [laɪn] .... ★★★★★

n. 線，排，行，線路，繩子

linear [ˈlɪnɪɚ] .... ★

adj. 直線的：linear arts 線條藝術

linen [ˈlɪnən] .... ★★

n. 亞麻布，亞麻布製品：Wash one's dirty linen at home. 家醜不可外揚。

liner [ˈlaɪnɚ] .... ★

n. 班船，班輪，班機，襯裏：ocean liner 遠洋班輪

lining [ˈlaɪnɪŋ] .... ★

n. 襯裏

ornament [ˈɔrnəmənt] .... ★★★

n. 裝飾品

v. 裝修：The babies ornament her ankles, which dangle from her pant legs. 孩子們圍繞在她那隨著褲腿搖晃的腳邊。

pad [pæd] .... ★★★

n. 墊，襯墊，便條本

v. 填塞：After washing the wound, the nurse began to put a clean pad of cotton over it. 護士把傷口沖洗之後，開始在上面貼了一塊乾淨的紗布墊。

peg [pɛg] .... ★

n. 衣鉤，衣夾

pocket [ˈpɑkɪt] .... ★★★★★

n. 衣袋，小袋

adj. 袖珍的，小型的：a pocket calculator 口袋型計算器

v. 把…裝入袋内：I locked the door and pocketed the key. 我鎖上門，然後把鑰匙放進了衣袋。

ribbon [ˈrɪbən] .... ★★★

n. 帶，緞帶，絲帶

robe [rob] .... ★★
n. 長袍，長衣：a bath robe 浴袍

seam [sim] .... ★
n. 縫，接縫：He searches for a lost coin in the seams of his trousers. 他在長褲接縫處找一枚遺失的錢幣。

sew [so] .... ★★★
v. 縫（紉）：His mother was sewing on this button with special strong thread. 他的母親用特別結實的線縫這個扣子。

shirt [ʃɜt] .... ★★★★
n. 襯衫

shirtsleeve [`ʃɜtˌsliv] .... ★★★★★
adj. 只穿襯衫的，隨便的
n. 襯衫袖子：He dined in shirtsleeves. 他不穿外套進餐。

silk [sɪlk] .... ★★★★
n. 絲綢：Silk Road 絲路

sleeve [sliv] .... ★★★
n. 袖子，唱片套

sock [sɑk] .... ★★★
n. 短襪：pull one's socks up （非正式用法）努力提高自己的成績

stocking [`stɑkɪŋ] .... ★★★
n. 長襪

substratum [sʌb`stretəm] .... ★
n. 襯底，基底：a substratum of rock 底層岩石

sweater [`swɛtɚ] .... ★★★
n. 毛線衣，（厚）運動衫

tailor [`telɚ] .... ★★★
n. 裁縫
v. 裁剪，縫製：The best tailor tailored her. 一流的裁縫為她縫製衣服。

textile [`tɛkstaɪl] .... ★★★
adj. 紡織的
n. 紡織品：Textiles are among the most important relics found in the ruins of ancient households. 紡織品是在古代家庭中發現存留下來的最重要的遺跡。

texture [`tɛkstʃɚ] .... ★★★
n. （織物的）組織，結構，質地，（材料等的）構造，構成，實質

textured [`tɛkstʃɚd] .... ★★★
adj. 結構的

thread [θrɛd] .... ★★★★
n. 線，線索，頭緒，思路
v. 穿線，穿過：thread one's way through 穿過（街道、人群、森林等）

tissue [`tɪʃu] .... ★★★
n. 〔生物〕組織

trousers [`traʊzɚz] .... ★★★
n. 褲子

underwear [`ʌndɚˌwɛr] .... ★
n. 內衣

veil [vel] .... ★
n. ①（婦女的）面紗，面罩②遮蓋物，蒂
v. 用面紗掩蓋，掩飾

velvet [`vɛlvɪt] .... ★★
n. 絲絨，天鵝絨
adj. 絲絨製的，柔軟的

vest [vɛst] .... ★★★
n. 背心，馬甲，汗衫，內衣：a thick, down vest 厚實的羽毛背心

wardrobe [`wɔrdˌrob] .... ★
n. 大衣櫃，立櫃

wear [wɛr] .... ★★★★★
v. 穿著，戴著，留著，蓄著：He wears a long hair. 他留一頭長髮。

wool [wʊl] .... ★★★
n. 羊毛，毛線，毛織品

woolen [`wʊlɪn] .... ★★★
adj. 羊毛的，羊毛製的，毛織的

03

居住類相關辭彙
Vocabulary of Living

accommodate [ə`kɑmə͵det] .... ★★
v. 供應，容納：Chicago's O'Hare International Airport accommodates forty-four million passengers per year. 芝加哥的歐海爾國際機場每年可以供4,400萬乘客過往。

accommodation [ə͵kɑmə`deʃən] .... ★★★
n. 住宿，膳宿：It is said that the accommodations of this hotel are limited to 600 people. 據說這家旅館最多只能提供600人住宿。

auditorium [͵ɔdə`torɪəm] .... ★
n. 大禮堂

avenue [`ævə͵nju] .... ★★★★
n. 林蔭大道，大街，途徑，手段：That is Madison Avenue. 那就是麥迪森大道。

balcony [`bælkənɪ] .... ★★★
n. 陽臺

bed [bɛd] .... ★★★★★
n. 床（位）
【片語】①go to bed 去睡覺 ②make the bed 整理床鋪

bedroom [`bɛd͵rum] .... ★★★★★
n. 臥室

bench [bɛntʃ] .... ★★★★
n. 長凳，工作臺，臺，座

broom [brum] .... ★★★
n. 掃帚

carpet [`kɑrpɪt] .... ★★★
n. 地毯

ceiling [`silɪŋ] .... ★★★
n. 天花板，平頂，雲層高度：He has a low ceiling of tolerance. 他的肚量很小。

cellar [`sɛlə] .... ★★
n. 地窖，地下室
v. 把…藏入地窖（酒窖）：The wine has been cellared for ten years. 這酒在地窖裡存了十年。

cottage [`kɑtɪdʒ] .... ★★★★
n. 農舍，小屋

Life 生活類名稱總匯

couch [kaʊtʃ] .... ★★
n. 睡椅，臥榻
v. 措辭，表達：couch their protests in diplomatic language 以外交辭令來表達他們的抗議

courtyard [ˈkortˏjɑrd] .... ★★★
n. 庭院，院子

crib [krɪb] .... ★
n. 有欄杆的兒童小床

curtain [ˈkɝtn] .... ★★★★
n. 窗簾，門簾，幕（布）

door [dor] .... ★★★★★
n. 門

doorway [ˈdorˏwe] .... ★★★★★
n. 門，門道

dormitory [ˈdɔrməˏtorɪ] .... ★★★
n. 宿舍

dwell [dwɛl] .... ★★
v. 居住：Rotifers are microorganism that dwell in quiet waters and live on algae. 輪蟲是生長在平靜的水中並以海藻為食的微生物。

dwelling [ˈdwɛlɪŋ] .... ★★
n. 住所

embellish [ɪmˈbɛlɪʃ] .... ★
v. 裝飾，修飾：Just tell the truth and don't embellish the story by any means. 〔喻〕你只要說實話，千萬不要加油添醋。

floor [flor] .... ★★★★★
n. 地板，（樓房的）層

furniture [ˈfɝnɪtʃɚ] .... ★★★★
n. 傢俱

garnish [ˈgɑrnɪʃ] .... ★
v. 加裝飾：The turkey was served with a garnish of parsley. 這火雞上面配上了芹菜做點綴。

hedge [hɛdʒ] .... ★★★
n. 籬笆

home [hom] .... ★★★★★
n. 家，家鄉，本國
adv. 在家：Everything goes well at home, but everything goes hard out. 在家千般好，出門萬事難。
【片語】①at home 在家，在國內 ②go home 回家

house [haʊs] .... ★★★★★
n. 住宅，房子

housewife [ˈhaʊsˏwaɪf] .... ★★★★★
n. 家庭主婦

hut [hʌt] .... ★★★★
n. 小屋，棚屋
v. （使）住進小屋

inhabit [ɪnˈhæbɪt] .... ★★★
v. 居住於，棲息於：Anthropologists believe that in the sixteenth century a few thousand Inuits inhabited northern Canada. 人類學家相信，在16世紀有幾千位因紐特人居住在加拿大北部。

inhabitant [ɪnˈhæbətənt] .... ★★★★★
v. 居民，住戶：San Francisco's Chinese community, comprising 67,000 inhabitants, is the largest concentration of Chinese outside of Asia. 舊金山的華人區共有67,000名居民，是亞洲以外最大的華人聚居區。

kitchen [ˈkɪtʃɪn] .... ★★★★★
n. 廚房

lavatory [ˈlævəˏtorɪ] .... ★★★
n. 盥洗室，廁所

lobby [ˈlɑbɪ] .... ★★★
n. 前廳，（會議）休息廳

lodge [lɑdʒ] .... ★★★★
v. 住宿，投宿：If a foreign object becomes lodged in the eye, medical help is necessary. 如果有異物進入到眼睛裏，就需要找醫生處理。

lodging [ˈlɑdʒɪŋ] .... ★★
n. 寄宿，住所，住宿：Youth hostels provide inexpensive lodging for young people throughout the US and other countries. 在美國和其他國家的青年旅館為青年提供便宜的住宿。

lounge [laʊndʒ] .... ★★
n. 休息室，客廳

mansion [ˈmænʃən] .... ★★
n. 大廈，大樓，宅第，官邸

mistletoe [ˈmɪsḷˌto] .... ★
n. 槲寄生（西方用作耶誕節的裝飾物）

pane [pen] .... ★
n. 窗格玻璃，方框

paper [ˈpepɚ] .... ★★
n. ①紙：a blank sheet of paper 一張白紙 ② 報紙：today's paper 今天的報紙

patio [ˈpɑtɪˌo] .... ★
n. 院子，天井：coffee drying patio 咖啡豆曬場

perch [pɝtʃ] .... ★★
n. 棲木，棲息處
v. 棲息，停歇：The child perched the glass on the edge of the counter. 這孩子把玻璃放在櫃檯的邊緣。

pillow [ˈpɪlo] .... ★★★
n. 枕頭

porch [portʃ] .... ★★
n. 門廊

primer [ˈprɪmɚ] .... ★★★★
n. 入門

pub [pʌb] .... ★★★
n. 小酒店，小旅館

quilt [kwɪlt] .... ★★★★
n. 被子

辨析 Analyze

accommodate, inhabit, lodge, reside

1　**accommodate** *vt.*「為…提供住宿，容納，使適應，順應」，意為「為…提供住宿」時基本可與lodge互換；而accommodate...to...則意為「使適應，順應」：We were accommodated/lodged in a small room on the third floor. 我們被安排住在三樓的一個小房間裡。

2　**inhabit** *vt.*「居住於，（動物）棲居於」，其衍生的名詞有 inhabitant（居民，住戶）：No one has inhabited that island for over 100 years. 那個島已經有100多年沒人居住了。

3　**lodge** *vt. & vi.*「暫住，借宿，供…臨時住宿」，可當不及物動詞，當及物動詞時，基本可與accommodate互換：The travelers lodge in motels every night. 這些旅行者晚上都住在汽車旅館。

4　**reside** *vi.*「居住，定居」，可指臨時住宿，相當於lodge；也可指長期居住，相當於live；其衍生的名詞有resident（居民，定居者）和residence（住處，住宅）；片語reside in意為「（性質）在於」，相當於lie in：Jim resided/lodged at the Grand Hyatt Hotel. 吉姆住在君悅大飯店。

生活類名稱總匯

Life

reside [rɪˋzaɪd] .... ★★

v. 居住：A number of the Mikasuki Indians still reside on their reservation in northern Florida. 有一部分米加蘇基印第安人仍然居住在佛羅里達州北部，那是他們祖先保留下來的地方。

residence [ˋrɛzədəns] .... ★★★★

n. 住處，住宅：a residence in the country 在鄉間的住處

resident [ˋrɛzədənt] .... ★★★★

adj. 居住的，常駐的

n. 居民：Many residents of the apartment complain objection to noisy neighbors. 該棟公寓住宅的許多居民都不喜歡吵鬧的鄰居。

residential [ˏrɛzəˋdɛnʃəl] .... ★★★★

adj. 居住的：Their residential building is located next to the park. 他們的住宅大樓座落於公園旁。

roof [ruf] .... ★★★★★

n. 屋頂，車頂，房頂

room [rum] .... ★★★★★

n. ①房間，室，空間，地方：There is only standing room in the bus. 公共汽車上只剩站位了。②餘地：There is no room for doubt. 沒有懷疑的餘地。

scarf [skɑrf] .... ★

n. 圍巾，頭巾

shack [ʃæk] .... ★

n. 小木屋，小室

sheet [ʃit] .... ★★★★★

n. ①被單：a soft bed with clean sheets 鋪著乾淨床單的軟床②（一）張，（一）片，薄片：a sheet of glass 一片玻璃

sill [sɪl] .... ★

n. 門檻，窗臺

terrace [ˋtɛrəs] .... ★★

n. 平臺，臺階，陽臺

threshold [ˋθrɛʃhold] .... ★★

n. 開端，開始，入門，門檻，產生效果或造成影響的下限：The sound was so loud that it was on the threshold of pain. 聲音大得開始讓人受不了。

villa [ˋvɪlə] ....★

n. 別墅

village [ˋvɪlɪdʒ] .... ★★★★★

n. 村，村莊

wall [wɔl] .... ★★★★★

n. 牆壁：We built a wooden wall around our garden. 我們在花園周圍蓋了木牆。
【片語】the Great Wall 長城

window [ˋwɪndo] .... ★★★★★

n. 窗，視窗

04

綜合相關辭彙

Vocabulary of Synthesis

birthday [ˈbɝθˌde] .... ★★★
n. 生日：Do you often get presents on your birthday?
你過生日時常收到禮物嗎？
【片語】①Happy birthday to you! 生日快樂！②hold a
birthday party 舉行生日派對

blond [blɑnd] .... ★
n. 金髮碧眼的人
adj. 金髮碧眼的

café [kəˈfe] .... ★★★
n. 咖啡館，小餐廳

camera [ˈkæmərə] .... ★★★★
n. 照相機

candle [ˈkændl̩] .... ★★★★
n. 蠟燭

cane [ken] .... ★★
n. 手杖，（藤、竹的）莖
v. 鞭笞，鞭打：English schoolmasters used to cane
the boys as a punishment. 英國的小學老師過去常用
鞭打男學生作為懲罰。

canvas [ˈkænvəs] .... ★★
n. 帆布，帆布油畫

chore [tʃor] .... ★
n.(pl.)家庭雜務

cob [kɑb] .... ★
n. 圓塊

comb [kom] .... ★★★
n. 梳子
v. 梳理：She is combing her hair. 她正在梳頭。

cup [kʌp] .... ★★★★★
n. ①杯子②（一）杯（的容量）③獎盃：a prize cup
獎盃

cupboard [ˈkʌbəd] .... ★★★
n. 碗櫃，小櫥

cushion [ˈkuʃən] .... ★★★
n. 墊層：an air cushion 氣墊
v. 緩解：Nothing can cushion the blow. 沒有什麼能減
輕打擊。

Life 生活類名稱總匯

drawer [ˋdrɔɚ] .... ★★★
n. 抽屜

fence [fɛns] .... ★★
n. 柵欄，圍欄，籬笆

fork [fɔrk] .... ★★★
n. ①餐叉：a knife and fork 一副刀叉②耙：
A fork is a gardening tool. 耙是一種園藝工
具。③分叉，岔路口：a fork in the road 路
的分岔口

garbage [ˋgɑrbɪdʒ] .... ★★★
n. 廢料，垃圾，餿水：garbage collection 收
集垃圾

glass [glæs] .... ★★★★★
n. ①玻璃：Glass breaks easily. 玻璃易碎。②
玻璃杯：He fills the glasses with beer. 他在
玻璃杯裡裝滿了啤酒。③鏡子，眼鏡：Is it
true that the glasses are helpful to eyes? 眼
鏡真的對眼睛有益嗎？

jug [dʒʌg] .... ★
n. 帶柄水罐，大壺：a jug of water 一壺水

kettle [ˋkɛtl̩] .... ★
n. 水壺

kiosk [kɪˋɑsk] .... ★★★★★
n. 小亭

knife [naɪf] .... ★★★
n. 刀，餐刀

knob [nɑb] .... ★★★
n. 旋鈕，門把，拉手，把手：This machine
has lots of knobs on it. Which one starts it?
這機器上有許多旋鈕，哪一個是開關？

ladder [ˋlædɚ] .... ★★★
n. 梯子

latch [lætʃ] .... ★
n. 門閂：The door is on the latch. 門上著閂。
vt. 用門閂將門關上：The door won't latch
properly. 這門關不緊。

laundry [ˋlɔndrɪ] .... ★★★
n. 洗衣房，待洗衣物，所洗衣物：laundry
resistant 耐水洗的

ledge [lɛdʒ] .... ★★★★★
n. 壁架，突出物，暗礁：a window ledge 窗臺

lid [lɪd] .... ★★★
n. 蓋，蓋子：the lid of a pot 壺蓋

litter [ˋlɪtɚ] .... ★
n. 四處亂丟的東西，廢物，廢紙
v. 亂扔，亂丟：Selfish picnickers litter the
beach with food wrappers. 自私的野餐者在
海灘亂扔包裝紙，使海灘雜亂不堪。

luggage [ˋlʌgɪdʒ] .... ★★★
n. 行李

mattress [ˋmætrɪs] .... ★
n. 床墊

mirror [ˋmɪrɚ] .... ★★
n. 鏡
v. 反照，反射：Do these opinions mirror what
people are thinking? 這些觀點能反映人們所
想的嗎？

napkin [ˋnæpkɪn] .... ★
n. 餐巾（紙）：paper napkin 餐巾紙

needle [ˋnidl̩] .... ★★★
n. 針，針狀物，指針，磁針：She used a
needle to sew the button onto the shirt. 她
用針把扣子縫到襯衫上。

offal [ˋɔfl̩] .... ★
n. 垃圾，廢物：inedible offal 非食用內臟

overshoe [ˋovɚˏʃu] .... ★★★★
n. 套鞋，膠鞋

palace [ˋpælɪs] .... ★★★★★
n. 宮殿：Buckingham Palace 英國白金漢宮

pan [pæn] .... ★★★★
n. 平底鍋，盤子

pantry [ˋpæntrɪ] .... ★★★★
n. 食品櫃，餐具室

park [pɑrk] .... ★★★★★
n. 公園

plate [plet] .... ★★★★
n. 盤子，盆子

211

pond [pɑnd] .... ★★★
n. 池塘

pool [pul] .... ★★★★
n. 水池，水潭

pot [pɑt] .... ★★★
n. 罐，壺：a clay pot 陶罐

razor [ˈrezɚ] .... ★★★★★
n. 剃刀：on a razor edge 處於險境

rubbish [ˈrʌbɪʃ] .... ★★★
n. 垃圾

rug [rʌg] .... ★★★
n. 小地毯，毛毯

rustic [ˈrʌstɪk] .... ★★★
adj. 鄉村的，粗糙的：rustic gloves and boots 結實的手套和靴子

saddle [ˈsædl̩] .... ★★★★
v. 使…負擔：He saddled his parents with debts. 他讓父母背上了債務。

sandal [ˈsændl̩] .... ★★★★★
n. 涼鞋，便鞋：straw sandals 草鞋

sewage [ˈsjuɪdʒ] .... ★★★
n. 污水，污物：sewage purification 污水淨化

sewer [ˈsuɚ] .... ★★★
n. 陰溝，下水道：sewer gas 陰溝氣味

soap [sop] .... ★★★
n. 肥皂：a bar of soap 一條肥皂

spade [sped] .... ★★★
n. 鐵鍬，鏟子

spoon [spun] .... ★★★
n. 湯匙

stair [stɛr] .... ★★★★★
n. 樓梯

stitch [stɪtʃ] .... ★
n. 一針，針腳
v. 縫：to stitch a button onto a shirt 把紐扣縫在襯衫上

stool [stul] .... ★★
n. 凳子

stove [stov] .... ★★★
n. 爐子，火爐

suitcase [ˈsutˌkes] .... ★★★
n. 小提箱，小型行李箱

table [ˈtebl̩] .... ★★★★★
n. 桌子，餐桌

television (TV) [ˈtɛləˌvɪʒən] .... ★★★★★
n. 電視

tent [tɛnt] .... ★★★★
n. 帳篷

辨析 Analyze

dish, plate, tray

1 **dish** *n.* 「碟子，盤子」，指（小）碟子，還指一道菜：Clear the table and wash the dishes. 去擦桌子，洗餐具。

2 **plate** *n.* 「盤子」，指（大）盤子，還指金屬牌、平板、地球的板塊等：Our food is served on plates. 我們的食物是裝在盤子裡端上來的。

3 **tray** *n.* 「托盤」，指用來遞送碟子、盤子的托盤：The waiters carry the dishes on trays. 服務生用托盤端菜。

toilet [ˈtɔɪlɪt] .... ★★★
n. 廁所，盥洗室

torch [tɔrtʃ] .... ★★★
n. 火把，火炬，手電筒

trash [træʃ] .... ★★★
n. 垃圾

tray [tre] .... ★★★
n. 盤，托盤，碟：The waitress brought drinks
on a tray. 女服務生用盤子端來了飲料。

trolley [ˈtrɑlɪ] .... ★
n. 手推車，小車，無軌電車

umbrella [ʌmˈbrɛlə] .... ★★★
n. ①傘，雨傘，陽傘②庇護，保護傘

upstairs [ˈʌpˈstɛrz] .... ★★★★
adv. 在樓上，往樓上：Upstairs there were
three little bedrooms. 樓上有3間小臥室。
adj. 樓上的：Neighbors watched from their
upstairs windows. 鄰居們從他們樓上的窗
戶觀看。

utensil [juˈtɛnsl̩] ....★
n. 炊具，用具，器皿：cooking utensils 烹飪
用具

vase [ves] .... ★★★
n. 瓶子，花瓶

vault [vɔlt] .... ★★
n. 拱形圓屋頂，地窖
v. 跳躍：He vaulted into a position of wealth.
他一夕致富。

video [ˈvɪdɪˌo] .... ★★★★★
n. 錄影機
adj. 錄影的：a video channel 電視頻道

videophone [ˈvɪdɪofon] .... ★★★★★
n. 電視電話

videotape [ˈvɪdɪoˌtep] .... ★★★★★
n. 錄影磁帶

wallet [ˈwɑlɪt] .... ★★★
n. 皮夾，錢包

yard [jɑrd] .... ★★★★★
n. ①（英美長度單位）碼（=3英尺）②院子，場
地：a farm yard 農家院子

Unit 10
時空類名稱總匯
Time & Space

01

時間相關辭彙

Vocabulary of Time

(1)日、週、月、季、年相關辭彙

A.M./a.m. .... ★★★★★
adv. 上午，中午之前：catch the 8 a.m. train from Vancouver 搭早上八點從溫哥華來的那班列車

afternoon [ˈæftɚˈnun] .... ★★★★★
n. 下午
【片語】in the afternoon 在下午

anniversary [ˌænəˈvɝsərɪ] .... ★★★
n. 週年，週年紀念（日）

annual [ˈænjʊəl] .... ★★★★★
adj. 週年的，一年年的，每年的，年度的：The company issues an annual report every March. 這家公司每年三月發佈年度報告。

annually [ˈænjʊəlɪ] .... ★★
adv. 每年地：The Springarn Medal is awarded annually for achievement in the fields of arts, sciences, government, and entertainment. Springarn 獎章每年獎勵藝術、科學、管理和娛樂領域的成就。

April [ˈeprəl] .... ★★★★★
n. 四月

August [ˈɔgəst] .... ★★★★★
n. 八月

autumn [ˈɔtəm] .... ★★★★
n. 秋

daily [ˈdelɪ] .... ★★★★★
adj. 每日的：He gets a daily wage. 他拿日薪。
adv. 每日：She goes there twice daily. 她每天去兩次。
n. 日報：America Daily《美國日報》

dawn [dɔn] .... ★★★★
n. ①黎明，拂曉：Roosters crow at dawn. 公雞在黎明啼叫。②開始：The war ended and we looked forward to the dawn of happier days. 戰爭結束了，我們盼望著幸福日子的來臨。

v. ①破曉：The day was just dawning. 天才剛亮。②開始發展，出現：It has just dawned upon me that there is another solution. 我剛剛想到還有另一種解決辦法。

day [de] .... ★★★★★
n. ①白晝，白天：We work during the day and sleep during the night. 我們白天工作，晚上睡覺。② (一) 天：I will see my aunt in a few days time. 過幾天我就能見到我嬸嬸了。
【片語】① in the old days 從前② the other day 前幾天，有一天③ the day after tomorrow 後天

daylight [ˋdeˌlaɪt] .... ★★★
n. 日光，白晝

daytime [ˋdeˌtaɪm] .... ★★★
n. 白天，日間

December [dɪˋsɛmbɚ] .... ★★★★★
n. 十二月

evening [ˋivnɪŋ] .... ★★★★
n. 傍晚，晚上【片語】in the evening 傍晚

February [ˋfɛbruˌɛrɪ] .... ★★★★★
n. 二月

Friday [ˋfraɪˌde] .... ★★★★★
n. 星期五

hour [aʊr] .... ★★★★★
n. 小時

January [ˋdʒænjuˌɛrɪ] .... ★★★★★
n. 一月

July [dʒuˋlaɪ] .... ★★★★★
n. 七月

May [me] .... ★★★★★
n. 五月

midday [ˋmɪdˌde] .... ★★★
n. 正／中午

midnight [ˋmɪdˌnaɪt] .... ★★★★
n. 午夜：It rained at midnight. 半夜下雨了。

minute [ˋmɪnɪt] .... ★★★★★
adj. 微小的：Living things consist of minute structures called cells. 構成生物的微小結構體叫做細胞。

Monday [ˋmʌnde] .... ★★★★★
n. 星期一

month [mʌnθ] .... ★★★★★
n. 月份

morning [ˋmɔrnɪŋ] .... ★★★★★
n. 早晨，早上：Good morning! 早安！

night [naɪt] .... ★★★★★
n. 夜，夜間，黑夜

nocturnal [nɑkˋtɝnl̩] .... ★
adj. 夜間的：nocturnal habits 熬夜的習慣

November [noˋvɛmbɚ] .... ★★★★★
n. 十一月

October [ɑkˋtobɚ] .... ★★★★★
n. 十月

o'clock [əˋklɑk] .... ★★★★★
adv. …點鐘：I had breakfast at seven o'clock this morning. 我今天早上七點吃早餐。

Saturday [ˋzætɚde] .... ★★★★★
n. 星期六

season [ˋsizn̩] .... ★★★★★
n. 季，季節，時間

September [sɛpˋtɛmbɚ] .... ★★★★★
n. 九月

spring [sprɪŋ] .... ★★★★★
n. 泉水
v. 跳躍，出現，發生：A group of American colonists calling themselves the Sons of Liberty spring up in protest against the *Stamp Act* of 1765. 在1765年，出現了一群自稱為自由之子的美國殖民者抗議《印花法》。

summer [ˋsʌmɚ] .... ★★★★★
n. 夏天，夏季

Time & Space

Sunday [ˈsʌnde] .... ★★★★★
n. 星期日

Thursday [ˈθɝzde] .... ★★★
n. 星期四

time [taɪm] .... ★★★★★
n. ①時間，時候，時刻：What's the time? 幾
點了？②時間，光陰：Time waits no man.
歲月不留人。③時期，時代：Times are
getting worse. 時機愈來愈糟。④（一）次／
回：I've been to London one time. 我去過
倫敦一次。
【片語】① all the time 一直，不斷地，始終②
in time 及時，適時③ on time 準時

timetable [ˈtaɪmˌtebl̩] .... ★★★★★
n. 時間表，時刻表，課程表

today [təˈde] .... ★★★★★
n. ①今天：Today is Friday. 今天星期五。②
現在，當前：Young people of today have
many interests. 現代年輕人有很多的興趣。

tomorrow [təˈmɔro] .... ★★★
n. 明天：She'll be in plane this time tomorrow.
她明天這個時候就在飛機上了。
【片語】Tomorrow comes never.〔諺〕明日不
再來。

Tuesday [ˈtjuzde] .... ★★★★★
n. 星期二

Wednesday [ˈwɛnzde] .... ★★★
n. 星期三

week [wik] .... ★★★★★
n. 一週，星期

weekend [ˈwikˈɛnd] .... ★★★
n. 週末

weekly [ˈwiklɪ] .... ★★★★★
adj. 每週的，一週一次的：weekly visits 每週
的訪問
adv. 一週一次地：The magazine is issued
weekly. 這種雜誌每週一期。
n. 週報

winter [ˈwɪntɚ] .... ★★★★★
n. 冬天，冬季

year [jɪr] .... ★★★★★
n. 年，年份

yesterday [ˈjɛstɚde] .... ★★★★★
n. 昨天

(2)過去、現在、將來相關辭彙

current [ˈkɝənt] .... ★★★★★
adj. 現今的：current English 當代英語；
current money 通用的貨幣

elapse [ɪˈlæps] .... ★★
v. （時間）消逝：Five months have elapsed
since he joined the army. 自從他當了兵以
後，已經五個月過去了。

future [ˈfjutʃɚ] .... ★★★★
n. 將來，未來：All will be well in future. 以後
什麼都會好的。

later [ˈletɚ] .... ★★★★★
adv. ①後來：Later on we realized she had
gone. 後來我們發現她已走了。②過一會
兒：I'll call you later. 我等一下再打給你。

medieval [ˌmidɪˈivəl] .... ★
adj. 中世紀的，古老的：parents with a
medieval attitude toward dating 父母對於
約會的保守態度

modern [ˈmɑdɚn] .... ★★★★★
adj. 現代的，新式的：What do you think of
modern art? 你怎麼看現代藝術？

noon [nun] .... ★★★★
n. 中午，正午：What are you doing at noon
yesterday? 昨天中午你在幹什麼？
【片語】at noon 在中午

nowadays [ˈnaʊəˌdez] .... ★★★
adv. （常用於與過去相比）現今，如今：
Nowadays we mostly watch TV. 現今我們
主要是看電視。

obsolescent [ˌɑbsəˈlɛsn̩t] .... ★

adj. 即將過時的：Traditional handicraft techniques are being steadily improved and some obsolescent equipment are obsoleting. 傳統的手工藝技術不斷革新，一些過時的設備也在淘汰。

due [dju] .... ★★★★

adj. 到期的：The loan is due this month. 貸款這個月到期。

permanence [ˈpɝmənəns] .... ★★★★

n. 永久（性），持久（性）：permanence of color 保色性，permanence of ink 墨水的持久性

permanent [ˈpɝmənənt] .... ★★★

adj. 永久的：a permanent address 永久地址；permanent secretary to the president 總統的永久秘書

perpetuate [pɚˈpɛtʃʊˌet] .... ★★★★★

v. 使⋯永恆，使⋯延續：The new library will perpetuate its founder's great love of learning. 這座新圖書館將紀念其創建人對學習的熱愛。

span [spæn] .... ★★★

n. 短時間，一段時間，全長，跨度，跨距：a bridge that spans the gorge 橫跨峽谷的橋樑；a career that spanned 40 years 持續四十年的事業

terminal [ˈtɝmən̩] .... ★★★

n. 終端，終點（站），中轉油庫，總站，電腦終端

adj. 終端的，學期的：a terminal exam 期末考

(3)不定時間相關辭彙

age [edʒ] .... ★★★★★

v. 老化：His face hadn't aged even though he was over fifty. 他雖然已年過五十，但臉上並不顯老。

aged [ˈedʒɪd] .... ★★★★★

adj. 陳年的，老年的：an aged, worn-out carpet 破舊的地毯

ago [əˈgo] .... ★★★★★

adv. 以前：She died two years ago. 她兩年前死了。

【片語】① long ago 很久以前② a moment ago 剛才

ancient [ˈenʃənt] .... ★★★★★

adj. 古代的，古老的：There are many sorts of ancient legends concerned with how life began on Earth. 關於地球上生命的起源有各種各樣古老的傳說。

antiquity [ænˈtɪkwətɪ] .... ★★★

n. 古代：in remote Greek antiquity 在遙遠的古希臘

archaic [ɑrˈkeɪk] .... ★★

adj. 古老的："Proven" is the archaic form of the past participle of "prove" and should not be used. 「proven」是「prove」一詞過去分詞的古舊形式，不該被使用。

B.C./BC .... ★★★★

adv. 西元前

calendar [ˈkæləndɚ] .... ★★★★★

n. 日曆，月曆：Their five-year-old son is able to use the calendar to count how many days it is to his birthday. 他們五歲的兒子能用日曆算出還有多少天到他的生日。

clock [klɑk] .... ★★★★★

n. 鐘

clockwise [ˈklɑkˌwaɪz] .... ★

adv. 順時針方向地

adj. 順時針方向的：counter clockwise 逆時針（轉）的；full clockwise 順時針轉滿一圈的

contemporary [kənˈtɛmpəˌrɛrɪ] ..... ★★★★

adj. 當代的，同時代的：contemporary furniture 當代傢俱

n. 同代人，同輩：He and I were contemporaries at school. 他和我是同期同學。

date [det] .... ★★★★★
n. 日期，年代：Date of birth：20 November, 1987 出生日期：1987年11月20日

dated [ˋdetɪd] .... ★★★★★
adj. 有年紀的，陳舊的

duration [djuˋreʃən] .... ★★★
n. 期間，持久，持續時間：The duration of one cycle of a circadian rhythm is approximately twenty four hours. 生理節奏的一個循環期大約是24小時。

during [ˋdjurɪŋ] .... ★★★★★
prep. 在…期間：He says that he wants Mr. Wang to give Tom some work to do during the holiday. 他說他想要王先生在假日時給湯姆一些工作。

early [ˋɝlɪ] .... ★★★★★
adv. 早的，初期：This winter snow came earlier than usual. 今年冬雪比往年早。
adj. 早的，早期的，及早的：You are early today. 你今天真早。

epoch [ˋɛpək] .... ★
n. 紀元，時代

era [ˋɪrə] .... ★★★★
n. 時代，紀元

eternal [ɪˋtɝnl] .... ★★
adj. 永恆的：Eternal life to the revolutionary martyrs! 革命先烈永垂不朽！

eternity [ɪˋtɝnətɪ] .... ★★
n. 永恆：to wait in the dentist's office for an eternity 在牙醫診所裡等待永恆

everlasting [ɛvɚˋlæstɪŋ] .... ★★
adj. 永久的：everlasting friendship 永恆的友誼

former [ˋfɔmɚ] .... ★★★★★
adj. 以前的：a former ambassador 前任大使

formerly [ˋfɔrmɚlɪ] .... ★★
adv. 從前，以前：Formerly, in the United States, many nurses worked as private duty nurse rather than in hospitals. 以前在美國有許多護士從事私人護理，不是在醫院裡工作。

hitherto [hɪðɚˋtu] .... ★★
adj. 迄今：The weather, which had hitherto been sunny and mild, suddenly turned cold. 迄今一直晴朗溫暖的天氣突然變冷了。

instant [ˋɪnstənt] .... ★★★★★
n. 瞬間，時刻：She paused an instant in the doorway. 她在通道裡停了片刻。
adj. ①立即的，即刻的：The novel was an instant importance. 這部小說一舉成名。②緊急的，急迫的：a matter of instant important 緊急的事情③（食品）即溶的，方便的：instant coffee 即溶咖啡

instantaneous [ɪnstənˋtenɪəs] .... ★
adj. 瞬間的，即刻的：an instantaneous reply to my letter 對我的信件即刻回覆

juncture [ˋdʒʌŋktʃɚ] .... ★
n. 時刻，結合點：At this juncture in our nation's affairs, we need solidarity. 國家事務在這種關鍵時刻，我們需要團結。

late [let] .... ★★★★★
adj. 遲的，晚的，晚期的：Juliet was late for class the day before yesterday. 茱麗葉前天上學遲到了。
【片語】be late for... 遲了，晚了
adv. 遲，晚：We always go to bed late on Saturday night. 星期六晚上我們總是很晚才睡。

lately [ˋletlɪ] .... ★★★★
adv. 最近：It is only/just lately that I got a copy of the novel. 最近我才拿到這一本小說。

meanwhile [ˋminʌhwaɪl] .... ★★★★
adv. 與此同時：She is cutting the grass; meanwhile her husband is planting roses. 她在修草皮，而她丈夫正在種玫瑰。

n. 其間，其時

moment [ˈmomənt] .... ★★★★★
n. 瞬間，片刻，時刻：There is not a moment to be late. 刻不容緩。
【片語】① the moment (that) 一…就② just a moment 等一會兒

momentary [ˈmomənˌtɛrɪ] .... ★
adj. 那間的，頃刻的，短暫的：He was momentarily unable to speak with excitement. 他激動得一時說不出話來了。

occasional [əˈkeʒənḷ] .... ★★★★
adv. 偶然的，臨時的：He took an occasional glass of wine. 他偶爾喝杯酒。

occasionally [əˈkeʒənḷɪ] .... ★★★★
adv. 偶然地：Occasionally, unusual creatures are washed to the shore, but they are rarely caught out at sea. 一些奇特的生物偶然被沖到岸上來，卻很少在海上被捕捉到。

often [ˈɔfən] .... ★★★★★
adv. 經常，常常：How often does the bus run? 公車多久一班？

periodic [ˌpɪrɪˈɑdɪk] .... ★
adj. 週期的：a periodic fit of cleaning up one's desk 不時地清理桌子

periodical [ˌpɪrɪˈɑdɪkḷ] .... ★★
n. 期刊，雜誌：acdamic periodical 學術期刊

periodicity [ˌpɪrɪəˈdɪsətɪ] .... ★★
n. 週期性，週期數：the periodicity of economic crises 經濟危機的週期

perpetually [pɚˈpɛtʃʊəlɪ] .... ★★
adv. 永遠地，不斷地，持久地：Throughout most of their lives, human beings perpetually learn and increase their mental capacities. 人類在一生當中，通常會不斷學習來增加其腦容量。

phase [fez] .... ★★★★
n. 階段

prehistoric [ˌprihɪsˈtɔrɪk] .... ★
adj. 史前的，遠古的：Fertile soil deposited by prehistoric glaciers is found in all parts of Ohio except the southeast. 人們在俄亥俄州（除東南部以外）的所有地區都發現了史前冰河所沉積的肥沃土壤。

previously [ˈpriviəslɪ] .... ★★★★
adv. 以前，從前：In 1975 the United States Army began to assign women to positions previously classified as having combat status. 在1975年，美國軍隊開始把女兵安排到以前被劃分為具有作戰性質的職位上來。

recent [ˈrisn̩t] .... ★★★★★
adj. 最近的：The American sold some arms to the Taiwanese according to a recent newspaper. 根據最近的消息，美國人將一些武器賣給了臺灣人。

recently [ˈrisn̩tlɪ] .... ★★★★★
ad. 最近地：The company has recently acquired a new office building in central Boston. 這家公司最近在波士頓市中心買了一幢新的辦公大樓。

simultaneity [ˌsaɪmḷtəˈnɪətɪ] .... ★★★★★
n. 同時性，同時發生或存在

simultaneous [ˌsaɪmḷˈteniəs] ..... ★★★★★
adj. 同時的，同時發生的：The two simultaneous shots sounded like one. 同時發出的兩聲槍響聽起來像一聲。

simultaneously [saɪməlˈteniəslɪ] ★★★★★
adv. 同時地：Glass-fiber cables can carry hundreds of telephone conversations simultaneously. 玻璃光纖電纜能夠讓數百通電話同時通話。

since [sɪns] .... ★★★★★
prep. 自從，從…以來：Since seeing you I have had good news. 自從遇見了你，我就有了好消息。

conj. ①從…以來，自從：How have you been since I saw you last time? 自上次見面以來，你還好嗎？②因為，既然：Since this way doesn't work, let's try another. 既然這樣行不通，我們就換種方法吧。

adv. 後來，自那以後：We have become friends since. 後來我們成朋友了。

soon [sun] .... ★★★★★
adv. 不久，即刻，早，快：You will soon be better. 你不久就會好轉的。
【片語】① as soon as 一…就…② sooner or later 遲早

sporadic [spəˈrædɪk] .... ★
adj. 零星的：a sporadic example 偶發的例子

stage [stedʒ] .... ★★★★★
n. ①階段，時期：Just now he is in the enthusiastic stage. 目前他正處於狂熱階段。
②舞臺，戲劇：When we got to the light again, it was like walking on to stage of a theater. 當我們再走到光亮處，就像踏在一個戲院的舞臺上。
【片語】(go) on the stage 當演員

subsequently [ˈsʌbsɪˌkwɛntlɪ] .... ★★
adv. 隨後；後來：Vice-President Lyndon Johnson became President of the United States following the death of John F. Kennedy and was subsequently elected to a full term in 1964. 副總統頓杜·詹森在甘迺迪總統遇刺後成為總統，並且隨後在1964年當選為總統。

temporal [ˈtɛmpərəl] .... ★★★★
adj. 一時的，暫時的：our temporal existence 我們短暫的存在

temporary [ˈtɛmpəˌrɛrɪ] .... ★★★★
adj. 臨時的：temporary employment 臨時工作

transient [ˈtrænʃənt] .... ★
adj. 短暫的，過路的：the transient beauty of youth 短暫的青春年華

transitory [ˈtrænsəˌtorɪ] .... ★
adj. 短暫的

unbounded [ʌnˈbaʊndɪd] .... ★★★★★
adj. 無限的：unbounded enthusiasm 狂放不羈的熱情

辨析 Analyze

phase, stage

1 **phase** *n.*「階段，時期，面，方面」，指發展或成長中的一個階段、時期，時間相對較長，介詞用in：His illness was discovered in an early phase. 他的病是在早期發現的。

2 **stage** *n.*「階段，時期，舞臺」，指發展或成長中的一個特定時刻或狀態，時間相對較短，介詞用at或in，也指一段路程：The baby has reached the talking stage. 這個嬰兒到了說話的階段。

02

空間相關辭彙

Vocabulary of Space

(1)空間相關辭彙

here [hɪr] .... ★★★★★
adv. ①這裡，在這裡：Can we put our coats here? 我
們把大衣放到這兒可以嗎？②從這裡，到這裡：
Here comes the bus. 汽車來了。
【片語】here and there 到處，處處

scope [skop] .... ★★★★
n. 範圍，餘地：What is the scope of your undertaking?
你的工作範圍是什麼？

space [spes] .... ★★★★★
n. ①空地，場地：time and space 時空②空間，太空：
Nowdays, space is no longer an unknown field. 如
今，太空已不再是一個未知的領域了。③篇幅：
His composition has occupied so much space that
there is no enough left. 他的作文占去了很大篇幅，
以致沒多少地方可寫字。④間隔，距離：Written
communication across the intervening space was
accomplished. 跨地域的書面往來已經完成。
v. 把…分隔開：Houses spaced as irregular as pins on
a map have been built up. 宛如在地圖上插針般、佈
局毫無規劃的房屋已經蓋好了。

(2)地方、中間、旁邊相關辭彙

amid(st) [əˋmɪd(st)] .... ★★★★
prep. 在…當中：move among the guests amidst easy
laughter and animated gestures 帶著輕鬆的笑
聲，並做著熱烈的手勢在來客當中周旋

among(st) [əˋmʌŋ(st)] .... ★★★★
prep. 在…之中，在中間：The building stands among
trees. 大樓聳立在樹叢中。

apart [əˋpɑrt] .... ★★★★
adv. ①相間隔：The two restaurants are three miles
apart. 這兩家餐廳相隔3英里。②分離，分開：I
rushed in and tried to pull the dogs apart. 我衝了
進去，並設法把兩條狗拉開。
【片語】apart from ①除…外（別無）②除…外（尚
有）

breadth [brɛdθ] .... ★★★
n. 廣度，寬度，幅度：breadth of mind 心胸的寬廣

intermediate [ˌɪntə`midɪət] .... ★★★★
adj. 中級的：Gray is intermediate between black and white. 灰色介於黑色和白色之間。

interoffice [ˌɪntə`ɔfɪs] .... ★★★★
adj. 局間的：an interoffice memo 各辦公室間的備忘錄；interoffice conferences 辦公室會議

interplanetary [ˌɪntə`plænəˌtɛrɪ] .... ★★★★
adj. 星際的，行星的：an interplanetary journey in a space ship 乘太空船作星際旅行

left [lɛft] .... ★★★★★
adj. 左邊的：Some people write with the left hand. 有些人用左手寫字。
adv. 左邊地：Turn left! 向左轉！
n. 左，左邊

medial [`midɪəl] .... ★★★★★
adj. ①中間的，中央的②平均的，一般的

middle [`mɪdl] .... ★★★★★
adj. 中部，中間，當中：The twins sit in the middle of classroom. 這對雙胞胎坐在教室中間。
【片語】in the middle of 在…當中，在…中途

midst [mɪdst] .... ★★★★★
n. 中部，中間，當中

overhead [`ovəˌhɛd] .... ★★★
adj. 在頭頂上的，架空的：an overhead bridge 天橋

place [ples] .... ★★★★★
n. 地方，地點：The people took places. 大家就位了。
【片語】① take one's place 代替某人的職務，坐某人的座位② take place 發生，進行③ take the place of 代替

side [saɪd] .... ★★★★★
n. 側面，旁邊：You can see many beautiful shop windows on both sides of street on your way to school. 在你去學校的路上，你可以看到許多漂亮的商店櫥窗。
【片語】by the side of... 在…旁邊

sidewalk [`saɪdˌwɔk] .... ★★★
n. 人行道

sideways [`saɪdˌwez] .... ★★★
adv. 斜著，橫著，從旁邊：Many insects chew by moving their jaws sideways. 許多昆蟲都斜著嘴咀嚼。

site [saɪt] .... ★★★★★
n. 地點

spot [spɑt] .... ★★★★★
v. 認出
n. 地點，污點：The osprey fly above the water and when it spots a fish it swoops down to catch it. 魚鷹在水面飛行，發現魚時就會俯衝下去捕捉。

(3)上下、前後、左右相關辭彙

above [ə`bʌv] .... ★★★
adv. ①在上方：Look at the clouds above. 瞧頭頂的雲彩。②在前面（書，頁等）：See the examples above. 見上述例子。
prep. 在…上方，（數量、價格等）大於…：There is nothing in this shop above fifty dollars. 這店裡沒有超過50元的商品。
　【片語】above all 最重要的，首要的

after [`æftə] .... ★★★★★
prep. 在…之後：Just after six the rain began to fall. 剛過六點，就開始下雨了。
conj. 在…後：I arrived after he left. 我在他離開後才到達。
adv. 以後，後來：John came last Tuesday, and I arrived the day after. 約翰上週二來，我隔天到達。
　【片語】after all 終究，畢竟

afterwards [ˈæftəwədz] .... ★★★
adv. 以後，後來：Let's have the dinner first and eat the dessert afterwards. 我們先用餐，然後再吃甜點。

along [əˈlɔŋ] .... ★★★★★
prep. 沿著，順著：We went for a walk along the road. 我們沿街散步。
adv. 向前，和…一起，一同：We came along with some friends. 我們和幾個朋友來。
【片語】come along! = come on! 來吧！／過來！

around [əˈraʊnd] .... ★★★★★
adv. ①各處，到處：The children are running around. 孩子們四處奔跑。②周圍，在附近：Is there any body around? 這裡有人嗎？
【片語】all around 到處，四周
prep. 在…周圍，在…附近，在…各地：We're going for a walk around the town. 我們要到城裡各處走走。

back [bæk] .... ★★★★★
n. 背（面），後面：Take care your back. 留意你後面。
【片語】in the back (of) 最裡面的，在最後面的
adv. ①在後，向後：Stand back, please. 請往後站。②回，回復：Put the book back, please. 請把書放回原處。

backdrop [ˈbækˌdrɑp] .... ★★★★★
n. 背景

background [ˈbækˌgraʊd] .... ★★★★★
n. 背景

backward(s) [ˈbækwəd(z)] .... ★★★
adv. 退步，相反：Without a backward glance, he walked away. 他頭也不回地走了。
adj. 退步的，相反的：The technology was backward, but the system worked. 雖然技術落後，但這個系統仍在用。

downcast [ˈdaʊnˌkæst] .... ★★★
adj. 沮喪的：Ashamed of his mistake, he stood with downcast eyes. 羞於他的錯誤，他眼睛下垂站著。

downstairs [ˌdaʊnˈstɛrz] .... ★★★
adv. 在樓下，住樓下：He went downstairs to breakfast. 他下樓吃早飯。
adj. 樓下的：the downstairs room 樓下的房間

downtown [ˌdaʊnˈtaʊn] .... ★★★★★
adv. 往／在商業區或鬧區：We went downtown yesterday. 我們昨天去了一趟市區。
adj. 商業區的，鬧區的：downtown restaurants 位於鬧區的餐館

downward(s) [ˈdaʊnwəd(z)] .... ★★★
adj. 向下的，下行的：a downward slope 下坡
adv. ①向下行，下行地：He laid the picture downward on the table. 他將那幅畫面朝下放在桌上。②趨向沒落

forth [forθ] .... ★★★★★
adv. 向前：The sun came forth from behind the cloud. 太陽從雲後露出來。

forward(s) [ˈfɔrwəd(z)] .... ★★★★★
adv. ①向前，前進：If he goes forward any more, he will find the secret. 如果他再前進一點，他就會發現秘密。②將來，今後：From the day forward he disappeared in the world. 從那天以後，他從這個世界消失了。

near [nɪr] .... ★★★★★
adj. 近的，接近的：Christmas is near. 聖誕節快到了。
adv. 接近：Come near and listen to me. 靠近一點聽我說。
prep. 靠近，在…旁：She is standing near the window. 她正站在窗戶旁。

nearby [ˈnɪrˌbaɪ] .... ★★★
adj. 附近的：a nearby village 附近的村莊
adv. 在附近：A football match is being played nearby. 附近正在舉行一場足球賽。

nearly [ˋnɪrlɪ] .... ★★★★★

adv. 幾乎：Although the lunar orbit is nearly circular, it is more accurately described as an ellipse around the Earth. 儘管月球的公轉軌道近乎圓形，但是更準確地講，它是一個橢圓形。

past [pæst] .... ★★★★★

prep. ①（指時間）過：I get up at half past five every morning. 我們每天早上五點半起床。②走過某處：The bus drove past the city hall. 公共汽車經過市政府。

adj. 過去的，從前的：Never forget the past suffering. 絕不要忘記過去的苦難。

n. 過去，昔日

prior [ˋpraɪɚ] .... ★★★

adv. 在…之前：A prior engagement will preclude me from coming. 我因有約在先，不能來了。

under [ˋʌndɚ] .... ★★★★★

prep. ①在…下方，在…下面：He is standing under a tree. 他正站在樹下。②以下，之下，少於，低於：I can't sell it under 200 dollars. 低於200元我不賣。③在…情況下，由於：The matter is under consideration. 這件事正在考慮之中。④（指狀態）在…之中：Your clock is under repair. 你的鬧鐘正在修理。

underground .... ★★★

adj. [ˋʌndɚˏɡraʊnd] ①地面下的：an underground railway 地下鐵 ②地下的，秘密的：He is an underground spy working in that foreign country. 他是在外國工作的秘密間諜。

n. [ˋʌndɚˏɡraʊnd] 地下鐵道，地鐵

adv. [ˏʌndɚˋɡraʊnd] ①在地下：They dug a tunnel underground. 他們在地下挖了條隧道。②暗中，秘密的：The meeting is held underground. 會議秘密召開。

underneath [ˏʌndɚˋniθ] .... ★★★

adv. 在後面，在下層，在下面：They looked down from the bridge at the water underneath. 他們從橋上觀看下面的水。

prep. 在…下面，在…之下：She sat underneath the tree in the shade. 她坐在樹蔭下。

n. 下部，下面：the underneath of a sofa 沙發的底部

upward [ˋʌpwɚd] .... ★★★★

adj. 向上的：A tree grows upward while its roots grow down. 樹往上長，而它的根往下長。

adv. （又作upwards）向上，往上，…以上：He happened to look upward. 他碰巧向上看。

辨析
Analyze

almost, nearly

1 **almost** *ad.* 「幾乎，差不多」，指相差無幾，有非常接近之意。在肯定句中可與 nearly 換用，語氣比 nearly 強。almost 不與 not 連用，可與 no、none、nothing、never 連用，也可用在 more than 或 too 前：It's almost nine miles from here to downtown Chicago. 從這兒到芝加哥的商業區差不多九英里遠。

2 **nearly** *ad.* 「幾乎，差不多」，指接近，往往強調不足部分，常與數字連用，只可與 not 連用表示否定：When the bus got in, it was nearly midnight. 公車進站時幾乎是半夜了。

(4)內外、遠近相關辭彙

distant [ˈdɪstənt] .... ★★★★★
adj. 遠的：It is difficult to get young people to plan for their old age, which seems very distant to them. 讓年輕人為他們的老年生活計畫是比較困難的，因為那看起來如此之遙遠。

external [ɪkˈstɜnəl] .... ★★★★
adj. 外部的：An internal sense of righteousness dwindles into an external concern for reputation. 內心的正義感變成對外在名譽的關心。

far [fɑr] .... ★★★★★
adj. 遙遠，久遠：On this way you have gone too far to return. 在這條路上你已走得太遠而不能回頭了。
adv. 遠，遙遠，久遠：The story took place far long ago. 故事發生在很久以前。
【片語】① far away 遠離② far from 遠非，毫不

farther [ˈfɑrðə] .... ★★★★
adv. ①更遠地：We can't go farther without a rest. 我們如不休息就無法再往前走了。②進一步：need farther help 需要進一步幫助
adj. 更遠的：on the farther bank of the river 在河的彼岸

inside [ˈɪnˈsaɪd] .... ★★★★★
prep. 在…裡面，在…內部：Let's go inside the house. 我們進屋去吧。
adj. 裡面的，內部：inside coat pockets 大衣內側口袋
adv. 在裡面，在內部：The children played inside all day. 孩子們整天在裡面玩。
n. 裡面，內部：the inside of the house 房子內部

intercity [ˌɪntəˈsɪtɪ] .... ★★★★★
adj. 城市間的，市際的：an intercity bus 市際公共汽車；intercity broadcasting network 城市間的廣播網

interior [ɪnˈtɪrɪə] .... ★★★★
n. 內部
adj. 內部的：interior decoration 室內裝潢；interior decorator 室內裝潢設計師；interior design 室內裝潢業

inward [ˈɪnwəd] .... ★★★
adj. 裡面的，內在的，向內的，內心的

inward(s) [ˈɪnwəd(z)] .... ★★★
adv. 向內，向中心：Her words were inwards and indistinct when she was in a state of half unconsciousness. 她處於半昏迷狀態時，說話的聲音低沉、模糊不清。

outdoor [ˈaʊtˌdor] .... ★★★
adj. 露天的，室外的：outdoor film show 露天電影放映

outside [ˈaʊtˈsaɪd] .... ★★★★★
n. 外面，外部
adj. 外表的，外部的：Don't judge a man from his outside look. 不要以貌取人。
adv. & prep. 在外面，向外面：Can we have our fish and chips outside? 我們可以在外面吃炸魚和薯條嗎？

outward(s) [ˈaʊtwəd(z)] .... ★★★★
adv. 在外，向外
adj. 外面的，顯著的：a concern with outward beauty rather than with inward reflections 更注重外在美而忽視內在思想品德

remote [rɪˈmot] .... ★★★★
adj. 遙遠的，遠程的：a remote relative 遠親

within [wɪˈðɪn] .... ★★★★★
prep. 在…裡面：live within one's income 量入為出
adv. 在內：be strong out but weak within 外強中乾

Unit 11
狀態、程度名稱總匯
Conditons & Degree

01

狀態、程度名稱總匯

狀態、穩定、動靜相關辭彙

Conditons & Degree

Vocabulary of Conditions

aspect [ˈæspɛkt] .... ★★★★★
n. 方面，樣子，外表：We must consider a problem in all its aspects. 我們必須全面考慮問題。

balance [ˈbæləns] .... ★★★★★
n. 平衡
v. 平衡：My accounts balance for the first time this year! 我的帳戶今年第一次出現收支平衡！

calm [kɑm] .... ★★★★
adj. ①平靜的，無風的：The sea is calm. 大海風平浪靜。②鎮靜的，鎮定的：He is always calm even in times of trouble. 他即使遇到麻煩，也是鎮定的。
v. 使平靜，使鎮定：The mother calmed her child. 母親使孩子安靜下來。

composed [kəmˈpozd] .... ★★★★★
adj. 鎮靜的

composure [kəmˈpoʒɚ] .... ★
n. 沉著，鎮靜：keep/lose one's composure 沉住／沉不住氣

exorbitant [ɪgˈzɔrbətənt] .... ★
adj. 過分的，過度的：The tourists can't bear the exorbitant prices of most souvenirs. 絕大多數的紀念品價格過高，遊客買不下手。

extravagant [ɪkˈstrævəgənt] .... ★
adj. 奢侈的，浪費的：She's very extravagant—she spends all her money on clothes. 她很奢侈，花掉了所有的錢來買衣服。

firm [fɝm] .... ★★★★★
adj. 堅挺的，結實的：Despite being hit by the car, the post was still firm. 柱子儘管被車撞了，仍然很穩固。

fix [fɪks] .... ★★★★★
v. 修理，安裝：Why don't you fix the door when you have so much free time? 你這麼空，幹嘛不修一下門呢？
【片語】fixed account 定期存款

fixed [fɪkst] .... ★★★★★
adj. 固定的：fixed assets 固定資產；fixed capital 固定資本；fixed charge 固定支出；fixed property 不動產；fixed rate 固定匯率；fixed star 恒星

Conditons & Degree

fixture [ˈfɪkstʃɚ] .... ★

n. 固定設備，固定在某地／某項工作的人：
volley ball fixtures 預定日期的排球賽

immobile [ɪmˈmobɪl] .... ★★★★★

adj. 固定的

inflexible [ɪnˈflɛksəbl] .... ★★★★★

adj. 堅定的：inflexible courage 不屈不撓的勇
氣；inflexible to threats 不為威脅所動

inordinate [ɪnˈɔrdn̩t] .... ★

adj. 無節制的，過度的：The employees make
inordinate demands. 員工們提出了無理的
要求。

instability [ˌɪnstəˈbɪlətɪ] .... ★

n. 不穩定性：the instability of human affairs
人事滄桑

invariable [ɪnˈvɛrɪəbl] .... ★★

adv. 不變地，總是

invariably [ɪnˈvɛrɪəblɪ] .... ★★

adv. 不變地，總是：Until about 1400 A.D. iron
was invariably smelted by the direct, or
bloomery process. 鐵直到西元 1400 年，
都是經由直接或煉鐵的過程來鑄造的。

mollify [ˈmɑləˌfaɪ] .... ★

v. 緩和：He bought his angry wife a gift, but
she refused to be mollified. 他買了一份禮物
送給生氣的太太，但她不肯就此息怒。

moor [mʊr] .... ★★

v. 使停泊，使停住，固定：moor a ship to a
dock 把船繫在碼頭上

olidly [ˈɔlɪdlɪ] .... ★★★★

adv. 牢固地

pacify [ˈpæsəˌfaɪ] .... ★★

n. 安撫，平息：The mother pacified her
crying baby. 母親哄著哭鬧的嬰兒。

peace [pis] .... ★★★★★

n. ①平靜，安寧：break the peace 打破寧靜
②和平，和睦：in times of peace 在和平年
代

peaceful [ˈpisfəl] .... ★★★★

adj. ①平靜的，安寧的，寧靜的：It's so
peaceful out here in the country. 這裡的
鄉間是多麼的寧靜。②和平的：We'll use
atomic energy for peaceful purposes. 我
們要和平地來利用原子能。

perennially [pəˈrɛnɪəlɪ] .... ★

adv. 終年，長年：Florida's perennially warm
climate and plentiful rainfall make the
state a center of citrus production. 佛羅里
達州長年溫暖多雨，非常適合柑橘類植物
生長。

placid [ˈplæsɪd] .... ★

adj. 安靜的：From an airplane, the grasslands
of the western prairie appear almost as
uniform as a placid sea. 從飛機上看，西
部大草原幾乎像海一樣平靜。

sedate [sɪˈdet] .... ★

adj. 安靜的：Betty is a sedate girl. 貝蒂是個恬
靜的女孩。

serene [səˈrin] .... ★

adj. 晴朗的，平靜的，沉靜的：serene skies
and a bright blue sea 晴朗的天空和亮藍
色的大海

serenity [səˈrɛnətɪ] .... ★

n. 安靜，從容

silence [ˈsaɪləns] .... ★★★★★

n. ①寂靜：He enjoys silence of the night.
他喜歡夜晚的寂靜。②沉默：He was in
silence during the quarrel of the negotiation.
他在談判的爭吵聲中，始終保持著沉默。

v. 使沉默，使安靜：Robin silenced him with
gesture. 羅賓示意要他安靜。

soothe [suð] .... ★★

v. 安慰，緩和，減輕：She soothed the child
who was afraid. 她使這個害怕的孩子平靜了
下來。

stability [stəˈbɪlətɪ] .... ★★

n. 穩定，穩定性，安定：light stability 光的穩
定性

231

stabilize [ˈsteblˌaɪz] .... ★★
v. 使堅定，使穩定，使安定：stabilize prices
穩定價格

stable [ˈstebl̩] .... ★★★★
adj. 穩定的，不變的，安定的
n. 馬廄，馬棚：No form of money has ever
proved completely satisfactory in terms of
providing a stable measure of value. 就提供
一種穩定的價值量度標準而言，沒有一種貨
幣能夠令人完全滿意。

static [ˈstætɪk] .... ★★★
adj. 靜的，靜態的：static electricity 靜電

stationary [ˈsteʃənˌɛrɪ] .... ★
adj. 固定的：If an object is suspended from
any point on the vertical line passing
through its center of gravity, the object will
remain stationary. 如果某一物體在通過其
重心的垂直線上的任一點被懸掛起來，那
麼該物體將保持靜止。

steadfast [ˈstɛdˌfæst] .... ★★★★
adj. 堅決的，堅定的，不變的：Emily Greene
Balch's steadfast labor for freedom and
for cooperation among individuals and
peoples brought her the Nobel Peace
Prize in 1946. 愛蜜莉・包奇為個人和民
族之間的合作而做出的不懈努力，讓她在
1946 年獲得了諾貝爾和平獎。

steadily [ˈstɛdəlɪ] .... ★★★★
adv. 穩定地，不斷地：The consumption of
condensed and evaporated milk has
steadily increased since they started
being commercially produced in 1856. 煉
乳從 1856 年開始商業化生產以來，其消費
量就不斷地增加。

steady [ˈstɛdɪ] .... ★★★★
v. 使穩定
adj. 穩固的：not very steady on one's leg 步
履不太穩定。

sturdy [ˈstɝdɪ] .... ★
adj. 不屈的，頑強的：to offer a sturdy
resistance 堅決地抵抗

tense [tɛns] .... ★★★
n. 時態
adj. 緊張的：The players were tense at the
start of the game. 隊員們在比賽開始時很
緊張。

tension [ˈtɛnʃən] .... ★★★★★
n. 緊張
v. 拉緊，繃緊：Tranquilizers are often used in
the treatment of tension. 鎮靜劑通常用於治
療情緒緊張。

tranquil [ˈtræŋkwɪl] .... ★
adj. 安靜的：Grandma Moses, a popular
painter, spent her life in a tranquil little
farming community. 摩西奶奶是一位受歡
迎的畫家，在一處寧靜的小農村度過了她
的一生。

unduly [ʌnˈdjulɪ] .... ★
adv. 過度地：unduly familiar with strangers 對
陌生人過度地親密

辨析 Analyze

stable, steady

stable 和 steady 都指「穩、平穩的、穩定的，還指人穩重的」，在指一種相對長期的狀態時，兩者基本可以互換：Keep your camera stable/steady while you take a picture. 照相時把相機拿穩／放穩。

辨析 Analyze

nervous, tense

1 **nervous** *a.* 「神經緊張的，情緒不安的，神經系統的，神經性的」，指人感到緊張的。The witness was extremely nervous/tense. 這個目擊者十分緊張。

2 **tense** *a.* 「緊張的，拉緊的，繃緊的」，指人感到緊張，也指身體某部位（如肌肉、面部）或物體（如繩子）繃緊或拉緊的，還指局勢或氣氛緊張的，如：a tense rope/muscle/situation/moment/face/expression 拉緊的繩子／緊縮的肌肉／緊張的情勢／緊張的時刻／緊張的臉／緊張的表情；There was a tense silence in the room. 房裡是一片緊張的沈默。

233

02

基礎、因果、方式、程度相關辭彙

Vocabulary of Base & Way

Conditons & Degree

absolute [ˈæbsəˌlut] .... ★★★★★

adj. 絕對的：The woman claimed her absolute ownership over the possessions. 這個女人宣稱她對這些財產有絕對擁有權。

base [bes] .... ★★★★★

n. ①基（礎），底（座）：the base of camp 燈座②基地；an air base 空軍基地

v. 把⋯建立在⋯上（後可接 on）：Scientific theories must be based on facts. 科學理論必須建立在事實基礎上。

basement [ˈbesmənt] .... ★

n. 地下室，底層

basic [ˈbesɪk] .... ★★★★★

adj. 基本的：The farm lacks even basic equipment. 該農場甚至連基本的設備也沒有。

n. 基本原理，實質性的東西：Let's stop chatting and get down to the basics. 我們別再閒聊了，做些要緊的事吧。

basin [ˈbesn̩] .... ★★★

n. 盆地：artesian basin 自流泉盆地

basis [ˈbesɪs] .... ★★★★★

n. （用於抽象意義）基礎，根據：The belief has no scientific basis whatever. 這一信念沒有任何科學根據。

【片語】on the basis of 根據⋯，在⋯的基礎上

bottom [ˈbɑtəm] .... ★★★★★

n. ①底部，基礎，根基：He is a good fellow at bottom. 他基本上是個好人。②海底，湖底，河床

categorical [ˌkætəˈgɔrɪkl̩] .... ★

adj. 絕對的，無條件的：categorical imperative 絕對良心律（康德所說的良心至上的道德觀）

cause [kɔz] .... ★★★★★

n. 事業，原因

v. 導致：The moderator invoked a rule causing the end of the debate. 仲裁人引用了一項規則，讓辯論結束。

countless [ˈkaʊntlɪs] .... ★★★★★

adj. 無數的：Over the years, countless storytellers have been narrating tales that entertain their listeners as well as teach them a lesson. 多年來，無數的說書人在娛樂聽眾的同時，也讓他們受到了教育。

elementary [ˌɛləˈmɛntərɪ] .... ★★★★
adj. 基本的，初級的：an elementary reading book for a child who is learning to read 為學習閱讀的兒童編的初級讀物

essential [ɪˈsɛnʃəl] .... ★★★★★
adj. 重要的，基本的：Potential computer buyers have come to expect versatility, energy efficiency, and simplicity as essential components of new equipment. 電腦的潛在的購買者都期望新機器能有多功能、低耗能和簡單結構的基本性能。

integral [ˈɪntəgrəl] ....★
adj. 組成的，完整的：Steel is an integral part of a modern skyscraper. 鋼鐵是現代摩天大廈的主幹。

maybe [ˈmebɪ] .... ★★★★
adv. 大概，或許：Maybe you are right. 或許你是對的。

means [minz] .... ★★★★★
n. 手段，方法，錢：In the early days of baseball, the game was played by young men of means and social position. 棒球運動在早期，是富有和有社會地位的年輕人從事的運動。

method [ˈmɛθəd] .... ★★★★★
n. 方法，辦法：modern teaching method 現代教學方法

mighty [ˈmaɪtɪ] .... ★★
adj. 巨大的：He struck the rock with a mighty blow of a hammer. 他用鐵鎚使勁地猛擊那塊岩石。

minimum [ˈmɪnəməm] .... ★★★★
n. 最小量，最低限度：How many people are aware that a dancer with the New York City Ballet typically wears out a minimum of two hundred pairs of toe shoes per year? 有多少人知道紐約市芭蕾舞團的舞者每年至少要穿破 200 雙鞋呢？

辨析 Analyze

basic, essential, fundamental

1 **basic** *a.*「基本的，基礎的，根本的」，指組成某物的主要或基本部分：The basic structure of a skyscraper is its steel frame-work. 摩天大樓的底基是鋼筋結構。

2 **essential** *a.*「必不可少的，非常重要的，本質的，實質的，基本的」，指有關事物核心部分的，也指「內在或本質上的」：I couldn't put together this computer because an essential piece was missing. 我無法將這部電腦組裝起來，因為少了一個主要的零件。

3 **fundamental** *a.*「基本的，根本的，基礎的」，一般指抽象事物，強調根源或最重要的部分，比 basic 更正式，有時可與 basic 互換：The Constitution is the fundamental law of our country. 憲法是我們國家的根本大法。

radical [ˋrædɪk!] .... ★★

adj. ①根本的，基本的：There is a radical fault in your design. 你的設計中有一個根本性的缺陷。②激進的，激進派的

n. 激進分子：Radicals are trying to overthrow the government. 激進派企圖推翻政府。

radically [ˋrædɪk!ɪ] .... ★★

adv. 根本地，激進地：If there are civilizations on other planets, they are likely to be radically different from ours. 如果其他星球上也有文明，那麼它們很可能和我們的文明有著根本的差異。

rather [ˋræðɚ] .... ★★★★★

adv. 相當，很：It's rather cold today. 今天相當冷。

reason [ˋrizṇ] .... ★★★★★

n. 原因

v. 推論：There is reason to believe that the accused did not commit this crime. 有理由相信被告沒有犯這項罪行。

reasonable [ˋriznəb!] .... ★★★★

adj. ①通情達理的，講道理的：a reasonable man通情達理的人②合理的，有道理的：It was quite reasonable to suppose that he wanted the money too. 合理的假設是他也想得到這筆錢。③公道的：The tickets cost a very reasonable 30 dollars. 這些票賣 30 美元是很合理的。

rudimentary [͵rudəˋmɛntəri] .... ★

adj. 根本的，低級的：Eyespots, the most rudimentary eyes, are found in protozoan flagellates, flatworms, and segmented worms. 單眼是最低級的眼睛，可以在原生鞭毛蟲、扁平蟲和節支蟲上發現。

sake [sek] .... ★★★★★

n. 緣故，原因：For the sake of safety, you must keep all medicines away from children. 為了安全，要把所有的藥都放在孩子們拿不到的地方。

underlying [͵ʌndɚˋlaɪɪŋ] .... ★★★★★

adj. 根本的，基礎的，潛在的：In contrast to history, the underlying principle of geography is not time but space, and the focus is not so much social as terrestrial. 與歷史相對照，地理的根本原理不是時間而是空間，其焦點也不如陸地那樣與社會相關。

way [we] .... ★★★★★

n. ①（通往某處的）道路，路線，方向：Hard work is the way to success. 勤奮是成功之路。②方法，方式：You can do it in this way. 你可以這樣做。

【片語】①by the way 順便提起②on one's/the way 在途中

辨析 Analyze

cause, reason

1　**cause** *n.* 「原因，起因」，指產生某事的起因：The cause of the forest fire was the fire-watcher's carelessness. 森林大火的起因是火災監測員的粗心大意。

2　**reason** *n.* 「理由，原因」，其用法是 the reason for (doing) sth. ：Give your reason for changing your mind. 請你把改變主意的理由說出來。

03

主炎、多少、大小、輕重相關辭彙

Vocabulary of Priority & Scale

big [bɪg] .... ★★★★★
adj. 大的，巨大的，重大的，重要的：His bag is big enough to hold all his books. 他的袋子大得足以裝下他所有的書。

bulk [bʌlk] .... ★★★
n. 物體，容積，大批

bulky [ˋbʌlkɪ] .... ★★★
adj. 龐大的，笨重的：a bulky sweater 寬大的毛線衣。

cardinal [ˋkɑrdnəl] .... ★★
adj. 首要的，基本的：This is a matter of cardinal significance. 這是非常重要的事。

chief [tʃif] .... ★★★★★
adj. 主要的，首要的：The President of the US is the chief executive of the country. 美國總統是該國的最高行政長官。
n. 領袖，首領：According to the Charter, the president is chief of the armed forces. 根據憲法規定，總統是三軍統帥。

chiefly [ˋtʃiflɪ] .... ★★★★★
adv. 主要地，多半地：Insect smells chiefly with their antennae. 昆蟲主要靠自己的觸角來嗅東西。

colossal [kəˋlɑsḷ] .... ★
adj. 巨大的：a colossal monument 巨大的紀念碑；a colossal accident 異常事故

considerable [kənˋsɪdərəbḷ] .... ★★★★★
adj. 相當的：Mary Mapes Dodge exercised considerable influence on children's literature in the late nineteenth century. 瑪利·道奇對 19 世紀末的兒童文學領域產生了相當大的影響。

crucial [ˋkruʃəl] .... ★★★
adj. 嚴重的，極重要的：at the crucial moment 在關鍵時刻，重要關頭，a crucial decision 極重要的決定

enormous [ɪˋnɔrməs] .... ★★★★
adj. 巨大的：When the first all-purpose computer was completed in 1946, no one could have foreseen the enormous impact it would have in the following years. 當第一臺多用途的電腦在 1946 年被生產出來之後，沒有人能夠預見它在隨後的幾年中產生的巨大影響。

extent [ɪkˈstɛnt] .... ★★★★★
n. 範圍，程度：Landowners are unaware of
the extent of their own holdings. 地主們不
知道他們擁有的土地的範圍。

fine [faɪn] .... ★★★★★
n. 罰金
adj. 細微的：There's an only very fine line
between punishment and cruelty. 在懲罰
和殘酷虐待之間只有一條很細微的分界
線。

flock [flɑk] .... ★★★★
n. (一) 群，大量
v. 群集，成群：Herons nest and roost in
flocks, but hunt for food alone. 蒼鷺在築巢
和棲息的時候是結群的，但獵食時是隻身進
行。

giant [ˈdʒaɪənt] .... ★★★★
adj. 巨大的
n. 巨物，巨人：Shakespeare is a giant
among writers. 莎士比亞是一位文壇巨匠。

gigantic [dʒaɪˈgæntɪk] .... ★★
adj. 巨大的：The new airplane looked like a
gigantic bird. 這架新飛機看起來像一隻巨
大的鳥。
〔近義詞〕colossal, enormous, huge,
immense, tremendous, vast

great [gret] .... ★★★★★
adj. ①大的，偉大的，重大的，極大的：
Alexander the Great 亞歷山大大帝 ②大量
的：a great number of people 許多人③重
要的：a great occasion 重要的場合
【片語】Great Britain 大不列顛；the Great
Wall 長城

greatly [ˈgretlɪ] .... ★★★★★
adv. 大大地，非常

heavy [ˈhɛvɪ] .... ★★★★★
adj. 重的，重型的：The bag is too heavy for
the little students. 對這些小學生來說，這
背包太重了。

huge [hjudʒ] .... ★★★★★
adj. 龐大的，巨大的：huge mountains 大山

immense [ɪˈmɛns] .... ★★★★
adj. 巨大的，無限的：Inside the Lincoln
Memorial is an immense stature of
Abraham Lincoln by Daniel Chester
Fronch. 在林肯紀念堂裡有一尊由丹尼
爾·佛洛奇製作的亞伯拉罕·林肯的巨大
雕像。

importance [ɪmˈpɔrtṇs] .... ★★★★★
adj. 重大的，重要的：Confidence is very
important for a young man. 對年輕人來
說，自信心是十分重要的。

important [ɪmˈpɔrtṇt] .... ★★★★★
adj. ①重要的，重大的：an important meeting
一個重要的會議②有勢力的，有地位
的：the most important person in the
government 政府中最有勢力的人

inferior [ɪnˈfɪrɪə] .... ★★★★
adj. 次的，低劣的，下級的，低等的
n. 下級，部下，晚輩，(地位) 低下的人：No
inferior products should be allowed to pass.
決不允許放過任何次級品。

infinite [ˈɪnfənɪt] .... ★★★★
adj. 無限／窮／盡的：The universe is infinite.
宇宙是無邊無際的。
n. 無限

innumerable [ɪˈnjumərəbḷ] .... ★★
adj. 無數的：The different parts of the cotton
plant are utilized in the manufacture of
innumerable commodities. 棉花的各個部
分可以用來製造無數的商品。

jot [dʒɑt] .... ★
n. 一點兒，(最) 少量
vt. 草草記下

large [lɑrdʒ] .... ★★★★★
adj. 大的，廣大的，大規模的：A large
number of people have died from traffic
accidents. 已有許多人死於交通事故。

leading [ˈlidɪŋ] .... ★★★★★
adj. 指導的，最主要的：Insect pests are
among the leading causes of crop failure.
害蟲是導致農作物減產的主要因素之一。

238

least [list] .... ★★★★★

adj. 最少的，最小的：He has the least interest in sport. 他對體育毫無興趣。
【片語】① at least 至少② in the least 絲毫，一點兒

adv. 最少，最小：He was one of the least known of the modern poets. 他是鮮為人知的現代詩人中的一位。

less [lɛs] .... ★★★★★

adj. 更少的，更小的：a less famous scientist 一位不太著名的科學家

adv. 更少地，更小地：I hope the next train will be less crowded. 我希望下班列車不會太擠。
【片語】no less than ①多達：No less than one thousand people came. 來者多達一千。②恰好，正是：Good heavens! It's a person no less than the President. 天哪！那人正是總統。

lightly [ˈlaɪtlɪ] .... ★★★★

adv. 輕輕地，容易地，不費力地：apply paint lightly 輕輕塗了一層漆

little [ˈlɪtl] .... ★★★★★

adj. ①小的，幼小的：There is little water in that little glass. 那小杯子裡幾乎沒有水。②一點兒，幾乎沒有：He is little better than a dead man. 他跟死人沒什麼兩樣。

n. 沒有多少，少量：Bob said he knew little about the matter. 鮑伯說他對此事知之甚少。
【片語】a little 一點，少量：There is a little bread on the plate. 盤子裡有些麵包。

adv. 毫不，幾乎不：I ate little for breakfast. 我早餐幾乎沒吃什麼。

lot [lɑt] .... ★★★★★

n. 許多：There are lots of men, there are lots of experiences. 每個人都有不同的經歷。
【片語】① a lot 許多，大量② a lot of = lots of 許多，大量

magnificent [mægˈnɪfəsənt] .... ★★★★

adj. 壯麗的，華麗的：The magnificent scene of the waterfall is a perfect delight to the eye. 瀑布的宏偉景象真是好看極了。

magnitude [ˈmægnəˌtjud] .... ★★

n. 大小，量，數量，重要性：I want to know the magnitude of this equipment. 我想知道這個設備的大小。

main [men] .... ★★★★★

adj. 主要的：The main problem lies in your confidence. 主要問題在於你的自信。

mainly [ˈmenlɪ] .... ★★★★

adv. 大體上，主要地

mainstream [ˈmenˌstrim] .... ★★★★

n. 主流：You need not accept the nominee's ideology, only be able to locate it in the American mainstream. 你不需要接受被提名者的意識型態，只要將其思想置於美國的思潮主流中就行了。

major [ˈmedʒɚ] .... ★★★★★

n. 專業

v. 主修

adj. 主要的：Glassmaking was the first major industry in the United States. 玻璃製造是美國的早期工業之一。

majority [məˈdʒɔrətɪ] .... ★★★★

n. 多數，大多數：The majority of children in our class have brown eyes; only three have blue eyes. 我們班大多數孩子是棕色眼睛，只有三位是藍眼睛。

manifold [ˈmænəˌfold] .... ★★

adj. 多樣的，多方面的：His interests are manifold. 他的興趣廣泛。

many [ˈmɛnɪ] .... ★★★★★

adj. 許多的，多的：How many cases of cigarettes can you sell in a day? 你一天賣幾盒煙？

pron. 許多人，許多：Many have bad eyesight. 許多人的視力都不好。

marginal [ˈmɑrdʒɪnl] .... ★

adj. 邊際的：There has been a marginal improvement in the firm's sales. 該公司的銷路已稍有好轉。

mass [mæs] .... ★★★★★
n. ①許多，大量：His studio is a mass of books. 他的書房裡滿是書。②團，塊，堆：A great mass of rock blocked the road. 一塊大石頭堵住了道路。③群眾，民眾：There're masses of people waiting at the airport. 大批的群眾在機場等候。④質量：A litre of air has less mass than a litre of water. 1 升空氣比 1 升水的質量小。

massive [`mæsɪv] .... ★★★
adj. 巨大的：The eagle's nest is a massive structure of sticks lined with leaves and grass. 鷹巢是由樹葉和草堆在枝條上所造起來的巨大建物。

miniature [`mɪnɪətʃə] .... ★
n. 縮影，縮圖：a miniature railway（玩具）小鐵道

miniaturization [ˌmɪnɪətʃərɪ`zeʃən] .... ★
n. 小型化

minor [`maɪnə] .... ★★★★
adj. ①較少的，較小的：a minor operation小手術②較次要的：She played a minor part in the play. 她在這部電影中演配角。

minority [maɪ`nɔrətɪ] .... ★★★★
n. 少數，少數民族：The nation wants peace; only a minority want(s) the war to continue. 全國人民要和平，只有少數人希望繼續打仗。

momentous [mo`mɛntəs] .... ★
adj. 極重要的：a momentous occasion 重大時刻

monstrous [`mɑnstrəs] .... ★★
adj. 惡魔般的，可怕的，極惡的：They complain that the monstrous edifices interfere with television reception. 他們抱怨說，那些怪物般的龐大建築干擾了電視接收。

most [most] .... ★★★★★
adj. ①最多的：Who has the most books? 誰的書最多？②多數的，大部分的：Most people in England like talking about weather. 大多數英國人喜歡談論天氣。
adv. 最，最多，很，十分：She draws most carefully in the class. 她在班上是畫得最認真的。
n. 大多數，大部分

mostly [`mostlɪ] .... ★★★★
adv. 多半地，通常：The Americans use their cars mostly for their jobs. 美國人開車主要是為了上班。

multitude [`mʌltətjud] .... ★★
n. 眾多：a great multitude of people 一大群人

numerous [`njumərəs] .... ★★★★★
adj. 眾多的：Billie Jean King won numerous tennis championships and led the campaign for women's parity with men in tournament prizes. 貝利·金贏得了許多網球比賽的冠軍，並且領導女性在錦標賽獎項上與男子爭平等的運動。

old [old] .... ★★★★★
adj. ①年老的：The old woman is his mother. 這位老太太是他的母親。②舊的：This is an old photo of my sister. 這是我妹妹的一張舊照片。③古老的：This bridge is over three hundred years old. 這座橋有三百多年的歷史了。

petty [`pɛtɪ] .... ★★
adj. 細小的，次要的：petty bourgeois 小資產階級

principal [`prɪnsəpl̩] .... ★★★★★
n. 校長
adj. 重要的：It is generally believed that the principal ancestor of the domestic cat is the Libyan Desert cat. 人們普遍相信家貓的主要祖先是利比亞沙漠中的貓。

prodigious [prə`dɪdʒəs] .... ★
adj. 巨大的：the young Mozart's prodigious talents 小莫札特驚人的天賦

quiet [ˈkwaɪət] .... ★★★★★

adj. 安靜的，平靜的：She spent a quiet evening reading at home. 她在家看書度過了一個恬靜的晚上。

scale [skel] .... ★★★★★

v. 攀登

n. 規模，尺度，秤，鱗片：Any public demonstrations on a large scale without the permission of the city authorities are antisocial. 沒有市政當局的允許，舉行大規模遊行示威會妨害社會秩序。

seldom [ˈsɛldəm] .... ★★★★

adv. 很少，不常：Very seldom does he eat any breakfast. 他很少吃早飯。

senior [ˈsinjɚ] .... ★★★★★

n. 〔美〕大四學生，〔英〕（大學）高年級生

adj. 年長的，資格老的，地位高的：She is senior to everyone else in the company. 她在公司裡的地位比其他人都高。

short [ʃɔrt] .... ★★★★★

adj. 短的，矮的：He is a short man, shorter than his wife. 他個子不高，比妻子還要矮。

【片語】for short 簡稱，簡略，簡言之

shortcut [ˈʃɔrtkʌt] .... ★

n. 捷徑

shortly [ˈʃɔrtlɪ] .... ★★★★

adv. ①立刻，不久：Very shortly after I joined the army I became a brave soldier. 我入伍不久就成為一名勇敢的戰士。②不耐煩地，簡短地：Mary answered shortly that she didn't care what I thought. 瑪麗不耐煩地回答說，她根本不在乎我怎麼想。

size [saɪz] .... ★★★★★

n. 大小，尺寸：What size do you want? 你想要多大尺碼？

small [smɔl] .... ★★★★★

adj. ①小的：She was rather small in stature. 她的身材相當嬌小。②少的：Pay small attention to the matter. 對這件事很少關心。

stroll [strol] .... ★

v. 漫步：They often stroll in the park. 他們經常在公園裡漫步。

subordinate [səˈbɔrdṇɪt] .... ★★

adj. 次要的，附屬的：The minority is subordinate to the majority. 少數服從多數。

tiny [ˈtaɪnɪ] .... ★★★★

adj. 小的，極小的：Hummingbirds are tiny creatures. 蜂鳥是一種極小的生物。

titanic [taɪˈtænɪk] .... ★

adj. 巨大有力的：a deepening sense that some titanic event lay just beyond the horizon 越來越強烈地感覺到一些重大的事件就要發生了

ton [tʌn] .... ★★★

n. ①噸：The Japanese extract ten million tons of coal each year from underwater mines. 日本人每年從水面下的礦山挖掘一萬噸煤。②（常用可數）大量，許多：I've still got tons of work to do. 我還有大量工作要做。

tremendous [trɪˈmɛndəs] .... ★★★★

adj. 巨大的，驚人的：Exploding stars burst unexpectedly with such tremendous energy that they hurl huge amounts of gas into space. 突然爆炸的恒星產生如此巨大的能量，以至於把大量的氣體衝向太空。

trifling [ˈtraɪflɪŋ] .... ★★

adj. 微小的

vast [væst] .... ★★★★★

adj. 巨大的，大量的：Vast amounts of money are being invested in the local market. 大量的資金被投入到當地市場。

whit [hwit] .... ★

n. 一點：There is not a whit of intelligence or understanding in your observations. 你的觀察沒有一點機智或聰慧。

enormous, giant, gigantic, huge, immense, tremendous, vast

1 **enormous** *a.*「巨大的,極大的,龐大的」,可用來形容平面的或立體的物體,可用於引申義:an enormous room/creature/crime/loss 寬敞的房間╱巨獸╱重罪╱重大損失

2 **huge** *a.*「龐大的,巨大的」,一般指立體的、(物體)巨大的,可用於引申義:a huge pile/balloon/audience/success 一大堆╱大型氣球╱大批聽眾╱巨大的成功

3 **giant** *a.*「巨大的」,指同類相比中巨大的,只用作定語,不能用作表語:The giant size packet gives you more for less money. 大號包裝經濟實惠。

4 **immense** *a.*「廣大的,巨大的」,可用來形容平面的或立體的物體,可用於引申義,與 enormous 基本通用:an immense ocean/statue 浩瀚的海洋╱巨型雕塑

5 **tremendous** *a.*「極大的,巨大的」,可形容立體的物體,但主要用來修飾抽象的事物:a tremendous wave/explosion/achievement 大浪╱巨大的爆炸╱極大的成就

6 **vast** *a.*「廣闊的,巨大的,浩瀚的」,指遼闊的、面積或數量巨大的,只可形容平面的物體:a vast desert/lake/land/property/fortune 遼闊的沙漠╱巨大湖泊╱廣闊的田野╱巨大的財產╱巨大的財富

7 **gigantic** *a.*「巨大的,龐大的」,可用來形容平面的或立體的物體,可用於引申義,與 enormous 基本通用:a gigantic country/skyscraper/appetite/feat 大國╱高樓大廈╱貪婪的胃口╱一次盛宴

状態、程度名詞總匯

Conditons & Degree

04

難易、高低、長、寬相關辭彙

Vocabulary of Length

ascetic [əˋsɛtɪk] .... ★
adj. 苦行的：He is determined to lead an ascetic life. 他決心要過苦行的生活。

broad [brɔd] .... ★★★★★
adj. ①寬闊的，廣闊的：the broad ocean 遼闊的海洋 ②廣泛的，廣大的：He has a broader range of interests than her. 他的興趣比她廣泛。③寬容的，豁達的：a man of broad mind 寬宏大量的人

broadcast [ˋbrɔdˏkæst] .... ★★★★
v. 在廣播節目中講話，播音：BBC broadcasts on different frequencies. 英國廣播公司以不同的頻率進行廣播。
n. 廣播

broaden [ˋbrɔdn̩] .... ★
v. 放寬，使寬闊：The original canal was twice broadened for the larger modern boats. 原本的運河被拓寬了兩倍，以適應現代的船隻。

commodious [kəˋmodɪəs] .... ★
adj. 寬敞的：a commodious house 一座寬敞的房子

difficult [ˋdɪfəˏkəlt] .... ★★★★★
adj. 困難的，艱難的：Nothing is difficult to a man who has a will. 世上無難事，只怕有心人。

difficulty [ˋdɪfəˏkʌltɪ] .... ★★★★★
n. ①困難：If you knew the difficulties I am in. 你不知道我遭遇了什麼困難。②困境：He did it, but with difficulty. 他做了，但頗為費力。
【片語】in difficulties 處境困難：The family is in difficulty. 這個家庭陷入困境。

easy [ˋizɪ] .... ★★★★★
adj. 容易，不費力的，安逸的，寬裕的：Easier said than done. 說比做容易。
【片語】take it easy 別著急

elder [ˋɛldɚ] .... ★★★★
adj. 年齡較大的，年長的：My elder brother is in America. 我哥哥在美國。
n. 長者，長輩

elderly [ˋɛldɚlɪ] .... ★★★
adj. 較老的，年長的：He's rather active for an elderly man. 就一個老年人來說，他可是相當活躍。
n. (the-) 到了晚年的人，較老的人

Conditons & Degree

eldest [ˈɛldɪst] .... ★★★★★
adj. 最年長
n. 年紀最大的人

height [haɪt] .... ★★★★★
n. ①高，高度，身高：He was of medium height. 他中等身高。②高處，高地：at heights 在高處 ③頂點：the height of luxury 極其豪華

high [haɪ] .... ★★★★★
adj. 高的，高級的，高尚的：a high official 高級官員
adv. 高高地：The plane flies higher and higher. 飛機越飛越高。

highlight [ˈhaɪˌlaɪt] .... ★★★
v. 突出顯示，強調：Charles Whecler's paintings often highlight the sharp edges and geometrical shapes of machines. 查爾斯·懷克勒的畫經常強調機器的尖銳棱角和幾何形狀。

highly [ˈhaɪlɪ] .... ★★★★
adv. ①高（指地位、等級等）：The executives of our company are highly paid. 我們公司經理的薪水都很高。②高度地，很，非常 ③贊許地

laborious [ləˈborɪəs] .... ★★★★
adj. 勤勞的，費力的，艱難的：spent many laborious hours on the project 在這項工程上耗費了長期的艱辛勞動

length [lɛŋθ] .... ★★★★★
n. ①長，長度，距離：It is ten metres in length. 它 10 米長。②一段，一節：He tied the dog with a length of rope. 他用一段繩子把狗拴住了。
【片語】at length 最終，終於：At length he returned. 他終於回來了。

lower [ˈloɚ] .... ★★★★★
adj. ①較低的，低等的：lower class 下層階級 ②下游的：the lower Nile River 尼羅河下游流域
v. 放下，降下，放低：Flags were lowered to half. 降半旗（表示哀悼）

narrow [ˈnæro] .... ★★★★★
adj. 狹窄的，範圍小的，眼光短淺的：The steps are rather narrow. 這臺階相當窄。

round [raʊnd] .... ★★★★★
adj. 圓的，球形的：The earth is round. 地球是圓的。
prep. 圍繞：The moon moves around the earth. 月亮繞著地球轉。

roundabout [ˈraʊndəˌbaʊt] .... ★
adj. 迂迴的，轉彎抹角的
n. 環狀交叉路：This conclusion was reached in a roundabout but nevertheless perfectly reliable way. 這個結論是間接得出的，但還是相當可靠的。

shaft [ʃæft] .... ★★
n. 軸，柄：the shaft of an arrow 箭身

shape [ʃep] .... ★★★★★
n. ①形狀，外形：You can spin-dry this sweater and it will still retain its shape. 這種毛衣可用脫水機脫水，形狀仍然不變。②狀況，狀態：He looked in good shape. 他看起來很健康。
v. 形成，使成形：The children liked shaping snow into figures of people. 孩子們喜歡堆雪人。

tall [tɔl] .... ★★★★★
adj. 高的：How tall are you? 你多高？

wide [waɪd] .... ★★★★★
adv. 寬闊的，寬大的，寬廣的：She stood there with wide eyes. 她睜大眼睛站在那裡。

widen [ˈwaɪdn] .... ★★★
v. ①加寬，放寬：widen the roads 拓寬道路 ②變寬：The river widens at its mouth. 河流在河口處變寬了。

widespread [ˈwaɪdˌsprɛd] .... ★★★
adj. 分佈廣的，蔓延的，普遍的，普通的，廣泛流傳的：a widespread disease 一種流行病

05

深淺、強烈、軟硬相關辭彙
Vocabulary of Degree

deep [dip] .... ★★★★★
adj. 深的，深刻的，深切的：We had to dig a deep hole to find water. 我們必須挖很深的洞才能找到水。
adv. 深深地：They carried out an experiment deep into the night. 他們一直進行實驗到深夜。

delicate [ˈdɛləkət] ....★★★★
adj. 精巧的，脆弱的：Forests are delicate systems that, if disturbed, can be permanently destroyed. 森林是脆弱的系統，一旦被擾亂，就會永久地遭到破壞。

ductile [ˈdʌktl̩] .... ★
adj. 柔軟的，馴良的：ductile metals 韌性金屬

fortify [ˈfɔrtəˌfaɪ] .... ★★★★★
v. 加強：After praying he faced his difficulties with a fortified spirit. 他祈禱之後，面對困難的勇氣增強了。

hard [hɑrd] .... ★★
adj. ①硬的，堅固的：a hard nut 堅果②困難的，艱苦的：The question is so hard that I can't answer it. 這問題太難了，我回答不了。
adv. ①努力地，猛烈地：He worked very hard. 他工作十分努力。②（下雨等）猛烈的：It is raining hard. 雨下得很大。

harden [ˈhɑrdn̩] .... ★★★
v. 使變硬，使堅固：Don't harden your heart against your own relatives. 〔喻〕對自己的親戚心腸不要太硬了（對待自己的親戚不要過於苛刻無情）。

hardy [ˈhɑrdɪ] .... ★★
adj. 強壯的，耐勞的

intense [ɪnˈtɛns] ....★★★★
adj. 非常的，緊張的：If treated with strong sulfuric acid and a small quantity of ferric chloride codeine compounds will emit an intense blue color. 可待因的混合物如果經過強硫酸和少量氯化鐵處理，就會發出強烈的藍光。

intensify [ɪnˈtɛnsəˌfaɪ] .... ★★★★★
v. 加強：The scientists have intensified their search for the new gene by working harder. 科學家們更加努力工作，加緊搜尋這種新的基因。

intensity [ɪnˈtɛnsətɪ] .... ★★★

n. 強度，強烈，緊張：go mad at the intensity of one's grief 因悲傷過度而發瘋

intensive [ɪnˈtɛnsɪv] .... ★★★

n. 集中的：Intensive care in hospitals is given to the seriously ill. 在醫院裡的重症病人得到了悉心護理。

lithe [laɪð] ....★

adj. 柔軟的，易彎的：a lithe ballet dancer 一個自然優雅的芭蕾舞者。

meek [mik] ....★

adj. 溫順的，柔和的：He could not say no to the request because he is a meek person. 他無法拒絕這個請求，因為他是一個溫順的人。

profoundly [prəˈfaʊndlɪ] .... ★★

adv. 深刻地，深度地：Laura Ingalls Wilder's books recall her experience of growing up in a pioneering family whose members were profoundly devoted to one another. 勞瑞‧威爾德的作品中回憶了他自己在成員相互深切地關懷、具有創新精神的家庭裡的成長過程。

rigid [ˈrɪdʒɪd] .... ★★★

adj. 嚴格的，僵化的：We have released the tense of the rigid and severe training. 我們已經減輕了這種乏味且嚴格的訓練的強度。

rigor [ˈrɪgɚ] ....★

n. 嚴格，嚴厲：The rigors of the winter in Russia is often described by Mongol. 蒙古人經常會描述俄羅斯的冬天是多麼的寒冷難當。

rigorous [ˈrɪgərəs] ....★

adj. 嚴厲的，嚴峻的：a rigorous program to restore physical fitness 恢復身體健康的嚴格計畫

robust [rəˈbʌst] ....★

adj. 強壯的：His robust strength was a counterpoise to the disease. 他身體強壯，抵抗住了這種疾病。

shallow [ˈʃælo] .... ★★★

adj. 淺的：The sea is shallow here. 這兒的海水很淺。

soft [sɔft] .... ★★★★★

adj. 軟的，柔軟的，柔和的：a soft chair 一張軟椅

stiff [stɪf] .... ★★★

adj. 硬的，僵直的：Hemp, a harsh, stiff fiber, comes from a plant that grows in both hot and mild climates. 大麻是一種結實、堅硬的纖維，在溫熱環境中生長。

strict [strɪkt] .... ★★★

adj. ①嚴格的，嚴厲的：Parents were strict in Victorian times. 維多利亞時代的父母是嚴厲的。②嚴重的，精確的：the strict meaning of a word 一個字的確切涵義 ③完全的，不折不扣的：She was a strict vegetarian. 她是個不折不扣的素食者。

strong [strɔŋ] .... ★★★★★

adj. 強大的，強壯的：He has a strong sense of responsibility. 他有強烈的責任感。

vehemence [ˈviəməns] ....★

n. 熱切，激烈：the vehemence of anger 盛怒

vehement [ˈviəmənt] ....★

adj. 猛烈的，激烈的：He spoke with vehement eloquence in defense of his client. 他為他的委託人激烈辯護。

rigid, rigorous, stiff, strict

1 **rigid** *a.*「嚴格的,死板的,剛硬的,僵硬的」,指制度、紀律、要求、標準嚴格的,也指固執己見而不變通的,還指挺直的、即使折斷也不能彎曲的,中性詞:The requirements for membership are rigid. 對會員資格的要求是嚴格的。

2 **rigorous** *a.*「嚴密的,縝密的,嚴格的,嚴厲的」,指訓練嚴格的、懲罰嚴厲的,還指計算或研究等嚴密的、縝密的,褒義詞:The training involves rigorous exercises and punishment. 這種訓練包括嚴格的操練和嚴厲的懲罰。

3 **stiff** *a.*「硬的,僵直的,不靈活的,拘謹的,生硬的,艱難的,費勁的」,指關節或肌肉僵硬,也指材料(如紙張、布料、塑膠、金屬等)硬的,還指人際交流中態度或行為生硬的,貶義詞:My back was stiff after sitting for so many hours. 我坐了好幾個小時,背都僵硬了。

4 **strict** *a.*「嚴格的,嚴厲的,嚴謹的,精確的」,指嚴格的,不僅可指物而且可指人,褒義詞:The rule/discipline is very strict. 規定/紀律很嚴格。

狀態、程度

06

Conditons & Degree

厚薄、充實、空虛、空白相關辭彙

Vocabulary of Vacuity

capacious [kə`peʃəs] .... ★
adj. 容量大的：a man of capacious mind 心胸開闊的人

elite [e`lit] .... ★★★★★
n. 精華，精英：In addition to notions of social equality there was much emphasis on the role of elite and of heroes within them. 除了社會平等概念之外，還強調精英和英雄們在當中所起的作用。

empty [`ɛmptɪ] .... ★★★★★
adj. 空的：At night these busy streets during the day become empty. 這些白天繁忙的街道，在夜晚是空無行人車輛。

essence [`ɛsn̩s] .... ★★
n. 本質，實質，要素，精華：The essence of his religious teaching is love for all men. 他宣揚的宗教教義要旨是熱愛世人。

facet [`fæsɪt] .... ★★★★★
n. 方面，平面：Every facet of a symphony orchestra's performance is the responsibility of the conductor. 交響樂樂團表演的各方面都跟指揮有關。

facetious [fə`siʃəs] .... ★
adj. 幽默的，滑稽的：He was so facetious that he turned everything into a joke. 他非常好笑，把一切都變成了戲謔。

forlorn [fə`lɔrn] .... ★
adj. 絕望的，被遺棄的：forlorn of all hope 沒有任何希望

full [fʊl] .... ★★★★★
adj. ①滿的，充滿的：He can eat a full box of apples. 他能吃掉整箱的蘋果。②完全，充分：The train was travelling at full speed. 火車正在全速前進。
【片語】be full of 充滿…的

fully [`fʊlɪ] .... ★★★★★
adv. ①完全地，充分地，徹底地：The day is closing in and the gas is lighted，but it not yet fully effective, for it is not quite dark. 這時候，天色漸暗，煤氣燈已經點了起來，但還沒有充分發揮作用，因為天色還不算黑。②整整地，足足，至少

hollow [`hɑlo] .... ★★★★
adj. ①空的，中空的：a hollow tube 空管子②空間的，空虛的：hollow promises 空口諾言

indeed [ɪnˈdid] .... ★★★★
adv. ①真正地，當然：A friend in need is a friend indeed. 患難見真情。②確實，實在：He is indeed the man we want. 他確實是我們所需要的人。

margin [ˈmɑrdʒɪn] .... ★★★
n. 頁邊的空白，欄外：They have always had to make do with relatively small profit margins. 他們總是得設法應付較少的利潤。

rim [rɪm] ....★
n. 邊緣：a pattern round the rim of a plate 盤子邊緣的圖案

blank [blæŋk] .... ★★★★★
adj. ①空白的，空著的（常指表面無字跡）：a blank sheet of paper 一張白紙②茫然的，無表情的：There was a blank look on his face. 他臉上毫無表情。
n. ①空白：My mind was a total blank. 我腦中一片空白。②空白表格，空白處：Fill out the blanks. 填空。

slender [ˈslɛndɚ] .... ★★★
adj. ①苗條的，修長的：the girl's slender waist 女孩苗條的腰身。②微薄的：With such slender resources, they could not hope to achieve their games. 他們的財力這樣微薄，無法指望能在比賽中取得好成績。

slight [slaɪt] .... ★★★★★
adj. 輕微的，微小的：Aneroid barometers are able to show much slighter changes in the atmosphere than mercury barometers. 無液氣壓計比水銀氣壓計更能反映出細微的變化。

slightly [ˈslaɪtlɪ] .... ★★★★
adv. 稍微地，輕微地，有一點，稍許：A baby's blood has slightly more hemoglobin than that of an adult. 嬰兒血液中的血紅素比成人略高。

slim [slɪm] .... ★★★
adj. 細長的，苗條的：Many gymnasts do special exercises to remain slim and fit. 許多體操運動員進行特別的訓練來使身體苗條健康。

sunken [ˈsʌŋkən] ....★
adj. 沉沒的：His cheeks were sunken from hunger. 他的面頰因饑餓而凹陷。

辨析
Analyze

edge, margin, rim

1 **edge** *n.* 「邊，棱，邊緣，刀口，刃」，既指平面的、又指立體的物體邊緣：He fell off the edge of the cliff. 他從懸崖的邊掉下去了。

2 **margin** *n.* 「頁邊空白，邊，邊緣」，指一平面的邊緣地帶：The students write notes in the margin of the books. 學生們在書的邊緣空白處寫筆記。

3 **rim** *n.* 「（圓形物體的）邊，緣」：The rims of the glasses are made of plastics. 這副眼鏡的邊框是塑膠做的。

superficial [ˌsupəˈfɪʃəl] .... ★★★
adj. 表面的，膚淺的：He made only a few superficial changes in the manuscript. 他只在手稿中做幾處無關緊要的小更改。

surface [ˈsɜfɪs] .... ★★★★★
n. 表面：The lake is with a smooth surface. 湖面平靜。
【片語】surface mail 平信：I haven't ever posted a surface mail. 我從沒寄過平信。

vacancy [ˈvekənsɪ] .... ★★★
n. 空虛，空間，空隙，空位，空額：Sorry, no vacancies. 不好意思，沒空房了。（指旅館客滿）

vacant [ˈvekənt] .... ★★★
adj. 空的，未被佔用的：Many city dwellers are turning vacant lots into thriving gardens. 許多城市居民正將一塊塊空著的土地變成繁榮的花園。

vacation [veˈkeʃən] .... ★★★
n. 假期

vanity [ˈvænətɪ] .... ★★★★
n. 虛榮心

void [vɔɪd] .... ★★
adj. ①空的，空虛的：The desert stretching away before the traveler seemed frighteningly void. 在旅行者面前延展出去的沙漠空蕩得讓人害怕。②無效的，無用的：The treaty was declared void. 該條約被宣佈無效。
【片語】void of 沒有…

辨析
Analyze

blank, empty, hollow, vacant, void

1. **blank** *a.* 「空白的，空著的，茫然的，無表情的」，指沒有寫字或印刷的，用於引申時指表情茫然：Please write your name in the blank space at the top of the page. 請把你的名字寫在這一頁最上面的空白處。

2. **empty** *a.* 「空的，空間的，空虛的，寂寥的」，常用詞，用法較廣，多指某個空間（如房間、口袋、箱子、手中、街道上）沒有人或物存在，也可用於引申用法：Our voices echoed in the empty hall. 我們的聲音在空空蕩蕩的大廳裡迴響。

3. **hollow** *a.* 「空的，中空的，凹陷的，（聲音）沉悶的，虛偽的，空虛的」，指某個物體非實心而是空心的或是陷下去的，也可用於引申：The trunk of the old tree is hollow. 這棵老樹的樹幹是空的。

4. **vacant** *a.* 「未被佔用的，空著的，（職位、工作等）空缺的，（神情等）茫然的，（心靈）空虛的」，指房間、座位、餐桌、計程車、停車場、職位、工作等尚未被人佔有或佔用的，也可用於引申：Do you know of a vacant apartment? 你知道是否有未租出去的公寓房間？

5. **void** *a.* 「沒有的，缺乏的，無效的」，多用於 be void of，意為「沒有的，缺乏的」，整個片語相當於 lack，多指缺乏意義、興趣：That part of the town is completely void of interest for visitors. 該城鎮的那一部分，對於來訪者而言是索然無味。

07

短缺、富裕、興衰相關辭彙

Vocabulary of Fullness

abound [əˋbaʊnd] .... ★
v. 盛產，充滿：The area abounds in wild game. 這個地區到處是野生動物。

abundance [əˋbaʊndəns] .... ★★
n. 豐富，充裕：Sand is found in abundance on the seashore and is often blown inland to form sand hills and dunes. 沙在海灘隨處可見，經常被吹到內陸，形成山崗和沙丘。

abundant [əˋbaʊndənt] .... ★★★
adj. 充裕的：Calcium, the body's most abundant mineral, works with phosphorus in maintaining the skeletal system. 鈣是人體內最豐富的礦物質，與磷一同維持著骨骼系統。

adequate [ˋædəkwɪt] .... ★★★
adj. 足夠的：One of California's greatest problems is to provide adequate water for the needs of its expanding population. 加州最大的問題之一是滿足日益膨脹的人口的用水問題。

affluence [ˋæflʊəns] .... ★
n. 豐富，富裕，流入：Heavy traffic on the Mississippi River brought affluence to Iowa, until the mid nineteenth century, when the arrival of the railroads diverted river shipping. 直到 19 世紀中葉鐵路運輸的興起取代水運之前，密西西比河上繁忙的水路運輸一直為愛荷華州帶來財富。

ample [ˋæmpl̩] .... ★★
adj. 充足的：The city's many cultural and sports facilities offer ample recreation. 這座城市的許多文藝與運動設施提供了充足的休閒活動。

barren [ˋbærən] .... ★★
adj. 貧瘠的，不毛的，不育的：The barren soil of the Rocky Mountains provides few nutrients to the grasses growing there. 落磯山脈上貧瘠的土壤，對在那裡生長的草提供不了多少營養。

boom [bʊm] .... ★★★
n. 隆隆聲，繁榮：This boom in adult education, in turn, helps to raise the intellectual standard of the whole country. 這股成人教育的熱潮，反倒有助於提升整個國家的文化水準。

dearth [dɝθ] .... ★★★
n. 缺乏，供應不足：There is a dearth of water in some countries. 一些國家有缺水的問題。

deficiency [dɪˋfɪʃənsɪ] .... ★
n. 缺乏，不足：a deficiency of protein 蛋白質不足；deficiency disease 營養缺乏病

deficient [dɪˋfɪʃənt] .... ★★
adj. 缺乏的，不足的

deluxe [dɪˋlʌks] .... ★★★
adj. 豪華的，華麗的

demerit [diˋmɛrɪt] .... ★
n. 缺點：merits and demerits 優點和缺點，是非曲直

destitution [ˌdɛstəˋtjuʃən] .... ★★
n. 窮困，缺乏，貧窮

enough [əˋnʌf] .... ★★★★★
adj. 足夠的，充分的：There are enough people to pick the pears. 有足夠的人可採梨子。
pron. 足夠，充分：I have enough to bear! 我受夠了！
adv. 足夠地，充分地：He is old enough to join the army. 他的年齡夠大了，可以去當兵了。

fertile [ˋfɝtl] .... ★★
adj. 肥沃的，多產的：A large area of desert was reformed to turn to fertile soil in the northwest region. 在西北地方有一大片沙漠，經過改良變成了肥沃的土地。

fertility [fɝˋtɪlətɪ] .... ★★
n. 肥料

flourish [ˋflɝɪʃ] .... ★★★★
vi. 茂盛，繁榮，興旺：The firm is flourishing. 這家公司生意興隆。
vt. 揮動（以引起注意）：He stormed into the office, flourishing a letter of complaint. 他揮舞著一封投訴信衝進了辦公室。

generosity [ˌdʒɛnəˋrɑsətɪ] .... ★★
n. 慷慨，大方：Uncommon generosity causes neglect rather than ingratitude. 罕見的慷慨引起的是怠慢而不是忘恩負義。

generous [ˋdʒɛnərəs] .... ★★★★
adj. 慷慨的，大方的，豐盛的：The young heiress was so generous that she gave all her money away in a couple of years. 年輕的女繼承人過於大方，不到幾年就把錢都花光了。

generously [ˋdʒɛnərəslɪ] .... ★★★★
adv. 寬大地："Next time, I won't treat you so generously if I were to catch you plagiarizing again in writing your dissertation," the professor warned him. 教授警告他說：「下次如果我再發現你在寫論文的時候抄襲，我就不會這麼客氣了。」

impoverishment [ɪmˋpɑvərɪmənt] .... ★
n. 貧乏：absolute impoverishment 絕對貧困化

indigent [ˋɪndədʒənt] .... ★
adj. 貧窮的：Tourism has made the indigent local people wealthy. 旅遊業使得當地的許多窮人變得富有了。

insufficient [ˌɪnsəˋfɪʃənt] .... ★
adj. 不足的：Fainting, or a temporary loss of consciousness, may be brought about by an insufficient supply of oxygen to the brain. 昏厥或暫時性的神智不清，可能是由於大腦供氧不足而引起的。

lack [læk] .... ★★★★★
v. 缺乏，不足，沒有：It seems that he lacks confidence. 看來他信心不足。
n. 缺乏

lavish [ˋlævɪʃ] .... ★
adj. 豐富的，浪費的：The critics were lavish with their praise. 評論家們大大地讚美。

luxuriant [lʌgˋʒurɪənt] .... ★
adj. 茂盛的，多產的：Luxuriant forests covered the hillside. 山坡上長滿茂密的樹林。

luxurious [lʌgˋʒurɪəs] .... ★
adj. 奢侈的：a luxurious hotel 豪華的旅館

luxury [ˋlʌkʃərɪ] .... ★★★
n. 奢侈，奢侈品，豪華：Cream cakes are no longer a luxury. 奶油蛋糕再也不是奢侈品了。

needy [ˋnidɪ] .... ★
adj. 貧窮的：a needy family 貧窮人家

opulence [ˋɑpjələns] .... ★
n. 財富，富裕：Beds were originally symbols of opulence found only in the homes of the nobility. 床鋪最初是貴族家庭財富的象徵。

plentiful [ˋplɛntɪfəl] .... ★★★
adj. 富裕的，豐富的：Coal is a plentiful source of energy in the world. 煤是世界上儲量豐富的能源。

plight [plaɪt] .... ★
n. （惡劣的）情勢，困境：be in a sorry/pitiable/wretched plight 處境困窘

plump [plʌmp] .... ★
adj. 豐滿的：the baby's plump arms 嬰兒圓胖的手臂

poor [pur] .... ★★★★★
adj. ①貧困的，窮的：We are poor now, but we will not always be poor. 我們現在窮，但我們不會永遠這麼窮。②可憐的：The poor little girl began to cry. 那可憐的小女孩哭了起來。③低劣的：We can't attribute every defaults to our poor memory. 我們不能把每次失約都歸因於記性不好。

poverty [ˋpɑvətɪ] .... ★★★★★
n. 貧窮，貧困：It was not poverty, but a concern for simplicity that kept Puritan churches unadorned. 清教徒是出於簡樸而非出於貧困，把他們的教堂弄得樸實。

profuse [prəˋfjus] .... ★
adj. 極其豐富的：They were profuse in their compliments 他們毫不吝惜地誇獎。

prosper [ˋprɑspɚ] .... ★★★★
v. 昌盛，成功：The newly developed satellite town is prospering with each passing day. 這座新發展起來的衛星城市蒸蒸日上。

prosperity [prɑsˋpɛrətɪ] .... ★★★★
adj. 富裕的，昌盛的，繁榮的：After the war, a period of prosperity began. 在戰爭結束後，開始了一段繁榮時期。

prosperous [ˋprɑspərəs] .... ★★★
adj. 繁榮的：a prosperous moment to make a decision 做決定的有利時機

辨析 Analyze

rare, scarce

1　**rare** *a.*「稀有的，罕見的，冷僻的，珍奇的，出類拔萃的」，指少有的、罕見的、稀有的，尤指動植物、礦物、文物等，常含有珍貴的意思：Friends like him are rare. 像他那樣的朋友不多。

2　**scarce** *a.*「缺乏的，不足的，稀少的，罕見的」，常與供給和價格有關：Fruit is scarce and dear in this season. 這個季節水果少，價格貴。

ration [ˈræʃən] .... ★★★

n. 定量，配給量：During the recent petroleum embargo, motor fuels had to be rationed. 在最近的石油禁運期間，汽機車用油不得不進行配給供應。

rich [rɪtʃ] .... ★★★★★

adj. 有錢的：Most of the people in rich country are getting richer and richer. 富國的大多數人越來越富有。

scanty [ˈskæntɪ] .... ★★★

adj. 貧乏的：The potato crop was rather scanty this year. 今年馬鈴薯歉收。

scarce [skɛrs] .... ★★★★

adj. 缺乏的，不足的：Chromium is a comparatively scarce element, existing only in natural compounds. 鉻是一種相對稀少的元素，僅存在於天然化合物中。

scarcity [ˈskɛrsətɪ] .... ★

n. 缺乏：Having looked to Government for bread, on the first scarcity they will turn and bite the hand that fed them. 他們依靠政府給予麵包，稍有不足時，將轉身撕咬那隻曾撫養他們的手。

shortage [ˈʃɔrtɪdʒ] .... ★★★

n. 不足，缺少，短缺：In the developed countries, there's a great shortage of labor/work force. 已開發國家非常缺乏勞動力。

shortcoming [ˈʃɔrtˌkʌmɪŋ] .... ★★★

n. 短處，缺點：Not being punctuated is his greatest shortcoming. 他最大的缺點是不守時。

sufficient [səˈfɪʃənt] .... ★★★★★

adj. 足夠的，充分的：There is sufficient evidence to indicate that the brain can detect specific levels of amino acids in the blood. 有充分的證據證明大腦可以測出血液中氨基酸的具體含量。

sufficiently [səˈfɪʃəntlɪ] .... ★★★★

adv. 足夠地，充分地

thrive [θraɪv] .... ★★★

v. 興旺，繁榮：Some species of bacteria and fungi thrive on simple compounds such as alcohol. 有些細菌和真菌在像酒精這類簡單的化合物中就能繁殖了。

want [wɑnt] .... ★★★★★

vt. ①（想）要：Ask him what he wants. 問問他想要什麼。②需要；應該，必須：The house wants a new coat paint. 這房子需要重新油漆。③欠缺，缺少

vi. 需要，缺少

n. ①需要，必需品，②缺乏

【片語】① be found wanting 發現某人沒有勇氣，不夠好 ② be wanting 缺… ③ in want 生活困難 ④ in want of 缺乏 ⑤ for want of（由於）缺少

wealth [wɛlθ] .... ★★★★★

n. 富有，財富，豐富，大量，富裕，豐饒：The father passed on the family's wealth to his son. 這位父親把大筆家產傳給兒子。

wealthy [ˈwɛlθɪ] .... ★★★

adj. 富裕的，富庶的：If we want everyone to be healthy, wealthy and happy, strict birth control is quite essential. 如果我們想讓每個人都能過健康、富裕和幸福的生活，就必須實行嚴格的生育控制。

辨析 Analyze

lack, want

1 **lack** *vt.* 「缺乏」，指缺少、缺乏：I lack the courage to do it. 我沒有勇氣做這件事情。

2 **want** *vt.* 「缺少，缺乏，需要」，指缺少並需要：His reply wants politeness. 他的回答很沒禮貌。

辨析 Analyze

abundant, adequate, ample, enough, sufficient

1 **abundant** *a.* 「大量的，充足的，豐富的」，文學意味較濃，固定片語有 be abundant in/with（有豐富的，有大量的）：Cultural life is more varied and abundant in big cities. 大城市的文化生活比較豐富多元。

2 **adequate** *a.* 「足夠的」，正式用語，強調數量多、可以滿足需要：The supply of computers is not adequate to the demand. 電腦供不應求。

3 **ample** *a.* 「足夠的，寬敞的，面積大的」，正式用語：There is ample room for forty desks here. 這裡很寬敞，足以放下 40 張書桌。

4 **enough** *a.* 「足夠的」，普通用語，含有不多不少、恰好滿足需要的意義：There is room enough to spare for another 10 people in the train. 火車上即使再上來 10 個人，也不會顯得很擁擠。

5 **sufficient** *a.* 「足夠的」，正式用語，指數量多、能滿足某種特殊需求，特別是精神上的需求：He has acquired sufficient proficiency to read French literary works. 他已學得足夠的能力閱讀法國的文學作品。

255

08

真假、利弊、有無、價值相關辭彙

Vocabulary of Values

artifact [ˈɑrtɪˌfækt] .... ★★★★★

n. 人工製造，製造物（尤指史前古器物）：
Archeologists debated on the significance of the
artifacts discovered in the ruins of Asia Minor and
came to no conclusion. 考古學家對在小亞細亞廢墟
中發現的史前古器物的意義發生了爭論，不過未獲結
論。

artificial [ˌɑrtəˈfɪʃəl] .... ★★★

adj. 非自然的，人工的，人造的：artificial leather 人造
皮；artificial price controls 人為的物價控制

authentic [ɔˈθɛntɪk] .... ★

adj. 可靠的，有依據的，真實的：an authentic news
report 可靠的新聞報導。

deserve [dɪˈzɜv] .... ★★★★★

v. 應得：The contribution he made deserved to be
rewarded. 他做出的貢獻應該得到獎勵。

desirable [dɪˈzaɪrəbl] .... ★★★★

adj. 理想的，如意的：This brand of home computers
has many desirable features. 這種牌子的家用電腦
具有許多理想的性能。

dummy [ˈdʌmɪ] .... ★★

n. 仿造品，假的東西

fact [fækt] .... ★★★★★

n. 事實，實際：No one can deny the fact that the
moon goes round the earth. 沒人能否認月亮繞地球
轉這個事實。

【片語】① as a matter of fact 事實上，其實② in fact
實際上，其實

false [fɔls] .... ★★★★★

adj. ①不真實的，錯誤的：false ideas 錯誤的觀念②
假的，偽造的：false hair 假髮③虛偽的：give a
false impression 給人一種虛偽的印象

falsification [ˈfɔlsəfəˈkeʃən] .... ★★★

n. 弄虛作假，偽造，歪曲

falsity [ˈfɔsətɪ] .... ★★★★★

n. 不真實：the falsity of an ally 盟友的背信棄義

flaw [flɔ] .... ★

n. 缺點，瑕疵，裂隙：Small flaws in an object show
that it is handmade. 物品上的小裂縫表明它是手工製
作的。

forte [fort] .... ★★
n. 長處：Games are his forte; he plays tennis and football excellently. 體育運動是他的專長，他打網球和踢足球都非常厲害。

genuine [ˈdʒɛnjʊɪn] .... ★★★★
adj. 真實的：All genuine knowledge originates in direct experience. 一切真知都源自於直接經驗。

invaluable [ɪnˈvæljəbl̩] .... ★
adj. 無價的：invaluable paintings 千金難買的繪畫作品；invaluable help 巨大的幫助。

merit [ˈmɛrɪt] .... ★★★★
n. 優點：The merit of a sales tax is that it decreases government reliance on income taxes. 銷售稅的優點是讓政府減少了對所得稅的依賴。

meritorious [ˌmɛrəˈtorɪəs] .... ★★★★
adj. 有功勞的：He wrote a meritorious theme about his visit to the cotton mill. 他寫了一篇對他參觀棉紡織廠有價值的論文。

naught [nɔt] .... ★
n. 零，無：All their work was for naught. 他們所有的工作都白做了。

precious [ˈprɛʃəs] .... ★★★★
adj. 寶貴的，珍貴的：precious words 珍貴的話

real [ˈriəl] .... ★★★★★
adj. ①真的，真實的：real feelings 真正的感情②實際的，現實的：That is the real reason for the absence. 那是缺席的實際原因。

reality [rɪˈælətɪ] .... ★★★★★
n. ①現實，實現：We have to face reality. 我們必須面對現實。②真實：I don't doubt the reality of his story. 我不懷疑他的故事的真實性。

really [ˈrɪəlɪ] .... ★★★★★
adv. 確實，實在，真正地，果然：I really miss you. 我真的很想你。

辨析 Analyze

artificial, fake, false, man-made, mock

1 **artificial** *a.*「人造的，人工的」，指不是天然的，強調非自然性，如：artificial teeth/leg/lake/silk/light 人工假牙／義腿／人工湖／人工絲／人造光；還指「人為的；假的，矯揉造作的」：artificial smile 做作的笑

2 **fake** *a.*「假的，偽造的，冒充的」，指看來像真的，其實是假的，有欺騙的意味，強調偽造的：People hate fake commodities. 人們討厭仿冒品。

3 **false** *a.*「不真實的，錯誤的，假的，偽造的」，可指非自然的，但主要指與事實不相符的、虛假的、錯誤的：Is this statement true or false? 這種說法是對還是錯？

4 **man-made** *a.*「人造的，人工的」，強調人造的，尤指人造（衛星）：a man-made satellite 人造衛星；There is a man-made / an artificial lake in my hometown. 我的家鄉有一個人工湖。

5 **mock** *a.*「假的，假裝的，模擬的，演習的」，一般指不以欺騙為目的的假裝或類比：The army training exercises ended with a mock battle. 軍隊的訓練以一場模擬戰結束了。

substantive [ˈsʌbstəntɪv] .... ★★★
adj. 實質性的：a substantive law 實體法；
　　substantive right 基本人權

tangible [ˈtændʒəbl̩] .... ★
v. 可見的，確實的：tangible asset 有形財產；
　　a tangible roughness of the skin 皮膚確實很
　　粗糙

trivial [ˈtrɪvɪəl] .... ★
adj. 微不足道的：trivial matters 瑣事；the
　　trivial round 日常生活事宜或職責

true [tru] .... ★★★★★
adj. ①真實的，真正的：Is that news true? 那
　　條消息是真的嗎？②忠實的，忠誠的：He
　　is true to his word. 他信守諾言。

truly [ˈtrulɪ] .... ★★★★★
adv. 真正地，忠實地

unblemished [ʌnˈblɛmɪʃt] .... ★
adj. 潔白的，無瑕疵的：an unblemished life
　　沒有污點的人生

valuable [ˈvæljuəbl̩] .... ★★★★
adj. 有價值的，昂貴的：This advice is
　　valuable. 這個建議很有價值。

value [ˈvælju] .... ★★★★★
n. 價值，重要性：Money doesn't have value.
　　錢沒有價值。
v. ①尊重，重視：Which do you value most,
　　wealth or health? 你重視財富還是健康？
　　②評價，給⋯估價：They had their jewels
　　valued. 他們為自己的寶石估價。

without [wɪðˈaʊt] .... ★★★★★
prep. 沒有，缺乏：I cannot do without my
　　glasses. 我沒有眼鏡做不了事。

辨析
Analyze

actual, authentic, genuine, real, true, virtual

1　**actual** *a.*「實際的，事實上的，真實
的」，指事物實際已發生和存在，並非謠
傳或假定的：The actual result does differ
from their predictions. 實際結果的確與他
們預想的不同。

2　**authentic** *a.*「真的，真正的，可靠的，
可信的」，指正宗的、道地的、來源真實
的：This is the authentic document. 這是
真實的文件。

3　**genuine** *a.*「真的，非人造的，真誠
的，真心的」，指與所說的、所宣稱的、
所宣傳的是一致的：The ring is made of
genuine/real gold. 這枚戒指是真金的。

4　**real** *a.*「真的，真正的，真實的，現
實的」，著重指客觀存在，強調真實
性：We need real help, not just oral
promises. 我們需要實際幫助，而不是口
頭的許諾。

5　**true** *a.*「真實的，確實的，真正的，
真的，忠誠的，忠實的，準確的，精確
的」，指與實際或真實情況相符，正確
的：What you said was quite true. 你所
說的非常正確。

6　**virtual** *a.*「實質上的，事實上的，實際
上的」，指區別於表面現象的：Because
the government was weak, the army
became the virtual ruler of the country. 由
於政府軟弱，軍隊成了這個國家實際上的
統治者。

worth [wɝθ] .... ★★★★★

adj. 值得…，有…價值：What is it worth? 它值多少錢？

【片語】be worth doing 值得…：The film is worth seeing. 這部電影值得一看。

worthy [ˈwɝðɪ] .... ★★★★★

adj. 有價值的：He is worthy of our praise. 他值得我們表揚。

辨析 Analyze

invaluable, priceless, valuable, valueless

1 **invaluable** *a.* 「非常寶貴的，極為貴重的，無價的」，比 valuable 語氣重：These manuscripts are invaluable / very valuable to scholars and should be in a museum. 這些手稿對於學者們十分珍貴，應當珍藏在博物館裡。

2 **priceless** *a.* 「非常寶貴的，極為貴重的，無價的」，比 valuable 語氣要重，多指商品，也可用於引申：He owned many priceless antiques. 他擁有許多極為珍貴的古玩。

3 **valuable** *a.* 「貴重的，有價值的」，常用語：Her suggestions are always valuable. 她的建議一向非常有價值。

4 **valueless** *a.* 「不值錢的、毫無價值的」，是 valuable、invaluable和priceless的反義詞：The ring is made of brass. It is valueless. 這枚戒指是黃銅做的，不值錢。

辨析 Analyze

worth, worthy, worthwhile

worth、worthy 和 worthwhile 都是形容詞，指「值得的，值…」，其主要區別在於句型不同。

1 **worth** 的句型為 be worth + 錢／名詞／動名詞／代詞：The watch is worth $120. 這隻錶值 120 美元。

2 **worthy** 有以下種用法：① be worthy of + 名詞／代詞（相當於be worth + 名詞／代詞）：The subject is worthy of careful study. 這個主題值得仔細研究。② worthy 做定語：Mathematics is an important and worthy subject. 數學是一個重要的、有價值的學科。

3 **worthwhile** 有以下種用法：①名詞／動名詞／不定詞 + be worthwhile：The subject / Studying the subject / To study the subject is worthwhile. 這個主題值得研究。② It is worthwhile + 動名詞／不定詞：It is worthwhile studying the subject / to study the subject. 這個主題值得研究。③ worthwhile 做定語：Mathematics is an important and worthwhile subject. 數學是一個重要的、有價值的學科。

09

新舊、傳統、流行相關辭彙

Vocabulary of Trends

conventional [kən`vɛʃənl] .... ★★★
adj. 傳統的，習俗的：The psychiatrist Karen Horney deviated from conventional Freudian analysis by emphasizing environmental and cultural, rather than biological, factors in the genesis of a neurosis. 精神病學家凱琳‧霍尼沒有依照傳統的佛洛依德學說分析強調生物性因素對神經症起源的影響，而是強調環境和文化因素。

currently [`kɜəntlɪ] .... ★★
adv. 現在，目前

fashionable [`fæʃənəbl] .... ★★★
adj. 流行的，時髦的：Short skirts are fashionable now. 現在短裙是蔚為風潮。

outdated [ˌaʊt`detɪd] .... ★★★
adj. 過時的，不流行的：Her ideas on education are rather outdated now. 她的教育思想現在看來很陳腐。

popular [`pɑpjələ] .... ★★★★★
adj. ①流行的，通俗的，大眾的：popular belief大眾的信念②廣受歡迎的，有名的：Swimming is very popular with all ages. 游泳受到各個年齡層人們的歡迎。

popularity [ˌpɑpjə`lærətɪ] .... ★
n. 普及，流行，名望：enjoy/win general popularity 享有盛名，受歡迎，深負眾望

prevail [prɪ`vel] ....★★★★
v. 流行，盛行：In the Pacific Northwest, as climate and topography vary, so do the species that prevail in the forests. 在太平洋的西北部，隨著氣候和地形的變化，森林中普遍的生物種類也在變化著。

prevalent [`prɛvələnt] .... ★
adj. 普遍的，流行的：According to a belief prevalent in many places, a small, forked stick referred to as a divine rod is able to locate subterranean springs. 根據一個在許多地方都流行的說法，用一根分岔的「小神棒」能夠找到地下泉水。

rag [ræg] .... ★★★
n. 破布，碎布：wipe hands on a rag 用抹布擦手

ragged [ˋrægɪd] .... ★★★

adj. 襤褸的，破爛的：clothes as ragged as a
　　scarecrow's. 衣服像稻草人一樣破爛不堪

tradition [trəˋdɪʃən] .... ★★★★★

n. 傳統，慣例

traditionally [trəˋdɪʃənlɪ] .... ★★★★

adv. 傳統地，按慣例地

veteran [ˋvɛtərən] .... ★★★★

n. 老兵，老手

adj. 陳舊的，舊式的：The veteran workers
　　and model workers are held in high/great
　　esteem in this company. 老員工和模範員
　　工在這間公司深受尊敬。

vogue [vog] ....★

n. 流行：This kind of dress had a great vogue
　　in New York. 這種裙子在紐約很流行。

10

秘密、巧合、公開相關辭彙

Vocabulary of Chances

accidental [ˌæksəˈdɛntl̩] .... ★★★
adj. 偶然的：The rate of accidental death has decreased since last year. 去年以來，意外事故的死亡率降低了。

anonymous [əˈnɑnəməs] .... ★★★
adj. 匿名的：Most traditional folk songs are of anonymous origin. 大多數傳統民歌起源不詳。

cipher [ˈsaɪfɚ] .... ★
n. 暗號，密碼

clandestine [klænˈdɛstɪn] .... ★
adj. 秘密的：clandestine dealings 秘密交易

coincide [ˌkoɪnˈsaɪd] .... ★
v. 相符合，巧合，同時發生：The initial appearance of the silver three-cent piece coincided with the first issue of three-cent stamps in 1851. 1851 年，三分銀幣與三分郵票都正好同時出現與發行。

conspiracy [kənˈspɪrəsɪ] .... ★
n. 陰謀

cryptic [ˈkrɪptɪk] .... ★
adj. 神秘的，隱藏的：a cryptic remark 涵義隱晦的話

event [ɪˈvɛnt] .... ★★★★★
n. 事件，事變，大事，活動，比賽項目：Coming events cost their shadows before. 〔諺〕未來之事先有徵兆。

eventful [ɪˈvɛntfəl] .... ★★★★★
adj. 多事的：an eventful year 多事之秋。

fair [fɛr] .... ★★★★★
adj. 公平的，正義的

fairly [ˈfɛrlɪ] .... ★★★★
adv. ①相當，還算：This is a fairly easy book. 這是一本相當淺顯的書。②公正地：come by some thing fairly 光明正大地獲取事物

fortuitous [fɔrˈtjuətəs] .... ★
adj. 偶然的，意外的

freedom [ˈfridəm] .... ★★★★★
n. 自由

freeway [ˈfrɪˌwe] .... ★★★★★
n. 高速公路

haphazard [͵hæpˋhæzɚd] ....★

adj. 偶然的，隨便的：At first glance, a forest appears to be a haphazard collection of trees, shrubs, vines, and flowers. 乍看之下，森林似乎是由樹、灌木、藤蔓和花隨意拼湊起來的集合體。

happen [ˋhæpən] .... ★★★★★

v. ①發生：When did the accident happen? 事故是何時發生的？②碰巧，恰好：I happened to meet her on the street. 我碰巧在街上遇見她。

incident [ˋɪnsədn̩t] .... ★★★★

n. 發生的事：That was one of the strange incidents in my life. 那是我一生中奇怪的事情之一。

incidentally [͵ɪnsəˋdɛntl̩ɪ] .... ★

adv. 偶然地，順便地：The Jamestown settlers explored trading, and only incidentally investigated traces of a lost colony on Roanoke Island. 詹姆士鎮的移民主要是探究貿易，只是在偶然之下才研究了洛亞諾克島已不復存在的殖民地蹤跡。

meeting [ˋmitɪŋ] .... ★★★★★

n. 會議，集會：She always speaks first at a meeting. 她總是在會議上第一個發言。
【片語】at a meeting 在會議上

munificent [mjuˋnɪfəsn̩t] .... ★

adj. 慷慨的：a munificent gift 一份厚禮

random [ˋrændəm] .... ★★

n. 隨機，隨意

adj. 隨機的，任意的：The outcome was a result of a series of random decisions. 這個結果是由一系列隨意的決定產生的。

secret [ˋsikrɪt] .... ★★★★★

adj. 秘密的，機密的：secret negotiation 秘密談判

n. 秘密：The results of the experiments remained a secret. 多項試驗的結果仍舊保密。

secretary [ˋsɛkrə͵tɛrɪ] .... ★★★★★

n. ①秘書，書記：A secretary is often a female. 秘書常為女性。②部長，大臣：the Foreign secretary〔英〕外交大臣

unconventional [͵ʌnkənˋvɛnʃənl̩] ....★

adj. 破例的，自由的

weirdly [ˋwɪrdlɪ] ....★

adv. 奇特地，不可思議地：The Badlands National Park was established in South Dakota to preserve this weirdly beautiful region. 南達科塔的巴蘭德斯國家公園是建來保護這一極美麗的地區的。

辨析
Analyze

accident, event, incident

1 **accident** *n.* 「事故」，指出乎意料之外的不幸事件：Twenty-five people were killed in this traffic accident. 在這場交通事故中有 25 個人喪生。

2 **event** *n.* 「事件，大事，比賽項目」，指有歷史意義的重大事件（中性詞）：The American Civil War is generally regarded as one of the greatest events in the American history. 南北戰爭常被認為是美國歷史上最重大的事件之一。

3 **incident** *n.* 「發生的事，事件，事變」，多指涉及到暴力的重大事件：The president often troubled by ordinary incidents at school. 校長常被學校的日常瑣事所困擾。

狀態、程度

11

狀態、程度名稱總匯

美麗、純潔、骯髒、粗俗、禮貌相關辭彙

Vocabulary of Appearance

Conditons & Degree

beautiful [`bjutəfəl] .... ★★★★★
adj. 美（好）的：How beautiful these painting are! 這些繪畫好漂亮！

beautifully [`bjutəfəlɪ] .... ★★★★★
adv. 出色地，美好地：She can play the piano quite beautifully. 她能彈一手好鋼琴。

beauty [`bjutɪ] .... ★★★★★
n. 美，美麗：He is a person of great beauty. 他長得很好看。

blemish [`blɛmɪʃ] .... ★
n. 玷污
v. 玷污：a face blemished by a scar 臉因疤痕破相

courteous [`kɜtjəs] .... ★
adj. 有禮貌的，謙恭的

decorate [`dɛkəˌret] .... ★★★
v. 裝飾，裝潢，佈置：to decorate a street with flags 用旗幟裝飾街道

defile [dɪ`faɪl] .... ★
v. 弄污：Rivers are often defiled by waste from factories. 河水常受工廠的廢棄物污染。

dignified [`dɪgnəˌfaɪd] .... ★
adj. 尊嚴的，高貴的

dignify [`dɪgnəˌfaɪ] .... ★
v. 使尊榮，使顯貴：He would not dignify the insulting question with a response. 他對無禮的問題不予回應。
n. 尊嚴

dignity [`dɪgnətɪ] .... ★★
n. ①莊嚴，端莊 ②尊嚴，高貴

dingy [`dɪndʒɪ] .... ★
adj. 昏暗的，骯髒的

dirt [dɜt] .... ★★★
n. 污垢：His clothes were covered with dirt. 他的衣服上滿是髒東西。

dirty [`dɜtɪ] .... ★★★★
adj. 弄髒的：We must have our dirty clothes washed. 我們得把髒衣服洗了。
v. 弄髒，弄污：Don't dirty your new coat. 別把你的新外套弄髒了。

emaciate [ɪˈmeʃˌet] .... ★

v. 使消瘦：A long illness had emaciated my father. 長期臥病使我父親消瘦了許多。

emaciated [ɪˈmeʃˌetɪd] .... ★

adj. 瘦弱的，憔悴的

exquisite [ˈɛkskwɪzɪt] .... ★

adj. 精美的，靈敏的：He has exquisite tastes and manners. 他有高尚的品味和舉止。

filth [fɪlθ] .... ★

n. 汙物，污穢：I don't know how you can read such filth. 我不知道你怎麼會去讀這種廢物。

fleck [flɛk] .... ★

n. 斑點，微粒：brown flecks on the skin 皮膚上的褐色斑點

frowzy [ˈfraʊzɪ] .... ★

adj. 不整潔的，臭的：frowzy clothes 髒衣服；a frowzy professor 邋遢的教授

haggard [ˈhægəd] .... ★

adj. 憔悴的：Don't lose so much weight, or you will look haggard. 別瘦太多，不然你會變得很憔悴的。

handsome [ˈhænsəm] .... ★★★★

adj. ①（男）漂亮的，英俊的：a handsome boy 帥哥②（女）端莊的，健美的，好看的：a handsome girl 美女③相當大的，可觀的：a handsome pay 可觀的報酬

humorous [ˈhjumərəs] .... ★★★

adj. 幽默的：a humorous story 幽默故事

hygiene [ˈhaɪdʒin] .... ★

n. 衛生：Codex Committee on Food Hygiene 食品衛生規範委員會

impeccable [ɪmˈpɛkəbl̩] .... ★

adj. 無瑕的

impunity [ɪmˈpjunətɪ] .... ★

n. 免罰：He behaved badly with impunity as he knew the teacher was weak. 他表現不好卻沒有受到懲罰，因為他知道老師軟弱可欺。

impure [ɪmˈpjʊr] .... ★★★★★

adj. 髒的，不純潔的：impure motives 不純的動機；impure thoughts 壞念頭；impure language 下流話

impurity [ɪmˈpjʊrətɪ] .... ★★★★★

n. 雜質

indecent [ɪnˈdisn̩t] .... ★

adj. 淫穢的：indecent talk 下流話；leave in indecent haste 很不禮貌地急忙離開；indecent exposure 有傷風化的暴露

indecorous [ɪnˈdɛkərəs] .... ★★★

adj. 不合禮節的

indignity [ɪnˈdɪgnətɪ] .... ★★★★★

n. 侮辱：put an indignity upon somebody 貶損某人的尊嚴，侮辱某人；subject somebody to indignities 貶損某人的尊嚴，侮辱某人。

innocent [ˈɪnəsn̩t] .... ★★★★

adj. 清白的，幼稚的：Can you provide any evidence that he was innocent of the crime? 你有證據證明他沒有犯罪嗎？

insolent [ˈɪnsələnt] .... ★

adj. 傲慢的，無理的

mean [min] .... ★★★★★

v. 意欲

adj. 卑鄙的：They have an air of freedom, and they have not a dreary commitment to mean ambitions or love of comfort. 他們有一種奔放不羈的風度，沒有一味獻身卑鄙的野心目標或迷戀舒適生活。

messy [ˈmɛsɪ] .... ★★★

adj. 骯髒的，凌亂的：I can't find anything on this messy desk. 我在這張亂七八糟的桌子上什麼也找不到。

noble [ˈnobl̩] .... ★★★★★

adj. ①高尚的，宏偉的：fight for a noble cause 為高尚的事業奮鬥②貴族的，高尚的：a noble family 貴族家庭

peerless [ˈpɪrlɪs] .... ★★★★

adj. 無與倫比的：a peerless beauty 絕代佳人

polite [pəˋlaɪt] .... ★★★
adj. 有禮貌的，客氣的：To be polite to people is proper. 待人有禮貌是正確的。

pretty [ˋprɪtɪ] .... ★★★★★
adj. 漂亮的，秀麗的：She looked pretty in her green dress. 她身著綠色服裝，看上去挺漂亮。
adv. 相當地，頗：I thought the plan was pretty good. 我認為這計畫相當不錯。

pure [pjʊr] .... ★★★★★
adj. ①純的，純潔的：a dress of pure silk一件純絲衣裙②純理論的，抽象的：pure physics 理論物理③完全的，十足的：He shut his eyes in pure bliss. 他閉上了眼睛，感到十分幸福。

rude [rud] .... ★★★★
adj. ①粗魯的，不禮貌的：Don't make rude remarks. 別說粗話。②粗糙的，粗陋的：I sat on the edge of one of the rude chairs. 我坐在一把破椅子的邊上。

smart [smɑrt] .... ★★★★
adj. 漂亮的，時髦的，聰明的，伶俐的
v. 劇痛，刺痛：It is believed that pigs are smarter than dogs. 豬比狗公認更聰明。

smartly [ˋsmɑrtlɪ] .... ★★★★
adv. 漂亮地，時髦地

sordid [ˋsɔrdɪd] .... ★
adj. 骯髒的：The poor family lived in a sordid hut. 這戶窮人家住在一個污穢的小屋裡。

tidy [ˋtaɪdɪ] .... ★★★
adj. 整潔的，整齊的：It's very difficult to keep a room tidy. 要保持房間整齊很困難的。
v. 使整潔，使整齊：You'd better tidy up yourself now. 你現在最好梳理一下。

ugly [ˋʌglɪ] .... ★★★★
adj. 難看的，醜陋的：She is ugly, but kind. 她很醜，但很溫柔。

vulgar [ˋvʌlgɚ] .... ★★
adj. 平庸的：the technical and vulgar names for an animal species 動物種類的科學名稱和通俗名稱

vulgarity [vʌlˋgærətɪ] .... ★★
n. 粗俗

12

次序、混亂、有效、無效相關辭彙

Vocabulary of Order

chaos ['keɑs] .... ★★★
n. 混亂：On the desk were a chaos of papers and unopened letters. 桌上是一堆雜亂的紙和未拆的信。

chaotic [ke'ɑtɪk] .... ★★★
adj. 雜亂無章的，混亂的：After a series of air raid, the traffic in the capital was chaotic. 首都在敵人連續空襲後，交通一片混亂。

clutter ['klʌtɚ] .... ★
n. 混亂
v. 使混亂：The room was cluttered up with old furniture. 房間裡亂七八糟地堆著舊傢俱。

disarray [ˌdɪsə're] .... ★
n. 雜亂，混亂：The enemy troops fled in disarray. 敵軍倉皇逃竄。
v. 雜亂，混亂：The child had disarrayed the books. 孩子把書弄亂了。

discombobulated [ˌdɪskəm'bɑbjəˌletɪd] .... ★
adj. 混亂的，破壞的：His plans were discombobulated by the turn of events. 由於事態轉變，他的計畫被打亂了。

disorder [dɪs'ɔrdɚ] .... ★★★★
n. 紊亂，混亂，騷亂，疾病，失調：The bandits fled in disorder when they heard that a regiment of soldiers were marching to their den. 土匪們在聽說有一個軍團的士兵正向其巢穴進軍後就四處潰逃了。

efficiency [ɪ'fɪʃənsɪ] .... ★★★
n. 效率，能力：Friction lowers the efficiency of a machine. 摩擦會減低機器的效率。

efficient [ɪ'fɪʃənt] .... ★★★★
adj. 有效率的：The mass production of goods resulting from the Industrial Revolution in the 1800's made person-to-person selling less efficient than mass distribution. 19 世紀初的工業革命使得大量配售比一對一的銷售更為有效。

invalid ['ɪnvəlɪd] .... ★
adj. 無效的，有病的：He helps to look after his grandfather who is an invalid. 他幫助照顧他病弱的祖父。

invalidate [ɪn'væləˌdet] .... ★
v. 使作廢

irregularity [ɪˌrɛgjəˈlærətɪ] .... ★

n. 不規則：found the firm's books riddled with irregularities 發現該公司的帳簿中到處都有不正當的地方

maze [mez] .... ★

n. 迷宮：a maze of government regulations 紛亂的政府條例

methodical [məˈθɑdɪkəl] .... ★★★★★

adj. 有條理的

methodology [ˌmɛθədˈɑlədʒɪ] ... ★★★★★

n. 條理，方法：the methodology of genetic studies 遺傳學研究的方法；an opinion poll marred by faulty methodology 觀點調查的效果被錯誤的方法破壞了

muddle [ˈmʌdl] .... ★★★

v. 使混亂：The lesson was not clear and it has muddled me. 這節課不清楚，把我弄糊塗了。

null [nʌl] .... ★

adj. 無效的，空的：render a contract null and void 使契約無效。

offhand [ˈɔfˈhænd] .... ★★★★★

adj. 臨時的，無準備的：I can't tell offhand how much it will cost. 我沒辦法立刻告訴你它值多少錢。

order [ˈɔrdə] .... ★★★★★

n. ①命令：The soldiers received an order to fire. 士兵接到開火的命令。②順序，秩序，正常狀態，整齊：Put these sentences in the right order. 將下列句子按正確順序組合起來。③訂購，訂貨單，等級：He placed an order for ten boxes of apples. 他訂購了10箱蘋果。④目的，意向：He studied hard in order to pass the exam. 他用功讀書以便能通過考試。⑤規則，秩序：To interrupt is not in order. 打斷別人的話會破壞秩序。

【片語】① in order 整齊，秩序井然：Put the books on your desk in order. 把你書桌上的書擺整齊。② in order that / in order to 為了，以便於：We started early in order that we can catch the scene of sunrise. 我們為了趕上日出的景色，提早出發。

v. 命令：He ordered that the work be started at once. 他命令立即開始工作。

probable [ˈprɑbəbl] .... ★★★

adj. 很可能的，大概的：It seems probable that be will arrive before dusk. 他看來很可能會在黃昏前到達。

probably [ˈprɑbəblɪ] .... ★★★★★

adv. 大概，或許，很可能：Probably he won't see you if you are leaving tomorrow. 如果你明天離開，他大概就見不到你了。

turmoil [ˈtɜmɔɪl] .... ★

n. 騷動，混亂：a country in turmoil over strikes 處於罷工混亂中的國家

vain [ven] .... ★★★★★

n. 徒勞，白費：The police tried in vain to break up the protest crowds. 警方企圖驅散抗議的人群，但沒有成功。

adj. 自負的，虛榮的：She's very vain about her good looks. 她為她姣好的容貌而自負。

valid [ˈvælɪd] .... ★★★

adj. 有效的，正當的：valid for three months 三個月內有效

辨析 Analyze

effective, efficient, valid

1 **effective** *a.*「有效的」，指行動、措施、計畫、藥物等有效力的：We must take effective measures to cut down the birthrate. 我們必須採取有效措施降低出生率。

2 **efficient** *a.*「效率高的，有能力的」，指人、管理、機器等工作效率高的、有效率的：A lawyer needs an efficient secretary. 律師需要效率高的秘書。

3 **valid** *a.*「有效的，具有法律效力的」，指證件、票、檔有法律效力的，還指理由、論點、推論、批評等「有根據的、有道理的」，反義詞是 void：You need a valid passport and visa to pass the Customs. 通過海關需要有效護照和簽證。

狀態、程度

13

安全、危險相關辭彙

Vocabulary of Safety & Danger

Conditons & Degree

crisis [ˋkraɪsɪs] .... ★★

n. ①危機：People in that country suffered a great loss during the economical crisis last year. 那個國家的人民在去年的經濟危機中遭受嚴重損失。②轉捩點，決定性時刻，緊急關頭：He's reached the crisis in his illness. 他的病情已到了關鍵階段。

danger [ˋdendʒɚ] .... ★★★★★

n. ①危險：There is always danger in a battle. 戰場上總是有危險。②危險事物，威脅：He looked around carefully for possible dangers. 他仔細察看四周有無危險。

【片語】① in danger 在危險中，垂危② out of danger 脫離危險。

dangerous [ˋdendʒərəs] .... ★★★★★

adj. 危險的：Aeroplanes have the reputation of being dangerous and even experienced travelers are intimidated by them. 飛機以危險著稱，即使有經驗的旅客也為之膽怯。

endanger [ɪnˋdendʒɚ] .... ★

v. 危害：The disappearance of lichens from an area gives warning of an endangered environment. 某地區苔蘚的消失是其環境受到危害的警訊。

fatalism [ˋfetl͵ɪzəm] .... ★

n. 宿命論

fate [fet] .... ★★★★★

n. 命運：I hoped to become a doctor, but fate has decided otherwise. 我本想當醫生的，不過命運卻使我不能如願。

fateful [ˋfetfəl] .... ★★★★★

adj. 重大的，預言性的，致命的：a fateful decision to counterattack 反擊的決定性決策

hazard [ˋhæzɚd] .... ★★★

n. 危險，公害：One major hazard of space travel is the radiation that exists beyond Earth's atmosphere. 地球大氣層外的輻射，是太空旅行的一項重要危害。

hazardous [ˋhæzɚdəs] .... ★★★

adj. 危險的：In chemical factories, employees sometimes receive extra pay for doing hazardous work. 在化工廠裡，員工有時會因為從事危險工作而獲得額外的報酬。

imminent [ˈɪmənənt] ....★

adj. 即將發生的：A darkened sky in the daytime is usually an indication that a storm is imminent. 白天陰暗的天空，通常預示著一場暴風雨即將來臨。

jeopardy [ˈdʒɛpədɪ] ....★

n. 危險：His foolish remark and behavior may put his whole future in jeopardy. 他愚蠢的言談和行為可能會毀了他一生的前程。

peril [ˈpɛrəl] ....★

n. 危機，危險的事物：Keep off peril! 遠離危險！

perilous [ˈpɛrələs] ....★

adj. 危險的：Anxiety is a reaction caused by fear of a situation that is felt to be threatening or perilous. 焦慮是一種在受到威脅或危險的情況下，由恐懼產生的反應。

reliability [rɪˌlaɪəˈbɪlətɪ] ....★★★

n. 可靠性

reliably [rɪˈlaɪəblɪ] ....★★★

adv. 可靠的，可信賴的：Communication satellites transmit information more reliably than do ordinary short-wave radios. 通訊衛星比普通短波無線電更能可靠地傳送資訊。

risk [rɪsk] ....★★★★★

v. 冒險：Although air travel has some risk, statistically it is much safer than any other means of mass transportation. 飛航旅行儘管有風險，不過從資料統計上來看，比其他任何方式的大眾運輸系統安全多了。

ruinous [ˈruɪnəs] ....★★★★★

adj. 災難性的：a ruinous habit 災難性的習慣

safe [sef] ....★★★★★

adj. 安全的：After days' walk, he got to a safe place in the end. 他經過幾天的跋涉，終於抵達一個安全的地方。

safety [ˈseftɪ] ....★★★★★

n. ①安全，保險：I am worried about the children's safety on these busy roads. 這幾條路上交通擁擠，我擔心孩子們的安全。②安全設備，保險裝置③安全場所

security [sɪˈkjurətɪ] ....★★★★

n. ①安全，保障：Security was tight during the President's visit. 總統來訪期間，保安工作十分嚴密。②抵押品：What can we offer as security for the loan? 我們可拿什麼抵押貸款呢？③證券：government securities 公債

辨析 Analyze

safety, security

1 **safety** *n.* 指「安全，保險」，較偏向指個人安全，做定語時修飾生活或生產中具體的裝置：safety belt/net/valve/lamp 安全帶／網／閥／燈；He was anxious about the safety of the children. 他擔心孩子們的安危。

2 **security** *n.* 指「安全，保障，抵押品，證券」，較偏向指公眾或國家安全，做定語時修飾相對抽象的事物：security measures/procedures 安全措施／程序；The Security Council is having a meeting to decide whether to send the UN Security Troops to the area. 安理會正在開會決定是否指派聯合國維和部隊至該地區。

14

光明、黑暗、陰影相關辭彙

Vocabulary of Brightness

bright [braɪt] .... ★★★★★
adj. ①明亮的，晴朗的，輝煌的：a bright sunny day
一個陽光明媚的日子②聰敏的，機靈的：A bright
boy learns quickly. 聰明的孩子學得快。③歡樂
的，美好的：Her face was bright with happiness.
她看起來喜氣洋洋。

brilliant [ˋbrɪljənt] ....★★★★
adj. 光輝的，耀眼的，卓越的：a brilliant color 鮮明的
顏色

dark [dark] .... ★★★★★
adj. ①黑暗的，暗的：It's too dark to read now. 現在看
書太暗了。②深色的，黑色的：He has dark hair.
他的頭髮是黑色的。

daze [ˋdez] .... ★★
v. 昏暈，使發昏，茫然：He looked dazed with drugs.
看樣子他好像因為服藥而頭暈。

dazzle [ˋdæzl] .... ★★
v. 使目眩，使迷惑：Such brilliant prospects almost
dazzled the young girl. 如此光明的前景幾乎迷惑了
那位女孩。

dazzling [ˋdæzlɪŋ] .... ★★
adj. 耀眼的：Andre Watts gave a dazzling
interpretation of Beethoven's *Emperor Concerto*.
安德·華茲出色地詮釋了貝多芬的鋼琴協奏曲《皇
帝》。

dim [dɪm] .... ★★★★
adj. 昏暗的，朦朧的：When telephone calls are
transmitted by satellite, a dim echo can often be
heard on the line. 電話訊號經由衛星傳送時，通常
會聽到微弱的回音。

fuzzy [ˋfʌzɪ] .... ★
adj. 有絨毛的，絨毛狀的，不清楚的：The television
picture is fuzzy tonight. 今晚的電視影像不穩定。

gloom [glum] .... ★★
n. 黑暗，憂愁：switch on a table lamp to banish the
gloom of a winter afternoon 打開檯燈驅除冬日下午
的昏暗

gloomy [ˈglumɪ] .... ★★
adj. 陰暗的，憂鬱的：He looked gloomy when he showed up this morning. 他今天早上來的時候，看起來很陰鬱。

obscure [əbˈskjʊr] .... ★★
v. 使變暗，使不顯著：The old man cactus is so-called because of the long, silvery hairs that totally obscure its leafless, columnar stem. 老頭仙人掌得名於其銀色的長絨毛，這種絨毛完全覆蓋住了其圓柱狀的無葉莖。

shade [ʃed] .... ★★★★
n. 陰影，差別：They sat in the shade. 他們坐在陰涼處。

shadow [ˈʃædo] .... ★★★★★
n. ①陰影，影子，蔭：I saw the shadow of a woman. 我看到一個女人的影子。②暗處，陰暗：He sat in the shadow. 他坐在暗處。

shadowy [ˈʃædəwɪ] .... ★
adj. 多蔭的，朦朧的，模糊的：a shadowy outline 模糊的輪廓

tinge [tɪndʒ] .... ★★★★★
n.（較淡的）色彩
v. 給⋯著色，染：Her cheeks are tinged with red. 她的雙頰泛紅暈。

辨析
Analyze

shade, shadow

1 **shade** *n.*「蔭，陰涼處」，強調溫度而不強調光線，也指色調、濃淡度，還指遮光物：He slept in the shade of the tree. 他在樹蔭下睡覺。

2 **shadow** *n.*「陰影，陰暗處」，強調光線而不強調溫度：The tree is showing a shadow on the ground. 這棵樹在地上投射出一片影子。

15

清晰、含糊、明顯相關辭彙

Vocabulary of Definition

ambiguous [æmˋbɪgjʊəs] .... ★

adj. 含糊不清的：His ambiguous directions misled us; we did not know which road to take. 他模糊的指示誤導了我們，我們不知道該走哪條路。

apparently [əˋpærəntlɪ] .... ★★★★

adv. 表面上，顯而易見地：The apparently homogeneous Dakota grasslands are actually a botanical garden of more than 400 types of grasses. 表面上整齊劃一的達科塔草原，實際上是一處擁有超過400種牧草的植物園。

ascertain [ˌæsɚˋten] .... ★★

v. 確定，查明：Biologists have ascertained that specialized cells convert chemical energy into mechanical energy. 生物學家們已經確認有特殊的細胞能將化學能轉化為機械能。

clarify [ˋklærəˌfaɪ] .... ★★★

v. 澄清，闡明：The government has time and again clarified its position on equal pay for women. 政府已經再次闡明對男女同工同酬的立場。

clarity [ˋklærətɪ] .... ★★★

n. 清楚，明晰：the clarity of the difficult problem by giving a full explanation 以充分的說明來解釋清楚那個難題。

distinct [dɪˋstɪŋkt] .... ★★★★

adj. 清楚的，顯著的，獨特的，迥然不同的：The school of Abstract Expressionism, developed during the mid-1940's, represented a distinct departure from artistic realism. 抽象表現主義學派在1940年代中期發展成熟，它意味著與藝術性的寫實主義劃清界線。

distinction [dɪˋstɪŋkʃən] .... ★★★★★

n. 區分，區別，差別：There is no appreciable distinction between the twins. 這對雙胞胎之間看不出有什麼明顯的差別。

distinguish [dɪˋstɪŋgwɪʃ] .... ★★★★★

v. 區別，分類，使顯出特色：They have distinguished themselves as dedicated social workers. 他們成為傑出又熱心奉獻的社會工作者。

dusk [dʌsk] .... ★★★★★

n. 黃昏，幽暗：It is difficult to see clearly at dusk. 在黃昏時很難看得清楚。

274

dusky [ˈdʌskɪ] .... ★★★★
adj. 微暗的，膚色黑的：dusky skin黑黝黝的
 肌膚；the dusky light of the forest 林中昏
 暗的光線

equivocal [ɪˈkwɪvək!] ....★
adj. 模棱兩可的，意義不清的：Lily's
 equivocal attitude toward John's proposal.
 莉莉對約翰向她求婚的曖昧態度

equivocate [ɪˈkwɪvəˌket] ....★
v. 說話模棱兩可，支吾

evident [ˈɛvədənt] .... ★★★
adj. 明顯的，明白的：The applause made it
 evident the play was a hit. 掌聲證明了該
 劇相當成功。

explicit [ɪkˈsplɪsɪt] ....★
adj. 詳盡的，清楚的：They were explicit in
 their criticism. 他們直截了當地表達了批
 評。

faint [fent] .... ★★★★★
adj. 昏暈的，模糊的，微弱的：I don't have
 the faintest idea of what you mean. 我一
 點也不懂你的意思。

illegible [ɪˈlɛdʒəb!] .... ★★★
adj. 難辨認的

indefinable [ˌɪndɪˈfaɪnəb!] ....★
adj. 難以說明的，不確定的：There's an
 indefinable air of tension at the meeting.
 會議上有種難以描述的緊張氣氛。

limpid [ˈlɪmpɪd] ....★
adj. 清澈的：writes in a limpid style 寫得明白
 易懂。

obvious [ˈɑbvɪəs] .... ★★★★
adj. 明顯的：Travel between time zones may
 result in obvious disturbances in normal
 sleep patterns and body rhythms. 在不同
 時區之間旅行，顯然會擾亂正常睡眠的模
 式和生理節奏。

opaque [oˈpek] ....★
adj. 不透明的：Some glass is so thick that it
 is opaque. 有些玻璃太厚了，無法透視。

plain [plen] .... ★★
n. 平原：vast plains 廣大的原野
adj. ①樸素的，無花紋的：She felt ashamed
 of her plain dress. 她為自己簡樸的穿著感
 到丟臉。②清晰的，明白的：a plain print
 字跡清晰的印刷

transparent [trænsˈpɛrənt] .... ★★★
adj. 透明的：Glass is a transparent material.
 玻璃是一種透明物。

vague [veg] .... ★★★★
adj. 模糊的，含糊的：His speeches are
 always too vague. 他的演講總是太含糊。

16

鬆緊、裸露相關辭彙

Vocabulary of Tightnss & Rareness

Conditons & Degree

bald [bɔld] .... ★
adj. 禿頭的，光禿的：a bald old man 禿頭的老人

bare [bɛr] .... ★★★★
v. 露出：The dog bared its teeth in the snarl. 那隻狗齜牙咧嘴咆哮著。
adj. 空的：Don't walk on that broken glass with bare feet. 不要光著腳走在那些碎玻璃上。

barely [`bɛrlɪ] .... ★★★
adv. 僅僅：The committee had barely entered into the matter when he felt dizzy. 委員會才剛開始討論此事，他就感到頭暈了。

compact [kəm`pækt] .... ★★
adj. 緊密的，小巧的
v. 使緊密，壓緊：In mountainous regions, much of the snow that falls is compacted into ice. 在山區，大量的雪積壓成冰。

dense [dɛns] .... ★★★
adj. 密集的：The earth's core is probably made of a dense material, possibly iron and nickel with small amounts of sulfur and silicon. 地核很可能是由鐵、鎳和小部分的硫與矽等所組成的。

density [`dɛnsətɪ] .... ★★★
n. 密度：the density of population 人口密度

fasten [`fæsn̩] .... ★★★★
v. 扣緊，紮牢，閂住：The original bobsled was merely a strip of animal skin pulled tight and fastened between smoothed strips of wood. 最原始的雪橇不過就是把一張獸皮繃緊並在兩根光滑的木條間綁牢。

flay [fle] .... ★
v. 剝…的皮，嚴責，苛評：The teacher flayed the idle students. 老師嚴懲那些懶惰的學生。

loose [lus] .... ★★★★
adj. 寬鬆的：a loose chair leg 鬆了的椅子腿

naked [`nekɪd] .... ★★★★
adj. 裸體的，毫無遮掩的：Granite crystals are large enough to be seen with the naked eye. 花崗岩晶體大得連肉眼都能看得見。

stringent [`strɪndʒənt] .... ★★★★★
adj. 嚴格的，迫切的：stringent necessity 緊急需要

tight [taɪt] .... ★★★★

adj. ①緊身的，貼身的：This pair of trousers
is too tight. 這條褲子太緊了。②緊的，
牢固的：The critical bolts are all tight
enough. 這些緊急門閂非常的緊。③（時
間）緊的：We have a tight schedule. 我
們的行程安排很緊。

adv. 緊緊地，牢牢地：Etta held the rope tight
in order to avoid falling down. 愛塔緊緊地
抓住繩子以免掉下去。

17

快慢、流暢、簡潔、和諧相關辭彙

Vocabulary of Fluidness

Conditons & Degree

according [əˈkɔrdɪŋ] .... ★★★★★
adv. 按照，根據：According to your words, the man must have died. 照你的說法，那人肯定死了。

compatible [kəmˈpætəbl̩] .... ★
adj. 相容的：Their marriage came to an end because they were simply not compatible with each other. 他們就是無法和睦相處，所以就離婚了。

congenial [kənˈdʒinjəl] .... ★
adj. 意氣相投的：In this small village he found few persons congenial to him. 他在這個小村子裡發現很少有人與他氣味相投。

congeniality [kəndʒiniˈælɪtɪ] .... ★
n. 志趣相投

cooperate [koˈɑpəˌret] .... ★★★
v. 合作，配合：The British cooperated with the French in building the new craft. 英、法兩國合作製造這種新型飛機。

cooperation [koˌɑpəˈreʃən] .... ★★★
n. 合作

coordinate [koˈɔrdn̩et] .... ★★★★
adj. 同等重要的，並列的：coordinate offices of a business 業務上同等的辦事處

coordination [koˌɔrdn̩ˈeʃən] .... ★★★★
n. 整理，協調：These dancers have poor coordination. 這些舞者的動作協調性不好。

coordinator [koˈɔrdn̩etɚ] .... ★★★★
n. 調度員，協調人，〔語〕並列連詞

discord [ˈdɪskɔrd] .... ★★★★★
n. 不和，不一致：Using extremely different decorating schemes in adjoining rooms may result in discord and a lack of unity in style. 在相鄰的房間中，用完全不同的佈置風格擺設的話，會產生不協調和整體感欠佳的感覺。

fast [fæst] .... ★★★★★
adj. 快的，迅速的，（鐘錶）快的：My watch is ten minutes fast. 我的錶快10分鐘。
【片語】fast food (restaurant) 速食（店）
adv. 快，迅速地：Don't run too fast, or else you will not run long. 別跑得太快，否則你跑不長久。

fluent [ˋfluənt] .... ★★★★
adj. 流利的，流暢的：speaks fluent French 說
一口流利的法語

fluid [ˋfluɪd] .... ★★★★
adj. 流動的，液體的
n. 液體，流質：Everyone seems to share in
an intricate set of lore from the past and
present whose deliciousness somehow
would be ruined if Britain were not a truly
fluid society. 每個人似乎都從過去到現在的
經歷中得到一套複雜多元的知識，如果英國
社會不是那麼易變，這種知識的美妙就將或
多或少地遭到破壞。

harmonious [harˋmonɪəs] .... ★
adj. 和諧的，協調的：a harmonious blend of
architectural styles 各種建築風格的完美結
合。

harmony [ˋharmənɪ] .... ★★★★
n. 和諧，和睦：In a beautiful picture there is
harmony between the different colors. 在這
張漂亮的圖畫中，不同的色彩相互調和。

incongruity [͵ɪnkɑnˋgruətɪ] .... ★
n. 不調和，不一致

incongruous [ɪnˋkɑngruəs] .... ★
adj. 不合適的，不協調的：The modern huge
building looks incongruous in that old-
fashioned village. 那棟現代化的高樓在那
古老的村莊裡看起來很不搭。

quick [kwɪk] .... ★★★★★
adj. 快的，迅速的：Could you find a quick
way of doing that? 你能找到做那件事情較
快的方法嗎？

rapid [ˋræpɪd] .... ★★★★
adj. 快的，迅速的：the rapid development of
industry 工業的迅速發展
n. 急流：There is another stretch of rapids. 又
出現一處急流。

slow [slo] .... ★★★★★
adj. 慢的，遲鈍的，不活潑的：She was very
slow to sing us a song. 她遲遲不肯為我們
唱首歌。

small [smɔl] .... ★★★★★
adj. 小的，少的：a small business 小本經營

sudden [ˋsʌdn̩] .... ★★★★★
adj. 突然的，意外的：All of a sudden she
began to laugh. 她突然間笑了起來。

suddenly [ˋsʌdn̩lɪ] .... ★★★★★
adv. 意外地，忽然：I suddenly remembered
that I hadn't locked the door. 我忽然想起
我沒有鎖門。

swift [swɪft] .... ★★★★
adj. 快速的，即時的：a swift runner 跑得很快
的人

swiftly [ˋswɪftlɪ] .... ★★★★
adv. 迅速地，敏捷地：Although it is commonly
believed that an ostrich hides its head
when confronted by danger, it actually
runs away swiftly. 儘管人們常都相信鴕鳥
在遇到危險時會把頭埋起來，但實際上它
會快速地逃開。

teamwork [ˋtim͵wɝk] .... ★★★★★
n. 協力，配合

unanimity [͵junəˋnɪmətɪ] .... ★
n. 同意，全體一致：achieve unanimity
through consultation 通過協商達成一致

unanimous [juˋnænəməs] .... ★
adj. 一致同意的，無異議的：He was elected
with unanimous approval. 他以全體一致同
意而獲選。

unconstant [ʌnˋkɑnstənt] .... ★★★★★
adj. 無常的，常變的

unidentified [͵ʌnaɪˋdɛntɪͅfaɪd] .... ★★★★★
adj. 身分不明的：an unidentified flying object
不明飛行物體

unify [ˋjunəͅfaɪ] .... ★★★★★
vi. 使成一體，統一：Spain was unified in the
16th century. 西班牙是在十六世紀統一的。

辨析
Analyze

fast, quick, rapid, swift

1 **fast** *adj.& adv.* 「快的，快速的；快，迅速地，緊緊地，牢固地」，形容移動中的物體速度很快：I took a fast plane. 我搭乘了一架快速飛機。

2 **quick** *a.* 「快的，迅速的，靈敏的，敏捷的，性急的，不耐煩的」，指迅速敏捷、反應快，也強調某事件突然發生或形容時間短促：He gave a quick answer to the question. 他立即回答了這個問題。

3 **rapid** *a.* 「快的，迅速的」，指運動的過程或結果快，比前兩詞語氣更為正式：A rapid river has a strong current. 湍急的河水水流很強。

4 **swift** *a.* 「迅速的，速度快的；敏捷的，反應快的」，指反應迅速、動作流暢，語氣較正式，略帶文學色彩：There was a swift change of plans. 多項計畫突然改變。

狀態、程度名稱總匯

18

直、彎、斜、角度相關辭彙

Vocabulary of Angles

bend [bɛnd] ....★★★★
v. ①使彎曲：They all bent their head. 他們都低下頭。
②使屈服：We will not bend to anyone. 我們不向任何人屈服。
n. 轉彎處：There is a sharp bend in the road. 路上有個急轉彎。

bent [bɛnt] ....★★★★
n. 傾向，愛好：She has a natural bent for music. 她有音樂天賦。

bias [ˋbaɪəs] ....★★★★★
n. 偏見：She has a strong musical bias. 她對音樂有強烈的偏好。
v. 使…偏離：His background biases him against foreigners. 他的經歷使他對外國人抱有偏見。

corner [ˋkɔrnɚ] ....★★★★★
n. 角落，街道拐角：The truck was coming round the corner near the school. 這輛卡車正開到學校附近的一個轉彎處。
【片語】① at the corner 在轉角處② in the corner 在角落裡

crook [krʊk] .... ★
n. 鉤子，〔俚〕騙子：She carried the parcel in the crook of her arm. 她把包裹夾在臂彎處。

crooked [ˋkrʊkɪd] .... ★
adj. 扭曲的，狡詐的：a crooked road 彎彎曲曲的道路

curve [kɝv] ....★★★★
v. 弄彎，使成曲線
n. 曲線，彎曲：The river curved round the hill. 河流繞山而過。

declivity [dɪˋklɪvətɪ] .... ★
n. 下傾的斜面：The degree of declivity of a beach depends on its sediment composition as well as on the action of waves across its surface. 一個海灘的傾斜程度取決於其沉積物的組成和其表面海浪活動的情況。

deflect [dɪˋflɛkt] .... ★
v. 使偏離：The Coriolis Force causes all moving projectiles on earth to be deflected from a straight line. 科氏力使地球上所有的發射物偏離直線飛行的軌道。

deform [dɪ'fɔrm] .... ★

v. 使變形：a body that had been deformed by disease 因疾病而導致畸形的身體

flexibility [ˌflɛksə'bɪlətɪ] .... ★★★

n. 適應性，靈活性：The flexibility of a man's muscles will lessen as he becomes old. 人變老的時候，肌肉的彈性將降低。

flexible ['flɛksəbl̩] .... ★★★

adj. 靈活的，變通的：Do you know why the wings of an airplane are flexible? 你知道飛機的機翼為什麼是靈活的？

gap [gæp] .... ★★★

n. 裂口，差距

lean [lin] .... ★★★★★

v. ①傾斜，屈身：The trees leant in the wind. 樹在風中搖曳。②靠，倚，依靠：He leant against the door. 他靠在門上。

adj. 瘦的，無脂肪的

loop [lup] .... ★★★

n. 圈，環，環孔

lopsided [lɑp'saɪdɪd] .... ★★★★★

adj. 傾斜的，不平衡的

perspective [pə'spɛktɪv] .... ★★★★

n. 透視，遠景，觀點：I tried to keep my perspective throughout the crisis. 我試圖在整個危機中保持洞察力。

ramp [ræmp] .... ★

n. 匝道，斜坡，斜面，發射裝置

slant [slænt] .... ★

n. 斜面

v. 傾斜：The report on the strike has been slanted. 關於這次罷工的報導遭到了扭曲。

slope [slop] .... ★★★★

n. 傾斜，斜面

v. 傾斜：The hill slopes steeply down to the town. 這座小山陡峭地向下傾斜直到城鎮上。

sloping ['slopɪŋ] .... ★★★★

adj. 成斜坡的，傾斜的：The earliest kind of desk was a box that had a sloping lid, under which there was storage space for writing materials. 最早的書桌是一個有著斜蓋的盒子，蓋子底下有空間可以放文具。

straight [stret] .... ★★★★

adj. 直的：Draw a straight line on the paper. 在紙上畫條直線。

adv. 直接：He will go straight to Singapore. 他將直接去新加坡。

straightforward [ˌstret'fɔrwəd] . ★★★★★

adj. 直爽的，坦率的

supple ['sʌpl̩] .... ★★★★

adj. 易彎曲的，柔順的：Because gymnasts exercise regularly, they have supple bodies. 體操運動員由於經常訓練，所以身體很柔軟。

transform [træns'fɔrm] .... ★★★★

v. 使變形，變換：She transformed the room by painting it. 她把房間上漆，使它為之一新。

transformation [ˌtrænsfə'meʃən] .... ★★

n. 轉化，轉變，改造，改革

upright ['ʌpˌraɪt] .... ★★★

adj. 垂直的，正直的：Gorillas usually walk on all fours but occasionally take a few steps in an upright position. 大猩猩通常用四肢走路，但偶爾也直立起來走個幾步。

vertical ['vɜtɪkl̩] .... ★★★

adj. 垂直的：Walls are usually vertical. 牆通常是垂直的。

zigzag ['zɪgzæg] .... ★

n. 之字形，鋸齒形：a zigzag path through the woods 林中彎彎曲曲的小道

19

尖銳、遲鈍、笨拙相關辭彙

Vocabulary of Sensitivity

acuity [ə'kjuətɪ] .... ★★★★
n. 尖銳（程度）：acuity of hearing 聽力敏感度

acumen [ə'kjumən] .... ★★★★
n. 敏銳：His business acumen helped him to succeed where others had failed. 他那敏銳的經營頭腦，讓他把別人搞不成功的事搞成功了。

acute [ə'kjut] .... ★★★★
adj. 敏銳的，（疾病）急性的：One of California's most acute problems is an inadequate water supply. 加州最急迫的問題之一是供水不足。

adept [ə'dɛpt] .... ★★★★★
adj. 擅長的：She was adept at irritating people. 她善於惹人生氣。

adroit [ə'drɔɪt] .... ★
adj. 靈巧的，機敏的：His adroit handling of the delicate situation pleased his employers. 他巧妙地處理了這一微妙的局面，讓他的老闆感到滿意。

agility [ə'dʒɪlətɪ] .... ★
n. 敏捷，活潑：The agility of the acrobat amazed and thrilled the audience. 這個雜技演員動作敏捷，讓觀眾驚歎不已。

awkward ['ɔkwəd] .... ★★★
adj. 笨拙的，尷尬的：There was an awkward silence, when no one knew what to say. 當沒人知道該說什麼時，就陷入了尷尬的沈默。

blunt [blʌnt] .... ★★★★★
adj. 遲鈍的：Too much alcohol makes your senses blunt. 大量喝酒會使你的感覺遲鈍。
v. 使…變鈍：blunt the enemy's attack 挫傷敵人的銳氣

clumsy ['klʌmzɪ] .... ★★★
adj. 笨拙的，蠢笨的：You are clumsy! You've knocked over my cup of coffee! 你真笨手笨腳！把我的這杯咖啡撞翻了！

crafty ['kræftɪ] .... ★★★★
adj. 靈巧的，巧妙的

dexterous ['dɛkstərəs] .... ★
adj. 靈巧的：dexterous fingers 靈巧的手指

elegant [ˈɛləgənt] .... ★★
adj.(舉止、服飾) 雅致的：an elegant writer 格調高尚的作家

expeditious [ˌɛkspɪˈdɪʃəs] .... ★★
adj. 敏捷的，迅速的：an expeditious answer to an inquiry 對提問迅速回答

facility [fəˈsɪlətɪ] .... ★★★★★
n. 熟練工具：an extreme facility in acquiring new dialects 在學習新方言上有著非凡資質

gauche [goʃ] .... ★
adj. 笨拙的，粗魯的

graceful [ˈgresfəl] .... ★★★
adj. 優美的，文雅的：England's slow and graceful economic collapse 英國緩慢又體面的經濟衰退

inert [ɪnˈɝt] .... ★
adj. 不活潑的，遲鈍的：Helium and neon are inert gases. 氦和氖都是惰性氣體。

moron [ˈmorɑn] .... ★
n. 低能兒，白癡

nimble [ˈnɪmbl] .... ★
a. 輕的，靈敏的：a nimble leap 敏捷的一躍；have a nimble tongue 能言善道；have a nimble mind 十分伶俐

ponderous [ˈpɑndərəs] .... ★★
a. 沉重的，笨重的：a ponderous burden 沉重的負擔；ponderous furniture 笨重的傢俱

sharp [ʃɑrp] .... ★★★★★
adj. ①鋒利的，銳利的：The knife is sharp. 這把刀很鋒利。②輪廓分明的，鮮明的：Sharp fresh footprints in the snow. 雪地上新留下輪廓分明的腳印。③敏銳的，機警的：His sharp eyes would ever miss it. 他的眼睛敏銳，不會錯過它的。④急劇的，猛烈的：Sales of the car have a sharp rising recently. 近來，汽車的銷量劇增。⑤刺耳的：Her voice was so sharp. 她的聲音非常刺耳。
adv. 整：His train came in at eight sharp. 他搭乘的火車在八點整準時到來。

sharpen [ˈʃɑrpn] .... ★
v. 削尖，使敏銳：to sharpen a knife 磨刀

subtle [ˈsʌtl] .... ★★
adj. 微妙的，精巧的，細微的，稀薄的，敏感的：a subtle distinction 微妙的差別

辨析
Analyze

awkward, clumsy, embarrassed

1 **awkward** a.「難操縱的，使用不便的，笨拙的，不靈巧的，尷尬的，棘手的」：The machine is awkward to handle. 這部機器操作起來不方便。

2 **clumsy** a.「笨拙的，簡陋的，不得體的，無策略的」，強調人的手腳不靈活：A clumsy person often knocks things down or bumps into things. 一個笨手笨腳的人經常打翻東西或撞到東西。

3 **embarrassed** a.「尷尬的」，一般用人來作主語：I felt embarrassed. 我感到尷尬。

subtlety [ˈsʌtḷtɪ] .... ★★
n. 微妙，敏銳，細微的區別

tenuous [ˈtɛnjʊəs] .... ★
adj. 細的，稀薄的：the tenuous air at a great height 高空的稀薄空氣

torpid [ˈtɔrpɪd] .... ★
adj. 遲鈍的，不活潑的

touchy [ˈtʌtʃɪ] .... ★★★★★
adj. 易怒的，棘手的：a touchy situation 微妙的形勢

辨析
Analyze

elegant, graceful, gracious

1 **elegant** a.「優美的，文雅的，講究的」，既可指人內在的修養，又可指物外表的雅致，但一般不形容動作；還指簡練的、簡潔的：She is elegant in her manners. 她的言談舉止十分優雅。

2 **graceful** a.「優美的，優雅的，得體的」，指人或人的動作優美的、優雅的，不能形容物體：She just isn't graceful enough to be a dancer. 她的動作就是不夠優雅，不適合跳舞。

3 **gracious** a.「親切的，和藹的，優美的，雅致的，雍容華貴的」，指對人和藹可親、彬彬有禮、不擺架子，還指物體美麗雅致：She was the most gracious hostess I've ever known. 她是我遇到的最和藹的女主人。

辨析
Analyze

acute, keen, sharp

1 **acute** a.「嚴重的，激烈的，敏銳的，（疾病）急性的」，常指人體五官或智力的敏銳、感覺的劇烈、或疾病急性發作：Dogs have an acute sense of smell. 狗有敏銳的嗅覺。

2 **keen** a.「鋒利的，激烈的，強烈的，敏銳的，敏捷的，熱心的，渴望的」，可修飾器具、興趣、感官、性格等，be keen on 意為「喜歡」：I have a knife with a keen edge. 我有一把鋒利的刀。

3 **sharp** a.「鋒利的，銳利的，尖的，輪廓分明的，鮮明的，敏銳的，機警的，急劇的，猛烈的，刺耳的，刺鼻的」，可用來修飾器具、感覺、味道：The robber carried a very sharp knife. 搶劫犯身上帶著一把非常鋒利的刀。

20

單雙、個別相關辭彙

Conditons & Degree

Vocabulary of Numbers

alone [ə'lon] .... ★★★★★

adj. 單獨的：In the large public gardens of Germany, there are special paths for children and "alone ladies". 在德國的大公園裡，有專供兒童和「單身女士」行走的小徑。

desolate ['dɛslɪt] .... ★★

adj. 荒涼的：Large areas of Alaskan land remain desolate due to the harsh climate. 阿拉斯加由於氣候惡劣，大部分的土地仍是荒涼的。

double ['dʌbl̩] .... ★★★★★

adj. 雙的，兩倍的：a double bed 雙人床

n. 雙，兩倍：Jeff has two apples, Lisa has double. 傑夫有兩顆蘋果，麗莎的是他的兩倍。

dual ['djəl] .... ★★★★★

adj. 二重的，兩層的：dual controls for pilot and copilot 飛行員與副飛行員複式操縱裝置

half [hæf] .... ★★★★★

n. 半，一半：It is half past three. 現在是三點半。

【片語】by halves 打退堂鼓，半途而廢

adj. 二分之一的，半個的：I have been in Seattle for half a year. 我來西雅圖已經半年了。

halve [hæv] .... ★

v. 對分，平攤：The twins halve everything. 這對雙胞胎把任何東西都對半分享。

individual [ˌɪndə'vɪdʒuəl] .... ★★★★★

adj. 個人的，個別的，個體的，單獨的，獨特的

n. 個人，個體，不可分割的實體：The rights of the individual are considered to be the most important in a free society. 在自由的社會裡，個人權利公認為是最重要的。

isolate ['aɪsl̩et] .... ★★★

v. 使隔離：One-room schoolhouses can still be found in isolated areas of North America where there are no other schools for many miles. 在北美方圓幾英里都沒有其他學校的偏遠地區，人們還是可以發現多所只有一間房子的校舍。

lonely ['lonlɪ] .... ★★★★

adj. ①孤獨的，寂寞的：a lonely widow 孤獨的寡婦②荒涼的，人跡稀少的：a lonely village 荒涼的村莊

mere [mɪr] .... ★★★★★
adj. ①僅僅的，只不過的：She is a mere
　　child. 她只不過是個孩子。②純粹的：a
　　mere nobody 十足的小人物

neither [ˈniðɚ] .... ★★★★★
adj. 兩者都不：Neither one is right. 兩者都不
　　正確。
pron. 兩者（都不）：Neither of his parents
　　knows English. 他父母都不懂英語。
conj. & adv. 也不：
He has never been to London, and neither
have I. 他從未去過倫敦，我也沒有。
【片語】neither...nor... 既不…，也不…

odd [ɑd] .... ★★★★
adj. 單的，單數的，帶零頭的，零星的，奇怪
　　的，古怪的：He found the antique shop
　　in an odd corner of town. 他在一個小鎮的
　　偏僻角落裡發現了這間古玩店。

only [ˈonlɪ] .... ★★★★★
adv. 僅僅，只不過：When he joined the army,
　　he is only sixteen. 他當兵時才16歲。
adj. 唯一的，僅有的：Young Tom is in school
　　for only three months. 小湯姆僅上了3個月
　　的學。

pair [pɛr] .... ★★★★★
n. 一對，一雙，一副：The students practice
　　English dialogue in pairs. 學生們兩個一組
　　練習英語對話。
　　【片語】in pairs 成雙地
adj. 一對，一雙，一副

personal [ˈpɝsṇl̩] .... ★★★★★
adj. ①個人的，私人的：father' personal chair
　　父親的專用椅子 ②親自的：The minister
　　made a personal visit to the scene of the
　　fighting. 部長親臨戰線視察。③針對個人
　　的，有關私人的：personal problems 個人
　　問題

personality [ˌpɝsṇˈælətɪ] .... ★★★★
n. 人格，個性：He won the election more on
　　personality than on capability. 他以人品而非
　　能力贏得了競選。

辨析
Analyze

individual, personal, private

1 **individual** a. 「個人的，個別的，單獨
的」，強調不是普遍的或整體的，如：
individual liberties/duties/prize/tastes/
style 個人的自由／責任／獎項／品味／
風格；A teacher cannot give individual
attention to each student if the class is
too large. 如果班級太大，老師不可能每
個學生都能注意到。

2 **personal** a. 「個人的，私人的，親自
的，針對個人的，有關私人的，涉及隱
私的」，指自己的、親自的，而不是他
人的，也指涉及到個人或私人的：The
document was drawn under his personal
guidance. 這份文件是在他親自指導下起
草的。

3 **private** a. 「個人的，私人的，秘密的，
私下的，私立的，私營的」，強調不是
公有或集體所有的。This is my private/
personal view. 這是我個人的觀點。

personally [ˈpɝsn̩lɪ] .... ★★★★
adv. 就自己而言：Personally, I think he is dishonest, but many people trust him. 就我個人而言，我認為他不誠實，可是有許多人信任他。

plural [ˈplʊrəl] .... ★★★
n. 複數
adj. 複數的

respective [rɪˈspɛktɪv] .... ★★★★
adj. 分別的，各自的：successful in their respective fields 在他們各自的領域都取得成功

single [ˈsɪŋɡl̩] .... ★★★★★
adj. 單人的，單個的，單一的：Alexander had a single purpose, namely to make money. 亞歷山大有一個目標，那就是賺錢。

singular [ˈsɪŋɡjələ] .... ★★★★
adj. 單數的，獨個的，非凡，異常：an event singular in history 歷史上獨一無二的事件

sole [sol] .... ★★★★
adj. 惟一的：You have to follow the guide whose sole interest is to cover all spots according to his strict schedule. 你得跟著導遊走，而導遊的惟一興趣就是按照他那一成不變的時間表，走過所有風景點。

solely [ˈsollɪ] .... ★★★
adv. 單獨地：did it solely for love 完全為了愛而做

solitary [ˈsɑləˌtɛrɪ] .... ★
adj. 單一的，單獨的：Father usually goes for a solitary walk. 父親通常獨自一人散步。

solitude [ˈsɑləˌtjud] .... ★★★★★
n. 與外界隔絕：Since she is a famous painter, Georgia O'Keeffe's solitude is often interrupted by visitors who want to meet her. 喬治・歐姬芙是一位出名的畫家，所以其獨居的生活常受希望見到她的訪客打擾。

twin [twɪn] .... ★★★★
adj. 雙的，成對的，孿生的
n. 孿生子，兩個相像的人或物之一

辨析 Analyze

alone, lonely, solitary

1 **alone** *a. & ad.* 「單獨的／地」，指客觀上獨自一人、無人做伴。做形容詞時，只可用作表語或後置定語：Her father lives alone in the countryside. 她父親獨自在鄉下生活。

2 **lonely** *a.* 「孤獨的，寂寞的」，強調主觀上、心理上的寂寞、傷感，可用作表語或定語，但不能做副詞：Though I was alone, I was not lonely. 雖然只是我一個人，但我不感到孤獨。

3 **solitary** *a.* 「單獨的，獨自的，單個的，唯一的，孤獨的」，其同義詞分別為 only 和 lonely：He spent many a solitary/lonely night. 他度過了許多孤獨的夜晚。

unique [juˋnɪk] .... ★★★★

adj. 獨一無二的：In his novels, Upton Sinclair showed his unique genius for recreating social history. 辛克萊在他的小說中顯露了其再現社會歷史的獨特天賦。

uniqueness [juˋniknɪs] .... ★★★★

n. 獨一無二的事物：The uniqueness of that building is shaped because all the others like it were destroyed. 那座建築很獨特，因為所有相像的其他建築都毀壞了。

21

狀態、程度名稱總匯

生疏、生熟相關辭彙

Vocabulary of Familiarity

Conditons & Degree

alienate [ˋeljənˏet] .... ★★

v. 使疏遠：The prime minister's policy alienated many benches. 首相的政策使許多議員敬而遠之。

familiar [fəˋmɪljə] .... ★★★★★

adj. ①熟悉的，通曉的：She has become familiar with the house. 她已經熟悉了這間房子。②親近的：After that, I avoided his presence as I felt he was becoming too familiar with me. 從那以後，他一在場我就迴避，因為我覺得他對我太親近了。

familiarity [fəˏmɪlɪˋærətɪ] .... ★★★★★

n. 熟悉，通曉：His familiarity with many rarely used languages surprised us all. 他通曉多種不常使用的語言，讓我們大家都感到驚訝。

intimacy [ˋɪntəməsɪ] .... ★★★★

n. 熟悉，親近：His intimacy with Japan makes him the likely choice as ambassador to that country. 他是日本通，很可能會被委派為該國駐日大使。

intimate [ˋɪntəmɪt] .... ★★★★

adj. 親密的

v. 暗示：Social reformer Jacob Riis's efforts to improve the rundown neighborhoods of New York City were aided by his intimate friend, Theodore Roosevelt. 社會改革家傑柯布・里斯改善紐約市鄰近破落街區的努力，得到了其好友羅斯福的幫助。

raw [rɔ] .... ★★★★

adj. 生的，未煮熟的，未加工的，原始的，未處理的：raw data 第一手資料

22

奇特、怪異、意外相關辭彙 Vocabulary of Strangeness

abnormally [æb'nɔrməlɪ] .... ★

adv. 異常地：Myopia can be the result of an abnormally thick eyeball or the distortion of the lens of the eye. 近視可能是眼球厚度異常或晶體變形的結果。

anomalous [ə'nɑmələs] .... ★★★★★

adj. 反常的：He was placed in the anomalous position of seeming to approve procedures which he despised. 他處境異常，看來只好同意原來不屑一顧的安排。

anomaly [ə'nɑmǝlɪ] .... ★★★★★

n. 異例，異常，變態：A bird that cannot fly is on anomaly. 不能飛的鳥是異常的。

erratic [ɪ'rætɪk] .... ★

adj. 古怪的，不穩定的：erratic behavior 古怪的行為

peculiarity [pɪˌkjulɪ'ærətɪ] .... ★★

n. 獨特性，特色：One of his peculiarities is that his eyes are not the same color. 他的特點之一是兩隻眼睛顏色不一樣。

quaint [kwent] .... ★

adj. 奇異的，不凡的：There is something almost quaint in the image of Irish organized crime, something that calls to mind old movies with Jimmy Cagney. 在愛爾蘭組織犯罪的影像中，有一個近乎離奇古怪的東西，讓人想起了吉米‧卡格尼的老式電影。

queer [kwɪr] .... ★★

adj. 奇怪的，古怪的：to speak a queer language 說一種奇特的語言。

v. 損害

strange [strendʒ] .... ★★★★★

adj. ①奇怪的，奇異的：The food looks strange but is good. 這種食物看起來很古怪，但吃起來不錯。②陌生的，生疏的，異鄉的：She is still strange to city life. 她還是過不慣城市的生活。

stranger ['strendʒɚ] .... ★★★★★

n. 陌生人，外地人，外國人

uncanny [ʌn'kænɪ] .... ★

adj. 不可思議的，離奇的

291

辨析 Analyze

curious, odd, peculiar, queer, strange

1 **curious** *a.* 「奇特的，稀奇的；好奇的，好求知的」，指奇異、獨特而引起注意或探索：He has a curious scar on his chest. 他胸口有塊奇特的疤。

2 **odd** *a.* 「奇特的，古怪的」，指反常而使人感到困惑或奇異：What seemed odd to me was that I saw snow in Miami. 讓我感到稀奇的是我居然在邁阿密看到了雪。

3 **peculiar** *a.* 「奇怪的，古怪的，特有的，獨具的，獨特的」，指奇特的、古怪的、陌生的（貶義詞），還指獨特的、特有的（中性詞）：This drink tastes peculiar. 這種飲料嚐起來很獨特。

4 **queer** *a.* 「奇怪的，異常的」，較老的用法，中性詞，還指生病的、頭暈的：It had a queer flavor, rather sweet at first, then slightly bitter. 這東西味道很怪，先是很甜，然後有點苦。

5 **strange** *a.* 「奇怪的，奇異的，陌生的，生疏的」，指未曾見過而使人感到新奇、生疏，常用語：Strange customs prevail among the inhabitants. 這些居民中盛行一些奇怪的風俗。

23

合適、可能、成敗相關辭彙

Vocabulary of Possbility

appropriate [əˋproprɪˏet] .... ★★★★★
adj. 適當的，恰當的：Screaming is not an appropriate response to the situation. 尖叫不是在這種情況下的恰當反應。

approximately [əˋprɑksəmɪtlɪ] .... ★★
adv. 近似地：In the phenomenon of atomic fission, the nucleus is split into two pieces of approximately equal mass. 在原子裂變的現象中，原子核分裂成幾乎相等的兩塊。

chance [tʃæns] .... ★★★★★
n. ①機會，機遇：a good chance of going abroad 出國的好機會②可能性
【片語】① by chance 偶然，碰巧② take a chance 冒險，投機

contingent [kənˋtɪndʒənt] .... ★
adj. 可能發生的：Whether or not we arrive on time is contingent on the weather. 我們是否準時到達，要視天氣情況而定。

fail [fel] .... ★★★★★
v. 失敗，不及格：She never fails to write to her mother once a month. 她每月給母親寫封信，從未間斷過。
【片語】fail an exam 考試不及格

failure [ˋfeljɚ] .... ★★★★
n. ①失敗：His plans ended in failure. 他的計畫以失敗告終。②失敗的人或事：As a writer, he was a failure. 他是一個失敗的作家。

feasible [ˋfizəbḷ] .... ★★★
adj. 切實可行的：His plan should succeed, for it seems quite feasible. 他的計畫似乎相當切實可行，應該能成功。

fit [fɪt] .... ★★★★★
adj. 合適的
v. 配合：The architect Frank believed that a building should be designed to fit its function and its location. 建築師法蘭克相信，建築物應該依據其功用和所處位置來設計。

improper [ɪmˋprɑpɚ] .... ★
adj. 不適當的，不合適的：an act improper to the occasion 不合時宜的行為；put something to an improper use 誤用

impropriety [ˌɪmprəˈpraɪətɪ] .... ★
n. 不適當

ineligible [ɪnˈɛlɪdʒəbl̩] .... ★
adj. 無資格的，不適當的：He was ineligible
　　to vote, because he didn't belong to the
　　club. 他不是那個俱樂部的成員，所以不具
　　投票資格。

medium [ˈmidɪəm] .... ★★★★
n. 媒介，中間
adj. 中等的：He writes stories, but the theatre
　　is his favorite medium. 他寫小說，不過戲
　　劇文學是他最喜愛的藝術形式。

negative [ˈnɛɡətɪv] .... ★★★
adj. 否定的，消極的，反面的，負的，陰性
　　的：Life is full of overwhelming odds. You
　　can't really eliminate the negatives but
　　you can diminish them. 生活充滿了無法抵
　　擋的機會，你不可能全然消滅那些負面的
　　因素，但是你能弱化它們。

opportunity [ˌɑpɚˈtjunətɪ] .... ★★★★★
n. 機會：The Fulbright Scholar-in-Residence
　　Program gives colleges and universities in
　　the United States the opportunity to host
　　visiting scholars from other countries. 富布
　　萊特方案基金的「駐地學人方案」，為美國
　　的學院和大學提供了吸引其他國家訪問學人
　　的機會。

optimum [ˈɑptəməm] .... ★
adj. 最優的

perhaps [pɚˈhæps] .... ★★★★★
adv. 或許，也許，恐怕："Perhaps I'll just buy
　　a jacket," said the young man. 年輕人說：
　　「也許我只是想買一件夾克。」

perverse [pɚˈvɝs] .... ★
adj. 不正當的，反常的，任性的：perverse
　　youngster 任性的年輕人。

plausible [ˈplɔzəbl̩] .... ★★★★★
adj. 似乎合理的：the plausible talk of a
　　salesperson 推銷員的花言巧語

possibility [ˌpɑsəˈbɪlətɪ] .... ★★★★
n. ①可能（性）：The possibility of man's
　　travelling to the moon has been proved. 人
　　類漫遊月球的可能性已經被證實了。②可
　　能的事：The general would not accept the
　　defeat as a possibility. 將軍不會接受失敗的
　　可能性。

possible [ˈpɑsəbl̩] .... ★★★★★
adj. 可能的，做得到的：I would like to see
　　him as soon as possible, please. 我想儘
　　快見到他。
【片語】as...as possible 盡可能

possibly [ˈpɑsəblɪ] .... ★★★★★
adv. ①可能地，合理地：I'll do all I possibly
　　can. 我將盡力去做。②也許，或者

辨析
Analyze

chance, opportunity

1 **chance** *n.* 「機會，機遇」，指偶然機
會，中性詞，如 by chance（偶然），
stand a chance of doing sth.（大有希
望）：It's the chance of a lifetime. 這是
一生難得的機會。

2 **opportunity** *n.* 「機會」，指良好的時
機、契機、有機會做希望做的事，褒義
詞：We are glad to have this wonderful
opportunity of discussing the matter with
Professor Wang. 我們很高興能有此絕佳
的機會和王教授討論此事。

potent [ˈpotn̩t] .... ★★★★
adj. 強有力的，有全權的：Do potent drugs work on the common cold? 特效藥是否能治療普通的感冒？

potential [pəˈtɛnʃəl] .... ★★★★
adj. 可能的，潛在的
n. 潛力：Every seed is a potential plant. 每粒種子都可能長成植物。

practicable [ˈpræktɪkəbl̩] .... ★
adj. 能實行的，行得通的，適用的：a practicable plan 可行的計畫

practical [ˈpræktɪkl̩] .... ★★★★★
adj. 實踐的，實用的：George Washington Carver discovered hundreds of practical applications for the peanut, the sweet potato, and the soybean. 喬治‧華盛頓‧卡瓦發現了數百種關於花生、甘薯和黃豆的實用用法。

proper [ˈprɑpɚ] .... ★★★★★
adj. ①適當的，恰當的：He's never had a proper job. 他一直沒有一份合適的工作。②合乎體統的，正當的：It wasn't proper for a man to cry. 以前男人哭泣是不成體統的。③本身的：By the time I got to the village proper, everyone was out to meet me. 當我到達這個村子時，所有的人都出來迎接我。

properly [ˈprɑpɚlɪ] .... ★★★★
adv. ①適當地，正當地：I'm learning Italian, but I still can't speak it properly. 我正在學義大利語，但還說不好。②嚴格地（說來）

qualified [ˈkwɑləˌfaɪd] .... ★★★★
adj. 合格的：She gave qualified agreement. 她有條件地同意了。

succeed [səkˈsid] .... ★★★★★
v. ①成功：May you succeed. 祝你成功。②接著發生，繼承：He should succeed to the estate by law. 根據法律，他應繼承產業。③接替，接…之後：Who will succeed him as our teacher? 誰接替他當我們的老師呢？

success [səkˈsɛs] .... ★★★★★
n. 成功，成就，成功的事：He has had three successes in his life. 他一生中取得了三次成功。

successful [səkˈsɛsfəl] .... ★★★★★
adj. 成功的：James Madison was successful in his campaign for President of the United States in 1808. 詹姆斯‧麥迪遜在1808年的美國總統競選中當選。

successor [səkˈsɛsɚ] .... ★★★★★
n. 繼承人：appoint a successor to a headmaster 任命校長繼承人

suit [sut] .... ★★★★★
v. ①合適，適中：His coat suits him perfectly. 他的外套很適合他。②中…的意：You should say something that suits her. 你應說些合她意的話。
n. ①一套衣服／西服：He always worn an expensive gray suit. 他總穿著一套昂貴的灰色西服。②起訴，訴訟：a civil suit 民事訴訟

suitable [ˈsutəbl̩] .... ★★★★
adj. 適合的：This toy is not suitable for young children. 這個玩具不適合小孩玩。

unbecoming [ˌʌnbɪˈkʌmɪŋ] .... ★★★
adj. 不配的，不適當的：unbecoming conduct of an officer 不符合官員身份的行為

unfit [ʌnˈfɪt] .... ★
adj. 不適於的，不適當的

unseemly [ʌnˈsimlɪ] .... ★
adj. 不合適的

uprising [ˈʌpˌraɪzɪŋ] .... ★
n. 叛亂：peasant uprising 農民起義

295

辨析
Analyze

appropriate, fit, proper, suitable

1 **appropriate** *a.*「適合的，恰當的」，正式用語，強調適合某種場合：Short skirts are not appropriate for the formal dinner. 正式的宴會不適合穿短裙。

2 **fit** *a.*「相稱的，稱職的，適合的」，普通用語，表示適合某種目的或某種用途，也可指「健康的」：Mr. Smith is not fit for the position. 史密斯先生不適合這份工作。

3 **proper** *a.*「合適的，恰當的」，強調符合風俗習慣、道德標準，還指「固有的，本身的，正派的」：You must use proper language in the company of ladies. 和女士們在一起時你說話要得體。

4 **suitable** *a.*「合適的，適宜的」，表明符合某種目的、某種場合的要求：We must find a suitable day for the meeting. 我們必須找一個合適的日期開會。

狀態、程度名稱總匯

24

能力、能夠相關辭彙

Vocabulary of Capability

ability [ə'bɪlətɪ] .... ★★★★★
n. ①能力，智能：He has enough ability to manage the business. 他有能力管理企業。②能耐，才能，才幹：Washington had great ability as a general. 華盛頓具有非凡的才能擔當將軍一職。

able ['ebḷ] .... ★★★★★
adj. 能夠，有能力的：He is an able man. 他是個能幹的人。
【片語】be able to do sth. 能夠／有能力做某事

capability [ˌkepə'bɪlətɪ] .... ★★
n. 能力：The little girl has great capability as a singer and should be trained. 這個小女孩很有當歌手的才華，應該加以訓練。

capable ['kepəbḷ] .... ★★★★★
adj. 有能力的：That mob's capable of any crime. 那個暴徒什麼勾當都幹得出來。

capacity [kə'pæsətɪ] .... ★★★★★
n. 能力，容量，容積，能量，資格：Algae vary in their capacity to tolerate salinity changes. 藻類忍受鹽分變化的能力各不相同。

competence ['kɑmpətəns] .... ★★
〔記〕{com（同）+ pet（要求）+ ence（性質，程度）}
n. 能力，勝任，稱職：communication competence 交際能力

competent ['kɑmpətənt] .... ★★★
adj. 能勝任的：If you want to learn English, you must first find a competent teacher. 如果你想學習英文，必須先找一位稱職的教師。

enable [ɪn'ebḷ] .... ★★★★★
v. 使能夠：Part-time employment gives students valuable experience and sometimes enables them to pay their college tuition. 課餘打工能夠豐富大學生的人生經歷，有時候還能幫助他們繳納大學學費。

energetic [ˌɛnə'dʒɛtɪk] .... ★
adj. 有力的，精力旺盛的

energetically [ˌɛnəˈdʒɛtɪkḷɪ] .... ★

adv. 積極地，精力旺盛地：As part of his domestic policy, known as the New Frontier, President Kennedy energetically advocated the accelerated development of the United States space program. 作為國內政策的一部分，即著名的新國境政策，甘迺迪總統積極地倡導加速美國太空計畫的發展。

energize [ˈɛnəˌdʒaɪz] .... ★

v. 供給能量，使活躍：His childhood haunted and energized him. 他的童年時常縈繞在他心頭，並使他奮發向上且精力充沛。

energy [ˈɛnədʒɪ] .... ★★★★★

n. ①精力，活力：He's full of energy. 他精力充沛。②能，能量：electrical energy 電能

faculty [ˈfækḷtɪ] .... ★★★★★

n. 才能，本領，能力，全體教員，院，系，學院或大學的系、科：These girls have the faculty to learn languages easily. 這幾個女孩擅長學習語言。

genius [ˈdʒinjəs] .... ★★★★

n. 天才，創造能力，才華：Einstein was a genius. 愛因斯坦是一個天才。

incapacitate [ˌɪnkəˈpæsəˌtet] .... ★★

v. 使…不能：It is believed the arthritis incapacitates more people than does any other chronic disorder. 很多人相信比起其他慢性病來，關節炎危害到了更廣泛的人群。

incompetent [ɪnˈkɑmpətənt] .... ★★

adj. 不稱職的：He is a total incompetent. 他是一個毫無能力的人。

proficient [prəˈfɪʃənt] .... ★

adj. 熟練的，精通的：She is proficient at/in figure skating. 她精於花式溜冰。

skill [skɪl] .... ★★★★★

n. ①技能，技巧，手藝：make a living with a skill 以技藝謀生 ②熟練：She plays the piano with skill. 她鋼琴彈得很好。

skillful [ˈskɪlfəl] .... ★★★

adj. 熟練的：He is a skillful and effortless mechanic. 他是一位很有技巧、駕輕就熟的機械修理工。

talent [ˈtælənt] .... ★★★★

n. 天才，才能，人才：My sister has a talent for music. 我妹妹有音樂才華。

unable [ʌnˈebḷ] .... ★★★★★

adj. 不能的，不會的：He was unable to sleep at night because of anxiety. 他內心焦慮，晚上難以入睡。

辨析
Analyze

ability, capacity

1 **ability** *n.*「能力，本領；才能，才智」，指做某事的能力，可以通過學習或鍛鍊而獲得，後接不定詞，其形容詞結構為 to be able to do sth.：I admire her simply for her ability to speak English so fluently. 我羨慕她，只因她的英語是那麼的流利。

2 **capacity** *n.*「能力，才能；容量，容積」，指學習、理解能力，後跟不定式或介詞for/of：Human beings were born with a capacity to learn / for learning / of learning a language. 人類生來就有學習語言的能力。

25

聰明、伶俐、精明相關辭彙

Vocabulary of Smartness

agile [ˈædʒaɪl] .... ★★
adj. 敏捷的，活潑輕快的：The boy escaped with an agile leap. 這男孩敏捷地一跳，逃脫了。

alert [əˈlɝt] ....★★★★
adj. 機敏的：The hostess remained standing, alert to everyone's drink needs. 女主人一直站著，隨時準備給大家斟酒。

astute [əˈstjut] .... ★
adj. 機敏的，狡猾的：play the most astute politics 玩弄最狡猾的權術

canny [ˈkænɪ] .... ★★
adj. 精明的，節儉的

clever [ˈklɛvɚ] ....★★★★
n. (指人或動物) 聰明的，機靈的：He is clever at English. 他擅長英語。

daft [dæft] .... ★★★
adj. 愚笨的，瘋狂的

deft [dɛft] .... ★
adj. 靈巧的，熟練的：deft hands 巧手

humble [ˈhʌmbl] ....★★★★
adj. 地位低下的，恭順的，謙卑的：The doctor was humble about his work, although he cured many people. 這位醫生雖然治好了許多人的病，但仍很謙遜。

idiot [ˈɪdɪət] .... ★
n. 白癡，傻子：Idiot! You've dropped my watch. 傻瓜，你把我的錶弄掉了。

idiotic [ˌɪdɪˈɑtɪk] .... ★
adj. 愚蠢的

ingenious [ɪnˈdʒinjəs] .... ★★
adj. 機靈的，製作精巧的：Duke's ingenious orchestration techniques made him perhaps the most remarkable artist that jazz has produced. 杜克天才的管弦樂曲技，使得他成為迄今為止也許是有爵士樂以來最偉大的藝術家。

insane [ɪnˈsen] .... ★
adj. 發狂的，精神錯亂的：He must be insane to drive his car so fast. 他把車開得這麼快，一定是瘋了。

intelligent [ɪnˋtɛlədʒənt] .... ★★★★
adj. 聰明的：Can you say that dolphins are much more intelligent than other animals? 你能說海豚比其他動物聰明得多嗎？

intelligible [ɪnˋtɛlədʒəbl] .... ★★★★
adj. 可理解的：an intelligible set of directions 一套易於理解的說明

responsive [rɪˋspɑnsɪv] .... ★★★★
adj. 敏感的，易引起反應的：She is responsive to kindness. 她易受善心所感動。

sane [sen] .... ★
adj. 理智的，健全的：I don't think a sane person would drive as dangerously as he did. 我想，一個神智清醒的人是不會像他那樣危險地開車的。

sensitivity [ˏsɛnsəˋtɪvətɪ] .... ★
n. 敏感（性），靈敏度：sensitivity training 感受能力訓練

shrewd [ʃrud] .... ★
adj. 精明的：shrewd business men 精明的商人

silly [ˋsɪlɪ] .... ★★★★
adj. 傻的，糊塗的：Mary is silly girl. 瑪麗是個傻女孩。

stupid [ˋstjupɪd] .... ★★★★
adj. 愚蠢的，蠢笨的：What a stupid idea! 多麼愚蠢的想法！

tact [tækt] .... ★
n. 老練，機智：A minister of foreign affairs who lacks tact is a dangerous man. 一個缺乏機智的外交部長是個很危險的人物。

tactless [ˋtæktlɪs] .... ★
adj. 沒有策略的：It was rather tactless for me to ask such a question. 我竟問出這麼個問題，實在是沒有大腦。

wisdom [ˋwɪzdəm] .... ★★★★★
n. ①智慧，明智：the collect wisdom of the mass 群眾的集體智慧②古訓，至理名言：the wisdom of the ancients 古人的名言

wise [waɪz] .... ★★★★★
adj. 智慧的，聰明的：a wise man 聰明的人

wit [wɪt] .... ★★★★
n. 智力，才智，智慧：He had the wit to telephone the police. 他機智地報了警。

witty [ˋwɪtɪ] .... ★
adj. 機智的，風趣的：a witty sculpture 別出心裁的雕塑品

26

饑渴、疲勞、活潑、沉悶相關辭彙 Vocabulary of Vigor

bleak [blik] .... ★★★★★
adj. 荒涼的：A bleak landscape is the most characteristic feature of his paintings. 他的畫最典型的特徵是荒涼的風景。

briskly [ˋbrɪsklɪ] .... ★
adv. 活潑的，輕快的：Health experts say that walking briskly strengthens the heart and lungs. 健康專家指出，快步行走可以增進心肺健康。

debilitating [dɪˋbɪləˏtetɪŋ] .... ★
adj. 衰弱的：a debilitating climate 使人虛弱無力的氣候

desirous [dɪˋzaɪrəs] .... ★★★★★
adj. 渴望的：Both sides were desirous of finding a quick solution to the problem. 雙方都渴望找到迅速解決問題的辦法。

doleful [ˋdolfəl] .... ★
adj. 悲哀的：a doleful loss 令人悲傷的損失

dreary [ˋdrɪrɪ] .... ★
adj. 陰鬱的，沉悶的：cheer a dreary mind 使憂鬱寡歡的心情振作起來

dull [dʌl] .... ★★★★
adj. ①枯燥的：a dull book 枯燥無味的書②（色彩等）不鮮明的，晦暗的：a dull color 晦暗的色彩③陰沈的：dull weather 陰沈的天氣④（聲音）低沈的，沉悶的：a dull thunder 低沈的雷聲⑤愚鈍的：a dull mind 遲鈍的頭腦⑥鈍的：A knife with a dull edge 鈍刀

enervate [ˋɛnɚˏvet] .... ★
v. 使衰退：The luxury enervates and destroys nations. 「奢侈」使民族萎靡不振並致毀滅。

exhaust [ɪgˋzɔst] .... ★★★★
v. 使疲倦：I think we've exhausted this subject; let's go on to the next. 我想我們已經竭盡所能地討論了這一問題，我們談下一個吧。

exuberant [ɪgˋzjubərənt] .... ★

adj. ①（人）充滿活力的：The exuberant young man never ego tripped, never grabbed the spotlight. 這個充滿活力的年輕人從不謀私利，從不出風頭。②（植物）茂盛的：The plant with exuberant foliage was evocative of spring. 枝葉茂盛的植物讓人想起了春天。

famish [ˋfæmɪʃ] .... ★

v. 使…挨餓：You are all resolved rather to die than to famish. 你們都下了決心，寧願死也不願挨餓。

fatigue [fəˋtig] .... ★★★

n. 疲乏，勞累：the fatigue of a long hike 一次長途跋涉的勞累

feeble [fibl] .... ★★★★

adj. 微弱的：By feeble contractions, the jellyfish propels itself along, buoyed up by the surrounding water. 水母藉由微弱的收縮向前划動，靠周圍的水浮起來。

frail [frel] .... ★

adj. 脆弱的，意志薄弱的：In her late seventies, too frail to continue her arduous farm work, Anna Mary Moses began painting simple scenes of rural life. 安・摩西七十多歲了，由於太過虛弱做不了辛苦的農活，開始畫關於鄉村生活的簡單畫作。

impotence [ˋɪmpətəns] .... ★

n. 無效，無力，虛弱

indefatigable [͵ɪndɪˋfætɪgəbl] .... ★

adj. 不疲倦的

inexhaustible [͵ɪnɪgˋzɔstəbl] ...... ★★★★★

adj. 用不完的，無窮無盡的：an inexhaustible supply of coal 用之不竭的煤炭供應

languid [ˋlæŋgwɪd] .... ★

adj. 精神不振的：The extreme heat made everyone quite languid. 高溫使人們無精打采。

languish [ˋlæŋgwɪʃ] .... ★

v. 變衰弱

malnutrition [͵mælnjuˋtrɪʃən] .... ★

n. 營養不良

naughty [ˋnɔltɪ] .... ★

adj. 頑皮的，淘氣的：The naughty boy devised a plan for winning the entrance tickets to the football match. 這個淘氣的男孩想出一種巧妙的辦法，來得到足球比賽的入場券。

picturesque [͵pɪktʃəˋrɛsk] .... ★★★★★

adj. 如畫般的，生動的：a picturesque village 景色如畫的村莊；a picturesque account 十分生動的敘述

realistic [rɪəˋlɪstɪk] .... ★

adj. 逼真的：She gave us a realistic appraisal of our chances. 她對我們的機會做了一個現實的評估。

starvation [stɑrˋveʃən] .... ★★★★

n. 饑餓，餓死：I'm on a starvation diet. 我正進行饑餓減肥法。

starve [stɑrv] .... ★★★★

v. 挨餓，（使）餓死：The poor dog starved to death. 那隻可憐的狗餓死了。

stocky [ˋstɑkɪ] .... ★★★★★

adj. 結實的，粗短的：stocky young trees 粗短的小樹。

thirst [θɝst] .... ★★★

n. ①渴，口渴②渴望，熱望
v. ①感到口渴②渴望，熱望

thirsty [ˋθɝstɪ] .... ★★★

adj. 口渴的，口乾的：It makes me feel thirsty! 它讓我感到口渴！

tire/tyre [taɪr] .... ★★★★★

n. 輪胎

vivid [ˋvɪvɪd] .... ★★★
adj. 生動的：Because of its vivid yellow, black and orange coloring, the emperor penguin stands out against the usually bleak landscape of its habitat. 由於國王企鵝擁有鮮豔的黃、黑、橙的色彩，在常顯得很陰冷的棲息地上顯得很突出。

vividness [ˋvɪvɪdnɪs] .... ★★★
n. 生動

weak [wik] .... ★★★★★
adj. ①虛弱的，無力的：too weak to walk 太虛弱走不動②（能力等）弱的，差的：weak in English 不擅長英語③微弱的，淡薄的，稀薄的：weak tea 淡茶

wearily [ˋwɪrɪlɪ] ....★
adv. 疲倦地，厭倦地

辨析 Analyze

faint, feeble, wea

1 faint *a.*「不清楚的，模糊的，隱約的，無力的，微弱的，微小的，眩暈的」，指力量虛弱到快要支持不住了的，還指聲音、氣味、顏色、光線、風、希望等微弱或微小：Her breathing grew faint. 她的呼吸變得微弱。The sound/smell/color/light became fainter than before. 聲音／氣味／顏色／光線變得比先前要小／淡／弱一些。

2 feeble *a.*「虛弱的，衰弱的，無力的」，指因年紀、疾病而虛弱，正式用語：The old woman is too feeble/weak to do her own shopping. 那位老婦人身體太虛弱，不能自己去買東西。

3 weak *a.*「虛弱的，無力的，（能力等）弱的，差的，微弱的，淡薄的，稀薄的」，指身體、意志、精神等虛弱，也指力量薄弱，還指聲音微弱，是普通用語：My mother is weak both in mind and in body. 我的母親身心衰弱。

303

27

忙碌、輕閒、謹慎相關辭彙

Conditons & Degree

Vocabulary of Busyness & Carefulness

busy [ˈbɪzɪ] .... ★★★★★
adj. 忙的，繁忙的：Did he had a busy day yesterday? 昨天他忙了一天嗎？
【片語】①be busy doing sth. 忙於做某事②be busy with sth. 忙於某事

careful [ˈkɛrfəl] .... ★★★★
adj. ①仔細的，小心的：Be careful not to break the eggs. 當心，別打破了雞蛋。②細緻的，精心的：careful reading 細心閱讀
【片語】be careful (of) 當心，小心

careless [ˈkɛrlɪs] .... ★★★
adj. 粗心的，粗枝大葉的，漫不經心的：He maintained a hard, careless deportment. 他保持一種漠不關心的嚴酷態度。

caution [ˈkɔʃən] .... ★★
n. 小心，謹慎，告誡，警告
v. 告誡，警告：Agricultural experts always caution farmers to irrigate in regions receiving only light rainfall. 農業專家一向告誡少雨地區的農民要進行灌溉。

cautious [ˈkɔʃəs] .... ★
adj. 小心的，謹慎的：The schoolboys are more cautious not to make any mistakes in spelling than ever before. 男學生們在拼寫時比以前更加小心，以避免發生錯誤。

chary [ˈtʃɛrɪ] .... ★
adj. 謹慎的：be chary of the risks involved 對涉入的風險小心翼翼

circumspect [ˈsɝkəmˌspɛkt] .... ★★★★★
adj. 慎重的，小心的：A circumspect person is heedful of circumstances and potential consequences. 一個慎重的人會留心各種情況及可能的後果。

comfort [ˈkʌmfɚt] .... ★★★★★
n. ①舒適，安逸：He lived in comfort. 他生活舒適。②安慰，慰問：His kind words gave me comfort. 他親切的話語給了我安慰。
v. ①使…舒適：The nurse comforted the child by tidying up his bed. 護士為孩子整理床鋪讓他舒服一些。②安慰：I tried to comfort her after her mother's death. 她母親去世後，我試著安慰她。

cozy [ˈkozɪ] .... ★

adj. 舒適的：Certain colors when incorporated into the décor of a room can produce a cozy atmosphere. 某些顏色組合用於室內裝潢時，會產生令人舒適的感覺。

deliberately [dɪˈlɪbərɪtlɪ] .... ★★

adv. 認真地，故意地：They attempted deliberately to provoke an enraged Black community. 他們蓄意挑釁被激怒的黑人公眾。

discreet [dɪˈskrit] .... ★

adj. 慎重的，謹慎的：My secretary is very discreet. She never tells anyone unconcerned anything about the company's business. 我的秘書很謹慎，有關公司的業務從不對任何無關的人談起。

discretion [dɪˈskrɛʃən] .... ★

n. 判斷力，慎重：All the decisions were left to our discretion. 所有的決定都由我們自行做出。

easily [ˈizɪlɪ] .... ★★★★★

adv. 容易地，不費力地

headlong [ˈhɛd.lɔŋ] .... ★

adj. 魯莽的：The runner slid headlong into third base. 跑壘者一頭滑進了三壘。

hectic [ˈhɛtɪk] .... ★

adj. 忙碌的，發熱的：a hectic life 緊張忙碌的生活

idle [ˈaɪdḷ] .... ★★★★

adj. 閒散的，閒置的，無用的，無效的：Men are left idle when machines break down. 機器壞了時，工人們便無事可做了。

v. 空費，虛度：idle the afternoon away 虛度一個下午。

imprudent [ɪmˈprudn̩t] .... ★

adj. 輕率的，不謹慎的：By today's standards, early farmers were imprudent because they planted the same crop repeatedly, exhausting the soil after a few harvests. 依照今天的標準來判斷，早期農民持續種植一種作物的做法是不可取的，因為這樣會讓土壤在幾季之後失去養分。

indolent [ˈɪndələnt] .... ★

adj. 懶惰的：humid, indolent weather 令人困倦的潮濕天氣

industrious [ɪnˈdʌstrɪəs] .... ★

adj. 勤勉的：The Chinese are an industrious nation. 華人是勤勞的民族。

lazy [ˈlezɪ] .... ★★★

adj. 懶惰的，懶散的：The lazy student never did his homework on time. 這個懶惰的學生從沒按時寫家庭作業。

leisure [ˈliʒɚ] .... ★★★★

n. 空暇，空閒，安逸：Labor laws enacted during the early twentieth century gave workers more leisure time. 在 20 世紀初頒佈實施的勞動法，讓工人擁有更多的空閒時間。

meticulously [məˈtɪkjələslɪ] .... ★

adv. 很仔細地：The secretary opened the mail meticulously, being cautious of anthrax spores. 秘書小心翼翼地打開郵件，擔心裡面會有炭疽病菌。

parsimony [ˈpɑrsəˌmonɪ] .... ★

n. 過分節儉

provident [ˈprɑvədənt] .... ★★★★★

adj. 有遠見的，節儉的：He is provident of his money. 他用錢很節省。

prudent [ˈprudn̩t] .... ★★

adj. 謹慎的：It's prudent to take a thick coat in cold weather when you go out. 在寒冷的天氣下外出時，謹慎點帶件厚外套。

rash [ræʃ] .... ★★★

adj. 輕率的，魯莽的：a rash young man 魯
莽的年輕人；be rash enough 膽敢；rash
advance 冒進

n. ①疹，熱疹：a heat rash 熱疹 ②（短期內）
爆發的一連串：a rash of robberies last
month 上月接二連三發生的搶劫案

rashly [ˈræʃlɪ] .... ★

adv. 魯莽地，輕率地：Some people jumped
rashly to the conclusion that the product
will not be welcomed. 有些人輕率地得出
結論，認為這項產品不會受歡迎。

recklessly [ˈrɛklɪslɪ] .... ★

adv. 魯莽地：The man was sent to prison for
driving recklessly. 這個男子因為駕車魯莽
而被判刑。

sluggish [ˈslʌgɪʃ] .... ★

adj. 怠惰的：The lizard called the Gila
monster is ordinarily sluggish and clumsy.
這種叫做毒蜥的蜥蜴通常既懶又笨。

scrupulously [ˈskrupjələslɪ] .... ★

ad. 嚴謹地，講究地：To avoid contamination,
surgeons wash their hands scrupulously
before starting each operation. 外科醫生
為了防止感染，在手術開始之前要仔細洗
手。

28

相同、相反、相關類相關辭彙

Vocabulary of Identity

adverse [æd'vɜs] .... ★★★★★
adj. 敵對的，不利的：Allergy is an adverse reaction of the body to certain substances. 過敏是身體對某些物質的不良反應。

affinity [ə'fɪnətɪ] .... ★
n. 類似之處，密切關係：A strange affinity attracts opposite natures. 一股奇怪的吸引力把性質相反的東西吸引在一起。

analogize [ə'næləˌdʒaɪz] .... ★
v. 類推，用類似法說明：Light traditionally is analogized with intellectual brilliance. 光向來被比擬成「智慧之光」。

analogous [ə'næləgəs] .... ★
adj. 類似的：This proposal was analogous to/with the one we discussed at the last meeting. 這項提案與在我們上次會議討論過的那份提案相似。

analogy [ə'nælədʒɪ] .... ★
n. 類似，類推：The fear of smallpox, which terrified the eighteenth century, has no analogy today. 在整個十八世紀裡對天花的恐懼，如今沒有可以與之相比的。

con [kɑn] .... ★
adv. 從反面，反面地：argue pro and con for hours 正反兩面辯論數小時；the pros and cons 贊成票和反對票。

contrary ['kɑntrɛrɪ] .... ★★★★★
adj. 相反的，矛盾的：In the United States the judiciary decides whether or not congressional enactments are contrary to the principles of the Constitution. 在美國，由司法部來判斷國會制定的政策是否與憲法的基本條款相矛盾。
n. 相反，反面

conversion [kən'vɜʃən] .... ★★
n. 轉交，轉化，改建：data conversion 資料轉換；digital-to-image conversion 數字對圖像轉換

convert [kən'vɜt] .... ★★★★
v. 轉換：I want to convert some Hong Kong Dollars into US Dollars. 我想把一些港幣換成美元。

correlate [ˈkɔrəˌlet] .... ★

v. 相關聯：Research workers find it hard to correlate the two sets of figures. 研究人員發現這兩組數字很難互相關聯。

correspondence [ˌkɔrəˈspɑndəns] ★★★★

n. 通訊員，記者：He is a correspondence of Reuters. 他是路透社的通訊員。

corresponding [ˌkɔrəˈspɑndɪŋ] .... ★★★

adj. 相應的：a high corporate position and its corresponding problems 高度自治的狀況及其伴隨的問題

different [ˈdɪfərənt] .... ★★★★★

adj. ①差異的，不同的：They are different people with the same name. 他們是同名不同人。②各種的：I called three different times, but he was out. 我在 3 個不同時間打電話給他，他都不在家。

discrepancy [dɪˈskrɛpənsɪ] .... ★

n. 差異，不一致：The two reports have a number of discrepancies. 這兩項報告有幾處不一致。

discriminate [dɪˈskrɪməˌnet] .... ★★

v. ①區別，辨別：You must try to discriminate between facts and opinions. 你必須設法把事實和看法區分開來。②有差別地對待：Law should not discriminate against any person. 法律不應當歧視任何人。

discrimination [dɪˌskrɪməˈneʃən] .... ★★

n. 歧視：Discrimination against women is not allowed. 歧視婦女是不允許的。

dissimilar [dɪˈsɪmələ] .... ★★★★★

adj. 不相似的，不同的：people with dissimilar tastes 有不同愛好的人

diverse [daɪˈvɝs] .... ★★★★

adj. 不同的：Felt is a fabric with diverse uses such as thermal insulation and soundproofing. 氈是一種可以隔熱和隔音的多用途織物。

diversify [daɪˈvɝsəˌfaɪ] .... ★★★★

v. 使…多樣化：A factory must try to diversify for further development. 一間工廠要獲得進一步發展，就要努力使產品多樣化。

equal [ˈikwəl] .... ★★★★★

adj. ①相同的，同等的，平等的：Equal pay for equal work. 同工同酬。②勝任，有能力：She is equal to that work. 她能勝任那份工作。

equal [ˈikwəl] .... ★★★★★

adj. 相等的，同樣的：We think that Mary is equal to the needs of the job. 我們認為瑪莉符合這項工作的需求。

equality [ˈikwələtɪ] .... ★★★★

n. 平等，相等

equalize [ˈikwəlaɪz] .... ★★★★

v. 使相等：He equalized the responsibilities of the staff members. 他使工作人員都承擔相同的責任。

equate [ɪˈkwet] .... ★★★★

v. 使相等，視為同等：Nowadays, many people equate passing examinations with being educated. 當今很多人把考試及格視為受過了教育。

equivalent [ɪˈkwɪvələnt] .... ★★★★

adj. 相等的

n. 等同品：In terms of precipitation, ten inches of snow is the equivalent of an inch of rain. 按降雨量來說，十英寸的降雪相當於一英寸的降雨。

homogeneous [ˌhoməˈdʒinɪəs] ...... ★★★★

adj. 同類的，相似的：a tight-knit, homogeneous society 一個緊密相連的同種社會

identical [aɪˈdɛntɪk]] .... ★★★

adj. 同一的：We are identical in our views of what should be done. 我們對應當怎麼辦的看法是一致的。

incompatible [ˌɪnkəmˋpætəb!] .... ★

adj. 不相容的：Water is incompatible with fire. 水火不相容。

interplay [ˋɪntɚ͵ple] .... ★ ★ ★ ★

n. 相互影響，相互作用：the interplay of light and shadow光影交錯

inverse [ɪnˋvɝs] .... ★

adj. 反的：an inverse network 倒置（電）網路

invert [ɪnˋvɝt] .... ★

v. 倒轉：The little boy caught the insect by inverting his cup over it. 小男孩把杯子倒過來，抓住了那隻昆蟲。

irrelevant [ɪˋrɛləvənt] .... ★ ★ ★ ★

adj. 不相干的：mentioned several irrelevant facts before finally coming to the point 在最後談到重點之前，先說了幾項不相關的事實

like [laɪk] .... ★ ★ ★ ★

v. ①喜歡：I like washing in cold water. 我喜歡冷水浴。②希望，想要：I'd like to have a talk with you. 我想跟你談談。

prep. 像，如，跟…一樣：The girls looks like their father. 女孩們長得很像她們的父親。

likewise [ˋlaɪk͵waɪz] .... ★ ★ ★

adv. 同樣地，也，而且，照樣：Some have little power to do good, and have likewise little strength to resist evil. 一些沒有能力去做善事的人，同樣也沒有什麼力量抵擋邪惡。

mutual [ˋmjutʃʊəl] .... ★ ★ ★

adj. 相互的，共同的：to give mutual support and inspiration 相互支持並鼓舞

reciprocal [rɪˋsɪprək!] .... ★

adj. 相互的，交往的：reciprocal agreements to abolish customs duties 取消關稅互惠的協定

relate [rɪˋlet] .... ★ ★ ★ ★ ★

v. ①有關聯：I want to ask you a question that relates to electricity. 我想問你一個與電有關的問題。②使互相關聯：I can't relate what he does to what he says. 我沒法把他的舉止和言行連在一起。③敘述，講述：He related the story of his escape from the enemy. 他講述從敵人那裡逃出來的故事。

relation [rɪˋleʃən] .... ★ ★ ★ ★ ★

n. ①關係，聯繫：the relation between wages and prices 薪水和價格之間的關係 ②親屬，親戚：You might invite all your relations to the dinner party. 你可以請你所有的親戚來參加晚宴。

【片語】in relation to ①有關，關於，涉及 ②與…相比

relationship [rɪˋleʃən͵ʃɪp] .... ★ ★ ★ ★ ★

n.（相互）關係，聯繫，親戚：The teacher has a very good relationship with her students. 這位老師和學生們關係良好。

relevant [ˋrɛləvənt] .... ★ ★ ★ ★

adj. 有關的，貼切的：relevant details 相關細節；not relevant to the present question 和目前問題無關

resemble [rɪˋzɛmb!] .... ★ ★ ★ ★

v. 像，類似：In his mathematics, Archimedes employed methods that resembled those of contemporary integral calculus. 阿基米德在他的數學中，運用的方法和當代積分的方法類似。

reverse [rɪˋvɝs] .... ★ ★ ★ ★

v. 顛倒，反轉，改變，使倒退

n. 反面，背面，相反：All along we thought Sue was older than Bill, but just the reverse was true. 我們一直認為蘇的年紀比比爾大，而事實恰恰相反。

same [sem] .... ★★★★★
adj. 相同的，一樣的：Father sits in the same chair every evening. 父親每天晚上都坐在同一把椅子上。
pron. 同樣的人，同樣的事物：All the newspapers say the same. 報紙上說的都一樣。

similar [ˋsɪmələ] .... ★★★★★
adj. 相似的，類似的：Pears is similar in colour to orange. 梨與橘子的顏色相似。
【片語】be similar to 與⋯相似

tally [ˋtælɪ] .... ★
v. 符合：Your account tallies with mine. 你的帳目和我的帳目相符。

turnover [ˋtɝ͵novɚ] .... ★★★★★
n. 翻倒，翻轉，顛倒

uniform [ˋjunə͵fɔrm] .... ★★★★
n. 制服，軍服
adj. 一致的，一律的，一樣的，不變的，均勻的：Until the late nineteenth century, there was no uniform system of time-keeping in the United States. 美國直到十九世紀末期才有統一的計時系統。

uniformity [͵junəˋfɔrmətɪ] .... ★
n. 統一，一致性，一樣，一律，均勻

unlike [ʌnˋlaɪk] .... ★★★★
adj. 不相似的，不同的：She is unlike her mother. 她不像她媽媽。
prep. 不像⋯，和⋯不同：Rose, unlike Susan, was a careful girl. 蘿絲和蘇珊不同，是個細心的女生。

辨析 Analyze

alike, identical, like, likely, same, similar

1 **alike** *a. & adv.* 「相像的／地，相同的／地」，形容詞只能作表語：The two sisters are very much alike. 姐妹倆長很像。

2 **identical** *a.* 「相同的，相等的，同一的」，指完全一樣的，常用 be identical to/with：The fingerprints of no two persons are identical. 沒有兩個人的指紋是完全相同的。

3 **like** *a. & prep.* 「相像的，相似的」，形容詞通常作前置定語：His car is like mine. 他的小汽車和我的很像。

4 **likely** *a.* 「可能的，合適的」，可作表語或定語：It is likely to rain. 看來要下雨了。

5 **same** *a.* 「相同的，同樣的，同一的」，指完全一樣的，幾乎總是與定冠詞 the 連用，常用 be the same as：Your bike is the same as mine. 你的自行車跟我的一樣。

6 **similar** *a.* 「相似的，類似的」，指相似但不完全一樣，常用 be similar to：Gold is similar to brass in colour. 金子和黃銅的顏色相似。

29

冷、熱、酸、甜相關辭彙

Vocabulary of Taste

acrid [ˈækrɪd] .... ★

adj. 苦澀的，辛辣的：Wild raspberries have a more acrid smell than do cultivated raspberries. 野生的黑莓比人工種植的黑莓更苦澀。

cool [kul] .... ★★★★★

adj. 涼的，涼爽的

frigid [ˈfrɪgɪd] .... ★

adj. 嚴寒的，冷淡的：a frigid refusal to a request 冷酷地拒絕請求

hardheaded [ˈhɑrdˌhɛdɪd] .... ★★★★★

adj. 冷靜的，頑固的

hot [hɑt] .... ★★★★★

adj. 熱的：The coffee is too hot to drink. 咖啡太燙沒辦法喝。

incandescent [ˌɪnkænˈdɛsn̩t] .... ★

n. 白熾，白熱

adj. 白熱的，白熾的：incandescent lamp 白熾燈；an incandescent filament 白熱燈絲

pungent [ˈpʌndʒənt] .... ★

adj. 辛辣的：The bulb of the garlic plant has a very pungent flavor and can be used to season foods. 蒜瓣有股辛辣的味道，可以用來調味食物。

sweet [swit] .... ★★★★★

adj. 甜的，親切的：It's very sweet of you to say so. 你這麼說真貼心。

n. 糖果：Children love sweets. 孩子們喜歡糖果。

30

平常、普通、極端、傑出相關辭彙

Vocabulary of Achievement

状態、程度名稱總匯

Conditons & Degree

common [ˈkɑmən] .... ★★★★★

adj. 普通的，一般的：Your daughter's trouble is very common these days. 你女兒的麻煩現在極常見。
【片語】in common 共同的／地

drastic [ˈdræstɪk] .... ★

adj. 激烈的，嚴厲的：the drastic measure of amputating the entire leg 截除整條腿的極端療法

excellent [ˈɛksḷənt] .... ★★★★★

adj. 優秀的，傑出的：She is an excellent hitter and able to drive the ball beyond 200 meters. 她是個優秀的打擊手，能把球擊出二百米以外。

exceptional [ɪkˈsɛpʃənḷ] .... ★★

adj. 卓越的，例外的：All her children are clever, but the youngest daughter is really exceptional. 她的孩子們都很聰明，但最小的女兒尤為突出。

extraordinary [ɪkˈstrɔrdṇ‚ɛrɪ] .... ★★★★★

adj. 非常的，非凡的，特別的：a man of extraordinary talents 有著驚人才能的人

extreme [ɪkˈstrim] .... ★★★★★

adj. ①極度的，極端的：in extreme pain極度的痛苦② 盡頭的，末端的：the extreme edge of a field 田地邊界

n. 極端：go to extremes 走到極端

extremely [ɪkˈstrimlɪ] .... ★★★★

adv. 非常，極其：Bounded by the Arctic Ocean on the north, the state of Alaska is often extremely cold. 阿拉斯加州北面與北極海相鄰，非常寒冷。

foremost [ˈforˌmost] .... ★★

adj. 最初的，第一流的：In 1965 California replaced New York as the foremost state in the export of manufactured goods. 加州於1965年取代紐約成為成品出口量最大的州。

general [ˈdʒɛnərəl] .... ★★★★★

adj. 普通的：Unlike opera, oratorio in general is based on a religious subject and is performed without scenery or stage action. 宗教劇不同於歌劇，一般是基於宗教主題而且沒有舞臺佈景或舞臺表演的。

grand [grænd] .... ★★★★★
adj. 盛大的，壯麗的：a grand old face that
bespeaks suffering but not defeat 一張帶
著受苦而非屈服表情的高貴蒼老面孔

matchless [`mætʃlɪs] .... ★★★★★
adj. 無與倫比的：Critics have never been
able to find adequate praise for Marian
Anderson's matchless contral to voice. 評
論家對瑪麗安‧安德森無與倫比的女高音
備加讚美。

mediocre [`midɪ,okɚ] .... ★
adj. 平常的，普通的：The student tried hard,
but his work is mediocre. 這個學生很用
功，但學業平庸。

normal [`nɔrml] .... ★★★★
adj. ①正常的，平常的：It's normal to feel
depressed sometimes. 有時感到抑鬱是
很正常的。②正規的：to receive normal
training 接受正規訓練

ordinary [`ɔrdn,ɛrɪ] .... ★★★★★
adj. 普通的，平凡的，平常的

outstanding [`aut`stændɪŋ] .... ★★★
adj. 顯著的，傑出的：Alvar Aalto is
considered one of the outstanding
architects of the twentieth century. 阿瓦‧
奧圖被認為是20世紀最傑出的建築師之
一。

predominate [prɪ`dɑmə,net] .... ★
v. 佔優勢，支配：Good predominates over
evil in many works of literature. 在許多文學
作品中是正義戰勝邪惡。

preeminence [prɪ`ɛmɪnəns] .... ★
n. 卓越，突出：The preeminence of the
newspaper as a daily source of information
has been undermined as a result of the
rapid expansion of the audiovisual media.
隨著視聽媒體快速發展，報紙作為每日消息
來源的卓越地位被日漸淡化了。

prominent [`prɑmənənt] .... ★★★
adj. 卓越的，突出的：The State of
Connecticut played a prominent role in
the Revolutionary War. 康乃狄克州在美國
獨立戰爭中扮演了傑出的角色。

辨析 Analyze

grand, magnificent, splendid

1 **grand** *a.*「宏偉的，壯麗的」，指建築
物或自然景觀規模宏大、莊嚴雄偉，還指
「重大的，重要的，極好的」等，詞義較
廣：This is a grand view of mountains.
壯麗的群山景色。

2 **magnificent** *a.*「壯麗的，宏偉的，
豪華的，華麗的，極好的」，指富麗堂
皇，不但宏偉而且常給人以華麗之感：
What could be more grand/magnificent/
splendid than Buckingham Palace? 有什
麼建築能比白金漢宮更雄偉壯麗呢？

3 **splendid** *a.*「輝煌的，壯麗的，豪華
的，極好的」，指才華出眾，成就輝煌，
也可指雄偉美麗或光輝燦爛：He made a
splendid record in the army. 他在軍隊中
有輝煌的經歷。

protrude [pro`trud] .... ★

v. 突出：The policeman saw a gun protruding from the man's pocket. 員警看到一支槍從那男人的口袋裡突出。

remarkable [rɪ`mɑrkəbḷ] .... ★★★★★

adj. 值得注意的：Your work has been remarkable this week. 你這星期的工作很出色。

spectacle [`spɛktəkḷ] .... ★★★★

n. 奇觀，景象：He drank too much and made a spectacle of himself. 他喝得過多，當眾出醜。

spectacular [spɛk`tækjələ] .... ★★★

adj. 引人入勝的，壯觀的：a spectacular achievement in science 科學上的一項驚人成就

splendid [`splɛndɪd] .... ★★★★

adj. 燦爛的，輝煌的：The splendid image of the Queen Elizabeth will forever live in the hearts of the people. 伊莉莎白女皇的光輝形象會永遠留在人民的心裡。

splendor [`splɛndə] .... ★★★★

n. 光彩，壯麗：An eighteenth-century traveler to Annapolis reported on the splendor of this southern city. 一個18世紀到安納波利斯的旅行者，描述了這座南方城市的壯麗。

superb [su`pɝb] .... ★★★

adj. 壯麗的，超級的：This play is a superb job. 這齣戲是一部出色的作品。

surpass [sɚ`pæs] .... ★★

v. 超過，超越，勝過：His qualifications surpass the job requirements. 他的條件超出了這項工作的需求。

transcend [træn`sɛnd] .... ★★★★★

v. 超越：One never can see the thing in itself, because the mind does not transcend phenomena. 一個人永遠不可能看出事物自身的本質，因為思想無法超越現象。

universal [ˌjunə`vɝsḷ] .... ★★★★★

adj. 宇宙的，普遍的：Personal computers are of universal interest; everyone is learning how to use them. 個人電腦大家都感興趣，每個人都在學習怎樣使用它。

辨析 Analyze

common, general, ordinary, usual

1 **common** *a.* 「平常的，普通的，共同的，公共的」，強調共同性，普通性，如：a common error 司空見慣的錯誤；Jason is a given name which is very common in US. 「Jason」在美國是一個很常見的名字。

2 **general** *a.* 「一般的，普通的，總的，普通的，全體的，籠統的，大體的」，強調普遍性，較少有例外：What you said just now expressed the general opinion of the public. 你剛才所說的表達了大眾的普遍看法。

3 **ordinary** *a.* 「通常的，普通的，平常的，平庸的，平淡的」，強調平常、很一般，其反義詞為 extraordinary（不平常的，非凡的）：We are all ordinary people. 我們都是普通人。

4 **usual** *a.* 「通常的，慣常的」，強調常見性、習慣性：Tea is the usual drink of the local people. 茶是當地人常喝的飲料。

universally [ˌjunəˈvɝsḷɪ] .... ★★
adv. 普遍地

unusual [ʌnˈjuʒəl] .... ★★★★
adj. ①不平常的，少有的：It was unusual
for me to come at two or three in the
morning. 對我來說，在凌晨兩三點鐘回家
是少有的。②與眾不同的，獨特的：I liked
that unusual painting. 我喜歡那幅與眾不
同的畫。

usual [ˈjuʒəl] .... ★★★★★
adj. 通常的，平常的：She got up earlier
yesterday than usual. 她昨天比平常起得
早。
【片語】as usual 像平常一樣，照例

usually [ˈjuʒəlɪ] .... ★★★★★
adv. 一般情況下，平常，通常：How do you
usually go to school? 你平時怎麼上學？

utmost [ˈʌtˌmost] .... ★★★★
adj. 最大的，極度的，最遠的：He did his
utmost to stop his sister marrying that
man. 他盡全力阻止他的妹妹和那人結婚。
n. 極限，極度，最大可能，最大限度：to do
one's utmost 竭盡全力

wonderful [ˈwʌndəfəl] .... ★★★★★
adj. 奇妙的，極好的：It's simply wonderful! 簡
直妙極了！

31

自私、慷慨、虛偽相關辭彙

Conditions & Degree — Vocabulary of Personality

altruism [ˈæltruˌɪzəm] .... ★
n. 利他主義：Altruism is the opposite of egoism. 利他主義和利己主義相反。

charitable [ˈtʃærətəbl] .... ★★★★
adj. 慷慨的，慈善的：a charitable club 慈善團體

charity [ˈtʃærətɪ] .... ★★★★
n. 施捨，慈善事業

cunning [ˈkʌnɪŋ] .... ★
adj. 狡猾的，可愛的：The fox has developed a high degree of cunning in eluding pursuers. 狐狸已演化出一種在躲避追擊者時所具備的高度狡詐功力。

decent [ˈdisnt] .... ★★★
adj. 正派的，體面的：decent behavior 正當的行為

designing [dɪˈzaɪnɪŋ] .... ★★★★★
adj. 狡猾的，蓄意的：According to the clues, this is a designing crime. 種種跡象表明這是一樁蓄意犯罪。

devious [ˈdivɪəs] .... ★
adj. 曲折的：His devious nature was shown in half-lies and small dishonesties. 他不正直的天性表現在小謊話及微小的不誠實行為中。

devoid [dɪˈvɔɪd] .... ★★★★★
adj. 缺乏的：Anna preferred to dance on a stage devoid of scenery. 安娜比較喜歡在沒有佈景的舞臺上跳舞。

egalitarian [ɪˌgælɪˈtɛrɪən] .... ★★★★★
adj. 平均主義的：Egalitarian means affirming, promoting, and is characterized by belief in equal political, economic, social, and civil rights for all people. 平等主義堅持、促進以及相信全人類在政治、經濟、社會和公民權利方面是平等的。

fidelity [fɪˈdɛlətɪ] .... ★
n. 忠誠：The rosemary plant is an emblem of fidelity and remembrance. 迷迭香這種植物是忠誠和紀念的象徵。

forthright [forθˈraɪt] .... ★★★★★
adj. 直接的，立即的：His forthright behavior shows that he's honest, but he seems rude to some people. 他的直率行為說明他是個誠實的人，可是似乎有些人認為他很粗魯。

frank [fræŋk] .... ★★★★★
adj. 坦白的，直率的：Will you be quite frank
　　with me about this matter? 你能不能在這
　　個問題上對我坦誠？

gentility [dʒɛnˈtɪlətɪ] .... ★★★★★
n. 有教養，文雅：shabby gentility 擺闊氣，裝
　　體面

guileless [ˈgaɪllɪs] .... ★
adj. 不狡猾的，誠實的

honest [ˈɑnɪst] .... ★★★★★
adj. 誠實的，正直的：an honest attitude 誠實
　　的態度

ignoble [ɪgˈnobl̩] .... ★★★★
adj. 卑微的

ignominious [ˌɪgnəˈmɪnɪəs] .... ★★★★
adj. 可恥的，不名譽的：The young people
　　huddled with their sodden gritty towels
　　and ignominious goosebumps inside the
　　gray-shingled bathhouse. 身上起滿難看的
　　雞皮疙瘩的年輕人，裹著佈滿沙粒的濕毛
　　巾，擠在灰色木瓦的澡堂裡。

insincere [ˌɪnsɪnˈsɪr] .... ★★★★★
adj. 不真誠的

loyal [ˈlɔɪəl] .... ★★★
adj. 忠誠的，忠貞的

loyalty [ˈlɔɪltɪ] .... ★★★
n. 忠誠，忠心：The government was sure of
　　the people's loyalty. 政府相信人民的忠誠。

miser [ˈmaɪzɚ] .... ★
n. 守財奴，吝嗇鬼

miserly [ˈmaɪzɚlɪ] .... ★
adj. 吝嗇的：The miserly millionaire refused
　　to part with any of his money. 那個吝嗇的
　　百萬富翁連點錢都不願意花。

probity [ˈprobətɪ] .... ★★★★★
n. 正直：He was a gentlemanly Georgian, a
　　person of early American probity. 他是一個
　　紳士型的喬治亞人，一個具備早期美式德行
　　的人。

sincere [sɪnˈsɪr] .... ★★★
adj. 誠摯的，真誠的，誠懇的：The apology
　　was sincere. 這個道歉是真誠的。

skimpy [ˈskɪmpɪ] .... ★
adj. 吝嗇的，太少的：a skimpy meal 不夠吃
　　的一頓飯

sly [slaɪ] .... ★★★
adj. 狡猾的，躲躲閃閃的：The fruit seller was
　　sly; he put his best fruit in front but gave
　　people bad ones from behind. 這個賣水果
　　的人很狡詐，把最好的水果放在前面，可
　　是從後面給顧客壞水果。

snob [snɑb] .... ★
n. 勢利小人：A snob is someone who judges
　　all things according to their social rating. 勢
　　利小人就是從他們的社會地位衡量一切事情
　　的人。

snobbish [ˈsnɑbɪʃ] .... ★
adj. 勢利的：People are often snobbish
　　without being aware of. 人經常沒有意識到
　　自己是勢利的。

stingy [ˈstɪndʒɪ] .... ★★★
adj. 缺乏的，吝嗇的：a stingy meal太少的
　　飯；stingy with details about the past 有
　　關過去的細節很少

vicious [ˈvɪʃəs] .... ★
adj. 邪惡的，不道德的，惡性的，惡毒的：
　　vicious circle 惡性循環

wicked [ˈwɪkɪd] .... ★★★★
adj. ①邪惡的，惡劣的，缺德的：It was
　　wicked of you to torment the cat. 你折磨
　　那隻可憐的貓真缺德。②淘氣的，頑皮
　　的：She gave me a wicked look. 她調皮
　　地朝我看了一眼。

32

Conditons & Degree

直接間接、簡單複雜、方便麻煩相關辭彙

Vocabulary of Convenience

abstruse [æb`strus] .... ★

adj. 深奧的：She read abstruse works in philosophy. 她在讀深奧的哲學著作。

brief [brif] .... ★★★★★

adj. 簡短的，簡潔的：a brief note 便條；a brief stay 小住

【片語】in brief 簡單地說

v. 向…簡要介紹：He briefed the commander on the enemy's strength. 他向司令官簡報敵人的兵力。

briefcase [`brif͵kes] .... ★

n. （扁平的）公事包

briefly [`brifli] .... ★★★★★

adv. 簡短地

complex [`kɑmplɛks] .... ★★★★

adj. 複雜的：Fitting astronauts into their pressure suits is a delicate and complex task. 讓太空人穿上有壓力的衣服是一件複雜細緻的工作。

n. 綜合體

complexion [kəm`plɛkʃən] .... ★★

n. 膚色

complexity [kəm`plɛksəti] .... ★

n. 複雜（性）：a maze of bureaucratic and legalistic complexities 官僚主義兼墨守成規

complicate [`kɑmplə͵ket] .... ★★

v. 使複雜，使陷入：Don't complicate life for me! 不要為我把生活搞複雜了！

concise [kən`saɪs] .... ★★★★★

adj. 簡明的：You are expected to present a concise treatment of this subject in the remaining time. 你最好在剩下的時間裡提出這一問題的簡明解決方案。

convenience [kən`vinjəns] .... ★★★

v. 為…提供方便

n. 方便，便利：We'll try our best to offer all services that promote the customer's convenience. 我們儘量提供各種服務使顧客便利。

direct [də`rɛkt] .... ★★★★★

adj. 直接的

v. 引導：Before his appointment to the United States Supreme Court in 1967, Thurgood Marshall had directed a team of lawyers representing the plaintiff in a landmark desegregation case. 桑哥德‧馬歇爾在1967年被指派到美國最高法院之前，曾經指導一個律師隊伍，在一樁劃時代的廢除種族歧視的案子中為原告辯護。

direction [dəˋrɛkʃən] .... ★★★★★
n. ①方向，方位：When the police arrived, the crowed scattered in all direction. 當警方到來時，人群四下散開。②說明，指令：The directions are on the label. 標籤上有說明。

directly [dəˋrɛktlɪ] .... ★★★★★
adv. ①直接地，筆直地：He was looking directly at us. 他直盯著我們看。②立即，馬上：He'll be here directly. 他即刻就到。

director [dəˋrɛktə] .... ★★★★★
n. ①指導者，主管：He serves as a director in the institute. 他是這個機構的主管。②董事：the Board of Directors 董事會③導演：the director of movie 這部電影的導演

elusive [ɪˋlusɪv] ....★
adj. 難懂的，躲避的：Failures are more finely etched in our minds than triumphs, and success is an elusive, if not mythic, goal in our demanding society. 失敗比勝利更容易烙印在我們心中，成功如果不是幻想，在我們這個有所需求的社會是一個難以理解的目標。

idyllic [aɪˋdɪlɪk] ....★
adj. 田園詩般的：an idyllic vacation in a seashore cottage 在海邊的小屋度過田園詩般的假期

indirect [ˌɪndəˋrɛkt] .... ★★★
adj. 間接的，迂迴的：indirect speech 間接引語

intricate [ˋɪntrəkɪt] ....★
adj. 錯綜複雜的，難懂的：The construction of large modern building is an especially intricate operation. 建造大型的現代建築物是一項特別複雜的工作。

simple [ˋsɪmpl] .... ★★★★★
adj. ①簡單的：He set out his ideas in simple words. 他簡要地闡述了他的思想。②樸素的：Everything in his room is simple. 他房裡的所有東西都很樸素。

辨析 Analyze

brief, compact, concise

1 **brief** *a.* 「簡短的，簡潔的」，常用詞，較為口語化，還指「短暫的，短時間的」：I'll be brief and to the point. 我簡要地說幾句，只講重點。

2 **compact** *a.* 「緊湊的，小巧的，緊密的，堅實的」，正式用語，指擺設、佈局等緊湊，還指文風簡潔，一般做定語：She has a very compact kitchen. 她有一間小巧的廚房。

3 **concise** *a.* 「簡明的，簡要的」，正式用語，只用於指語言文字簡明扼要：a concise dictionary 簡明字典；The letter that I wrote to my boyfriend was very concise. 我寫給男朋友的那封信非常簡明扼要。

simplicity [sɪmˋplɪsətɪ] .... ★★★★
n. 簡單，單純，質樸

simplify [ˋsɪmpləˏfaɪ] .... ★★★
v. 簡化，使單純：The English in this story
　　has been simplified to make it easier to
　　understand. 這個故事的英語已經簡化過，
　　更容易理解了。

simply [ˋsɪmplɪ] .... ★★★★★
adv. 簡單地：We should express our ideas
　　simply and accurately. 我們應當簡單準確
　　地表述我們的思想。

sophisticated [səˋfɪstɪˏketɪd] .... ★★★
adj. 老於世故的，老練的，很複雜的，高級
　　的，尖端的

33

altogether [ˌɔltəˈgɛðɚ] .... ★★★★
adv. ①完全，全部地：I don't altogether agree with her. 我與她的意見不完全一致。②總的來說，總之：Altogether the holiday was disappointing. 總之，假期很掃興。③總共：I owe you 1,000 dollars altogether. 我共欠你1,000美元。

completely [kəmˈplitlɪ] .... ★★★★★
adv. 十分，完全

comprehensive [ˌkɑmprɪˈhɛnsɪv] .... ★★★★
adj. 綜合的，有理解力的：The state government gave a very comprehensive explanation of its plans for the development of electronic industry. 州政府詳盡解釋電子工業發展的計畫。

entire [ɪnˈtaɪr] .... ★★★★★
adj. 全部的，整個的：He enjoys our entire confidence. 他受到我們的絕對信任。

generally [ˈdʒɛnərəlɪ] .... ★★★★★
adv. 廣泛地，一般地：Mosquitoes generally breed in swampy areas. 蚊子一般是在潮濕的地區繁殖。

intersect [ˌɪntɚˈsɛkt] .... ★★★★★
v. 相交：The road intersects the highway a mile from here. 這條路在離這兒一英里的地方與公路相交。

overall [ˈovɚˌɔl] .... ★★★★
adj. 全面的，綜合的：Like painters, art photographers are usually concerned with color, shape, texture, and overall composition in their work. 攝影師和油漆匠一樣，通常在作品中會考量顏色、形狀、紋理和全面的組合。

part [pɑrt] .... ★★★★★
n. 部分，局部：the parts of the body 身體的各個部分
【片語】①do one's part 盡自己的職責，盡自己的一份力量②take part in 參與，參加③in part 在某種程度上，部分地

partial [ˈpɑrʃəl] .... ★★★
adj. 部分的，偏袒的：The plan calls for partial deployment of missiles. 這個計畫要求撤除部分導彈。

partially [ˈpɑrʃəlɪ] .... ★★★
adv. 部分地，不公平地：The driver is partially to blame for the accident. 司機對那次車禍應負部分責任。

particular [pəˋtɪkjələ] .... ★★★★★
adj. ①特別的，特殊的：He took particular trouble to get it right. 他特別費力把它弄好。②特定的，個別的：It happened on that particular day. 事情就發生在那一天。【片語】in particular 尤其，特別
n. 細節，詳情：For particulars, please contact our local office. 欲知詳情，請洽詢我駐當地機構。

partly [ˋpɑrtlɪ] .... ★★★
adv. 在一定程度上，部分地，不完全地：I admit that what you say is partly true. 我承認你說的話一部分是真的。

piecemeal [ˋpisˌmil] .... ★★★★
adj & adv. 零碎的／地：
The college buildings were put together piecemeal. 大學的建築是一幢幢慢慢建起來的。

portion [ˋporʃən] .... ★★★★★
n. 一部分：The major portion of writer Juian's work was in social criticism. 作家朱利安的大部分作品都遭到了社會上的批評。

section [ˋsɛkʃən] .... ★★★★★
n. 一段，一部分，（文章等的）節，部，科，處，組，斷面：One section of the class was reading and the other section was writing. 班上的一部分人在看書，另一部分人在寫東西。

segment [ˋsɛgmənt] .... ★★
n. 部分，片段：The community college is the most rapidly growing segment of higher education in the United States. 在美國高等教育中，社區大學是增長最快的一個部分。

slice [slaɪs] .... ★★★
n. ①薄片，切片 ②一份，部分

total [ˋtotḷ] .... ★★★★★
n. 總和：a grand total 總計
v. 全部的，全體的：The total number of the students in the school is about 4,000. 該校學生人數總計4,000名。

totality [toˋtælɪtɪ] .... ★★★★★
n. 全體，總數，完全：He was appalled by the totality of the destruction. 他對於徹底的破壞感到震驚。

whole [hol] .... ★★★★★
n. 全部，整體：The whole of my money was stolen. 我全部的錢都被偷走了。
【片語】on the whole 總的來說，大體上
adj. ①全部的，全體的：I waited for a whole hour. 我整整等了一個小時。②完整的，無缺的：There isn't a whole plate in the house. 這家竟沒有一個完整的盤子。

fraction, fragment, part, portion, section, segment

1 **fraction** *n.*「小部分，片斷，分數」，強調小，常指微不足道的一部分：She's careful with her money, and spends only a fraction of her earnings. 她花錢謹慎，只用她收入的一小部分。

2 **fragment** *n.*「碎片，碎塊，斷片」，指話語、文章當中的一部分，還指物體的碎片：He overheard fragments of their conversation. 他無意中聽到了他們談話時的隻字片語。

3 **part** *n.*「一部分，部分，零件，角色，作用」，指整體而言的部分，用法較廣，可以是具體的，也可以是抽象的：Only a part of the work was finished. 工作只完成了一部分。

4 **portion** *n.*「一部分，一份」，指占多少比例的一份：A portion of each school day is devoted to English. 學校每一天都把一部分時間專用來上英語課。

5 **section** *n.*「部分，章節；部門」，指整體中的各組成部分或從整體中分開的一部分，如 eight equal sections（8等份）；還指「截面，剖面」，如 a section of tissue/stem（一塊組織切片／一根莖的截面）：Her section/portion of the heritage amounted to $50,000. 她所得的那份遺產達5萬美元。

6 **segment** *n.*「部分，斷片，（橘子等的）瓣」，指線段或圓的一部分：The runner went faster on the middle segment of the course. 那個賽跑的人在中間這一段路跑得快些。

34

優劣、對錯、正常、反常相關辭彙

Conditons & Degree

Vocabulary of Evaluation

advantage [əd'væntɪdʒ] .... ★★★★★
n. 好處，有利條件，優點，利益：The camel's hump is of most advantage to it in conditions of drought. 在乾旱的情況下，駝峰對駱駝的好處非常大。

badly ['bædlɪ] .... ★★★★★
adv. 壞，糟，惡劣地，嚴重地：He went to school though his arm ached badly. 他雖然手臂痛得厲害，仍堅持上學。

best [bɛst] .... ★★★★★
n. 最好的人或物：He is the best in his class. 他是班上最優秀的。
【片語】① do one's best 盡力，盡最大努力② make the best of 充分利用，妥善處理③ in one's best 盛裝
adj. 最好的：The book is the best for the middle school students. 這本書最適合中學生讀。

better ['bɛtɚ] .... ★★★★★
adj. (good 的比較級）較好的，更好的，（健康狀況）有所好轉的：The man is better than his brother. 這人比他哥好。
【片語】① for the better 好轉，向好的方向發展② get the better of 戰勝，在…占上風③ had better 最好（還是）（後接原型動詞）

defect [dɪ'fɛkt] .... ★★★
n. 缺陷：defects in a system of education 教育制度上的缺陷

defection [dɪ'fɛkʃən] .... ★★★
n. 背叛，缺陷：a sudden defection of courage 突然失去勇氣

defective [dɪ'fɛktɪv] .... ★★★
adj. 有缺陷的：He is defective in moral sense. 他無法分辨邪正。

fallible ['fæləbl] .... ★★★★★
adj. 易錯的：Human beings are only fallible. 人類本身易犯錯誤。

fault [fɔlt] .... ★★★★
n. ①（不可數）過失，過錯：It's not my fault. 這不是我的錯。②缺點，毛病：He loves me in spite of all my faults. 雖然我有種種缺點，他仍愛我。③故障：There is a fault in the engine. 引擎故障了。
【片語】find fault 埋怨，挑剔

faulty [ˈfɔltɪ] .... ★★★
adj. 有錯誤的，有缺點的，有欠缺的，不完善的：a faulty design 不完善的設計方案；faulty coal 劣質煤；faulty insulator 故障絕緣體

finery [ˈfaɪnərɪ] .... ★★
n. 美麗的服裝，美觀的裝飾品

good [gʊd] .... ★★★★★
adj. 良好的，合適的，有益的：It's very good! 太好了!
【片語】be good at 善於，擅長

mistake [mɪˈstek] .... ★★★★★
n. 錯誤，過失，誤會：There must be some mistakes. 一定有些錯誤。
【片語】① by mistake 錯誤地② make a mistake 犯錯誤，出錯

nice [naɪs] .... ★★★★★
adj. 令人愉快的，美好的：Nice to see you. 見到你真高興。

pervert [pəˈvɝt] .... ★
v. 導入歧途，曲解：an analysis that perverts the meaning of the poem 曲解這首詩涵義的分析

righteous [ˈraɪtʃəs] .... ★★★★★
adj. 正義的，正直的：righteous anger 義憤

super [ˈsupə] .... ★★★★
adj. 極好的，超級的：I'll be a super secretary for you. 我將成為你的超級秘書。

superior [səˈpɪrɪə] .... ★★★★★
n. 上級，長官，長者，優勝者
adj. 更好的，較好的，優越的，優秀的，高級的：This western restaurant is superior to the one we went to last week. 這家西餐廳比我們上星期去的那一家好。

superiority [səpɪrɪˈɔrətɪ] .... ★★
n. 優勢，優越（性）：superiority in strength 實力方面的優勢

terrific [təˈrɪfɪk] .... ★★★
adj. 極好的，非常的，極度的：a terrific party 了不起的宴會

辨析 Analyze

defect, error, fault, flaw, shortcoming

1 **defect** *n.* 「缺點，缺陷，過失」，指有缺陷、不完善：With all defects the little play has a real charm. 這齣短劇儘管有些缺點，仍頗具魅力。

2 **error** *n.* 「錯誤，謬誤，缺陷」，與 mistake 是同義詞，但偏重指說話、書寫、打字、計算、操作等不符合標準的技術性錯誤：I've made some errors in grammar. 我犯了一些文法錯誤。

3 **fault** *n.* 「缺點，毛病」，指各種缺點、缺陷和性格上的毛病，尤指追究過失和挑毛病：My parents are always finding fault with me. 我的父母總是愛挑我的錯。

4 **flaw** *n.* 「缺點，瑕疵」，指本質上、結構上的小毛病、瑕疵：It is a large diamond, but it has a flaw. 這是一顆大鑽石，但有瑕疵。

5 **shortcoming** *n.* 「短處，不足」，較為婉轉：He is a man with many shortcomings. 他這個人有不少缺點。

worse [wɝs] .... ★★★★★

adj. 更壞的，較差的：Your work is bad but mine is worse. 你的工作不好，但我的更差。

adv. 較壞，較差：You are making things worse. 你把事情弄得更糟了。

worst [wɝst] .... ★★★★★
　　　（bad的最高級）

adj. 最壞的，最差的：the worst storm in five years. 5年來最大的暴風雨

adv. 最壞，最差：Tom did badly, Frank did worse, and I did worst. 湯姆做得不好，法蘭克更差，而我最爛。

wrong [rɔŋ] .... ★★★★★

adj. ①錯誤的，不正確的：Sorry, you have the wrong number. 你撥錯電話號碼了。②不道德的，不正當的：Telling lies is wrong. 說謊是不對的。

【片語】be wrong with... 出毛病，不順心

35

精確、粗糙、平滑相關辭彙
Vocabulary of Precision

accuracy [ˈækjərəsɪ] .... ★★★
n. 準確，精確，準確度：The newly invented rifle is of high accuracy. 新研製出來的步槍準確度很高。

accurate [ˈækjərɪt] .... ★★★
adj. 準確的，正確的：Orchids are regarded as the largest family of flowering plants, although it is not possible to give an accurate estimate of the family's size. 蘭花被認為是開花植物中最大的一類，然而這一類植物的規模到底有多大，人們很難有一個準確的估計。

coarse [kors] .... ★★★
adj. 粗糙的：coarse talk 粗魯的談話

exact [ɪgˈzækt] .... ★★★★
adj. 確切的，精確的：Give me his exact words. 把他的話一字不漏地告訴我。

exacting [ɪgˈzæktɪŋ] .... ★★★★
adj. 費力的：an exacting microbe 對生存條件要求極高的微生物；Volunteers are needed for an exacting assignment. 我們需要志願者承擔一項艱巨任務。

exactly [ɪgˈzæktlɪ] .... ★★★★★
adv. ①確切地，精確，恰好②正是，就是

exhaustive [ɪgˈzɔstɪv] .... ★★★★
adj. 無遺漏的，徹底的：an exhaustive lecture on a certain subject 對於某一課題的詳盡講解

harsh [hɑrʃ] .... ★★★
adj. 嚴厲的，刺耳的：The harsh winter slowed the production of all industrial products. 寒冷的冬天使得所有工業產品的產量都下降了。

inaccuracy [ɪnˈækjərəsɪ] .... ★
n. 不精確性：There is a slight inaccuracy in this design. 這張設計圖中有一點不大準確。

inaccurate [ɪnˈækjərət] .... ★
adj. 不精確的：This thermometer is inaccurate. 這支溫度計不準確。

pinpoint [ˈpɪnˌpɔɪnt] .... ★★★★
vt. 精確地發現目標：Can you pinpoint it on the map for me? 你能幫我在地圖上標出它的準確位置嗎？

precise [prɪˈsaɪs] .... ★★★
adj. 周密的，精確的：Annie Oakley became famous as one of the world's most precise sharpshooters. 安妮・奧克利成為世界上最準確的射手之一而聞名。

precisely [prɪˈsaɪslɪ] .... ★★★
adv. 正好，恰恰：Inferior equipment was precisely the reason some hikers refused to continue the climb. 一些登山者不願繼續登山，正是由於設備低劣所致。

rough [rʌf] .... ★★★★
adj. 大致的，不平的，粗暴的：Amphibians have moist, scaleless skin that may be either soft and smooth or rough and gritty. 兩棲類動物都有潮濕的無鱗皮膚，可能很柔軟光滑，也可能很粗糙。

rugged [ˈrʌgɪd] .... ★★★
adj. 粗糙的，不平的：the rugged face of the old sailor 老水手滿是皺紋的臉

辨析
Analyze

accurate, exact , precise

1 **accurate** *a.*「準確的，精確的」，常指與標準相符合，著眼點是誤差小：The guidance system is accurate within a few yards. 制導系統的準確性保持在誤差幾碼之內。

2 **exact** *a.*「精確的，正確的，確切的」，強調每個細節的確切無誤：Give me the exact words of my parents. 把我父母的話一字不漏地告訴我。

3 **precise** *a.*「精確的，準確的」，多指儀器的精密和敘述正確無誤：This instrument is capable of extremely precise measurement. 這部儀器計量極其精確。

辨析
Analyze

coarse, rough

1 **coarse** *a.*「粗的，粗糙的，粗劣的，粗俗的」，指材料表面粗糙、內部結構鬆散，也指鹽、糖、沙等的顆粒不細，還指產品加工不精：The clothes were made of coarse materials. 這些衣服是粗布料子做的。

2 **rough** *a.*「粗糙的，粗暴的，粗野的，粗略的，大致的」，指紙張、材料、道路、海洋等的表面粗糙、不平坦：The old worker's hands are rough. 這個老工人的手很粗糙。

smooth [smuð] .... ★★★★
adj. 平穩的，光滑的，平滑的：a smooth ride
　　in a good car 坐在好汽車上兜風

tentative [`tɛntətɪv] .... ★★★★★
adj. 實驗性，暫時的：This is just a tentative
　　schedule. 這僅僅是個試驗性的計畫表。

36

新鮮、陳舊相關辭彙

Vocabulary of Freshness

fresh [frɛʃ] .... ★★★★★
adj. ①新的，新進的：a boy fresh from school 剛從學校畢業的男孩。②新鮮的：fresh milk 新鮮牛奶③新穎的，有獨創性的④（水）淡的：fresh water 淡水

freshman [ˈfrɛʃmən] .... ★★★★★
n. （大學）一年級學生：in my freshman year 我一年級；a freshman senator 任期未滿一年的議員

hackneyed [ˈhæknɪd] .... ★
a. 平凡的，陳腐的：a hackneyed phrase 陳腐之詞

obsolete [ˈɑbsəlit] .... ★★★★★
adj. 過時的：That manufacturing method is obsolete. 那種製造方法已經過時了。

shabby [ˈʃæbɪ] .... ★
adj. 襤褸的，破舊的：shabby clothes 破舊的衣服

stale [stel] .... ★★★
adj. 陳腐的，陳舊的：stale news 陳舊的新聞

37

嚴厲、嚴格相關辭彙

Vocabulary of Severeness

austere [ɔˋstɪr] .... ★
adj. 嚴厲的：His austere demeanor prevented us from engaging in our usual frivolous activities. 他嚴肅的舉止使我們無法從事平常輕鬆的活動。

serious [ˋsɪrɪəs] .... ★★★★★
adj. 嚴肅的，認真的：This is a serious political story, not an entertainment. 這是一篇嚴肅的政治報導，不是供消遣的。

severe [səˋvɪr] ....★★★★
adj. 嚴重的，嚴肅的：The severe teacher has gone abroad; you can breathe freely again. 要求嚴苛的教師已經出國了，你可以再度自由呼吸了。

solemn [ˋsɑləm] ....★★★★
adj. ①莊嚴的，隆重的：a solemn protest 嚴正的抗議 ②嚴肅的：He staked his life on the fulfilling of this solemn charge. 他不惜犧牲生命去達成這一嚴肅的使命。

solemnly [ˋsɑləmlɪ] ....★★★★
adv. 莊嚴的，隆重的：Even today, when discussing the sinking of the Titanic, survivors tend to speak solemnly of their ordeal. 即便在今天談起鐵達尼號沉船事件時，倖存者還是會嚴肅地談起他們那段苦難的經歷。

辨析
Analyze

serious, solemn

1 **serious** *a.*「嚴重的，危急的，重要的，重大的，認真的，嚴肅的，莊嚴的」，指行為、風格等嚴肅的，也指態度認真的、當真的，還指嚴重的，比 solemn 更常用：Don't mind him. He is not serious. 別在意，他不是當真的。

2 **solemn** *a.*「嚴肅的，莊嚴的，隆重的」，多指外表嚴肅的，也指行為、風格等嚴肅的，還指莊嚴的、隆重的，正式用語：He looks solemn/serious and never smiles. 他看起來很嚴肅，從來不笑。

狀態、程度

Unit 12
運動、變化名稱總匯
Exercise & Change

01

變化、調整、更新相關辭彙

Vocabulary of Change

abbreviation [əˌbrivɪˋeʃən] .... ★

n. 縮寫式，節略，縮寫：Abbreviation of words is sometimes not acceptable in formal writing. 字的縮寫有時在正式文體中是不被允許的。

adapt [əˋdæpt] ....★★★★

v. （使）適應，改編：Some species of animals have become extinct because they could not adapt to the changing environment. 有一些動物因為不能適應環境的變化，已經絕種了。

adaptable [əˋdæptəbḷ] ....★★★★

adj. 能適應的，可改寫的：soil and climate adaptable to the growth of grapes 適於葡萄生長的土壤和氣候

adaptation [ˌædæpˋteʃən] ....★★★★

n. 適應，改寫：As aquatic plants moved millions of years ago from the ocean to the land, they underwent a number of adaptations. 隨著水生植物幾百萬年前從海洋遷移到陸地，牠們經歷了許多變化。Radioadaptation of books requires skill. 將書本改編成無線電廣播節目需要技巧。

adjust [əˋdʒʌst] .... ★★★

v. 調節，使適於：adjust the economy to a new pattern 調節經濟，使之適合於新的格局

alternate .... ★★
[ˋɔltənɪt]

adj. 交替的：alternate stripes of blue and white 藍白相間的條紋

n. 替代物：We have several alternates on our team. 我們隊有幾個替補隊員。
[ˋɔltənet]

v. 輪流：Good harvests alternate with bad. 豐收與歉收交替更迭。

alternating [ˋɔltənetɪŋ] .... ★★

adj. 交流的：alternating current 交流電

alternator [ˋɔltənetə] .... ★★

n. 交流發電機

become [bɪˋkʌm] .... ★★★★★

v. 成為，變得：It's becoming warmer and warmer. 天氣變得越來越暖和。

bleach [blitʃ] ....★

v. 去色，漂白：Did you bleach this tablecloth? 你把這塊桌布漂白了嗎？

n. 漂白劑

change [tʃendʒ] ....★★★★★

v. 改變，更換：The village has changed a lot since we visited it last year. 這個村子自從我們去年參觀以來，發生了很大的變化。

【片語】① change into 變成，使成為② change one's mind 改變主意

n. ①變化：make a change in the plan. 更動計畫②零錢，找零：Here is your change. 這是找給你的錢。

correct [kə`rɛkt] ....★★★★★

adj. 正確的

v. 糾正：If predictions made by industrial engineers are correct, plastic will continue to replace many natural materials. 如果工業工程師的預設正確的話，那麼塑膠將會取代許多天然物質。

correctly [kə`rɛktlɪ] ....★★

adv. 正確地

fickle [`fɪkl̩] ....★

adj. 多變的：It's the third time that he changed his mind; he's so fickle! 這是他第三次改變主意，他這人太反覆無常了！

mutation [mju`teʃən] ....★

n. 變化：mutation plural 母音變化構成的複數（如由 man 變出的 men 等）

operate [`ɑpə.ret] ....★★★★★

v. 操縱：Drug dealers operate in residential and urban areas. 毒品販賣者在住宅區和市區進行販賣。

operation [ɑpə`reʃən] ....★★★★★

n. 操作，工作，手術，運轉，運算：The skillful operation of a computer is hard. 熟練地操作電腦很難。

operational [ɑpə`reʃən̩l] ....★★★

adj. 可使用的，用手操作的：De facto apartheid is still operational even in the "new" African nations. 即使在「新興的」非洲國家裡，種族隔離仍然存在。

辨析 Analyze

adapt, adjust, adopt

1 **adapt** vt. & vi. 「（使）…適應，（使）…適合，改編」，指調整使適應新的情況，用於 adapt oneself to 或 adapt sth. for 句型中：This is an English book adapted for middle-school students. 這是一本為中學生改編的英語書。

2 **adjust** vt. 「校正，調整，調節，改變…以適應」，常指機械方面的調整，使其相互協調；片語 adjust oneself to 的意思等同於片語 adapt oneself to：Children can adjust the seat to their height. 小孩可根據他們的身高調整座位。

3 **adopt** vt. 「採取，採用，採納，正式通過，批准，收養」，指採用或採納外來的東西：He is an adopted son of the couple. 他是那對夫婦的養子。

operative [ˈɑpərətɪv] .... ★★★★
adj. 工作著的，起作用的：Two major tendencies are operative in the American political system. 在美國的政治體系中以兩種主要潮流為主。

rectify [ˈrɛktəˌfaɪ] .... ★
v. 糾正，整頓：Alice Hamilton helped bring about legislation aimed at rectifying factory conditions detrimental to the health of workers. 愛麗絲・漢米爾頓幫助立法機構立法，糾正對工人身體有害的工廠工作環境。

rehabilitate [ˌrihəˈbɪləˌtet] .... ★
v. 恢復：He has been rehabilitated in public esteem. 公眾已恢復對他的敬重。

synchronize [ˈsɪŋkrənaɪz] .... ★
v. 同時發生：They synchronized their steps. 他們將步伐調整一致。

unalterable [ʌnˈɔltərəbḷ] .... ★★★★
adj. 不變的，不可變更的：the unalterable season of bitter cold in Siberia 西伯利亞無法改變的酷寒天氣

variable [ˈvɛrɪəbḷ] .... ★★★★
n. 變數

variant [ˈvɛrɪənt] .... ★★★★
adj. 不同的
n. 變數：variant spellings of a word 一個字的不同拼法

variation [ˌvɛrɪˈeʃən] .... ★★★★★
n. 變化，變動：The water table fluctuates from season to season and year to year because it is affected by climatic variations. 地下水位由於受到氣候變動的影響，一年四季、年復一年地波動。

variety [vəˈraɪətɪ] .... ★★★★★
n. ①多樣化，變化：She didn't like the work because it lacked variety, she was doing the same things all the time. 她不喜歡這工作，因為它單調乏味，一天到晚都做著同樣的事情。②種類，品種

various [ˈvɛrɪəs] .... ★★★★★
adj. ①不同的，各種各樣的：There were various questions he wanted to ask. 他有各種各樣的問題要問。There are various colors to choose from. 有各種各樣的顏色可供選擇。②多方面的：for various reasons 由於種種原因

vary [ˈvɛrɪ] .... ★★★★
v. 改變：The molecular and structural arrangements of the components in a composite material can vary greatly. 複合物成分的分子和結構排列可以有多種變化。

辨析 Analyze

variable, varied, various

1 **variable** *a.*「易變的，多變的，可變的」，指變化不定的，還指可變的、可調的：Weather in England is variable. 英格蘭的天氣變化無常。

2 **varied** *a.*「各種不同的，各種各樣的」，可形容靜態的或同時存在的事物，但還指變化很多的、有種種變化的，強調歷時的變化：His excuses are many and varied/various. 他有很多各種各樣的藉口。

3 **various** *a.*「各種不同的，各種各樣的，多方面的」，一般用來形容靜態或同時存在的事物。

辨析 Analyze

alter, change, convert, transform, vary

1 **alter** *vt.*「改變，改動，變更」，指某一方面或某一部分的變化，改變後基本保持原物、原樣：She has to alter the dress because it is too large. 衣服太大，她不得不把它改一下。

2 **change** *vt & vi.*「變化，改變」，常用語，強調有明顯的差異：Mary has changed her mind. 瑪麗已改變了主意。

3 **convert** *vt & vi.*「（使）轉變，（使）轉化，（使）改變信仰或態度等」，強調形態、目的的轉變：He converted euros into dollars. 他把歐元換為美元。

4 **vary** *vt. & vi.*「變化，有不同，呈差異，改變，使不同」，常指不發生質的變化，在數量、品種、價格和式樣上產生不規則變化或多樣化，可指變來變去：Prices of meat vary with the season. 肉品的價格隨季節變化。

02

組成、包含、除外相關辭彙

Vocabulary of Composition

compose [kəmˈpoz] .... ★★★★★

v. 寫作，作曲，由…組成 (of)：The modern operas composed by Philip Glass have received a great deal of attention from reviewers and the public. 由菲利普・格拉斯所譜曲的現代歌劇受到了評論家和普通大眾的廣泛關注。

comprise [kəmˈpraɪz] .... ★★★

v. 包括：Rodents comprise one-fifth of the entire mammal population. 齧齒動物占整類哺乳動物的五分之一。

constitute [ˈkɑnstəˌtjut] .... ★★★★

v. 構成，組成：Silicon constitutes about 28 percent of the Earth's crust. 地殼中矽的含量大約占28%。

constitution [ˌkɑnstəˈtjuʃən] .... ★★★★★

n. 構成，結構，成分，體格，體質，憲法：According to the American Constitution, presidential elections are held every four years. 按照美國憲法，總統每四年選舉一次。

contain [kənˈten] .... ★★★★★

v. ①包含，容納，裝有：The house contains five rooms. 這間房子有5個房間。②等於，相等於：A gallon contains eight pints. 一加侖等於八品脫。

container [kənˈtenɚ] .... ★★★

n. 容器

containerize [kənˈtenɚˌaɪz] .... ★★★

v. 用貨櫃運貨，將（貨物）裝入貨櫃

depot [ˈdipo] .... ★

v. 容納

n. 倉庫：blood depot 血庫

eliminate [ɪˈlɪməˌnet] .... ★★★★

v. 排除，消除，消滅：She has been eliminated from the swimming race because she did not win any of the practice races. 她在訓練中沒有得到名次，已被取消了游泳比賽的資格。

elimination [ɪˌlɪməˈneʃən] .... ★★★

n. 排除，消滅

enlist [ɪnˈlɪst] .... ★★★★★
v. 徵召，招募：Having enlisted in the in
August 1918, Johnson was made a
provisional sergeant a month later. 詹森在
1918年8月被招募到海軍軍團後，在隨後的
一個月後成為臨時中士。

except [ɪkˈsɛpt] .... ★★★★★
prep. 除…之外：He goes to the library every
day except when he is not well. 他除了
身體不舒服外，每天都去圖書館。

exception [ɪkˈsɛpʃən] .... ★★★★
adj. 例外：We praised them all, with two
exceptions. 我們稱讚了他們所有的人，只
有兩個例外。

exclude [ɪkˈsklud] .... ★★★★
v. 把…排除在外：In 1840 Lucretia Mott and
Elizabeth Stanton were excluded from the
World's Anti-Slavery Convention merely
because they were women. 僅僅因為露克瑞
莎・摩特和伊莉莎白・斯坦頓身為女性，就
被 1840 年的世界反奴隸制大會所驅逐。

exclusion [ɪkˈskluʒən] .... ★★★
n. 除外，拒絕：A leading member should
never concentrate all his attention on one
or two problems, to the exclusion of others.
一個領導人不能把全部注意力只集中在一兩
個問題上而不顧其他問題。

exclusive [ɪkˈsklusɪv] .... ★★★★
adj. 排外的，獨佔的：Twenty-five percent
of Ecuador's population speak Quechua
exclusively. 厄瓜多爾25%的人口只說蓋楚
瓦族語。

group [grʊp] .... ★★★★★
n. 群，組

implicate [ˈɪmplɪˌket] .... ★★★
v. 牽連：The police found a letter which
implicated him in the robbery. 警方發現了一
封信，而把他牽連到搶劫案中。

implication [ˌɪmplɪˈkeʃən] .... ★★★
n. 牽連，關係，含意，暗示，（常用複）推
斷，結論：He smiled, but the implication
was that he didn't believe me. 他微微一笑，
但暗示著他不相信我的話。

ingredient [ɪnˈgridɪənt] .... ★★★
n. 原料，成分

integrate [ˈɪntəˌgret] .... ★★
v. 使結合，使併入：Peter's architectural
designs of integrate the structure and its
environment. 彼得的建築設計把建築物與周
圍環境結合起來了。

integration [ˌɪntəˈgreʃən] .... ★★
n. 結合，〔美〕取消種族隔離：the integration
of races in the US 美國的種族大熔爐

integrity [ɪnˈtɛgrətɪ] .... ★★
n. 正直，完整性：The ancient temple and the
pagoda are still there, but not in its integrity.
那座古老的廟宇和塔還在，但是不完整了。

involve [ɪnˈvɑlv] .... ★★★★★
v. 捲入，連累，涉及，包含：a story that
completely involved me for the rest of the
evening. 這個故事讓我在那天晚上完全沉浸
於其中。

irreconcilable [ɪˈrɛkənˌsaɪləbl] ....★
adj. 不能妥協的：irreconcilable enemies 不能
和解的敵人

unite [juˈnaɪt] ....★
v.（使）聯合，（使）團結，（使）結合：They
united to form a club. 他們聯合組成了一個
俱樂部。

辨析
Analyze

compose, comprise, constitute, contain, include, involve

1 **compose** *vt.*「組成，構成，創作（樂曲、詩歌等）」，如果是部分組成某個整體用compose，如果是整體由部分組成則用片語be composed of（由…組成）：Twelve men compose a jury. 十二個人組成一個陪審團。

2 **comprise** *vt.*「包含，包括，由…組成，構成，組成」，一是指整體包含構成某一整體的全部內容，相當於consist of、be made up of 或be composed of；二是指部分構成整體或占一定的比例：The United Kingdom comprises England, Wales, Scotland and Northern Ireland. 英國包括英格蘭、蘇格蘭、威爾斯以及北愛爾蘭。

3 **constitute** *vt.*「組成，構成，形成」，一是指部分構成整體（通常有數字）；二是指等同於，不能指整體包含部分：This constitutes a direct threat to their country. 這對他們的國家形成了一個直接的威脅。

4 **contain** *vt.*「包含，容納」，一是指同類的東西裝在或包含在一個容器或一個有形的整體中，二是指被包含的部分往往混合在一起：Pig iron may contain 5% of carbon. 生鐵中可含5%的碳。

5 **include** *vt.*「包括，包含」，與contain相比，include 包含的部分往往是較為分散的、獨立存在的人或物；與comprise相比，include 所包含的只是整體的一部分內容：Our five-cities tour includes a visit to Berlin and Paris. 我們的五城之旅包括柏林、巴黎之行。

6 **involve** *vt.*「包括，涉及」，著重指由於某種必然關聯而包括、涉及到，常用句型有 be involved in（陷入，被捲入）：House keeping involves cooking, washing dishes, sweeping and cleaning etc. 做家事包括煮飯、洗碗、掃地和清洗等等。

運動、變化類名稱總匯

03

聚集、連接、交換、分離相關辭彙

Vocabulary of Relation

運動、變化

accumulate [əˋkjumjəˏlet] .... ★★★

v. 積聚：While they were away on vacation, they allowed their mail to accumulate at the post office. 他們外出度假期間，郵件都堆積在郵局。

adhere [ədˋhɪr] .... ★★

v. 黏著，堅持：I will adhere to this opinion until I am proven to be wrong. 我將堅持這個意見，直到被證明錯了。

adherent [ədˋhɪrənt] .... ★★

n. 信奉者：Being still a student, basketball player Lew Alcindor became an adherent of Islam and in 1971 changed his name to Kareen Abdul-Jabbar. 當籃球運動員 Lew Alcindor 還是個學生時，他成為一名伊斯蘭教教徒，並在 1971 年改名為 Kareen Abdul-Jabbar。

adhesive [ədˋhisɪv] .... ★

adj. 黏著的：He feels an adhesive dread, a sudden acquaintance with the darker side of mankind. 他感到一種無法忘卻的恐懼，一種對人類黑暗面的突然認識.

n. 黏合劑

affix [əˋfɪks] .... ★★★

vt. ①附加：Please affix your signature to the agreement. 請在這份協議上簽字。②貼上：You should affix a label to the package. 你應該在這個包裹上貼上標籤。③蓋印：Affix a seal to the document. 在這份文件上蓋上印章。

aggregate [ˋægrɪˏget] .... ★

n. 總數

adj. 合計的，總的：The aggregate wealth of this country is staggering to the imagination. 這個國家富有得令人難以想像。

amass [əˋmæs] .... ★★★★★

v. 收集，積聚：The miser's aim is to amass and hoard as much gold as possible. 這個守財奴的目的是要盡可能地積聚金子。

appendix [əˋpɛndɪks] .... ★★

n. 附錄：two appendixes to a book 書的兩個附錄

341

assemble [əˋsɛmbḷ] .... ★★★★
v. 聚集：As a gift to the United States
from France, the Statue of Liberty was
assembled and dedicated in 1886. 自由女神
像是法國在1886年組裝並且贈送給美國的禮
物。

assembly [əˋsɛmblɪ] .... ★★★★★
n. 集會：New England town meetings, in their
most highly developed form, are assemblies
of the voter's. 新英格蘭市鎮會議的最高形態
是選舉人集會。

attach [əˋtætʃ] .... ★★★★★
v. 附加，隸屬，繫，縛，相連，綁上，把
（重點）放在：They gained influence by
attaching themselves to prominent city
institutions. 他們通過與著名的城市機構之
間的聯繫而獲得威望。We attached several
riders to the document. 我們在主文件上加了
幾條附文。

attachment [əˋtætʃmənt] .... ★★
n. 連接物，附件：an attachment for an
electric drill 電鑽的附件

blend [blɛnd] .... ★★★
v. 混合：In the groundbreaking musical play
Oklahoma, Agnes successfully blended
story, dancing, and popular music into a
unified work. 在具有開拓性的音樂劇《奧克
拉荷馬》中，埃格尼斯成功地將故事情節、
舞蹈及流行音樂融為一體。
n. 混合

coherent [koˋhɪrənt] ....★
adj. 連貫的：We found the professor's talk on
nuclear reactors quite coherent. 我們發現
這位教授對核反應的講述十分連貫。

cohesion [koˋhiʒən] ....★
n. 附著（力），結合，凝聚力：The most
important thing is more cohesion within the
party to win the next general election. 要想
贏得下屆大選的勝利，最重要的是我們黨内
要更加團結。

cohesive [koˋhisɪv] ....★
adj. 有凝聚力的：cohesive force 凝聚力，内
聚力，黏合力

collect [kəˋlɛkt] .... ★★★★★
v. ①收集，聚集：He collect a crowd of
children around him. 他周圍聚集了一群
孩子。②領取，接走：collect a child from
school 從學校接孩子③收（帳、稅等）：
collect taxes 收稅④聚集，堆積

collection [kəˋlɛkʃən] .... ★★★★★
n. ①收藏品，收集的東西：Bob took his insect
collection to school. 鮑伯把他收集的昆蟲
帶到學校。②收取，收集：We're holding a
collection for Tom's retirement present. 我
們正在為湯姆退休購買禮物而湊錢。③聚
積，積聚

collective [kəˋlɛktɪv] .... ★★★★
n. 集體
adj. 集體的，共同的：our collective mistakes
我們大家共同所犯的錯誤

combination [͵kɑmbəˋneʃən] .... ★★★★
n. 化合，組合：After the general election,
a combination of parties formed the new
government. 各政黨在大選後，聯合組成了
新政府。

combine [kəmˋbaɪn] .... ★★★★★
v. 結合，化合：We must combine theory with
practice. 我們必須把理論和實踐相結合。

concentrate [ˋkɑnsɛn͵tret] .... ★★★★
v. 集中，濃縮：Myra began her career as an
illustrator, but later concentrated on murals
and stained glass. 瑪伊拉以插圖畫家作為
第一職業，但是後來致力於壁畫和玻璃畫創
作。

concentration [͵kɑnsɛnˋtreʃən] .... ★★★
n. （精神等）集中，濃度：The largest
concentrations of iron ore are found in the
sedimentary deposits of the earth's crust.
鐵礦石主要聚集在地殼的沈積岩中。

condensation [ˌkɑndɛnˈseʃən] .... ★★★
n. 壓縮，冷凝，凝聚：There was condensation on the windows. 玻璃窗上凝結著水珠。

condense [kənˈdɛns] .... ★★★
v. 凝結，壓縮，精簡：A long story may be condensed into a few sentences. 一個長篇故事可縮短成幾句話。

congregate [ˈkɑngrɪˌget] .... ★
v. 聚集：Although dolphins sometimes swim singly or in pairs, they usually congregate in large herds, often numbering in the hundreds. 儘管海豚有時候單獨或成對遊動，但它們經常聚集成群，數量往往達數百隻。

conjunction [kənˈdʒʌŋkʃən] .... ★★★
n. 連接詞

consolidate [kənˈsɑləˌdet] .... ★
v. 合併：Several small businesses are planning to consolidate to form a large powerful company. 幾家小企業正計畫合併成一家實力雄厚的大公司。

convene [kənˈvin] .... ★
v. 集合：The graduate students will convene in the Student Union. 研究生將在學生會集會。

converge [kənˈvɝdʒ] .... ★
v. 聚集：The beam of light converges at a certain point. 這束光線集中於某一點。

discrete [dɪˈskrit] .... ★
adj. 不連續的，離散的：uniformly discrete 一致離散的

discretionary [dɪˈskrɛʃənˌɛrɪ] .... ★★
adj. 任意的，自由決定的

divide [dəˈvaɪd] .... ★★★★★
v. 分割，〔數〕除：On some minor points members of the committee divide with one another. 在一些細節問題上，委員們意見各不相同。

focus [ˈfokəs] .... ★★★★★
n. 中心，焦點，焦距
v. 聚焦，集中：He was forever taken aback by (New York's) pervasive atmosphere of purposefulness—the tight focus of its drivers, the brisk intensity of its pedestrians. 他非常驚訝於（紐約）彌漫的那種以「目的」為導向的氣氛——司機高度集中以及行人節奏快速的步伐。

gang [gæŋ] .... ★★★★
n. 一幫，一群：The gang was planning a robbery of a bank. 這夥歹徒正在計畫搶劫一家銀行。

辨析 Analyze

assemble, gather

1 **assemble** *vt. & vi.*「集合，聚集，召集，裝配」，一般不用於抽象的事物：Assemble your papers and put them in this file. 把你的文件收起來放進這檔案夾內。

2 **gather** *vt. & vi.*「聚集，集合，收集，採集」，既可指具體的事物，也可指抽象的事物；還指「逐漸增加（速度或力量）」：He gathered his experiences and wrote a book. 他把自己的經歷加以收集整理並寫了一本書。

gangster [ˈɡæŋstɚ] .... ★
n. 暴徒，歹徒：a gangster film 幫派片

gather [ˈɡæðɚ] .... ★ ★ ★ ★ ★
v. ①聚集，集合：A crowd soon gathered around him. 不久一群人聚集在他的周圍。②收穫，採集：Gather some flowers for me. 請為我採集些花。③逐漸增加：gather information 收集消息④猜想，推測：What did you gather from his statement? 你猜想他的聲明是什麼意思？

inclination [ˌɪnkləˈneʃən] .... ★ ★
n. 傾向，愛好：I have no inclination to be a doctor. 我不想當醫生。

inclined [ɪnˈklaɪnd] .... ★ ★ ★ ★
adj. 傾向…的：I am inclined to be ill after eating fish. 我吃完魚後就想吐。

intercept [ˌɪntɚˈsɛpt] .... ★
v. 中途攔截，阻止：The parcels of drugs were intercepted by the Customs House before they were delivered. 成包的毒品在運到前被海關截獲了。

joint [dʒɔɪnt] .... ★ ★ ★ ★ ★
n. 關節，骨節，接合處，接縫
adj. 聯合的，共同的，共有的，連接的：The conservation of Utah's natural resources is the joint responsibility of federal and state agencies. 對猶他州自然資源的保護是州和聯邦政府機構共同的責任。

jumble [ˈdʒʌmbl] .... ★
v. 混雜：How can I find that letter when all your papers are jumbled up like this? 你的文件像這樣亂成一堆，我怎麼能找到那封信呢？

junction [ˈdʒʌŋkʃən] .... ★
n. 連接，會合處：The hydraulic power station stands at the junction of two rivers. 水力發電站位於兩條河流的會合處。

knit [nɪt] .... ★ ★
v. 編織，接合，黏合：The two edges of that broken bone will knit together smoothly. 骨折的地方將接合得很好。

liaison [ˌlɪəˈzɑn] .... ★
n. 聯絡：served as the President's liaison with Congress 作總統與議會的橋樑

辨析 Analyze

blend, mingle, mix

1 **blend** *vt. & vi.* 「（使）混合，（使）混雜」，強調容和在一起以求得某種品質：The coffees we sell here are carefully blended. 我們這裡出售的各種咖啡都是仔細混合而成的。

2 **mingle** *vt. & vi.* 「混合」，指兩個以上的東西混合，各種留其原有性質：When the policeman wanted to catch the robber, he mingled with the crowd at once. 當警察想抓住盜賊時，盜賊立即混入人群中。

3 **mix** *vt. & vi.* 「混合」，指兩種以上的東西相混，變成難以區分的狀態：We can't mix oil with water. 我們不能將油與水相混合。

link [lɪŋk] .... ★★★★★

v. 連接，聯繫：The road links all the new towns. 這條馬路通到所有的新城鎮。

n. 環，節，聯繫：There's a link between smoking and lung cancer. 吸煙和肺癌有關係。

merge [mɝdʒ] .... ★★★★★

v. 合併：The three companies will merge. 這三家公司將要合併。

mingle [ˈmɪŋgl] .... ★★

v. 混合，加入：a speech of praise mingled with blame 褒貶兼有的發言

mix [mɪks] .... ★★★★★

v. ①使混合，攪和：You can't mix oil and water. 你不能使油和水混合在一起。②混淆，搞混：mix black with white 混淆黑白 ③相混合：Oil doesn't mix with water. 油不溶於水。

【片語】① mix up 攪勻，拌和② mix up with 把…和…混淆，把…看做是

rally [ˈrælɪ] .... ★★★

v. 召集，恢復：The stock market declined, then rallied. 股市下跌了，接著又漲回了。

rend [rɛnd] .... ★

v. 分離，撕破：An explosion rent the air. 一聲爆炸劃破長空。

segregate [ˈsɛgrɪˌget] .... ★

v. 隔離，分離：The doctor segregated the child sick with scarlet fever. 醫生把患猩紅熱的孩子隔離起來。

separate .... ★★★★★

adj. [ˈsɛprɪt] 分離的，單獨的，獨立的

v. [ˈsɛpəˌret] 分開，隔離：separate A from B 將 A 與 B 分開

辨析 Analyze

assembly, conference, congress, meeting, rally, session

1 **assembly** *n.* 「大會，集會，議會」，常指群眾集會或立法界、宗教界會議：the General Assembly 聯合國大會，a national assembly 國民大會；還指「組裝，裝配」：assembly line 生產線

2 **conference** *n.* 「會議」，指正式會議，尤指年度會議和記者招待會：press conference 記者招待會

3 **congress** *n.* 「代表大會，國會，議會」：The US Congress is made up of the Senate and the House of Representatives. 美國國會由參議院和眾議院構成。

4 **meeting** *n.* 「會議」，指各類大小會議，是常用語：Our team had a meeting in the classroom yesterday. 昨天我們團隊在教室裡開了一個會。

5 **rally** *n.* 「集會，群眾大會」，指有目的的群眾集會，還指「汽車拉力賽」：Thousands of people in the city of Beijing staged anti-war rallies. 幾千名北京群眾舉行了反戰集會。

6 **session** *n.* 指「一屆會議」：This year's session of Congress is unusually short. 今年國會的會期特別短。

separately [ˈsɛpərɪtlɪ] .... ★★★
adv. 分離地，分別地：They arrived together but left separately. 他們一起到達，但分別離開。

split [splɪt] .... ★★★★
v. ①被撕裂，裂開：Three people died when their car split in two. 當他們的車被撞成兩截時，有三人死亡。②分裂：The government split apart on how to deal with the situation. 政府對如何處理這一局面產生了分歧。③劈開：split fire wood 劈柴 ④使分裂：a quarrel which split the labor party 使工黨分裂的一場爭論
n. 分裂，裂口

synthesis [ˈsɪnθəsɪs] .... ★
n. 合成，綜合：The genetic material DNA contains coded information for the synthesis of proteins. DNA 的遺傳物質有蛋白質合成的編碼資訊。

synthesize [ˈsɪnθəˌsaɪz] .... ★
v. （人工）合成：The main features of the telegraph were developed by two inventors, but it was Samuel Morse who successfully synthesized their ideas. 電報的主要特點是由兩個人發明的，但是山謬爾‧摩斯成功地把他們的想法結合在一起。

synthetic [sɪnˈθɛtɪk] .... ★★★
adj. 綜合的，合成的：Before the advent of synthetic fibers, people had to rely entirely on natural products for making fabrics. 人們在合成纖維發明之前，得完全依靠天然產品來製作纖維。

weave [wiv] .... ★★★
v. 編，織，編織，紡織，迂迴行進：Weaving is an art among the Navaho of Arizona and New Mexico. 編織是亞利桑那州和新墨西哥州的納瓦霍人的一種藝術。

weaver [ˈwivɚ] .... ★
n. 紡織工人

weld [wɛld] .... ★★★
v. 焊接，鍛接：He welded the broken rod. 他焊接一根斷了的桿子。

辨析
Analyze

knit, spin, weave

1 **knit** *vt. & vi.*「編結，編織」，指織毛衣、毛褲、圍巾等：She spent her spare time knitting sweaters. 她用業餘時間織毛衣。

2 **spin** *vt. & vi.*「紡（紗），織（網），快速旋轉，眩暈」，多指紡紗、紡線：Yarn has been spun in this city for hundreds of years. 這座城市已有數百年紡紗的歷史。

3 **weave** *v.*「編，織」，指織布、織網、編藍子、編羅筐等：She is weaving a rug/basket. 她正在織地毯／編藍子。

divide, isolate, part, segregate, separate

1 **divide** *vt.*「分開，分配」，指把整體劃分為若干部分，尤其指平均劃分、分成等份或數學上的除，也可指自然分開：We divided the money equally. 我們把錢平分了。

2 **isolate** *vt.*「使隔離，使孤立」，強調把少數或小部分與多數或整體分開：The US has sought to isolate Cuba both economically and politically. 美國一直謀求在經濟和政治上孤立古巴。

3 **part** *vt. & vi.*「（使）分開」，指（把）原來在一起或原來是一體的人或物分開，詞義與 separate 接近，但一般不用於否定句和被動語態：We parted at the airport. 我們在機場分開。

4 **segregate** *vt.*「使隔離、使分開」，尤其指由於種族、性別、宗教等原因把一群人與另一群人分開、隔離：Blacks used to be segregated from whites in churches, schools and colleges. 黑人曾經因種族隔離而與白人上不同的教堂和學校。

5 **separate** *vt. & vi.*「（使）分離，（使）分開」，強調把原來靠近或在一起的東西或人分開，也可指因自然障礙而隔離，常與 from 連用：I'm sorry you two have to be separated. 對不起，你們兩位得分開。

347

04

傾向、打破、破壞相關辭彙

Vocabulary of Tendence & Breaks

apt [æpt] .... ★★

adj. 有…傾向的，貼切的，恰當的：Plants apt to suffer from drought can hardly grow in this area. 習性懼旱的植物很難在這個地區生長。

arduous [ˋɑrdʒuəs] .... ★

adj. 險峻的，困難的：The scientific conquest of fusion energy is proved to be an arduous task. 以科學克服核融合產生的能量是一項艱難的工作。

breach [britʃ] .... ★★★★★

n. 破裂：The breach between "serious" and commercial artists first became apparent in the nineteenth century. 「嚴肅」藝術家與商業藝術家之間關係的破裂在19世紀首次變得十分明顯。

break [brek] .... ★★★★★

v. ①打破：Who broke the window? 誰打破了窗戶？②損壞：My watch is broken. 我的手錶壞了。③破壞，違反：break the law 犯法；break a promise 食言，違約④中止，中斷：They decided to break their journey. 他們決定中止旅程。⑤破，斷裂：The window broke into pieces. 窗戶破成了碎片。

【片語】① break away 突然離開，強行逃脫② break down 損壞③ break in 闖入；插嘴④ break into 強行闖入⑤ break off 中止，中斷⑥ break out 爆發，突然出現，使…逃脫，使…逃走⑦ break through 突圍，破碎⑧ break up 打碎，破碎，終止，結束

n. （課間）休息時間：have/take a break 休息一下

breakdown [ˋbrek͵daʊn] .... ★★

n. 崩潰，倒塌，失敗，細目：The first step in planning a marketing strategy for a new product is to analyze the breakdown of sales figures for competitive products. 新產品市場策略規劃的第一步，是分析競爭產品銷售額的細目。

breaker [ˋbrekɚ] .... ★★★

n. 電流斷路器

breakfast [ˋbrɛkfəst] .... ★★★★★

n. 早餐

breakthrough [ˋbrek͵θru] .... ★

n. 突破，驚人的進展

brittle [ˈbrɪtl̩] .... ★

adj. 易碎的：Galena, the first chief ore of lead, is a brittle, lead-gray mineral with a metallic luster. 方鉛礦作為首要的鉛礦石，是一種具有金屬色澤的鉛灰色易碎礦物。

broken [ˈbrokən] .... ★ ★ ★ ★ ★

adj. 打碎的：She was weeping for a broken vase. 她為一個碎裂的花瓶哭泣。

collapse [kəˈlæps] .... ★ ★ ★

n. 倒塌，崩潰

counterproductive [ˈkaʊntəprəˈdʌktɪv] ... ★

adj. 反生產的：Violation of the court order would be counterproductive. 破壞法庭秩序將無益於勝訴。

crush [krʌʃ] .... ★ ★ ★ ★

v. 榨，擠，壓碎：to crush one's way through the crowd 擠過人群

damage [ˈdæmɪdʒ] .... ★ ★ ★ ★

n. ①毀壞，損害：The storm caused great damage. 暴風雨造成了巨大的損失。②（常作複數）損害賠償金：The court ordered him to pay 1,000 dollars damages to the person he had hurt. 法庭判他賠償他所傷害的人1,000美元。

v. 毀壞，損害：Quarrels damaged their marriage. 爭吵毀掉了他們的婚姻。

debris [dəˈbri] .... ★

n. 碎片：glacial debris 冰河的岩屑

demolish [dɪˈmɑlɪʃ] .... ★

v. 破壞：All these old houses are going to be demolished. 所有這些舊房屋都快要拆除了。

destroy [dɪˈstrɔɪ] .... ★ ★ ★ ★ ★

v. ①破壞，毀滅：The forest was destroyed by fire. 森林被大火所毀。②消滅：go all out and be sure to destroy the enemy intruders 全力以赴，務必殲滅入侵的敵人

destruction [dɪˈstrʌkʃən] .... ★ ★ ★ ★ ★

n. 破壞，毀滅：The fire caused the destruction of my books. 這場大火使我的藏書被毀壞。

destructive [dɪˈstrʌktɪv] .... ★

adj. 破壞（性）的，危害的：Now a negative finance policy could be destructive to the economy. 現在消極的財政政策可能對經濟不利。

detach [dɪˈtætʃ] .... ★ ★

v. 分開，分遣：The accountant detached a check from the checkbook and gave it to me. 會計從支票簿上撕下一張支票遞給我。

detached [dɪˈtætʃt] .... ★ ★

adj. 分離的，公正的：The Smiths own a house with a detached garage. 史密斯家擁有一幢有獨立車庫的房子。

detriment [ˈdɛtrəmənt] .... ★

n. 損害：She took a long leave without detriment to her career. 她請了長假但不會對她的事業造成損害。

detrimental [dɛtrəˈmɛntl̩] .... ★

adj. 有害的，有損的：Such activities would be detrimental to our interest. 這種行為有損於我們的利益。

devastate [ˈdɛvəsˌtet] .... ★

v. 使荒廢，破壞：A long war devastated Europe. 長期的戰爭破壞了歐洲。

devour [dɪˈvaʊr] .... ★ ★

v. 吞食，吞沒，毀滅：A female mantis does not hesitate to devour her own mate if she is hungry. 一個雌性螳螂在饑餓的時候會毫不猶豫地吞下她的雄性夥伴。

disable [dɪsˈebl̩] .... ★ ★ ★

v. 使喪失能力，使傷殘：His illness totally disabled him from following his vocation. 他的疾病使他完全喪失了就業的能力。

disadvantage [ˌdɪsəˈvæntɪdʒ] .... ★★★

n. 不利，不利條件，損失，損害：His inability to speak English puts him at a disadvantage when he attends international conferences. 他不會說英語，這使他在參加國際會議時處於不利的地位。

disfigure [dɪsˈfɪgjɚ] .... ★

v. 破壞：disfigure one's face by a deep cut 深深的傷痕使臉色很難看

disrupt [dɪsˈrʌpt] .... ★★★

v. 使中斷，使分裂：Our efforts in the garden were disrupted by an early frost. 一場早霜中斷了我們在花園裡的成果。

disunite [ˌdɪsjuˈnaɪt] .... ★★★★★

v. 使分離：to disunite the links of a chain 拆開一條鐵鏈的鏈環

diverge [daɪˈvɝdʒ] .... ★

v. 分歧，差異：I'm afraid our opinions diverge from each other on the direction of investment. 恐怕我們在投資方向的見解不同。

divergent [daɪˈvɝdʒənt] .... ★

adj. 分叉的，分歧的：a divergent opinion 不同的意見

division [dəˈvɪʒən] .... ★★★★★

n. 分，分割，分裂，部分，部門，除法：The river forms the division between the heavy industrial and light industrial areas of the city. 這條河成了這座城市重工業區和輕工業區的分界線。

fraction [ˈfrækʃən] .... ★★★

n. 片段，分數：Mother's careful with her money, and spends only a fraction of her earnings. 母親用錢很審慎，只花自己收入很小的一部分。

fracture [ˈfræktʃɚ] .... ★

n. 斷裂，骨折：a sudden and irreparable fracture of the established order 本已確立的秩序突然而無法挽救地破裂

fragile [ˈfrædʒəl] .... ★

adj. 脆弱的，體制弱的：I'm feeling rather fragile after all that beer last night. 我昨晚喝了啤酒，現在感到軟弱無力。

fragment [ˈfrægmənt] .... ★★★★

n. 碎片，破布：Palynologists, who study spores and pollen, also examine tiny fragments of animals and plants found in sediment. 孢粉學家是研究孢子和花粉的人，同時還研究在沉積物中發現的細小動植物碎片。

辨析
Analyze

delicate, fragile

1 delicate *a.*「精美，雅致」，指人的身體纖弱易病，指器官或物體纖嫩易損，引申義為微妙的、怡人的：He has been in delicate health for several years. 幾年來，他的身體健康狀況相當不好。

2 fragile *a.*「易碎的，虛弱的」，指易碎的、虛弱的，更接近貶義：Thin glass is fragile. 薄的玻璃易碎。

fragmentary [ˈfræɡmənˌtɛrɪ] .... ★★★
adj. 碎片的，不連續的：a picture that emerges from fragmentary information 由拼湊不完整的資訊而畫出的畫

indiscriminate [ˌɪndɪˈskrɪmənɪt] ★★★★★
adj. 不加區別的：In *Silent Spring*, Rachel Carson forcefully descried the indiscriminate use of pesticides. 卡森在《寂靜的春天》一書中，有力地指出了對殺蟲劑的濫用。

indistinguishable [ˌɪndɪˈstɪɡwɪʃəbḷ] ★★★
adj. 不能區別的，難區別的，無特徵的：indistinguishable twins 難以分辨的雙胞胎

liable [ˈlaɪəbḷ] .... ★★★
adj. 有…傾向的，易於…的，有責任的，有義務的：liable to criminal charges 可能被提起刑事訴訟的

overthrow [ˌovɚˈθro] .... ★★★★★
v. 推翻，廢除，顛覆：overthrow slavery 廢除奴隸制度

perish [ˈpɛrɪʃ] .... ★★
v. 死亡，枯萎，腐朽：Must the Christ perish in torment in every age to save those who have no imagination? 基督必須每年為拯救那些缺乏想像力的人們受一次死亡的折磨嗎？

perishable [ˈpɛrɪʃəbḷ] .... ★★
adj. 容易腐爛的：Fruits are perishable in transit. 水果在運途中容易腐爛。

piece [pis] .... ★★★★★
n. （一）件，（一）片，（一）篇
【片語】a piece of 一張／片／塊：a piece of paper 一張紙

prejudice [ˈprɛdʒədɪs] .... ★★★★
v. 使抱偏見
n. 偏見，成見，侵害，損害：A judge must be free from prejudice. 法官不應存在偏見。

prone [pron] .... ★★★★★
adj. 傾向於…的：Children of poor health are very prone to colds in winter. 體弱的孩子在冬天易患感冒。

辨析 Analyze

apt, liable, prone

1 **apt** *a.*「易於…的，有…傾向的」，用作這一意義時只做表語，其唯一句型為 be apt to do sth.，還指「恰當的，適宜的；聰明的，反應敏捷的」：He is apt/liable to lose his temper. 他易於發怒。

2 **liable** *a.*「易於…的，有…傾向的，易患…病的」，句型一：be liable to do sth. 意為「易於…的，有…傾向的」；句型二：be liable to sth. 意為「易患…病的」；句型三：be liable for sth. 則意為「有法律責任的，有義務的」：One is more liable/prone/apt to make mistakes when one is tired. 人累了的時候容易犯錯誤。

3 **prone** *a.*「易於…的，很可能…的」，貶義詞，多指不好的事情，有兩個句型：be prone to do sth. 和 be prone to sth.，見以上兩例。

propensity [prəˈpɛnsətɪ] .... ★

n. 傾向：a propensity to extravagance (for gambling) 奢華（賭博）的癖好

ravage [ˈrævɪdʒ] .... ★

v. 掠奪，破壞：The forest fire ravaged many miles of country. 森林大火使數英里範圍的農村遭到破壞。

ruin [ˈruɪn] .... ★ ★ ★ ★ ★

v. 使毀壞，毀壞：You are ruining your health. 你在糟蹋你的身體。

n. ①毀滅，毀壞：Drink was your father's ruin. 酒毀了你父親。②廢墟，遺跡：the ruins of an ancient castle 古城堡的遺跡

rupture [ˈrʌptʃɚ] .... ★

n. 破裂，決裂：the rupture between the two neighbouring countries 兩個鄰國的斷交

sabotage [ˈsæbə͵tɑʒ] .... ★

n. 破壞活動，故意毀壞：The secret agent was arrested on a charge of sabotage. 密探因犯下蓄意破壞罪被捕。

v. 破壞：Enemy agents sabotaged the arms factory. 敵人的間諜蓄意破壞了軍工廠。

spoil [spɔɪl] .... ★ ★ ★ ★

v. 損壞，糟蹋，寵壞：Ice can be used to keep food from spoiling. 冰可以防止食物腐壞。

tarnish [ˈtɑrnɪʃ] .... ★

v. 使晦暗，敗壞（名譽）：The copper pot has become tarnished after many years of neglect. 該銅壺由於多年未擦拭而變得顏色灰暗。

tend [tɛnd] .... ★ ★ ★ ★ ★

v. ①易於，往往會：I tend to wake up early in the morning. 我早晨往往早醒。②表示致歉或委婉：I tend to think that's a good solution. 我傾向於認為那是個好的解決辦法。

v. 照管，護理：tend the sick and wounded 護理傷者與病人

tendency [ˈtɛndənsɪ] .... ★ ★ ★ ★

n. 趨勢，脾性，修養：His tendency to utter acrimonious remarks alienated his roommates. 他老是說話尖刻，同寢室的人和他疏遠了。

trend [trɛnd] .... ★ ★ ★ ★

n. 傾向，趨勢：the latest trend in fashion 服裝界最新潮流

wreck [rɛk] .... ★ ★ ★ ★

v. ①破壞，毀壞：You'll wreck your digestion if you swallow your food that way. 你如此狼吞虎嚥，一定會壞了你的消化系統。②造成…失事，使遇難：The train was wrecked. 火車失事了。

n. ①失事，失事的船或飛機，殘骸：The wreck lay 1,000 meters below the surface of the sea. 船的殘骸在離海平面 1,000 米的海底。②受到嚴重損害的人：If these anxieties continue she will become a nervous wreck. 如果她繼續焦慮下去，她會得精神病。

wreckage [ˈrɛkɪdʒ] .... ★ ★ ★

n. （船隻等）失事，遭難，毀壞：the wreckage of the plane after the crash 飛機墜落後的殘骸

damage, destroy, harm, hurt, injure, spoil, wound, wreck

1 **damage** *vt.*「損害，毀壞」，指部分地損壞、損害物體或身體的一部分，使之失去完整性等：Her heart was slightly damaged as a result of her long illness. 她由於長期生病，心臟受到輕微損傷。

2 **destroy** *vt.*「破壞，摧毀，消滅」，指完全摧毀：The bombs destroyed two buildings and damaged several others. 炸彈摧毀了兩座建築並使其他幾座受損。

3 **harm** *vt.*「傷害，損害，危害」，指對物體、身體、名聲、形象的損害，強調痛苦的後果，其動作有一定的延續過程，如 to harm the eyes/reputation/image/crops：Smoking harms your health. 抽煙傷身。

4 **hurt** *vt.*「使受傷，危害，損害，傷…的感情」；*vi.*「引起疼痛」。指肉體和情感上的傷害，強調痛苦和苦惱，沒有 injure 正式：Several people were seriously hurt/injured in the accident. 有幾個人在事故中受重傷。

5 **injure** *vt.*「傷害，損害，損傷」，指對人的身體、機能、感情、容貌、名聲等的傷害，如 to injure one's health/legs/reputation/feelings：The injured were taken to the hospital. 傷者被送到了醫院。

6 **spoil** *vt. & vi.*「損壞，破壞，寵壞，溺愛」，指損壞某人、某物、某事（但仍然存在），使之不再有作用、吸引力、舒適感：The countryside has been spoiled by the new freeway. 這片農村被新修的高速公路破壞了。

6 **ruin** *vt.*「使毀滅，使毀壞」，指徹底毀壞：The rain ruined our holiday. 下雨毀了我們的假期。

7 **wound** *vt.*「使受傷，傷害」，指刀傷、槍傷：Several soldiers were wounded in the battle. 有幾個士兵在戰鬥中受傷。

8 **wreck** *vt.*「破壞，毀壞，使失事」，多指船隻、車輛被毀或遇難，也可引申指抽象事物（計畫、希望、健康等）被毀：The ship was wrecked in the storm. 這艘船在暴風雨中失事。

05

爆炸、燃燒、熄滅相關辭彙

Vocabulary of Burns

bake [bek] .... ★★★

v. 烤，烘，焙：Do you like baked chicken? 你喜歡吃烤雞嗎？

bang [bæŋ] .... ★★★

n. ①（突發的）巨響，槍聲，爆炸聲：We heard the bang of a gun. 我們聽到一聲槍響。②（發出砰的一聲的）猛撞：He fell down and got a bang on the head. 他摔倒了，腦袋砰地撞了一下。

v. ①發出砰的一聲，砰砰作響：The guns banged away. 槍砰砰作響。②（砰砰）猛擊，猛撞：There is someone banging at the door. 有人在用力敲門。

bask [bæsk] .... ★★★★★

v. 取暖，曝曬，沐浴於：He basked in his employer's approval. 他受到雇主的讚許而得意洋洋。

blast [blæst] .... ★★★★

n. 一陣（風）

v. 爆破：They're trying to blast away the hill to pave the way for the new highway. 他們試圖炸掉這座小山丘來鋪設新公路。

blaze [blez] .... ★★

n. 火焰，火光

v. 燃燒：Lights were blazing and men were running here and there; they had just discovered that a prisoner had escaped. 燈光強烈耀眼，人們跑來跑去，他們剛剛發現有個戰俘逃掉了。

blazing [ˈblezɪŋ] .... ★★

adj. 燃燒的：pick cotton in the blazing summer 在炎熱的夏天採棉花

broil [brɔɪl] .... ★★★

v. 烤（肉），酷熱：to broil a chicken 烤一隻雞

burn [bɝn] .... ★★★★★

v. ①燃燒，燒著：Dry wood burn easily. 乾柴易燃。②燒，點燃：Big steamer burns oil instead of coal. 大汽船燒油而不是燒煤。③燒毀，燒傷：He burn his finger. 他燒傷了手指。

【片語】① burn out 燒光，燒毀② burn up 燒光，燒毀

n. 燒傷，灼傷：They suffered severe burns. 他們被嚴重燒傷。

burning [ˋbɝnɪŋ] .... ★★★★★
adj. 燃燒的，強烈的：a burning house 正在燃燒的房子

burnish [ˋbɝnɪʃ] .... ★★★★★
n. 光澤，光亮，光滑：a high burnish 很亮的光澤
v. 磨光，使光滑

burst [bɝst] .... ★★★★★
v. ①使爆裂：The boy burst the balloon. 這孩子把氣球弄爆了。②爆炸，爆裂：The balloon burst. 氣球爆了。③突然發作，突然出現：The storm burst and we all got wet. 暴風雨突然降臨，我們全被淋濕了。
n. 爆炸，爆裂：the burst of a bomb 炸彈的爆炸

combustible [kəmˋbʌstəbl] .... ★
adj. 易燃的：Petrol is highly combustible, so smoking is strictly forbidden during the handling of it. 汽油極易燃燒，處理時嚴格禁止吸煙。

combustion [kəmˋbʌstʃən] .... ★
n. 燃燒，點火：Combustion within the populace slowly built up to the point of revolution. 群眾的憤怒已到了一觸即會引發革命的程度。

conflagration [͵kɑnfləˋgreʃən] .... ★
n. 大火

explode [ɪkˋsplod] .... ★★★
v. 爆炸：The population level in this area has exploded during the past 12 years. 在過去的十二年中，這一地區的人口一直劇增。

explosion [ɪkˋsploʒən] .... ★★★
n. 爆炸，爆發：After the explosion of the storehouse the storekeeper was dazed. 倉庫爆炸後，倉庫管理員感到昏昏然。

explosive [ɪkˋsplosɪv] .... ★★★
adj. 爆炸的
n. 炸藥：If explosives are used, vibrations will cause the roof of the mine to collapse. 如果用炸藥，震動會使礦井崩塌。

extinct [ɪkˋstɪŋkt] .... ★
adj. 熄滅的，滅絕的：Some of the species of birds are extinct. 有幾種鳥類已經絕種了。

extinction [ɪkˋstɪŋkʃən] .... ★
n. 滅絕：The most effective agent in the extinction of species is the pressure of other species. 在種族滅絕中影響最大的是來自其他種族的壓力。

辨析
Analyze

burst, explode

1 **burst** vt. & vi.「使爆裂，爆炸，爆裂，擠滿，充滿」，作為不及物動詞指因火藥、氣體、蒸汽等內部能量的突然釋放而引起爆炸，還指因裝的東西太多而擠破、擠裂；作為及物動詞指使容器、血管、提包、口袋、堤防等破裂，而不指火藥爆炸：The bag of flour burst as I was carrying it. 這一袋麵粉在我扛的時候破裂了。

2 **explode** vt. & vi.「（使）爆炸，（使）爆發，激增」，主要指因火藥、氣體、蒸汽等內部能量的暫態釋放而引起爆炸：The boiler exploded/burst and many people were injured in the accident. 鍋爐爆炸，致使很多人在事故中受傷。

extinguish [ɪkˈstɪŋgwɪʃ] .... ★★

v. 熄滅，消滅：She was extinguished by her
sister. 她的妹妹使她相形見絀。

fulminate [ˈfʌlməˌnet] .... ★

v. 猛烈爆發：to fulminate against the crime 嚴
厲掃蕩猖獗的犯罪行為

gust [gʌst] .... ★

n. 陣風：A gust of wind blew the leaves along.
一陣狂風把樹葉刮起來。

ignite [ɪgˈnaɪt] .... ★

v. 使燃著：A burning match applied to paper
will make it ignite. 燃著的火柴可以將紙引
燃。

ignition [ɪgˈnɪʃən] .... ★

n. 發火，點火：turn on the ignition 開點火開
關

kindle [ˈkɪndl̩] .... ★★

v. 燃起，激起：Her eyes kindled with
excitement. 她興奮得兩眼閃閃發光。

scorch [skɔrtʃ] .... ★

v. 烤焦，使褪色：I scorched my dress with
the iron. 我用熨斗熨衣服時燙壞了我的衣
服。

sear [sɪr] .... ★

v. 燒灼：His soul has been seared by
injustice. 他的心靈因受屈辱而受了傷。

singe [sɪndʒ] .... ★★★★★

v. 微燒，燙焦：If the iron is too hot you'll
singe that nightdress. 如果熨斗過熱，就會
把睡衣燙焦。

運動、變化類名稱總匯

06

前進、促進、改進相關辭彙

Vocabulary of Advances

accessible [æk`sɛsəbl] .... ★ ★ ★ ★ ★
adj. 能進去的，可以理解的：Bone and ivory are light, strong, and accessible materials for Inuit artists. 骨頭和象牙對因紐特的藝術家來說是質輕、堅固和容易獲得的材料。

advance [əd`væns] .... ★ ★ ★ ★ ★
v. 提出，前進：As the autumn advanced, he became worse. 秋深了，他的情況變得更加糟糕。

advanced [əd`vænst] .... ★ ★ ★ ★ ★
adj. 先進的，高級的，在前面的：advanced mathematics 高等數學

advancement [əd`vænsmənt] .... ★ ★ ★ ★ ★
n. 進步，改進，提高，推進：the advancement of learning 學術的進步

ebb [ɛb] .... ★
v. 退潮，衰退：He's on sixty, so his strength is slowly ebbing away. 〔喻〕他快六十歲了，所以體力在漸漸衰退。

emend [ɪ`mɛnd] .... ★ ★ ★ ★ ★
v. 修訂：emend a faulty text of a book 修訂書中一篇錯誤百出的課文

halt [hɔlt] ....★ ★ ★ ★
v. 停止，躊躇：No one can halt the advance of history. 誰也阻擋不了歷史的前進。

improve [ɪm`pruv] .... ★ ★ ★ ★ ★
v. ①改進，改善：It will improve your pronunciation. 這將會改進你的發音。②改善，變得更好：His health is improving. 他的健康逐步好轉。

improvement [ɪm`pruvmənt] .... ★ ★ ★ ★ ★
n. ①改進，增進：I can not see any improvement in your writing. 我看不出你的寫作進步了。②改進處：None of the improvements has cost much. 這些改善花費都不多。

modulate [`mɑdʒəˌlet] .... ★
v. 調整：Because noises modulate radio frequency, radio stations use a band of frequencies to prevent interference with other stations. 由於噪音會影響廣播頻率，所以廣播站會用一個波段來避開其他廣播站的影響。

357

progress [prəˋgrɛs] .... ★★★★★
v. 前進，發展：work on the new building progressed at a rapid rate 快速地修建新建築

progressive [prəˋgrɛsɪv] .... ★★★
adj. 進步的，前進的，發展的：a progressive politician 進步主義的政客

propel [prəˋpɛl] .... ★
v. 推進，促進：In North America, the first canoes were constructed from logs and propelled by means of wooden paddles. 在北美，第一艘獨木舟是用圓木造成的，並且用木槳來划行。

propulsion [prəˋpʌlʃən] .... ★
n. 推動，驅動，推進（器）

reform [ɹɪˋfɔrm] .... ★★★★
v. 改革，革新：During the 1840's, Dorothea Dix was a leader in the movement for the reform of prison conditions. 在1840年代，狄克斯領導改革監獄環境。

remedial [rɪˋmidɪəl] .... ★★★★
adj. 補救的，糾正的，修補用的：to do remedial exercises for a weak back 為有病的背部作矯正復健

renovate [ˋrɛnəˌvet] .... ★★★★★
v. 革新

revise [rɪˋvaɪz] .... ★★★★
v. 修訂：The revised proposals were debated. 這些經過修訂的提案仍在爭論之中。

revision [rɪˋvɪʒən] .... ★★★★
n. ①修訂，修改，修正②修訂本，修訂版③複習，溫習

revolution [ˌrɛvəˋluʃən] .... ★★★★★
n. 革命，旋轉，轉數

revolutionary [ˌrɛvəˋluʃənˌɛrɪ] .... ★★★
adj. 革命的，大變革的，革新的
n. 革命者

revolutionize [ˌrɛvəˋluʃənˌaɪz] .... ★★★
v. 使革命化，徹底改革：The invention of the computer revolutionized business procedures. 電腦的發明徹底改變了商業的流程。

transition [trænˋzɪʃən] .... ★★
n. 轉變，變遷，過渡：the frequent transition of weather 天氣的變化無常

07

恢復、重複、代替相關辭彙

Vocabulary of Variation

corrective [kəˋrɛktɪv] .... ★★★★
adj. 校正的，補償的：corrective action 改正行動

displace [dɪsˋples] .... ★
v. 取代，轉移：He displaced a bone in his knee in the crash with another player. 他與另一名運動員相撞時，膝部有一塊骨頭移位了。

displacement [dɪsˋplesmənt] .... ★
n. 位移：absolute displacement 絕對位移

indemnity [ɪnˋdɛmnɪti] .... ★
n. 補償：a letter of indemnity 賠償保證書

instead [ɪnˋstɛd] .... ★★★★★
adv. 代替，頂替：Why don't you come and play volleyball instead? 你何不出來打排球呢？
【片語】instead of 代替…，而不是

recover [rɪˋkʌvɚ] .... ★★★★★
v. 恢復：Chemists at Oak Ridge National Laboratory in Tennessee have developed a process for recovering silver from liquid photographic wastes. 在田納西州橡樹山國家實驗室的化學家，發明了一種從洗相水中恢復銀的方法。

recycle [riˋsaɪk̩l] .... ★★★★★
v. （使）再循環，重複利用，回收：The recycling of aluminum conserves ninety-five percent of the energy needed to make new metal. 鋁的回收使用節約了95%的新金屬製造所需的能源。

reiterate [riˋɪtəˌret] .... ★
v. 重述

relapse [rɪˋlæps] .... ★
v. 復發，回復：relapse into coma 再次昏迷；relapse into obscurity 變得默默無聞

repeat [rɪˋpit] .... ★★★★★
v. 重複，重說，重做：He repeated several times that he was busy. 他一再地說他很忙。
n. 重複

repetition [ˌrɛpɪˋtɪʃən] .... ★★★
n. 重複，反復：I want no repetition of your bad behavior. 我不希望你重複惡劣的行為。

replace [rɪ`ples] .... ★★★★★
v. ①替代，取代：Tom bought a new sweater to replace the one he lost. 湯姆買了件新毛衣取代他弄丟的那件。②把…放回原處：She replaced the receiver. 她把聽筒放回原處。

reproducibility [ˌriprə`djusˌbɪlətɪ] .... ★★
n. 再生長（性），再複製（性）

restate [ri`stet] .... ★★★★★
v. 重申

restore [rɪ`stor] .... ★★★★★
v. 恢復：restore law and order 恢復法律和秩序

retrieve [rɪ`triv] .... ★★★★★
v. 重新找回：The large red ants can dig as deep as ten feet to establish nests and retrieve soil for their mounds. 大紅蟻能夠挖深達10英尺的洞建巢穴，並且找回挖出的土蓋蟻丘。

revert [rɪ`vɝt] .... ★★★★★
n. 回復：The money will revert to the bank in six months. 這筆錢將在6個月後返還給銀行。

revive [rɪ`vaɪv] .... ★★
v. 復活：The fresh air soon revived him. 新鮮空氣很快就使他甦醒過來。

substitute [`sʌbstəˌtjut] .... ★★★★
n. 代替人，代替物，代用品
v. 用…代替，代替，代：Two substitutes were used during the football games. 該足球比賽中用了兩名替補隊員。

supersede [ˌsupɚ`sid] .... ★★★★★
v. 替代：The use of machinery has superseded manual labor. 機器的使用已經取代了人力。

supplant [sə`plænt] .... ★
v. 排擠，取代：The word processor has largely supplanted electric typewriters. 文字處理程式已很大程度上取代了打字機。

辨析 Analyze

displace, replace, substitute

1　**displace** *vt.*「取代，代替」，常用句型為A displace B（A代替B）：Television has displaced motion pictures as America's most popular form of entertainment. 電視已經取代了電影，成為美國最普及的娛樂形式。

2　**replace** *vt.*「代替，更換」，指取代、替代、替換，還指「歸還、放回原處」，常用句型 replace B with A（用A代替B）：We can replace steel with plastics in making these parts. 我們製造這些零件時，可以用塑膠來替代鋼材。

3　**substitute** *vt.*「代替，代以」，常用句型為 substitute A for B（用A代替B）：We can substitute plastics for steel in making these parts. 我們製造這些零件時，可以用塑膠來替代鋼材。

運動、變化類名稱總匯

08

繼續、保持、堅持相關辭彙

Vocabulary of Keeping

clinch [klɪntʃ] .... ★

v. 釘牢，揪住：The offer of more money clinched her. She agrees to take the job as the assistant to the managing director. 由於薪酬增加而達成協定，她同意擔任總經理工作助手。

cling [klɪŋ] .... ★★★★★

v. 黏附：Starfish cling to stones by the suction of their innumerable tube feet. 海星藉著其無數管狀腳的吸力吸附到石頭上。

constant [ˈkɑnstənt] ....★★★★

adj. ①不斷的，連續發生的：Matter is in constant motion and constant change. 物質總是不斷運動，不斷變化。②始終如一的：constant temperature 恒溫③忠實的：He is constant to his friends. 他對朋友很忠實。

n. 常數，恒量：the circular constant 圓周率

constantly [ˈkɑnstəntlɪ] ....★★★★

adv. 不變地：Erosion is a general term for the process by which the top layer of soil is constantly being worn away. 侵蝕一般是指一個表層土不斷流失的過程。

continually [kənˈtɪnjʊəlɪ] .... ★★★

adv. 不斷地：The telephone has been ringing continually in the office all morning. 整個早上辦公室的電話鈴聲不斷。

continue [kənˈtɪnjʊ] .... ★★★★★

v. 繼續，延伸：The road continues for miles. 路延伸了好幾英里。

continuous [kənˈtɪnjʊəs] ....★★★★

adj. 連續不斷的，不斷延伸的：a continuous hot weather 持續高溫的天氣

incessant [ɪnˈsɛsn̩t] .... ★

adj. 不斷的：The high-pitched noises were incessant. 尖銳的雜訊不絕於耳。

incoherent [ˌɪnkoˈhɪrənt] .... ★★★★★

adj. 不連貫的：The old man became incoherent as the disease got worse. 老人隨著病情加重，變得語無倫次了。

insist [ɪnˋsɪst] .... ★★★★
v. 主張，堅持說：We all insist that we will not rest until we finish the work. 大家都堅決要求不完工就不休息。

insistent [ɪnˋsɪstənt] .... ★
adj. 堅持的：The dean's very insistent that they should finish the papers in time. 系主任非常堅決地要求他們按時完成論文。

irrepressible [ˌɪrɪˋprɛsḷ] .... ★★★★★
adj. 不可壓制的，難以征服的：irrepressible laughter 抑制不住的笑聲

irresistible [ˌɪrɪˋzɪstəbḷ] .... ★★★★★
adj. 不可抗拒的：irresistible beauty 無法抗拒的美麗

keep [kip] .... ★★★★★
v. ①保存，保守，保留：I will keep the secret. 我將保守秘密。②保持，繼續，遵守，守護：Keep still while I take your picture. 我拍照時你不要動。
【片語】① keep (on) doing sth. 繼續做某事② keep up with 跟上，不落在後面

maintain [menˋten] .... ★★★★★
v. 堅持認為，維持：Central City, Colorado, has maintained its famous opera house partly to remind visitors of the city's opulence in the gold mining days. 科羅拉多州的中心城市保留其著名歌劇院的部分，以讓遊客回味淘金年代曾有的輝煌。

maintenance [ˋmentəənəs] .... ★★★★
n. 保持，維修：cost of maintenance 維修費

persevere [ˌpɝsəˋvɪr] .... ★
v. 堅持，不屈不撓：persevere in one's studies 孜孜不倦地學習

persist [pɚˋsɪst] .... ★★★★
vi. ①堅持不懈，執意：They persisted in finishing the journey in spite of the bad weather. 儘管天氣惡劣，他們仍堅持要走完這段路程。②持續，繼續存在：The tradition has persisted to this day. 這傳統一直延續至今。

persistently [pɚˋsɪstəntlɪ] .... ★
adv. 堅持不懈地，固執地：Brooks Adams failed to find the universal law of commerce that he persistently sought. 布魯克斯·亞當斯雖堅持不懈地探索，還是未能找到商業的普世準則。

pursue [pɚˋsu] .... ★★★
v. 追逐，追擊，追求，從事，進行，繼續：The falcon is a type of hawk that is trained to pursue game in the sport called falconry. 獵鷹是一種被訓練來參加追逐獵物的體育項目「獵鷹訓練術」的鷹類。

辨析
Analyze

continual, continuous

1 **continuous** *a.*「連續不斷的，不斷延伸的」，指時間上和空間上完全的連續，強調無間斷性，無論從整體還是從局部看都是連續的：After eight continuous hours of working, I feel extremely tired. 連續工作八小時後，我感到累極了。

2 **continual** *a.*「不間斷的，不停的，多次重複的，頻頻的」，指有間斷的連續，或者說從整體上看是連續的，從局部上看是有間隔的。有時含有貶意：Continual dropping water wears away a stone. 滴水穿石。

renew [rɪ`nju] .... ★★★★
v. ①（使）更新，恢復：We renew our strength in sleep. 我們在睡眠中恢復體力。②重新開始，繼續：In the morning the enemy renewed their attack. 早上敵人重新開始進攻。

reprogrammable [ˌri`progræməbl̩] .... ★
adj. 可重新編寫程式的

reservation [ˌrɛzə`veʃən] .... ★★★
n. 保留，保留意見，預定，預訂：If you want to go to the concert, you'll have to make a reservation, or there will be no tickets. 如果你想去聽音樂會，你得事先訂票，否則會沒有票的。

resume [rɪ`zjum] .... ★★★★
v. 繼續：After a long lunch hour, business resumes as usual. 漫長的午飯時間過後，工作又重新開始。

retain [rɪ`ten] .... ★★★★
v. 保留，記住：In 1896 George Washington Carver became director of the Department of Agricultural and Industrial Institute, a position he retained for the rest of his life. 喬治‧卡瓦於1896年成為農業部和國防部部長，一個他終生從事的職務。

sequence [`sikwəns] .... ★★★★
n. 序列：A computer will always follow the same sequence when solving a problem, no matter how complicated that problem may be. 電腦不管所處理的問題有多複雜，總是按照相同的次序來處理問題。

succession [sək`sɛʃən] .... ★★★★
n. 連續，順序性，系列，繼任，繼承：a succession of one-man stalls offered soft drinks 不停提供飲料的一人售貨亭

successive [sək`sɛsɪv] .... ★★★
adj. 連續的：the government successive to the fallen monarchy 接替了垮臺的君主制的政府

sustain [sə`sten] .... ★★★★★
v. 支撐，維持：The principal difference between singing and speaking is that in singing vowel sounds are sustained and given a precise pitch. 唱歌和說話的主要區別是在唱歌的時候母音需要持續，並且要有一個準確的音調。

09

過程、開始相關辭彙

Vocabulary of Process

agenda [ə`dʒɛndə] .... ★★★★★

n. 議程：We had so much difficulty agreeing upon an agenda that there was very little time for the meeting. 我們在議程的決定上發生許多紛爭，以致於開會的時間很短暫。

antecedent [͵æntə`sidənt] .... ★★★★

adj. 先行的，先成的，前提的：That was antecedent to this event. 那是在這件事之前。

begin [bɪ`ɡɪn] .... ★★★★★

v. 開始：When did life begin on this earth? 地球上的生命始於什麼時候？

【片語】begin with 用…開頭

beginning [bɪ`ɡɪnɪŋ] .... ★★★★★

n. ①開始，開端：We think of this as a good beginning. 我們認為這是一個良好的開端。②起源，早期階段：Did democracy have its beginnings in Athens? 民主制度是創始於雅典嗎？

commence [kə`mɛns] .... ★★

v. 開始，獲得學位：The students of history will commence in arts when they graduate. 歷史系所的學生畢業時將獲文科學位。

course [kors] .... ★★★★★

n. ①課程，教程：The college offers courses in science. 該學院開設自然科學課程。②過程，進程：the curse of world history 世界歷史的進程③（一）道（菜）：a dinner of six courses 6道菜的晚餐④路程，路線

【片語】① in the course of 在…期間，在…過程中② of course 當然，自然

cradle [`kredl̩] .... ★★

n. 搖籃，發源地：Greece was the cradle of Western culture. 希臘是西方文化的發源地。

derive [dɪ`raɪv] .... ★★★★

v. 導出，從…（得到），衍生，起源，由來：Paper derives its name from the papyrus plant. 紙的名字是由紙紗草這種植物而來。

drive [draɪv] .... ★★★★★

v. ①駕駛：They drove to the company. 他們驅車前往公司。②驅使，趕：drive the mice out of room 把老鼠趕出房間

fold [fold] .... ★★★★
v. 折疊：fold a letter 折信
n. 褶痕：a dress hanging in loose folds 有寬鬆褶皺的連衣裙

fountain [ˈfaʊntɪn] .... ★★★★
n. 泉水，噴泉，噴水池

hew [hju] .... ★
v. 砍伐，開闢：He hewed out an important position for himself in the company. 他在公司中為自己佔據了重要的職位。

inaugurate [ɪnˈɔɡjəˌret] .... ★
v. 開始，使就職：inaugurate a president 舉行總統就職典禮

incipient [ɪnˈsɪpɪənt] .... ★
adj. 初期的：detect incipient tumors 發現早期腫瘤

initial [ɪˈnɪʃəl] .... ★★★★
adj. 初始的：The initial response to the proposal surprised the officials. 對該提議最初的反應使官員們感到吃驚。

initiate [ɪˈnɪʃɪˌet] .... ★★
v. 開始，創始，啓蒙：The term "New Deal" applies to the program of reform and recovery initiated by President Franklin D. Roosevelt. 用於描述革新和恢復的「新政」一詞，是由富蘭克林‧羅斯福總統創造的。

initiative [ɪˈnɪʃətɪv] .... ★★★★
adj. 創始的，起始的
n. 第一步，創始，主動精神，首創：He helped me on his own initiative. 他主動幫助我。

launch [lɔntʃ] .... ★★★★
v. 發射，投射，發動，使升空：The year 1962 saw the launching of a major satellite. 1962 年曾經發射了一顆大型人造衛星。

original [əˈrɪdʒənl] .... ★★★★★
adj. 最初的，獨創的：Later models of the car retained many features of the original. 新近的汽車樣式保持了許多從前產品的特徵。

originally [əˈrɪdʒənlɪ] .... ★★★★★
adv. 本來，最初：I live here now, but I wonder who lived here originally? 我現在住在這，但是我想知道最初是誰住在這兒的？

originate [əˈrɪdʒəˌnet] .... ★★
v. 發起：The quarrel originated in a misunderstanding. 爭吵是由於誤解而引起的。

pioneer [ˌpaɪəˈnɪr] .... ★★★
n. 先驅，開拓者：He was the pioneer of the revolution. 他是革命的先驅者。

precede [priˈsid] .... ★★
v. 先於，領先：Because light travels more quickly than sound, a rumble of thunder never precedes a bolt of lightning. 由於光比聲音傳播的速度快，所以對人們來說，隆隆的雷聲永遠不會比閃電先到。

primarily [praɪˈmɛrəlɪ] .... ★★★★
adv. 首先，首要地，只要地：Natural adhesives are primarily of animal or vegetable origin. 天然黏合劑主要來自於動物或植物。

primary [ˈpraɪˌmɛrɪ] .... ★★★★
adj. 最初的，重要的：The Social Insurance Number (SIN) card is the primary mode of identification for Canadians. 社會保險號碼卡是加拿大人的主要身份識別工具。

primitive [ˈprɪmətɪv] .... ★★★★
adj. 原始的，最初的：Primitive man made tools from sharp stones and animal bones. 原始人用尖石塊和動物的骨製造工具。

procedure [prəˈsidʒɚ] .... ★★★★★
n. 過程，程式，手續：The new work procedure is a great improvement on/over the old one. 新的工作流程比起過去是大幅地改善。

proceed [prəˈsid] .... ★★★★★
v. 進行：He proceeded to his destination. 他繼續向終點前進。

resource [rɪˋsors] .... ★★★★★
n. ①資源，財力：Oil is Kuwait's most important natural resources. 石油是科威特最重要的自然資源。②謀略，應付辦法：Robinson Crusoe was a man of great resource. 魯賓遜是一個足智多謀的人。

preceding [prɪˋsidɪŋ] .... ★★★★
adj. 在前的，在先的，前面的：In the preceding chapter, we talked about the importance of attracting foreign capital. 在上一章中，我們談了吸引外資的重要性。

proceeding [prɪˋsidɪŋ] .... ★★★★
n. 進行，進程，程序

process [ˋprɑsɛs] .... ★★★★★
n. 過程
v. 處理：The firm is now in the process of moving the main equipment to a new place. 公司目前正在把主要設備遷到新地址去。

processor [ˋprɑsɛsɚ] .... ★★★★★
n. 加工者，處理程序，資訊處理機

source [sors] .... ★★★★★
n. 源，源泉，根源：Bad food is a source of illness. 壞了的食物是疾病之源。

original [əˋrɪdʒ[]l] .... ★★★★★
〔記〕{origin（起源）+ al（有關的）}
adj. ①起初的，原來的：the original plan 原計畫 ②獨創的，新穎的：original ideas 新穎的意見 ③原版的，原件：an original edition 原版
n. 原件，原作：to read Mark Twain's works in the original 閱讀馬克‧吐溫的原著

sponsor [ˋspɑnsɚ] .... ★★★★★
n. 發起人，主辦者，保證人，資助人
v. 發起，主辦：The exhibition was sponsored by the Society of Culture. 這個展覽會是由文化學會主辦的。

spontaneous [spɑnˋtenɪəs] .... ★
adj. 自發，本能的：The eruption of a volcano is spontaneous. 火山爆發是自發的。

start [stɑrt] .... ★★★★★
v. 開始，著手：We start lessons at 8 a.m. 我們上午八點開始上課。
【片語】start doing / to do sth. 開始做某事

undergo [ˏʌndɚˋgo] .... ★★★★
v. 經歷，遭受：Through exposure to air, water and organic matter, rocks undergo changes known as weathering. 岩石由於暴露在空氣、水和有機物質中，會受到「風化」的改變。

precede, proceed

1 **precede** *vt.* 「走在…之前，先於」，指存在或發生在某人或某事之前、先於（指時間，靜態），還指走在…之前（指空間，動態）；與 proceed 相比，precede 強調（順序上）「在…之前」：The Greek civilization preceded the Roman one. 希臘文明先於羅馬文明。

2 **proceed** *vi.* 「進行，繼續下去，（沿特定路線）行進，（朝特定方向）前進」，與precede相比，proceed 強調（方向上）「向前」：The train proceeded at the same speed as before. 火車以先前同樣的速度行駛。

origin, resource, source

1 **origin** *n.* 「起源，來源，起因，出身，血統」，指根源、來源、起源，強調歷史的久遠，也指事故等的起因，還指種族出身（此意多用複數）：the origin of the word/civilization/human species 詞源／文明起源／人類起源；The family is Irish by origin. 這一家是愛爾蘭血統。

2 **resource** *n.* 指「資源，財力」，常用複數：natural/oil/water resources 自然資源／石油資源／水資源；We must make the best possible use of our financial resources. 我們必須盡最大可能來善用我們的財力。

3 **source** *n.* 「源（泉），發源地，來源，出處」，指事物或事情的根源、來源、起源、原因，強調持續的存在：Where is the source of River Thames? 泰晤士河發源自何處？

10

完成、結束、停滯、目標相關辭彙

Vocabulary of Ends & Results

accomplished [əˋkɑmplɪʃt] .... ★★★★★
adj. 完成的，熟練的：accept something as an
accomplished fact 把某事當成既成事實予以
接受；be accomplished in/at the left-handed
manipulation of the dinner fork 熟練地用左手使用
餐叉

accomplishment [əˋkɑmplɪʃmənt] .... ★★★★★
n. 完成，達到，實行：She is known for her
accomplishment in improving the country's
hospitals. 她在改進國內醫院方面卓有成績而著名。

achieve [əˋtʃiv] .... ★★★★★
v. 完成，實現，達到：The only movement he could
achieve was a trivial flutter of the left eyelid. 他所能
做出的惟一動作就是左眼瞼微微一顫。

attain [əˋten] ....★★★★
v. 獲得，達到：The tree has attained to a great height.
樹已經長得很高了。

attainment [əˋtenmənt] ....★★★★
n. 成就：notions difficult of attainment 難以實現的設想

close [kloz] .... ★★★★★
adv. 緊密地
adj. 親密的：English has a close affinity to German. 英
語和德語很相近。

complete [kəmˋplit] .... ★★★★★
adj. 完成的：He was in complete accord with the
verdict. 他完全同意此次裁決。
v. 完成：When will the work on the highway be
completed? 公路什麼時候能完工？

consequence [ˋkɑnsəˏkwɛns] .... ★★★★★
n. 後果，影響，結果，重要性：In the system of ethics
known as utilitarianism, the rightness or wrongs of
an action is judged by its consequences. 在功利主
義的道德規範中，一個行為的正確與否是由其產生的
結果來判斷的。

consequently [ˋkɑnsəˏkwɛntlɪ] .... ★★★★
adv. 因而，所以，從而：Mr. Foster has never been to
U.K. Consequently he knows very little about U.K.
福斯特先生從未去過英國，所以對英國瞭解得很
少。

culminate [ˈkʌlmə‿net] .... ★★★★★
vi. (以⋯) 告終：The argument culminated in hand fight. 爭論以大打出手而告終。

culmination [ˌkʌlmə‿neʃən] .... ★
n. 頂點

degenerate .... ★
adj. [dɪˈdʒɛnə‿rɪt] 墮落的
v. [dɪˈdʒɛnə‿ret] 退步：old water pipes that are degenerating with age 年久失修而逐漸失去功用的水管；a dispute that degenerated into a brawl 演變為爭吵的辯論

destination [ˌdɛstə‿neʃən] .... ★★★
n. 目的地：It took us all day to reach our destination. 我們花了一整天才到達目的地。

enclosure [ɪnˈkloʒɚ] .... ★
n. 圍繞，圍欄，圍場，附件：There's a special enclosure where you can look at the horses before the race starts. 這裡有一處特殊的圍場，在比賽前你可以先看看馬。

end [ɛnd] .... ★★★★★
n. ①端，稍：One end of the stick is black, the other is red. 那棍子一端是黑的，一端是紅的。②結尾，結束：At the end of last term, Claire won the prize for study. 上學期末，柯蕾爾獲得了獎學金。
【片語】in the end 最後

ending [ˈɛndɪŋ] .... ★★★★
n. 結局，結尾，終結：Children like stories with happy endings. 小孩子喜歡結局圓滿的故事。

endless [ˈɛndlɪs] .... ★★★
adj. 無止境的：The aircraft was able to fly over the endless white plains without difficulty. 飛機能夠毫無困難地飛越這一望無際的茫茫雪原。

eventual [ɪˈvɛntʃʊəl] .... ★★★★
adj. 最後的：the eventual success of his efforts 他努力的最後成果

辨析 Analyze

accomplish, attain, complete, finish, fulfill

1. **accomplish** *vt.* 「完成」，強調成功地完成或做了某事，後接名詞作賓語：I tried and tried again but accomplished nothing. 我試了又試，但是一無所獲。

2. **attain** *vt.* 「達到，獲得」，在指達到目標和取得成績時與fulfill或accomplish是同義詞：I hope you will attain your object/end/objectives/ambition. 我希望你達到你的目標／實現你的抱負。

3. **complete** *vt. & vi.* 「完成，結束，使完整，使完全」，較正式用語，指完成了指定的任務，尤其指完成工程項目：The building will be completed in two years. 該大樓兩年後完工。

4. **finish** *vt.* 「完成」，非正式用語，後跟名詞或動名詞：I haven't finished my homework yet. 我作業還未做完。

5. **fulfill** *vt.* 「完成，履行，實現，滿足（條件等）」，用法較廣，後接名詞作賓語：I'll fulfill my task/obligation/duty to the best of my ability. 我將盡我最大努力完成我的任務／職責。

Exercise & Change

expire [ɪk`spaɪr] .... ★★

v. 失效，斷氣：My membership in the club has expired. 我的俱樂部會員資格已過期了。The patient expired early this morning. 那個患者是凌晨斷氣的。

final [`faɪnl] .... ★★★★★

adj. 最後的：The final thing she did before she left the house was to lock the door. 她離開房子前做的最後一件事是鎖門。

finally [`faɪnlɪ] .... ★★★★★

adv. 最後，不可更改地：After several delays, the plane finally left at six o'clock. 飛機幾經耽擱，終於在六點起飛。

finish [`fɪnɪʃ] .... ★★★★★

v. 結束，完成：Have you finished reading the book? 這本書你看完了嗎？

fulfill [fʊl`fɪl] .... ★★★★★

v. 完成，履行：She fulfilled herself both as a qualified mother and as a successful painter. 她充分發揮了自己的才能，既是一個稱職的母親又是一個成功的畫家。

fulfilling [fʊl`fɪlɪŋ] .... ★★★★★

adj. 能充分發揮自己才能的

fulfillment [fʊl`fɪlmənt] .... ★★★★★

n. 實現，完成，結束：a sense of fulfillment 滿足感

goal [gol] .... ★★★★★

n. 終點，球門，目標，目的：Since rhetoric is the art of calculated polemic and has persuasion as its goal, can't it be considered a verbal science? 既然修辭學是精心計畫的爭論藝術，以說服人為目的，那麼可以稱其為言語的科學嗎？

influx [`ɪnflʌks] .... ★

n. 流入，灌輸：There was a sudden influx of household electric products into the market. 大批家用電氣產品突然湧進市場。

last [læst] .... ★★★★★

adj. ①最後的，惟一剩下的：Why doesn't he use the lift for the last three floors? 他為什麼不搭電梯上最後三層樓呢？②上一個的，去（年），昨天的：They've lived here for the last two years. 他們最近兩年一直住在這裡。

【片語】at last 最後，終於

adv. 最後，最後一次：When he stole last he was caught at once. 當他最後一次偷竊時，立即被抓了起來。

辨析
Analyze

eventually, finally, last, lastly

1 **eventually** adv. 「最終，終於」，指經過長時間的耽誤或困難之後：He worked so hard that eventually he made himself ill. 他拼命工作，最終病倒了。

2 **finally** adv. 「最後」，指長時間之後最終（相當於in the end），也指作為一系列步驟中的最後一步：I tried hard and finally I managed it. 我盡力去做，最後獲得了成功。

3 **last** adv. 「最後」，強調先後順序，與別人或別的東西比起來是最後，也可跟finally一樣指一系列中步驟中的最後一步：Our horse came last in the race. 我們的馬是賽馬的最後一名。

4 **lastly** adv. 「最後」，一般指列舉事物時的最後項目：There are three reasons：first(ly)…，second(ly)…，and lastly… 共有三個原因，第一…，第二…，第三…。

v. 持續：In Australia, autumn lasts from February to April. 在澳洲，秋季從二月延續到四月。

lasting [ˈlæstɪŋ] .... ★★★★★
adj. 持久：The works of Walt Whitman had a lasting effect on the development of modern American poetry. 華特‧惠特曼的作品在美國現代詩歌的發展上具有持久的影響力。

motif [moˈtif] ....★
n. 主題，主旨：In her compositions for musical theater, Agnes De Mille uses many specifically American motifs. 艾格妮斯‧德米勒在為音樂廳設計的時候，運用了許多美國化的主題。

motivation [ˌmotəˈveʃən] .... ★★★
n. 動機：Motivation is a primary factor in learning. 動機是學習的一個主要因素。

motive [ˈmotɪv] .... ★★★★
n. 動機，目的
adj. 發動的，運動的：We should know what the author's motives are. 我們應該知道作者的意圖。

object [ˈɑbdʒɪkt] .... ★★★★★
n. ①物體，實物：Tell me the name of the objects in this laboratory. 告訴我這實驗室裡物體的名稱。②目的，目標：study with the object of obtaining more knowledge 為獲得更多知識而學習。③對象：an object of respect 受尊敬的對象④賓語
v. 反對，異議：All the farmers of that village object to the new airport. 村裡所有農民都反對修建新機場。

objection [əbˈdʒɪkʃən] .... ★★★★
n. 反對，異議：He has a strong objection to getting up early. 他強烈反對早起。

辨析 Analyze

aim, goal, object, objective, purpose, target

1 **aim** *n.* 「目的，目標，意圖，瞄準，對準」，指具體而有明確的目標，或較小而近期的目的：I went to Taipei with the aim to see my girlfriend. 我去臺北是要看看我的女朋友。

2 **goal** *n.* 「目的，目標，球門，進球得分」，指需要經過努力奮鬥才能達到的目的或目標：His goal in life is to become a great musician. 他人生的目標是當一名偉大的音樂家。

3 **object** *n.* 「目標，目的，對象，物體」，指個人決定的目標和願望，尤指情感、思想或行動的物件：The object of our search now is a murderer. 我們現在的搜查目標是一名殺人犯。

4 **objective** *n.* 「目標，目的」，指這一詞義時與 object 是同義詞：Her object/objective is to get a college education. 她的目標是接受大學教育。

5 **purpose** *n.* 「目的，意圖，用途，效果」，指希望達到的某種具體目的或意圖，既是行為的出發點又是行動的歸宿：These boys came here with the sole purpose of making trouble. 這些男孩來這兒的意圖只是為了搗亂。

6 **target** *n.* 「目標，物件，靶子」，指某種具體活動要達到的指標或軍事目標：We do not have a target for attack. 我們沒有攻擊目標。

objective [əbˋdʒɛktɪv] .... ★★★★

n. 目標

adj. 客觀的：to take an objective view of a situation 對形勢持客觀的看法

outcome [ˋaʊtͺkʌm] .... ★★★

n. 後果，成果：The outcome of their discussion is still unknown. 他們討論的結果仍然不清楚。

pause [pɔz] .... ★★★★★

v. 暫停，中止：He paused to sweep sweat with a handkerchief. 他停下來用手帕擦汗。

n. 暫停，中止：a pause in the competition 比賽暫停

perform [pɚˋfɔrm] .... ★★★★★

v. ①做，履行：perform a contract 履行合約 ②演出，表演：He will be performing at the piano. 他將演奏鋼琴。

performance [pɚˋfɔrməns] .... ★★★★★

n. 性能，表演，操作，行為，執行，完成：The performances are on the 5th and 6th of this month. 演出是在這個月的5號和6號。

performer [pɚˋfɔrmɚ] .... ★★★★★

n. ①表演者，演奏者②履／執行者

result [rɪˋzʌlt] .... ★★★★★

n. ①成績，效果：Lucy got good results because of her hard work. 露西努力用功，因而獲得了好成績。②結果：His illness is the result of bad food. 他的病因在於吃了壞了的食物。

【片語】as a result of 由於，因為

shut [ʃʌt] .... ★★★★★

v. 關閉：Shut the door, please. 請把門關上。

shutter [ˋʃʌtɚ] ....★

n. 快門，（攝影機和放映機上的）遮光器，百葉窗：The shop front is fitted with rolling shutters. 那店面裝上了捲門。

stop [stɑp] .... ★★★★★

v. 停止，阻止，阻撓，中止：Nothing will stop us from going there. 什麼也不會阻止我去那裡。

【片語】① stop sb. from doing sth. 阻止某人做某事② stop doing sth. 停止做某事③ stop to do 停下來做某事

辨析
Analyze

cease, halt, pause, stop

1 **cease** *vt. & vi.* 「終止，停止」，主要指停止一種狀態或終止一種行為，這種動作或狀態短時間內再次出現的可能性較小，甚至永遠不復存在；多用於書面語；其句型為 cease to do / doing sth.：The animal has ceased to exist. 這種動物已經不存在了。

2 **halt** *vt. & vi* 「（使）停住，（使）停止」，強調行動完全停止，但一般不指狀態的終止：The tired soldiers halted for a short rest. 疲憊的士兵們停下休息一會兒。

3 **pause** *vi.* 「暫停」，多用於指說話或走路等停頓一下、暫停一下，還指答錄機等的暫停鍵：The president paused until it was interpreted. 總統停了一下，等說過的話被翻譯完。

4 **stop** *vt. & vi.* 「停止，中斷，塞住，堵塞，阻止」，主要指停止正在進行的動作或行為，這種動作隨時可能再啟動；一般不指狀態的終止，其後跟不定式或動名詞時意義不同：When she saw me, she stopped to talk with me. 她見到我便停下來跟我說話。

n. ①停車站：Where is the nearest bus stop? 最近的公車站在哪兒？②停止，中止：After two or three stops, we arrived in Toronto. 過了兩、三站後，我們到達了多倫多。

suspend [sə`spɛnd] .... ★★★★
v. 懸吊：We saw smoke suspended in the still air. 我們看見煙懸浮在靜止的空氣中。

suspender [sə`spɛndə] .... ★★★★
n. 吊襪帶

target [`tɑrgɪt] .... ★★★★
n. 靶子，目標：The hunter's target was a wild animal. 這個獵人的目標是一隻野獸。

terminate [`tɝmə͵net] .... ★★
v. 終止：Glaciers terminate where the rate of ice loss is equivalent to the forward advance of the glacier. 冰河在融冰和冰河前進速度相等的地方終止。

ultimate [`ʌltəmɪt] .... ★★★★
adj. ①極端的，最大的，最高的：the ultimate ends of the world 天涯海角 ②最後的，最終的：the ultimate result of one's actions 行為的最後結果
n. 終極，頂點，極限

ultimately [`ʌltəmɪtlɪ] .... ★★★★
adv. 最後，終於：Ultimately people rely on science to gain an understanding of biological phenomena. 人們最終依靠科學來理解生物現象。

辨析 Analyze

final, last, ultimate

1 **final** *a.*「最後的，最終的」。多用以指空間順序，還指具有決定性的。
The final answer to this mysterious question is still to be found. 對這個神秘問題的最終答案還有待於探索。

2 **last** *a.*「剛過去的，最後的，最終的，結論性的」，既可指空間順序，也可指時間順序，。從選擇或可能性的角度看，還指「最不可能的，最不合適的」。Their last visit to us was in December. 他們上次來拜訪我們是在十二月。

3 **ultimate** *a.*「最後的，最終的」，正式用語，具有文學意味，可用於修飾抽象的事物，還指「最大的，最根本的」。The explorers discovered the ultimate source of the Nile. 探測人員找到了尼羅河的最終源頭。

11

延期、到達、離開相關辭彙

Vocabulary of Arrival & Departure

Exercise & Change 運動、變化類名稱總匯

abandon [ə`bændən] ....★★★★

v. 拋棄，放棄：Sophonishba P. Breckinridge, the first woman admitted to the bar in Kentucky, eventually abandoned her legal career and became a social worker. 第一位被肯塔基州法律界承認的女性 Sophonishba P. Breckinridge，最終放棄了她的律師職業而成為了一名社會工作者。

adjourn [ə`dʒɝn] .... ★

v. 延期，休會：The meeting was adjourned until April 14. 會議延至4月14日舉行。

arrival [ə`raɪvl] ....★★★★

n. ①到達，到來：On arrival at the hotel please call me. 到旅館後，請打電話給我。②到達者，到達物：Late arrival must wait in the corridor for a while. 遲到者必須在走廊裡稍等片刻。

arrive [ə`raɪv] .... ★★★★★

v. 到達，來到 ：She arrived by train. 她乘火車到達了。

【片語】arrive at（小地方）/ in （大地方）

away [ə`we] .... ★★★★★

adv. 離開，遠離：Put them away, please. 請把它們收拾好。

【片語】① be away from 遠離② go/run away 走／跑開

defer [dɪ`fɝ] .... ★

v. 延期：We can't defer the action until Mrs. Thomas returns. 我們不能把活動延到湯瑪斯夫人回來以後。

delay [dɪ`le] .... ★★★★★

v. 延遲，耽擱，延誤：The letter was delayed for three days by the train accident. 這次火車事故使這封信耽擱了三天。

depart [dɪ`part] .... ★★★★★

v. 離開，出發：When does the next plane depart? 下一班飛機什麼時候起飛？

departure [dɪ`partʃɚ] ....★★★★

n. 離開，出發：The departure of the plane was delayed. 飛機起飛的時間延後了。

digressive [daɪ`grɛsɪv] ....★★

adj. 離題的，枝節的：a digressive orator 離題的演說家

lag [læg] .... ★★★

n. 落後：He wondered darkly at how great a lag there was between his thinking and his actions. 他暗自驚訝自己在思想和行動上有如此大的差距。

leave [liv] .... ★★★★★

v. ①離開，出發：What time will you leave home to go to the station? 你什麼時候離家去火車站？②留下，剩下，忘記：All has gone, and nothing was left in the world. 一切都過去了，什麼也沒有留下。

linger [ˈlɪŋɚ] .... ★★

v. 逗留，徘徊，拖延：We lingered away the whole summer at the beach. 我們在海灘上消磨掉整個夏天。

postpone [postˈpon] .... ★★★

v. 延遲，延緩：We postponed the match from March 5th to March 19th. 我們把比賽從3月5日延到3月19日舉行。

prolonged [prəˈlɔŋd] .... ★★

adj. 拖長的，長時期的：Pianist Duke Ellington was the first musician to compose prolonged jazz works. 鋼琴家艾靈頓公爵是第一位譜長篇爵士樂的音樂家。

protract [proˈtrækt] .... ★

v. 延長：disputants who needlessly protracted the negotiations 那些不需要延長談判時間的爭論者

reach [ritʃ] .... ★★★★★

v. ①抵達，達到：It took five days for the letter to reach me. 過了5天，我才收到信。②伸出，搆到：I can't reach ceiling. 我摸不到天花板。③達到，延伸：The merchant reaches for a packet of tea. 那商人伸手拿了一包茶葉。

n. 能達到的範圍

retard [rɪˈtɑrd] .... ★

v. 延遲：Cold retards the growth of plants. 寒冷的氣候延緩了農作物的生長。

wait [wet] .... ★★★★★

v. 等，等待，等候：I waited for her to put on her school clothes. 我等她穿上校服。

【片語】wait for 等候

waiter [ˈwetɚ] .... ★★★

n. ①等候者②男侍者，男服務員

waitress [ˈwetrɪs] .... ★★★

n. （餐廳的）女侍者，女服務員

辨析 Analyze

delay, detain, postpone

1 **delay** *vt. & vi.* 「耽擱，延遲」，指耽擱、延遲，主、客觀原因皆可，及物、不及物動詞皆可：The dense fog delayed the plane's landing for two hours. 濃霧使飛機延遲了兩個小時才降落。

2 **detain** *vt.* 「拘留，扣留」，指耽擱（某人），只用人做賓語，也可指「拘留」：Allow me to detain you for a moment. 請允許我延誤您一點時間。

3 **postpone** *vt.* 「延遲，延期」，指主動延期、延遲，只用物做賓語：We have postponed the party for two days—until Sunday. 我們把晚會延了兩天，到星期天舉行。

12

增加、減少、取消相關辭彙

運動、變化類名稱總匯

Exercise & Change

Vocabulary of Increase & Decrease

abate [ə`bet] .... ★
v. 減少：The ship sailed when the storm abated. 當風暴減弱時，船啓航了。

abolish [ə`bɑlɪʃ] .... ★★
v. 廢棄，取消：They voted to abolish slavery. 他們投票廢除奴隸制。

abridge [ə`brɪdʒ] .... ★
v. 縮短，刪節：The airplane abridges distance. 飛機縮短了距離。

alleviate [ə`livɪˌet] .... ★
v. 使減輕：This should alleviate the pain; if it does not, we shall have to use stronger drugs. 這藥應能使痛苦減輕，如果無效的話，我們就要用更強的藥了。

annul [ə`nʌl] .... ★★★★★
v. 廢除，取消：The parents of the eloped couple tried to annul the marriage. 這對私奔情侶的父母試圖取消這門婚事。

cancel [`kænsl̩] .... ★★★
v. 取消，抵消：Today's decline in stock price canceled out yesterday's gain. 今天股票價格下跌，抵消了昨天的收益。

cancellation [ˌkænsl̩`eʃən] .... ★★★
n. 抵消，取消

constrict [kən`strɪkt] .... ★★★★★
v. 收緊，壓縮：Cold air causes the arteries around the heart to constrict. 冷空氣使心臟周圍的動脈收縮。

curt [kɝt] .... ★
adj. 簡短的，草率的：a curt answer 草率的回答

curtail [kɝ`tel] .... ★
v. 縮減：to curtail public spending 縮減公共支出

detract [dɪ`trækt] .... ★★★★★
v. 去掉，減損：This is a decorating scheme that detracts but does not enhance. 這是一個不但沒增色反而更糟的裝修計畫。

disuse [dɪs`juz] .... ★★★★★
v. 廢棄：disuse the original complex form 不用複雜形式

dwindle [ˋdwɪndl̩] .... ★★★★★
v. 減少：The Appalachians stretch south from the St. Lawrence valley, dwindling away in Alabama. 阿帕拉契人的居住地從聖勞倫斯峽谷向南延伸，逐漸從阿拉巴馬州消滅。

enhance [ɪnˋhæns] .... ★★★★★
v. 增加：With the aid of new technology and innovative procedures, meteorologists have enhanced their understanding of atmospheric conditions and weather systems. 氣象學家在新技術和創新程式的輔助下，提高了對大氣情況和天氣系統的理解能力。

excess [ɪkˋsɛs] .... ★★★★
n. 過度
adj. 過度的：to try to avoid engaging in emotional excesses such as hysteria and fits of temper 儘量避免陷於像歇斯底里這樣的感情衝動

excessive [ɪkˋsɛsɪv] .... ★★★
adj. 過多的，極度的：Exposure to excessive amounts of noise can cause hearing loss. 暴露在極度的噪音中會導致聽覺減退。

extra [ˋɛkstrə] .... ★★★★
adj. 額外的，外加的：without extra charge 沒有額外費用
adv. 特別地：extra large shirt 特大號襯衫

n. （常用複數）額外的事物，另外的費用：Her regular school fees are $43 a term, music and dancing are extra. 她的固定學費是每學期43美元，音樂和舞蹈另行收費。

heighten [ˋhaɪtn̩] ....★
v. 提高，加高：heighten an effect 增強效果

increase .... ★★★★★
n. [ˋɪnkris] 增加，增長，增強：There was a steady increase in production. 生產穩定成長。
v. [ɪnˋkris] 增加，增長，增強：The government has increased taxation. 政府已經增加了稅收。

irrevocable [ɪˋrɛvəkəbl̩] ....★
adj. 不能取消的：In the days leading up to the American Revolution, both the colonies and the British Crown were reluctant to take the final irrevocable step. 在最終導致美國革命的日子裡，各個殖民地和英國王室都不願意採取最後無可逆轉的措施。

maximize [ˋmæksəˏmaɪz] .... ★★★
v. 使增加／擴大到最大限度：the ideal of maximizing opportunity through the equalizing of educational opportunity 通過均等受教育的機會來最大幅度擴大機會的理想

maximum [ˋmæksəməm] .... ★★★
n. 最大量，最高值
adj. 最大的，最高的：What's the maximum distance you've swum? 你游過的最遠距離是多少？

辨析
Analyze

abolish, cancel

1　**abolish** *vt.*「徹底廢除，廢止」，相當於 do away with，指廢除長期存在的制度、法律或習慣：It was Abraham Lincoln who abolished the American slavery. 是林肯廢除了美國的奴隸制度。

2　**cancel** *vt.*「取消，廢除，抵消，刪去，劃掉」，相當於call off，指取消事先安排好的事情：Tom cancelled his trip to India due to the accident. 湯姆由於這場事故，取消了他的印度之行。

mitigate [ˋmɪtəˌget] .... ★

v. 緩和，減輕：The judge said that nothing could mitigate the cruelty with which the stepmother had treated the girl. 法官說沒有任何理由可以把那個殘忍虐待女孩的繼母減輕罪責。

multiple [ˋmʌltəpḷ] .... ★★

adj. 多樣的，多重的：a man of multiple interests 興趣廣泛的人。

multiplication [ˌmʌltəpləˋkeʃən] .... ★

n. 乘法：multiplication table 九九乘法表

multiply [ˋmʌltəplaɪ] .... ★★★

v. 使相乘，乘，增加，繁殖：When animals have more food, they generally multiply faster. 動物如果吃得多，通常繁殖也快。

pressurize [ˋprɛʃəˌraɪz] .... ★★★★

v. 使密封，對…加壓，使增壓：The government have pressurized the farmers into producing more milk. 政府對農民施加壓力，使他們增加牛奶的產量。

promote [prəˋmot] .... ★★★★★

v. 促進，升職：The young army officer was promoted (to the rank of) captain. 那個年輕的陸軍軍官已被提拔為上尉。

prompt [prɑmpt] .... ★★★★

v. 促使，激起：Harvest time prompts celebrators into a dancer of thanks for the gifts of the earth. 收穫季節的到來使歡慶的人們跳起感謝大地恩賜的舞蹈。

adj. 敏捷的，迅速的：She was prompt to dismiss any suspicious I might have had. 她很快就打消了我心存的疑慮。

reduce [rɪˋdjus] .... ★★★★★

v. 減少，簡化：The cylindrical shape of a cactus reduces moisture loss. 圓柱狀的仙人掌減少了水分的散失。

reduction [rɪˋdʌkʃən] .... ★★★★

n. 減少，縮小，縮減：a reduction of 12 percent in violent crime 暴力犯罪率下降十二個百分點

refuel [riˋfjuəl] .... ★★★★★

v. 加燃料：The plane refueled at Singapore and flew on. 那架飛機在新加坡加油後繼續飛行。

辨析
Analyze

excess, excessive, extra, surplus

1 **excess** *a.*「過多的，過分的」，指多餘而又不想要或超過規定的，一般只用作定語，偏向貶義：The excess furniture was stored in the basement. 多餘的傢俱存放在地下室。

2 **excessive** *a.*「過多的，過分的，過度的」，指多餘到過分或有害程度的，貶義詞：John's wife left him because of his excessive drinking. 約翰因為酗酒，妻子離開了他。

3 **extra** *a.*「額外的，外加的，多餘的」，指工作或生活上需要另加的、額外的，中性詞，偏向褒義：The store hired extra clerks for Christmas. 這家商店招聘額外的員工應付聖誕節。

4 **surplus** *a.*「過剩的，多餘的」，指需要上多餘的，尤指供給關係上剩餘的：They sold surplus goods at low prices. 他們把剩餘的貨物以低價售出。

replenish [rɪ'plɛnɪʃ] ....★
v. 補充：The music will replenish my weary
soul. 音樂使我疲憊的精神充滿活力。

scissors ['sɪzəz] ....★★★
n. （一把）剪刀：a pair of scissors 一把剪刀

shorten ['ʃɔrtn] ....★
v. 縮短，減少：to shorten a dress 把衣服改短

subtract [səb'trækt] ....★★★
v. 減去

subtractive [səb'træktɪv] ....★★★
adj. 減少性的

taper ['tepɚ] ....★
v. 逐漸變細，逐漸減少：The storm finally
tapered off. 風暴漸漸平息下去。

supplement ['sʌpləmənt] ....★★★★★
n. ①增補（物），補充（物）：She has been ill
and must have supplements to her ordinary
food. 她生病了，必須在平常飲食外吃點營
養品。②增刊：The newspaper publishes a
special travel supplement once a month. 報
紙每月發行一份旅遊特刊。

v. 增補，補充：He supplemented his earnings
by taking a night job. 他為了增加收入，找了
份夜間工作。

wane [wen] ....★
v. 衰減：From now until December 21, the
winter equinox, the hours of daylight will
wane. 從現在開始到12月21日的冬至為止，
白晝的時間將逐漸減少。

辨析
Analyze

immediate, instant, prompt

immediate、**instant**、**prompt** 都表示「立即的，立刻的」，指間隔時間很短：
a(n) immediate/instant/prompt answer（立即答覆）；此外它們各有其特有的詞義：

1 **immediate** *a.*「直接的，當前的」，指
時間或空間上沒有距離或間隔，可用於引
申用法：His immediate neighbors felt it
their duty to call the police. 他的鄰居感到
有責任打電話報警。

2 **instant** *a.*「瞬間的」，指一刻也不耽
擱，比immediate或 prompt更快；還指
「（食品）即溶的，方便的」：instant

coffee/noodle 即溶咖啡／泡麵；The
accident caused their instant deaths. 事
故使他們當即喪命。

3 **prompt** *a.*「迅速的，敏捷的」，指動
作的過程很快：This worker is always
prompt in his duties. 這個工人總是迅速完
成任務。

13

轉移、搖擺、流動相關辭彙

Vocabulary of Moves

agitate [ˈædʒəˌtet] .... ★★
v. 煽動：His fiery remarks agitated the already angry mob. 他激烈的言論煽動了本已憤怒的群眾。

bleed [blid] .... ★★★
v. 流血：The cut on my arm bleed for a long time. 我手臂上的傷口流了好長時間的血。

budge [bʌdʒ] .... ★★★★★
v. 移動：I can't budge this rock. 我搬不動這塊岩石。

carry [ˈkærɪ] .... ★★★★★
v. ①運送，搬運：I can't carry it. Help me, Dad. 我搬不動它，爸爸，幫我。②攜帶：He always carries a small box in his hand. 他手中總是拿著一個小盒子。
【片語】① carry on doing sth. 繼續做某事② carry out 實施，實行③ carry through 完成

carryall [ˈkærɪˌɔl] .... ★★★★★
n. 一種載客汽車，軍用大轎車：Carryall is a closed automobile with two lengthwise seats facing each other. 客車是一種有兩排縱長的相對座位的封閉式汽車.

cease [sis] .... ★★★★★
n. 停止，終止：without cease 不停止
v. 停止，終止：The old man ceased breathing. 老人停止呼吸。

ceaseless [ˈsislɪs] .... ★★★★★
adj. 不停的：The ceaseless rain was bad for the crops. 綿綿不斷的雨對穀物有害。

circuitous [səˈkjuɪtəs] .... ★★★★
adj. 迂迴的：to take a circuitous route 繞遠路

circulate [ˈsɝkjəˌlet] .... ★★★
v. (使)循環，散佈，傳播：Blood circulates round the body. 血液在全身循環。

circulation [ˌsɝkjəˈleʃən] .... ★★
n. 循環，流通，發行：His book has been taken out of circulation. 他的書已經不發行了。

divert [daɪˈvɝt] .... ★★
v. 轉移，(使)轉向，(使)轉移：The government is planning to divert the river to supply water for the town. 政府正計畫改變河道為那座城鎮供水。

drift [drɪft] .... ★★★★
v. 漂，漂流，漂移：The cutters seem to be drifting around the bay. 快艇看起來似乎在海灣附近漂泊。

effuse [ɛˋfjuz] .... ★
v. 流出，散佈：The drawing room effused an atmosphere of unhappiness. 客廳中瀰漫著一種不愉快的氣氛。

emigrate [ˋɛməˏgret] .... ★
v. 移民（移出）

emigration [ˏɛməˋgreʃən] .... ★
n. 移居，（總稱）移民：emigration policy 移民政策

flighty [ˋflaɪtɪ] .... ★★★★★
adj. 輕浮的：She is too flighty to take care of young children. 她太不負責任，不能照顧小孩。

float [flot] .... ★★★★
v. （使）漂浮：Wood floats on water. 木頭漂浮在水上。
n. 浮動，漂浮

flow [flo] .... ★★★★★
v. ①流（動）：Rivers flow into the sea. 百川歸海。②（衣服、頭髮）飄拂：Her hair flowed over her shoulders. 她的頭髮飄垂在肩上。

fluctuate [ˋflʌktʃuˏet] .... ★
v. （使）波動：The price of vegetables and fruits fluctuates according to the season. 蔬菜和水果的價格隨季節而波動。

gush [gʌʃ] .... ★
v. 湧出：Clear water gushed into the irrigational channel. 清澈的水湧進了灌溉渠道。

immigrate [ˋɪməˏgret] .... ★
v. 移居入境：Britain immigrated many colonists to the New World. 英國把大量殖民者移居到了新大陸。

itinerant [ɪˋtɪnərənt] .... ★
adj. 巡迴的，流動的：Itinerant preachers played an important role in United States religious history. 巡迴的佈道者在美國宗教歷史中扮演過重要的角色。

jar [dʒɑr] .... ★★★
v. 震動：The fall jarred every bone in my body. 這一跤摔得我渾身骨頭痛。

jolt [dʒolt] .... ★
v. 搖動：Her angry words jolted him out of the belief that she loved him. 她憤怒的話令他震驚，使他明白她不再愛自己了。

levitate [ˋlɛvəˏtet] .... ★
v. 浮動，漂浮，懸浮：levitating field 浮力場

levitation [ˏlɛvəˋteʃən] .... ★
n. 漂浮，懸浮：levitation melting 懸熔法

辨析
Analyze

drift, float

1 **drift** *vi.*「漂流，漂泊」，指在水面漂流或空氣中飄流，強調動態，可用於引申義：The rubber raft drifted out to sea. 這艘橡皮筏向大海漂去。

2 **float** *vi.*「浮動，漂流」，指在水面漂浮、漂流或空氣中飄浮、飄流，靜態、動態均可，可用於引申義：Wood usually floats. 木頭一般會浮起。

migrate [`maɪˌgret] .... ★★★

v. 遷移，移居：When birds migrate, they sometimes fly in formation. 鳥類在遷徙時有時會組成隊形飛行。

mobile [`mobɪl] .... ★★★★

adj. 機動的，活動的，運動的，流動的：The mobile medical team will soon be here. 巡迴醫療隊不久就要到這兒來。

mobility [mo`bɪlətɪ] .... ★★★★

n. 可動性，流動性

mobilize [`mobˌlaɪz] .... ★

v. 動員：to mobilize the country's economic resources 調動國家的經濟資源

motion [`moʃən] .... ★★★★★

n. 運動：The motion of ocean water varies at different depths below the surface. 洋面以下水流的變化隨著所處的深度而不同。

motionless [`moʃənlɪs] .... ★★★★★

adj. 不動的，靜止的：The cat sat motionless. 這隻貓蹲著不動。

move [muv] .... ★★★★★

v. 移動，搬動，遷移："Move along, please!" said the conductor. 售票員說：「請往裡面走！」

oscillation [ˌɑsə`leʃən] .... ★

n. 震盪，波動：the duration of oscillation 振盪期間

overflow [ˌovɚ`flo] .... ★

v. 從…中溢出：The lake overflowed till all the villages in the neighborhood were awash. 湖水氾濫使得周圍的所有村莊都被水淹沒了。

quake [kwek] .... ★

v. 地震，震動：The ground quaked under his feet. 大地在他的腳下震動。

quaver [`kwevɚ] .... ★★★★★

v. 發抖，顫抖，用顫聲說或唱：She said in a quavering voice. 她用一種顫抖的聲音說著。

quiver [`kwɪvɚ] .... ★★

v. 振動：The bridge quivered as the truck crossed it. 這座橋在卡車通過時有點顫動。

remove [rɪ`muv] .... ★★★★★

v. 移動，搬開，脫掉：His name was removed from consideration. 他的名字被排除在考慮的範圍之外。

辨析 Analyze

emigrate, immigrate, migrate

1 **emigrate** *vi.*「移民，移居」，一般指移居到國外去：Einstein emigrated from Germany to the United States. 愛因斯坦從德國移居到美國。

2 **immigrate** *vi.*「移民，移居」，一般指從他國移居進來：Einstein immigrated from Germany to the United States. 愛因斯坦從德國移居到美國。（從美國的角度看）

3 **migrate** *vi.*「移居，遷徙」，指候鳥等動物的遷徙，也指人移居：In winter many birds migrate to warmer areas. 冬天，許多鳥類遷徙到溫暖的地區。

rock [rɑk] .... ★★★★★

n. ①岩石，礁石：cut a road through rock 鑿岩築路②（常 pl.）暗礁，災難，危險：see rocks ahead 看到前途堪憂

roll [rol] .... ★★★★★

v. 滾動，打滾：Stones rolled down the hill. 石塊滾下山。

【片語】rock and roll 搖滾樂

roller [`rolɚ] .... ★★★

n. 滾筒，壓路機

rotate [`rotet] .... ★★★

v. 旋轉，轉動：Today a typical Corn Belt farm has from 80 to 120 acres of land, on which the farmer grows mainly corn, rotated every few years with soybeans. 目前典型的玉米帶農場通常在80到120英畝的地域範圍，其中農民主要種植玉米，間隔幾年種黃豆。

shake [ʃek] .... ★★★★★

v. 搖動，振動：The victim described the enemy's bombardment in a voice shaking with emotion. 受害者用激動發抖的聲音描述了敵人轟炸的經過。

shift [ʃɪft] .... ★★★★

v. ①移動，轉移：He shifted the chair close to the bed. 他把椅子向床邊挪近了一些。②改變，轉變：The balance has to be shifted towards developing agriculture. 這個平衡必須打破，使其向農業發展。

n. ①轉換，轉變：The sudden shift in the wind warned of the coming storm. 風向突然轉變，預示著暴風雨的來臨。②（換或輪）班：He chose the night shift. 他選擇了夜班。

shock [ʃɑk] .... ★★★★★

n. ①震動，衝擊：There was a severe shock of earthquake. 這裡發生了一次劇烈的地震。②震驚，驚愕：I recovered very gradually from the shock of her death. 過了好久，我才從她死亡的噩耗中回神。③休克：She was taken to hospital suffering from shock after the crash. 失事後，她處於休克狀態被送往醫院。④電震，電擊

v. ①（使）震驚：She was deeply shocked by the bad news. 這個壞消息令她十分震驚。②（使）震動：The earth was shocked by the bomb explosion. 炸彈的爆炸震動了大地。

辨析
Analyze

glide, slide, slip

1　**glide** *vi.* 「滑行，滑動，滑翔」，指在空中滑翔；也用於引申義，指像飛行一樣在表面滑行，故介詞一般不用on，而用over；相關名詞有glider（滑翔機）：The plane glided the last few miles to the airport. 飛機在最後幾英里飛向機場。

2　**slide** *vt. & vi.* 「（使）滑動，（使）下滑；（使）悄悄地移動」，指呈接觸狀態在光滑面上移動，如a sliding door（拉門）；動詞意為「滑動，滑板，滑梯，幻燈片」：It is fun to slide on the ice. 在冰上滑行很有意思。

3　**slip** *vt. & vi.* 「滑（倒），滑落，溜走，下降，跌落，悄悄放進」，指非有意地失去平衡或依著狀態，往往有一段空中下墜的狀態，還指其他引申用法；指「悄悄放進」時可與slide互換：I slipped on the ice and hurt my leg. 我在冰上滑了一跤，把腿摔傷了。

slide [slaɪd] .... ★★★★

n. ①滑坡，滑道：There are a few ski slide. 有幾條滑雪道。②滑（動）：The van went into a slide on the ice. 貨車在冰上打滑。③幻燈片：The color slides showed the rice fields in Bangkok. 彩色幻燈片展示了曼谷的稻田。

v. （使）滑動，（使）滑行：slide on the ice 在冰上滑行

slip [slɪp] .... ★★★★★

v. ①滑（倒），滑落：I slipped on the snow and sprained my ankle. 我在雪地裡滑倒，扭傷了腳踝。②溜走：I hope we can slip away before her notice. 我希望我們在她注意之前能溜走。

n. 疏忽，筆誤：That remark was a slip of the tongue. 那句話是口誤。

slipper [ˋslɪpɚ] .... ★★★

n. 拖鞋，便鞋：a pair of slippers （一雙）拖鞋

slippery [ˋslɪpərɪ] .... ★★★

adj. 滑的，使人滑跌的：a slippery floor 光滑的地板

spin [spɪn] .... ★★★★

v. 旋轉，自轉，紡紗，結網，吐絲：Most tachometers measure the speed of rotation of a spinning shaft or wheel in terms of revolutions per minute. 大多數轉速計是測量旋轉的桿或輪每分鐘所轉的圈數。

stagger [ˋstægɚ] .... ★★

v. 蹣跚：The wounded man staggered along. 受傷的人蹣跚地走路。

stay [ste] .... ★★★★★

v. 停留，暫住：Can you stay for dinner? 你能留下來吃晚飯嗎？

【片語】stay up 熬夜，不睡，通宵達旦

n. 逗留，停留：I'd like to go and see some places during my stay here. 在這兒逗留期間，我想去看一些地方。

swing [swɪŋ] .... ★★★★

n. ①擺動，搖擺：The swing of the pendulum. 鐘擺的擺動。②鞦韆：A little girl sat on the swing in the park swinging. 一個小女孩坐在公園的鞦韆上盪著玩。③擺動，搖擺：The lantern swung in the wind. 燈籠隨風晃動。④轉動，轉彎：The highway swings north around the end of the mountain. 公路在山盡頭向北轉了。

v. 使擺動，使轉動：Commander Ram arrived, swinging a stick. 拉姆司令揮舞著一根手杖來了。

辨析
Analyze

sway, swing

1 **sway** *vt. & vi.* 「（使）搖擺，（使）搖動」，指（使）搖擺，常指樹枝、輪船的擺動，也指人走路或跳舞時左右搖擺（比較典型的如時裝模特走路的樣子）；還指使改變看法，使動搖：The branches of the tree were swaying/swinging in the wind. 樹枝在風中搖擺。

2 **swing** *vt. & vi.* 「（使）搖擺，（使）搖盪」，指（使）擺動，即一個物體固定在一個點上做相對較有規律的前後或左右運動，如鐘擺的擺動、走路時兩臂的擺動、盪鞦韆等，還指（使）旋轉、（使）突然轉向：Our arms swing as we walk. 我們走路時兩臂擺動。

swirl [swɝl] .... ★

v. 旋轉：Tornadoes are rapidly swirling columns of air that are common in the Midwestern United States. 龍捲風是高速旋轉的氣流柱，在美國中西部很常見。

switch [swɪtʃ] .... ★★★

n. 電閘，開關，旋轉，枝條，鞭子：There is a switch on the wall for turning on the lights. 牆上有一個電燈開關。

v. 接通 (on)，接通電流，關掉 (off)；轉變，轉向：I used to cook on electricity, but I've switched to gas. 我過去用電煮飯，但現已換成用瓦斯了。

transfer [trænsˋfɝ] .... ★★★★

v. 牽動，調動，變換，傳輸，換車，轉讓，過戶：His employer transferred him to another office. 老闆把他調到另一間辦公室。

tuck [tʌk] .... ★★

n. （衣袖等的）褶

v. 捲起，塞進：She tucked in the covers on the bed. 她捲好床上的被子。

turn [tɝn] .... ★★★★★

v. ①（使）轉，轉動，旋轉：The Earth turns around the sun. 地球繞著太陽轉。②翻轉：The wind turned the car upside down. 風把汽車吹翻了。③翻滾，翻動：Please open your books and turn to page 45. 打開書，翻到第45頁。④使變化，變成：His hair has turned grey. 他的頭髮變白了。

【片語】①by turns 依次，輪流② in turn 按順序③ turn on/off 打開／關上（電器）④ turn to 求助於

vibrate [ˋvaɪbret] .... ★★★

v. 擺動，震動：The bus vibrated when the driver started the engine. 當司機發動了引擎時，公共汽車震動著。

vibration [vaɪˋbreʃən] .... ★★★

n. 震動：There is so much vibration on a ship that one cannot write. 船上的震動大得使人無法寫字。

wag [wæg] .... ★

v. 搖，擺：The dog wagged its tail with pleasure. 狗高興地搖尾巴。

辨析
Analyze

rock, shake, vibrate

1 **rock** *vt. & vi.* 「搖動」，指速度相對不快的前後或左右的搖動、搖晃：She rocked the baby in her arms. 她把嬰兒抱在懷中輕輕搖著。

2 **shake** *vt. & vi.* 「搖動，（使）顫抖，震動」，指快速反覆前後或左右搖動、搖晃，常用詞：His hand shook as he signed the paper. 他簽署文件時，手在發抖。

3 **vibrate** *vt. & vi.* 「（使）振動，（使）搖擺」，指小幅度快速震動、顫動、振動，多用於科技文體：The ship's engine caused the whole ship to vibrate. 輪船的引擎使整條船振動。

wave [wev] .... ★★★★★
v. ①揮動，向…揮手或物示意：wave one's
hand at sb. 向某人揮手示意②揮手示意：
Bill waved to me. 比爾向我揮手致意。③波
動，飄動：flags waving in the wind 在微風
中飄動的旗幟
n. ①波浪，波濤：The waves run high. 波濤
洶湧。②（手等的）揮動：with a wave of a
hand 揮動一下手

wavelength [ˈwevˌlɛŋθ] .... ★★★
n. 波長

waver [ˈwevɚ] ....★
v. 動搖，猶豫：He wavered over buying a
house . 他在購買房屋上猶豫不決。

whirl [hwɜl] .... ★★
vt. 使旋轉：He whirled his partner round the
dance floor. 他帶著舞伴環繞舞池旋轉。
vi. 眩暈：After meeting so many new people,
my head was whirling. 會見這麼多陌生人，
我頭都昏了。

wield [wild] ....★
v. 支配，控制：to wield power 掌握權力

wobble [ˈwɑb!] ....★
v. 搖晃，搖擺，晃動：The front wheels of the
car wobble. 汽車的前輪搖擺。

wobbly [ˈwɑblɪ] ....★
adj. 搖擺的：wobbly line 彎彎曲曲的線條

辨析
Analyze

revolve, rotate, spin, turn, whirl

1 **revolve** *vt. & vi.*「旋轉」，指自轉、圍
繞…轉、使轉動，與 rotate 基本可以互換
使用。

2 **rotate** *vt. & vi.*「旋轉」，指自轉、圍
繞…轉、使轉動，與revolve 基本可以互
換使用；此外還指輪流當班工作：The
metal disc rotates/revolves/turns at high
speed. 這個金屬圓盤高速旋轉。

3 **spin** *vt. & vi.*「（使）旋轉」，指（使）
快速旋轉，也指眩暈，還指紡紗：The ice
skater was spinning faster and faster. 這
個溜冰的人越轉越快。

4 **turn** *vt. & vi.*「旋轉，轉動，翻轉，扭
轉（使）轉向，（使）變化，（使）變
成」，是常用語：The Earth turns on its
axis. 地球繞著自軸旋轉。

5 **whirl** *vi.*「旋轉，急轉」，擬聲字，使人
想起呼呼的響聲，文學意味較濃；還指
發暈：The fan blades whirled in the hot
room. 風扇葉子在悶熱的房間裡呼呼地
轉。

運動、變化類名稱總匯

14

腐爛、稀釋、蒸發、吸收相關辭彙

Vocabulary of Moisture

absorb [əbˋsɔrb] .... ★★★★
v. 吸引，吸收，併吞：The game absorbed the boy completely. 這個男孩完全被遊戲吸引住了。

assimilate [əˋsɪmḷͺet] .... ★★★★★
v. 吸收：Food is assimilated and converted into organic tissues through a process known as metabolism. 食物被吸收，並經新陳代謝作用轉變為有機組織。

assimilation [əͺsɪmḷˋeʃən] .... ★★★★★
n. 吸收：Technological advancement depends on the rapid assimilation of new ideas. 技術進步有賴於吸收進步的新思想。

boil [bɔɪl] .... ★★★★
v. 沸騰，蒸發，汽化，起泡：Those sweet potatoes have been boiling away for 20 minutes. 那些甘薯已經煮沸二十分鐘了。

boiler [ˋbɔɪlɚ] .... ★
n. 鍋爐

damp [dæmp] .... ★★★
adj. 潮濕的，有濕氣的：I don't like to sleep between damp sheets. 我不喜歡睡在潮濕的被單裡。
v. 使潮濕，使變弱，使沮喪：Nothing could dump his spirits. 任何事都不能掃他的興。

dampen [ˋdæmpən] .... ★★★
v. 使潮濕，使沮喪：The camp supplies dampened during the long rainy season. 營地的補給品在漫長的雨季裡變潮濕了。

dank [dæŋk] .... ★
adj. 陰濕的：Alligators still exist in some of the dank swamps and bayous of Alabama's coastal regions. 短吻鱷仍在阿拉巴馬州沿海地區一些潮濕的沼澤中生存著。

decay [dɪˋke] .... ★★★★
v. 腐敗：When insects feed on decaying plant material in a compost pile, they help turn it into useful garden soil. 昆蟲在堆肥上吞食腐敗的植物，有助於把這些植物變成有用的土壤。

deteriorate [dɪˋtɪrɪəͺret] .... ★
v. 腐化，敗壞：The situation is bound to deteriorate. 情況肯定會變糟。

diffuse [dɪˈfjuz] .... ★★★★★
v. 傳播，擴散：The colors of the sunset were diffused across the sky. 日落時分的霞光佈滿天空。

disseminate [dɪˈsɛməˌnet] .... ★
v. 散佈，傳播：The National Science Foundation disseminates information related to scientific research. 國家科學基金會發佈與科學研究有關的資訊。

dissemination [dɪˌsɛməˈneʃən] .... ★
n. 傳播：information dissemination 資訊傳播

drench [drɛntʃ] .... ★
v. 使淋透：I was drenched in the storm. 我在暴風雨中淋得濕透。

emit [ɪˈmɪt] .... ★★★
v. 散發，發射，放出：A cathode emits electrons in a controlled environment. 陰極在受控制的環境下會發射出電子。

erode [ɪˈrod] .... ★★★★★
v. 腐蝕：Long enduring war often erodes popular morality. 長期的和平常常會腐蝕大眾的道德觀。

erupt [ɪˈrʌpt] .... ★★★★★
v. 爆發：Mount St. Helens erupted in March 1980 after one hundred twenty-three years of silence. 聖海倫斯山在沉寂了120年後於1980年3月爆發。

eruption [ɪˈrʌpʃən] .... ★★★★★
n. 爆發

evaporate [ɪˈvæpəˌret] .... ★
n. 蒸發（作用）：The pool of water on the playground evaporated in the sun. 操場水坑裡的水在陽光下蒸發了。

impervious [ɪmˈpɜvɪəs] .... ★
adj. 不能滲透的：This material is impervious to gases and liquids. 氣體和液體都透不過這種物質。

leak [lik] .... ★★★
v. 洩露：a damaged reactor leaking radioactivity into the atmosphere 一座損壞的反應爐向大氣洩露出放射性物質

permeate [ˈpɜmɪˌet] .... ★★★★★
v. 滲透，透過：Neon light is utilized in airport beacons because it can permeate fog. 氖燈被用於機場的燈塔上，因為它能透射霧氣。

辨析 Analyze

decay, deteriorate, rot, spoil

1 **decay** *vi.*「腐爛，腐朽，衰敗，衰退，衰落」，指由於化學反應而變壞或腐爛，也可用於引申義：The fruit / His teeth / The old books began to decay. 這些水果／他的牙齒／這些舊書開始腐爛。

2 **deteriorate** *vi.*「惡化，變壞，變糟」，常與抽象事物連用，不強調化學變化：His health / Their relations began to deteriorate. 他的健康／他們的關係開始惡化。

3 **rot** *vt. & vi.*「（使）腐爛，（使）腐朽」，強調在自然過程中腐爛、變壞，也可指生活腐敗、生活墮落：A fallen tree soon rots. 倒塌的樹很快就腐爛了。

4 **spoil** *vt. & vi.*「損壞，破壞，寵壞，溺愛」，多指食物變質，也可指寵壞、溺愛：Some kinds of food soon spoil. 有些食品變質得很快。

pervade [pəˈved] .... ★★★★★
v. 遍佈，彌漫：The air is pervaded by a smell (of the smoke). 空氣中瀰漫著一股（煙的）氣味。

pour [por] .... ★★★★★
v. ①灌，倒，注：a machine that pours grain into sacks 一部把糧食灌到袋子裡的機器 ②傾洩，流出：The rain poured through a hole in the roof. 雨水從屋頂上的一個洞流出。

quench [kwɛntʃ] .... ★
v. 熄滅，撲滅，解（渴）：The disapproval of my colleagues quenched my enthusiasm for the plan. 同事們的反對減低了我對這項計畫的熱情。

radiate [ˈredɪet] .... ★
v. 散發，發光，輻射：All the roads radiate from the center of the town. 所有的路都是從市中心輻射出來的。

rot [rɑt] .... ★★★
v. 腐爛：One could see the blackened areas where the branches had rotted off. 人們可以在污穢骯髒的地區看見樹枝因腐爛而脫落。

rotten [ˈrɑtn̩] .... ★★★
adj. 腐爛的：The fish is rotten; you must not eat it. 這條魚已經壞了，你千萬不能吃。

saturate [ˈsætʃəˌret] .... ★
v. 浸透：The recollection was saturated with sunshine. 回憶中充滿了陽光。

soak [sok] .... ★★★★
v. ①浸泡，使濕透：Soak the material for several hours in cold water. 把原料浸泡冷水裡幾個小時。②滲透：The blood soaked through his bandage. 血滲透了他的繃帶。

splash [splæʃ] .... ★★
v. 濺，潑：The children splashed in the pool. 孩子們在水池裡戲水。

spout [spaʊt] .... ★
v. 噴出，湧出：The lava spouted out of the volcano. 熔岩從火山噴發出來。

spray [spre] .... ★★★
n. 噴霧：a spray of water 水花飛濺
v. 噴霧：The seed was sprayed over the ground in huge quantities by airplanes. 飛機把這些種子大量地撒在地面上。

sprinkle [ˈsprɪŋkl̩] .... ★★
n. 灑，噴，淋，噴水：She sprinkled sugar on the cakes. 她把糖撒在蛋糕上。

辨析 Analyze

dip, saturate, soak

1. **dip** vt.「浸，蘸」，指將某物浸入液體並迅速拿出，還指落下、下降：He dipped his brush in the ink. 他把畫筆在墨水裡蘸了一下。

2. **saturate** vt.「使濕透」，指浸透，還指使飽和、使充滿，正式用語，常用於引申用法：The ground was saturated with water. 這塊土地飽含水分。

3. **soak** vt.「浸泡，濕透」，指長時間浸泡，還指（使）濕透、滲透：If you want to take out the stain, soak the cloth in cold water. 如果你想要把污漬洗掉，把布在冷水裡泡一下。

spurt [spɝt] .... ★
v. 噴出，湧出：Blood spurted out from the wound. 血從傷口湧出。

steep [stip] .... ★★★
adj. 陡直的，陡峭的，陡的，急劇（升降）的：The steep rock seems to be growing at an angle. 這塊陡直的岩石似乎在以一定角度生長。

submerge [səb`mɝdʒ] .... ★★★
v. 浸沒，淹沒：The Weddell seal of Antarctica can dive to a depth of about 1,600 feet and remain submerged for as long as an hour and ten minutes. 南極洲的維得爾海豹能潛到水面下1,600英尺處，並能在水下最長待上1小時又10分鐘。

transpire [træn`spaɪr] .... ★
v. 發散，排出，洩露：It was transpired that the fire was caused by a careless smoker. 據傳這場大火是由一位粗心的吸煙者造成的。

trickle [`trɪkl̩] .... ★★★★
n. 滴，細流
v. 滴，淌：Blood trickled from the wound. 血從傷口一滴滴流出。

辨析
Analyze

overflow, pour, spill, splash

1 **overflow** *vt. & vi.* 「滿得外溢，外流，氾濫」，指由於液體或鹽、沙等超過容器的容量而溢出：The river overflowed (its banks). 這條河氾濫了。

2 **pour** *vt. & vi.* 「灌，倒，注，傾瀉，流出」，指有意識地把液體或鹽、沙等倒出或倒入：Jim poured some water into a glass. 吉姆把水倒在杯子裡。

3 **spill** *vt. & vi.* 「（使）溢出，（使）灑落」，指由於不小心而潑出：I've spilt coffee all down my shirt. 我把咖啡都潑到襯衫上了。

4 **splash** *vt. & vi.* 「濺，潑」，指（水）向外濺，往⋯上面濺／潑：Children love to splash (water over each other) in the swimming pool. 孩子們喜歡在游泳池（互相）潑水。

15

呼吸、餵養、生死相關辭彙

Vocabulary of Life & Death

adopt [əˈdɑpt] .... ★★★★★
v. 採用，收養：New York was the first United States metropolis to adopt zoning laws. 紐約是美國最早採用城市區劃法的大都市。

alive [əˈlaɪv] .... ★★★★★
adj. 活著的，有活力的：Is his grandfather still alive? 他的祖父還在世嗎？

breath [brɛθ] .... ★★★★★
n. 氣息，呼吸：He drew/took a deep breath. 他深深地吸了口氣。
【片語】① catch one's breath 喘氣，鬆口氣，（因激動或恐懼）屏息② out of breath 喘不過氣來

breathalyzer [ˈrɛθəˌlaɪzɚ] .... ★
n. （測醉用的）呼吸分析器

breathe [brið] .... ★★★★★
vi. 呼吸，喘氣：He was breathing hard after climbing up the stairs. 他爬上樓梯後，吃力地喘著氣。

dead [dɛd] .... ★★★★★
adv. 完全地：You can be dead sure of my innocence. 你絕對可以相信我是無辜的。

deadline [ˈdɛdˌlaɪn] .... ★★★
adv. 期限：application deadline 申請截止日期；bid deadline 投標截止日期

deadly [ˈdɛdlɪ] .... ★★★★
adj. 致命的，極度的：Fog is the sailor's deadly enemy. 霧是航海者的天敵。

death [dɛθ] .... ★★★★★
n. 死亡，滅亡，毀滅

defunct [dɪˈfʌŋkt] .... ★
adj. 死的：a defunct political organization 解散了的政治組織

demise [dɪˈmaɪz] .... ★★★★★
n. 死亡：The introduction of the trolley car signaled the gradual demise of the bus. 有軌電車的引進意味著公車將漸漸消失。

die [daɪ] .... ★★★★★
v. 死亡：William died from an accident. 威廉死於意外事故。
【片語】① die from 因（傷）而死② die of 因（病，餓）而死

drown [draʊn] .... ★★★★
v. 溺死，把…淹死，淹沒：people who drowned their troubles in drink 借酒澆愁的人們；screams that were drowned out by the passing train 被經過的火車蓋過的尖叫聲

dying [ˋdaɪɪŋ] .... ★★★★
adj. 垂死的，臨終的

enrich [ɪnˋrɪtʃ] .... ★★
v. 豐富：Glittering tears enriched her eyes. 閃爍的淚光使她的雙眼更加美麗。

enrichment [ɪnˋrɪtʃmənt] .... ★★
n. 豐富，增添裝飾

exhale [ɛksˋhel] .... ★
v. 呼出，發出，散發：chimneys exhaling dense smoke 煙囪中冒出濃煙

exist [ɪgˋzɪst] .... ★★★★★
v. 生存：Wealth and poverty exist in every demographic category. 富裕和貧窮存在於所有人口統計分類中。

existence [ɪgˋzɪstəns] .... ★★★★★
n. ①存在：Henry doesn't believe in the existence of God. 亨利不相信上帝的存在。②生存，生活（方式）：I have never heard anything so silly during my whole existence. 我一生中未聽過有這麼傻的事。

feed [fid] .... ★★★★★
vt. ①餵（著），飼（養）：Have you fed chicken? 你餵過雞了嗎？②向…提供：Two moving belts feed the machine with raw material. 兩條轉動的傳送帶輸送原料給機器。
【片語】be fed up (with) 對…感到厭煩
vi. 吃飼料：The horses were feeding in the meadows. 馬在草地上吃草。

feedback [ˋfid͵bæk] .... ★★★★
n. 反應，回饋：to ask the students for feedback on the new curriculum 徵求學生對新課程的反應

gasp [gæsp] .... ★★★★
v. 氣喘，喘息：The swimmer came out of the water and gasped for breath. 游泳的人從水裡浮出來喘口氣。

lethal [ˋliθəl] .... ★
adj. 致命的：accusations lethal to the candidate's image 對候選人形象極其有害的指控

life [laɪf] .... ★★★★★
n. ①生命：Treasure your life and keep away from drugs. 珍惜生命，遠離毒品。②一生，生涯：Would you love her for your whole life? 你會愛她一輩子嗎？③生活，生計：Life is not easy. 生活是艱辛的。

live [lɪv] .... ★★★★★
v. ①居住：We have lived here for quite a number of years. 我們在這兒住了好些年了。②生活，生存：Man, animals and plants cannot live without water. 人類、動物和植物離開了水，將無法生存下去。

lively [ˋlaɪvlɪ] .... ★★★★
adj. ①充滿活力的，活潑的：a lively song 輕快的歌曲②逼真的，栩栩如生的：lively colors 鮮豔的色彩

living [ˋlɪvɪŋ] .... ★★★★★
adj. 活的，活著的：Was your grandmother still living when the doctor arrived? 醫生到達的時候，你祖母還活著嗎？
n. 生活：Such hard living can ruin his health. 這樣沉重的生活會搞垮他的身體。

mortal [ˋmɔrtl̩] .... ★★★★
n. 凡人：All mortals must die. 人終有一死。
adj. 終有一死的

naturalize [ˋnætʃərə͵laɪz] .... ★
v. 採納（外國的東西），使入國籍：He was naturalized after living in Italy for many years. 他在義大利生活了多年以後入了義大利國籍。

nourishment [ˋnɝɪʃmənt] .... ★★★★★
n. 食物，滋養品

nurture [ˈnɝtʃɚ] ....★
v. 養育：nurture a student's talent 培養學生的才能

nutriment [ˈnjutrəmənt] ....★★★★
n. 營養品

pant [pænt] ....★★
n. 喘氣
v. 喘，氣喘吁吁地說：I panted my congratulations to the winner of the race. 我上氣不接下氣地向賽跑的贏家道賀。

respiration [ˌrɛspəˈreʃən] ....★★★★★
n. 呼吸：The process of respiration consists of two independent actions, inhaling and exhaling. 呼吸過程是由兩個獨立的動作 吸氣和呼氣」完成的。

respiratory [rɪˈspaɪrəˌtorɪ] ....★★★★★
adj. 呼吸（作用）的：respiratory organs 呼吸器官

辨析
Analyze

alive, live, lively, living

1 **alive** *a.*「活著的」，與 dead 相對，作表語或後置定語：He is still alive among people. 他仍然活在人們的心中。

2 **live** *a. & ad.*「活的，有生命力的，精力充沛的」，常常做定語，還可表示「實況轉播」：He is a live young man. 他是一個充滿生機的年輕人。

3 **lively** *a.*「活躍的，充滿生機的」：Although he is very old, his imagination is still very lively. 他雖然年紀大了，但想像力仍很活躍。

4 **living** *a.*「活著的（人），活生生的（事物）」，與 dead 相對，作前置定語：English is a living language. 英語是一種正在使用中的語言。

16

並排、平行、擁擠相關辭彙

Vocabulary of Arrangement

Exercise & Change

arrange [əˋrendʒ] .... ★★★★★

v. 排列：The term "composition" refers to the way the components of a drawing are arranged by the artist. 「構圖」這個術語指的是畫家排列圖畫各部分的方式。

congested [kənˋdʒɛstɪd] .... ★

adj. 擁擠的：The main streets in the center of the city are always very congested. 城市中心的主要街道總是很擁擠。

crowd [kraʊd] .... ★★★★★

n. 群，人群，群眾

v. ①聚集，群集：They all crowded round the teacher. 他們都圍在教師周圍。②擠滿，擁擠：The stadium were crowded with spectators. 運動場擠滿了觀眾。

overcrowd [ˌovəˋkraʊd] .... ★★★★★

v. 擠滿，使太擁擠：The hall was overcrowded long before the performance began. 演出開始前，大廳早已擠得水洩不通了。

parallel [ˋpærəˌlɛl] ....★★★★

v. 與…平行，匹敵

n. 類似點，類似處：Numerous parallels exist between Ernest Hemingway's life and the lives of his characters. 海明威的一生與其筆下創作的人物命運有許多相似之處。

range [rendʒ] .... ★★★★★

n. 範圍，距離，分類，(行，路)程，飛越距離，區域，排列，連續，(山)脈，爐

v. 排列，整理，整隊，(事物等在一定範圍內)變動：Ranging from solitary to gregarious, beaked whales may travel in schools of several hundred during the breeding season. 喙鯨從獨處到群居，可能在哺育季節幾百個一群地游動。

raze [rez] .... ★

v. 摧殘：The old school was razed to ground, and a new one was built. 那所舊學校被完全拆掉，並蓋了一所新的。

slit [slɪt] .... ★

n. 狹長切口，細長裂縫

v. 切開，截開，縱割：I slit open the letter with a knife. 我用一把小刀把信裁開。

suffuse [sə`fjuz] .... ★

v. 充滿：The sky above the roof is suffused with deep colors. 屋簷上的天空浸染了深深的顏色。

throng [θrɔŋ] .... ★★★★★

n. 群眾

v. 擠進，塞滿：commuters thronging the subway platform 擠滿地鐵月臺的通勤乘客

17

刺激、活躍、冒險、背叛相關辭彙

Vocabulary of Adventure

adventure [ədˋvɛntʃɚ] .... ★★★★★
n. 冒險，奇遇，驚險活動：The network has access to four percent of the prime time for adventure and mysteries. 那家電視臺播放的冒險和懸疑節目占去4%的黃金時間。

adventuresome [ədˋvɛntʃɚsəm] .... ★★★★★
adj. 愛冒險的：The adventuresome traveler sparely survived in his last trip to Alps. 這個愛冒險的旅行家在上次的阿爾卑斯山之旅中差點喪生。

betray [brˋtre] .... ★★
v. 背叛，洩露：Her face betrayed her nervousness. 她的面部表情顯露出她很緊張。

deviate [ˋdivɪˏet] .... ★
v. 出軌，離題：Human behaviors cannot deviate from certain rules. 人的行為不能夠違背某些原則。

deviation [ˏdivɪˋeʃən] .... ★
n. 偏差，差數，誤差：Vice was a deviation from our nature. 不道德行為就是背離我們生活常規的行為。

rebel [rɪˋbɛl] .... ★★★★
v. 謀反，叛徒，反感：She rebelled at the unwelcome suggestion. 她對這不受歡迎的建議感到反感。

rebellion [rɪˋbɛljən] .... ★★
n. 造反，叛亂，反抗：When a lot of people rebel, there is a rebellion. 當許多人產生反感後，就會反抗。

traitor [ˋtretɚ] .... ★★
n. 叛徒，賣國賊：a hidden traitor 內奸

treachery [ˋtrɛtʃərɪ] .... ★
n. 背信棄義，背叛

treason [ˋtrizn̩] .... ★★
n. 通敵，叛國罪：a case of treason 叛國案

venture [ˋvɛntʃɚ] .... ★★★★★
v. 冒險，冒昧：I would venture to guess that Anon, who wrote so many poems without signing them, was often a woman. 我冒昧地猜測，寫下如此多詩歌的無名氏多半是個女人。

18

妨礙、碰擊、打擾相關辭彙

Vocabulary of Disturbance

annoy [ə'nɔɪ] .... ★★★

v. 使惱怒，打擾：She was annoyed at/with his lighthearted attitude. 她對他那種若無其事的態度感到討厭。

balk [bɔk] .... ★

v. 妨礙：The kidnapping attempt was balked by the police. 綁架的企圖被警方所阻礙。

bother [ˈbɑðɚ] .... ★★★

v. ①打擾，煩擾 ：If you don't mind, I'll bother you to lend me some money. 如果你不介意，麻煩你借我點錢。②麻煩 ：Don't bother about getting dinner for him, he have eaten good food at a restaurant. 不用麻煩為他做飯了，人家已經在餐廳裡吃好吃的了。

n. 麻煩

butt [bʌt] .... ★

n. 末端：a cigar butt 煙蒂；a candle butt 蠟燭頭

clog [klɑg] .... ★

v. 填塞：The early symptoms of measles resemble those of the common cold, including a cough, clogged sinuses, and red, irritated eyes. 麻疹早期的症狀類似普通感冒，患者會咳嗽、鼻竇阻塞、眼睛發紅、酸痛。

collide [kə'laɪd] .... ★

v. 碰撞，衝突，抵觸：Whale sharks are not aggressive, but they have been known to collide with boats. 鯨鯊沒有攻擊性，但是他們卻會和船隻相撞。

collision [kə'lɪʒən] .... ★★★

n. （車、船等的）碰撞：Both of the drivers were injured in the collision. 在撞車事故中，兩個司機都受傷了。

conflict [ˈkɑnflɪkt] .... ★★★★★

v. 牴觸，衝突，矛盾：All these actions conflicted with the universally accepted laws. 所有的這些行動都與普世公認的法則相牴觸。

運動、變化

containment [kən`temənt] .... ★★★★★

n. 抑制，遏制政策：The containment is a policy of checking the expansion or influence of a hostile power or ideology, as by the creation of strategic alliances or support of client states in areas of conflict or unrest. 遏制政策是一種遏制敵對勢力或意識形態擴張或影響的政策，像是締結戰略性同盟或支援衝突或動盪地區的被保護國。

defy [dɪ`faɪ] .... ★★

v. 蔑視，反抗：to defy the court order by leaving the country 以出國逃避法院程序

derange [dɪ`rendʒ] .... ★

v. 擾亂：The woman's mind has been deranged for many years. 那女人已精神錯亂很多年了。

deter [dɪ`tɝ] .... ★★★★

v. 阻止，嚇住：Despite of the poor weather conditions, the delivery people could not be deterred from their work. 儘管天氣很惡劣，搬運工還是不能停止自己的工作。

disarrange [ˌdɪsə`rendʒ] .... ★

v. 擾亂：The incident was sufficient to disarrange her whole life. 那一事件足以使她一生受到擾亂。

distract [dɪ`strækt] .... ★★

v. 分散（心思），打擾：The school students were distracted by the noise outside the classroom. 教室外面的喧鬧聲使學生們不能集中注意力。

disturb [dɪs`tɝb] .... ★★★★

v. 擾亂，妨礙，打擾，使不安：When disturbed, a sea anemone retracts its tentacles and shortens its body so that it resembles a lump on a rock. 海葵被打擾時，就會收縮觸角和身體，看起來就像石頭上突起的一塊。

disturbance [dɪs`tɝbəns] .... ★★

n. 動亂，騷亂，干擾：There has been a disturbance in the street; somebody has been hurted. 街上發生了一陣騷亂，有人被打傷了。

辨析 Analyze

annoy, bother, disturb, trouble

1 **annoy** *vt.*「使生氣，使惱火」，指使人煩惱或生氣：We were annoyed to learn that we would not be able to catch the train. 聽說趕不上火車，我們感到很煩惱。

2 **bother** *vt. & vi.*「打擾，使麻煩」，指受干擾而感到不安或煩惱，也指打擾或麻煩他人：He did not want to tell me exactly what it was that bothered him. 他不想告訴我究竟是什麼使他煩惱。

3 **disturb** *vt.*「打擾」，指妨礙他人的工作，學習或生活而使他人感到焦慮，心中不平靜或心慌意亂：That letter disturbed my mother greatly. 那封信使我母親很不安。

4 **trouble** *vt. & vi.*「使煩惱，使苦惱，麻煩，（使）費神」，指因干擾使人不適、不方便、苦惱或不安，有時可與bother換用：He was greatly troubled about his daughter's behavior. 他為女兒的行為感到非常煩惱。

encumber [ɪnˈkʌmbə] .... ★

v. 阻礙，妨礙：a hiker who was encumbered with a heavy pack 一個為沉重背包所累的徒步旅行者，一生總為責任義務所累的人

friction [ˈfrɪkʃən] .... ★

n. 摩擦：The constant friction between the young couple finally caused divorce. 小夫妻之間經常的衝突終於導致了離婚。

hamper [ˈhæmpə] .... ★

v. 妨礙：The boy was hampered by a stone. 男孩被石頭絆了一下。

handicap [ˈhændɪˌkæp] .... ★

v. 妨礙，使不利：Over 20 million women in the United States are handicapped. 在美國有2,000萬的婦女有某方面的障礙。

n. 妨礙，不利條件

harass [ˈhærəs] .... ★

v. 侵擾：The landlord harassed tenants who were behind in their rent. 房東不斷地騷擾拖欠房租的房客。

hinder [ˈhɪndə] .... ★★★★★

v. 妨礙：Too much calcium can hinder a child's growth. 鈣質過多會妨礙孩子的成長。

hurdle [ˈhɜdl̩] .... ★

n. 籬笆，障礙，欄

impact [ˈɪmpækt] .... ★★★★★

n. 影響作用：The storm's impact on the area's economy will not be known for several months. 這場暴風雨對該地區經濟的影響程度要在幾個月後才能得知。。

v. 衝擊

interfere [ˌɪntəˈfɪr] .... ★★★★

n. 干涉，干預，妨礙：Some plants contain substances that interfere with the digestive processes of animals. 某些植物含有的物質會影響到動物的消化過程。

interference [ˌɪntəˈfɪrəns] .... ★★★

n. 干涉，干預，妨礙：interference colors 干擾色；interference wave 干擾波

interlude [ˈɪntəˌljud] .... ★

n. 間隔，插曲：interludes of bright weather 間隔的晴朗天氣

interrupt [ˌɪntəˈrʌpt] .... ★★★★

v. 打斷，插嘴：Traffic in the city was interrupted by a snowstorm. 市內交通被暴風雪所阻斷。

interval [ˈɪntəvl̩] .... ★★★★

n. 間隔，空隙，間歇：There was a long interval before he answered the telephone. 他隔了好久才回了電話。

辨析 Analyze

interfere, intervene

1. **interfere** *vi.*「干涉，介入，阻礙，干擾」，指無理干涉，尤指干涉主權範圍內的事。片語 interfere with 意為干擾、妨礙，語氣較弱；interfere in 意為干涉，語氣較強：The noise interfered with my study. 噪音妨礙了我的學習。

2. **intervene** *vi.*「干涉，干預，干擾，阻撓」，指為了預防或改變結果而進行干預，intervene between 意為調停，intervene in 意為干預；總的來說，intervene 的語氣比 interfere 要弱一些：His task is to intervene between people who are disputing. 他的任務是調停人們之間的糾紛。

intervene [ˌɪntəˈvin] .... ★★★★

v. 干涉：They refused to intervene in the quarrel. 他們拒絕干涉那場爭吵。

intrude [ɪnˈtrud] .... ★★★★★

v. 侵擾：intrude one's views upon others 強迫他人採納自己的意見

intrusion [ɪnˈtruʒən] .... ★★★★★

n. 打擾，侵入：The film star claimed that the police action was an intrusion on her private life. 電影明星聲稱警方的行動侵犯她的私生活。

obstacle [ˈɑbstəkl] .... ★★★★

n. 障礙：The tendency of the human body to reject foreign matter is the main obstacle to successful tissue transplantation. 人體對進入體內的異物的排斥性，是阻礙組織移植成功的主因。

obstruct [əbˈstrʌkt] .... ★★★★★

v. 阻礙，妨礙：Protein intake should be high enough to obstruct water loss and the loss of body tissue. 蛋白質的攝入量應該高到足以阻止人體組織及水分消耗。

prevent [prɪˈvɛnt] .... ★★★★★

v. ①阻礙：Almost all maritime countries have some organized means of preventing accidents at sea and assisting the shipwrecked. 幾乎所有有海事活動的國家，都有某種防止海上事故和救助失事船舶的機制。②預防，防止：What can we do to prevent the spreading of the disease? 我們能做些什麼事防止這種疾病散佈呢？

repulse [rɪˈpʌls] .... ★

v. 排斥，擊退：He repulse an unreasonable request. 他拒絕不合理的要求。

repulsion [rɪˈpʌlʃən] .... ★

n. 拒絕，排斥，推斥：repulsion at the sight of a diseased animal 看到生病的動物感到厭惡

repulsive [rɪˈpʌlsɪv] .... ★

adj. 排斥的：a repulsive force 排斥力

smash [smæʃ] .... ★★

v. ①打碎，摧毀，粉碎，使破滅：The final setback smashed all his hope of success. 最後一次失敗使他成功的希望完全破滅。②猛力衝擊：The angry lawyer smashed his fist against the desk. 憤怒的律師揮拳猛擊書桌。

【片語】smash into 猛撞上

stunt [stʌnt] .... ★

v. 阻礙：The disease, rust, stunts a plant's growth and leads to the destruction of the plant. 鏽病阻礙植物生長並會導致其死亡。

tamper [ˈtæmpɚ] .... ★

v. 干預：tamper with the will 篡改遺囑；tampering with the timing mechanism of the safe 胡亂撥弄保險箱的計時裝置

thump [θʌmp] .... ★

v. 重擊：The shutters thumped the wall in the wind. 百葉窗在風中砰砰地碰在牆上。

運動、變化類名稱總匯

19

分散、驅散、開除相關辭彙

Vocabulary of Separation

banish [`bænɪʃ] .... ★
vt. ①流放，放逐②消除，排除（顧慮，恐懼等）

disintegrate [dɪsˋɪntəgret] .... ★★★★★
v. 分離，分化，分解，使分裂，蛻變，衰變，使瓦解：
During nuclear fission, uranium atoms disintegrate
into lighter elements. 在核分裂過程中，鈾原子分裂
成更輕的物質。

disperse [dɪˋspɜs] .... ★★
v. 散開，散去：A gust of wind dispersed the smoke
from the stove. 一陣風把爐子裡產生的煙吹散了。

evacuate [ɪˋvækjʊet] .... ★
v. 疏散，使⋯空：Molly Brown was labeled
"unsinkable" after she helped to evacuated
passengers from the ill-fated ship the Titanic. 茉莉·
布朗在救出了慘遭厄運的鐵達尼號的乘客之後，被譽
為「不沉之人」。

expulsion [ɪkˋspʌlʃən] .... ★
n. 驅逐，排出：an expulsion order 驅逐出境的命令；
the expulsion of somebody from school 開除某人學
籍；the expulsion of air from the lungs 從肺中排出
空氣

impel [ɪmˋpɛl] .... ★★★★★
v. 驅使：We were impelled by circumstances to take a
stand. 我們因形勢所迫而採取一個立場。

revoke [rɪˋvok] .... ★★★★★
v. 取消，撤回：As a result of the accident, the police
revoked his driver's license. 由於一次事故，警方吊
銷了他的駕駛執照。

scatter [`skætɚ] .... ★★★★
v. 分散：The farmer scattered the corn in the yard for
the hens. 農民把穀子撒在院子裡餵母雞。

secede [sɪˋsid] .... ★
v. 退出，脫離

seclusion [sɪˋkluʒən] .... ★
n. 歸隱，隔離：She lives in seclusion apart from her
friends. 她遠離朋友，過著隱居生活。

shatter [ˋʃætɚ] .... ★★
n. 碎片
v. 使粉碎，破碎：The glass shattered when I dropped
it. 我把玻璃摔成了碎片。

20

Exercise & Change

尋找、發現、檢查、規定相關辭彙

Vocabulary of Finds & Rules

chase [tʃes] ....★★★★
v. 追趕，追求：The Johnsons' cat likes to chase the mice as if it were playing with them. 詹森家的貓喜歡追逐老鼠，好像牠在跟牠們鬧著玩似的。
n. 追趕，追求

ferret [ˈfɛrɪt] ....★
v. 搜索：ferret out the solution to a mystery 發現了謎底

find [faɪnd] ....★★★★★
v. ①找到，發現：I can't find my boots. 我找不到我的靴子。②發覺，感到：We found her to be dishonest. 我們發現她不誠實。
【片語】find out 查明，發現，瞭解

glean [glin] ....★
v. 收集：records from which historians glean their knowledge 歷史學家們用以從中收集資訊的記錄

grope [grop] ....★
v. 摸索：He groped for the door handle in the dark. 他摸著黑找門把。

insoluble [ɪnˈsɑljəbl̩] ....★
adj. 不能解決的，不可溶解的：insoluble matter 不可溶物質

inspect [ɪnˈspɛkt] ....★★★
v. 檢查，視察：The government sent somebody to inspect our school. 政府派人來視察我們學校。

inspection [ɪnˈspɛkʃən] ....★★★★
n. 視察，檢查：On closer inspection, it was found to be false. 經過更仔細的檢查，發現那是假的。

inspector [ɪnˈspɛktɚ] ....★★
n. 檢查員，監察員，巡官：The School Inspector visited our school. 督學視察了我們學校。

research [rɪˈsɝtʃ] ....★
n. 研究，調查：I was doing some research on Indian literature. 我正在研究一些印度文學。
v. 研究，調查：research on a subject 研究一個課題

resolve [rɪˈzɑlv] .... ★★★★★

v. 決定：By 1847 the residents of Oregon and the Hudson Bay Company had resolved all of their disputes over the control of the state. 到1847年，奧勒岡州的居民和哈得遜海灣公司已經解決了對州控制權的所有相關問題。

resolved [rɪˈzɑlvd] .... ★★★★★

adj. 下定決心的

review [rɪˈvju] .... ★★★★★

n. ①評論：I hope your new book gets good reviews. 我希望你的新書能獲得好評。②回顧，檢討，複查：After careful review of political events, he decided not to vote at all. 他認真回顧了多項政治事件後，決定不去投票了。③複習：general review 總複習

v. ①細查，審核：By law, state prisons must be reviewed once a year. 根據法律規定，國家監獄必須每年審核一次。②回顧，檢討，複查：He reviewed the whole of his past life. 他回顧了他過去的全部生活。③複習：You ought to review your lessons regularly. 你應該定期複習功課。④評論（作品等）：Susan has reviewed *The Times*. 蘇珊已經為《時代週刊》寫了評論。

search [sɜtʃ] .... ★★★★★

v. 搜，尋，探查：He glanced around the small room, searching for a place to sit. 他環視小屋，找個地方坐下。

n. 搜尋，探查：We eventually found the keys after a long search. 我們經過長時間的尋找，終於找到了鑰匙。

seek [sik] .... ★★★★★

v. ①尋找，追求：He went to seek the lawyer's advice. 他徵求律師的意見。②（+動詞不定式）試圖，企圖：I want to seek shelter from rain. 我想找個躲雨的地方。

stipulate [ˈstɪpjəˌlet] ....★

v. 約定，規定：stipulate a date of payment and a price 規定付款日和價格

trace [tres] .... ★★★★★

n. 痕跡

v. 跟蹤，追溯：Nineteenth-century scholars tried to trace the origins of modern languages to ancient Hebrew. 19世紀的學者們試圖從古希伯來語中找到現代語言的起源。

辨析
Analyze

chase, pursue, search, seek

1 **chase** *vt. & vi.* 「追逐，追捕，追求」，指快速追逐以達到抓住或趕走的目的，一般指具體的動作而不指抽象的事物：I saw a hunter chasing a fox on his horse. 我看見一個獵人騎著馬追趕一隻狐狸。

2 **pursue** *vt.* 「追趕，追蹤，追求」，正式用語，既指追趕或追捕某人，又指目標追求，還指「繼續，從事」：Two policemen pursued the robber down the street. 兩個警察沿街追捕那個搶劫犯。

3 **search** *vt.* 「搜索，尋找，探查」，指仔細、徹底地搜尋；常用「search … for…」句型，把搜索或尋找的地點作為賓語，for後面則接搜索或尋找的物件或目標：The police were searching the woods for the thief. 警方在搜查樹林，尋找那個小偷。

4 **seek** *vt.* 「尋求，追求，徵求（意見），請求（幫助）」，既可指對具體事物的尋找，也可以指對抽象事物的追求，把尋求或追求的物件作為賓語：I want to seek shelter from rain.

403

21

剩餘、補充、倖存相關辭彙

Exercise & Change

Vocabulary of Addition

---

overkill [ˈovɚˌkɪl] .... ★

n. 過多：government overkill in dealing with dissent 政府在處理不同意見時的過度行為

redundant [rɪˈdʌndənt] .... ★★★★

adj. 過多的，冗長的：redundant population in the cities 城市中的過多人口

remain [rɪˈmen] .... ★★★★★

v. ①剩下，餘留：It only remains for me to say that I'm wrong. 我能說的只有我錯了。②留待，尚需：One hazard remained to be overcome. 還有一項危險需要克服。③仍然是，依舊是：The result of these experiments remains a secret. 這些實驗的結果仍然是秘密。

n. ①殘餘，餘額：They discovered the remains of a dinosaur. 他們發現了恐龍的殘骸。②遺跡：Roman remains 羅馬遺跡

remainder [rɪˈmendɚ] .... ★★

n. 剩餘，剩餘物：I will go ahead with three of you, and the remainder can wait here. 我將和你們三個向前走，剩下的人可以在這裡等。

residual [rɪˈzɪdʒʊəl] .... ★

adj. 殘餘的：Some residual problems were very difficult to resolve. 有些剩餘的問題很難解決。

slag [slæg] .... ★

n. 渣滓：a slag brick 礦渣磚

spare [spɛr] .... ★★★★★

adj. 多餘的，剩下的，備用的：He devoted every spare moment to his hobby. 他將他所有的閒暇時間都用於個人愛好上了。

subsidiary [səbˈsɪdɪˌɛrɪ] .... ★

n. 支流

adj. 輔助的，附屬的：The Texas Opera Theater was established as a subsidiary of the Houston Grand Opera in order to give young singers performing experience. 德克薩斯歌劇院是作為休士頓大歌劇院的輔助設施而建的，提供給年輕的歌唱家表演的機會。

surplus [ˈsɝpləs] .... ★★★

n. 過剩，剩餘（物資）

adj. 過剩的：President Jefferson approved the idea of using surplus revenues of the government to promote the interests of commerce, industry, agriculture, and education. 傑佛遜總統以剩餘的政府稅收來促進商業、工業、農業和教育的發展。

survival [sɚˈvaɪvḷ] .... ★★★

n. 倖存，生存，倖存者，殘存物：The future survival of the bald eagle is still an important American ecological concern. 未來禿鷹的生存仍然是美國生態上的一個問題。

survive [sɚˈvaɪv] .... ★★

v. ①活下來，倖存：Numerous houses in the 18th century survived. 許多18世紀的房子倖存下來了。②從⋯中逃出，從（困境中）挺過來：Fishes are known to survive conditions well below freezing point. 魚類以能在冰點以下生存自如而出名。③比⋯活得長：Only his son survived him. 只有他兒子活得比他長。

辨析
Analyze

remain, retain

1 **remain** *vi.* 「仍然是，依舊是，留下，逗留，停留，剩餘，餘留，留待，尚需」，指剩下、留下、還有（不及物動詞），還指待在某地、繼續存在、一直是（連繫動詞，等於 continue to be）：After the fire, nothing remains of the house. 火災之後，房子燒光了。

2 **retain** *vt.* 「保持，保留」，還指記住、記得，及物動詞：China dishes retain heat longer than metal pans. 瓷盤比金屬平底鍋保溫。

405

22

落下、舉起、超出、來臨相關辭彙

Exercise & Change

Vocabulary of downs & ups

ascend [əˋsɛnd] .... ★★
v. 攀登，登高，追溯：The airplane ascended into the cloud. 飛機飛入雲端。

ascent [əˋsɛnt] .... ★★
n. 攀登，上升：the ascent of man from his primitive state to modern civilization 人類從原始狀態到現代文明狀態的進化

crash [kræʃ] .... ★★★★★
v. 撞碎：The elephant crashed through the forest. 大象衝進森林。

decadence [ˋdɛkədəns] .... ★★★★
n. 衰落，頹廢

descent [dɪˋsɛnt] .... ★★
n. 下降，降下，出身，家世：In Mississippi many individuals of Acadian descent, called Cajuns, still maintain a separate folk culture. 在密西西比州的許多阿卡迪亞人後裔，又稱為移居美國路易士安納州的法人後裔，仍然保留著一個獨立的民間文化。

drop [drɑp] .... ★★★★★
v. ①（使）滴下，（使）落下：He dropped his stick in the relay. 他在接力賽中掉了棒。②下降，降低：The temperature dropped suddenly. 氣溫突然降低。
【片語】drop in (on sb.) 偶然拜訪
n. 滴：a drop of water 一滴水

droplet [ˋdrɑplɪt] .... ★★★★★
n. 小滴

elevate [ˋɛləͺvet] .... ★★
v. 提高（思想），擡高：John Singleton Copley elevated the status of American portraiture through his series of paintings of notable eighteenth-century New Englanders. 約翰‧柯普利以著名的18世紀新英格蘭人的系列畫，使美國的肖像畫法水準得以提升。

exalt [ɪgˋzɔlt] .... ★
v. 稱讚，提升：The temple of Ephesus, one of the seven wonders of the ancient world, was built to exalt Artemis, the goddess of nature. 古代世界的七大奇蹟之一的埃弗斯廟是建來歌頌自然女神阿蒂米斯的。

exalted [ɪgˈzɔltɪd] .... ★

adj. 尊貴的，興奮的：He has an exalted sense of his importance to the project. 他誇大自己在這個項目中的重要性。

fall [fɔl] .... ★★★★★

v. ①跌倒：The old man has fallen off a ladder and hurt himself. 那老人從梯子上跌下來受了傷。②下降，減弱，墜落：The rain is falling hard. 雨下得正大。
【片語】① fall ill 生病② fall in love with sb. 愛上某人

n. 秋季：She left there in the fall of that year. 她那年的秋季離開了這裡。

forthcoming [ˌforθˈkʌmɪŋ] .... ★

adj. 即將到來的：When she was asked why she was absent for the party, no answer was forthcoming. 她被問到為什麼沒來參加晚會時，不作任何回答。

hike [haɪk] .... ★

v. 上升：Shopkeepers hiked their prices for the tourist trade. 店鋪老闆對觀光客大幅提高價錢。

hoist [hɔɪst] .... ★

v. 升起

n. 吊車：The sailors hoisted the flag and the ship was ready to start on a long voyage. 水手們升起船上的旗子，輪船準備啟程遠航。

precipitate [prɪˈsɪpəˌtet] .... ★

v. 猛然落下，突然陷入，引發：Meteorologists predict that, due to the greenhouse effect, the gradual warming of the Earth's atmosphere will precipitate large-scale flooding in coastal areas. 氣象學家預言，由於溫室效應，逐漸變暖的地球大氣將會引發沿海地區大規模的洪水。

rise [raɪz] .... ★★★★★

v. ①升起，上升：Clouds of birds rose from the tree tops. 一大群鳥從樹頂上飛上天空。②起立：He rose to greet the visitors. 他起身迎接客人。③上漲，增高：Prices rose by 10%. 價格上漲了一成。④起義，奮起：The settlers rose in revolt. 移民們奮起反抗。

n. ①上漲，增高：a rise in the cost of living 生活費用增加②起源，發生：the rise of a river 河的源頭
【片語】give rise to 引起，導致，為…的原因

sink [sɪŋk] .... ★★★★★

n. 水槽，水池

v. （使）下沉，（使）降低，（使）下垂：She sank back in her chair and sipped her drink. 她坐回椅子上，啜了口飲料。

slump [slʌmp] .... ★

v. 猛然落下：a stock market slump 股市暴跌

辨析
Analyze

arise, arouse, raise, rise

1 **arise** *vi.* 「產生，出現，發生」，常指麻煩、困難、問題產生：A new problem has arisen. 一個新的問題產生了。

2 **arouse** *vt.* 「引起，激起，喚起，喚醒」，指透過刺激引起反應：Her behavior aroused suspicion of the policeman. 她的舉動引起警察的懷疑。

3 **raise** *vt.* 「舉起，提高，提升」，指把事物向高處抬起：The blocks can raise the table eight inches. 這些磚塊可以把桌子擡高8英寸。

4 **rise** *vi.* 「升起，上升，起立，起床，上漲，增高，增加」，指事物本身由低處向高處移動：The sun rises in the east and sets in the west. 日出東方，日落西山。

23

增大、擴展、縮小相關辭彙

Vocabulary of Broadening & Reducing

Exercise & Change

運動、變化類名稱總匯

add [æd] .... ★★★★★
v. ①添加（後接sth. to sth.）：If the coffee is too strong, add some sugar. 假如咖啡太濃，就多加些糖。②進一步說或寫："And don't forget it," she added. 她又說道：「別忘了。」③增添（後可接 to）：His illness had added to their difficulties. 他的病給他們增加了困難。
【片語】add up to 合計達

amplification [͵æmpləfəˋkeʃən] .... ★★★
n. 擴大，放大：the amplification of knowledge 增廣見聞；a few final remarks added in amplification of an account 用以進一步闡明某一說法的附加結束語

amplify [ˋæmplə͵faɪ] .... ★★★
v. 放大：His attempts to amplify upon his remarks were drowned out by the jeers of the audience. 觀眾的嘲笑打消了他想詳述意見的意圖。

amplitude [ˋæmplə͵tjud] .... ★★★
n. 廣闊，豐富，（物理學名詞）振幅

augment [ɔgˋmɛnt] .... ★
v. 增大，增加：Ms. White augments her income by typing thesis and dissertation. 懷特小姐靠列印碩士論文和博士論文來增加她的收入。

booster [ˋbustɚ] .... ★★★
n. 起飛發動機，助推器

compress [kəmˋprɛs] .... ★★★
v. 壓縮，濃縮，壓擠：Wood blocks may compress a great deal under pressure. 木塊受壓時可縮小很多。

compression [kəmˋprɛʃən] .... ★★★
n. 壓縮，濃縮：compression ignition（發動機）壓縮點火；compression stroke 壓縮衝程

contract [ˋkɑntrækt] .... ★★★★★
v. 收縮，感染：Metal contracts as it cools. 金屬遇冷收縮。

contraction [kənˋtrækʃən] .... ★★★★★
n. 收縮："Won't" is a contraction of "will not". 「won't」是「will not」的縮寫。

dilate [daɪˋlet] .... ★
v. 使膨脹，使擴大：The pupils of your eyes dilate when you enter a dark room. 當你進入暗室時，眼睛的瞳孔就會擴大。

diminish [dəˋmɪnɪʃ] .... ★★
v. 減少，縮小

diminutive [dəˋmɪnjətɪv] .... ★
adj. 小的：The needlelike leaves of the giant redwood tree are diminutive, each scarcely a quarter of an inch long. 巨型紅木樹的針狀葉子很小，每片不足四分之一英尺長。

enlarge [ɪnˋlɑrdʒ] .... ★★★★
v. 擴大，放大，增大：We're enlarging the production scale to produce more and better computers. 我們在擴充生產規模以便生產出更多更好的電腦。

expand [ɪkˋspænd] .... ★★★★
v. 擴張：Today in the United States, adult education facilities face rising demand created by expanding leisure time. 今天在美國，成人教育設施面臨由於休閒時間增多所增加的需求。

expansion [ɪkˋspænʃən] .... ★★★
n. 擴大，擴充，發展，膨脹：His big book is an expansion of the little book he wrote before. 他的大本書是他以前寫的小本書的擴充版。

expansive [ɪkˋspænsɪv] .... ★★★
adj. 廣闊的，可擴張的，可膨脹的：After he'd had a few drinks, Charles became very expansive. 查理喝了幾杯酒，話就滔滔不絕了。

extension [ɪkˋstɛnʃən] .... ★★★★★
n. 延伸：We built an extension onto the school, so now we have two more classrooms. 我們把學校擴建，因此現在我們又多了兩間教室。

extensive [ɪkˋstɛnsɪv] .... ★★★★
adj. 大量的，廣泛的：The test is very extensive. 這次考試的範圍很大。

辨析 Analyze

compress, condense, contract, shrink

1. **compress** *vt.* 「壓緊，壓縮」，指把某物體擠壓到較小的空間，還指把文章等縮短：air-compressor 空氣壓縮機；They compressed the cotton into a bale. 他們把棉花擠成一包。

2. **condense** *vt. & vi.* 「（使）冷凝，（使）凝結，濃縮，壓縮，減縮」，指將蒸汽凝結成水，還指把水蒸發掉而使濃度增加：condensed water 蒸餾水；Moisture in the atmosphere condensed into dew during the night. 空氣中的水蒸氣在夜晚凝結成露珠。

3. **contract** *vi.* 「縮小，收縮」，多指金屬、肌肉等固體的收縮，也指縮成一團，還指「訂合同，簽（約）」：When he got worried, he contracted his brows. 他著急時就緊皺眉頭。

4. **shrink** *vt. & vi.* 「（使）起皺，（使）收縮，退縮，畏縮」，指布料、衣物等縮水，還可用於引申用法：Woolen cloth shrinks in hot water. / Washing wool cloth in hot water will shrink it. 毛料用熱水洗會縮水。

extensively [ɪkˈstɛnsɪvlɪ] .... ★★★★
adv. 廣泛地：For one to two years before
Election Day, a candidate for the
presidency of the United States travels
extensively around the country debating
national and international issues. 美國總
統選舉日到來前的一至兩年之內，候選人
在國內四處巡遊，辯論國內和國際問題。

shrink [ʃrɪŋk] .... ★★★★
v. 收縮：If wool is submerged in hot water, it
tends to shrink. 如果把羊毛浸在熱水中，它
就會縮水。

sprawl [sprɔl] .... ★
n. 擴展
v. 蔓延，伸開手腳：suburbs that sprawl out
into the countryside 向鄉間擴展的市郊；
sprawling on the sofa 平躺在沙發上

spread [sprɛd] .... ★★★★★
v. 伸開，展開：Please spread the coat over
bed. 請把衣服展開放在床上。

stretch [strɛtʃ] .... ★
n. 一段路程，路段，一段時間，伸展，範圍，
一片
v. 伸展，延伸，拉長：This material was just
stretched a little longer. 這種材料只能拉長
一點點。

width [wɪdθ] .... ★★★
n. 寬度，廣闊：What is the width of this
material? 這種材料有多寬？

24

隱藏、出現、消失、衝突相關辭彙

Vocabulary of Hide or Hair

arise [əˋraɪz] .... ★★★★★
v. ①出現，發現：How did the quarrel arise? 爭吵是怎麼發生的？②由…引起，起源於（後可接from / out of）：There are problems arising from the lack of communication. 有一些問題是由於缺乏相互溝通而引起的。

disappear [ˌdɪsəˋpɪr] .... ★★★★★
v. 不見，消失：The snow soon disappeared. 雪很快就消融了。

dissemble [dɪˋsɛmbl̩] .... ★★★★★
v. 隱藏，偽裝：dissemble anger with a smile 用微笑掩飾憤怒；dissemble understanding 裝出理解的樣子

divulge [dəˋvʌldʒ] .... ★
v. 宣佈，洩露：News men divulged that the two countries had met together secretly several times before they arrived at the peaceful agreement. 據新聞記者透露，這兩個國家在達成和平協議前已經秘密接觸多次了。

emerge [ɪˋmɝdʒ] ....★★★★
v. 出現：The Abstract Expressionist movement emerged in New York City in the 1940's. 抽象表現主義運動是於1940年代在紐約市出現的。

emergence [ɪˋmɝdʒəns] ....★★★★
n. 顯露，出現，發生，上升：The issue of loose construction versus strict construction of the United States Constitution contributed to the emergence of political parties. 對於美國政體要採鬆散建制或嚴密建制的爭論使得不同的黨派出現了。

emergency [ɪˋmɝdʒənsɪ] ....★★★★
n. 緊急情況，突然事件：The hospital has to treat emergencies such as car accidents. 這個醫院處理諸如車禍一類的急診。

exposure [ɪkˋspoʒɚ] .... ★★★
n. 曝光：These two pictures were taken with different exposures. 這兩張照片的曝光時間不同。

fade [fed] ....★★★★
v. 褪色，凋謝，（顏色）褪去，消失：Because of their chemical structure, synthetic dyes generally fade more slowly than natural ones. 合成染料由於其化學結構，一般比天然染料褪色要慢得多。

411

lurk [lɝk] .... ★

v. 躲藏：The villagers reported that the lion from the zoo was still lurking in nearby areas. 村民們報告說那隻逃出動物園的獅子還躲在附近。

pose [poz] .... ★★

v. 構成，(使)擺好姿勢：to pose an argument 提出議論

position [pəˋzɪʃən] .... ★★

n. ①位置：They tell the time by the position of the sun. 他們根據太陽的位置來判斷時間。②職位，職務：top management position 高階管理職位③姿勢，姿態：I helped her to a sitting position. 我幫她坐好。④見解，立場：What is their position on the proposal? 他們對此提案有何見解？

reveal [rɪˋvil] .... ★★★★★

v. 展現，揭露：For the wrath of God is revealed from Heaven. 上帝的憤怒是從天國顯露的。

revelation [ˌrɛvḷˋeʃən] .... ★★★★★

n. 顯示，揭露：Her true nature was a revelation to me. 她的真實性格對我而言是一項新發現。

uncover [ʌnˋkʌvɚ] .... ★★★

v. 揭開…的蓋子，揭露，移去覆蓋物：Many fossils are uncovered by changes in the surface of the earth. 許多化石隨著地表面暴露而顯現出來。

vanish [ˋvænɪʃ] .... ★★★★

v. 消失：I thought it would rain, but the clouds have vanished and it's a fine day. 我原以為要下雨了，可是雲散去後，是個好天氣。

辨析 Analyze

disappear, fade, vanish

1 **disappear** *vi.*「消失，不見」，常用語，用法很廣：That species disappeared in the 1970's. 該物種在1970年代消失了。

2 **fade** *vi.*「褪色，逐漸消失」，指逐漸消失、消退，尤指褪色、凋謝：As evening came the coastline faded into darkness. 夜幕降臨，海岸線漸漸消失在黑暗中。

3 **vanish** *vi.*「突然不見，消失，不復存在，絕跡」，指迅速消失：With a wave of his hand the magician made the rabbit vanish. 魔術師一揮手，把兔子變不見了。

辨析
Analyze

disclose, discover,
expose, reveal,
uncover

1 **disclose** *vt.*「揭露，洩露，披露」，指
透露原來有意對公眾保密的資訊，正式
用語：The secret was disclosed to the
public. 這個秘密已公諸於世。

2 **discover** *vt.*「發現，找到，發覺」：
Columbus discovered America in 1492.
哥倫布在1492年發現了美洲。

3 **expose** *vt.*「使暴露，顯露，揭露」，指
把隱蔽的東西暴露出來，還指暴露在危險
中、感受某種文化、膠捲曝光等，偏向貶
義：The soldiers in the open field were
exposed to risks / to the enemy's gunfire.
在開放空間的這些士兵暴露在危險之中／
敵人炮火之下。

4 **reveal** *vt.*「揭示，洩露」，指顯露出
（秘密的東西）、洩露、暴露、透露
等，中性詞：He drew the curtain and
revealed the map behind it. 他拉開廉子，
露出裡面的地圖。

5 **uncover** *vt.*「揭露，暴露」，指揭露、
暴露，還指揭開…的蓋子等：It was two
reporters who discovered and uncovered
the whole plot. 是兩名記者發現並揭露了
這整起陰謀。

12
運動，變化

25

模仿、發生、按照相關辭彙

Exercise & Change

Vocabulary of Happening

develop [dɪˋvɛləp] .... ★★★★★

v. 發展，產生，成長：The project began with a good premise but developed without imagination. 這項方案由一個好的前提開始，但在進展的過程中卻缺乏想像力。

development [dɪˋvɛləpmənt] .... ★★★★★

n. ①發展，形成，開發，研製：He is engaged in the development of his business. 他正致力於發展事業。②生長，進化：the great development of chest muscles in birds 異常發達的鳥類胸肌③事態發展，新情況：the latest development in foreign affairs 外交上的最新發展

disillusion [ˏdɪsɪˋluʒən] .... ★

n. 覺醒，幻滅

v. 使覺醒，使幻滅：They had thought that the new colony would be a paradise, but they were soon disillusioned. 他們原以為新殖民地是個天堂，但不久便從這幻想中覺醒了。

engender [ɪnˋdʒɛndə] .... ★

v. 產生：Not every cloud engenders a storm. 並非每片雲都能生成一場風暴。

evolution [ˏɛvəˋluʃən] .... ★★★★

n. 漸進，進化，演化：The evolution of heat from the sun is inestimable. 從太陽中放射出的熱是無法估計的。

evolutionary [ˏɛvəˋluʃənˏɛrɪ] .... ★★★★

adj. 進化的

evolve [ɪˋvɑlv] .... ★★★

v. 使進化，使發展：Biological oceanographers study how organisms live in the sea and how various species evolve and adapt to their environment. 海洋生物學家研究生物體在海洋中如何生存，以及各種各樣的生物是如何進化而適應環境的。

exert [ɪgˋzɝt] .... ★★★

v. 盡（力），施加（壓力等），發揮，運用：That council member has been exerting a lot of pressure on the company to accept the raw material of low quality. 那個市議員一直在對這間公司施加很大的壓力，要該公司接受這批劣質原料。

exertion [ɪgˋzɝʃən] .... ★★★
n. 盡力：increased exertion 加緊努力；too
　　much exertion to breathe 呼吸吃力

generate [ˋdʒɛnəˌret] .... ★★★★
v. 造成：The lantern fish generates light as it
　　swims about in the depths of the ocean. 燈
　　籠魚在深水中游動時會發光。

generating [ˋdʒɛnəˌretɪŋ] .... ★★★★
adj. 產生（電）的：generating station/plant
　　發電站／廠

generation [ˌdʒɛnəˋreʃən] .... ★★★★★
n. 一代，世代，產生：We belong to the same
　　generation. 我們是同世代的人。

imitate [ˋɪməˌtet] .... ★★★
v. 模仿：The modern process for making
　　rayon imitates the silkworm's method. 現代
　　人造纖維的製作過程是模仿蠶的吐絲方法而
　　來的。

imitation [ˌɪməˋteʃən] .... ★★
n. 模仿，仿效：His imitation of that singer is
　　perfect. 他模仿那位歌手模仿得維妙維肖。

mimicry [ˋmɪmɪkrɪ] ....★
n. 模仿，擬態：aggressive mimicry 模擬攻擊

occur [əˋkɝ] .... ★★★★★
v. ①發生，發現，存在：When did the
　　accident occur? 事故是什麼時候發生的？②
　　被想起，被想到：A good idea has occurred
　　to me. 我有一個好主意。

occurrence [əˋkɝəns] .... ★★★
n. 發生，出現，事件，事故：daily
　　occurrences 日常發生的事

pop [pɑp] .... ★★★★
n. 流行音樂，砰的一聲

simulate [ˋsɪmjəˌlet] .... ★★★★★
v. 偽裝，扮演：simulate death 裝死

415

26

生產、製造、建立、解決相關辭彙

Vocabulary of Production

Exercise & Change

construct [kən`strʌkt] ....★★★★
v. 建造，構造：to construct a hexagon within a circle 在圓内作一個六邊形

create [krɪ`et] ....★★★★★
v. ①創造，創作：The *Bible* says that God creates the world. 《聖經》說上帝創造了世界。②引起，產生：It's bound to create trouble sooner or later. 這肯定遲早會引起麻煩。

erect [ɪ`rɛkt] ....★★★★
v. 建設，直立：Serious singers support their vocal production by sitting or standing with their torsos erected. 嚴肅音樂的歌唱家藉著坐直或站直身體來幫助發聲。

establish [ə`stæblɪʃ] ....★★★★★
v. 建立，設立，創辦，確立，使確認：The Girl Scouts of America was established by Juliette Gordon Low in 1912. 美國女童子軍是由朱莉特‧羅在1912年創立的。

established [ə`stæblɪʃt] ....★★★★★
adj. 確認的：an established fact 既成事實； an established invalid 慢性病人

establishment [ɪs`tæblɪʃmənt] ....★★★★★
n. 建立的機構或組織，設立：These two hotels are both excellent establishments. 這兩家旅館都是出色的商業機構。

found [faʊnd] ....★★★★★
v. 創立，創辦，創建：The company was founded in 1983. 這家公司建立於1983年。

foundation [faʊn`deʃən] ....★★★★★
n. 基礎，地基，建立，創辦，基金：Observation and description provide the foundation for the study of psychology. 觀察和描述是研究心理學的基礎。

grow [gro] ....★★★★★
v. ①生長，發育，增長，發展，漸漸變得：Truth never grows old. 真理是永恆的。②種植，栽培：Chinese farmers grow rice, wheat and corn. 中國農民種植稻子、小麥和玉米。
【片語】grow up 成熟，成年，形成，興起

innovation [ˌɪnəˈveʃən] .... ★★
n. 改革，革新：The use of wild animals in circuses was an innovation first introduced in the United States. 把野生動物用來從事馬戲表演是最初引進美國的一項革新。

manual [ˈmænjʊəl] .... ★★★★
adj. 用手的，人工作業的，手工的：manual work 手工勞動

manufacture [ˌmænjəˈfækʃɚ] ..... ★★★★★
v. （大量）製造，加工：His books seem to have been manufactured rather than composed. 他的作品像是以機器製造出來的，而不是創作的。
n. （大量）製造，產品，製造人，製造商

produce .... ★★★★★
v. [prəˈdjus] ①生產，製造，產生：This drug has produced terrible effects on children. 這種藥物已經在兒童身上產生了不良的作用。②顯示，出示：He couldn't produce any evidence. 他拿不出任何證據。
n. [ˈprɑdjus] 產品，農產品

product [ˈprɑdəkt] .... ★★★★★
n. ①產品，產物：Important products of south Africa are fruits and gold. 南非的主要產品為水果和黃金。②乘出的數：The product of 3 multiplied by 2 multiplied by 6 is 36. 3×2×6 ＝36

production [prəˈdʌkʃən] .... ★★★★★
n. ①生產，產量：The production has increased in this factory. 這家工廠的產量增加了。②產品，作品：early production 早期作品

productive [prəˈdʌktɪv] .... ★★
adj. 生產的，多產的，豐饒的，富饒的：a productive force 生產力

productivity [ˌprodʌkˈtɪvətɪ] .... ★★
n. 生產率

reclaim [rɪˈklem] .... ★★★★★
v. 開墾，收回：reclaim valuable materials from wastes 從廢物中回收有價值的材料

solvable [ˈsɑlvəbl] .... ★★★★
adj. 可解釋的，可解決的：solvable problems 可以解決的問題

27

鑄造、精煉、安裝、維修相關辭彙

Vocabulary of Construction

amend [əˋmɛnd] .... ★

v. 修正，改進：amend the UN Charter 修改聯合國憲章

fabricate [ˋfæbrɪˏket] .... ★

v. 製造，偽造：The reason he gave for his absence was obviously fabricated. 他所說的缺席理由顯然是編造的。

install [ɪnˋstɔl] .... ★★★★★

v. 安裝，設置：I installed myself in front of the fire. 我在爐火前就坐。

installation [ˏɪnstəˋleʃən] .... ★★★★★

n. （整套）裝置，安裝

mend [mɛnd] .... ★★★

v. 改正，修正，改進：In 1893, Williams became the first surgeon to mend a tear in the pericardium, the sac around the heart. 威廉斯於1893年成為第一個做心包膜（包在心臟上的囊）破損修補手術的人。

modify [ˋmɑdəˏfaɪ] .... ★★★

v. 修改：The equipment may be modified to produce VCD sets. 這套設備經過改裝可以用來生產影音光碟機。

patch [pætʃ] .... ★★★★

n. 小片，小塊，補丁：The twinkling of the stars is caused by warm and cool patches of air drifting through the Earth's atmosphere. 我們看到的星星閃爍現象，是由地球大氣層的冷氣流和熱氣流相互流動而產生的。

v. 補，修補

prune [prun] .... ★

v. 修剪：The rose may grow as a low bush or as a tree, depending on how it is pruned. 根據修剪情況的不同，玫瑰可以成為低矮的灌木，也能成為樹一般高的植物。

repair [rɪˋpɛr] .... ★★★★

n. 修理，修補：He has left his car for repairs in the garage. 他把汽車留在車庫裡等待修理。

v. ①修理，修補：No one knows how to repair the engine. 沒有人知道怎樣修理這部發動機。②補救，糾正：repair a mistake 補救錯誤

smelt [smɛlt] .... ★★★★

v. 冶煉：smelt copper 煉銅

28

分類、總結相關辭彙

Vocabulary of Classes & Summary

absorbing [əb`sɔrbɪŋ] .... ★★★★
adj. 引人入勝的：These topics are absorbing to almost anyone. 這些主題幾乎能吸引任何人。

analyse/analyze [`ænḷˌaɪz] .... ★★★
v. 分析，分解：The chemist analysed the new tonic and found it containing poison. 藥劑師對這種新補藥化驗分析，發現有毒。

analysis [ə`næləsɪs] .... ★★★★★
n. 分析：Each chapter of the book is an analysis of a well-known painting. 書的每一章就是一幅名畫的分析介紹。

classification [ˌklæsəfə`keʃən] .... ★★★★
n. 分類：climatic classification 氣候分類

classify [`klæsəˌfaɪ] .... ★★★
v. 分類，分等，劃分：Annie Jump Cannon's job as an assistant at the Harvard University observatory was to classify stars according to their spectra. 安妮・康儂在哈佛大學實驗室當助手時的工作，是按照光譜來劃分恒星。

conclude [kən`klud] .... ★★★★★
v. 推斷出，斷定，結束：The doctor concluded that the patient's disease was cancer. 醫生斷定病人患的是癌症。

conclusion [kən`kluʒən] .... ★★★★★
n. ①結論，推論：I came to the conclusion that she was lying. 我推斷她是在說謊。②結尾：I found the conclusion of his book very interesting. 我覺得他的書的結語很有意思。③締造，議定

conclusive [kən`klusɪv] .... ★★★★★
adj. 決定性的，最後的：conclusive evidence/proof 確證，真憑實據，結論性的證據

dissection [dɪ`sɛkʃən] .... ★★
n. 解剖，切開

inconclusive [ˌɪnkən`klusɪv] .... ★★★★★
adj. 非結論性的：The jury found the evidence against the prisoner inconclusive and acquitted him. 陪審團發現控告囚犯的罪證不確鑿，所以釋放了他。

運動、變化

Unit 13
肢體動作名稱總匯
Movement

01

工作、行為、從事相關辭彙

Vocabulary of Behavior & Work

behave [bɪˋhev] ....★★★★

v. ①表現，舉止，舉動：You should behave better. 你應該表現得好一些。②（機器等）運轉，開動：How is your new car behaving? 你的新車還好開嗎？③檢查（自己的）行為（後接反身代詞做賓語）

behavior [bɪˋhevjɚ] ....★★★★★

n. 行為：A child's behavior often changes in the presence of strangers. 小孩子在有陌生人的情況下，行為舉止常常不一樣。

deed [did] ....★★★★★

n. ①行為，行動：be rewarded for one's good deeds 因做善事而得到報答②功勳：deeds of arms 戰功③契約：Do you have the deed to the house? 你有這間房子的契約嗎？

errand [ˋɛrənd] ....★★

n. 差使，差事：The boy quickly went on an errand with money clasped in his hands. 男孩手中握著錢快速地跑出去買東西。

induction [ɪnˋdʌkʃən] ....★

n. 感應，入門：induction into the presidency 總統就任儀式；induction principle 歸納法原則；air induction 吸氣

inductive [ɪnˋdʌktɪv] ....★

adj. 感應的，誘導的：inductive reasoning 歸納推理；the inductive capacity 電感容量，電容

manner [ˋmænɚ] ....★★★★★

n. ①方式，方法：a meal prepared in the Chinese manner 中式餐②態度，舉止：He has a pleasant manner. 他的舉止得宜。③禮貌，規矩：It's bad manners to eat like that. 那樣吃東西很不禮貌。

misdeed [mɪsˋdid] ....★★★★★

n. 不檢行為：The selection committee decided to overlook his past misdeeds. 甄選委員會決定不追究他過去的不檢行為。

occupancy [ˋɑkjəpənsɪ] ....★★★★

n. 佔有，居住：during the occupancy of his post 在他任職期間

occupation [ˌɑkjəˈpeʃən] .... ★★★★
n. 佔領，佔有，職業，工作：Alice Hamilton was one of the first doctors to study the relation between one's health and one's occupation. 艾麗絲‧漢米爾頓是最早研究人體健康和其職業之間關係的醫生之一。

occupational [ˌɑkjəˈpeʃənl̩] .... ★★★★
adj. 與職業有關的，職業的：an occupational disease 職業病

profession [prəˈfɛʃən] .... ★★★★
n. 職業，自由職業：I don't know what profession would suit me. 我不知道什麼職業適合我。

professional [prəˈfɛʃənl̩] .... ★★★★★
adj. 職業的，專業的，專門的
n. 專業人員，內行，專家：For professional footballers, injuries are an occupational hazard. 對於職業足球運動員來說，受傷是職業本身帶來的危險。

task [tæsk] .... ★★★★★
n. 任務，工作，作業：fulfill a task 完成一項任務

undertake [ˌʌndəˈtek] .... ★★★★★
v. 從事，進行：During her husband's presidency, Jacqueline Kennedy undertook the coordination of the White House restoration. 賈桂琳‧甘迺迪在她丈夫的總統任內，進行了白宮修繕的協調工作。

work [wɝk] .... ★★★★★
n. ①工作，勞動：Many workers are out of work. 許多工人下班了。②職業，工作，差事：I have to apply for the work. 我不得不應徵那份工作。③（用作複數，後接單數動詞）工廠：The works produced soap. 該工廠生產肥皂。
v. ①工作，勞動，做事，幹活：We ought to keep healthy, study hard and work well. 我們應該保持健康、認真唸書及努力工作。②（機器）運轉，發動：The lift doesn't work. 這部電梯壞了。③（某事物，如計畫、方法、藥等）有效，起作用，行得通：Your idea just won't work. 你的想法是行不通的。④（通過努力）創造出，完成，做出，造成⑤捏成，揉，搓（成）

【片語】① at work 在工作，忙於② work out 解決，計算出，解答出

workshop [ˈwɝkˌʃɑp] .... ★★★★
n. 車間，工作，作坊；研討會，講習班：a summer workshop in short story writing 短篇小說寫作的暑期班

辨析 Analyze

employment, job, occupation, profession, work

1. **employment** *n.* 「職業，雇傭」，指謀生手段的就業、職業，與失業相對應，不可數名詞：He is out of employment, so he is seeking employment. 他失業了，正在找工作。

2. **job** *n.* 「工作」，指職業，也指具體的一件工作，還指責任等，用法很廣，可數名詞：Eventually, Mary got a job as a waitress. 瑪麗最後找到了一個服務生的工作。

3. **occupation** *n.* 「從事的活動」，指職業，一般用於填表、瞭解資訊等，還指佔領等：Please state your name, address and occupation. 請說您的名字、地址和職業。

4. **profession** *n.* 「職業，自由職業」，指知識型職業：She intends to make teaching her profession. 她想當個教師。

5. **work** *n.* 「工作，勞動」，指工作、勞動、職業、學習等，用法很廣，不可數名詞：The broken window must be the work of that boy. 那扇破窗肯定是那個男孩子的傑作。

肢體動作

02

花費、節省、吃、喝、咬相關辭彙

Vocabulary of Expense

Movement

肢體動作名稱總匯

austerity [ɔ'stɛrətɪ] .... ★
n. 節儉，嚴峻：A peculiar austerity marked almost all his judgments of men and actions. 他對於人及行為的判斷，幾乎都帶著一種特殊的苛刻。

avarice ['ævərɪs] .... ★
n. 貪婪：She agreed to marry the aged millionaire more because of avarice than because of love. 她答應嫁給這個年邁的百萬富翁，貪婪的成分多於愛情。

avaricious [ævə'rɪʃəs] .... ★
adj. 貪婪的，貪心的：Winston became quite avaricious in his late life. 溫斯頓在他的晚年變得相當貪婪。

avid ['ævɪd] .... ★
adj. 熱切的，貪婪的：Double Eagle, the first transatlantic balloon, was greeted by avid crowds in France. 第一隻橫渡大西洋的熱氣球「雙鷹」，受到法國熱情群眾的歡迎。

bite [baɪt] .... ★★★★★
v. 咬，叮：Giant shovels are biting off big chunks from the hill. 巨型挖土機正把小山頭一大口一大口地鏟掉。
n. 一口，咬，叮

blow [blo] .... ★★★★★
n. 一擊，打擊
v. 吹，噴（水，氣）：The winds blow across the sea, pushing little waves into bigger and bigger ones. 風吹過海面，把小的波浪推向前，形成越來越大的波浪。

chew [tʃu] .... ★★★
n. 咀嚼，玩味：We chew our food well before we swallow it. 我們在吞下食物之前要細細咀嚼。

consume [kən'sjum] .... ★★★★
v. 消費，消耗：Crayfish, small freshwater crustacean similar to lobsters, are consumed by inhabitants of the Mississippi River Basin. 小龍蝦是一種像龍蝦的小型淡水生甲殼類動物，為密西西比河盆地的居民所食用。

consumer [kən'sjumə] .... ★★★★
n. 顧客，消費者：The consumers complained about the poor quality of the electronic products. 消費者抱怨電子產品品質低劣。

consumption [kən'sʌmpʃən] .... ★★★★

n. 消費（量），消耗：The nation's consumption of coal decreased continuously last year. 去年該國的耗煤量持續下降。

cost [kɔst] .... ★★★★★

v. 價值，花費：This book costs me twenty dollars. 這本書花了我 20 元。

covetous ['kʌvɪtəs] .... ★

adj. 貪心的：covetous of learning 渴望學習

dip [dɪp] .... ★★★

v. 醮，浸：The old professor dipped his one finger into the liquid, then showed it to the students. 老教授將一根手指伸進液體，然後向學生們展示了一下。

eat [it] .... ★★★★★

v. 吃，喝（湯）：He ate an apple after lunch. 他在午飯後吃了個蘋果。

【片語】eat up 吃完，吃光

economize [ɪ'kɑnəmaɪz] .... ★★★★★

v. 節儉：The best that can be said of this method is that it economizes on thought. 這種方法最好的一點是它不費腦筋。

engulf [ɪn'gʌlf] .... ★

v. 吞沒，吞食：The spring tide engulfed the beach houses. 春潮淹沒了海灘上的房子。

expend [ɪk'spɛnd] .... ★★★★

v. 消費：Every effort seemed to expend her spirit's force. 每一次的努力看起來都像是耗盡了她的精力。

expenditure [ɪk'spɛndɪtʃɚ] .... ★★

n. 支出，消費，經費：administrative expenditure 行政開支

expense [ɪk'spɛns] .... ★★★★

n. ①花費：A car for a family is not worth the expense. 對一個家庭來說，花大錢買這輛汽車是不值得的。②費用：travel expense 旅行費用

expensive [ɪk'spɛnsɪv] .... ★★★

adj. 昂貴的，費用大的：Any illness of the poor is the most expensive misfortune. 窮人生一點病都是極大的不幸。

frugal ['frugl] .... ★

adj. 節約的：a frugal supper of bread and cheese 只有麵包和乳酪的晚餐

frugality [fru'gæləti] .... ★

n. 節約，簡樸

gnaw [nɔ] .... ★

v. 啃，咬：Hunger gnawed at the prisoners. 饑餓折磨著犯人們。

gobble ['gɑbl] .... ★

v. 吞食，狼吞虎嚥：The children gobbled up their food and rushed out to play. 孩子們急急忙忙吞下食物，便跑出去玩了。

gorge [gɔrdʒ] .... ★

n. 峽谷

v. 塞飽：gorge themselves with candy 用糖果塞飽

greed [grid] .... ★

n. 貪婪，貪心：Many attach to competition the stigma of selfish greed. 許多人把競爭和自私貪婪的恥辱連在一起。

greedy ['gridɪ] .... ★★★

adj. 貪婪的，渴望的：greedy for the opportunity to prove their ability 渴望證明他們能力的機會

gulp [gʌlp] .... ★

v. 梗塞，吞咽：to gulp down a cup of tea 一口氣喝下一杯茶

imbibe [ɪm'baɪb] .... ★

v. 飲：Plants imbibe nourishment usually through their leaves and roots. 植物通常經由葉和根吸收養分。

improvident [ɪm'prɑvədənt] .... ★

adj. 浪費的

lick [lɪk] .... ★★★

v. 舔：The cat cleaned itself by licking its hair. 貓舔身上的毛使自己乾淨。

nibble [`nɪbḷ] .... ★

v. 細咬：Cactus plants have spines that prevent animals from nibbling them. 仙人掌類植物的刺可以防止其被動物吃掉。

prodigal [`prɑdɪgḷ] .... ★

adj. 浪費的：The country has been prodigal of its forests. 這個國家的森林正遭受過度的採伐。

ravenous [`rævɪnəs] .... ★

adj. 極餓的，貪婪的：ravenous for power 對權力極其嚮往的

savings [`sevɪŋz] .... ★★★★

n. 儲蓄：He used his savings to buy the car. 他用存的錢買了這輛車。

smoke [smok] .... ★★★★★

n. 煙，煙塵

v. 抽煙：I don't smoke but he smokes cigar. 我不抽煙，但他抽雪茄。

【片語】No smoking! 禁止吸煙！

sniff [snɪf] .... ★★

v. 用鼻子吸，嗅，聞：When she had stopped crying, she sniffed and dried her eyes. 她停止哭泣，抽著鼻子擦乾眼淚。

snore [snor] .... ★★

v. 打呼嚕，打鼾：Grandfather was snoring. 爺爺在打著呼。

spend [spɛnd] .... ★★★★★

v. ①用錢，花費：What did you spend for that book? 那本書你花了多少錢？②度過，消磨：I have spent all day looking for you. 我花了一整天找你。

squander [`skwɑndɚ] .... ★

v. 揮霍，浪費：Poor planning led him to squander his entire fortune. 他因為缺乏規劃性，花光了全部財產。

suck [sʌk] .... ★★★★★

v. 吸，吮：Ken was sucking an orange. 肯在吸柳橙汁。

swallow [`swɑlo] .... ★★★★

n. 燕子

v. 吞下，咽下，吞咽，併吞，取消：She swallowed some milk. 她喝下了幾口牛奶。

thrift [θrɪft] .... ★

n. 節儉，節約：To practice thrift is a virtue. 節儉是一種美德。

thrifty [`θrɪftɪ] .... ★

adj. 節儉的，節約的：a thrifty housewife 勤儉持家的主婦；a thrifty tree 枝葉繁茂的樹

waste [west] .... ★★★★★

v. 浪費，未充分利用：waste one's time and money on paying bribes 將時間和金錢浪費於賄賂

n. ①浪費，糟踏：What (a) waste of energy! 這真是浪費體力！②廢料，棄物：toxic waste 有毒廢物

adj. ①廢棄的，丟棄的，無用的：waste paper 廢紙②荒蕪的：waste land 荒蕪的土地

肢體動作名稱總匯

Movement

03

行走、跑步、跳躍、爬、通過、鍛鍊、飛相關辭彙

Vocabulary of Physical Activities

across [əˋkrɔs] .... ★★★★★
prep. ①橫越，穿過：Go across the street. 穿過這條馬路。②在…對面，在…另一面：The post office is just across the street. 郵局在馬路對面。
adv. 橫過，穿過，橫斷：You must come across and see me. 你一定要過來看我。

act [ækt] .... ★★★★★
n. 行為，動作：The thief is caught in the act. 小偷被逮個正著。
vt. 表演：He acted Hamlet very well. 他扮演哈姆雷特極其出色。

action [ˋækʃən] .... ★★★★★
n. 作用，行動：The women, though trained in military tactics, are not sent into action. 這些婦女雖然受過戰術訓練，但並沒被派去打仗。

active [ˋæktɪv] .... ★★★★★
adj. 活動的，活躍的：Marginal mines that are active only when prices are high. 邊境的礦井只有在價錢高的時候才會運作。

activity [ˋæktɪvətɪ] .... ★★★★★
n. 能動性，活動：There are not quite so much activity in the gold market. 黃金市場交易不怎麼熱絡。

bounce [baʊns] .... ★★★
v. 使反射，彈回，發射：The children were bouncing a ball. 孩子們在拍皮球。

bound [baʊnd] .... ★★★★★
v. 跳躍，跳著跑：His heart bounded with joy. 他高興得心臟砰砰直跳。
adj. 負有義務的
n. 範圍，界限：Within the bounds of given data, the biographer seeks to illuminate factual information about a person and transform it into insight. 傳記作者在給定的資料範圍內，試圖闡釋某個人的真實情形，並且將其轉化為可理解的文字。

climb [klaɪm] .... ★★★★
v. 攀登，爬：climb (up) the tree 爬樹

crawl [krɔl] .... ★★★★
v. 爬行，慢行：The baby crawled towards his mother. 嬰孩向他媽媽爬去。

creep [krip] .... ★★★
v. 爬行，躡手躡腳地走動：Starfish, five-armed sea creatures, creep across coral reefs by using suckers on the bottom of their arms. 海星是一種有五隻手臂的海洋動物，以手臂底部的吸附器官在珊瑚上爬行。

crisscross [ˈkrɪsˌkrɔs] .... ★★★★★
v. 交叉：crisscrossed the country on a speech tour 在全國巡迴演說

dive [daɪv] .... ★★★
v. 潛水，跳水
n. 潛水，跳水：A traditional way of gathering oysters is to dive from small boats and collect them from the bottom of the ocean. 採集牡蠣的傳統方法是從小船潛入水中，在海底採集。

diver [ˈdaɪvɚ] .... ★★★
n. 潛水者，跳水者：a tall diver who excelled in performing the jackknife 擅長表演鐮刀式跳水的高大跳水者

exercise [ˈɛksɚˌsaɪz] .... ★★★★★
n. ①練習，習題：I did exercises in English grammar. 我做了英語文法練習。②訓練，鍛煉：Walking is a kind of good exercise. 散步是一種很好的運動形式。

fluster [ˈflʌstɚ] .... ★★
v. 使慌亂
n. 慌張：She was put in a fluster by the unexpected guests. 不速之客的到來弄得她很慌張。

flutter [ˈflʌtɚ] .... ★★
v. 拍翅，振翼，飄動：She fluttered her bristly black lashes as swiftly as butterflies' wings. 她如蝴蝶翅膀一般閃著她濃密的睫毛。

fly [flaɪ] .... ★★★★★
v. ①飛行：Some birds are flying in the air. 一些鳥正在天空中飛翔。②乘飛機飛行：They flew from London to Pairs last Saturday. 他們上週六從倫敦飛往巴黎。③空運（乘客，貨物）：He flew his car to New York. 他把他的轎車空運到紐約。

辨析
Analyze

act, action, acting, activity, conduct, deed

1 **act** n.「行動，做事，舉止，表現」，常指瞬間的、不可分的一個動作，還指較為抽象的某種行為：He was caught in the act of stealing. 他偷東西時被逮個正著。

2 **action** n.「行動，行動過程」，強調動作的過程，還可表示抽象概念，體現在固定搭配上：Actions speak louder than words. 坐而言不如起而行。

3 **acting** n.「表演，演出」：His acting was quite first-rate. 他的表演是一流的。

4 **activity** n.「活動」，指做某項具體的活動，常用複數，如social activities（社交活動）：When I was attending college, there were a lot of recreational activities. 我上大學的時候，文藝娛樂活動很豐富。

5 **conduct** n.「舉止，行為」，指從道義上和行為準則上看正確與否的行為：She described his conduct as disgusting. 她把他的行為說成是令人反感的。

6 **deed** n.「行為，事蹟」，一是指與言語相對應的行為，二是指良好的、英勇的行為：Deeds, not words, are needed. 需要的是行動，而不是言語。

肢體動作名稱總匯

Movement

428

gallop [ˈgæləp] .... ★

n. 奔跑：Events were proceeding at a gallop. 事情正在迅速進行之中。

glide [glaɪd] .... ★★★

v. 滑動，溜走：a submarine gliding through the water 潛艇在水中自由行駛

hobble [ˈhɑbl̩] .... ★★★

v. 跛行，束縛雙腿（尤指馬腿）：The horse has been hobbled so that it can't run away. 馬的兩條腿被綁住了，所以跑不了。

hop [hɑp] .... ★★

v. 跳躍：hop a ditch two feet wide 跳過兩英尺寬的水溝

hover [ˈhʌvɚ] .... ★★

v. 徘徊，躊躇，翱翔，盤旋：hovering around the speaker's podium 在演講臺邊徘徊

jog [dʒɑg] .... ★

v. 慢跑：Many old people go jogging in the park in the early morning. 許多老年人在大清早到公園去慢跑。

jump [dʒʌmp] .... ★★★★★

v. ①跳躍：The children jumped for joy. 孩子們歡呼雀躍。②猛漲，猛增：The price of steel jumped sharply last year. 去年鋼材的價格急劇上漲。③跳過，越過：The horse jumped the fence. 馬跳過了柵欄。

n. ①跳，躍：long jump / high jump 跳遠／跳高②猛漲，激增：the jump of profits 利潤劇增

kneel [nil] .... ★★★

v. 跪，跪下：She knelt down to pull a weed from the flowerbed. 她跪下來從花壇裡拔了根草。

leap [lip] .... ★★★★★

n. 飛躍，跳躍：Salmon have been known to leap up waterfall as high as eleven feet in their journey to the places where they spawn. 鮭魚因能夠在到達產卵地途中跳過高達 11 英尺的瀑布而聞名。

lie [laɪ] .... ★★★★★

v. ①躺下，平放，位於：He lay awake all night thinking of the problem. 他琢磨著問題，徹夜未眠。②說謊：It's not necessary that I lie to you. 我沒必要對你說謊。

n. 謊言，謊話

participant [pɑrˈtɪsəpənt] .... ★★

n. 參加者：participant observation（社會學家與其研究對象共同生活所進行的）現場觀察研究

participate [pɑrˈtɪsəˌpet] .... ★★★★

v. 參加，參與：If only I could participate in your good fortune. 要是我能分享你的好運就好了。

participation [pɑrˌtɪsəˈpeʃən] .... ★★

n. 參加，參與：workers' participation in management 勞工參加管理

participative [pɑrˈtɪsəˌpetɪv] .... ★★

adj. 提供參加機會的

prance [præns] .... ★

vi.（馬）騰躍：The children pranced about with delight. 孩子們高興得活蹦亂跳。

ramble [ˈræmbl̩] .... ★

v. 漫步：They rambled along the woodland paths. 他們沿著林中小徑漫步。

roam [rom] .... ★

v. 漫步，漫遊：Millions of bison roamed over the prairies from Canada to Central Mexico. 數百萬的美洲野牛從加拿大的大草原上漫遊到墨西哥中部的大草原。

rush [rʌʃ] .... ★★★★★

v. ①衝，奔，急速流動：The children rushed out into the garden. 孩子們衝進花園裡。②倉促行動：There is plenty of time, we needn't rush. 時間充足，我們不必急急忙忙。③匆忙地做：People were rushing to buy the newspaper. 人們急著去買報紙。④催促：Don't rush me, let me think about it. 別催我，讓我想一想這件事。

n. 衝，急速行動

adj.（交通）繁忙的：during the rush hours 在
　（交通）尖峰時間

scramble [ˋskræmbl̩] .... ★
v. 爬，攀登：The children scrambled up the
　hill. 孩子們爬上了這座小山。

shackle [ˋʃækl̩] .... ★
v. 加桎梏，束縛：economic shackles that
　precluded further investment 阻止進一步投
　資的經濟障礙

shuffle [ˋʃʌfl̩] .... ★
v. 攪亂，混合：shuffle cards 洗牌；shuffle the
　cards〔喻〕改變機構人事，改變政策

skim [skɪm] .... ★★★
v. 略讀，掠過：The swallows were skimming
　over the water. 燕子正掠過水面。

skip [skɪp] .... ★★★★
vt. ①跳過②遺漏③不吃，誤掉
vi. ①跳，蹦②跳繩③略過

stray [stre] .... ★★
adj. 漂泊的，走失的：a stray dog 流浪狗

stride [straɪd] .... ★★
adj. 跨越：He strode angrily into the
　classroom. 他氣憤地跨進教室。

stumble [ˋstʌmbl̩] .... ★★
v. 絆（跌），絆倒，絆一下腳：She stumbled
　and hurt herself. 她跌倒了，摔傷了自己。

through [θru] .... ★★★★★
prep. ①穿越，穿過，通過：The river flows
　through the city from west to east. 這條
　河從西向東穿越城市。②從頭到尾，從開
　始到結束：He stayed there through the
　winter. 他在那待了一個冬天。
adv. 從頭到尾，自始至終：He read the new
　Chinese textbook through. 他把新的中文
　課本讀了一遍。

辨析
Analyze

hop, jump, leap, plunge, skip參見hop

1　**hop** *vt. & vi.*「單足跳，齊足跳躍，跳上
交通工具」：The rabbit hopped across
the field. 兔子跳著穿過田野。

2　**jump** *vt. & vi.*「跳躍，越過，跳過」，
指向上跳、向下跳、向前跳，常用語，
可用於引申義：to jump across a stream
/ over a ditch / into the river / out of the
water / through the window 跳過一條小河
／跳過一條溝／跳進溪裡／跳出水／跳進
窗裡

3　**leap** *vt. & vi.*「跳躍，衝，越過」，尤
指一大段的跳躍：The monkeys leaped
from tree to tree. 這些猴子從一棵樹跳到
另一棵樹上。

4　**plunge** *vt. & vi.*「縱身投入，一頭進入，
（猛地）把…投入或刺進」，指猛地跳
進、栽下、浸入、陷入，還指猛跌、突
降：He plunged his dirty hands into the
water. 他把一雙髒手放到水中。

5　**skip** *vi.*「跳，蹦跳，跳繩，跳過，略
過，漏過」，指輕快敏捷地跳，可用於引
申義：The little girl is skipping rope. 那個
小女孩在跳繩。

throughout [θru`aʊt] .... ★★★★★

prep. 遍及，貫穿：I could feel the tension throughout her body. 我能感覺到她全身緊張。

adv. 到處，自始至終，貫穿全部地：Throughout the journey, Rose remained silent. 柔絲在整趟旅程中，一直保持沈默。

tramp [træmp] .... ★★

v. 步行，跋涉：tramp the fields 走過田野

transfix [træns`fɪks] .... ★

v. 刺穿：transfix an enemy with a sword 用刺刀刺穿敵人

trot [trɑt] .... ★

v. (馬) 小跑，慢跑：The horse trotted along the road. 馬沿著路小跑。

trudge [trʌdʒ] .... ★

v. 跋涉，吃力地走：He trudged the deserted road for hours. 他沿著荒蕪的路走了數小時。

tumble [`tʌmbl̩] .... ★★

v. 摔跤，跌倒，打滾，翻騰，翻筋斗：She tumbled downstairs. 她從樓梯上摔了下來。

via [`vaɪə] .... ★★★★

prep. 經過，通過，經由：Archaeologists think that Native American originally reached the North American Continent via the Bering Strait between ten and twenty thousand years ago. 考古學家認為，美洲原住民原本是在一萬到兩萬年以前經由白令海峽到達北美大陸的。

waddle [`wɑdl̩] .... ★

v. 蹣跚而行：The ducks waddled across the road. 鴨群搖搖擺擺地穿過道路。

wade [wed] .... ★★

v. 跋涉：I've finally managed to wade through that boring book I had to read. 我終於吃力地讀完了必須讀的那本討厭的書。

walk [wɔk] .... ★★★★★

v. 走，步行：Miss Raegon walks to the church every Sunday. 雷根小姐每個禮拜天都會走去教堂。

n. 步行，散步：Our school is about ten minutes' walk from my house. 我們學校離我家大概要走十分鐘。

wand [wɑnd] .... ★★★★★

n. 棒，指揮棒，魔杖

wander [`wɑndɚ] .... ★★★★

v. ①漫遊，漫步：wander over the countryside 在鄉間漫步②失神，(神智) 恍惚：His mind is wandering. 他心不在焉。

04

看、聽、說、喊、叫相關辭彙 Vocabulary of Senses

accent [ˈæksɛnt] .... ★★★
n. ①重音：In the word "today" the accent is on the second syllable. 「today」這個單字的重音落在第二個音節上。②腔調，口音：From your accent, I judge you are a man of some education. 從你的言語判斷，你是個受過教育的人。

accentuate [ækˈsɛntʃuˌet] .... ★★★
v. 重讀，強調：The lack of furniture accentuated the feeling of space. 缺少傢俱更使人覺得空間大。

aloud [əˈlaʊd] .... ★★★★
adv. 出聲地，大聲地：He read the text aloud. 他大聲朗讀課文。

audience [ˈɔdɪəns] .... ★★★★★
n. 觀眾：The more plays he sees, the better an audience he becomes. 戲看得越多，就越有好的鑑賞力。

audiovisual [ˌɔdɪoˈvɪʒuəl] .... ★★★★
adj. 視聽的

auditory [ˈɔdəˌtorɪ] .... ★
adj. 聽覺的，聲音的：Long-horned grasshoppers have auditory organs on their forelegs. 長角蚱蜢在它們的前腿上有聽覺器官。

aural [ˈɔrəl] .... ★★★
adj. 聽覺的：a musical with plenty of visual and aural appeal 一齣悅人耳目的音樂喜劇

browse [braʊz] .... ★★★★★
v. 流覽（書刊等），吃嫩枝／草等，放牧：to browse through some books 流覽群書；goats browsing on shrubs 在灌木叢吃草的山羊

buzz [bʌz] .... ★
n. 嗡嗡聲，蜂鳴器
v. （蜜蜂）嗡嗡叫：The crowd buzzed with excitement. 群眾很興奮，嘰嘰喳喳交頭接耳。

chat [tʃæt] .... ★★★
v. 閒談：The two friends sat in a corner and chatted about the price of stocks and shares. 兩個朋友坐在角落裡，閒聊股票行情。

chatter [ˈtʃætə] .... ★★
v. 喋喋不休，饒舌：The teacher told the
children to stop chattering in class. 老師叫
孩子們在課堂上不要嘰嘰喳喳講話。

chirp [tʃɝp] .... ★★★
v. 啾啾（蟲和鳥的叫聲）

cry [kraɪ] .... ★★★★★
v. ①哭（泣），流淚：It's no use crying over
spilt milk. 後悔是沒有用的。②叫，喊：He
cried that he had found the key. 他喊著他找
到鑰匙了。
n. ①哭泣，哭聲：The old lady cried when
she thought of the past. 老婦人想到過去便
哭了。②叫喊，喊聲：We heared a cry for
help. 我們聽到求救的喊聲。

declaim [dɪˈklem] .... ★★★★★
v. 朗誦，演講：declaim love lyrics to an
audience of more than one thousand 向千
餘聽眾朗誦愛情詩

discourse [ˈdɪskors] .... ★★
n. 演講，論文：The scholar discoursed at
great length on the poetic style of John
Keats. 那位學者詳細講述了約翰·濟慈的詩
歌風格。

eavesdropper [ˈivzˌdrɑpə] .... ★
n. 屋簷，茅草簷，凸出的邊緣

exclaim [ɪksˈklem] .... ★★★★★
v. 呼喊，驚叫：The children exclaimed with
excitement. 孩子們激動地喊了起來

exclamation [ˌɛkskləˈmeʃən] .... ★★
n. 叫喊，感歎

gabble [ˈgæbl̩] .... ★
v. 急促而不清楚地說出：Mary gabbled out her
prayers and jumped into bed. 瑪麗急匆匆說
過祈禱詞後就跳上了床。

glance [glæns] .... ★★★★★
v. 看一眼，掃視：glance at the clock 匆匆看
一眼鐘
n. 一瞥，掃視：take a glance at the
newspaper headlines 流覽報上的頭條消息

gossip [ˈgɑsəp] .... ★★
n. 閒話

growl [graʊl] .... ★★
n. 嗥叫，咆哮

hear [hɪr] .... ★★★★★
v. ①聽，聽見：He heard a strange sound in
the dark. 他在黑暗裡聽到一些奇怪的聲音。
②聽說，得知：I'm sorry to hear the news.
聽到這個消息我非常遺憾。
【片語】hear from 收到…的來信

hiss [hɪs] .... ★
n. 嘶嘶聲
v. 發出嘶嘶聲：The audience booed and
hissed. 觀眾們發出噓聲。

howl [haʊl] .... ★★
v. 咆哮：The dog howled when it was shut in
the house. 狗被關在屋子裡時，叫了起來。

hubbub [ˈhʌbʌb] .... ★
n. 嘈雜

hurrah [həˈrɑ] .... ★
int . 萬歲，好哇

invisible [ɪnˈvɪzəbl̩] .... ★★★★
adj. 看不見的，無形的：It was so cloudy that
the top of the mountain was invisible. 天
陰陰的，看不見山頂。

listen [ˈlɪsn̩] .... ★★★★★
v. 聽，聽從：At the mid night of December
31, people always listen for the clock to
announce the new year. 人們總是在 12 月
31 日午夜時分等待著時鐘報新年。
【片語】listen to 聽

loud [laʊd] .... ★★★★★
adj. 響亮的，大聲的：a loud voice 洪亮的嗓音
adv. 響亮地，大聲地：Can you speak louder?
你能說大聲一點嗎？

mutter [ˈmʌtə] .... ★★
v. 低語，咕噥：He muttered something to his
mother about losing his wallet. 他低聲向他
母親說了弄丟皮夾的事。
【片語】mutter against / at 小聲抱怨

433

noise [nɔɪz] .... ★★★★★
n. 喧聲，雜訊，吵嚷聲：The noise of traffic kept him awake. 車馬喧鬧使他難以入睡。

noisy [ˈnɔɪzɪ] .... ★★★
adj. 喧鬧的，嘈雜的：They all looked at a big and noisy machine in another corner of the work shop. 他們都看著工作室另一個角落裡的一臺吵雜的大機器。

oral [ˈorəl] .... ★★★★
adj. 口頭的，口述的，口的：Sequoya, a Native American who was born in 1770, formed an alphabet of eighty-six letters that enabled him to put the oral Cherokee language into writing. 西昆亞是一個在 1770 年出生的美洲印第安人，他創造了一套 86 個字母的字母系統，從而把卻洛奇族的口頭語言用書寫的形式表現了出來。

oration [oˈreʃən] .... ★★★★★
n. 演說：make an oration 演說

orator [ˈɔrətɚ] .... ★★★
n. 演講者

overhear [ˌovɚˈhɪr] .... ★
v. 偶然聽到，從旁聽到

peck [pɛk] .... ★
v. 啄起：The young lady's only pecking at her food; what's wrong with her? 那位小姐吃東西一小口一小口的，她怎麼啦？

roar [ror] .... ★★★★
v. 吼叫，咆哮，轟鳴：The crowd roared their approval. 群眾高聲喊叫表示同意。

say [se] .... ★★★★★
v. 說，講：He said that he was tired. 他說他累了。

scan [skæn] .... ★★★
v. 流覽，掃描：Migrating wild geese scan the ground for possible danger before they land. 遷徙中的野雁在落地之前，會對地面可能存在的危險進行一番審視。

scream [skrim] .... ★★★★
v. 尖叫，發出刺耳的聲音：She was screaming by hysterically. 她歇斯里地尖叫。
n. 尖叫聲，刺耳的聲音

screech [skritʃ] .... ★
v. 發出尖銳刺耳的叫聲：The car tires screeched on the road as it turned too fast. 當汽車轉彎轉太快時，輪胎會在路上發出尖銳刺耳的聲音。

scrutinize [ˈskrutn̩ˌaɪz] .... ★
v. 細察：The jeweler scrutinized the diamond for flaws. 寶石商人仔細察看鑽石有無瑕疵。

see [si] .... ★★★★★
v. ①看見：Can I see your licence, please? 我能看看你的執照嗎？②理解，領會：Do you see what I mean? 你懂我的意思嗎？③會見，訪問：I'm glad to see you. 很高興和你見面。
【片語】see sb. off 為某人送行

shout [ʃaut] .... ★★★★★
v. 呼喊，呼叫：Don't shout at me like that! 別對我那樣大叫！

shriek [ʃrik] .... ★★
v. 尖叫，叫喊：She shrieked in fear. 她驚怕得尖聲叫喊。
n. 尖叫，叫喊

shrill [ʃrɪl] .... ★★
adj. 尖銳的，刺耳的
v. 尖叫：the shrill wail of a siren 警笛的尖嘯

shrilly [ˈʃrɪlɪ] .... ★★
adv. 尖聲地

sigh [saɪ] .... ★★★★★
n. 歎息："I wish I had finished this work," she said with a sigh. 她歎口氣說：「我是希望我完成了這項工作。」

sightseeing [ˈsaɪtˌsiŋ] .... ★★★
n. 觀光，遊覽：a sightseeing bus 遊覽車

sing [sɪŋ] .... ★★★★★
v. 唱，演唱：She sang a pop song for us. 她
為我們唱了一首流行歌曲。

speaker [ˋspikɚ] .... ★★★
n. ①說話人，演講者②揚聲器

splutter [ˋsplʌtɚ] .... ★
v.（因激動等）氣急敗壞地說：She spluttered
a few words of apology to me. 她語無倫次
地向我道歉。

squeak [skwik] .... ★
v.（老鼠或物體）發出吱吱聲：We heard the
squeaks of the rocking chair. 我們聽見搖椅
吱吱響。

squeaky [ˋskwiki] .... ★
adj. 吱吱響的，輾軋聲的：squeaky shoes 嘎
吱作響的鞋

stammer [ˋstæmɚ] .... ★
n. 口吃，結巴
v. 結結巴巴地說："Th-th-thank you," he
stammered. 他結結巴巴地說：「謝…謝謝
你。」

stare [stɛr] .... ★★★★★
v. 盯視，凝視：They stared into each other's
miserable eyes. 他們彼此痛苦地凝視。

talk [tɔk] .... ★★★★★
v. 說話，講：I want to talk about something to
you. 我想跟你說件事。
n. ①談話，會談：The teacher has a talk with
him. 老師和他談了話。②演講，講話：I
heard his talk on the radio last night. 我昨天
晚上在收音機上聽到了他說的話。

辨析 Analyze

gaze, glance, glare, glimpse, peer, stare

1 **gaze** vi.「凝視，注視」，不及物動詞，
指出於羨慕、好奇等原因長時間地注視，
通常不會引起對方反感：The boy loved
this painting and gazed at it for a long
time. 那男孩喜歡這幅畫，所以盯著它看
了很長一段時間。

2 **glance** vi.「看一眼，掃視」，不及物動
詞，作名詞時常用於片語 take a glance
at：He always glances at the headlines
in the newspaper before going to bed. 他
睡覺前，總是匆匆看了一下報紙的頭版頭
條新聞。

3 **glare** vi.「怒目而視」，還指「發射
強光，發出刺眼的光線」：That father
glared at his son as he spoke. 那位父親
說話時怒目瞪著他的兒子。

4 **glimpse** vt.「看一眼，瞥見」，及物
動詞，作名詞時常用於片語 catch / get a
glimpse of：We glimpsed the charming
mountain views through the windows of
our train. 我們從火車窗戶瞥見迷人的山
景。

5 **peer** vi.「仔細看，費力地看」，有時含
有不禮貌的意味；做名詞意為「同等地位
的人」：They were used to being peered
at on arriving in a strange town. 到一個陌
生的城鎮就被人盯著看，他們對此已經習
慣了。

6 **stare** vi.「盯著，凝視」，不及物動詞，
指出於好奇、無禮睜大眼睛看或盯著看，
有時會引起反感：They all stared with
astonishment. 他們都驚異地瞪著眼。

tell [tɛl] .... ★ ★ ★ ★ ★
v. ①（+ that + 子句或 + to）（用語言文字）告知，告訴，講述，敘述：Will you tell me how to do it? 你可以告訴我怎麼做這件事嗎？②警告，告訴，要求，命令

unaccented [ʌnˈæksɛntɪd] .... ★
adj. 無重音的，非重讀的：an unaccented part 非重音的部份

visibility [ˌvɪzəˈbɪlətɪ] .... ★ ★ ★ ★
n. 清晰程度，能見度：poor visibility 能見度差

visual [ˈvɪʒuəl] .... ★ ★ ★ ★
adj.（肉眼）可見的，視力的：visual knowledge of a place 對一個地方的實地觀察

visualize [ˈvɪʒuəˌlaɪz] .... ★ ★ ★ ★
v. 目測，想像出：He tried to visualize the scene as it was described 他盡力設想所描繪的場景。

watch [wɑtʃ] .... ★ ★ ★ ★ ★
v. 注視，監視：Do you often watch television? 你常看電視嗎？
n. 看守

whisper [ˈhwɪspɚ] .... ★ ★ ★ ★ ★
v. 低語，耳語：whisper to sb. 對某人說話
n. 低語：He answered in a whisper. 他低聲回答。

whistle [ˈhwɪsl̩] .... ★ ★ ★ ★
v. 吹口哨，鳴笛：He whistled the song. 他用口哨吹了這首歌。

yell [jɛl] .... ★
v. 大叫：He yelled at her to be careful. 他大聲叫她注意。

yelp [jɛlp] .... ★
v. 喊叫：The dog yelped with pain. 狗疼得叫了起來。

辨析 Analyze

fancy, imagine, visualize

1 **fancy** *vt.*「猜想，以為，想像，設想，想要，喜歡」，指認為、相信時，沒有太大把握，文學意味較濃：She fancied she heard a noise downstairs. 她以為她聽到樓下有什麼動靜。

2 **imagine** *vt.*「設想，想像，料想，猜想」，比 fancy 的把握性更小，並有設身處地地想一想的意思：Try to imagine you are on a spaceship. 試著想像一下你正在太空船上。

3 **visualize** *vt.*「設想，想像」，是設身處地想一想的意思，在這個詞義上可與 imagine 互換：Try to visualize a bright future / sailing through the sky on a cloud. 試著想像一下光明的未來／在空中駕雲翱翔。

05

提及、陳述、讀與寫、描述相關辭彙

Vocabulary of Writing & Statements

annotate [ˈænoˌtet] .... ★

v. 註解：In the appendix to the novel, the critic sought to annotate many of the esoteric references. 在這本小說的附錄中，評論家嘗試對許多較難懂的附註加以註解。

delineate [dɪˈlɪnɪˌet] .... ★

v. 刻畫，記述：He delineated the State of Texas on the map with a red pencil. 他用紅鉛筆在地圖上畫出德克薩斯州的邊境。

depict [dɪˈpɪkt] .... ★★★★★

v. 描寫，敘述：Embroidery depicting scenic views became popular in the United States toward the end of the eighteenth century. 在 18 世紀末，有著自然風景的刺繡在美國流行起來。

describe [dɪˈskraɪb] .... ★★★★★

v. 形容，描寫：Words can't describe the beauty of the scene. 景色之美，非筆墨所能形容。

description [dɪˈskrɪpʃən] .... ★★★★★

n. ①描寫，形容：His article contains brief descriptions of some of his ideas. 他在那篇文章中簡要介紹了自己的一些觀點。②種類，性質：Events of this description occurred daily. 這類事情每天都會發生。

detailed [ˈdiˈteld] .... ★★★★★

adj. 詳細的，明細的：a detailed report on the state of the economy 關於經濟狀況的詳細報告

dictate [ˈdɪktet] .... ★★★

v. 聽寫，口授，口述：The union leaders are trying to dictate their demands to the employer. 工會領導群正設法迫使雇主接受他們的要求。

dictation [dɪkˈteʃən] .... ★★★

n. 口述，聽寫，口授，筆錄：The teacher gave us an English dictation. 老師讓我們作了一次英語聽寫。

elucidate [ɪˈlusəˌdet] .... ★

v. 闡明，說明：Please elucidate the reasons for your action. 請說明你採取行動的理由。

endorse [ɪnˈdɔrs] .... ★★★★★

v. 確認，贊同，支持：We can't endorse her recent statements. 我們不同意她最近的聲明。

engrave [ɪn'grev] .... ★★★

vt. ①刻上：His memorial was engraved on the stone. 紀念他的碑文刻在石碑上。②銘記：The terrible scene was engraved on his memory. 那可怕的情景銘記在他的記憶中。

enunciate [ɪ'nʌnsɪet] .... ★

v. 闡明，清晰發音：Actors learn how to enunciate clearly in the theatrical college. 演員在戲劇學院學習如何清晰發音。

exemplify [ɪg'zɛmpləˌfaɪ] .... ★

v. 例證，例示：The recent oil price rises exemplify the difficulties which the motor industry is now facing. 最近的石油漲價是汽車工業現在面臨困難的一個例子。

explain [ɪk'splen] .... ★★★★★

v. 解釋，說明：Before the facts, you needn't explain it any more. 事實面前，你不必再解釋什麼了。

explanation [ɛksplə'neʃən] .... ★★★★★

n. 解釋，說明：No explanation will be needed. 不需任何解釋。

exponent [ɪk'sponənt] .... ★★★★★

n. 解釋者，指數：Our senator is an exponent of free trade. 我們的參議員是一個自由貿易的擁護者。

illustrate ['ɪləstret] .... ★★★★★

v. 說明：In economics, graphs are used to illustrate functions. 在經濟學中，圖表被用來解釋函數。

illustration [ɪlʌs'treʃən] .... ★★★★

n. 說明，圖解，實例，插圖：Before the invention of photoengraving, steel and copperplate engraving served as the principal means of reproducing illustrations. 在照相凸版印刷發明之前，鋼和銅板印刷雕版是製作插圖的主要手段。

interpret [ɪn'tɝprɪt] .... ★★★★

v. 解釋，口譯，說明，闡明，把⋯理解為：I interpret his answer as a refusal. 我把他的回答理解為拒絕。

interpretation [ɪntɝprɪ'teʃən] .... ★★★★

n. 解釋，說明，翻譯：different interpretations of the same facts 同一事實的不同解釋

interpreter [ɪn'tɝprɪtɚ] .... ★★

n. 譯員，口譯者：An actor is an interpreter of other men's words, often a soul which wishes to reveal itself to the world. 演員是他人話語的口譯員，通常是一個希望向世界展示自己的人物。

interrelated [ɪntərɪ'letɪd] .... ★★★★★

adj. 互相聯繫的

interrogate [ɪn'tɛrəˌget] .... ★

v. 審問，詢問：interrogate the witness 訊問證人

mention ['mɛnʃən] .... ★★★★★

n. 主張

v. 提及：Because the tree was mentioned in a newspaper, the number of visitors to Frinley has now increased. 因為這棵樹在一家報紙報導過，所以參觀弗林利的人數現在增多了。

narrate [næ'ret] .... ★

v. 敘述：The story is well narrated. 這故事敘述得很好。

narrator [næ'retɚ] .... ★

n. 講述者

opinion [ə'pɪnjən] .... ★★★★★

n. 意見，看法，主張，見解：The world is not run by thought, nor by imagination, but by opinion. 世界不是依思想和想像而轉移，而是因觀念而生生不息。

paradox ['pærəˌdɑks] .... ★★★

n. 反論，矛盾，似非而可能是的說法：It is a paradox that in such a rich country there should be so many poor people. 這樣富有的國家中有那麼多窮人是矛盾的現象。

proposal [prə'pozl] .... ★★★★★

n. 提案，建議：agree to a proposal 同意某項建議／提案

proposition [ˌprɑpəˈzɪʃən] .... ★★
n. 主張，陳述，提議，建議

read [rid] .... ★★★★★
v. 朗讀，閱讀：I read the story in the newspaper. 我是在報上讀到這個故事的。
【片語】① read aloud 朗讀② read out 讀出聲來，朗讀

record [ˈrɛkəd] .... ★★★★★
n. 記錄，檔案，唱片：He holds the world's record for the high jump. 他保持世界跳高記錄。

recorder [rɪˈkɔrdə] .... ★★★
n. ①記錄員②答錄機，記錄器

refer [rɪˈfɜ] .... ★★★★★
v. ①提到，涉及：When I said that some people were stupid I was not referring to you. 我說有些人愚蠢但不是指你。②參考，查閱：She could make a new dish without referring to a cooking book. 她可以不參考食譜就做出一道新的菜色。③引…去參考（或查詢）：I was referred to the Inquiry Desk. 人家叫我去問詢詢處。
【片語】①refer to....as 把…稱作，把…當作② refer to 查閱，涉及，提到，把…提交

specify [ˈspɛsəˌfaɪ] .... ★★★★
v. 詳述，指定：It is specified that they be included in the will. 條件是他們要列入遺囑中。

view [vju] .... ★★★★★
n. 景色，眼界，觀點：It's only my personal view. 這是我個人的觀點。
【片語】come into view 進入視線

viewer [ˈvjuə] .... ★★★★★
n. 觀察者，觀察器

viewpoint [ˈvjuˌpɔɪnt] .... ★★★
n. 觀察點，視點，觀點，看法，見解：From my viewpoint I think we should help him. 以我的觀點我認為我們應該幫助他。

write [raɪt] .... ★★★★★
v. ①寫，書寫：What did he write about in his letter? 他在信裡寫了什麼？②寫（書、著作、話劇等），寫作：Mr. Johnson has written a lot of books. 強森先生寫了不少書。③寫信，寫信給：He wrote me the news. 他寫信告訴了我那消息。
【片語】write down 寫下，記下

06

說謊、哭、笑相關辭彙

Vocabulary of Lies, Cries & Laughs

amuse [ə`mjuz] .... ★★★★
v. ①逗樂，逗笑：Her story amused her grandmother. 她的故事把她的外婆逗笑了。②提供…娛樂：Jack amused himself by throwing peanut into the dog's month. 傑克往狗的嘴巴裡扔花生，以此取樂。

giggle [`gɪgḷ] .... ★★
vi. 咯咯笑，傻笑：The girls whispered and giggled together. 女孩們咯咯地笑著說悄悄話。
n. 咯咯笑，傻笑

grin [grɪn] .... ★★
v. 咧著嘴笑：I grinned my approval. 我咧嘴一笑表示讚許。

laugh [læf] .... ★★★★★
v. 譏笑：The ignorant person is likely to laugh at the others. 那個無知的人喜歡嘲笑他人。
【片語】laugh at sb. 嘲笑某人
n. 笑聲：He gave a loud laugh. 他大聲地笑了。

laughter [`læftɚ] .... ★★★★
n. 笑，笑聲：burst into laughter 哈哈大笑起來

liar [`laɪɚ] .... ★★★
n. 說謊的人

nonsense [`nɑnsɛns] .... ★★★★
n. 胡說，廢話

smile [smaɪl] .... ★★★★★
v. 微笑：She smiled a strange smile. 她發出奇怪的微笑。
n. 微笑：Mr. Smith answered with a smile. 史密斯先生笑著答覆。

sob [sɑb] .... ★★
v. 哭泣，嗚咽
n. 啜泣（聲），嗚咽（聲）

weep [wip] .... ★★★★★
v. ①哭泣，流淚：She lost control of her feelings and began to weep. 她控制不住自己的情緒，哭了起來。②悲歎，哀悼：Don't weep for the dead for they are at peace. 別為死者傷心，因為他們已經安息。

07

睡、夢、醒、姿勢相關辭彙

Vocabulary of Sleep & Dream

asleep [əˋslip] .... ★★★★
adj. 睡著的：The baby is asleep. 嬰兒睡著了。

dream [drim] .... ★★★★★
n. 夢，夢想，幻想：awake from a dream 從夢中醒來
v. 做夢，夢想：I dreamed about you last night. 昨晚我夢見你了。
【片語】dream up 想像出

gesture [ˋdʒɛstʃɚ] .... ★★★★
n. 姿勢，手勢，姿態
v. 做手勢：He gestured angrily. 他氣憤地比手勢。

sleep [slip] .... ★★★★★
v. 睡：Milk will help you sleep. 牛奶會幫助你入睡。
n. 睡眠：How many hours' sleep do you need? 你需要睡多少小時？
【片語】go to sleep 入睡

sleepy [ˋslipɪ] .... ★★★
adj. ①想睡的②寂靜的③懶散的

wake [wek] .... ★★★★★
v. 醒來，喚醒：What time do you want to be waken up? 你想要在什麼時候被叫醒？
【片語】wake (sb.) up （使）醒來

yawn [jɔn] .... ★★★
v. 打哈欠：I felt so sleepy that I couldn't stop yawning. 我感到很睏，所以一直打呵欠。
n. 哈欠

辨析
Analyze

asleep, sleepy

1 **asleep** *a.*「睡著，熟睡」，多用作表語：My daughter is fast asleep in the room. 我的女兒在房裡睡得正香。

2 **sleepy** *a.*「想睡的」，即可用作表語，又可用作定語：Many students feel sleepy when they are having classes. 很多學生上課時打瞌睡。

肢體動作

08

點頭、鼓掌、眨眼相關辭彙

Vocabulary of Nodding, Clapping & Winking

applaud [əˋplɔd] .... ★★★★★
v. 喝彩，歡呼：The ideal listener has been humorously described as a person who applauds vigorously. 「理想的聽眾」被幽默地描述成熱烈鼓掌喝彩的人。

beckon [ˋbɛkṇ] .... ★
v. 召喚：An entirely new era, the era of intellectual economy, is beckoning us on. 一個嶄新的知識經濟時代正在召喚我們繼續前進。

blink [blɪŋk] .... ★
v. 眨眼：All toads and frogs blink when they swallow. 所有的蟾蜍和青蛙在吞嚥時都會眨眼。

blinker [ˋblɪŋkɚ] .... ★
n.（馬的）眼罩

bow [bo] .... ★★★★★
n.（小提琴的）弓
v. 彎腰，屈服：I can't agree with you but I bow to your greater experience and knowledge. 我不同意你的意見，但我佩服你比我豐富的經驗和知識。

clap [klæp] .... ★★★
v. ①拍手：The audience clapped after his speech. 聽眾在他演講完後鼓掌。②拍擊：He clapped his son on the back. 他在他兒子背上拍了一下。
n. 拍手，鼓掌

fishy [ˋfɪʃɪ] .... ★★★★★
adj. 值得懷疑的：It's a fishy story that a tramp deposited quite a lot of money in the bank yesterday. 很難相信一個流浪漢昨天在銀行裡存了不少錢。

frown [fraʊn] .... ★★★★
v. 皺眉，反對：The teacher frowned angrily at the noisy class. 老師生氣地對那班吵吵嚷嚷的學生皺起眉頭。

nod [nɑd] .... ★★★★
v. ①點（頭），點頭表示：She nodded her head to me. 她向我點頭。②點頭同意，點頭示意：We nodded in agreement with him. 我們點頭對他表示贊同。③瞌睡，打盹：I nodded off in my chair. 我在椅子上打盹。
n. ①點頭同意，點頭示意：He gave me a nod. 他向我點頭。②瞌睡，打盹

rap [ræp] .... ★ ★

v. 責難，敲擊：He rapped the table with his fist. 他用拳頭重擊桌子。

rapacious [rəˋpeʃəs] .... ★

adj. 貪婪的，強奪的：rapacious pirates 搶劫的海盜

slap [slæp] .... ★ ★ ★

v. 掌擊，拍：The doctor slapped the hysterical child to make him calmer. 醫生拍了拍那個歇斯底里的孩子，使他靜下來。

spit [spɪt] .... ★ ★ ★

v. ①吐唾沫或痰：No spitting in public places! 公共場所禁止隨地吐痰。②吐出：He took out a cigar, bit off the end and spit it out. 他拿出一支雪茄，咬下尾端，然後吐了出來。

n. 唾液

09

放棄、撤退、逃跑相關辭彙

Vocabulary of Withdrawal

abdicate [ˋæbdəˌket] .... ★

v. 放棄權利：When Edward VIII abdicated the British throne, he surprised the entire world. 當愛德華八世放棄英國王位時，全世界都為之震驚。

banish [ˋbænɪʃ] .... ★

v. 驅逐出境：political foes banished by the dictator 被獨裁者放逐的政敵

disband [dɪsˋbænd] .... ★★★

v. 解散（軍隊）：The army was disbanded when the war ended. 戰爭結束後，軍隊被裁減了。

discard [dɪsˋkɑrd] .... ★★★

v. 丟棄：The library discarded all its old magazines. 這個圖書館清理掉了所有的舊書。

dissipate [ˋdɪsəˌpet] .... ★

v. 驅散，消散：If a way could be found to dissipate the fog that often settles over airports, air travel would probably be safer. 如果能有辦法驅散機場裡常常揮散不去的霧，那麼空中旅行就會變得更加安全。

escape [əˋskep] .... ★★★★★

v. 避免，逃避：There is a strange odor in the air. The gas must have been escaping somewhere. 空氣中有股奇怪的味道，一定是什麼地方瓦斯漏氣了。

exile [ˋɛksaɪl] .... ★★

v. 流放

n. 放逐，被流放者：He had been exiled for five years. 他已經流放五年了。

flee [fli] .... ★★★★★

v. 逃跑：During the United States Civil War, many people in the South were forced to flee their homes. 在美國內戰期間，許多南方人被迫背井離鄉。

forsake [fəˋsek] .... ★★★★

v. 遺棄，拋棄，摒絕：For financial reasons, scientists are often compelled to forsake their research. 許多科學家由於財務原因，常被迫放棄了他們的研究。

hustle [ˋhʌsl̩] .... ★

v. 驅趕：Mother hustled the children off to school lest they should be late. 母親催促著孩子們趕快上學以免遲到。

quit [kwɪt] .... ★★★★
v. ①停止，放棄：Jack doesn't want to quit smoking. 傑克不想戒煙。②辭（職）：A month later he quit and went home to Japan. 一個月後他辭掉工作回日本去了。

recede [rɪˋsid] .... ★★★★★
v. 退去，退遠：With the passage of time, my unhappy memories of the place receded. 隨著時間的推移，我對那地方不愉快的記憶變得模糊了。

recoil [rɪˋkɔɪl] .... ★
v. 後退，退縮：recoil from doing something對做某事畏縮不前；A gun recoils after being fired. 槍在射擊後向後彈。

relinquish [rɪˋlɪŋkwɪʃ] .... ★
v. 放棄：Do you think he will relinquish his seat in the Senate? 你認為他會放棄他的參議員席位嗎？

renounce [rɪˋnaʊns] .... ★★★★★
v. 放棄，否認：He renounced his claim to the property. 他宣佈正式放棄財產所有權。

resignation [ˌrɛzɪgˋneʃən] .... ★
n. 辭職，辭呈，聽從，屈從：give / hand in one's resignation 遞交辭呈

retract [rɪˋtrækt] .... ★★★★★
v. 收回，撤回：A cat can retract its claws. 貓能縮回爪子。

setback [ˋsɛtˌbæk] .... ★★★★★
n. 挫傷

waiver [ˋwevɚ] .... ★
n. 放棄，棄權：waiver of obligation 免除債務

withdraw [wɪðˋdrɔ] .... ★★★★
v. 取回：to withdraw $500 from a bank account 從銀行帳戶提取500美元

withdrawal [wɪðˋdrɔəl] .... ★★★★
n. 收回，退出，撤退，取消：Our chief representative's withdrawal was construed as a protest. 我們首席代表的退場被看作是一種抗議。

10

進、出、放置、堆積相關辭彙

Movement

肢體動作名稱總匯

Vocabulary of In & Out

enter [ˈɛntɚ] .... ★★★★★
v. 走入，進入，加入，登記：She entered her name
　　for the high jump. 她報名參加跳高比賽。
【片語】enter into 討論，開始

export [ɪksˈport] .... ★★★★★
v. 輸出，出口：export raw material 出口原料
n. 出口（物）：grain export 糧食出口

fill [fɪl] .... ★★★★★
v. 填滿，充滿：I was filled with pleasure when I saw
　　my old friend. 我看見我的老朋友時，心中充滿了喜
　　悅。
【片語】fill in / out 填充，填寫

heap [hip] .... ★★★★
n. 堆，大量，許多
v. 堆積，裝滿：His books lay in a heap on the floor of
　　the living room. 他的書疊成一堆放在客廳的地板上。

input [ˈɪnˌput] .... ★★★★
n. ①輸入：press the input button 按輸入鈕②投入
　　的資金（或物資）：We must not forget the sales
　　department's input. 我們不能忘記行銷部的投入。

lay [le] .... ★★★★★
v. ①放置，放下：He laid the bag on the ground. 他
　　把包包放在地上。②鋪，砌，鋪設：She laid a new
　　carpet in the bedroom. 她在臥室裡鋪設了新地毯。
　　③設置，佈置：She laid the table for dinner. 她整理
　　桌子準備吃飯。
【片語】① lay aside 把…擱置一旁；留存，儲蓄② lay
down 放下③ lay off（臨時性）解雇④ lay out 安排，佈
置，設計，擺出，展開

layer [ˈleɚ] .... ★★★★
n. 層，地層，階層，金屬：a layer of dust on the
　　windowsill 窗臺上的一層灰塵；a cake with four
　　layers 四層蛋糕

out [aut] .... ★★★★★
adv. 離開，向外，在外：I'm afraid his out at the
　　moment. 我想他現在出去了。
【片語】out of 在…外，從…裡頭出來

overlap [ˈovɚˌlæp] .... ★
v. 重疊：The style in these two books largely overlaps.
　　這兩本書的風格有許多一致之處。

pile [paɪl] .... ★★★★
n. 一堆，一疊：a pile of sand 一堆沙子
v. （把…）堆積：Her hair was piled high on
her head. 她的頭髮高高地束在頭上。

plunge [plʌndʒ] .... ★★★★
v. 投入：Plunge the lobsters, head first, into a
large pot of rapidly boiling salted water把龍
蝦頭朝下，扔進一大鍋滾燙的鹽水中。

repel [rɪˋpɛl] .... ★
v. 擊退：Bodies with like electrical charges
repel each other, and those with unlike
charges attract each other. 相同電荷的物體
相互排斥，不同電荷的物體相互吸引。

stack [stæk] .... ★★★★★
n. （草）堆，一堆，大量，大宗：a stack of
books 一大堆書； a stack of papers 一堆報
紙
v. 堆積，堆起：to stack (up) books 囤積書

辨析
Analyze

heap, pile, stack

1 **heap** *n. & vt.* 「（一）堆，大量，許
多」，指一大堆不整齊的東西（如垃圾、
髒衣服），偏向貶義，也可用作動詞，意
為「（使）成堆，堆起」：This heap of
dirty clothes is for the laundry. 這堆髒衣
服是要送洗的。

2 **pile** *n. & vt.* 「一堆，一疊」，尤指堆放
整齊的東西，中性詞，也可用作動詞，
意為「堆積」：a pile of books / papers /
letters 一堆書／一疊報紙／一疊信件：He
has already sorted the documents and
put them out in piles on his desk. 他已經
把文件整理好，整齊地堆放在桌子上了。

3 **stack** *n. & vt.* 「整齊的一疊（或一
堆）」，指一堆整齊的東西，也可用作
動詞，意為「把…疊成堆，堆放於」：a
stack of letters / hay / boxes 一疊信件／
一堆乾草／一堆盒子：They left me with
a stack of dirty dishes. 他們給我留下了一
堆髒盤子。

447

11

肢體動作名稱總匯

努力、勤奮、準備相關辭彙

Vocabulary of Diligence

Movement

assiduous [əˋsɪdʒuəs] .... ★

adj. 勤勉的：Through assiduous research work in museums and libraries, some very rare drawings have been recovered for this exhibition. 經過博物館和圖書館的辛勤研究努力，一些非常珍貴的畫為了這次展出已修復了。

diligent [ˋdɪlədʒənt] .... ★

adj. 勤勉的，勤奮的：Though he's not clever, he's a diligent worker and has often done well in the examinations. 他雖然不聰明，卻很勤奮，所以考試常常取得好成績。

effort [ˋɛfət] .... ★★★★★

n. 盡力，努力，成就：Ralph Bunche won a Nobel Prize in 1950 for his peacemaking efforts as a United Nations diplomat. 羅夫·邦區因在擔任聯合國特使期間為和平努力，於 1950 年獲頒諾貝爾和平獎。

elaborate .... ★★★

v. [ɪˋlæbəˏret] 精心製作，詳細闡述：The chairman just wanted the facts. You don't need to elaborate on them. 主席只想瞭解事實，你不必多加闡釋。

adj. [ɪˋlæbərɪt] 精心構思的：The Underground Railroad was an elaborate network of safe houses organized to help slaves escape from bondage before the Civil War. 地下鐵路是美國南北戰爭時，為了幫助奴隸逃脫而精心設計的一種安全藏身網。

emulate [ˋɛmjəˏlet] .... ★

v. 與⋯競爭，仿效：John tried to emulate his older sister. 約翰試著仿效他的姊姊。

endeavor [ɪnˋdɛvə] .... ★★

n. 努力，盡力，力圖：After many years of unsuccessfully endeavoring to form his own orchestra, Glenn Miller finally achieved world fame in 1939 as a big band leader. 格蘭·米勒在經過多年努力組建自己的管弦樂團卻不成功的情況下，終於在1939年成為一位世界級的大型樂團領導人。

flounder [ˋflaundə] .... ★

v. 掙扎，躊躇：The boy floundered in the water till someone jumped in to save him. 男孩在水中拼命掙扎，直到有人跳入水中把他救起。

preliminary [prɪˋlɪməˌnɛrɪ] .... ★★★
adj. 初步的，初級的，預備的：The preliminary carving of Iroquois masks was done on living trees because it was believed that, by this means, the masks would also have life. 易洛魁族人雕刻面具的初始階段是在活樹上進行的，因為據說這樣獲得的面具才有生命。

preparation [ˌprɛpəˋreʃən] .... ★★★★★
n. ①準備（工作），預備：The meeting will require a lot of preparation. 這次會議需要大量的準備工作。②（藥品）配製

prepare [prɪˋpɛr] .... ★★★★★
v. 準備，預備：A room has been prepared for you. 已經為你準備好了一個房間。

reinforce [ˌriɪnˋfɔrs] .... ★★★
v. 加強，鞏固：Monkeys constantly groom one another, thus reinforcing the social bonds necessary to their survival. 猴子經常相互梳理毛髮，進而加強生存所必須的社會連結。

strenuous [ˋstrɛnjʊəs] ....★
adj. 辛苦的：Eleonora R. Sears, the nineteenth-century athlete and philanthropist, demonstrated that women could successfully participate in strenuous sports. 19 世紀的運動員及慈善家愛蓮諾拉，證明女子能夠從事劇烈的運動並且能夠取得好成績。

strive [straɪv] .... ★★
v. 努力，奮鬥，力求：strive against injustice 反抗不公正

struggle [ˋstrʌg!] .... ★★★★★
v. 鬥爭，奮鬥，努力：We should give them support as they struggle to build a more prosperous society. 當他們努力建立一個更繁榮的社會時，我們應予以支持。
n. 鬥爭，奮鬥，努力

toil [tɔɪl] ....★
n. 辛苦，勞累：A bit of the blackest bread is the sole recompense and the sole profit attaching to so arduous a toil. 一小塊黑得不能再黑的麵包是艱苦的工作的惟一補償和收益。

try [traɪ] .... ★★★★★
v. 試圖，努力：I tried mending my shoes myself. 我試著自己修鞋。
【片語】① try to do sth. 設法做某事② try on 試穿

bundle [ˈbʌndl̩] .... ★★★★
n. 捆，束，包：a bundle of clothes 一捆衣服

chain [tʃen] .... ★★★★★
n. ①鏈，鏈條②鐐銬③一連串，連鎖：a chain of events 一連串的事件
v. 用鏈條栓住：They chained the dog to a tree. 他們用鏈條把狗拴在樹上。

chop [tʃɑp] .... ★★★
n. 排骨
v. 砍：The old man chopped the block of wood into two with a single blow. 這老人用一把斧頭把木塊劈成兩半。

clip [klɪp] .... ★★
v. 夾住，修剪
n. 夾子，鉗子：Since fingernails can be easily clipped, they are a convenient resource for those who wish to measure levels of trace elements in the body. 指甲由於很容易被剪掉，因此對那些想檢測體內微量元素的人來說，是方便的檢測來源。

coil [kɔɪl] .... ★★★
n. 盤繞
v. 卷：The dragon coiled round the column. 龍盤繞在柱上。

cord [kɔrd] .... ★★★
n. 軟電線，細繩，索：the vocal cords 聲帶

cram [kræm] .... ★
v. 填塞，倉促用功：The hall was crammed with many people standing. 這大廳裡擠滿了站著的人。

cut [kʌt] .... ★★★★★
v. ①切割，剪，砍，削：Please cut the apple into two. 請把蘋果切成兩半。②削減，刪節：The power country agreed to cut it's army. 這個有權勢的國家同意裁軍。
n. ①切割，剪，砍，削：The pig can never avoid a cut. 豬難免挨一刀。②削減，刪節：We must learn to make a cut in price. 我們得學會殺價。③切口，傷口：The cut on his finger has completely healed. 他手指上的傷口完好了。

encompass [ɪnˈkʌmpəs] .... ★★★★★
v. 包圍，環繞：a reservoir encompassed by mountains 群山環繞的水庫

impale [ɪmˈpel] .... ★

v. 刺穿，刺住：The boy fell out of the window and was impaled on the fence. 男孩從窗子跌下來，被籬笆刺傷了。

insert [ɪnˈsɝt] .... ★★★

v. 插入：A cultured pearl is made by inserting tiny bead inside an oyster. 人工養殖的珍珠是以在牡蠣中放置小珠子而生成的。

lash [læʃ] .... ★

v. 鞭打：The man lashed the donkey but it would not go any faster. 這人用鞭子抽驢子，可是牠無法跑更快了。

mess [mɛs] .... ★★★

n. 混亂，混雜，髒亂：With divorce and bankruptcy, his personal life was in a mess. 離婚和破產的官司使得他的私人生活陷入一片混亂當中。

mince [mɪns] .... ★

v. 切碎，裝腔作勢：He does not mince matters / his words. 他是有話直說的。

mow [mo] .... ★

v. 割：mow the lawn 除草

muffler [ˈmʌflɚ] .... ★

n. 消音器

pack [pæk] .... ★★★★★

v. ①捆紮，把…打包：Have you packed your things? 你的東西打包好了嗎？②使…擠在一起，塞滿：The moment the door was opened, people began to pack the hall. 門剛打開，人群就湧進了大廳。

n. 包，小盒

penetrate [ˈpɛnəˌtret] .... ★

v. 刺穿，進入：Automobile experts have shown that halogen headlights penetrate thick fog more effectively than traditional incandescent headlights and thus help to reduce accidents. 汽車專家已經發現車前的鹵素燈光比傳統的白熾車燈光更能穿透濃霧，因而有助於減少交通事故發生。

辨析 Analyze

pack, package, packet, parcel, sack

1 **pack** *n.*「包，小盒，包裹」，指一包（東西），尤指在背上背或駄的東西，還指小盒子：a pack of cigarettes/cards/gum 一盒香煙／一盒牌／一盒口香糖；The climber carried some food in a pack on his back. 那個登山者在背上的背包裡裝著一些食物。

2 **package** *n.*「包裹，包裝」，指一包（東西）、貨物的包裝容器（如紙盒、紙箱）：a package of books/clothes/tea/sugar/candies 一包書／衣服／茶／糖／糖果；還指一些計畫、方案：If you want to use the device properly, follow the directions on the package. 要正確使用這一裝置，請按包裝盒上的說明操作。

3 **packet** *n.*「小包，小盒」，指一小包（茶葉或香煙等）、一袋（信封等）：a packet of tea/letters/envelopes 一包茶／信／信封

4 **parcel** *n.*「小包，包裹」，指一包（東西），尤指（郵政）包裹：Send this parcel via airmail. 把這個包裹寄航空郵件。

5 **sack** *n.*「麻袋，包」，指麻袋、大包、牛皮紙袋：a sack of potatoes/fruit/grain/rice/vegetables 一（大）包馬鈴薯／水果／糧食／米／蔬菜

perforate [ˈpɝfəˌret] .... ★

v. 穿孔，打眼：An arrow has a sharp, pointed head with which it perforates its target. 箭有著尖銳的箭頭可以穿透靶子。

pierce [pɪrs] .... ★★★★★

v. 穿透，戳穿，洞察：Large glowing yellow eyes pierced the darkness. 一雙大而發光的黃眼睛穿透了黑暗。

poke [pok] .... ★

v. 戳，刺，伸（頭等）：A seal poked its head out of the water. 一隻海豹把頭探出了水面。

prick [prɪk] .... ★

v. 刺，戳

n. 刺孔，刺傷：She pricked herself when passing a thread through the hole of a needle. 她在穿針線時被針紮了一下。

reel [ril] .... ★★

n. 捲筒，線軸

v. 卷，繞：reel in a large fish 釣上一條大魚

sack [sæk] .... ★★★★

n. 袋，麻袋：The potatoes were put into sacks. 馬鈴薯裝進了麻袋。

sheathe [ʃið] .... ★

v. （將刀劍）入鞘

shed [ʃɛd] .... ★★★★

n. 棚子，車庫

v. 脫落，脫去，流出，流下，解釋：Some trees shed their leaves in cold weather. 有些樹在寒冷的天氣裡落葉。

squash [skwɑʃ] .... ★

v. 壓碎

n. 南瓜：When squashed, the stem and leaves of the jewelweed exude a juice that will soothe some skin irritations. 鳳仙花的莖和葉在被壓碎時，會滲出一種能治療皮膚疾病的汁液。

squeeze [skwiz] .... ★★★

v. 擠：The children squeezed together to make room for me to sit down. 孩子們擠在一起以便騰出空間來讓我坐下。

stab [stæb] .... ★

v. 刺，戳：He stabbed the woman with a knife and she died. 他用小刀把這位婦女刺死了。

stick [stɪk] .... ★★★★★

n. 棍，棒，手杖

v. ①刺，戳：She stuck her finger with a needle. 她用針刺傷了手指。②黏貼，貼上：He forgot to stick a stamp on the letter. 他忘了在信上貼郵票。③被黏住：The gum stuck to fingers. 口香糖黏在手指上了。

辨析
Analyze

streak, strip, stripe

1 **streak** *n.*「條紋，條痕」，指不小心弄出的一條紋、條痕，是從平面角度看的：There was a streak of blood on his cheek. 他臉上有一道血印。

2 **strip** *n.*「條，條紋，條狀物」，指窄條，是從立體角度看的，還指狹長的土地或飛機跑道：He tore the cloth into strips to make a mop. 他把布撕成一條條做拖把。

3 **stripe** *n.*「條紋」，指天生的或有意做出的條紋，是從平面角度看的：Tigers have orange fur with black stripes. 老虎橙色的皮毛上有著黑色的條紋。

【片語】① stick to 黏貼在…上，緊跟，緊隨，堅持，忠於，信守② stick out 伸出，空出，堅持到底，繼續

sting [stɪŋ] .... ★★★
v. 螫，刺，叮：The red spot on his arm is a sting. 他手臂上的小紅點是蟲叮的傷痕。

strap [stræp] .... ★★★
n. 皮帶
v. 用帶子捆：He strapped the bag onto his bicycle. 他用帶子把袋子捆在自行車上。

strip [strɪp] .... ★★★★
n. 條帶
v. 剝，奪去：He stripped the paper off the wall. 他把紙從牆上撕去。John stripped off his shirt. 約翰脫掉了襯衫。

stripe [straɪp] .... ★★★
n. 條紋：A tiger has stripes. 老虎（身上）有條紋。

tangle [ˈtæŋg!] .... ★★
v. 使纏結，使糾纏：tangled affair 亂成一團的事物

thrust [θrʌst] .... ★★★★
v. ①插，推：Edward thrust his hands into his pockets. 愛德華把手插進口袋。②刺，戳：He thrust the knife into the enemy's heart. 他把刀刺進敵人的胸膛。
n. ①戳，刺：He gave me a thrust on the back. 他朝我後背刺一刀。②要點，要旨：the main thrust of robot research. 機器人研究的主要方向。③推力：The direction of thrust of rockets and their power are controlled by computers. 火箭及其動力系統的推力方向是由電腦控制的。

tie [taɪ] .... ★★★★★
v. ①拴，繫，捆：The old man tied the dog to the tree. 那個老人把狗拴在樹上。②把…打結，繫上：He is tying his necktie. 他正在打領帶。
n. ①領帶，領結：He took off his jacket and loosened his tie. 他脫了夾克，解鬆了領帶。②紐帶，聯繫：They want to loose their ties with Britain. 他們想要解開和英國的緊密關係。③束縛，牽連：She feels her little son a tie. 她覺得她的小兒子是個累贅。

trim [trɪm] .... ★★★
v. 整理，修剪，裝飾：She trimmed his hair. 她替他修剪頭髮。

辨析
Analyze

bind, fasten, tie

1 **bind** vt. 「捆綁，捆紮，使結合，使黏合，約束，裝訂」，指用繩索等線狀的東西捆綁起來（兩者緊挨著），還可用作比喻，表示關係密切：They bound his legs and arms so that he couldn't escape. 他們把他的手腳綁起來，使他逃不了。

2 **fasten** vt. 「紮牢，繫牢」，指用某種方式固定，使其不會鬆開（不一定用繩索）：Have you fastened all the doors and windows? 你把所有的門窗關牢沒？

3 **tie** vt. 「栓，紮，捆，把…打結，連接，使有關聯」，指用繩將兩個物體連在一起（可以有一段距離），有時用作比喻，表示有關聯：The boy tied the cow to a small tree. 小孩將牛栓在一棵小樹上。

n. 整理，修剪，裝飾：My hair needs trim. 我的頭髮該剪了。

adj. 整齊的，整潔的：a trim hedge 修整好的籬笆

twist [twɪst] .... ★★★★
v. 搓，撚，撚，扭，扭曲，歪曲，曲解：String is made of threads twisted together. 繩子是把線撚在一起做成的。

n. 扭轉，扭彎，扭，撚，搓：a road full of twists and turns 彎彎曲曲的路

undo [ʌnˈdu] .... ★★★
v. 取消，解開，打開：She undid the string round the parcel. 她解開了繞在包裹上的繩子。

wind [waɪnd] .... ★★★★
vt. ①繞，纏，裹②上發條
vi. ①迂迴前進②捲曲，纏繞
【片語】① wind off 纏開，捲開 ② wind up 結束，上緊發條 ③ wind sb. up 使振奮，使氣惱 ④ wind down （鐘錶）越走越慢，（人）放鬆，鬆弛

辨析 Analyze

chop, clip, cut, trim

1 **chop** *vt.*「砍，劈，斬」，指用斧或其他有刃的工具重複性地用力砍、劈或剁，其相應名詞有 chopper（砍刀）：We are going to chop down some of the old apple trees; they've almost stopped producing fruit. 我們打算砍掉一些蘋果樹，這些樹幾乎不結果實了。

2 **clip** *vt.*「剪，修剪」，指剪短頭髮、指甲、羊毛等：The farmers are clipping the sheep's wool. 農民在剪羊毛。

3 **cut** *vt.*「割，切，剪」，還可指切斷關係等，詳見以上該詞條的用法：Mum asked me to go into the kitchen and cut a plate of ham. 母親要我到廚房去切一盤火腿。

4 **trim** *vt.*「修剪，整修，削減，刪減，裝飾」，指為了美化而修剪花木、頭髮、鬍子等：The bushes need trimming. 這些灌木需要修剪。

辨析 Analyze

twist, wind

1 **twist** *vt. & vi.*「使纏繞，使盤繞，轉動，旋轉，撚，搓，歪曲，扭傷」，指扭、撚、反覆折彎或纏繞，也指編繩索、辮子，還指路、河蜿蜒：Don't twist my arm. 別撚我的手臂。

2 **wind** *vt.*「繞，纏，（給…）上發條」，指反覆纏繞、環繞，尤指繞毛線團或上發條，還指路、河蜿蜒：She wound the wool into a ball. 她把毛線繞成一個毛線團。

Movement 肢體動作名稱總匯

13

應得、偷盜、搶劫相關辭彙

Vocabulary of Theft

accredit [ə'krɛdɪt] .... ★★★★★
v. 歸功於…：They have accredited the landslide victory of the election to the rich and influential sponsors. 他們將選舉中獲得的壓倒性勝利歸功於富裕且影響力大的贊助商們。

burglar ['bɝglɚ] .... ★
n. 夜盜，竊賊

due [dju] .... ★★★★★
adj. 預期的，應得的，到期的：Their plane is due in 15 minutes. 他們的飛機預定在 15 分鐘後到達。

pilferage ['pɪlfrɪdʒ] .... ★
n. 偷竊

theft [θɛft] .... ★★
n. 偷竊：When she discovered the theft of her bag, she went to the police. 當她發現錢包被偷時，她便報警了。

thief [θif] .... ★★★★
n. 賊，小偷

14

推、拉、拿取、投、拋、撫摸相關辭彙

Vocabulary of Pushing & Pulling

bring [brɪŋ] .... ★★★★★
v. ①拿來，帶來：Bring me some water, please! 請幫我拿些水來；Bring your friends with you. 把你的朋友帶來。②引起，導致：This sad news brought tears into her eyes. 這個壞消息讓她流下了眼淚。
【片語】① bring about 帶來，造成② bring down 打倒，降低③ bring forward 提出，提議④ bring out 出版，推出，使顯出⑤ bring up 教育，培養

cast [kæst] .... ★★★★★
v. 投，擲，拋，鑄造：Laser light beamed onto glass fibers casts a characteristic pattern. 投射到玻璃光纖上的雷射光線射出一個特殊的圖案。

clamp [klæmp] .... ★
v. 夾：Try to clamp these two blocks of wood together. 試著把這兩塊木頭夾在一起。

dab [dæb] .... ★
v. 輕拍：He dabbed the wound on her arm gently with cotton wool. 他用脫脂棉輕擦她手臂上的傷口。

dangle [`dæŋgl̩] .... ★★★★★
v. 懸擺：The leaves dangled in the wind. 樹葉迎風搖擺。

dart [dɑrt] .... ★★
v. 投擲，猛衝
n. 標槍，猛衝：The child made a sudden dart across the road. 那小孩突然橫越馬路。

dash [dæʃ] ....★★★★
v. 衝，猛衝，突進：The wolf dashed through the woods. 狼突然跑進樹林中。

dig [dɪg] ....★★★★
v. 挖，掘：Some boys dug a hole on the hill. 一些小男孩在山上挖了個洞。

drag [dræg] ....★★★★
v. 拖動：Mother had to drag me to the dentist. 媽媽不得不硬拖我去看牙醫。He dragged the truth out of the reluctant witness 他迫使不情願的目擊者講出事實。

excavate [`ɛkskəˌvet] .... ★
v. 挖掘：The workmen excavated a hole in the wall to let the sewage pipe pass through. 工人們在牆上挖了個洞讓污水管通過。

exhume [ɪgˈzjum] .... ★

v. 掘出：exhume a body from an ancient tomb 從古墓中掘出屍體；exhume an old play 發掘舊劇本

extract [ɪkˈstrækt] .... ★★

v. 取出，提取，推斷出（原理等），摘錄：After crude oil is extracted from a well, it is usually piped to a refinery. 當原油從油井中提取出來後，通常被輸送到精煉廠。

n. 摘錄，節錄：She read me a few extracts from her own new novel. 她把自己新的小說念了幾段給我聽。

extraction [ɪkˈstrækʃən] .... ★

n. 提煉，提取：Her teeth are so bad that she needs three extractions. 她牙齒壞得非常嚴重，得拔掉三顆。

feel [fil] .... ★★★★★

v. ①感覺，覺得：I feel something biting me. 我感到什麼東西在咬我。②摸，觸：I can't feel where the candle is. 我摸不到蠟燭在哪兒。

【片語】feel like 想要

fetch [fɛtʃ] .... ★★★★

v. 拿來，請來，帶來：The puppy fetched the stick that we had tossed. 小狗啣回了我們扔掉的棍子。

finger [ˈfɪŋgɚ] .... ★★★★★

n. 手指

fling [flɪŋ] .... ★★

v. 投，拋，擲：Don't fling your clothes about on the chair; hang them up. 別把衣服亂扔在椅子上，把它們掛起來。

haul [hɔl] .... ★★

v. 拖拽，拖運：Raised for its milk, meat, and hide, the reindeer is also used to haul things from place to place. 人們飼養馴鹿不僅用來獲取奶、肉和毛皮，而且還用它們運輸東西到別處。

heave [hiv] .... ★★★

v. 用力舉起，拖：The storm heaved the sea into mountainous waves. 風暴在海面上掀起萬丈波濤。

hold [hold] .... ★★★★★

v. ①拿著，握住：He is holding his hat on his head because the wind is so strong. 因為風太大了，他按住頭上的帽子。②舉行：We shall hold a meeting this evening. 今晚我們要開會。

【片語】① hold back 阻止② hold on 別掛（電話），堅持下去③ hold up 舉起，擡起，停滯

hurl [hɝl] .... ★★

v. 猛投，猛衝：He hurled the brick through the window. 他用力把磚頭丟進窗戶。

jerk [dʒɝk] .... ★★

v. 急拉，抽搐：She jerked out the knife that was stuck in the wood. 她把戳在木頭裡的刀猛地拔了出來。

lift [lɪft] .... ★★★★★

v. ①提，舉：Can you lift the box with one hand? 你能用一隻手把這個箱子舉起來嗎？②消極，消失：The fog lifted and the sun came out. 霧消散了，太陽出來了。③上升，升為：His voice lifted suddenly. 他的聲音猛地提高。

n. 電梯：He took the lift to the 5th floor. 他乘電梯到了 5 樓。

lock [lɑk] .... ★★★★★

n. 鎖：She changed all the locks after the burglary. 盜竊發生後她更換了所有的鎖。

v. （被）鎖上：The door won't lock to. 門無法鎖上。

pull [pʊl] .... ★★★★★

v. 拉，拖，拽：Pull your chair up to the desk. 把椅子拉到桌子旁邊來。

【片語】① pull on 穿，戴：Pulling on his hat, he went out of door. 他戴上帽子出門。② pull off 脫衣、帽：The guest pulled off their coat after they enter the hall. 客人們走進大廳後，脫掉了外衣。

n. 拉，拖，拉力，牽引力：Give the rope a pull. 把繩子拉一下。

push [pʊʃ] .... ★★★★★
v. 推：You should apologize for you had pushed me. 你推了我，應該要道歉。
n. 推，推力，促進，推進：Give the gate a push and it will open. 用力推一下門就會開。

pushy [ˋpʊʃɪ] .... ★★★★★
adj. 有衝勁的，愛干涉的

put [pʊt] .... ★★★★★
v. 放，擺：He put the books on the shelf. 他把書放在書架上。
【片語】① put away 把…收起來，放好② put down 記下，放下③ put off 延期④ put on 穿上，戴上，演出，上演，增加（體重）：put on weight 發胖⑤ put up 舉起，抬起，掛起

send [sɛnd] .... ★★★★★
v. ①送，寄：The child was tired, so I sent him to bed. 孩子累了，於是我將他送上床。②派遣，打發：Please send these people away. 請把這些人打發走吧。
【片語】① send for 派人去請，召喚，索取② send away 攆走，開除，解雇

sensory [ˋsɛnsərɪ] ....★
adj. 感覺的：sensory nervous system 感覺神經系統

sensuous [ˋsɛnʃʊəs] ....★
adj. 感覺的，美感的：a sensuous painting 一幅有美感的繪畫

shove [ʃʌv] ....★
v. 推擠：to shove a boat into the water 把船推到水裡

辨析
Analyze

cast, fling, hurl, pitch, throw, toss

1 **cast** *vt.* 「投，扔，投射（光、視線等）」，與throw同義，但更強調目的性，有更多的固定搭配詞和抽象的涵義，其動作的方向多為向下：I saw many peasants casting seed on the field. 我看到很多農民在田裡撒種子。

2 **fling** *vt.* 「（用力地）扔，擲，丟」，指用力扔，但不一定扔得很遠：The carpenter angrily flung aside his tools and would work no longer. 這個木匠氣憤地把工具扔到一邊，不再工作了。

3 **hurl** *vt.* 「猛投，力扔」，指用力向遠處扔：The last competitor hurled the shot 193 meters. 最後一位選手將鉛球投了 193 米。

4 **pitch** *vt. & vi.* 「投擲，扔」，指向上或向前投、扔：He pitched the ball to the other end of the court. 他把球投到球場的那一邊。

5 **throw** *vt.* 「扔，投」，常用詞，用法很廣：He threw a ball at me. 他把一個球向我扔過來。

6 **toss** *vt.* 「投，扔，拋」，指輕輕地向上拋或向上拋較輕的東西：The children tossed the ball to each other. 孩子們把球相互拋來拋去。

肢體動作名稱總匯

Movement

strain [stren] .... ★★★★

n. ①過勞，極度緊張：suffer from mental strain 精神極度緊張②張力，應變：stand any strain 承受任何拉力

v. ①盡力使用，使緊張：strain one's eyes 全神貫注地看。②拉緊，繃緊：They both strain the rope. 他倆都拉緊了繩子。③扭傷，拉傷：He strained his foot. 他把腳扭傷了。④盡力，努力：His eyes strained to catch a glimpse of the hero. 他努力望去要看一看這位英雄。

take [tek] .... ★★★★★

v. ①拿，攜帶：Who has taken my umbrella? 誰拿走我的傘？②帶（往某處）：Will this road take me to the post office? 這條路能到郵局嗎？③做某個動作，進行某種活動：The old man takes a walk every morning. 那老人每天早晨都會去散步。④花費（時間）：The game took five hours. 這場比賽花了 5 個小時。⑤吃，喝，吸入，服用：Take this medicine after each meal. 每次飯後服用此藥。⑥乘車（船）：He took a plane to Beijing. 他乘飛機前往北京。

【片語】① take a walk 散步② take a rest 休息③ take down 取下④ take exercise 鍛煉⑤ take off 脫掉，起飛⑥ take out 取出⑦ take medicine 吃藥⑧ take turns 依次，輪流

辨析 Analyze

drag, draw, haul, pull, tow, trail, tug

1. **drag** *vt.* 「拖，拉，拖著腳步走」，指拖，拽，其動作需要克服較大的阻力，如在地面上或泥水中等：Drag the chair over here so that I can stand on it. 把椅子拖過來，我好站在上面。

2. **draw** *vt.* 「拖，拉，拔出，取出」，指平穩地拖、拉、划：The engine drew the train out of the station. 火車頭牽引著火車駛出車站。

3. **haul** *vt.* 「拖，拉，拖運」，指拖、拉笨重的東西：The tractor hauled the logs out of the forest. 拖拉機把木頭從森林拖出來。

4. **pull** *vt.* 「拖，拉，拔」，常用語，用法很廣：She pulled his sleeve to get his attention. 她扯了扯他的一隻袖子以引起他注意。

5. **tow** *vt.* 「拖，拉，牽引」，指用繩索拖，尤其是用一種交通工具拖另外一種交通工具：We towed the damaged car to the nearest garage. 我們把損壞的車拖到最近的修理廠。

6. **trail** *vt.* 「跟蹤，追蹤」，指有物體拖隨在後面，還指跟蹤、跟隨：She walked slowly along the path, with her skirt trailing in the mud. 她沿著小路慢慢走著，裙子拖在泥水裡。

7. **tug** *vt.* 「用力拖拉」，指用力拖、拉：The horse tugged harder, and finally the log began to move. 那匹馬使勁拉，最後把木頭拉動了。

throw [θro] .... ★★★★★

v. 擲，扔，拋，投：She threw an angry eye
at me. 她生氣地看了我一眼。

【片語】throw away 扔掉，拋棄

toss [tɔs] .... ★★

v. 向上扔，向上擲，搖擺，顛簸，輾轉反側：
They tossed the ball to each other. 他們把
球互相丟來丟去。

tow [to] ....★

v. 拖引，牽引：We towed the car to the
garage. 我們把車子拖到了車庫。

tug [tʌg] .... ★★★

v. 用力拉，猛拉，拖拉：The small child
tugged at her sleeve to try and get her
attention. 這個小孩子用力拉她的一隻袖子，
以引起她的注意。

Movement 肢體動作名稱總匯

15

清潔、切割、弄髒相關辭彙

Vocabulary of Cleaning & Cutting

bath [bæθ] .... ★★★★
n. ①浴，洗澡②浴缸
【片語】have/take a bath 洗個澡
v.（為…）洗澡：The mother had to bath her baby. 這位媽媽得幫孩子洗澡。

bathe [beð] .... ★★★
v. ①幫…洗澡：She bathed the babies. 她幫嬰兒們洗澡。②洗澡：Some boys don't like to bathe. 有些男孩子不喜歡洗澡。③游泳：On hot days we often to bathe in the river. 我們在熱天常去河裡游泳。

bathroom [ˈbæθˌrum] .... ★★★
n. 浴室

brush [brʌʃ] .... ★★★★
n. ①刷子，毛刷：a boot / shoe brush 鞋刷②畫筆
v. ①刷，擦，撢，拂：brush one's teeth 刷牙②擦過，掠過：He brushed past me in a rude way. 他冒失地從我身邊擦身而過。
【片語】brush up 溫習，複習

clean [klin] .... ★★★★★
v. 清掃，打掃：Once the museum staff cleans out the drawers, the curator may store the shells there. 當博物館工作人員把抽屜清乾淨之後，館長就可以把貝殼放在那裡了。

cleanse [klɛnz] .... ★★★★★
v. 使清潔：The nurse cleansed the wound for the injured before stitching it. 護士先把傷者的傷口處理乾淨後再縫合。

clear [klɪr] .... ★★★★★
adj. ①清晰的，清楚的：They reason is very clear. 理由很清楚。②晴朗的，清澈的，明亮的：a clear day 晴天③暢通的，無阻的：The road is clear. 道路暢通無阻。
adv. 清楚，清晰，明白：speak loud and clear 說話聲音洪亮而清楚
v. ①打掃，清除：clear the ground 掃地②使清楚，使明白：The president's statement cleared the air of guessing. 總統的聲明澄清了種種猜測。
【片語】① clear away 使…清除掉，收拾② clear up 使變清，放晴，清理

contaminate [kən'tæmənet] ...... ★★★★★

v. 污染：In some cases, the organisms that cause blood poisoning enter the bloodstream through contaminated needles or other improperly sterilized instruments. 在某種情況下，那些使血液感染的有機體，是由感染的針頭或其他未完全消毒的醫療器具進入到血管中的。

contamination [kən,tæmə'neʃən] ★★★★★

n. 污染：Groundwater, a resource that exists everywhere beneath the Earth's surface, is under increasing risk of contamination and overuse. 儲藏於地表下方的地下水資源，越來越受到污染和過量使用的威脅。

delete [dɪ'lit] .... ★★★

v. 刪除：References to places of battle were deleted from soldiers' letters during the war. 在戰時，士兵們的信件中提到作戰地點的地方均被刪掉。

eradicate [ɪ'rædɪ,ket] .... ★

v. 根除：The Salk vaccine is a major factor in the fight to eradicate polio. 沙克疫苗在根除脊髓灰質炎之戰中起到了主要作用。

erase [ɪ'res] .... ★

v. 消除：Unconsciousness erased the details of the accident from her memory. 昏迷抹去了她對事故細節的記憶。

immerse [ɪ'mɝs] .... ★

v. 沉浸，為…施洗禮：The professor was so immersed in her work that she didn't notice me. 教授在專心工作，所以沒注意到我。

indivisible [,ɪndə'vɪzəb!] .... ★★★★★

adj. 不可分割的：an indivisible union of states 不可分離的國家聯盟

mop [mɑp] .... ★

n. 拖把：The housemaid comes to mop our kitchen floor twice a week. 女傭每週兩次到我家來拖洗廚房地板。

vt. 用拖把拖洗，擦，揩

polish ['pɑlɪʃ] .... ★★★★

n. 亮光劑，上光蠟

v. 擦亮，拋光，磨光，改善：Boxwood is close-grained, hard, and polishes nicely when waxed. 黃楊木紋路緻密，質地堅硬，並且在打蠟之後非常光亮。

pollutant [pə'lutənt] .... ★★★

n. 污染物質

pollute [pə'lut] .... ★★★

v. 污染：Churches and altars were polluted by atrocious murders. 教堂和聖壇被兇殘的謀殺褻瀆了。

pollution [pə'luʃən] .... ★★★

n. 污染，玷污：Pollution in the air reduced the visibility near the airport. 空氣中的污染降低了機場附近的能見度。

purification [,pjʊrəfə'keʃən] .... ★★★★★

n. 純化，淨化

rinse [rɪns] .... ★

v. 涮，漂洗，清洗

n. 洗髮水，染髮劑：I rinsed the clothes I had washed. 我把洗過的衣服沖洗乾淨。

rub [rʌb] .... ★★★★

v. 擦，摩擦：She rubbed the window with a cloth. 她用一塊布擦窗戶。

rubber ['rʌbɚ] .... ★★★

n. ①橡皮：He used a rubber to wipe out mistakes. 他用橡皮擦去錯字。②橡膠製品 ③膠鞋

adj. 橡膠的：rubber gloves 橡膠手套

scrape [skrep] .... ★★★

n. 擦痕，擦傷，刮痕／屑

v. 刮，擦，刮去：Scrape the mud off your shoes with this knife. 用這把小刀把你鞋上的土刮去。

scrub [skrʌb] .... ★

n. 刷洗，擦洗

肢體動作名稱總匯

Movement

v. 刷洗，擦洗：Although she scrubbed the old pot thoroughly, she could not make it look completely clean. 儘管她使勁擦洗了那個舊壺子，但還是無法讓它看起來完全乾淨。

sever [ˈsɛvə] .... ★★★★★
v. 分開，斷絕：The rope severed under the strain. 繩子在拉緊後斷了。

shave [ʃev] .... ★★★
v. ①剃，刮，刨，削：She shaved her legs' hair. 她刮掉腿上的毛。②修面，刮臉：He shaved off his beard. 他刮掉了鬍子。
n. 刮臉

shear [ʃɪr] .... ★★★
v. 修剪：shearing a hedge 修剪樹籬

smear [smɪr] .... ★
v. 塗，弄髒：The child's face was smeared with chocolate. 這個孩子的臉上抹得到處都是巧克力。

stain [sten] .... ★★★★
n. 污點，瑕疵
v. 著色，染色：Ravaged by pollution and war, many famous monuments have become eroded and stained. 許多著名的紀念碑由於受到污染和戰爭的破壞，都變得消蝕無色了。

stainless [ˈstenlɪs] .... ★
adj. 不鏽的，沒有污點的：stainless steel 不鏽鋼

sweep [swip] .... ★★★★★
v. ①掃，打掃，拂去：He swept the books from the table. 他清理了桌上的書。②（風）吹，（浪等）沖：The wind swept the street. 風吹過街道。③掃掠：A great wave of fear swept the country. 一場恐慌掃掠了全國。④快速移動：When the front door was open, the children swept in. 前門剛開，孩子們就衝了進去。

tint [tɪnt] .... ★
v. 染色

wash [wɑʃ] .... ★★★★★
v. 洗，洗滌：I wash my own clothes. 我自己洗衣服。

wipe [waɪp] .... ★★★★
v. 擦，揩，拭：Please wipe up the table. 請把桌子擦乾淨。

肢體動作 13

16

預防、避免、掩飾、遮蓋相關辭彙 Vocabulary of Prevention & Coverage

abstain [əb`sten] .... ★
v. 戒絕：He was kidnapped after refusing to abstain from politics. 他拒絕退出政壇後就被綁架了。

abstinence [`æbstənəns] .... ★
n. 禁戒，節制：abstinence from participation in social affairs 戒絕參與社交活動

assuage [ə`swedʒ] .... ★
v. 緩和：Nothing could assuage his anger. 沒有任何事情能夠平息他的怒氣。

avert [ə`vɝt] .... ★★★★★
v. 轉移，避免，防止：Many highway accidents can be averted by courtesy. 互相禮讓可以避免公路上的許多交通事故。

avoid [ə`vɔɪd] .... ★★★★★
v. 避免，迴避，躲開：I crossed the street to avoid meeting him, but he saw me and came running towards me. 我穿越馬路以避開他，但他看到了我並朝我跑過來。

beforehand [bɪ`for.hænd] .... ★
adv. 事先：If you wanted soup for lunch, you should have told me beforehand. 你要是中午想喝湯，應該事先就告訴我。

conceal [kən`sil] .... ★★★★★
v. 把…隱藏起來：He concealed the sweets in his pocket. 他把甜食藏在口袋裡。

cover [`kʌvɚ] .... ★★★★★
v. 包括，報導：to take out a new policy that will cover all our camera equipment 提出能保障我們所有攝影器材的新政策；Two reporters covered the news story. 兩名記者負責報導這則新聞。

eschew [ɪs`tʃu] .... ★
v. 避開，遠離：A wise person eschews bad company. 聰明人遠避惡友。

evade [ɪ`ved] .... ★★★★★
v. 逃避，迴避：The released criminal always tries to evade the police. 被釋放的罪犯總試著躲避警方。

evasion [ɪ`veʒən] .... ★★★★★
n. 逃避：The fox's clever evasion of the dogs. 狐狸狡猾地躲避狗。

evasive [ɪ'vesɪv] .... ★★★★★
adj. 逃避的，推諉的：took evasive action 採
　　取逃避行動

exodus ['ɛksədəs] .... ★
n. 大批離去：capital exodus 資本逃避

hide [haɪd] .... ★★★★★
v. ①把…藏起來，隱藏：The boy hid the book
　　under his bed. 這個男孩把書藏到了床下。
　　②隱瞞，遮掩：Clouds hide the sun. 雲彩
　　遮住了太陽。③（躲）藏，隱埋：She hid
　　behind the door. 她藏在門後。

hush [hʌʃ] .... ★★
n. 沉沒，靜寂
v. 掩蓋
int. 噓：The President tried to hush up the
　　fact that his adviser had lied. 總統試圖掩
　　蓋他的顧問說謊的事實。

mask [mæsk] .... ★★★★
v. ①用面具遮住，遮蓋：The surgeon masked
　　his face before performing the operation. 外
　　科醫生在動手術以前戴上了口罩。②掩飾，
　　掩蓋：His smile masked his anger. 他的微
　　笑掩飾了他的憤怒。
n. ①面具，面罩，口罩：The dancers at the
　　ball wore colorful masks. 參加舞會的人們
　　戴著色彩斑斕的面具。②假面具，偽裝：
　　under a / the mask of friendship 在友誼的假
　　面具下

precaution [prɪ'kɔʃən] .... ★★★
n. 預防，謹慎，警惕：He took every
　　precaution but still got a bad deal on that
　　used car. 他處處小心但還是在二手車交易中
　　吃了虧。

precautionary [prɪ'kɔʃənˌɛrɪ] .... ★★★
adj. 預防的：take precautionary measures 採
　　取預防措施

preclude [prɪ'klud] .... ★★★★★
v. 排除，防止：Modesty precludes me from
　　accepting the honor. 謙遜使我拒絕這項榮
　　譽。

secrete [sɪ'krit] .... ★★★★★
v. 藏匿，私行侵吞，分泌：Penguins do not
　　suffer from the cold in Antarctica because
　　their feathers secrete a protective oil. 企鵝
　　在南極不會凍傷，因為牠們的羽毛能分泌出
　　一層保護性的油脂。

shun [ʃʌn] ....★
v. 避開：In many societies the person who
　　fails to conform to conventional behavior is
　　likely to be shunned by others. 在許多社會
　　裡，人們很可能會避開不遵守傳統習俗的
　　人。

sidestep ['saɪdˌstɛp] .... ★★★★★
v. 迴避，閃過

465

17

坐、休息相關辭彙

Vocabulary of Sit & Rest

Movement 肢體動作名稱總匯

recess [rɪˋsɛs] .... ★★★
n. 休息，凹處

rest [rɛst] .... ★★★★★
n. ①休息，睡眠，停止，靜止：He must not work so hard, and he'd better take a rest for three days. 他不能再拼命工作了，最好是休息個 3 天。②剩餘部分，其餘：He took ten and gave the rest of apples to others. 他拿了 10 顆蘋果，剩下的給別人。③其餘的人（或物）：Three of us will go, the rest are to stay here. 我們 3 個人去，其餘人留在這兒。
【片語】have/take a rest 休息
v. ①休息：He stopped to rest his horse. 他停下來讓馬休息一下。②睡，放，（使）擱在：He is so tired that he rested on the grass and soon went to sleep. 他太累了，以至於躺在草地上不久就睡著了。

seat [sit] .... ★★★★★
n. 座位，底座：All the seats in the room were empty. 屋子裡所有的位子都空著。

sit [sɪt] .... ★★★★★
v. （使）坐，（使）就坐：Please sit down. 請坐下。

stand [stænd] .... ★★★★★
v. 忍受：My aunt said that she couldn't stand being kept waiting. 我姑姑說她無法忍受等待。

stoop [stup] .... ★★★★
v. 彎腰，俯身：He stooped to look under the table. 他彎腰往桌下看。

18

調查、審查相關辭彙
Vocabulary of Checking

audit [ˈɔdɪt] .... ★

v. 審查：Independent accountants audit the company annually. 獨立的會計師每年審查公司帳目。

n. 查帳

audition [ɔˈdɪʃən] .... ★

n. 試聽，面試：She would have her audition in front of the director. 她將在導演面前試演。

auditor [ˈɔdɪtɚ] .... ★

n. 審計員，旁聽者

censor [ˈsɛnsɚ] .... ★

v. 檢查

n. 檢查員：The censor in a dictatorship is authorized to examine books, films, or other material and to remove or suppress what is considered morally, politically, or otherwise objectionable. 獨裁國家的審查員負責審查書籍、電影或其他資料，並刪去或削減在道德上、政治上或其他方面不宜的內容。

check [tʃɛk] .... ★★★★★

v. 檢查，核對：Please check over the speech draft and correct the mistakes, if any. 請把演講稿檢查一遍，如果有錯誤，請改正過來。

19

追、捉、抓、拍打相關辭彙

Vocabulary of Chasing & Hitting

baste [best] .... ★★★★★
v. 毆打，公開責罵

beat [bit] .... ★★★★★
adj. 疲倦的：I'm deadly beat after going through all
　　this mass of details of the case! 我看完一大堆關於
　　這個案件的細節後，簡直快累死了！
v. 攪打，攪拌：Cream of tartar, a weak acid, can be
　　added to egg whites to help them foam when they
　　are beaten. 酒石英是一種弱酸，可以在攪打蛋白時
　　加入來產生泡沫。

captive [ˋkæptɪv] .... ★★
n. 俘虜
adj. 被俘虜的，被監禁的：Lying in my hospital bed, I
　　was a captive audience to these uninteresting old
　　stories. 我躺在醫院裡，只好乖乖當個聽眾，聽那
　　些乏味的舊故事。

captivity [kæpˋtɪvətɪ] .... ★★
n. 囚禁，拘留：They were in captivity for a month. 他
　　們已被監禁一個月了。

capture [ˋkæptʃɚ] .... ★★★★
v. ①捕獲，俘獲：We captured them alive. 我們活捉
　　了他們。②奪得，攻佔：Tom was so clever that he
　　captured most the prizes at school. 湯姆聰明極了，
　　所以他得到了學校裡大部分的獎品。
n. 捕獲，俘獲：He played dead to escape capture by
　　the enemy. 他裝死以免遭敵人俘虜。

catch [kætʃ] .... ★★★★★
v. ①接住：Hi, catch the frisbee. 喂，接住飛盤。②捉
　　住：Cats like to catch mice. 貓喜歡捉老鼠。③趕上
　　（車輛）：Hurry up, or you won't catch the early
　　bus. 快一點，否則你會趕不上早班公車。④患（病
　　等）：catch a cold 著涼，傷風
【片語】catch up with 趕上

catching [ˋkætʃɪŋ] .... ★★★★★
adj. 迷人的，傳染的：Bad colds are catching. 惡性感
　　冒是有傳染性的。

clutch [klʌtʃ] .... ★★
v. 抓住，掌握，攫：He clutched at the branch but
　　could not reach it. 他想抓住那根樹枝，但是搆不著。

expedite [ˈɛkspɪˌdaɪt] .... ★★

v. 加速，派出，暢通：That will expedite the project. 那將加速工程的進展。

fell [fɛl] .... ★★

v. 砍伐：fell a tree 砍倒一棵樹

flap [flæp] .... ★

n. 垂下物，帽邊，袋蓋，拍動

v. 拍打，拍動：The sails flapped in the wind and the boat went ahead smoothly. 帆迎風拍打著，小船順利地向前行駛。

flip [flɪp] .... ★

v. （用手指）彈，投，翻滾：flip over a card 敏捷地翻牌

grab [græb] .... ★★★

v. 攫取，抓住：He grabbed my coat and hat and left. 他拿了我的衣服和帽子就離開了

grasp [græsp] .... ★★★★

v. 理解：That is a problem really beyond my grasp. 這個問題我實在無法理解。

grip [grɪp] .... ★★★★

n. 握緊：He kept a firm grip on his children. 他管小孩管得很嚴。

hit [hɪt] .... ★★★★★

v. ①打擊，擊中：He hit the thief on the head. 他擊中了小偷的頭部。②碰撞：The car hit the wall. 汽車撞在牆上。

n. ①成功而風行一時的事物：The film became a hit overnight. 這部影片一夜間走紅。②擊中：He gave me a hit on the head. 他擊中了我的頭部。③到達，完成：At last we hit the main road. 我們終於到達了主要公路。

kick [kɪk] .... ★★★★

v. 踢：The boy kicked the ball. 那個小男孩踢球。

knock [nɑk] .... ★★★★★

v. 敲，敲打，碰撞：She knocked his head against a tree. 她把他的頭往樹上撞。
【片語】knock at 敲…

n. 敲擊

overtake [ˌovɚˈtek] .... ★★★

v. 追上，趕上，超過：American journalists often overstake a situation to make the news more stimulating. 美國記者經常誇大報導，讓新聞更加刺激。

pat [pæt] .... ★★★★

v. 輕拍，輕打：pat a ball 拍球

n. 輕拍，輕打：He gave the dog a pat as he walked past. 他走過那裡時，輕輕拍了狗一下。

pinch [pɪntʃ] .... ★★★★

v. 擰，捏，夾：A year and half of the blockade has pinched Germany. 一年半的封鎖使德國經濟萎縮。

punch [pʌntʃ] .... ★★★

n. 重擊，打孔：He punched two holes in the tin of oil, and then poured it out. 他在油筒上打了兩個孔，然後把油倒出。

pursuit [pɚˈsut] .... ★★★★

n. 追趕，尋求，職業，工作：*Invisible Man* by Ralph Ellison is about a young black man's pursuit of identity in modern America. 艾利森的作品《隱形人》，是一篇描述一位黑人青年在現代的美國尋求認同感的故事。

scratch [skrætʃ] .... ★★★

v. 撓，抓，扒：He scratched the insect bite on his leg (with his nails). 他（用指甲）搔著腿上被蟲咬的地方。

n. 撓，抓，抓痕，起跑線，起步線：a scratch on her hand 她手上的抓痕

seize [siz] .... ★★★★★

v. 奪取，捕獲：Scott seized the opportunity to present his proposal to the director. 史考特抓住機會，向主管提出了自己的建議。

slug [slʌg] .... ★★★★★

n. 慢吞吞的人或物

v. 猛擊：slug sb. on the nose 一拳打在某人的鼻子上

stun [stʌn] .... ★★

v. 使昏暈，使目瞪口呆：A serious burn can stun and weaken the victim. 嚴重的燒傷會讓患者感到驚恐和虛弱。

swoop [swup] .... ★

v. 猛撲：The bird swooped down to the lake. 這隻鳥猛撲到湖上。

tap [tæp] .... ★★★

n. ①塞子，水龍頭②輕叩，輕拍

v. ①利用，開發：Scientists have found a new way of tapping the sun's energy. 科學家們發現了利用太陽能的新方法。②輕叩，輕拍：She tapped on the glass partition. 她輕輕地叩著玻璃隔牆。

thrash [θræʃ] .... ★

v. 打，鞭打，翻騰，猛烈擺動，翻來覆去：The fishes thrashed around in the net. 魚在網裡活蹦亂跳。

辨析
Analyze

catch, clasp, clutch, grab, grasp, grip, hold, seize

catch、grab、seize描寫動態動作；clasp、grip、hold描寫靜態動作；grasp、clutch則既描寫動態動作也描寫靜態動作。

1　**catch** *vt. & vi.* 「抓住，接住，(使) 夾住」，詞義很廣，本義指伸手去抓、捉 (動態)：Catch the ball with both hands. 用雙手把球接住。

2　**clasp** *vt.* 「抱緊，緊握，扣住，扣緊」，強調緊緊抓住或用雙手／兩隻手臂緊緊抱住 (靜態)，部分詞義與 grip 意義較為接近：The sisters were clasped in each other's arms. 兩姊妹緊緊擁抱。

3　**clutch** *vt. & vi.* 「企圖抓住，抓緊，緊握」，當作「企圖抓住」時與 at 連用，用作「抓緊，緊握」時則是及物動詞，靜態或動態均可：The child clutched/clasped the doll tightly. 那孩子把玩具娃娃抱得緊緊的。

4　**grab** *vt. & vi.* 「抓取，攫取，抓住 (機會)」，指突然抓住 (動態)，與 seize 意義較為接近；作為不及物動詞與 at 連用，意為「抓 (住)，奪 (得)」，主要指瞬間抓住稍縱即逝的東西：The dog grabbed the meat and ran. 那條狗搶了肉就跑。

5　**grasp** *vt.* 「抓緊，抓牢」，常用詞，既可指伸手去抓 (動態)，又可指緊緊抓在手中 (靜態)，還指「理解，領會」：She grasped the letter and held it to her breast. 她抓住信，把信貼在胸前。

6　**grip** *vt.* 「握緊，抓牢」，強調緊緊抓住 (靜態)，還指「吸引…的注意力或想像力等」：The frightened child gripped its mother's arm. 這個受到驚嚇的孩子緊緊抓住媽媽的手臂。

7　**hold** *vt. & vi.* 「拿，握，擁有，持有；支撐」，詞義很廣，本義指用手握住 (靜態)：My father held my hand and tried to comfort me. 父親握住我的手試著安慰我。

8　**seize** *vt.* 「抓住，捉住，奪取，佔據」，指突然用力地抓住或奪取某物 (動態)，也可指抓住易流失的東西：She seized/grabbed the gun from him. 她從他手裡奪過槍。 Many people want to seize/grab/grasp an opportunity to make a lot of money. 很多人想抓住機會大賺一筆。

touch [tʌtʃ] .... ★★★★★

v. ①觸摸，碰到：One of the branches was touching the water. 一根樹枝正觸碰著水面。②觸動，感動：Her sad story touched him. 她悲慘的故事觸動了他。③涉及，論及：They touched many topics in their talk. 他們在談話中談到了許多問題。④觸摸，接觸：The two wires were touching. 兩根電線碰在一起了。

n. ①接觸，碰到：He managed to get a touch to the ball. 他成功地碰到了球。②少許，一點：There's a touch of frost in the air. 空氣中有些薄霧。

【片語】① in touch 聯繫，接觸② out of touch 失去聯繫③ touch on 談及，涉及④ touch up 潤色，改進，修飾⑤ keep in touch with 與…保持聯繫

whip [hwɪp] .... ★★★★

n. 鞭子

v. ①鞭打，抽打，鞭策：whip a horse 抽打馬②攪打（奶油、蛋等）成糊狀

辨析 Analyze

hit, knock, pat, rap, strike, tap

1 hit *vt. & vi.* 「打，擊，擊中，碰撞」，指用力敲打，也指撞擊，還指擊中目標、達到目標：The little boy hit him hard enough to blacken his eyes. 那個小男孩使勁打他，把他的眼睛都打青了。

2 knock *vt. & vi.* 「敲，打，碰撞，撞擊」，常用語，用法很廣：She knocked her head against the wall. 她把頭在牆上撞了一下。

3 pat *vt.* 「輕打，輕敲」，指反覆輕輕敲擊，有時含有鼓勵或喜愛之意：The couch patted the player on the back and said a few encouraging words. 教練在運動員背上輕輕拍了一下，說了幾句鼓勵的話。

4 rap *vt.* 「（輕而快地）敲擊，急敲」，指輕快地敲擊，強調頻率快：She rapped the desk with her pen and called for silence. 她用鋼筆在桌子上敲了幾下，請大家安靜。

5 strike *vt. & vi.* 「打，擊，敲」，指用力敲打、打擊，還指攻擊、襲擊：He struck the table angrily. 他生氣地敲桌子。

6 tap *vt. & vi.* 「輕叩，輕拍」，指輕輕敲擊，還指「利用，開發，竊聽」：He sat tapping his fingers on the arm of the chair. 他坐著用手指輕輕敲椅子的扶手。

20

保衛、抵抗、報復相關辭彙

Vocabulary of Guard & Revenge

baby-sit [ˈbebɪˌsɪt] .... ★★★★★
v. 看管（嬰孩）：Grandmother helps with washing
and baby-sitting. 奶奶幫忙照顧嬰兒，替嬰兒洗澡。

conservative [kənˈsɝvətɪv] .... ★
n. 保守的人
adj. 保守的：The researchers made a conservative
guess at the population of Tokyo. 研究人員對東京
的人口作了一項保守的估計。

conserve [kənˈsɝv] .... ★★★★★
v. 貯藏：He calls to conserve our national heritage in
face of bewildering change. 他呼籲大家，在面臨令
人手足無措的改變時，要保護我們的民族遺產。

escort [ˈɛskɔrt] .... ★★
v. 護送：The queen was escorted by the directors as
she toured the factory. 女王由董事們陪同參觀了工
廠。

guard [gɑrd] .... ★★★★★
n. 守衛，警衛，哨兵

preserve [prɪˈzɝv] .... ★★★★★
v. 保存：After years of research, Charles Drew
devised a procedure for preserving plasma. 查理經
過幾年的研究，發明出了保存血漿的辦法。

protect [prəˈtɛkt] .... ★★★★★
v. 保護，保衛：She had her umbrella to protect her
from the rain. 她有雨傘讓自己不會被雨淋。

react [rɪˈækt] .... ★★★★★
v. 反應，起反應，起作用，起反作用：The ability to
react to the environmental stimuli is a basic and
general characteristic of living organisms. 活的有機
體的一項基本特徵，是會對周圍環境反應。

reactivity [rɪˌækˌtɪvətɪ] .... ★★★★★
n. 反應，反作用（力）

revenge [rɪˈvɛndʒ] .... ★★
v. 報復，報仇：I broke Mary's pen by accident, and in
revenge she tore up my schoolwork. 我不小心弄壞
了瑪麗的鋼筆。她為了報復，撕掉了我的作業。

shield [ˈʃild] .... ★★★★
v. 庇護，保護：He shielded his eyes from the sun. 他
把手放在眼前遮住太陽光。

conserve, preserve, reserve

1 **conserve** *vt.*「保護，保藏，保存」，指保護資源，還指節省、留著以後再用：We must conserve our forest if we are to make sure of a future supply of wood. 如果我們要確保未來木材的供應，我們一定要保護森林資源。

2 **preserve** *vt.*「保護，維持，保存，保藏，醃製」，指加以保護使維持狀態、價值不變，還指使之不腐爛等：She dieted constantly in order to preserve her slender figure. 她經常節食以保持苗條的體態。

3 **reserve** *vt.*「保留，留存，預訂」，指保留權利、觀點，也指預訂房間、座位，還指留著以後再用：I reserve the right to make my own decisions. 我保留自己決定的權利。

defend, guard, protect, safeguard, shield

1 **defend** *vt.*「保衛，保護，辯護」，指採取積極措施，用武力手段抵禦外來進攻或危險，可用作引申義：That lawyer is defending Mr. Smith. 那位律師為史密斯先生辯護。

2 **guard** *vt.*「守衛，保護，防護」，作名詞意為衛兵、哨兵，作動詞指警惕地、小心地看守具體的目標：Two soldiers guarded the gate. 兩名衛兵把守大門。

3 **protect** *vt.*「保衛，保護」，常用語，指利用防護工具或措施使免受傷害或損害：It is the responsibility of adults to protect children. 保護兒童是成年人的職責。

4 **safeguard** *vt.*「保護，維護」，指防範未來的危險、使有保證：Put a good lock on your door to safeguard your property. 把你的門上好鎖以保證你的財產安全。

5 **shield** *vt.*「保護，防護」，作名詞為盾牌、保護物，作動詞指擋住、遮住、保護：He raised his arm to shield himself from the blow. 他舉起手臂擋住別人的毆打。

21

計畫、設計相關辭彙 Vocabulary of Planning

contrive [kən'traɪv] .... ★★★★★

v. 發明，設法：Colonial New Englanders contrived overlapping clapboard walls for their houses to keep out the cold winds. 新英格蘭的殖民者發明了重疊的隔板牆來保持室內的溫暖。

design [dɪ'zaɪn] .... ★★★★★

n. 設計，圖案

v. 設計：Navajo Indians create sand paintings by arranging grains of sand, ground-up minerals, and seeds of various colors into designs. 納瓦霍印第安人以排列沙子、石頭和各種顏色的種子創造出了沙畫。

devise [dɪ'vaɪz] .... ★★★

v. 計畫，發明：Astronauts are subjected to the most rigorous training that has ever been devised for human beings. 太空人所接受的嚴格訓練，是為人類所設計出的最苛嚴的實驗。

layout ['le,aʊt] .... ★★★

n. 規劃，設計：the layout of a factory 工廠的佈局

plan [plæn] .... ★★★★★

n. 計畫，規劃：You may need a plan to overcome your shortcomings step by step. 你可能需要訂一個計畫，來逐步克服你的缺點。

program(me) ['progræm] .... ★★★★★

n. 節目，程式表，說明書

project [prə'dʒɛkt] .... ★★★★★

v. 反射，投射，突出，規劃，放映

n. 方案，規劃，工程，專案：You current project is to build a garage next to your house. 你目前要做的就是在房子旁邊建一個車庫。

22

選擇、使用、引用、編造相關辭彙

Vocabulary of Choice & Use

alternative [ɔlˈtɝnətɪv] .... ★★★★
n. 選擇

adj. 兩者挑一的：the alternative plan of having a picnic or taking a boat trip 去野餐或者是乘船旅遊，二者只能選擇其一的計畫

choice [tʃɔɪs] .... ★★
n. ①選擇，抉擇：Make a careful choice of your friends. 擇友要慎重。②供選擇的東西，選擇：There is a big choice in this shop. 這家商店品種齊全。③入選者，精華：The choice of the enemy troops has been wiped out. 敵軍的主力部隊被殲滅了。

adj. 上等的，精選的：a choice apple 上等蘋果

choose [tʃuz] .... ★★★★★
v. 選擇：After a little time, she chose one of the most expensive dresses in the shop and handed it to an assistant. 她過了一會兒，選了店裡最貴的其中一件衣服，遞給一個店員。

cite [saɪt] .... ★★★★
v. 引用，舉例：Footnotes sometimes explain a word or an idea, but more often they merely cite the source of authority for what the author says. 註腳有時用來解釋一個字或一個概念，但是更常被用來引證作者觀點的來源。

concoct [kənˈkɑkt] .... ★
v. 編造，虛構，製造：When Thomas Edison was only twelve and working as a vendor on a train, he concocted a laboratory in the baggage car. 當愛迪生只有 12 歲並在火車上當小販的時候，在行李車廂裡造了一間實驗室。

optimize [ˈɑptəˌmaɪz] .... ★
v. 最佳化

option [ˈɑpʃən] .... ★★★★★
n. 選擇，取捨：The government has two options, to reduce spending or to increase taxes. 政府有兩種選擇，不是減少開支就是增加稅收。

pick [pɪk] .... ★★★★★

v. ①拾，採，摘：Will you pick some mushrooms for our supper? 你可以為我們的晚餐摘些蘑菇嗎？②挑選，選擇：He picked the biggest box to put away his books. 他選了一個最大的盒子裝他的書。③扒竊：I had my pocket picked in the train. 我在火車上被扒了。④（去）野餐：To pick is very popular in spring. 春天去野餐很流行。

【片語】pick up 撿起，拿起，挑選

picket [ˋpɪkɪt] .... ★

n. 尖木樁，一隊糾察：picket boat 哨船；picket line 警戒線，哨兵線，（罷工時的）糾察線

pickle [ˋpɪkl̩] .... ★

n. 醃製品，酸黃瓜

v. 醃製，醃漬

select [səˋlɛkt] .... ★★★★★

v. 選擇，挑選：He selected a pair of socks to match his suit. 他挑選了一雙與西裝相配的襪子。

adj. 精選的，選擇的：The captain needs a select crew for the dangerous job. 船長需要一批經過精心挑選的水手來做這項危險的工作。

selection [səˋlɛkʃən] .... ★★★★★

n. 選擇：There is a great selection of books on that topic. 在那個話題上有很多可供選擇的書論述。

selective [səˋlɛktɪv] .... ★★★★★

adj. 選擇的，挑選的：selective controls on goods 對商品的選擇性控制

share [ʃɛr] .... ★★★★★

n. 份，份額：This is my share of it. 這是我的一份。

v. 共用，分擔，分享：May she share you book? 她能看你的書嗎？

sift [sɪft] .... ★

v. 篩選，過濾：Snow sifted through a chin in the window. 雪從窗縫中飛進來。

sophistication [sə‚fɪstɪˋkeʃən] .... ★★★

n. 完善，改進

usage [ˋjusɪdʒ] .... ★★★★

n. 使用，用法，慣用法：modern English usage 現代英語用法

used .... ★★★★★

v. [juzd] used to do 過去常常

adj. [just] be/get used to 習慣於

辨析
Analyze

alternative, choice, selection

1 **alternative** *n.*「取捨，抉擇，供選擇的東西，選擇的自由，選擇的餘地」，常指從兩個物件中選擇一個：You have the alternative of leaving or staying. 你可以在去留之間選擇。

2 **choice** *n.*「選擇，選擇權，供選擇的東西」，指從多個物件中自由選擇：The enemy had no choice but to surrender. 敵人別無選擇只好投降。

3 **selection** *n.*「挑選」，主要指從多個對象中挑揀出最好的，selection 還可表示「選集」，如 Selections from Keats 濟慈詩選；The department store has a good selection of computers. 這家百貨商店有很多電腦可供挑選。

Movement 肢體動作名稱總匯

useful [ˈjusfəl] .... ★★★★★
adj. 有用的：It is useful to keep up to date.
跟上時代總是有益的。

useless [ˈjuslɪs] .... ★★★★
adj. 無效的：This is a useless knife—the
handle has broken! 這是把沒用的小刀，
刀柄壞了！

user [ˈjuzɚ] .... ★★★★★
n. 使用者，用戶

utilitarian [ˌjutɪləˈtɛrɪən] .... ★★★
adj. 功利的
n. 功利主義：utilitarian considerations in
industrial design 在企業佈局上的功利主義
考量

utilize [ˈjutḷˌaɪz] .... ★★★
v. 利用

Unit 14
情感心理活動名稱總匯
Feeling

01

感覺、精神、願意相關辭彙

Vocabulary of Feeling

conscious [ˈkɑnʃəs] .... ★★★★
adj. 有意識的：The patient remained fully conscious after the local anesthetic was administered. 該病人在被局部麻醉之後，仍能保持完全清醒。

consecutive [kənˈsɛkjʊtɪv] .... ★★★★★
adj. 連續的：Congressman Sam Rayburn's 25 consecutive terms in the House of Representatives marked one of the longest tenures of any representative in the United States history. 國會議員山姆‧雷伯在眾議院連續 25 年的任期，是美國歷史上最長的任期之一。

embalm [ɪmˈbɑm] .... ★
v. 銘記，使不朽：A precedent embalms a principle. 慣例標榜著法則。

feeling [ˈfilɪŋ] .... ★★★★★
n. ①感情：Have you hurt her feelings? 你傷了她的感情嗎？②感覺，知覺：a feeling of hunger 饑餓感

happiness [ˈhæpɪnɪs] .... ★★★★★
n. ①幸福②愉快，快樂

imposing [ɪmˈpozɪŋ] .... ★★★★
adj. ①令人難忘的：an imposing view 令人難忘的景色；an imposing figure 大人物，要人；an imposing gymnasium 壯麗的體育館②莊嚴的：Ocean waves can cut imposing cliffs along coastlines. 海浪能夠把海岸沿線的岩石沖刷成陡峭雄偉的懸崖。

impress [ɪmˈprɛs] .... ★★★★
v. ①給…深刻的印象，使銘記：The movie didn't impress me at all. 這部電影沒有讓我留下任何印象。②印，壓印：He impressed his seal on the painting. 他在畫上蓋上了他的印章。

impressive [ɪmˈprɛsɪv] .... ★★★
adj. 印象深刻的，感人的：The view from above was more impressive. 從上面看到的景色讓人印象更深。

inherent [ɪnˈhɪrənt] .... ★
adj. 固有的：He has an inherent love of beauty. 他天生愛美。

instinct [ˈɪnstɪŋkt] .... ★★★★
n. 本能，直覺，天性：Trust your instincts and do what you think is right. 相信你的直覺，按你自己認為對的去做。

instinctive [ɪnˈstɪŋktɪv] .... ★★★★
adj. 天生的，本能的：Learning to fly is instinctive in birds. 鳥兒學飛是出於本能。

internal [ɪnˈtɜnl] .... ★★★★
adj. 內在的：internal affairs 國內事務

intrinsic [ɪnˈtrɪnsɪk] .... ★★★★★
adj. 本質的，本身的：The intrinsic value of a coin is the value of the metal it is made of. 一枚錢幣本身的價值是依造幣用金屬的價值而定。

intuition [ˌɪntjuˈɪʃən] .... ★★★★★
n. 直覺

lofty [ˈlɔftɪ] .... ★★
adj. 高聳的，高尚的：Alaska boasts of several climates due to its lofty mountains, warm ocean currents, and frozen seas. 阿拉斯加因其高聳的山脈、溫暖的大洋海浪和冰凍的海水而擁有幾種不同的氣候。

perceive [pəˈsiv] .... ★★★★★
v. 察覺到，看見：I perceived that I could not make her change her mind. 我發覺我不能使她改變主意。

perception [pəˈsɛpʃən] .... ★★★★
n. 感覺，概念，理解力

perceptive [pəˈsɛptɪv] .... ★★★★
adj. 知覺的：Well known for her perceptive and tough-minded movie criticism, columnist Pauline Kael also possessed an extensive knowledge of the technical aspects of filmmaking. 專欄作家克爾因其敏銳和實際的評論而聞名，她同時還對電影製作技術有著廣泛的研究。

reluctant [rɪˈlʌktənt] .... ★★★
adj. 不情願的，勉強的：The mother was reluctant to give his son the key to her car. 這位母親不願意把車鑰匙給兒子。

sensation [sɛnˈseʃən] .... ★★★★★
n. 感覺，知覺，轟動，轟動一時的事物：The sensation of a "lump in one's throat" arises from an increased flow of blood into the tissues of the pharynx and larynx.「喉嚨中有腫塊」的感覺，是由於咽喉中的組織充血產生的。

辨析 Analyze

emotion, feeling, passion

1 **emotion** *n.*「情感，激情」，指外露的情感：The candidate addressed the crowd with emotion. 這個候選人情緒激昂地向人群發表演講。

2 **feeling** *n.*「感情，感覺」，指感覺、感情等，常用語：What he said reflected our feeling. 他的話反映了我們的感受。

3 **passion** *n.*「熱情，酷愛」，指強烈的感情或情感：Can't we talk about this with a little less passion? 我們談這件事情時能不能不要這麼激動？

sense [sɛns] .... ★★★★★

v. 覺得，意識到：The horse sensed danger and stopped. 那匹馬感覺到了危險，停下不走了。

n. ①感官，官感：He has lost his sense of smell. 他已沒了味覺。②感覺：He has a well developed musical sense. 他的音感非常好。③判斷力，見識：common sense 常識 ④意義，意見：The sense of the word is clear. 這個字的意義很清楚。

【片語】① come to one's senses 恢復理性，醒悟過來，甦醒過來② in a sense 從某種意義上來說③ make sense 講得通，有意義，言之有理

sensitive [ˈsɛnsətɪv] .... ★★★★

adj. 敏感的：Estuaries are extremely sensitive and ecologically important habitats providing breeding and feeding grounds for many life forms. 河口是極其敏感的地區，在生態上很重要，為許多生命型態提供了生長的環境。

sentiment [ˈsɛntəmənt] .... ★★

n. 感情，情緒，情操，意見：There's no place for sentiment in business. 做生意不能感情用事。

sentimental [ˌsɛntəˈmɛntl] .... ★★

adj. 傷感的，多愁善感的：The goose quill pen has a great sentimental appeal in this century's highly mechanized culture. 鵝毛筆在這個高度機械文化的世紀裡，給人一種非常傷感的感覺。

spirit [ˈspɪrɪt] .... ★★★★★

n. ①精神：She is here in body, but not in spirit. 她人在心不在。②氣概，志氣：The youth with great spirit is able to do something greater. 志向宏偉的青年能夠取得較大成就。③情緒，心情：You should face to the life with good spirits. 你應該精神飽滿地去面對生活。④酒精，烈酒：Spirits will do you harm. 烈酒對你有害。

spiritual [ˈspɪrɪtʃʊəl] .... ★★★★

adj. 精神（上）的，心靈的：Some people calls the Falungong "the spiritual movement". 有些人把法輪功稱為「精神運動」。

stamina [ˈstæmənə] .... ★

n. 體力，精力：Her lack of stamina made other contestants give up the race. 由於她體力不支，其他的競賽者便放棄了比賽。

temperament [ˈtɛmprəmənt] .... ★★★

n. 氣質，性情：an artistic temperament 藝術家的氣質

辨析
Analyze

instinct, intuition

1 **instinct** *n.*「本能，直覺，天性」，指生來即有的本能，是純客觀的：Most animals have an instinct to protect their young. 大多數動物都有保護自己幼兒的本能。

2 **intuition** *n.*「直覺」，指某種人在某種環境或條件下的直覺，有一定的主觀判斷：My intuition told me it was right. 我的直覺告訴我這是對的。

Feeling 情感心理活動名稱總匯

temperance [ˈtɛmprəns] .... ★★★★★
n. 節制，自制，戒酒：practice temperance in diet 節制飲食

temperate [ˈtɛmprɪt] .... ★★★
adj. 適度的，有節制的：The moist air of the Pacific Ocean brings a temperate climate to the West Coast of the United States. 太平洋的濕潤空氣為美國西海岸帶來了溫和的氣候。

touching [tʌtʃɪŋ] .... ★★★★★
adj. 動人的，令人感傷的：At the age of seventeen, Patty Duke won an Academy Award for her touching portrayal of Helen Keller in *The Miracle Worker*. 派蒂‧杜克 17 歲時，因為在《海倫‧凱倫傳》中感性地刻畫了海倫‧凱勒的形象而獲得了奧斯卡金像獎。

unconscious [ʌnˈkɑnʃəs] .... ★★★★
adj. 失去知覺的，不覺察的：After she hit her head she was unconscious for several minutes. 她撞到頭後，昏迷了幾分鐘。

vigorously [ˈvɪgərəslɪ] .... ★★★
adv. 強有力地：William Penn, the founder of Pennsylvania, vigorously defended the right of every citizen to freedom of choice in religion. 賓夕法尼亞州的創建人威廉‧佩恩，奮力捍衛每個公民宗教自由的權利。

voluntary [ˈvɑlənˌtɛrɪ] .... ★★★★
adj. 自願的，志願的，任意的：She is a voluntary worker at the hospital. 她是這家醫院的義工。

volunteer [ˌvɑlənˈtɪr] .... ★★★★
n. 志願者
adj. 自願的
v. 自願：My uncle volunteers his services to worthy causes. 我的叔叔自願為有價值的事業服務。

willing [ˈwɪlɪŋ] .... ★★★★★
adj. 願意的，樂意的，心甘情願的：He is quite willing to help her. 他很願意幫助她。

willingness [ˈwɪlɪŋnɪs] .... ★★★★★
n. 心願

02

記住、忘記、喚起相關辭彙

Vocabulary of Memory

arouse [ə`raʊz] .... ★★★
v. 喚起，激發：President's policy of cutting down expenditure aroused many protests. 總統的開支縮減政策激起了許多人的抗議。

conjure [`kʌndʒɚ] .... ★
v. 懇求，想像：I conjure you not to betray me. 我懇求你不要背棄我。

conjurer [`kʌndʒərɚ] .... ★
n. 變戲法的人

evoke [ɪ`vok] .... ★★★★★
v. 喚起：That old film evoked our father generation's memories of the years of the war. 那部老片喚起了我們的父執輩對戰爭年代的回憶。

forget [fɚ`gɛt] .... ★★★★★
v. 忘記，遺忘：Forgetting the history means betrayal. 忘記歷史意味著背叛。

memory [`mɛmərɪ] .... ★★★★★
n. ①記憶（力）：She has a good memory for figures. 她對數字有很好的記憶力。②回憶 (of)：memories of one's childhood 童年的回憶③紀念：This book is to the memory of the soldiers who died in the battle. 這本書是紀念那次戰鬥中犧牲的戰士們。④（電腦）記憶體：What kind of memory does the computer have? 這部電腦用什麼樣的記憶體？
【片語】in memory of 紀念

monument [`mɑnjəmənt] .... ★★★
n. 紀念碑，紀念館：This pillar is a monument to all those who died in the civil war. 這座紀念碑是獻給所有在內戰中犧牲的人的。

nostalgia [nɑs`tældʒɪə] .... ★
n. 思鄉，懷舊

oblivion [ə`blɪvɪən] .... ★
n. 忘卻，遺忘：The city has long passed into oblivion. 該城市早已湮沒在記憶裡。

recall [rɪ`kɔl] .... ★★★★★
v. 記憶，憶起：Recall the misery of the past and contrast it with the happiness of today. 想想過去的苦，對比今天的好日子。

recollect [ˌrɛkəˈlɛkt] .... ★★★★
v. 記憶，記得，追憶，回憶：I often recollect childhood days. 我經常回想起童年的日子。

recollection [ˌrɛkəˈlɛkʃən] .... ★★
n. 記起，回想：I have no recollection of that incident. 我記不起來那件事情了。

remembrance [rɪˈmɛmbrəns] .... ★★★★★
n. 記憶，回憶：Christians eat bread and drink wine in remembrance of Jesus. 基督徒吃麵包喝葡萄酒來紀念耶穌。

remind [rɪˈmaɪnd] .... ★★★★
v. 提醒：Please remind me again nearer to the time of the interview. 快要面試的時候請再提醒我一下。

辨析
Analyze

recall, remember, remind

1 **recall** *vt.*「回憶起，回想起，召回，叫回，收回，撤銷」，指主觀地、有意識地回憶起、回想起，指瞬間動作：He couldn't recall her features distinctly. 我無法清楚回想起她的特徵。

2 **remember** *vt. & vi.*「記得，記住」，指往事自然留存在記憶中，不需有意識或刻意追憶便可回想起來，可表示記憶的客觀延續狀態：He suddenly remembered that he had left the windows open. 他突然想起他沒把窗戶關上。

3 **remind** *vt.* 指「提醒，使…想起」，其常用句型有：remind sb. of sth. / remind sb. that... / remind sb. to do sth. ：That story you have just told reminds me of an experience I once had. 你剛才講的故事讓我想起以前的經歷。

03

印象、想像、思考 相關辭彙

Vocabulary of Thinking

brood [brud] .... ★★
n. 一窩孵出的雛雞或雛鳥
v. 沉思：Don't brood about it. 不要想太多。

conceit [kən`sit] .... ★
n. 自負，自大：An eccentric addition to the lobby is a life-size wooden horse, a 19th century conceit. 這個大廳中有一個古怪的附加物，是一匹與活馬大小相當的木馬，代表19世紀的自負。

conceive [kən`siv] .... ★★
v. 想像：The Empire State Building was conceived on a grander scale than previous skyscrapers. 帝國大廈被認為是比以前的其他摩天大樓都宏偉的建築。

consider [kən`sɪdə] .... ★★★★★
v. ①認為，把…看作：We all considered him a clever fellow. 我們都認為他很聰明。②考慮，細想：He considered whether he should do it. 他考慮是否該做這件事。③顧及，關心：He never considers other. 他從不為他人著想。④考慮，細想：Let me consider fully. 讓我充分考慮一下。

consideration [kənsɪdə`reʃən] .... ★★★★★
n. 考慮：The cost of consumption is the first consideration, as far as most ordinary people are concerned. 就多數普通百姓而言，首先要考慮的是消費品的價格。

erroneous [ɪ`ronɪəs] .... ★
adj. 錯誤的：The initial assumption was erroneous. 最初的假設是錯誤的。

fantastic [fæn`tæstɪk] .... ★★★
adj. 空想的，奇異的，古怪的：fantastic ideas about her own superiority 對自己懷有奇特的優越感

fantastically [fæn`tæstɪklɪ] .... ★★★
adv. 奇異地，異乎尋常地

fantasy [`fæntəsɪ] .... ★★★
n. 幻想，空想，怪念頭：The young man lives in a world of fantasy. 這個年輕人生活在幻想的世界裡。

figment [`fɪgmənt] .... ★★★★★
n. 虛構之事：just a figment of the imagination 只不過是虛構出來的事

illusion [ɪ`ljuʒən] .... ★★
n. 幻覺：I have no illusions about his ability.
我對他的能力不存幻想。

imaginary [ɪ`mædʒə͵nɛrɪ] .... ★★★
adj. 虛構的：Acting is defined as the ability to
react to imaginary stimuli. 演戲被定義為
對虛構的刺激的反應能力。

imaginative [ɪ`mædʒə͵netɪv] .... ★★★★★
adj. 富於想像的：an imaginative poet 富於想
像的詩人

imagine [ɪ`mædʒɪn] .... ★★★★★
v. 想像，設想，認為：I tried to imagine the
city when we talk about it. 當我們談論那座
城市時，我努力去想像它。

incisive [ɪn`saɪsɪv] .... ★
adj. 深刻的，尖銳的：an incisive and piquant
style of writing 鋒利、辛辣的寫作風格

inconceivable [͵ɪnkən`sivəbl] .... ★★★★★
adj. 不可思議的：It's almost inconceivable that
a handicapped girl is very independent
and lives all alone. 一個殘疾的女孩居然自
食其力，獨自生活，簡直難以想像。

insight [`ɪn͵saɪt] .... ★★★
n. 洞察力，洞悉，見識：You must have
insight into the international market. 你一定
對國際市場很熟悉。

meditate [`mɛdə͵tet] .... ★
v. 沉思，冥想，反省：She meditated for 2
days before giving her answer. 她考慮了兩
天才答覆。

meditative [`mɛdə͵tetɪv] .... ★
adj. 深思的

mirage [mə`rɑʒ] .... ★
n. 幻境：In a mirage the desert will mimic a
lake. 在海市蜃樓中，沙漠有時會現出湖泊
的形象。

muse [mjuz] .... ★★
v. 沉思，默想：Something must have
happened to her. She has been sitting there
musing for hours. 她一定發生什麼事了，一
連幾小時都坐在那裡沉思。

ponder [`pɑndɚ] .... ★★
v. 考慮，沉思：Bob ponders when he runs
out of money. 鮑伯花光了錢以後，陷入了沉
思。

regard [rɪ`gɑrd] .... ★★★★★
v. ①看待，把…看作為，對待：I regard it as
one of my masterpieces. 我把它看成我的傑
作之一。②尊重：She regards her parents
highly. 她很尊敬她的父母。
n. 敬意，致意，問候：Give my regards to
your parents. 代我向你的父母問好。
【片語】① as regards... 至於② with/in
regard to 關於，至於

辨析
Analyze

imaginary, imaginative

1 **imaginary** *a.*「想像中的，假想的，虛
構的」：This story is not real; it is only
imaginary. 這個故事不是真的，只是虛構
的。

2 **imaginative** *a.*「富有想像力的，愛想
像的」：One of our duties is to cultivate
the students' imaginative power. 我們的
職責之一就是要培養學生的想像力。

ruminate [ˋruməˌnet] .... ★
v. 沉思

seem [sim] .... ★★★★★
v. 好像，似乎：It seems as if it is going to rain. 看來要下雨了。

seemingly [ˋsimɪŋlɪ] .... ★★
adv. 表面上，似乎：In the street portraits of photographer Diane, a seemingly straightforward investigation of the city becomes an intense, introspective analysis of both subject and viewer. 在攝影家丹尼的街頭影像中，一個看似對城市的直觀調查變成了對主題和觀察者深刻自省的分析。

thinker [ˋθɪŋkɚ] .... ★★★★★
n. 思想家

thinking [ˋθɪŋkɪŋ] .... ★★★★★
adj. 思想的，有理性的
n. ①思想，思考 ②想法，見解

thought [θɔt] .... ★★★★★
n. ①想法，見解：His words were full of striking thoughts. 他的話語充滿了非凡的見解。②思考，思維，思想的活動：The youth are full of modern thought. 年輕人滿腦子現代思想。
【片語】on second thought 經重新考慮後，一轉念

vision [ˋvɪʒən] .... ★★★★★
n. 視覺，觀察，視力，想像力，幻想，幻影：She has good vision. 她的視力很好。

Feeling 情感心理活動名稱總匯

04

猜想、假定、假裝相關辭彙

Vocabulary of Supposition

allude [əˈlud] .... ★

v. 提及，暗指：Try not to allude to this matter in his presence because it annoys him. 他在的時候千萬別提這件事，他聽了會生氣。

allusion [əˈluʒən] .... ★

n. 引述，暗指：The allusions to mythological characters in Milton's poems bewilder the reader who has not studied Latin. 密爾頓的詩中對神話人物的引述，讓沒有學過拉丁文的讀者感到困惑。

assumption [əˈsʌmpʃən] .... ★★★

n. 就職，假設：The framework of the special theory of relativity can be constructed from the assumption of the absolute invariability of the speed of light. 特殊相對論的架構，可以由對光速的絕對不變性的假設來構成。

circumvent [ˌsɝkəmˈvɛnt] .... ★

v. 欺詐，以計謀勝過：The king tried to circumvent his enemies. 國王試圖用計謀戰勝敵人。

conjecture [kənˈdʒɛktʃɚ] .... ★

n. 推測，猜想，假想結論

v. 猜測，假設：Scientists conjecture the origin of the universe. 科學家們猜測宇宙的起源。

convenient [kənˈvinjənt] ....★★★★

adj. 便利的，方便的：The mall near our house is convenient to shopping. 我們家附近的購物中心買東西很方便。

disguise [dɪsˈgaɪz] .... ★★★★★

v. 裝扮，假裝，偽裝：disguise one's true intentions 掩蓋某人真正的意圖

n. 偽裝物，假裝，隱藏

dissimulate [dɪˈsɪmjəˌlet] .... ★★★★★

v. 假裝，掩飾：dissimulate fear 掩飾恐懼，強作鎮靜

ensure [ɪnˈʃʊr] ....★★★★

v. ①保證，擔保：We can't ensure success. 我們不能保證成功。②保護，使安全③獲得，保證得到：I cannot ensure you a good post. 我沒辦法保證你能夠得到一個好職位。

expedient [ɪkˈspidɪənt] .... ★★

adj. 權宜的，方便的：It is expedient that he should retire at once. 他最好還是立刻退休。

feign [fen] .... ★

v. 假裝：The hunter had to feign death when he suddenly found out that a bear was coming toward him. 獵人突然發現有隻熊正向他走來，只好裝死。

guess [gɛs] .... ★★★★★

v. 猜想，推測：Guess what I have brought for you. 猜猜我為你帶什麼來了。

hypothesis [haɪˈpɑθəsɪs] .... ★★

n. 假設：That's a quite interesting hypothesis. 那個假設十分有趣。

hypothetical [ˌhaɪpəˈθɛtɪkl̩] .... ★★

adj. 假說的，假想的：a hypothetical situation 一個假設的情形

incredulity [ˌɪnkrəˈdjulətɪ] .... ★

n. 懷疑：Just a few years ago, the very idea that a newborn baby had social behaviors would have been greeted with incredulity. 僅僅在幾年以前，認為新生嬰兒擁有社交行為能力的觀點會招致人們的懷疑。

inkling [ˈɪŋklɪŋ] .... ★★★★

n. 略知，模糊的想法，暗示：to have some inkling 略知一點；to have no inkling 一無所知

insinuate [ɪnˈsɪnjuˌet] .... ★

v. 迂迴進入，暗示：He insinuated his doubt of the reply. 他暗示對這答覆有著懷疑。

presumably [prɪˈzuməblɪ] .... ★★★

adv. 大概，推測起來：Presumably the bad weather has delayed the flight. 大概是天候不佳使飛機誤點了。

presume [prɪˈzum] .... ★★

v. 假定，假設：I presume from your speech that you are a foreigner. 從你說的話，我還以為你是個外國人呢。

presumption [prɪˈzʌmpʃən] .... ★★

n. 推定，猜想：There is a strong presumption in favor of the truthfulness of their statement. 有一個有力的根據足以推定他們所講的是真實的。

pretend [prɪˈtɛnd] .... ★★★★

v. 偽裝：You had to pretend conformity while privately pursuing high and dangerous nonconformist. 當你私底下追求崇高又危險的新教時，你仍得假裝信奉國教。

辨析
Analyze

assure, ensure, insure

1. **assure** *vt.* 「使確信，使放心，確保，保證…」，常用結構為assure sb. that 和 assure sb. of sth.。在用 assure sth. 這一句型時可與 ensure 互換：I can assure you that there is no danger living in this city. 我可以向你保證生活在這城市沒有危險。

2. **ensure** *vt.* 「保證，擔保，確保」，常用結構為「ensure sb. sth.」、「ensure that...」和「ensure sth.」：The sleeping pills will ensure you a good night's sleep. 這些安眠藥可以保證你夜裡睡個好覺。

3. **insure** *vt.* 「保險」：Insurance companies will insure ships and their cargoes against loss at sea. 保險公司會讓船隻及貨物保海上損失險。

情感心理活動名稱總匯

Feeling

provided [prəˋvaɪdɪd] .... ★ ★ ★ ★ ★

conj. 假如，若是：Provided there is no opposition, we shall hold the meeting here. 若沒有異議，我們就在這裡開會。

skeptical [ˋskɛptɪkl] .... ★

adj. 懷疑的：a skeptical attitude 懷疑的觀點；skeptical of political promises 對政治上的許諾產生懷疑

succinct [səkˋsɪŋkt] .... ★

adj. 簡明的，簡潔的：a succinct reply 簡明扼要的回答

suppose [səˋpoz] .... ★ ★ ★ ★ ★

v. 假設，推測：suppose a company has a new breakfast cereal that it wants to sell 假設有間公司想出售一種新的早餐麥片粥

supposedly [səˋpozdlɪ] .... ★ ★ ★ ★ ★

adv. 想像上，恐怕，按照規定：He was supposedly an American. 人們猜他是個美國人。

surmise [səˋmaɪz] .... ★ ★ ★ ★ ★

v. 臆測：Who would have surmised that by 1984 over twenty-four million families in the United States would have both parents in the work force? 誰料想得到，到了1984年，美國將會有2,400萬家庭的父母成為勞動力呢？

suspect [səˋspɛkt] .... ★ ★ ★ ★ ★

v. ①疑有，推測：I suspect that he may be right. 我想他可能是對的。②對…表示懷疑或不信任：She suspects everyone. 她懷疑每個人。③有懷疑

n. 嫌疑犯，可疑分子：The policeman was questioning a murder suspect. 警察正在偵訊謀殺嫌疑犯。

辨析
Analyze

assume, presume, suppose

1 **assume** *vt.*「假定，假設，臆斷」，多指根據假定事實做主觀推測，有時含有武斷的意思：How can you assume me to be responsible for it? 你怎麼能臆斷我對這事有責任呢？

2 **presume** *vt.*「揣測，假定，（沒有證據地）相信，認定，推定」，指根據經驗、理由或邏輯而假設或推測：I presume that you are hungry, so I'm making you some sandwiches. 我想你餓了，所以我正在為你做一些三明治。

3 **suppose** *vt.*「料想，猜想，以為，假定，假設」，常用語，指猜想或假定，用於試探性地陳述自己的看法：Let us suppose for a moment that what you say is true. 讓我們暫且假定你所說的是真的。

05

懷疑、相信、妒忌相關辭彙

begrudge [bɪˈgrʌdʒ] .... ★

v. 羨慕，嫉妒：She begrudged his youth. 她嫉妒他的年輕。

belief [bɪˈlif] .... ★★★★★

n. ①相信，信心，信任，信仰：He expressed his belief in the boy's honesty. 他說他相信這個孩子是誠實的。②信念，信條，教條：That man has a strong belief in God. 那個人對上帝堅信不疑。

believe [bɪˈliv] .... ★★★★★

v. ①相信，信仰 ：Some people believe in God. 有些人信仰上帝。②認為：He believed the fault lay with her. 他認為是她的錯。

confide [kənˈfaɪd] .... ★

v. 傾訴：One evening he came and confided to me that he had spent five years in prison. 有一天晚上，他來向我吐露他曾坐過五年的牢。

confidence [ˈkɑnfədəns] .... ★★★★★

n. 信心：It's a tragedy that one lacks confidence in himself. 一個人如果缺乏自信心，那就是悲劇。

confidential [ˌkɑnfəˈdɛnʃəl] .... ★★

adj. 機密的：a confidential order 密令

credulous [ˈkrɛdʒuləs] .... ★

adj. 輕信的：credulous superstition 幼稚的迷信

cynic [ˈsɪnɪk] .... ★

n. 憤世嫉俗者

cynical [ˈsɪnɪkl] .... ★

adj. 譏諷的，冷嘲熱諷的：a cynical distrust of friendly strangers 對和善的陌生人輕蔑的不信任

deem [dim] .... ★★

v. 認為：The epic, which makes great demands on a poet's knowledge and skill, has been deemed as the most ambitious of poetic forms. 史詩對詩人的知識和技巧要求最高，已被認為是詩體中最具挑戰性的一種。

definite [ˈdɛfənɪt] .... ★★★★

adj. 明確的，肯定的：An apprentice is a person who has agreed to work for a skilled craftsperson for a definite period of time in order to learn a trade. 學徒是一個為了學會某種手藝，而同意在一段確定的時間內為有技能的手藝師父工作的人。

doubt [daʊt] .... ★★★★

v. 懷疑：to doubt politicians when they make sweeping statements 懷疑政客含糊其辭的聲明

doubtful [ˋdaʊtfəl] .... ★★★

adj. 未確定的，不可靠的：the candidate's doubtful past 這位候選人令人質疑的過去

dubious [ˋdjubɪəs] .... ★

adj. 懷疑的：The result is still dubious. 結果尚未確定。

envious [ˋɛnvɪəs] .... ★★★★

adj. 嫉妒的：She was envious of her sister's beauty. 她嫉妒妹妹的美貌。

envy [ˋɛnvɪ] .... ★★★★

v. 妒忌（事物），羨慕（目標）：When I peruse the conquered fame of heroes and the victories of mighty generals, I do not envy the generals. 當我細細咀嚼那些英雄的盛名和偉大的將軍們的勝利時，我並不羨慕他們。

grudge [grʌdʒ] .... ★

v. 嫌惡

n. 惡意：I always feel she has a grudge against me. 我總覺得她對我懷恨在心。

grumpy [ˋgrʌmpɪ] .... ★

adj. 壞脾氣的，性情暴躁的：The grumpy man found fault with everything. 那個性情乖戾的人對什麼事都要找碴。

incredible [ɪnˋkrɛdəbl̩] .... ★★★

adj. 難以相信的：The microscope enables scientists to distinguish an incredible number and variety of bacteria. 顯微鏡可讓科學家區分出細菌令人難以置信的數量和種類。

jealous [ˋdʒɛləs] .... ★★★★

adj. 妒忌的，猜疑的：Sarah is one of Jane's friends, but she is jealous if Jane plays with other girls. 莎拉是珍的朋友，但是如果珍和別的女孩子一起玩，她就會吃醋。

jealousy [ˋdʒɛləsɪ] .... ★★

n. 妒忌：Jealousy and suspicion are eroding our friendship.〔喻〕嫉妒和猜疑在侵蝕我們的友誼。

malevolent [məˋlɛvələnt] .... ★

adj. 惡意的：malevolent stars 掃把星

malice [ˋmælɪs] .... ★★

n. 惡意：He did it through malice. 他做這件事是出於惡意。

辨析
Analyze

doubt, suspect

1 **doubt** vt. 「懷疑」，和suspect在有名詞做其賓語時都指懷疑某事的真實性：I doubt / suspect the truth of the report. 我懷疑該報告的真實性。

2 **suspect** vt. 後面接子句表示「認為⋯會，猜想⋯會」，其名詞子句只能由that引導，用作肯定語氣：I suspect that he will come. 我想他會來。句型suspect sb. of sth. 指懷疑某人做了某事：The police suspected him of murder / selling state secrets. 警方懷疑他犯謀殺罪／出賣國家機密。

malicious [mə`lɪʃəs] .... ★★
adj. 心毒的，懷惡意的：a malicious remark
懷有惡意的言語

perfect [`pɝfɪkt] .... ★★★★★
adj. 無瑕的，完好無損的：The weather during
the last few days has been perfect. 最近
幾天的天氣十分美好。

perfectly [`pɝfɪktlɪ] .... ★★★★★
adv. 很完全：She is perfectly capable of
taking care of herself. 她完全有能力照顧
自己。

suspicion [sə`spɪʃən] .... ★★★★
n. 懷疑：I have a suspicion that she is not
telling the truth. 我有些懷疑她講的不是真
話。

trust [trʌst] .... ★★★★★
v. ①信任，信賴：Everybody liked him and
trusted him. 每個人都喜歡他，也信賴他。
②託付，託交：She trusted her house to
the kind neighbor during her journey. 她在
旅行期間，把房子託付給熱心的鄰居看顧。
③敢於讓…做，對…放心：Next year I hope
the company will trust me with a bigger
budget. 明年我希望公司會信任我，把更大
的預算交給我做。④想，確信：I trust you
all like coffee. 我想你們都愛喝咖啡吧。
【片語】trust in 信賴，信任
n. 信任，信賴：Adam could feel his father's
trust in him. 亞當可以感覺到父親對自己的
信任。

unspecified [ʌn`spɛsəˌfaɪd] .... ★★★★★
adj. 未特別指出的：an unspecified wage 未協
定的薪水

辨析
Analyze

doubtful, dubious, suspicious

1 **doubtful** *a.* 「未定的，懷疑的」，指難
以預測的、不太可能的、對可能性感到懷
疑的，常接whether或that引導的子句：
I'm still doubtful whether I should accept
this job. 我仍然懷疑我是否應當接受這份
工作。

2 **dubious** *a.* 「懷疑的，猶豫不決的，無
把握的，有問題的，靠不住的」，指對真
實性、可能性、能力、動機、誠實等懷疑
的或沒有把握的，常用句型為be dubious
about / of sth. ：I'm dubious / doubtful
about my chances of success. 我懷疑我
成功的機會。

3 **suspicious** *a.* 「猜疑的，疑心的」，
指懷疑某人有罪或有錯的、可疑的，
比 dubious和doubtful的語氣要重：
His behavior that day made the police
suspicious. 他那天的行為引起了警方的懷
疑。

Feeling 情感心理活動名稱總匯

06

迷惑、驚奇、同情、抱歉相關辭彙

Vocabulary of Confusion, Amazement & Sympathy

amaze [əˋmez] ....★★★★
v. 使驚奇，使驚愕：What you have done amazed me so greatly. 你所做的事情使我大吃一驚。

amazed [əˋmezd] ....★★★★
adj. 驚愕的：I am amazed that he got the post. 我很驚訝他居然得到這個職位。

astonish [əˋstɑnɪʃ] ....★★★★
v. 使驚訝：I was astonished at his sudden appearance. 我對他突然出現感到驚訝。

astonished [əˋstɑnɪʃt] ....★★★★
adj. 驚訝的

astonishing [əˋstɑnɪʃɪŋ] ....★★★★
adj. 令人驚訝的，驚人的：In today's cars, computers can control engine performance with an astonishing degree of accuracy. 今日的汽車，電腦能以驚人的準確度控制引擎的運轉。

astonishment [əˋstɑnɪʃmənt] ....★★
n. 驚訝：The book races on from one astonishment to the next. 書中驚人的事一樁緊接著一樁出現。

astound [əˋstaʊnd] ....★
v. 使驚異：I was astounded at what I heard. 我聽到的事讓我大吃一驚。

befuddle [bɪˋfʌdl] ....★
v. 使昏亂：befuddle public with campaign promises 以競選時的許諾愚弄大眾

bewilder [bɪˋwɪldə] ....★★
v. 迷惑，把…弄糊塗：The twists and turns in the cave soon bewildered us. 蜿蜒繞行的洞穴很快就使我們失去了方向感。

blunder [ˋblʌndə] ....★
v. 犯大錯：Diplomatic misunderstandings can often be traced back to blunders in translation. 外交上的誤會往往可以追溯到翻譯上的錯誤。

captivate [ˋkæptə͵vet] ....★★
v. 迷惑：The schoolboys were captivated by the adventures of the heroes in the cartoon. 男學生們被卡通男主角的冒險經歷吸引住了。

charisma [kəˋrɪzmə] .... ★

n. 魅力，感召力：The television news program is famed for the charisma of its anchors. 該電視新聞節目以主持人的魅力而聞名。

charming [ˋtʃɑrmɪŋ] .... ★★

adj. 迷人的，可愛的：What a charming young man! 多麼討人喜歡的年輕人！

compassion [kəmˋpæʃən] .... ★★★

n. 憐憫，同情：Her heart was filled with compassion for the motherless children. 她對於沒有母親的孩子們充滿了憐憫心。

confound [kənˋfaund] .... ★

v. 使糊塗，迷惑：Poor writing often confounds the reader. 拙劣的文筆通常使讀者感到迷惑。

confuse [kənˋfjuz] .... ★★★★

v. 混淆：to confuse black and white 混淆黑白

crazy [ˋkrezɪ] .... ★★★★

adj. 狂熱的：He's crazy to drive his car so fast. 他把車開得這樣快，真是瘋了。

curiosity [ˏkjurɪˋɑsətɪ] .... ★★★★

n. 好奇心：He is full of curiosity. 他充滿了好奇心。

curious [ˋkjurɪəs] .... ★★★★★

adj. 好奇的：It is good to be curious about the world around you. 對周圍的世界感到好奇是件好事。

eccentric [ɪkˋsɛntrɪk] .... ★★★★★

adj. 古怪的：A daring experimentalist in Language, Gertrude Stein wrote in a style so eccentric that early critics were uncertain whether to take her seriously. 一位在語言方面大膽的實驗者葛盧德·史坦，其寫作風格如此古怪，以至於早期的評論家不知是否應嚴肅看待其作品。

elude [ɪˋlud] .... ★

v. 躲避，困惑：The actor's name eludes me for the moment. 該男演員的名字我一時想不起來。

embarrass [ɪmˋbærəs] .... ★★★

v. 使困惑：She was embarrassed by her friend's bad manners. 她朋友的粗魯舉止使她很難堪。

enchant [ɪnˋtʃænt] .... ★★

v. 施魔法於：The football fans were enchanted by / with the wonderful goal. 足球迷們為這個精彩的進球而欣喜若狂。

entangle [ɪnˋtæŋgl̩] .... ★

v. 使糾纏，使迷惑：The ropes were entangled so I was not able to untie the parcel. 繩子纏在一起了，所以我沒能解開包裹。

enthrall [ɪnˋθrɔl] .... ★

v. 迷惑，使服從：The boy was enthralled by the stories of adventure. 這男孩被冒險故事迷住了。

error [ˋɛrəˋ] .... ★★★★★

n. 錯誤，差錯：spelling errors 拼寫錯誤

fallacy [ˋfæləsɪ] .... ★★★★★

n. 謬誤，謬論：The fallacy has been exposed in its naked absurdity. 這謬論的荒誕性已被完全揭露。

fascinate [ˋfæsn̩et] .... ★★

v. 使迷惑：He's fascinated with Buddhist ceremonies. 他迷上了佛教的儀式。

fascinating [ˋfæsn̩etɪŋ] .... ★★★

adv. 迷人的：a fascinating shop window display 吸引人的商店櫥窗陳列

fuss [fʌs] .... ★★★

n. 忙亂，大驚小怪：There's sure to be a fuss when they find the window's broken. 他們發現窗子破了以後，一定會有麻煩。

fussy [ˋfʌsɪ] .... ★★★

adj. 過分挑剔的：He was always fussy about clothes. 他總是過分在意衣服。

gainful [ˋgenfəl] .... ★★★★★

adj. 有利的，有報酬的：gainful occupation 有報酬的職業

glamour [ˈglæmɚ] .... ★

n. 魅力：the glamour of foreign countries 異國的魅力；a woman with glamour 具有魅力的女人

heresy [ˈhɛrəsɪ] .... ★★★★★

n. 異端，邪說

hesitate [ˈhɛzəˌtet] .... ★★★★

v. 猶豫，躊躇：Though she hesitated for a moment, she finally went in and asked to see a dress that was in the window. 她儘管遲疑了片刻，但最後還是進了店，要求看一件在櫥窗裡的衣服。

indulge [ɪnˈdʌldʒ] .... ★★

v. 縱容，放任，縱情，沉迷，沉醉於：His father sometimes indulges in a cigarette. 他的父親有時喜歡抽一根煙。

indulgent [ɪnˈdʌldʒənt] .... ★★

adj. 縱容的：indulgent grandparents 溺愛孩子的（外）祖父母

intoxicate [ɪnˈtɑksəˌket] .... ★

v. 使陶醉，使中毒：be intoxicated by/with one's success 陶醉於自己的成功

irresolute [ɪˈrɛzəlut] .... ★

adj. 猶豫不決的：Irresolute persons make poor victors. 優柔寡斷的人不會成為勝利者。

marvelous [ˈmɑrvələs] .... ★★★

adj. 不可思議的，了不起的：the marvelous directional sense of migrating birds 候鳥非凡的方向感

miracle [ˈmɪrəkl̩] .... ★★★★

n. 奇蹟，令人驚異的人或事：Miracles are spontaneous, they cannot be summoned, but come of themselves. 奇蹟是自然發生的，不是被召喚來的，而是自己到來的。

novel [ˈnɑvl̩] .... ★★★★★

n. （長篇）小說：Do you have novels by Leo Tolstoy? 你有托爾斯泰寫的小說嗎？

adj. 新穎的，新奇的：a novel idea 新奇的想法

novelty [ˈnɑvl̩tɪ] .... ★

n. 新穎，新奇的事物：novelty goods 新奇商品；novelty shop 出售新奇物品的商店

pensive [ˈpɛnsɪv] .... ★★★

adj. 憂愁的，哀思的：The woman in this painting has a pensive smile. 這幅畫中的女人露出憂鬱的微笑。

perplex [pɚˈplɛks] .... ★★

v. 迷惑，困惑，難住：be perplexed for an answer 不知怎麼回答才好；perplex a man with questions 用問題難倒一個人

pity [ˈpɪtɪ] .... ★★★★★

v. （覺得）可憐，惋惜，同情：I pity your experience; I think it is not your fault. 我同情你的經歷，我想那不是你的錯。

n. 遺憾，憐憫：It's a pity to know that you can't come. 你不能來真是遺憾。

puzzle [ˈpʌzl̩] .... ★★★★

v. （使）迷惑，（使）為難：There was one sentence which puzzled me most. 有一句話最讓我不解。

n. ①測驗智力、技巧等的問題或遊戲，智力玩具，謎：No one has yet succeeded in explaining the puzzle of how life began. 沒人能夠說清楚生命是如何開始的。②難題，令人費解的事或人：The motive of the film makers remains a puzzle. 電影製片人的動機令人費解。

regret [rɪˈgrɛt] .... ★★★★

v. 懊悔，遺憾，抱歉：I regretted to inform you that you are to be dismissed next week. 我很遺憾地要告訴你，下個星期你將被開除。

n. 懊悔，遺憾，抱歉：I have never had any regrets over anything I've done. 我從不對自己所做的事感到遺憾。

情感心理活動

scruple [ˋskrupl̩] .... ★

v. 躊躇，顧及：A man who could make so vile a pun would not scruple to pick a pocket. 一個能說出如此惡劣的雙關語的人，是不會對偷竊錢包感到遲疑的。

sinister [ˋsɪnɪstɚ] .... ★

adj. 邪惡的，不詳的：a sinister look/plot 陰險的神情／陰謀；a sinister beginning 不吉祥的開端

sorry [ˋsɑrɪ] .... ★★★★★

adj. 遺憾的，對不起的，可憐的：I'm sorry that I can't come. 我很遺憾不能到場。

startle [ˋstɑrtl̩] .... ★★

n. 吃驚

v. 使大吃一驚：You startled me when you shouted. 你大叫的時候，嚇了我一跳。

surprise [səˋpraɪz] .... ★★★★★

n. 驚異，詫異：His visit is a surprise to the Greens. 他的到訪使格林一家感到意外。

v. 使驚愕，使驚駭，使驚奇，使詫異：All these things didn't surprise Tom for he had thought all of them. 這些事都沒有讓湯姆感到驚訝，因為他已經考慮到所有的這一切了。

surprising [səˋpraɪzɪŋ] .... ★★★

adj. 使人驚奇的，驚人的：He reacted with surprising speed. 他以驚人的速度反應。

surprisingly [səˋpraɪzɪŋlɪ] .... ★★★

adv. 驚人地，使人吃驚：It was surprisingly easy. 那事出乎意料地容易。

sympathetic [ˌsɪmpəˋθɛtɪk] .... ★★★

adj. 同情的，和諧的：When I told her why I was worried, she was very sympathetic. 當我告訴她我為何著急時，她很同情我。

sympathize [ˋsɪmpəθaɪz] .... ★★★

v. 同情，憐憫，共鳴，同感：I sympathized with the goals of the committee. 我對委員會的目標有同感。

sympathizer [ˋsɪmpəθaɪzɚ] .... ★★★

n. 同情（心），贊同，同感

vice [vaɪs] .... ★★★★★

adj. 副的，代替的：The president is ill, so the vice-president is acting on his behalf. 總裁病了，所以由副總裁代替他履行職責。

n. 罪惡，惡習，不道德行為，缺點，毛病：to tell vice from virtue 分辨善惡

辨析 Analyze

bewilder, confuse, puzzle

1 bewilder *vt.* 「使迷惑，使難住」，指使陷入一種驚奇或糊塗的地步，語氣較強：The old lady from the countryside was bewildered by the crowds and traffic in the big city. 那鄉下來的老太太看到大城市裡的人群及車輛就愣住了。

2 confuse *vt.* 「使困惑，把…弄糊塗，混淆，搞亂」，可指客觀上對幾種事物分辨不清，也可指內心困惑：Don't confuse Austria with Australia. 別把奧地利與澳大利亞弄混了。

3 puzzle *vt. & vi.* 「（使）迷惑，（使）為難，（使）苦思」，主要指內心困惑：I found his behavior very puzzling. 我覺得他的行為叫人難以理解。

07

肯定、否定、決定相關辭彙

Vocabulary of Pros & Cons

affirm [əˋfɝm] .... ★★
v. 斷言，批准，證實：He was affirmed as a candidate. 他被確認是候選人。

assert [əˋsɝt] .... ★★
v. 斷言，宣稱，維護：Formulated in 1823, the Monroe Doctrine asserted that America would no longer open to European colonization. 創立於1823年的門羅學說宣稱美國不再對歐洲拓殖者開放。

assertive [əˋsɝtɪv] .... ★
adj. ①武斷的：He speaks in an assertive tone. 他用武斷的口氣講話。②過分自信的：He is assertive to assign odd behaviour to ill health. 他武斷地把行為古怪的原因歸於健康不佳。

certain [ˋsɝtən] .... ★★★★★
adj. ①確實的，無疑的：The fact is certain. 事實確實如此。②肯定的，必然的：He is certain to succeed. 他一定會成功。③某一，某些：for a certain reason 出於某種理由

certainly [ˋsɝtənlɪ] .... ★★★★★
adv. ①一定，無疑：He'll certainly come. 他肯定會來的。②當然：Certainly I know this. 我當然知道此事。

cocksure [ˋkɑkˋʃʊr] .... ★
adj. 過於確信的：She was cocksure that she was able to do the job. 她堅信自己能勝任這項工作。

confident [ˋkɑnfədənt] .... ★★★
adj. 確信的，自信的：Peter is confident of winning the post as the assistant to the managing director. 彼得確信他能得到總經理助理的職位。

contradict [͵kɑntrəˋdɪkt] .... ★★
v. 反駁，抵觸：It's difficult to contradict someone politely. 彬彬有禮地駁斥別人是很難的。

contradiction [͵kɑntrəˋdɪkʃən] .... ★★★
n. 矛盾，反駁：It is a contradiction to say you know him but he's a stranger. 你說認識他，又說他是個陌生人，這是很矛盾的。

convince [kənˋvɪns] .... ★★★★★
v. 使信服，使確信：It took many hours to convince the court of his guilt. 花了幾個小時，法庭才相信他有罪。

convincing [kən'vɪnsɪŋ] .... ★★★★★
adj. 令人信服的：a convincing speech 令人信
　　服的演講

decide [dɪ'saɪd] .... ★★★★★
v. 決定：The judge will decide the case
　　tomorrow. 法官將在明天判決這個案子。

decisive [dɪ'saɪsɪv] .... ★★
adj. ①決定性的：Our air forces were decisive
　　in winning the war. 我們的空軍在贏得這
　　場戰爭中，起了決定性的作用。②堅決
　　的，果斷的：A man who is not decisive
　　cannot hold a position of responsibility. 一
　　個做事不果斷的人不能擔當重任。

determination [dɪˌtɜmə'neʃən] .... ★★★★
n. 決定，決心：The choice of a foster home
　　was left to the determination of the court. 選
　　擇寄養家庭的權利將交由法庭決定。

determine [dɪ'tɜmɪn] .... ★★★★★
v. 決定，下決心：The management
　　committee determines departmental policy.
　　管理委員會決定各部門的政策。

dispensable [dɪ'spɛnsəbl] .... ★★★★★
n. 可有可無的：dispensable items of personal
　　property 個人財產中不必要的項目

indefinite [ɪn'dɛfənɪt] .... ★
adj. 不明確的，不確定的：indefinite answer
　　含糊的答覆

indispensable [ˌɪndɪs'pɛnsəbl] .... ★★★
adj. 不可缺少的，必須的：In the Navajo
　　household, grandparents and other
　　relatives play indispensable roles in
　　raising children. 在納瓦霍人（美國最大
　　的印第安部落）的家庭中，祖父母以及其
　　他親戚在撫養孩子的過程中扮演必要的角
　　色。

inevitability [ɪnˌɛvətə'bɪlətɪ] .... ★
n. 不可避免，必然性

inevitable [ɪn'ɛvətəbl] .... ★★★
adj. 不可避免的，必然的：Mrs. Bell's
　　resignation is inevitable. 貝爾夫人辭職是
　　必然的。

infallible [ɪn'fæləbl] .... ★
adj. 必然的，不會錯的：an infallible remedy
　　肯定有效的藥方，可靠的補救辦法

irrefutable [ɪ'rɛfjutəbl] .... ★
adj. 無可辯駁的：irrefutable arguments 毋庸
　　置疑的論據

literally ['lɪtərəlɪ] .... ★★
adv. 確實地，不加誇獎地，逐字地，照字義：
　　There are people in the world who literally
　　do not know how to boil water. 世界上確
　　實有不知道該怎麼燒水的人。

necessary ['nɛsəˌsɛrɪ] .... ★★★★★
adj. 必需的，必要的：Sport is necessary to
　　health. 運動對健康是必要的。
　　【片語】if necessary 如果有必要

辨析
Analyze

affirm, assert

1 **affirm** vt. 「斷言」，指有一定根據或理
　由相信某事的真實性：It can be safely
　affirmed that the news is true. 可以斷言，
　這個消息是真的。

2 **assert** vt. 「斷言」，常含有主觀上以為
　是正確或真實的：The leader asserted
　that this could be done. 領導者宣稱這是
　可以做得到的。

necessitate [nɪˋsɛsəˌtet] .... ★★★★
v. 使成為必要：The increase in population necessitates a greater food supply. 人口的增加需要更多食物供應。

pending [ˋpɛndɪŋ] .... ★
adj. 未決定的：This matter must wait pending her return from London. 這件事必須等到她從倫敦回來後再處理。

persuade [pəˋswed] .... ★★★★
v. ①說服，勸服：Marsha was trying to persuade Posy to change her mind. 瑪莎試圖說服波西改變自己的觀點。②使相信：Even with the evidence, the police were not persuaded. 即使有了證據，警方也不相信。

persuasive [pəˋswesɪv] .... ★
adj. 有說服力的：a persuasive argument 令人信服的論據

positive [ˋpɑzətɪv] .... ★★★★
adj. 積極的：Light is a positive thing. 光明是正面之物。

punctual [ˋpʌŋktʃʊəl] .... ★★★
adj. 守時的：She is always punctual, but her friend is always late. 她總是很守時，可是她的朋友總是遲到。

quite [kwaɪt] .... ★★★★
adv. 非常，十分，相當：I have quite a lot of homework to do. 我還有很多作業要寫。
【片語】quite a few 相當多

resolute [ˋrɛzəˌlut] .... ★
adj. 堅決的：Despite dangers and difficulties, the soldiers were resolute. 儘管危險和困難並存，士兵們仍然非常堅決。

resolution [ˌrɛzəˋluʃən] .... ★★★★★
n. 決心，堅決，決定，決議：The resolution was passed at the previous plenary session. 決議在上次的全體會議上通過。

sheer [ʃɪr] .... ★★
adj. 純粹的，全然的：Our army was beaten by sheer weight of numbers. 我軍純粹是由於敵眾我寡才失敗的。

sure [ʃʊr] .... ★★★★★
adj. 肯定的，確信的：I think she's coming, but I'm not quite sure. 我想她會來的，不過我不敢太肯定。

suspense [səˋspɛns] .... ★★★★
n. 焦慮：The children's story writer known as Dr. Seuss proved that the simplest stories for children could have characterization and suspense. 兒童故事作家蘇士博士證明，即便是最簡單的兒童故事也可能有特色和懸疑感。

辨析 Analyze

convince, persuade

1 **convince** *vt.* 「使確信，使信服，說服」，強調講道理試圖使某人相信(try to convince)，其句型為convince sb. of sth. 或convince sb. + that子句：How can I convince you of my innocence? 我怎樣才能讓你相信我是無辜的呢？

2 **persuade** *vt.* 「說服，勸說，使相信」，強調成功地說服某人去做某事(successfully convince)，其句型為persuade sb. into doing / to do sth.：We finally persuaded the government into taking / to take immediate action. 我們最終說服了政府立即採取行動。

thorough [ˈθɝo] .... ★★★
adj. ①徹底的，完全的：Please give your room a thorough cleaning. 請徹底打掃一下你的房間。②仔細周到的，精心的：He is enormously thorough and full of inspiration. 他做事非常仔細周到且很能鼓舞人心。

thoroughness [ˈθɝonɪs] .... ★★★
n. 認真，徹底性

uncertain [ʌnˈsɝtn] .... ★★
adj. ①易變的，靠不住的：He is a man with an uncertain temper. 他是一個喜怒無常的人。②不確知的，不能斷定的：She was uncertain whether she continued or not. 她不能斷定繼續與否。
【片語】be uncertain of / about 對…沒把握，說不準

unshaken [ʌnˈʃekən] .... ★★★★★
adj. 堅決的，不動搖的

utterly [ˈʌtɚlɪ] .... ★★★★★
adv. 完全地：Many doctors and nurses were utterly convinced of the medicine's strength. 許多醫生和護士對藥物的力量深信不疑。

veto [ˈvito] ....★
n. 否決，否決權：Father put a veto upon our staying out late. 父親不許我們在外面逗留太晚。
v. 否決，禁止

辨析
Analyze

certain, definite, positive, sure

1 **certain** *a.*「肯定的，確信的，確實的，無疑的，某，某一」，既可用人做主語，也可用物做主語。表示「肯定的，確信的，確實的，無疑的」時只做表語，表示「某一」時只做定語：His information was by no means certain. 他的資訊一點也不確實。

2 **definite** *a.*「明確的，確定的，一定的，肯定的」，做表語時表示「肯定的」，在這個詞義上可與certain互換，做定語時一般表示「明確的，確定的」：It is definite / certain that he will take the job. 他肯定會接受這項工作。

3 **positive** *a.*「確實的，明確的，積極的，肯定的」，做表語時意為「肯定的」，一般只用人做主語，相當於 sure；做定語時意為「積極的，肯定的，明確的」：We have positive / sure knowledge that the earth moves around the sun. 我們明確地知道，地球環繞太陽運行。

4 **sure** *a.*「確信的，有把握的，一定的，必定的，可靠的，穩妥的」，做表語時意為「確信的，有把握的」，一般只用人做主語。做定語時意為「可靠的，穩妥的」：I'm sure / certain / definite / positive that he is honest. 我肯定他是誠實的。

08

同意、反對相關辭彙

Vocabulary of Yes & No

agree [əˋgri] .... ★★★★★
v. (+ to + v. / that / on / about / with) 同意，應允：
　　Everyone but you has agreed. 除了你，大家都同意
　　了。
【片語】agree to do sth. 同意做某事

agreeable [əˋgriəbḷ] ....★★
adj. 宜人的：an agreeable odor 宜人的氣味；The
　　　stewardesses are hired to be agreeable. 雇用空中
　　　小姐就是要她們和藹待客。

agreement [əˋgrimənt] .... ★★★★★
n. 同意，一致：No agreement seemed possible. 看來
　　不可能意見一致。

concur [kənˋkɝ] .... ★
v. 同意，同時發生：The *New Critics* concurred in their
　　emphasis on dealing with the text directly. 在著重於
　　直接論述原文的同時，《新批評家》誕生了。

concurrence [kənˋkɝəns] .... ★
n. 一致

concurrent [kənˋkɝənt] ....★★★★
adj. 同時發生的：concurrent insurance / policy（對於一
　　　投保物的）共同保險／契約；concurrent post 兼職

consensus [kənˋsɛnsəs] ....★★★★★
n. 一致：What is the consensus of opinion at the
　　afternoon meeting? 下午的會議上有什麼共識嗎？

consent [kənˋsɛnt] .... ★★★★★
v. 同意，答應：Has the minister consented to have his
　　speech printed? 部長已同意印發他的演講稿了嗎？
n. 同意，答應

contravene [ˌkɑntrəˋvin] .... ★
v. 反對，違反：Don't do anything that contravenes the
　　law of the country. 任何觸犯國家法律的事都不要做。

counter [ˋkauntɚ] .... ★★
n. 櫃檯，計算機
adj. 相對的，對立的：a method running counter to
　　　traditional techniques 與傳統技術相悖的方法

counterpart [ˋkauntɚˌpɑrt] ....★★★★
n. 相對物，極相似之物：The foreign minister is the
　　counterpart of the secretary of state. 外交部長是和
　　國務卿相同職等的人。

defiant [dɪˈfaɪənt] .... ★

adj. 大膽反抗的：a defiant manner 蔑視的樣子；The defiant child was punished. 這個不聽話的孩子受到了懲罰。

demur [dɪˈmɝ] .... ★

v. 躊躇，抗議：They never demured at the difficulty. 他們從不因困難而躊躇。

deprecate [ˈdɛprəˌket] .... ★

v. 抗議，抨擊：deprecate hasty action 反對匆忙行事

disagree [ˌdɪsəˈgri] .... ★★★

v. 意見分歧，不同意，不一致，不符：I disagreed with him about / over / as to how we ought to deal with the backward. 對於我們怎樣對待落後者，我和他持不同的看法。

disapproval [ˌdɪsəˈpruvl̩] .... ★★★★★

n. 不滿，不贊成，不同意：speak with disapproval of somebody's behavior 不贊成某人的行為

disapprove [ˌdɪsəˈpruv] .... ★★★★★

v. 不同意：The workers strongly disapprove of the firm's new methods on the assembly line. 員工們非常不贊成公司在裝配線採取的新方法。

discontented [ˌdɪskənˈtɛntɪd] ..... ★★★★★

adj. 不滿（足）的：Motion-picture actor James was known for his intense portrayals of discontented and rebellious young men. 電影演員詹姆斯以深刻表現出不滿又反叛的年輕人而出名。

grant [grænt] .... ★★★★★

v. 同意，允許，授予：The colonists obtained a charter that granted them the right to settle in the New world. 殖民者取得了一部能夠讓他們在新大陸定居的憲章。

n. 授予物，撥款，助學金

license / licence [ˈlaɪsn̩s] .... ★★★★

n. ①許可，特許：We make these goods under licence from the government. 我們製造這些物品是經過政府許可的。②許可證，執照：a driving licence 駕照

辨析 Analyze

agree, approve, consent

1 **agree** *vt. & vi.*「同意，贊成」，常表示原本有分歧，但經過協商達成一致。用法有 agree to sth.（同意某事），agree to do sth.（同意做某事），agree on sth.（就某事達成一致），agree with sth.（與某事相符），agree with sb.（同意某人的意見）：Do you agree to my arrangement? 你同意我的安排嗎？

2 **approve** *vt. & vi.*「贊成，同意；批准」，包括審批的涵義：Our request has been approved. 我們的請求已經被批准了。

3 **consent** *vi.*「准許，同意，贊成」，表示同意別人的請求或願意做某事。常與 to 搭配，句型為 consent to sth.（同意某事）或 consent to do sth.（同意做某事）。因此，其搭配詞比 agree 要少：Mary didn't consent / agreed to Tom's plan. 瑪麗不同意湯姆的計畫。

Feeling 情感心理活動名詞總匯

licensed ['laɪsn̩st] .... ★★★★
adj. 被許可的

oppose [ə'poz] .... ★★★★★
v. 反對，反抗：oppose the building of the airport 反對修建機場

opposed [ə'pozd] .... ★★★★★
adj. 反對的：Topeka, Kansas, was settled in 1854 by people opposed to slavery. 反對奴隸制度的人，於1854年在堪薩斯州的托皮卡住了下來。

opposite ['ɑpəzɪt] .... ★★★★★
prep. 對面：the house opposite the post office 在郵局對面的房子
adj. ①對面的：on the opposite side of the road 馬路對面②相反的，對立的：in the opposite direction 在反方向
n. 對立面，對立物：She was quite the opposite. 她正好相反。

permission [pə'mɪʃən] .... ★★★★★
n. 允許，許可，同意：Without your permission, I'll leave now. 你不准許的話，我現在就離開。

permissive [pə'mɪsɪv] .... ★★★★★
adj. 許可的，寬容的：She was a permissive mother. 她是一個有包容心的媽媽。

permit [pə'mɪt] .... ★★★★★
v. 允許：The climate and soil as far north as the Arctic Circle permit farmers to raise livestock and grow barley, potatoes, and other crops. 農民可以在遠到北極圈的氣候下和土壤上畜養家畜並種植大麥、馬鈴薯和其他作物。

ratify ['rætə,faɪ] .... ★
v. 批准，認可：Before an amendment can be added to the Constitution, it must be ratified by three-fourths of the state legislatures. 憲法修正案在被正式寫入憲法以前，必須得到州立法機關四分之三議員的認可。

traverse ['trævɜs] .... ★★
v. 走過，反對：Light from the Sun and distant stars traverses a vacuum in space. 從太陽和遙遠的恒星發出的光在真空中穿行。

09

反感、討厭相關辭彙

Vocabulary of Dislike

aggravating [ˈægrəˌvetɪŋ] .... ★★★★★

adj. 使人惱火的：How aggravating to be interrupted!
　　　 被打擾多令人生氣呀！

aversion [əˈvɝʃən] .... ★

n. 厭惡：Her aversion to alcohol consumption caused
　　 her to shun all social gatherings where such
　　 beverages would be served. 她對酒類消費的厭惡感
　　 使她避開所有可能有這類飲料的社交活動場所。

bicker [ˈbɪkə] .... ★

v. 爭吵：The two boys were always bickering with
　　 each other over their toy guns. 這兩個男孩總是互相
　　 為了玩具槍而爭吵。

bore [bor] .... ★★★★★

v. ①鑽孔，打眼，鑽探：This machine can bore
　　 through solid rock. 這部機器能鑽穿堅硬的岩石。
　　 ②煩擾，使厭煩（過去分詞當形容詞）：Three
　　 months after she lived in America she began to get
　　 bored and homesick. 她在美國住了三個月後，開始
　　 厭煩和想家。

n. 討厭的人，厭煩的事

boredom [ˈbordəm] .... ★★★★★

n. 煩惱，無聊：take up a hobby to relieve the
　　 boredom of retirement 養成一種嗜好以消除退休後
　　 的無聊

boring [ˈborɪŋ] .... ★★★★★

adj. 令人厭煩的
n. 鑽孔

brawl [brɔl] .... ★

v. 爭吵
n. 吵架，喧嚷：They got in quite a brawl. 他們大吵了
　　 一架。

carp [kɑrp] .... ★

n. 鯉魚
vi. 吹毛求疵：To carp in a disagreeable way 以令人不
　　 快的方式挑剔

complain [kəmˈplen] .... ★★★

v. 抱怨（後接about / of）：I have nothing to complain
　　 of. 我沒有什麼可抱怨的。

complaint [kəmˈplent] .... ★★★

n. 抱怨，怨言，控訴：If your neighbors are too noisy, then you have cause for complaint. 如果你的鄰居太吵，你就有理由投訴。

disgust [dɪsˈgʌst] .... ★★★★

v. 厭惡：We're all disgusted at the way her husband has treated her. 她的丈夫那樣對待她，使我們都感到厭惡。

domineering [ˌdɑməˈnɪrɪŋ] .... ★

adj. 盛氣凌人的，專權的：domineer over one's inferiors 對下屬盛氣凌人

grumble [ˈgrʌmbl] .... ★

v. 喃喃訴苦：She has nothing to grumble about. 她沒有什麼可抱怨的。

grunt [grʌnt] .... ★

v. 哼哼，作呼嚕聲，咕噥（著說出）：He merely grunted his approval. 他只是咕噥了一聲表示同意。

hate [het] .... ★★★★★

v. 憎恨，不喜歡，不願：She hates working at night. 她討厭在晚上工作。

hatred [ˈhetrɪd] .... ★★★★

n. 憎惡，憎恨：She looked at me with an expression of hatred. 她面帶憎恨看著我。

haughty [ˈhɔtɪ] .... ★★

adj. 傲慢的，輕蔑的：A haughty girl is always unpopular at school. 驕傲的女孩子在學校總是不受歡迎。

loath [loθ] .... ★

adj. 不喜歡的：The little girl was loath to leave her mother. 那小女孩不願離開她的母親。

loathe [loð] .... ★

v. 厭惡：You loathe the smell of greasy food when you are seasick. 當你暈船時，你會很討厭油膩食物的氣味。

moan [mon] .... ★★

n. 呻吟聲，悲歎聲：the horrible moan of the night wind 夜風的可怕哀鳴

nasty [ˈnæstɪ] .... ★

adj. 骯髒的，卑鄙的，下流的，令人討厭的
n. 討厭的人，令人不快的事：It is the business of museums to present us with nasties as well as with fine things. 博物館的職責是向我們展示好的事物，也展示壞的事物。

nuisance [ˈnjusns] .... ★★★

n. 損害，妨害，討厭的人或事物，麻煩事：The disruptive child was a nuisance to the class. 這個搗蛋的孩子令全班人討厭。

obscene [əbˈsin] .... ★

adj. 猥褻的：The way he writes about the disease that killed her is simply obscene. 他描寫她死於疾病的方式，簡直令人噁心。

pathetic [pəˈθɛtɪk] .... ★

adj. 淒婉動人的，可憐的：Every human being is pathetic. 人類都具有同情心。

unpleasant [ʌnˈplɛznt] .... ★★★

adj. 令人不快的，討厭的：He was very unpleasant to me when I asked him for his advice. 我向他求教，他卻對我極為無理。

10

意圖、希望、失望相關辭彙

Vocabulary of Desire

anticipate [ænˋtɪsəˏpet] ....★★★★
v. 預料，預期，期望：It is possible to anticipate when things will happen. 不可能預料事情何時會發生。

attempt [əˋtɛmpt] ....★★★★★
n.&v. 企圖，試圖，嘗試，努力：Farmers seldom attempt to cultivate every foot of their land. 農夫很少嘗試耕種他們的每一寸土地。

crave [krev] ....★★★★★
v. 渴求：crave for a person's pardon 懇求某人原諒；crave after sympathy 渴望同情

dejected [dɪˋdʒɛktɪd] ....★
adj. 失望的，沮喪的

desire [dɪˋzaɪr] ....★★★★★
v. 渴望，意欲：She desires that you (should) see her at once. 她要你立即去見她。

despondency [dɪˋspɑndənsɪ] ....★
n. 沮喪，失望：She shook her head in deep despondency. 她極度沮喪地搖搖頭。

disappoint [ˏdɪsəˋpɔɪnt] ....★★★★
v. 使失望：His carelessness disappointed me. 他的粗心大意使我失望。

eager [ˋigɚ] ....★★★★
adj. 渴望的，熱心的：They are eager for new skills so that they can be qualified for the jobs in various fields to which they are strange. 他們迫切想學新技術，讓自己能勝任各種陌生領域的工作。

expect [ɪkˋspɛkt] ....★★★
v. 期望，指望：You are expected to reply quickly. 期望你及早答覆。

expectation [ˏɛkspɛkˋteʃən] ....★★★★
n. 期待，期望，預期，預料，前程，可能性：a result that was beyond my expectation 出乎我意料的結果

hope [hop] ....★★★★★
n. 希望，期望：Where there is life there is hope. 哪裡有生命，就會有希望。
v. 希望，期望：We are hoping for some rain. 我們希望能下點雨。

intention [ɪnˈtɛnʃən] .... ★★★★
n. 意圖，動機，意向，目的：I began reading with the intention of finishing the book, but I never did. 我開始讀這本書時想讀完它，可是我從來就沒能讀完。

intentional [ɪnˈtɛnʃən!] .... ★★★★
adj. 有意的，故意的：an intentional slight 故意怠慢

luck [lʌk] .... ★★★★
n. 運氣，好運：I had the luck to find him at once. 我很幸運，立刻找到他了。

meaning [ˈminɪŋ] .... ★★★★★
n. 意義，意味，意圖：It has many meanings. 它有許多意思。

meaningful [ˈminɪŋfəl] .... ★★★★★
adj. 富有意義的，意味深長的：a meaningful experience 有意義的經驗

prospect [ˈprɑspɛkt] .... ★★★★
n. 前程，期望：There's not much prospect of Mr. Smith's being elected as Congressman. 史密斯先生當選國會議員的希望不大。

prospective [prəˈspɛktɪv] .... ★★★★
adj. 預期的：prospective advantages 預期的利益

purpose [ˈpɝpəs] .... ★★★★★
n. 目的，意圖，企圖，打算：Those, who want enjoyment will find it in the purpose they pursue. 那些想要得到快樂的人，一定會在他們追求的目標中尋求到它。

wish [wɪʃ] .... ★★★★★
v. ①真想，真希望，要是⋯多好，但願：I wish her out of trouble. 我希望她能擺脫麻煩。②祝願，祝賀：He wished me a good night. 他向我道晚安。

wistful [ˈwɪstfəl] .... ★★★★★
adj. 渴望的：a wistful expression 渴望的表情

yearn [jɝn] .... ★
v. 渴望：to yearn for an end to the war 盼望戰爭結束

辨析
Analyze

anticipate, expect

1 **anticipate** *vt.* 「期望，預料」，指以某種心情去期待某事發生，或預感將要發生什麼事，並沒有一定的根據：I anticipate great pleasure from my visit to Los Angeles. 我預料洛杉磯之行會非常愉快。

2 **expect** *vt.* 「期待」，指有一定的根據預見或期待某事一定會發生，也可指在心理上期待，是肯定性較強的常用詞：There is still no news from her for a long time, but we expect a letter soon. 儘管長時間沒有她的消息，但我們預料很快會有信來。

11

羞愧、懦弱、堅強、勇敢相關辭彙

Vocabulary of Cowardice & Braveness

Feeling

abashed [ə`bæʃt] .... ★

adj. 羞愧的，局促不安的：The boy was not abashed by the laughter of his classmates. 這個男孩並沒有因為同學的嘲笑而局促不安。

ashamed [ə`ʃemd] .... ★★★★

adj. 慚愧的，害臊的（後可接of）：He felt ashamed of having done so little work. 他為沒有做多少工作而感到慚愧。

bashful [`bæʃfəl] .... ★

adj. 害羞的，膽小的：be too bashful to speak to strangers 過於羞怯而不敢對陌生人說話

bigoted [`bɪgətɪd] .... ★

adj. 固執己見的：a bigoted person 固執的人；an outrageously bigoted viewpoint 異常偏執的觀點

blush [blʌʃ] .... ★★

v. 臉紅，害臊：She blushed as red as a rose. 她臉紅得像朵玫瑰花。

n. 臉紅，愧色：Spare my blushes. 別害我臉紅。

bold [bold] .... ★★★★★

adj. ①勇敢的，無畏的，進取的：I determined to be bold and speak the truth. 我決定要大膽講出真相。②冒昧的：Let me be so bold as to offer my suggestion. 請恕我冒昧提出個建議。③粗體（字）的，黑體（字）的：in bold type用黑體字④輪廓清楚的：a painting made with a few bold strokes of the brush 一幅筆觸遒勁的畫

boldly [`boldlɪ] .... ★★★★★

adv. 大膽地，勇敢地：The first half of the 1960's produced a cluster of significant books written by authors who stepped boldly outside their fields. 1960年代的前半期出版了一批有意義的書，是由那些勇敢跨出專業領域的作家寫的。

brave [brev] .... ★★★★★

adj. 勇敢的：The soldiers were brave in defense. 士兵們英勇抵抗。

courage [`kɝɪdʒ] .... ★★★★★

n. 勇氣，膽識：He had the courage to speak out his opinions. 他敢於說出自己的意見。

courageous [kə`redʒəs] .... ★★★★★

adj. 勇敢的，無畏的：a courageous deed 勇敢的行為

coward [ˈkaʊəd] .... ★★
n. 懦夫：a coward cry 膽怯害怕的叫聲

cower [ˈkaʊə] .... ★★★
v. 畏縮：The dog cowered when its master beat it. 那隻狗在主人揍牠時，縮成了一團。

dare [dɛr] .... ★★★★★
v. ①膽敢，竟敢：I wonder how he dares to do such a thing. 我想不透他怎麼敢做這種事。②向…挑戰：I dare you to say that again?你敢再說那件事？
aux. 敢，竟敢：Dare you jump down from the top of that wall? 你敢從那面牆上跳下來嗎？

daring [ˈdɛrɪŋ] .... ★★★
adj. 大膽的，勇敢的：He was awarded a medal for his daring deeds. 他因勇敢的行為獲得一枚獎章。

dastardly [ˈdæstədlɪ] .... ★
adj. 卑怯的

dauntless [ˈdɔntlɪs] .... ★
adj. 勇敢的：The hero was dauntless when facing danger. 英雄無畏於危險。

disgraced [dɪsˈgrest] .... ★★
adj. 不光彩，丟臉的：The family was disgraced by the scandal. 這個家庭由於醜聞而失去名望。

fearful [ˈfɪrfəl] .... ★★★★
adj. 可怕的：There has been a fearful accident several people have been killed. 發生了一件可怕的事故，有幾個人死了。

ferocious [fəˈroʃəs] .... ★★★★
adj. 兇猛的：Giant horned dinosaurs like triceratops were probably among the favorite prey of the ferocious "Tyrannosaurus rex". 三角龍之類的巨大有角恐龍，可能是兇猛的「暴龍王」最愛捕食的動物之一。

fierce [fɪrs] .... ★★★★
adj. 兇猛的，兇惡的，猛烈的，強烈的：The famous boxer killed a fierce wolf with his bare hands. 那位著名的拳擊手，赤手空拳打死了一頭兇猛的惡狼。

fiery [ˈfaɪərɪ] .... ★★★★
adj. 激烈的，燃燒似的：a fiery speech 一場激昂的演講

flimsy [ˈflɪmzɪ] .... ★
adj. 脆弱的，薄弱的：a flimsy excuse站不住腳的藉口

gallant [ˈgælənt] .... ★
adj. 英勇的：The officer is gallant in his behavior toward the woman. 該官員對這位女士獻殷勤。

headstrong [ˈhɛdˌstrɔŋ] .... ★★★★
adj. 頑固的：The members of Aaron Burr's family were noted for their passionate and headstrong temperament. 亞倫‧博家的成員以其充滿熱情和頑固的性格而著稱。

heroic [hɪˈroɪk] .... ★★★
adj. 英雄的，英勇的：His heroic action has left a deep impression on people's minds. 他英雄般的行為在人民心裡留下了深刻的印象。

heroine [ˈhɛroˌɪn] .... ★★★
n. 女英雄，女主角

humiliate [hjuˈmɪlɪˌet] .... ★
v. 屈辱，貶抑：Ann was humiliated by her friend's remarks. 朋友的話讓安感到難堪。

humiliation [hjuˌmɪlɪˈeʃən] .... ★
n. 羞辱

indomitable [ɪnˈdɑmətəbl̩] .... ★
adj. 不屈不撓的：an indomitable will 不屈不撓的毅力；indomitable courage 不屈不撓的勇氣

infamous [ˈɪnfəməs] .... ★★★★
adj. 臭名昭著的：an infamous deed 無恥的行為

infamy [ˈɪnfəmɪ] .... ★★★★★
n. 臭名昭著的行為：an infamy greater than
mutiny 比叛變更為可恥的行為

insurmountable [ˌɪnsəˈmauntəbḷ] .... ★
adj. 難以超越的：insurmountable difficulty 無
法克服的困難

intrepid [ɪnˈtrɛpɪd] .... ★
adj. 勇敢的

luster [ˈlʌstə] .... ★
n. 光彩，光澤：The award added luster to the
author's reputation. 該項獎勵為這名作家的
名譽增添光彩。

lusty [ˈlʌstɪ] .... ★
adj. 強壯的，有精神的：a lusty cry 強有力的吼
叫

majestic [məˈdʒɛstɪk] .... ★★
adj. 威武的，莊嚴的，高貴的：the majestic
Himalayas 氣勢雄偉的喜馬拉雅山

modest [ˈmɑdɪst] .... ★★★★
adj. ①適中的，不過分的：They were very
modest in their demands. 他們沒有過分
的要求。②謙虛的，謙恭的：The actor is
very modest about his success. 這個男演
員對自己的成就很謙虛。

modesty [ˈmɑdɪstɪ] .... ★
n. 謙虛：Modesty helps one to go forward,
whereas conceit makes one lag behind. 虛
心使人進步，而驕傲則使人落後。

obstinate [ˈɑbstənɪt] .... ★
adj. 固執的：The boy was obstinate and
would not listen to his father. 這個男孩很
頑固，不肯聽他父親的話。

pluck [plʌk] .... ★★
n. 勇氣：You had great pluck to talk to your
boss like that. 你敢那樣對老闆講話，真夠
有勇氣的。
v. 採，摘，拔，鼓起（勇氣），振作

shame [ʃem] .... ★★★★★
n. 假冒，虛偽
adj. 假冒的，虛偽的：His promise is shame.
他的承諾是假的。

shameful [ˈʃemfəl] .... ★★★★
adj. ①可恥的②不道德的，不體面的

shameless [ˈʃemlɪs] .... ★★★★★
adj. 無恥的：a shameless liar 厚顏無恥的說謊
者

辨析
Analyze

ashamed, shameful

ashamed與shameful之間的區別類似interested與interesting。

1 **ashamed** *a.* 「羞恥的，慚愧的，害臊
的」，指為自己或別人的言行感到羞愧，
只能做表語，一般只用人來做主語：After
he failed the exam, he felt ashamed of
himself. 他考試不及格，感到很羞愧。

2 **shameful** *a.* 「可恥的，不要臉的」，
指人或行為本身不光彩、不道德：The
mayor's shameful conduct was exposed
to the public. 市長的可恥行為被曝光了。

Feeling 情感心理活動名稱總匯

shy [ʃaɪ] .... ★★★
adj. 害羞的，膽小的：Bats are extremely shy creatures and avoid humans if at all possible. 蝙蝠是極其膽怯的生物，牠們會盡可能地避開人類。

sneak [snik] .... ★★★★
v. 潛行：The man sneaked about the place, watching for a chance to steal something. 那人在這兒鬼鬼祟祟的，想找機會偷東西。

stubborn [ˈstʌbən] .... ★
adj. 頑固的，頑強的：stubborn courage堅持不懈的勇氣

tenacious [tɪˈneʃəs] .... ★
adj. 抓住不放的，頑強的：a tenacious material 黏性很強的材料；a tenacious memory 很強的記憶力

terrible [ˈtɛrəbl] .... ★★★★
adj. ①可怕的，駭人的：a terrible accident 可怕的事故②極度的，厲害的：It's a terrible waste of their talents. 這是對他們才智的極大浪費。③很糟的，極壞的：terrible weather 壞天氣

terrify [ˈtɛrəˌfaɪ] .... ★★
v. 使恐嚇，使恐怖：In prehistoric times, eclipses of the Moon and Sun probably terrified people. 在史前時代，人們可能對日蝕和月蝕感到恐怖。

terror [ˈtɛrə] .... ★★★★★
n. 恐怖：a feeling of terror 恐怖的感覺

terrorist [ˈtɛrərɪst] .... ★★
n. 恐怖主義者

terrorize [ˈtɛrəˌraɪz] .... ★★
v. 使感到恐怖：President Bush assured the world that the American people would not be terrorized by terrorists' attacks. 布希總統向全世界保證，美國人民不會因為恐怖主義者的襲擊而害怕。

timid [ˈtɪmɪd] .... ★★
v. 膽怯的，羞怯的：The iguana is a slow, timid creature that can be caught without difficulty by hunters. 蜥蜴是一種行動緩慢又膽怯的生物，捕獵者可以不費吹灰之力抓到牠。

tough [tʌf] .... ★★★
adj. ①強壯的，堅強的，能吃苦耐勞的：You need to be tough surviving in the jungle. 在叢林生活需要吃苦耐勞的精神。②堅韌地，牢固的：Tough glass is needed for windscreens. 牢固的玻璃被用來做汽車擋風玻璃。③（肉等）老的：The steak is as tough as old leather belts. 這塊牛排老得像是舊皮帶。④困難的，艱苦的：It's tough to find a job. 找工作不容易。

undaunted [ʌnˈdɔntɪd] .... ★
adj. 無畏的，勇敢的

辨析 Analyze

horror, terror

1 **horror** *n.* 「恐怖，憎惡；令人恐怖或討厭的人或事」，指強烈的震撼和恐懼，強調外顯的表情，如 a horror film（恐怖片）：After the explosion she had a look of horror on her face. 爆炸後，她一臉是恐怖的神情。

2 **terror** *n.* 「恐怖，恐怖活動，引起恐怖的人或事」，指內心的恐懼、恐怖的氣氛、恐怖行動等，其衍生詞有 terrorism（恐怖主義），terrorist（恐怖分子）：The poor woman was trembling with terror. 這個可憐的女人怕得發抖。

12

熱情、仁慈、殘暴相關辭彙

Vocabulary of Kindness & Cruelty

affable [ˈæfəbl] .... ★

adj. 和藹可親的：Although he had a position of responsibility, he was an affable individual and could be reached by anyone with a complaint. 雖然他居於負責之職位，但他仍是個和藹可親的人，願意接受任何人的抱怨。

amiable [ˈemɪəbl] .... ★

adj. 友善的，和藹的：She has an amiable disposition. 她性情溫柔。

amicable [ˈæmɪkəbl] .... ★

adj. 和平的，和睦的：The dispute was settled in an amicable manner with no harsh words. 那場爭吵是在沒有粗暴語言的友善態度下化解的。

amity [ˈæmətɪ] .... ★★

n. 友好，親善關係

apathetic [ˌæpəˈθɛtɪk] .... ★

adj. 冷淡的：In the 1950's, college students in the United States were often criticized for being apathetic. 在1950年代，美國的大學生經常由於冷漠而受到指責。

ardent [ˈɑrdənt] .... ★

adj. 極熱心的，熱情的：Mahalia Jackson was noted for her vibrant, expressive voice and for her ardent interpretations of gospel music. 馬哈納‧傑克遜因富於表現力的生動嗓音以及對福音音樂熱情洋溢的演奏而著名。

ardor [ˈɑrdɚ] .... ★

n. 熱心：His ardor was contagious; soon everyone was eagerly working. 他的工作熱誠具有感染性，很快大家都熱衷於工作了。

aspiration [ˌæspəˈreʃən] .... ★

n. 熱望，渴望：As nineteenth-century American cultural aspirations expanded, women stepped into a new role as interpreters of art, both by writing works on art history and by teaching art. 隨著19世紀美國對文化的渴望膨脹，婦女開始成為藝術的詮釋者，並以撰寫藝術歷史著作和教授藝術步入了新的藝術詮釋角色。

aspire [əˈspaɪr] .... ★★★★★
v. 熱望：Broadcasters tried to abandon their native regional accents and aspire a BBC pronunciation. 廣播員們力圖去掉他們的鄉音，渴望達到英國廣播公司的發音標準。

barbarian [bɑrˈbɛrɪən] .... ★
n. 野蠻人

bland [blænd] .... ★★★★★
adj. 無刺激性的（食物等）：The criminal made a bland confession of guilt. 罪犯毫不在乎地承認犯罪。

brutal [ˈbrutl̩] .... ★★
adj. 野蠻的：a brutal attack 殘忍的攻擊

brutality [bruˈtælətɪ] .... ★★
n. 暴行，野蠻行為：willful brutality 有意做出的粗野動作

cordial [ˈkɔrdʒəl] .... ★
adj. 真誠的，誠懇的：Relations between the two countries have never been more cordial. 這兩國的關係達到了有史以來最好的階段。

cruel [ˈkruəl] .... ★★★★
adj. 殘忍的：He is cruel to animals. 他對動物很殘忍。

cruelty [ˈkruəltɪ] .... ★★★★
n. 殘忍，殘酷

辨析 Analyze

brutal, cruel, fierce, savage, violent, wild

1 **brutal** a. 「野獸般的，殘忍的」，尤指野獸般的殘忍：a brutal attack 野蠻的襲擊；The government put down an uprising with brutal force. 政府殘酷地鎮壓一場起義。

2 **cruel** a. 「殘酷的，殘忍的」，常用語：I do not want to be one of the cruel spectators of bullfight. 我可不想成為殘忍的鬥牛觀眾之一。

3 **fierce** a. 「兇殘的，殘酷的」，指人或動物的性情、行為兇殘可怕，也指暴風雨等自然現象「猛烈的，狂暴的」，還指「辯論、戰鬥等激烈的」，既可做定語，也可做表語：The wind was so fierce / violent that we could hardly stand up. 風勢猛烈，使得我們難以站穩。

4 **savage** a. 「殘暴的，兇猛的，粗魯的，未開化的，野蠻的」，指粗野毫無憐憫之情，還指動物兇猛，一般只做定語：The inhabitants in some mountain areas are still in the savage state. 有些山區居民仍處於未開化狀態。

5 **violent** a. 「暴力引起的，強暴的，猛烈的，劇烈的，強烈的」，指兇狠殘暴，強烈得難以控制，或有危險性和毀滅性。在描寫暴風雨等自然現象或辯論、戰鬥、發脾氣時基本上可與 fierce 互換，但一般不用於描寫動物：He gets very violent / fierce when he is drunk. 他喝醉酒時，變得非常兇暴。

6 **wild** a. 「野生的，未馴化的，荒涼的，荒蕪的，狂熱的，瘋狂的，憤怒的」，指舉止粗野、放蕩不堪，也指動物狂野，自然現象猛烈狂暴：A group of wild / savage youths vandalized the school. 一群粗野的小伙子破壞了這所學校。

enthusiasm [ɪnˈθjuzɪˌæzəm] .... ★★★★

n. 熱情：Theories about the existence and location of the lost continent of Atlantis have always generated conjecture and enthusiasm among archaeologists. 有關失落的大陸「亞特蘭提斯」的存在與位置的學說，總是能夠引起考古學家間的猜測和極大興趣。

enthusiastic [ɪnˌθjuzɪˈæstɪk] .... ★★★

adj. 熱心的，熱情的：Though too old to work much, the retired worker is very enthusiastic about neighborhood affairs. 這個退休工人雖因年老不能多操勞，但對社區工作可是非常熱心。

facile [ˈfæsl̩] .... ★

adj. 輕而易舉的，隨和的：a facile slogan devised by politicians政客所提出的缺乏誠意和深度的口號

fervent [ˈfɜvənt] .... ★

adj. 白熱的，強烈的：He's a fervent believer in free speech. 他是言論自由的熱烈信仰者

genial [ˈdʒinjəl] .... ★

adj. 和藹的：A genial boss may well increase the efficiency of his employees more greatly than a rigid one. 和藹可親的上司在增進其員工工作效率上，可能會強於苛嚴的上司。

gentle [ˈdʒɛntl̩] .... ★★★★★

adj. ①和藹的，溫和的：a gentle nature溫和的性情②輕柔的，徐緩的：a gentle touch輕輕的觸摸③不陡的，坡度小的：a gentle slope不太陡的斜坡

辨析
Analyze

gentle, mild, moderate, soft, tender

1 **gentle** *a.*「和藹的，溫和的，輕柔的，徐緩的」，指言談舉止、聲音、動作、風等和藹、溫和，也指坡度和緩的：Mary is very gentle; she never talks roughly. 瑪麗很溫柔，說起話來文雅不粗俗。

2 **mild** *a.*「溫和的，柔和的，溫暖的，暖和的，輕微的，不嚴重的」，指天氣、氣候、懲罰、疾病、言談舉止、化學成分（如肥皂、飲料）等溫和的：We have very mild climate here. 我們這裡的氣候溫和。

3 **moderate** *a.*「中等的，溫和的，穩健的，適度的」，如不快不慢、不熱不冷等，也是「小」的一種委婉的說法：The prices at the hotel are moderate. 這家旅館的價格不算高。

4 **soft** *a.*「軟的，柔軟的，細嫩的，溫和的，和藹的，柔弱的，嬌嫩的」，主要指感覺很柔軟、鬆軟，也指科技上物質的硬度小，並指聲音輕柔或顏色、光線等柔和的，還指力量、決定、行動軟弱：This silk scarf feels soft. 這條絲質圍巾摸起來很柔軟。

5 **tender** *a.*「柔嫩的」，主要指日常生活中肉、蔬菜、皮膚等質地很嫩，也指心腸軟的、柔情的（褒義詞），還指身體敏感易疼痛的：Her skin is tender, like a baby's. 她的皮膚很細膩，像嬰兒一樣。

情感心理活動名稱總匯

Feeling

gentleman [ˈdʒɛntl̩mən] .... ★★★★★

n. ①有身份的人，紳士：gentleman's agreement 君子協定②有教養的人，彬彬有禮的人③先生：Ladies and Gentleman! 各位女士，各位先生！

glorious [ˈglorɪəs] .... ★★★★

adj. 光榮的，壯麗的：Our country has a glorious past. 我們的國家有一段光輝的歷史。

grim [grɪm] .... ★★

adj. 冷酷的，不吉祥的：a grim and rainy day 一個陰暗的雨天

humane [hjuˈmen] .... ★★★★

adj. 仁慈的，親切的

impassioned [ɪmˈpæʃənd] .... ★

adj. 熱烈的：an impassioned plea for justice 對公正的強烈要求

impassive [ɪmˈpæsɪv] .... ★★★★

adj. 無感情的

impudent [ˈɪmpjədn̩t] .... ★

adj. 魯莽的：be (so) impudent enough / as to do... 竟然無恥到做…

indifferent [ɪnˈdɪfərənt] .... ★★★★

adj. 冷漠的，不積極的：It is quite indifferent to me whether you go or stay. 我對你的去留我不是很在意。

kind [kaɪnd] .... ★★★★★

adj. 仁慈的，和氣的，親切的，和善的：It was very kind of you to help us. 謝謝你好心幫助我們。

n. 種類：Things of a kind come together. 物以類聚。

【片語】①a kind of 一種，一類②all kinds of 各種各樣的

lenient [ˈlinjənt] .... ★

adj. 寬厚的：lenient parents 仁慈的父母；lenient rules 寬鬆的制度

listless [ˈlɪstlɪs] .... ★★★★★

adj. 冷漠的，無精打采的：to react to the latest crisis with listless resignation 對最近的危機的反應是無可奈何

mercy [ˈmɝsɪ] .... ★★★★★

n. 慈悲，仁慈，寬容：The man showed no mercy. 這個人沒有同情心。

【片語】at the mercy of 任憑…擺佈，完全受…支配

outrageous [autˈredʒəs] .... ★

adj. 暴亂的，不尋常的：He loved to dress in outrageous clothing. 他愛穿奇裝異服。

passion [ˈpæʃən] .... ★★★★★

n. 熱情，激情，愛好，激怒：As a boy, the historian Francis Parkinson had a passion for the wilderness. 歷史學家法蘭西斯・帕金森在孩提時代對荒野充滿了熱情。

passionate [ˈpæʃənɪt] .... ★★★★★

adj. 激怒的，激昂的：a passionate speech against injustice 一個反對不公正的激昂演講

passive [ˈpæsɪv] .... ★★★

adj. 被動的，消極的：In spite of my efforts, the boy remained passive. 儘管我很努力，那男孩還是提不起勁。

relentless [rɪˈlɛntlɪs] .... ★

adj. 無情的：relentless persecution 無情的迫害

savage [ˈsævɪdʒ] .... ★★★

n. 未開化的人

adj. 野蠻的，未開化的，兇惡的，殘暴的：The poor man received a savage beating from the thugs. 那可憐的人遭到暴徒的痛打。

tender [ˈtɛndɚ] .... ★★★★

adj. 細心的，考慮周到的，嬌嫩的：tender flowers 柔弱的花朵；a tender expression on her face 她臉上溫柔的表情

tenderness [ˈtɛndɚnɪs] .... ★★★★

n. 溫情

13

慌亂、緊急、懈怠相關辭彙

Vocabulary of Hurry

accelerate [æk`sɛləˌret] .... ★★★

v. 加速，促使：accelerate world peace 促進世界和平；Current demographic trends, such as the fall in the birth rate, should favor accelerating the economic growth in the long run. 目前的人口統計趨勢，如出生率的降低，從長遠來看將會有利於加速經濟增長。

accelerator [æk`sɛləˌretə] .... ★★★

n. 加速器，油門

cursory [`kɜsərɪ] .... ★

adj. 倉促的：give a cursory glance at the headlines in a newspaper 草草地看一眼報紙的頭版頭條新聞

haste [hest] ....★★★★

n. 匆忙，急速：Marry in haste and repent at leisure. 〔諺〕草率結婚後悔多。

v. 趕快，趕忙

hasten [`hesṇ] ....★★★★

v. 催促，趕緊：Modern nursing practices not only hasten the recovery of the sick but also promote better health through preventive medicine. 現代的護理措施不僅能加速病人康復，也能經由藥物預防來增進健康。

hasty [`hestɪ] .... ★★★

adj. 匆忙的：They shouldn't have made such a hasty decision. 他們本不該如此草率決定。

hurry [`hɜɪ] .... ★★★★★

v. （使）趕緊，（使）匆忙：No need to hurry. 不必匆忙。

n. 匆忙，倉促：In a hurry, he forget to leave his address. 他匆忙間忘了留下自己的住址。

【片語】①hurry up 趕快，迅速完成②in a hurry 匆忙，很快的

immediate [ɪ`midɪɪt] .... ★★★★★

adj. 立即的：A five-day week has found an immediate welcome and much popularity since officially adopted across the country. 五天工作制自從在全國正式實行以來，立刻受到了人們的歡迎。

impetuous [ɪm`pɛtʃʊəs] .... ★

adj. 猛烈的，衝動的：Youngsters are usually more impetuous than old people. 年輕人常比老年人急躁。

impulse [ˈɪmpʌls] .... ★★
n. 衝動，刺激：A sudden impulse of anger
　　arose in him. 他突然升起一股怒火。

impulsive [ɪmˈpʌlsɪv] .... ★★
adj. 易衝動的，任性的：an impulsive action
　　一時衝動的行為

slack [slæk] .... ★
n. 便褲，運動褲
adj. 鬆弛的，（繩子或鐵絲等）不緊的，淡季
　　的，蕭條的：The string around the parcel
　　was slack. 捆包裹的繩子很鬆。

slacken [ˈslækən] .... ★
v. 鬆弛：I slackened the line to let the fish
　　swim. 我放鬆了魚線讓魚游走。

slovenly [ˈslʌvənlɪ] .... ★
adj. 不潔的，馬虎的：Such slovenly work
　　habits will never produce good products.
　　這樣馬虎的工作習慣永遠生產不出優質產
　　品。

unhurried [ʌnˈhɝɪd] .... ★★★★★
adj. 不慌不忙的，從容不迫的

辨析
Analyze

accelerate, hasten, hurry, quicken

1　**accelerate** *vt. & vi.* 「（使）加快，
　　（使）增速」，側重正式用語或科技用
　　語：The car accelerated to 70 miles per
　　hour in a few seconds. 這輛車在幾秒鐘內
　　加速到了每小時70英里。

2　**hasten** *vt. & vi.* 「趕快，急忙，趕緊」，
　　做不及物動詞時常用於 hasten home / out
　　或 hasten to do sth.，做及物動詞時側重
　　客觀作用：She hurried/hastened away in
　　the opposite direction. 她匆忙地朝相反方
　　向走去。

3　**hurry** *vt. & vi.* 「匆忙，趕緊，使加快，
　　催促，急運，急派」，強調主觀意願，多
　　用人做主語，可用人或物做賓語：Don't
　　hurry the cook or she'll spoil the dinner.
　　不要催廚師，否則她會把晚餐搞砸。

4　**quicken** *vt. & vi.* 「加快」，指加快動作
　　（尤其是步伐）的頻率：He quickened
　　his steps / pace. 他加快了步伐。

14

欣賞、愛恨、滿意相關辭彙

Vocabulary of Love & Hatred

Feeling

情感心理活動名稱總匯

admirable [ˈædmərəbl̩] .... ★★★★
adj. 可敬的，極好的：The work is admirable for the vast labor it involved. 這部作品因工程浩大而令人讚賞。

admire [ədˈmaɪr] .... ★★★★
v. 欽佩，讚賞，羨慕（後接sb. / sth. for）：I admire her for her success in career. 我欽佩她在事業上的成就。

adore [əˈdor] .... ★★
v. 敬愛，極喜愛：People adore her for her noble character. 人們因為她的高貴品格而敬愛她。

affection [əˈfɛkʃən] .... ★★★★★
n. 慈愛，愛慕：Lorraine Hansberry acquired a deep affection for Africa and its people from her uncle William, a professor of African history at Harvard University. 蘿瑞‧漢斯柏利受到她一位在哈佛大學教非洲歷史的教授叔父威廉的影響，對非洲及其人民充滿了深厚的感情。

affectionate [əˈfɛkʃənɪt] .... ★★★★★
adj. 摯愛的，親切的：an affectionate brother 感情誠摯的兄弟

appreciate [əˈpriʃɪˌet] .... ★★★★
v. 重視，感激，讚賞：Doctors are highly appreciated in that country. 醫生在那個國家是受到高度重視的。

appreciation [əˌpriʃɪˈeʃən] .... ★★
n. 欣賞，感激，評價：Please allow me to express my appreciation to you for your help. 請允許我對您的幫助表示感謝。

content [kənˈtɛnt] .... ★★★★★
adj. 滿足的：The old couple seem content to sit in front of the television all night. 老夫婦倆似乎整夜坐在電視機前就心滿意足了。

elegance [ˈɛləgəns] .... ★★
n. 雅致：a woman of unstudied elegance 自然優雅的女子

fan [fæn] .... ★★★★
n. 扇子，狂熱者：the football fan 足球迷

favo(u)r [ˈfevɚ] .... ★★★★★

n. ①好感，喜愛：win favor with sb. 贏得某人的好感②贊同，支持：We will look with favor on your plan. 我們會支持你的計畫。③恩惠，好事：do sb. a favor 幫助某人④偏袒，偏愛：show favor toward neither party 對雙方均無偏袒⑤庇護：under favor of night 在黑夜掩護下

【片語】in favor of 贊同，支持

v. ①贊同，偏愛：favor late marriage 贊同晚婚②賜與，給與 (with)：kindly favor us with an early reply 請早日回覆③像：The child favors her father. 這孩子像爸爸。

favo(u)rite [ˈfevərɪt] .... ★★★★★

n. 最喜愛的人或物

adj. 特別喜歡的，中意的：Swimming is his favorite sport. 游泳是他最喜愛的運動。

fond [fɑnd] .... ★★★★

adj. ①喜愛的，喜歡的：be fond of music 愛好音樂②溺愛的，癡情的：a young wife with a fond husband 一名少婦與癡情丈夫

love [lʌv] .... ★★★★★

v. ①愛，熱愛：Love me, love my dog. 愛屋及烏。②愛好，喜歡：He simply loves to find mistakes. 他簡直就是喜歡找碴。

n. 愛，熱愛：Indeed, love is the prime motive of our existence. 的確，愛是我們生存的主要動力。

satisfaction [ˌsætɪsˈfækʃən] .... ★★★★

n. ①滿足，滿意：He looked at his work with satisfaction. 他滿意地看著自己的作品。②賠償（物），補償（物）

satisfactory [ˌsætɪsˈfæktərɪ] .... ★★★

adj. 令人滿意的：In fact, I'm sure that's the only satisfactory way out. 事實上，我確定那是惟一令人滿意的出路。

satisfy [ˈsætɪsˌfaɪ] .... ★★★★★

v. 滿足，使滿意：The foreign teacher was very satisfied with his students answer. 外籍教師對學生們的回答極為滿意。

worship [ˈwɝʃɪp] .... ★★★★

n. 崇拜（儀式）：A church is a place of worship. 教堂是做禮拜的地方。

v. 崇拜，敬仰，做禮拜：Where do you worship? 你到哪裡做禮拜？

辨析 Analyze

admire, adore, worship

1 **admire** *vt.* 「欽佩，讚賞，羨慕」，指對人或事物羨慕或讚不絕口：The guests admired the beautiful flowers in the garden of their hostess. 客人們對女主人花園中美麗的鮮花讚賞不已。

2 **adore** *vt.* 「崇拜，敬慕，愛慕」，指出自心中的崇拜或敬愛，在俗語中是「非常喜歡」的意思：The little boy adored/worshipped his father. 這個小男孩崇拜他的父親。

3 **worship** *vt.* 「崇拜，崇敬，敬奉，信奉」，指崇拜、鍾愛某人／某物或信奉神靈等，有虔誠的涵義，比adore更普通：Each religion worships God in its own way. 每個宗教都以各自的方式信奉上帝。

15

歡樂、興奮、煩惱相關辭彙

Vocabulary of Happiness & Worry

---

animated [ˈænəˌmetɪd] .... ★

adj. 有生氣的，熱烈的：Her animated expression indicated a keenness of intellect. 她生動的措辭顯示出其智力的敏銳。

bliss [blɪs] .... ★

n. 狂喜：What a bliss to be going on holiday. 度假真是樂趣無窮。

cheerful [ˈtʃɪrfəl] ....★★★★

adj. 快樂的，樂意的，使人振奮或高興的：He was always cheerful and honorable, a warrior for a good cause. 他一向快樂又誠實，是一個為美好的事業奮鬥的戰士。

delight [dɪˈlaɪt] ....★★★★★

n. ①快樂，高興：Music gives delight to us. 音樂使人愉快。②使人高興的東西或人：Gardening is my delight. 做園藝是我的樂事。
【片語】take (a) delight in 以⋯為樂

v. 使高興，使欣喜：Her singing delighted everyone. 她的歌聲令人歡喜。

disinterested [dɪsˈɪntərɪstɪd] .... ★

adj. 公正的，不關心的：His unwillingness to give five minutes of his time proves that he is disinterested in finding a solution to the problem. 他連五分鐘的時間都不願撥出，證明他對這個問題的解決方法不感興趣。

ecstasy [ˈɛkstəsɪ] .... ★

n. 恍惚，狂喜：Speechless with ecstasy, the little boys gazed at the toys. 小男孩們注視著那些玩具，高興得說不出話來。

enrapture [ɪnˈræptʃɚ] .... ★

v. 使狂喜，使出神：They were enraptured to meet the great film star. 他們和大名鼎鼎的電影明星見面後，欣喜若狂。

excite [ɪkˈsaɪt] ....★★★★★

v. ①使激動，使興奮：All were excited when hearing the good news. 所有人聽到好消息都很興奮。②引起，激起：excite a riot 引起暴動

excitement [ɪkˈsaɪtmənt] ....★★★★★

n. 激動，興奮，刺激：As the end of the game grew nearer, the crowd's excitement increased. 隨著比賽接近終場，觀眾越來越激動。

exultant [ɪgˋzʌltn̩t] .... ★

adj. 歡騰的，狂歡的：The exultant crowds were dancing in the square. 歡騰的人群在廣場上跳著舞。

frenzy [ˋfrɛnzɪ] .... ★

n. 狂熱：In a frenzy of hate he killed his enemy and revenged his father. 他在恨之入骨的衝動下把仇人殺了，為父親報了仇。

fun [fʌn] .... ★★★★★

n. ①玩笑，娛樂：The little dog is full of fun. 這隻小狗十分有趣。②有趣的人或事物：Tom is far from fun. 湯姆是個無趣的人。

gay [ge] .... ★★★★

adj. 快樂的，同性戀的：The people of the Middle Ages lived in a violent world, but they loved gay colors and rich decorations. 中世紀的人生活在充滿暴力的環境中，但是他們喜愛鮮豔的顏色和華貴的裝潢。

glad [glæd] .... ★★★★★

adj. 高興的，樂意的：He is glad about his new job. 他對新工作很滿意。

【片語】be glad to see / meet sb. 很高興見到某人

gleeful [ˋglifəl] .... ★

adj. 極高興的，興奮的：gleeful news 喜訊；in gleeful mood 高高興興地

hilarious [hɪˋlɛrɪəs] .... ★

adj. 高興的，熱鬧的：a hilarious joke 輕鬆的笑話

hilarity [hɪˋlærətɪ] .... ★

n. 歡鬧：the hilarity of a New Year's Eve celebration 跨年晚會的狂歡慶典

interest [ˋɪntərɪst] .... ★★★★★

n. 興趣，利息：Recently, there has again been great interest in the idea of a Channel Tunnel. 近來，人們對開鑿英吉利海峽隧道的想法又有了很大興趣。

interesting [ˋɪntərɪstɪŋ] .... ★★★★★

adj. 有趣的，引人入勝的：The students are interested in that interesting film. 學生們對那種有趣的電影很感興趣。

joy [dʒɔɪ] .... ★★★★★

n. ①歡欣，喜悅：She was filled with joy on seeing her son. 她看到她的兒子，非常高興。②樂事，趣事：She has been my friend throughout all the joys and sorrows of life. 她是我患難與共的朋友。

joyous [ˋdʒɔɪəs] .... ★★★★★

adj. 快樂的，高興的

merry [ˋmɛrɪ] .... ★★★★

adj. 歡樂的，愉快的：a merry smile 歡樂的笑容

pleasant [ˋplɛzənt] .... ★★★★

adj. 令人愉快的，討人喜歡的：a pleasant chat 令人愉快的談話

please [pliz] .... ★★★★★

v. ①請：Will you dance with me, please? 可以請你跳支舞嗎？②使愉快，使滿意：One can't please everybody. 一個人無法討好所有人。

pleasing [ˋplizɪŋ] .... ★★★★★

adj. 愉快的：The optical properties of a diamond give it the beauty that makes it pleasing as a gem. 鑽石的光學道具外觀美麗，看起來像美麗的寶石。

pleasure [ˋplɛʒɚ] .... ★★★★★

n. 快樂：One of the greatest pleasures of life is conversation. 生活中最大的樂事之一就是交談。

prefer [prɪˋfɝ] .... ★★★★★

v. 更喜歡，寧願：I prefer dogs to cats. 我比較喜歡狗而不是貓。

preferable [ˋprɛfərəbl̩] .... ★★★

adj. 更好的，可取的：Coffee is preferable to tea, I think. 我認為咖啡比茶更好。

523

preference [ˈprɛfərəns] .... ★★★
n. 偏愛，優先，優先權：A teacher should not
show preference for any one of his pupils.
老師不應偏愛任何一個學生。

radiant [ˈredɪənt] .... ★★
adj. 絢麗的，容光煥發的：In astronomy
the Little Dipper is the figure formed
by the seven most radiant stars in the
constellation Ursa Minor. 在天文學中，北
斗七星是由小熊星座中最亮的七顆星星組
成的。

rapture [ˈræptʃɚ] .... ★
n. 狂喜：listen with rapture 凝神靜聽

ravish [ˈrævɪʃ] .... ★
v. 強奪，使狂喜：The prince was ravished by
Cinderella's beauty. 王子被灰姑娘的美麗迷
住了。

readily [ˈrɛdɪlɪ] .... ★★★★
adv. 願意地，容易地：Once considered a rare
fruit, the avocado is now readily available
in most supermarkets. 曾經被看作是稀有
水果的鄂梨，現在在大多數的超級市場裡
隨處可見。

ready [ˈrɛdɪ] .... ★★★★★
adj. 準備好的，現成的：He always has a
ready answer. 他總有現成的答案。
【片語】be/get ready for 為⋯準備好

refresh [rɪˈfrɛʃ] .... ★★★
v. 使清新，恢復精神：A cool drink refreshed
me after my long walk. 我走了很長的一段路
之後，一杯冷飲讓我恢復了精神。

refreshment [rɪˈfrɛʃmənt] .... ★
n. 茶點，點心，恢復，爽快：We bought
refreshments at the football match. 我們在
足球比賽那兒買了食物和飲料。

rejoice [rɪˈdʒɔɪs] .... ★★★★★
v. 欣喜，高興：He rejoiced in his friend's
good fortune. 他為他朋友的好運而高興。

stimulate [ˈstɪmjəˌlet] .... ★★★★
v. 刺激，激勵，激發：The professor tried to
stimulate interest in archaeology by taking
his students on expeditions. 教授以帶領學
生參加探險的方式，來激發他們對考古學的
熱情。

stimulus [ˈstɪmjələs] .... ★★★★
n. 刺激，激發，促進，鼓舞，使興奮：Works
which were in themselves poor have often
proved a stimulus to the imagination. 本質
貧乏的作品常證明是想像力的刺激物。

tedious [ˈtidɪəs] .... ★★★
adj. 冗長乏味的，沉悶的：The study of law,
with its great number of cases, statutes,
and contracts, can be a tedious process.
由於有大量的案例、法令和契約，研究法
律可能會是一段非常乏味的過程。

tingle [ˈtɪŋgl̩] ....★
v. 刺痛，（因興奮）激動：The straw tingled.
稻草會刺痛人的。

16

悲觀相關辭彙 Vocabulary of Pessimism

afflict [əˋflɪkt] .... ★

v. 使痛苦，折磨：Unemployment afflicts 12 million workers in that country. 那個國家有120萬勞工深受失業之苦。

affliction [əˋflɪkʃən] .... ★

n. 折磨，苦惱：Caused by an ascorbic acid deficiency, scurvy was a serious human affliction until fairly recent times. 缺乏維生素C而引起的壞血病，直到不久以前還是人類的一大痛苦。

anxiety [æŋˋzaɪətɪ] .... ★★★★

n. 焦急，憂慮：We all felt anxiety when the prairie fire came close to town. 當草原大火將要延燒到市鎮時，我們都感到焦慮不安。

anxious [ˋæŋkʃəs] .... ★★★★★

adj. 渴望的：We were anxious for the news of your safe arrival. 我們都很想知道你是否平安到達。

despair [dɪˋspɛr] .... ★★★★

n. 絕望

v. 對…絕望，喪失信心：despair of success 毫無成功的希望

desperate [ˋdɛspərɪt] .... ★★★★

adj. 不顧一切的，絕望的：His failure made him desperate. 他因失敗鋌而走險。

dismal [ˋdɪzml̩] .... ★

adj. 沮喪的，陰暗的：dismal weather 陰沈的天氣；took a dismal view of the economy 對經濟抱著不樂觀的看法；a dismal book 乏味的書；a dismal performance on the cello 沉悶無趣的大提琴演奏

dismay [dɪsˋme] .... ★★

v. 使驚愕，使沮喪：She was dismayed to learn that her favorite dancer used drugs. 她得知她喜愛的舞蹈演員吸毒時，感到很失望。

downhearted [ˋdaʊnˋhɑrtɪd] .... ★★★

adj. 無精打采的

fraught [frɔt] .... ★

adj. 充滿的：Art Nouveau painters chose themes fraught with symbolism. 新藝術派畫家選擇充滿象徵主義的主題來創作。

fret [frɛt] .... ★
v. 激怒：fret your soul with crosses and with cares 用欺騙和憂慮來煩擾你的靈魂

frustrate [ˈfrʌsˌtret] .... ★★★
v. 破壞，挫敗（動名詞當形容詞）：After three hours' frustrating delay, the train at last arrived. 火車在三個小時令人厭煩的誤點後，終於到達了目的地。

frustration [ˌfrʌsˈtreʃən] .... ★★★
v. 挫敗，使感到灰心，阻撓：frustration of our design 我們計畫的失敗

harry [ˈhærɪ] .... ★
v. 掠奪，折磨：We have to harry him for money. 我們不得不常常纏著他要錢。

haunt [hɔnt] .... ★★
v. 縈繞於心，常到：the melancholy that haunts the composer's music 經常出現在那位作曲家音樂中的憂鬱感

trouble [ˈtrʌbl̩] .... ★★★★★
n. 困難，麻煩，憂慮，煩惱：We had no trouble (in) finding his office. 我們毫不費力就找到他的實驗室。

troublesome [ˈtrʌbl̩səm] .... ★★★
adj. 討厭的，麻煩的：Although wild flowers appeal to nature lovers, some of them are considered troublesome weeds by farmers. 儘管野花對熱愛自然的人很有吸引力，但是對於農民來說是令人討厭的雜草。

upset [ʌpˈsɛt] .... ★★★
adj. 難過的
vt. 使煩亂：James was upset because he had lost his ticket. 詹姆斯很煩躁，因為他把車票丟了。

vex [vɛks] .... ★★
v. 使煩惱：It vexes me to have to wait a long time for him. 要長時間等他真的很煩。

worried [ˈwɜɪd] .... ★★★★★
adj. 悶悶不樂的

worry [ˈwɜɪ] .... ★★★★
v. （使）擔心，（使）憂慮，（使）不安，（使）煩惱：Don't worry yourself about me. 你別為我擔心。
n. ①擔心，憂慮，不安，煩惱：It seems that she has got rid of worry. 她似乎已擺脫了煩惱。②使人擔心或不安的事：He doesn't want his own worry to affect the others. 他不想讓自己的煩惱影響別人。

辨析
Analyze

anxious, eager, worried

1 **anxious** *a.*「焦慮的，發愁的，令人焦急的」，強調焦急、擔心的情緒：Your father and mother are very anxious/worried about your sickness. 你爸爸媽媽很擔心你的病。

2 **eager** *a.*「渴望的，熱切的」，強調強烈的願望和熱切的情緒：The students were eager/anxious to see their new teacher. 學生渴望見到他們的新老師。

3 **worried** *a.*「發愁的，擔憂的」，強調發愁、煩惱、擔心的情緒：I'm somewhat worried that something might go wrong with our computer. 我有點擔心我們的電腦可能會出差錯。

Feeling 情感心理活動名稱總匯

17

悲傷、痛苦、幸福相關辭彙

Vocabulary of Grief & Happiness

ache [ek] .... ★★★
v. 痛，疼痛：My head aches. 我頭疼。
n. 疼痛（常用於複合詞）：headache 頭痛

addict [ə`dɪkt] .... ★
v. 對…有癮：He addicted himself to gambling. 他沉溺
於賭博。
n. 沉溺於…者：You are not much a TV addict, as I
remember. 我記得你不怎麼愛看電視的。

addicted [ə`dɪktɪd] .... ★
adj. 沉溺的，上癮的：He was an addicted traveler. 他
是個旅行迷。

adversity [əd`vɜsətɪ] .... ★★★★★
n. 不幸，逆境：A brave man smiles in the face of
adversity. 勇敢的人面臨大難而無懼色。

agonize [`æɡəˌnaɪz] .... ★★
v. 使受苦，使苦悶，感到極度痛苦：He agonized
himself with the thought. 他因為這一想法使自己陷入
了痛苦。

agony [`æɡənɪ] .... ★★
n. 極度痛苦，苦惱：The soldier suffered untold
agonies from a severe wound. 這個士兵因傷痛而承
受無法言語的痛苦。

anguish [`æŋɡwɪʃ] .... ★
n. 極度的痛苦，苦悶：She was in anguish over her
missing child. 她因孩子失蹤而痛苦。

catastrophe [kə`tæstrəfɪ] .... ★
n. 異常的災禍：Plants without leaves, such as algae
and fungi, are the first forms of life to grow back
after a natural catastrophe. 海藻和真菌等沒有葉子
的植物，是在自然的大災難之後最先重新生長起來的
生命類型。

deplore [dɪ`plor] .... ★
v. 悲痛，深悔：Some critics have praised James's
epic novel for their facts but deplored their
characterizations. 有些評論家讚揚了詹姆斯史詩體小
說中的史實部分，但對於其中的人物塑造感到可惜。

depress [dɪ`prɛs] .... ★★★
v. 使沮喪：He was depressed because he had not
passed his examinations. 他沒有通過考試，很沮
喪。

depression [dɪ`prɛʃən] .... ★★★
n. 蕭條，（地質）凹陷，沮喪：A holiday will get rid of his depression. 度假會讓他拋開抑鬱的情緒。

destiny [`dɛstənɪ] .... ★★
n. 命運：Marriage and death go by destiny. 婚姻與死亡都是命中註定的。

dilemma [də`lɛmə] .... ★
n. 左右為難，困境：Ph.D. students who haven't completed their dissertations by the time their fellowships expire face a difficult dilemma: whether to take out loans to support themselves, to try to work part-time at both a job and their research, or to give up on the degree entirely. 博士生們在學位攻讀期限終止時還沒有完成論文，就會面臨一種困境：要不拿貸款支持其學業，要不試著半工半讀，再不然就是徹底放棄學位。

distress [dɪ`strɛs] .... ★★★★★
v. 使苦惱，使痛苦
n. 苦惱，悲痛，危難，不幸：The mother was in great distress when her baby became ill. 那個母親的小孩子生病時，非常苦惱。

distressed [dɪ`strɛst] .... ★★★★★
adj. 痛苦的：the distressed parents of wayward youths 為任性的年輕人苦惱的父母

doom [dum] .... ★★
n. 命運，厄運：to go to one's doom 走向毀滅
v. 註定，命定

doomed [dumɪd] .... ★★★★★
adj. 命中註定的，註定失敗的

doomsday [`dumzˏde] .... ★
n. 最後的審判日，世界末日

fortunate [`fɔrtʃənɪt] .... ★★★★
adj. 幸運的：I was fortunate to catch today's last bus to the county at the last minute. 我在最後一分鐘趕上了今天最後一班去鄉下的巴士，真是幸運。

fortunately [`fɔrtʃənɪtlɪ] .... ★★★
adj. 幸運地，幸好

fortune [`fɔrtʃən] .... ★★★★★
n. ①機會，運氣：It's my fortune to be chosen to play for the school. 我真是好運，被選出代表學校參加比賽。②財富：He is a man of fortune. 他很有錢。

辨析 Analyze

destiny, doom, fate, fortune

1 **destiny** *n.* 「命運，天數」，指命運、命中註定的事情，中性詞，偏向貶義：Jack accepted his destiny without complaint. 傑克毫無怨言地接受了自己的命運。

2 **doom** *n.* 「註定，命定」，指厄運、末日等：Thousands of soldiers met their doom on this battlefield. 成千上萬的士兵在這個戰場上慘遭厄運。

3 **fate** *n.* 「命運」，指命運、命中註定的事情，中性詞：I have taken the examination but I don't know what my fate will be. 我參加了考試，但不知結果如何。

4 **fortune** *n.* 「財產，運氣」，指命運、運氣，中性詞，偏向褒義，可指算命，還可指財產：By good fortune he was not hurt. 他運氣不錯，沒有受傷。

Feeling 情感心理活動名稱總匯

grievance [ˈgrivəns] .... ★★
n. 不滿：to have a grievance against somebody 抱怨某人

grieve [griv] .... ★★
v. 悲傷：She is still grieving for her dead husband. 她仍為死去的丈夫傷心。

grieved [grivd] .... ★★
adj. 傷心的

grievous [ˈgrivəs] .... ★★
adj. 嚴重傷害的，引起痛苦的：The economic position was grievous. 經濟情況極為嚴峻。

grind [graɪnd] .... ★★★
v. 折磨，壓榨：Laws grind the poor, and rich men rule the law. 法律壓榨窮人，而富人統治著法律。

grinding [ˈgraɪndɪŋ] .... ★★★
adj. 難熬的：grinding toil 辛勞的工作；a grinding toothache 一陣難挨的牙痛

lament [ləˈmɛnt] .... ★★★
v. 悲傷，痛惜：He lamented his thoughtless acts. 他非常懊悔自己輕率的舉動。

melancholy [ˈmɛlənˌkɑlɪ] .... ★★
adj. 憂鬱的，悲傷的：She has been melancholy for nearly two weeks. 近兩週以來，她一直憂傷不已。
n. 憂鬱，悲傷

miserable [ˈmɪzərəbḷ] .... ★★★★
adj. 痛苦的，可憐的，粗劣的：to live in a miserable shack 住在簡陋的棚屋中

misery [ˈmɪzərɪ] .... ★★
n. 痛苦，苦惱：Our happiness or misery depends on our dispositions, and not on our circumstances. 我們的歡樂或痛苦是取決於我們的性情，不是我們的環境。

mishap [ˈmɪsˌhæp] .... ★
n. 災禍，不幸：A mishap prevented him from attending the routine meeting of the company. 他遇到一件不幸的事，不能來參加公司的例會。

sad [sæd] .... ★★★★★
adj. ①悲哀的，憂愁的：She is sad because her son is ill. 她的兒子病了，她很難過。②使人悲傷的：I learned the sad news by telephone. 我從電話中得知這個噩耗。

sadly [ˈsædlɪ] .... ★★★
adv. ①悲傷地：He walked sadly away. 他傷心地走開了。②不幸，可惜

sorrow [ˈsɑro] .... ★★★★★
n. 悲哀，悲痛：The people are in deed sorrow at the news. 人們對這則消息極為悲痛。

torment [ˈtɔrˌmɛnt] .... ★★
n. 痛苦
v. 折磨：to be tormented by toothache 受牙痛折磨

torture [ˈtɔrtʃə] .... ★★★★
n. 折磨，痛苦，拷問，拷打：to suffer torture from 受…折磨
v. 折磨，拷打

torturous [ˈtɔrtʃərəs] .... ★★★★
adj. 痛苦的

trying [ˈtraɪɪŋ] .... ★★★★★
adj. 難堪的，痛苦的：trying situation 尷尬的局面，難處的境況

unfortunately [ʌnˈfɔrtʃənɪtlɪ] .... ★★★★
adv. 不幸地：Unfortunately belts are worn only by a small percentage of drivers and passengers. 不幸的是，只有少數的駕駛和旅客會繫上安全帶。

woe [wo] .... ★★
n. 悲痛，苦惱：all her woe 她的滿腔悲痛

wretched [ˈrɛtʃɪd] .... ★★
adj. 不幸的，可憐的，卑鄙的：the wretched prisoners huddling in the stinking cages 全擠在惡臭牢籠裡的不幸囚犯

18

克制、憤怒、後悔相關辭彙

Vocabulary of Bearing & Fury

abide [ə`baɪd] ....★★
v. 遵守，忍受：The one thing he cannot abide is slacking. 惟一使他無法忍受的就是做事懶散。
【片語】 abide by 指遵守（法律、決定），信守（諾言等）

angry [`æŋgrɪ] ....★★★★★
adj. 憤怒的，生氣的 ：He was angry with the man upstairs. 他對樓上那人十分惱火。
【片語】 ①be angry at（對某人言行、某事）生氣，不滿②be angry with 生某人的氣 ③be angry about 對某事感到氣憤

chafe [tʃef] ....★
v. 擦傷，煩擾：He chafed under the loud noise from the nearly factory. 附近工廠的噪音使他煩躁不安。

concession [kən`sɛʃən] ....★★★
n. 讓步，遷就：The boss's promise to increase the workers' pay was a concession to the union demands. 老闆答應提高員工們的薪水，是對工會提出的要求讓步。

connivance [kə`naɪvəns] ....★
v. 縱容，共謀

connive [kə`naɪv] ....★
v. 縱容，默許：The student tried to connive with her friend to cheat in the examination. 那名學生企圖和她的朋友串謀考試作弊。

contrite [`kɑntraɪt] ....★
adj. 悔悟的：He participated the funeral of the victim with a humble and contrite heart. 他懷著謙恭悔罪的心參加了受害人的葬禮。

durable [`djurəbl] ....★★★
adj. 耐久的，耐用的：Beams made of teakwood are among the most durable, and some of them are functional after 1,000 years. 由柚木製成的樑柱是最耐用的，有些可以用1,000多年。

endurance [ɪn`djurəns] ....★
n. 耐久力，忍耐力：Through hard work and endurance, we will complete this project. 我們經由不懈的努力和辛勤的工作，將會完成這項方案。

endure [ɪnˈdjʊr] .... ★★★★
v. 忍受，容忍：Perhaps the greatest resource of the North American pioneers was their capacity to endure. 或許北美拓荒者最大的資源就是他們的忍耐力。We seek the truth, and will endure the consequences. 我們尋找真理，並將忍受一切後果。

enrage [ɪnˈredʒ] .... ★★★★★
v. 激怒：be enraged at/by somebody's conduct 對某人的行為極為憤怒；be enraged with somebody 對某人勃然大怒

exasperating [ɪgˈzæspəˌretɪŋ] .... ★
adj. 激怒人的，使人觸怒的：Parents sometimes find their children's conduct exasperating, and this may lead to arguments. 父母有時會覺得孩子的行為令人憤怒，而這可能會引起爭吵。

fortitude [ˈfɔrtəˌtjud] .... ★
n. 堅忍，剛毅：bear a calamity with fortitude 毅然忍受災禍

fume [fjum] .... ★★★★★
n. （濃烈或難聞的）煙，氣體：Air conditioning protects industrial workers against harmful fumes in the environment. 空調設備在對人體有害的氣體環境中，能夠保護企業員工。

furious [ˈfjʊrɪəs] .... ★★
adj. 狂怒的，狂暴的：There was a furious knocking at the door at midnight yesterday. 昨天半夜有人猛烈地敲門。

fury [ˈfjʊrɪ] .... ★★
n. 勃然大怒：fly into a fury for the slightest reason 為一點小事就發火

impatient [ɪmˈpeʃənt] .... ★★★
adj. 不耐煩的：He is impatient to know whether he has passed the final examinations or not. 他急於想知道他的期末考試是否都及格了。

incense [ˈɪnsɛns] .... ★
v. 激怒：Cruelty incenses kind people. 殘忍行為使心地善良的人們憤怒。

incentive [ɪnˈsɛntɪv] .... ★
n. 刺激，動機：Money is still a major incentive in most occupations. 在許多職業中，錢仍是主要的刺激因素。

indignant [ɪnˈdɪgnənt] .... ★
adj. 憤慨的，義憤的：I was indignant because I felt that I had been punished unfairly. 我非常憤慨，因為我覺得對我的懲罰是不公平的。The indignant passengers beat the pickpocket up. 憤怒的乘客們把那個扒手痛打了一頓。

indignation [ˌɪndɪgˈneʃən] .... ★★
n. 憤怒，憤慨：indignation at the injustice 對不公平感到憤慨

insufferable [ɪnˈsʌfərəbḷ] .... ★
adj. 難以忍受的：His insufferable insolence cost him many friends. 他那令人難以容忍的蠻橫態度使他失去了許多朋友。

irritable [ˈɪrɪtəbḷ] .... ★★
adj. 過敏的，易怒的：People who do not sleep enough tend to become irritable. 睡眠不足的人容易發火。

irritate [ˈɪrəˌtet] .... ★★
v. 激怒：A loud bossy voice irritates listeners. 又大又專橫的聲音讓聽眾惱火。

malcontent [ˈmælkənˌtɛnt] .... ★
n. 不平者，不滿者：immature malcontents who have long been sold out to conformity 長期慣於服從的不成熟反對者

mania [ˈmenɪə] .... ★
n. 癲狂，狂熱：He has a mania for (driving) fast cars. 他有開快車的癖好。

patience [ˈpeʃəns] .... ★★★★
n. 忍耐，耐心：I don't have the patience to hear your complaints. 我沒耐心聽你的抱怨。

patient [ˈpeʃənt] .... ★★★★★
adj. 忍耐的，容忍的：Be patient with a tired child. 對疲倦的小孩要有耐心。
【片語】 be patient of sth. 能忍受某事

n. 病人：The Smiths are patients of Dr. Quack. 庫瓦克醫生替史密斯全家人看病。

rage [redʒ] .... ★★★★★
n. 激怒，憤怒：The man in a rage was dead last night. 那個憤怒的男子昨晚死掉了。

refrain [rɪ'fren] .... ★★
v. 控制，忍住：refrain from crime 抑制犯罪；refrain from smoking 禁止吸煙

repent [rɪ'pɛnt] .... ★★
v. 悔過，後悔：You will repent very much having said those unkind works. 你會為自己說了那樣不友好的話後悔的。

resent [rɪ'zɛnt] .... ★
v. 憎恨：He resents criticism. 他怨恨批評。

spite [spaɪt] .... ★★★★★
n. 惡意：out of spite 出於惡意

【片語】in spite of 不顧，不管：In spite of what you say, I still believe he is a good person. 不管你說什麼，我還是相信他是好人。

spleen [splin] .... ★
n. 脾臟，憤怒：vent one's spleen 發洩怒氣

sullen ['sʌlɪn] .... ★
adj. 陰沈的：sullen skies 陰沈的天空

tolerable ['tɑlərəbl] .... ★★★
adj. 可容忍的：The pain was severe, but tolerable. 疼痛劇烈，但尚能忍受。

tolerance ['tɑlərəns] .... ★★★
n. 忍受，容忍

tolerant ['tɑlərənt] .... ★★★
adj. 寬容的，容忍的：This is a plants tolerant of extreme heat. 這是一種能夠忍受極端炎熱環境的植物。

辨析 Analyze

bear, endure, stand, tolerate, withstand

1 **bear** *vt.* 「忍受，忍耐」，常用語，指對消極事物的忍受，多用於否定句或疑問句：My wife can't bear my smoking in the living room. 我妻子受不了我在客廳裡抽煙。

2 **endure** *vt.* 「忍受，容忍」，常指長時間忍耐肉體或精神上較嚴重的病苦折磨：The old man could not endure the torture and committed suicide at last. 老人受不了這種折磨，終於自殺了。

3 **stand** *vt.* 「容忍，忍受，經受，經得起」，指「忍受」時可與bear互換：I can't stand the hot days in summer. 我受不了夏天炎熱的日子。

4 **tolerate** *vt.* 「容忍，忍受，容許，承認」，一般不指肉體上的忍受，而是指精神上的容忍，常用於肯定句：They tolerated the existence of opinions contrary to their own. 他們容忍／允許相反的觀點存在。

5 **withstand** *vt.* 「經受，承受，抵住」，指能夠抵擋或抵抗某種不利的環境：This cloth material will withstand repeated washings. 這種衣料經得起反覆清洗。

19

輕視、忽視、注意相關辭彙

Vocabulary of Ignorance & Notice

alarm [ə'lɑrm] .... ★★★★★
n. 警報，信號
v. 向…報警，使驚恐：the growing alarm at the rising crime rate among youths 青年犯罪率增加引起的與日俱增的憂慮； In the middle of the night，the sleeping campers were alarmed by a loud crash. 半夜裡，正在熟睡的露營者們被一聲巨響驚醒。

arrogance ['ærəgəns] .... ★
n. 傲慢：The arrogance of the nobility was resented by the middle class. 貴族的傲慢使中產階級感到憤恨。

arrogant ['ærəgənt] .... ★
adj. 傲慢的：It is your arrogant insistence that compelled me to do as you asked. 是你傲慢的堅持使我不得不按你的要求做。

attention [ə'tɛnʃən] .... ★★★★★
n. 注意，留心：call sb.'s attention to sth. 引起某人對某事的注意
【片語】pay attention to 注意…

attentive [ə'tɛntɪv] .... ★★★
adj. 注意的，留神的：He is attentive to what he is doing. 他很專心做現在的工作。

attitude ['ætətjud] .... ★★★★★
n. 看法，態度，姿態：take an attitude of wait and see toward a new administration 對新政府採取觀望態度

attract [ə'trækt] .... ★★★★
v. 吸引，引起…的注意 ：The light attracted a lot of mosquitoes. 亮光吸引了大量的蚊子。

attractive [ə'træktɪv] .... ★★★
adj. 有吸引力的，吸引的：The flower is the most attractive, most colorful, and most fragrant part of many plants. 花朵是許多植物最有吸引力、最有色彩和最芳香的部位。

belittle [bɪ'lɪtl̩] .... ★
v. 輕視：Although I do not wish to belittle your contribution, I feel we must place it in its proper perspective. 雖然我不願貶抑你的貢獻，但我覺得我們必須適當地對其評價。

beware [bɪ`wɛr] .... ★

v. 當心，謹防：Beware of the computer virus. 當心電腦病毒。

care [kɛr] .... ★★★★★

n. ①小心，照料：Do your homework with more care! 寫作業時要更仔細。②關心，愛護：The children have the best of care in the nursery school. 兒童們在托兒所裡受到最好的照顧。

v. ①關心，擔心，介意，計較：I don't care how far I'll have to go. 要走多遠我都不在乎。②喜歡，嚮往：I don't care to go there. 我不願意到那裡去。③關懷，照顧：He cares for no one. 他誰也不在乎。

casual [`kæʒʊəl] .... ★★★

adj. 非正式的，隨便的：The casual newspaper reader wouldn't like long articles on serious subjects every day. 休閒的報紙讀者不願每天看有關嚴肅主題的長篇文章。

concerned [kən`sɜnd] .... ★★★★

adj. 焦慮的：I am very concerned about her. 我非常掛念她。

conspicuous [kən`spɪkjʊəs] ...... ★★★★★

adj. 引人注目的：An individual nerve cell usually has a large cell body and a conspicuous nucleus. 單個神經細胞有一個大細胞體和一個明顯的細胞核。

contemn [kən`tɛm] .... ★

v. 蔑視

contempt [kən`tɛmpt] .... ★★

n. 輕蔑，藐視：He refused to answer in contempt of the rules of the court. 他藐視法院法規，拒絕回答。

contemptible [kən`tɛmptəbl] .... ★★

adj. 藐視的，傲慢的：It was contemptible of him to speak like that about a respected teacher! 他那樣議論一位受人尊敬的教師真是為人所不齒！

despicable [`dɛspɪkəbl] .... ★

adj. 可鄙的：It is despicable to desert your children. 你拋棄自己孩子的行為是卑劣的。

despise [dɪ`spaɪz] .... ★★★★

v. 輕視，蔑視：Don't cheat at examination, or your classmates will despise you. 考試不要作弊，否則同班同學會鄙視你的。

disdain [dɪs`den] .... ★

v. 輕視，不屑：Mrs. Grey disdained to answer her husband's rude remarks. 格雷太太對於丈夫那些無禮的話不屑回答。

n. 輕蔑

disparage [dɪ`spærɪdʒ] .... ★

v. 輕視，毀謗：This is not intended to disparage the advances in communication. 這不是故意要貶低通訊事業方面的發展。

disregard [ˌdɪsrɪ`gɑrd] .... ★★

v. 不管，不顧：Professor Smith continued his research work and disregarded his colleague's advice. 史密斯教授不顧同事的建議，繼續進行他的研究工作。

disrespectful [ˌdɪsrɪ`spɛktfəl] .... ★★★★★

adj. 無禮的，輕視的

emphatic [ɪm`fætɪk] .... ★★★★★

adj. 顯著的，強調的，有力的：He answered the question with an emphatic "No." 他用一個加強語氣的「不」字回答了這個問題。

engross [ɪn`gros] .... ★

v. 全神貫注於：Newton was so engrossed in his laboratory work that he often forgot to eat. 牛頓全神貫注地在實驗室工作，常常忘了吃飯。

engrossed [ɪn`grost] .... ★

adj. 全神貫注的

gaze [gez] .... ★★★★★
v. 凝視：After gazing at the display for several minutes, Mr. Taylor went back into his shop. 泰勒先生對此擺設凝視了幾分鐘之後，便回到店裡去了。

heedless [ˋhidlɪs] ....★
adj. 不留心的

ignore [ɪgˋnor] .... ★★★★
v. 忽視：Ignore the child if he misbehaves, and he'll soon stop. 小孩不乖時，別去理他，不久他就不鬧了。

neglect [nɪgˋlɛkt] .... ★★★★
v. 疏忽，忘記：The animals were thin and ill because the farmer had neglected them. 這些動物瘦弱有病，因為農夫一直忽略牠們。

negligent [ˋnɛglɪdʒənt] ....★
adj. 忽略的：be negligent of one's duties 怠忽職守

notable [ˋnotəbḷ] .... ★★
adj. 著名的，顯要的：Dr. Alfred Block's most notable work dealt with surgical shock and the regulation of circulation. 艾佛德‧布洛克醫生最主要的工作，是處理手術休克，使血液循環正常。

notably [ˋnotəblɪ] .... ★★
adv. 特別地，顯著地

notice [ˋnotɪs] .... ★★★★★
n. 佈告，通知，注意
v. 注意，留意，評價：The book will be noticed by readers. 這本書將受到讀者的注目。

noticeably [ˋnotɪsəblɪ] .... ★★★
adv. 清楚地，可注意到地：The degree of brilliance of the Star Algol changes noticeably every two and a half days. 大陵變星的亮度每2天半就會明顯變化。

observable [əbˋzɝvəbḷ] .... ★★★★
adj. 可觀察到的：observable phenomena 可觀察到的現象；an observable change in demeanor 可觀察到的態度上的變化

辨析
Analyze

ignore, neglect, overlook

1　**ignore** *vt.* 「不顧，不理，忽視」，指主觀上有意忽視、不理睬，一般接名詞做賓語：Prof. Burg heard my question, but he ignored it and talked about something else. 伯格教授聽見了我的問題，但他沒有理會，而是談了些別的東西。

2　**neglect** *vt.* 「忽視，忽略，疏忽」，指客觀上不注意而忽視、忽略、不好好照顧，可接名詞、動名詞、不定式做賓語：The secretary was careful enough not to neglect her duties. 這個秘書非常細心，不會忽略她的職責。

3　**overlook** *vt.* 「忽視，忽略，未注意到，寬恕，寬容」，指客觀上不注意而忽視、忽略，也指主觀上有意忽視並且原諒，還指「俯視、鳥瞰」：It is easy to overlook a small detail like that. 很容易忽略那樣的細節。

observance [əbˈzɝvəns] .... ★★★★★
n. 遵守：Consider how much intellect was needed in the architect, and how much observance of nature. 試想從事建築要多少聰明才智，要觀察多少自然現象。

observant [əbˈzɝvənt] .... ★★★★★
adj. 觀察力敏銳的：be observant of the traffic rules 嚴格遵守交通規則；be observant to avoid danger 注意避免危險；an observant boy 機警的男孩

observation [ˌɑbzɝˈveʃən] .... ★★★★★
n. 觀察，注意，監視，言論：Give me your observations on what happened. 把發生的事情向我報告一下。

observational [ˌɑbzɝˈveʃənl] ..... ★★★★★
adj. 觀察的，監視的

observe [əbˈzɝv] .... ★★★★★
v. 看到，遵守：Because it is so small and so close to the Sun, the planet Mercury has been extremely difficult to observe. 水星由於體積很小，又離太陽很近，所以要觀察非常困難。

overestimate [ˌovɝˈɛstəˌmet] .... ★
v. 估計過高：overestimate one's abilities 高估自己的能力

overlook [ˌovɝˈluk] .... ★★★
v. 俯瞰，眺望，看漏，忽略，寬容，放任：You have overlooked several of the mistakes in this work. 你忽略了這項工作中的幾個錯誤。

posture [ˈpɑstʃɝ] .... ★
n.（人體的）姿勢，（政府等的）立場態度：Those bases are essential to our military posture in the Middle East. 那些軍事基地對我們在中東的軍事立場十分重要。

stance [stæns] .... ★★★★★
n. 姿態，態度，（高爾夫球）擊球姿勢：Peru has also toughened its stance toward foreign investors. 秘魯對外國投資者的態度也轉趨強硬了。

trepidation [ˌtrɛpəˈdeʃən] .... ★
n. 驚恐，戰慄

underestimate [ˈʌndɝˈɛstəˌmet] .... ★
v. 低估

vigilant [ˈvɪdʒələnt] .... ★
adj. 警惕的，清醒的：The dog kept a vigilant guard over the house. 這隻狗警戒地守護著這所房屋。

vigor [ˈvɪgɝ] .... ★★
n. 精力：the vigor of youth = youthful vigor 年輕人的活力

warily [ˈwɛrəlɪ] .... ★
adv. 小心地

wary [ˈwɛrɪ] .... ★
adj. 機警小心的：The spies grew wary as they approached the sentry. 間諜們接近步哨時，提高了警覺心。

Feeling 情感心理活動名稱總匯

20

害怕、知道、認出、覺察相關辭彙

Vocabulary of Scaring & Knowing

acknowledge [əkˋnɑlɪdʒ] .... ★★★★★
v. 承認：When pressed for an answer, she
  acknowledged the existence of another motive for
  the crime. 她在逼供下，承認了犯案的另一個動機。

afraid [əˋfred] .... ★★★★★
adj. ① (+ to + v. / that / of) 怕，害怕的：She was
  afraid to go out at night. 她不敢晚上出去。
  ② (+ that 子句) 恐怕，擔心的（只用作表語）：
  He was weak and was afraid that he could not do
  the work. 他的身體很弱，擔心無法勝任這項工作。
  【片語】be afraid of 害怕

aware [əˋwɛr] .... ★★★★★
adj. 意識到的，知道的，曉得的：The principal didn't
  seem to be aware that there are so much dispute
  about the decision. 校長好像沒有意識到這個決定
  竟會有這麼多爭議。

cognizant [ˋkɑgnɪzənt] .... ★★★
adj. （與of連用）認識的，知曉的，察知的：He was
  cognizant of the truth. 他知道真相。

detect [dɪˋtɛkt] .... ★★★★
v. 探測，發覺：Security officials say that computer
  crime is easy to accomplish and hard to detect. 安全
  部門的官員指出，電腦犯罪易於成功，難於偵察。

detective [dɪˋtɛktɪv] .... ★★★
n. 偵探：Sherlock Holmes is a character in a most
  famous detective novel. 夏洛克・福爾摩斯是一部最
  著名的偵探小說中的人物。

disagreeable [͵dɪsəˋgriəbl̩] .... ★★★
adj. 不愉快的，討厭的：a disagreeable task 不合意的
  工作

discern [dɪˋzɝn] .... ★★
v. 辨明：Electronic telescopes enable astronomers to
  discern galaxies ten billion light-years away. 電子望
  遠鏡讓天文學家能夠看清幾百億光年以外的星體。

discernible [dɪˋsɝnəbl̩] .... ★★
adj. 可覺察的

dread [drɛd] .... ★★
v. 畏懼

n. 畏懼，恐怖：Most critics agree that the nineteenth-century writer Edgar Allan Poe created a sense of dread with extraordinary skill. 許多評論家都認為作家愛倫坡以超群的筆法寫出了一幕恐怖的場景。

dreadful [ˈdrɛdfəl] .... ★★
adj. 可怕的，討厭的：I've had a dreadful day — everything seems to have gone wrong. 我度過了很糟糕的一天，每件事好像都不對勁。

fear [fɪr] .... ★★★★★
n. 害怕，恐懼：They stood there in fear. 他們害怕地站在那兒。

v. 畏懼，害怕，擔心：These men are not to be feared. 這些人不可怕。

formidable [ˈfɔrmɪdəbḷ] .... ★★
adj. 傑出的，可怕的：Though a true hero, he was also a thoroughgoing bureaucrat and politician, a formidable combination. 他雖然是一個真正的英雄，但也是一個十足的官僚和政治家，一個不可思議的混合體。

fright [fraɪt] .... ★★
n. 驚嚇，恐怖：The loud thunder gave me a fright. 這聲響雷嚇了我一大跳。

frighten [ˈfraɪtṇ] .... ★★★★★
v. 使驚嚇，嚇唬：The suspect was frightened into confessing. 嫌疑犯在被逼供。

frightened [ˈfraɪtṇd] .... ★★★★★
adj. 受驚嚇的：be frightened out of one's life 嚇得要命

frightful [ˈfraɪtfəl] .... ★★
adj. 非常的，可怕的：Due to the unremitting efforts of the leaders of the two countries, a frightful disaster was avoided. 由於兩國領導人的不懈努力，避免了一次可怕的災難。

horrible [ˈhɔrəbḷ] .... ★★★★
adj. 可怕的，令人恐怖的

horror [ˈhɔrɚ] .... ★★★★★
n. 恐懼：He was filled with horror at the sight. 他看見那種情景嚇得發抖。

辨析
Analyze

dissolve, melt, resolve

1 **afraid** *a.*「害怕的」，常指心理上的害怕，懼怕的色彩較淡。只做表語，其用法為 be afraid of sth. 或 be afraid to do sth.，afraid 後接 that 子句意為恐怕、擔心：The little boy is afraid of dogs. 那個小男孩怕狗。

2 **fearful** *a.*「可怕的，嚇人的，不安的，憂慮的」，指嚇人的東西，相當於 frightening：There has been a fearful accident; several people have been killed. 發生了一場可怕的事故，有好幾個人喪生。

3 **frightened** *a.*「害怕的，受驚的」，指人感到害怕的，有強烈的、突然的或暫時的恐懼感：He was frightened at the thought of being laid off. 他一想到被解雇就很害怕。

misgiving [mɪsˈgɪvɪŋ] .... ★★★★★
n. 疑懼，疑慮：full of misgiving(s) 滿腦子疑
惑，十分不安

panic [ˈpænɪk] .... ★★
n. 恐慌：When the theater caught fire, there
was a panic. 劇院失火時，引起一陣恐慌。

recognition [ˌrɛkəgˈnɪʃən] .... ★★
n. 認識，承認：Henry received widespread
recognition for his naturalistic paintings of
plantation life. 亨利因其農莊生活的繪畫作
品筆法自然，得到了廣泛的認同。

recognize [ˈrɛkəgˌnaɪz] .... ★★★★★
v. 認識，認出，承認：Many people who are
colorblind cannot recognize different hues
of red and green. 很多色盲區分不出紅色和
綠色的色度。

scare [skɛr] .... ★★★★
v. 驚嚇，使受驚：The small animals were
scared when they saw a tiger walking
towards them. 小動物看到一隻老虎向牠們
走來時，驚恐不已。

unaware [ˌʌnəˈwɛr] .... ★★★★★
adj. 不知道的，不注意的，沒覺察到的：He is
unaware of the danger. 他沒有覺察到危
險。

undetected [ˌʌndɪˈtɛktɪd] .... ★★★★★
adj. 未被發現的

unknown [ʌnˈnon] .... ★★★★★
adj. 未知的，不知名的：She took me to
another unknown village. 她帶我到了另一
個陌生的村莊。

wonder [ˈwʌndə] .... ★★★★★
v. ①（對…）感到驚訝或詫異：I don't wonder
at her refusing to marry him. 她拒絕和他結
婚，我一點也不驚訝。②對…感到疑惑，想
知道：I wonder who he is? 我想知道他是
誰？
n. ①驚奇，驚異：They were filled with
wonder. 他們感到十分驚奇。②奇蹟，奇
事：The Great Wall is one of the wonders
of the world. 長城是世界奇蹟之一。
【片語】no wonder 難怪，怪不得

辨析
Analyze

percent, percentage, proportion, rate, ratio

1 **acknowledge** *vt.*「承認，承認…的
權威、權利、主張；確認；對…表示感
謝」：He acknowledged his complete
ignorance of the computer. 他承認他對電
腦一無所知。

2 **admit** *vt. & vi.*「承認，供認」，指在壓
力下不得不承認事實或錯誤，中性詞；還
指「准許…進入，准許…加入」：I admit
that I was wrong to do that. 我承認我那樣
做錯了。

3 **confess** *vt. & vi.*「供認，坦白，承
認」，多用於貶義；做不及物動詞
用時與連詞 to 連用：He admitted /
acknowledged / confessed his fault / guilt.
他承認了他的過錯／罪行。

4 **recognize** *vt.*「承認，確認，認可」，
指承認組織、政府、黨派、權利的合法
存在，也指承認成績、功勞等，還指「認
出，識別」等：Fifty-four countries have
recognized the new government. 已經有
54個國家承認了這個新政府。

Unit 15
人際互動名稱總匯
Relationship

01

交際、聯合、會合、討論相關辭彙

Relationship Vocabulary of Meetings

associate .... ★★★★★

v. [ə`soʃɪˌet] 聯合：Provocation will often cause an animal to attack an object not necessarily associated with the source of irritation. 挑釁通常會導致動物攻擊一個與憤怒原因沒有必然關聯的事物。

adj. [ə`soʃɪt] 合夥的：At the conference, I met many friends from associate organizations. 我在那次會議上，遇到了相關單位的許多朋友。

association [əˌsosɪ`eʃən] .... ★★★★★

n. 協會，關聯：Religion had an intimate association with alchemy during the Middle Ages. 在中世紀，宗教和煉金術有著密切的關係。

communicate [kə`mjunəˌket] .... ★★★★

v. ①通訊，交流，交際：I communicated with him regarding this matter. 我為了這件事和他聯絡。②傳達，傳播：They communicated the news to me. 他們向我傳達了消息。

communicative [kə`mjunəˌketɪv] ....★★★★

adj. 交際的，健談的

consort [`kɑnsɔrt] .... ★

v. 結交：Father is annoyed that his daughter consorts with all kinds of strangers. 女兒與各種來歷不明的人廝混在一起，父親很是惱火。

conversation [ˌkɑnvɚ`seʃən] .... ★★★★★

n. 會話，談話：Tom want a sincere conversation with you. 湯姆想和你來一次誠懇的會談。

discuss [dɪ`skʌs] .... ★★★★★

v. 商議，討論：This question will be answered after we discuss it in the coming meeting. 這個問題，我們將在即將召開的會議上討論之後答覆。

interaction [ˌɪntɚ`rækʃən] .... ★★★

n. 相互作用，相互影響：interaction of electrons 【物】電子的相互作用

interconnect [ˌɪntɚkə`nɛkt] .... ★

v. 使相互聯繫：They are closely interconnected. 他們彼此互相緊密關聯。

intercourse [ˈɪntəˌkors] .... ★★★★★

n. 交際，交往：Airplanes, good roads, and telephones make intercourse with different parts of the country far easier than it was 50 years ago. 飛機、良好的道路和電話讓國內各地之間的交流較五十年前遠為便利。

interdependent

[ˌɪntədɪˈpɛndənt] .... ★★★★★

adj. 互相依賴，互相關聯：Today, the mission of one institution can be accomplished only by recognizing that it lives in an interdependent world with conflicts and overlapping interests. 今天，一間機構只有認識到它是處在衝突、交互存在利益又是相互依存的世界裡，才能完成自己的任務。

02

人際互動類名稱總匯

建議、評論、辯論相關辭彙

Relationship

Vocabulary of Suggestion & Review

advice [ədˋvaɪs] .... ★★★★★

n. 建議，忠告：John went to the beach on the advice of the doctor. 約翰遵照醫生的建議，到海邊去了。

advisable [ədˋvaɪzəbl] .... ★★★

adj. 合理的：It is advisable that they go with a clearly defined goal in mind. 他們去的時候應該在心中有一個明確的目標。

advise [ədˋvaɪz] .... ★★★★

v. 忠告，通知：They strongly advised him to accept the offer. 他們極力勸他接受這個建議／報價。

adviser [ədˋvaɪzɚ] .... ★★★★

n. 導師，顧問：My adviser recommended me to apply to your program. 我的導師推薦我申請你們的課程。

advisory [ədˋvaɪzərɪ] .... ★★★★

adj. 顧問的，諮詢的：advisory committee 諮詢委員會

claim [klem] .... ★★★★★

v. 聲稱，斷言，索賠，要求：Did you claim on the insurance after your car accident? 你在車禍之後有沒有請領保險？

n. 要求，權利，所有權

cogent [ˋkodʒənt] .... ★

adj. 強有力的，有說服力的：a cogent argument 令人信服的證據

comment [ˋkɑmɛnt] .... ★★★★★

n. 評論，意見

v. 評論（後可接on / upon）：He refused to comment on the election result. 他拒絕評論選舉結果。

commentator [ˋkɑmənˌtetɚ] .... ★★★★★

n. 注釋者，評論員，實況廣播員：sports commentator 體育評論員

contend [kənˋtɛnd] .... ★★

v. 主張，宣稱，競爭：The official in the tax office contended that the shopkeeper was innocent. 稅務所的官員認為該店主是清白的。

debatable [dɪˋbetəbl] ....★★★★

adj. 爭論中的，未決定的：a debatable ground / land 爭執不定的邊界

debate [dɪˈbet] .... ★★★★

n. 爭論，辯論，辯論會：The tradition of unlimited debate of the United States Senate is very strong. 美國參議院不設限辯論的傳統非常盛行。

disprove [dɪsˈpruv] .... ★★★★★

v. 反駁，證明…有誤：He could not disprove the major contention of his opponents. 他無法駁倒對方的主要論點。

dispute [dɪˈspjut] .... ★★★★

n. 爭端，爭論，辯駁：Few disputes between neighbors cannot be settled outside the courtroom. 鄰里之間的爭端大都可以在法庭以外解決。

elect [ɪˈlɛkt] .... ★★★★★

v. 選舉，推選，選擇：He elected to become a lawyer. 他選擇當律師。

election [ɪˈlɛkʃən] .... ★★★★★

n. 選舉：When the election results were made known, the Secretary of the Democratic Party acknowledged that they had been defeated. 大選結果公佈後，民主黨的秘書承認他們已經敗選。

eloquence [ˈɛləkwəns] .... ★★

n. 雄辯：His eloquence did not avail against the facts. 他的雄辯在事實面前不起什麼作用。

eloquent [ˈɛləkwənt] .... ★★

adj. 雄辯的，有口才的：Abolitionist Frederick Douglas's eloquent speeches helped him achieve great success. 廢除主義者佛列德瑞克·道格拉斯口若懸河的演講，幫助他獲得了巨大的成功。

forensic [fəˈrɛnsɪk] .... ★

adj. 法庭的：The poor peasant's son worked his way through difficulties and finally became a specialist in forensic medicine. 那個貧苦農民的兒子歷經艱難困苦，終於成為一名法醫專家。

propriety [prəˈpraɪətɪ] .... ★★★★★

n. 適當：I doubt the propriety of this behavior. 我懷疑這樣做是否適當。

recommend [ˌrɛkəˈmɛnd] .... ★★★★★

v. 勸告，推薦：I recommended him for the job. 我曾推薦他做那項工作。

辨析
Analyze

advice, proposal, suggestion

1 **advice** *n.*「忠告，勸告」，不可數名詞，指專家建議或有益的經驗：You should eat on the doctor's advice. 你應遵照醫師的建議進食。

2 **proposal** *n.*「建議，提議」，指提出建議供參考或考慮；片語 make a proposal to sb. 意思則是向某人提議或向某人求婚：His proposal for peace has been accepted by the committee. 他的和平提議已經為委員會所接受。

3 **suggestion** *n.*「建議，提議」，普通用語：His suggestion didn't appeal to the students. 他的建議不吸引學生。

recommendation

[ˌrɛkəmɛnˋdeʃən] .... ★★★★★

n. 推薦，建議，勸告：I went to the new hotel on your recommendation. 經過你的介紹，我去了這家新旅館。

refutation [ˌrɛfjuˋteʃən] .... ★

n. 反駁

refute [rɪˋfjut] .... ★

v. 駁斥，反駁，駁倒：People refuted the results of the poll 人們不承認選舉結果的真實性。

remark [rɪˋmɑrk] .... ★★★★★

v. ①說，評論說：He remarked that it was getting dark. 他說天黑了。②評論，議論：Everybody remarked loudly on her absence. 大家都大聲議論著她的缺席。

n. 議論，談論，評論

retort [rɪˋtɔrt] .... ★★

v. 反駁："Of course not," she retorted. 她回嘴說：「當然不是。」

squabble [ˋskwɑbl̩] .... ★

n. 爭論，口角：The children were squabbling about who had won the game. 孩子們在為誰贏了比賽而爭吵。

suggestion [səˋdʒɛstʃən] .... ★★★★

n. ①建議，意見：Anyone has any other suggestions to make? 誰還有別的建議嗎？②細微的跡象：a suggestion of a smile 一絲微笑③暗示，聯想

人際互動名稱總匯

03

損壞、傷害、威脅、危害相關辭彙

Vocabulary of Damage & Danger

assassin [əˈsæsɪn] .... ★
n. 刺客：a character assassin 詆毀人格者

assassinate [əˈsæsɪˌet] .... ★
v. 暗殺，行刺

assassination [əˌsæsəˈneʃən] .... ★
n. 暗殺

deleterious [ˌdɛləˈtɪrɪəs] .... ★★★★★
adj. 有害的：Too much watering can be deleterious on plants. 太多水會對植物有害。

harm [hɑrm] .... ★★★★
n. 傷害，損害，危害：do sb. harm 傷害某人
v. 傷害，損害：There was a traffic accident in the street, but no one was harmed. 街上發生了一起交通事故，但沒人受傷。

harmful [ˈhɑrmfəl] .... ★★★
adj. 有害的：Follow the directions carefully, or this medicine may be harmful. 小心遵守指示，否則這藥可能有害。

hurt [hɜt] .... ★★★★★
vt. ①傷害，損害：Mike hurt his leg badly when he fell. 麥克跌了一跤，腿傷得很嚴重。②感情受到創傷：It hurts me to think that she even said such things to others. 我想到她竟對別人說這些事情就感到痛心。

impair [ɪmˈpɛr] .... ★★★★★
v. 損害：an injury that impaired my hearing 令我聽力受損的傷

injure [ˈɪndʒɚ] .... ★★★★
v. 傷害，損害，損傷：She was injured badly in an accident during the work. 她在一次工作意外中受了重傷。

injury [ˈɪndʒərɪ] .... ★★★★
n. 損害，傷害，毀壞：He escaped from the accident without injury. 他毫髮無傷地逃過一劫。

intimidate [ɪnˈtɪməˌdet] .... ★★★★
v. 恐嚇：He said he would never be intimidated by big names and authorities. 他說他絕不會為名人和權勢所嚇倒。

mangle [ˈmæŋgl̩] .... ★

v. 撕裂，毀壞

menace [ˈmɛnɪs] .... ★

v. 威嚇，脅迫：When menaced by a predator
in close proximity, a snake may suddenly
alter its behavior. 當一條蛇受到近處捕食者
的威脅時，它會突然變化行為。

mischief [ˈmɪstʃɪf] .... ★★

n. 損害，傷害，危害，惡作劇，搗蛋，胡鬧：
The broken window was the mischief of
vandals. 被打碎的窗戶是那些故意破壞公物
的人造成的。

persecute [ˈpɝsɪˌkjut] .... ★

v. 迫害：be persecuted by the reactionary
government 受到反動政府的迫害

04

獲勝、征服、打賭、獲得相關辭彙

Vocabulary of Gain & Bets

acquire [əˋkwaɪr] .... ★★★★★

v. 獲得：In the early 1850's, the City of New York acquired the land that was to become Central Park. 在1850年代初期，紐約市獲得了可建成中央公園的那塊土地。

acquisitive [əˋkwɪzətɪv] .... ★

adj. 貪得無厭的，可獲得的：In an acquisitive society, the form that selfishness predominantly takes is monetary greed. 在一個貪婪的社會裡，貪財是自私自利的顯著表現形式。

bet [bɛt] ....★★★★

v. ①以…打賭，與…打賭 ：He bet me ten dollars that I couldn't do it. 他和我賭10美元，賭我無法做那件事。②打賭

n. ①打賭 ：I will make a bet with you. 我要和你賭一賭。②賭金，賭注

gain [gen] .... ★★★★★

v. ①獲得：gain an advantage over a competitor 勝過對手，占上風②增加（體重）：gain weight 增加重量③（鐘錶）走快：The watch gains three minutes a day. 這錶一天快3分鐘。④受益，得益：gain from an experience 從經驗中得益

n. ①增進，增加：a gain in health 健康的增進②（常pl.）收益：make gains at other's expense 損人利己

gamble [ˋgæmbl̩] .... ★★

v. 賭博，投機：You are gambling with your health by continuing to smoke. 你繼續抽煙是把自己的健康當賭注。

overwhelm [͵ovɚˋhwɛlm] .... ★★

v. 壓倒，制服：The small craft was overwhelmed by the enormous waves. 小船被濤天巨浪打翻了。

reap [rip] .... ★★★★

v. 收割，收穫：She reaped large profits from her unique invention. 她從她那奇特的發明中獲得了很多益處。

subdue [səbˋdju] .... ★★

v. 征服，服從：subdue my excitement about the upcoming holiday 克制我因即將到來的節日而產生的興奮感

subjection [səbˋdʒɛkʃən] .... ★★★★★

n. 征服，服從：bring...under subjection 征服…

triumph [ˈtraɪəmf] .... ★★★★
n. （大）成功，（大）勝利

triumphant [traɪˈʌmfənt] .... ★
adj. 得勝的，得意洋洋的

victory [ˈvɪktərɪ] .... ★★★★★
n. 勝利

win [wɪn] .... ★★★★★
v. 贏得，獲得：I couldn't win her
understanding. 我無法得到她的諒解。

winner [ˈwɪnɚ] .... ★★★★
n. 獲勝者，成功者

辨析 Analyze

acquire, derive, gain, get, obtain, reap

1 acquire *vt.* 「取得，獲得，學到」，指經由努力和逐漸積累而獲得：During his 10 years' stay in America, he acquired a lot of knowledge about American culture. 他在美國居住的10年裡，瞭解了很多有關美國文化的知識。

2 derive *v.* 「取得，得到，追溯…的起源」，常與 from 連用，強調「從…得到」，其片語「derive from / be derived from」意為「起源於，來自」：He derives much pleasure from his books. 他從書中得到很大的樂趣。

3 gain *v.* 「獲得，增加，受益」，指透過努力奮鬥而獲得某種利益，還指「（鐘、錶）走快」：Their hard work gained them a good reputation. 他們的辛勤工作替自己贏得了好名聲。

4 get *vt.* 「得到，獲得」，是最常用的一個字，搭配詞極多，既可指主動獲得，也可指偶然得到：He got a book from his brother. 他從他的兄弟那裡得到一本書。

5 obtain *vi.* 「獲得，得到，通行，流行，存在」，指得到了渴望得到之物，含有滿足願望、達到目的之意，風格較為正式；還指「通行，流行，存在」：Anyone can obtain knowledge through his / her practice. 任何人都能透過實踐獲得知識。

6 reap *vt. & vi.* 「獲得，得到」，其本義為「收割，收穫」，其引申義為得到回報或報償：The child's behavior reaped praise. 那個孩子的行為得到了表揚。

人際互動名稱總匯

Relationship

05

介紹、說明、支持相關辭彙

Vocabulary of Introduction & Support

introduce [ˌɪntrəˋdjus] .... ★★★★★

v. ①介紹：The chairman introduced the lecturer to audience. 主持人把解說人介紹給聽眾。②引進，進入：Tea was introduced into Europe from China. 茶葉由中國傳入歐洲。③提出：introduce a motion 提出建議

introduction [ˌɪntrəˋdʌkʃən] .... ★★★★★

n. ①介紹②引進，傳入③採用（的東西）④導言⑤入門（書）

prop [prɑp] .... ★

v. 支持：Both woodpeckers and kangaroos prop themselves up with their tails. 啄木鳥和袋鼠都用尾巴來支撐自己的身體。

support [səˋport] .... ★★★★★

v. ①支持，擁護：A lot of building workers supported the strike. 許多建築工人支持罷工。②支撐，支承：He had to sit down, because his knees wouldn't support him any more. 他不得不坐下來，因為他的膝蓋再也支撐不住了。③供養，維持：He has a wife and three children to support. 他必須供養妻子和三個孩子。

n. ①支持：They failed to get trade union's support. 他們沒有得到工會的支持。②支撐：Most high buildings have steel supports. 大多數高樓大廈裡都有鋼鐵支架。③贍養費，資助：We are dependent on them for financial support. 我們依靠他們的財政資助。

supporter [səˋportə] .... ★★★★★

n. 支持者，支架，托器：He was an effective supporter of reform. 他是改革的有力支持者。

06

影響、強迫、強調相關辭彙

Vocabulary of Force & Emphasis

Relationship

affect [əˋfɛkt] .... ★★★★★
v. 影響，感動：Constant exposure to intense light affects the eyes adversely. 持續暴露在強光之下會損害眼睛。

allege [əˋlɛdʒ] .... ★★★★★
v. 宣稱，主張：It is alleged that he had worked for the enemy. 據說他曾為敵人工作過。

allegiance [əˋlidʒəns] .... ★
n. 忠誠：Ocean-going vessels have often used flags to indicate their national allegiance. 航海的船隻常懸掛旗幟來表示對自己國家的忠誠。

bearing [ˋbɛrɪŋ] .... ★★★★
n. 軸承，忍受，聯繫：What they have done has no bearing on the promotion of sales. 他們所做的事情與這次促銷活動毫無關聯。

compel [kəmˋpɛl] .... ★★★★★
v. 強迫：Juries that decide civil and criminal cases always deliberate in private and are not compelled to reveal their reasons for a decision. 判決民事和刑事案件的陪審團總是在私下商議，他人則無權強迫他們披露判決的理由。

compulsive [kəmˋpʌlsɪv] .... ★★★★★
adj. 強迫的，情不自禁的：Compulsive drinking is bad for one's health. 喝酒不加節制有害健康。

compulsory [kəmˋpʌlsərɪ] .... ★
adj. 義務的，必修的：After 1850, various states in the United States began to pass compulsory school attendance laws. 美國各州在1850年以後，都開始通過義務教育法令。

effect [ɪˋfɛkt] .... ★★★★★
n. 效果，印象：Plato's teachings had a profound effect on Aristotle. 柏拉圖的教學法對亞里斯多德產生了深遠的影響。

effectively [ɪˋfɛktɪvlɪ] .... ★★★★★
adv. 有效地，有影響地：Mr. Stewart is very much pleased because his instructions are carried out effectively by his subordinates. 史都華先生的屬下有效率地執行他的指示，他感到很滿意。

effectuate [ɪˈfɛktʃuˌet] .... ★★★★★
v. 使實現：Now we can begin to effectuate the cure. 現在我們能著手來治療這疾病了。

emphasis [ˈɛmfəsɪs] .... ★★★★
n. 強調，重點：a lecture on housekeeping with emphasis on neatness 一場強調整潔的客房管理演說

emphasize [ˈɛmfəˌsaɪz] .... ★★★★
v. 強調，著重：Writers of the Romantic period revolted against the rules of Classicism and emphasized the inherent goodness of the individual. 浪漫主義時期的作家反對古典主義的教條，強調個人天賦的善良。

imbue [ɪmˈbju] .... ★
v. 浸染，灌輸：A President should be imbued with a sense of responsibility for the nation. 一位總統應該充滿對國家的責任感。

impressionable [ɪmˈprɛʃənəbl] .... ★
adj. 易受影響的：Sixteen is a highly impressionable age. 十六歲是一個可塑性極強的年齡。

inflict [ɪnˈflɪkt] .... ★★★★★
v. 造成：Our army inflicted heavy losses on the enemy. 我軍重創敵人。

influence [ˈɪnfluəns] .... ★★★★★
v. 影響，感化
n. 影響，感化，勢力，權勢：Many women have had civilizing influence upon their husbands. 許多婦女對丈夫都具有影響力。

influential [ˌɪnfluˈɛnʃəl] .... ★★★
adj. 有影響的，有權勢的：The *Dial*, edited by Margaret Fulier, was among the first influential magazines published in the United States. 由 Margaret Fulier 編輯的「Dial」雜誌，是美國早期有影響力的雜誌之一。

overstress [ˈovəˈstrɛs] .... ★★★★★
v. 過於強調

underscore [ˌʌndəˈskor] .... ★★★★★
v. 在⋯下面劃線，強調：Last week's fire underscores the necessity of observing safety rules. 上星期的火災提醒人們要注意安全規則的必要性。

辨析
Analyze

affect, effect, influence

1 **affect** *vt.* 「影響」，常指對人或物產生具體或消極的影響，其相應的名詞為 effect：The dry weather has affected the production of the fruit. 乾旱影響了水果產量。

2 **effect** *vt.* 「實現，使生效，引起」，做動詞則與 affect 毫不相干；做名詞表示「結果，效果」：The snow effected a sharp drop in temperature. 下雪讓溫度急劇下降。

3 **influence** *vt. & n.* 「影響」，指產生潛移默化或長期的影響。這種影響可以是積極的，也可以是消極的：No students can avoid being influenced by their teachers. 學生都會受到老師的影響。

07

鼓勵、挑戰、處理、挑剔相關辭彙

Vocabulary of Incitation & Dealing

advocate .... ★★★★
n. [ˈædvəkɪt] 辯護者
v. [ˈædvəˌket] 擁護：The abolitionists advocated freedom for the slaves. 奴隸制度廢除論者提倡解放奴隸。

challenge [ˈtʃælɪndʒ] .... ★★★★★
n. 挑戰，挑戰書
v. 挑戰，激勵，要求：Their school challenged ours to a football match. 他們學校向我們學校挑戰，要來一場足球比賽。

cheer [tʃɪr] .... ★★★★
v. ①（使）振奮，（使）高興：Every one was cheered by the good news. 大家聽到這個好消息，都感到興奮。②歡呼，喝彩：The crowd cheered as the hero drove past. 英雄驅車經過時，人群發出了歡呼聲。
【片語】cheer up 高興起來，振作起來
n. 振奮，歡呼，喝彩

cope [kop] .... ★★★
v. 對付，妥善處理：She is not a competent driver and can't cope with driving in heavy traffic. 她不是個稱職的駕駛，在交通擁擠時就是開不好車。

deal [dil] .... ★★★★★
v. 處理：The United States is trying to deal with the serious problem brought on by the energy crisis. 美國正在著手處理因能源短缺引起的嚴重問題。
n. 交易

disposal [dɪˈspozl] .... ★★★
n. ①丟掉，清除：waste disposal 垃圾處理 ②排列，佈置：a pleasing disposal of plants and lawn 賞心悅目的植物和草坪佈置

dispose [dɪˈspoz] .... ★★★★
v. 處理，配置，傾向於：The circulatory system helps dispose of wastes that would harm the body if accumulated. 循環系統幫助處理那些一旦累積起來就會危害人體的廢物。

disposition [ˌdɪspəˈzɪʃən] .... ★★★★★
n. 性情：Maria Callas became one of the world's most widely known opera singers because of her musical talent, acting ability and fiery disposition. 瑪麗亞·卡拉斯因其音樂天賦、演出才能和火暴的脾氣，成為世界上最著名的歌劇演唱家之一。

encourage [ɪnˈkɝɪdʒ] .... ★★★★★

v. 鼓勵：The American Association of University Women encourages women to develop their intellectual talents. 美國大學婦女協會鼓勵婦女們提升自己的知識水準。

foment [foˈmɛnt] .... ★

v. 引發：Three sailors were fomenting a mutiny on the ship. 三個水手正在船上煽動叛變。

incite [ɪnˈsaɪt] .... ★★★★★

v. 引起，激起，煽動：His bravery incited the soldiers to fight continuously. 他的勇敢激勵士兵們繼續戰鬥下去。

inspiration [ˌɪnspəˈreʃən] .... ★★

n. 靈感，授意，妙想，鼓舞，激動：the inspiration from nature 大自然給予的靈感

inspire [ɪnˈspaɪr] .... ★★★★

v. 鼓舞，激起，感動，使產生靈感：Myths have inspired many of the world's greatest poets, artists, musicians and scientists. 世界上許多偉大的詩人、藝術家、音樂家以及科學家都是從神話獲得靈感的。

instigate [ˈɪnstəˌget] .... ★

v. 鼓動：He instigated the ending of a free working lunch in the company. 他鼓吹要讓公司的免費工作午餐走入歷史。

outrage [ˈaʊtˌredʒ] .... ★

v. 激怒，侵犯：I was surprised and outraged to see that she had gone ahead with her plans without consulting us first. 她未經商量就擅自按照她自己的計畫行事，對此我感到吃驚和憤怒。

patronage [ˈpætrənɪdʒ] .... ★

n. 贊助，資助：It seems our little establishment has finally been deemed worthy of the bank's patronage. 看來銀行終於認為值得資助我們這種小機構了。

praise [prez] .... ★★★★★

v. 讚揚，表揚：They praised his speech for its clarity and humour. 他們稱讚他的演講很清晰、幽默。

n. ①稱讚，表揚：Three entrants were singled out for special praise. 三位參賽者被挑選出來得到特殊表揚。②讚美的話：She finds it hard to give praises. 她想不出讚美的言詞。

prod [prɑd] .... ★

v. 刺激：Bob is lazy; he won't do any work if he's not prodded into it. 鮑伯很懶，不催促他是不肯做任何工作的。

provoke [prəˈvok] .... ★★

v. 激怒，煽動：The Southern attack on Fort Sumter near Charlston provoked a sharp response from the North, which led to the American Civil War. 南方軍隊對查爾斯敦附近的福特要塞進攻激怒了北方軍隊，從而引發了美國南北戰爭。

spur [spɝ] .... ★★★★

n. 鞍刺，馬刺，刺激，刺激物

v. 刺激，激勵，鼓舞：The *National Industrial Recovery Act* was designed to spur industry. 《國家工業復甦法》是為了刺激工業發展而設計的。

tackle [ˈtækl̩] .... ★★★★

v. 著手處理，對付：The question set by the teacher was so difficult that the pupils did not know how to tackle it. 老師提的問題太難了，學生們都不知道怎麼回答。

n. 用具，裝備，（足球）阻截隊員：fishing tackle 釣魚用具

transact [trænsˈækt] .... ★★

v. 處理：to transact business over the phone 在電話中進行交易

transaction [trænˈzækʃən] .... ★★

n. 處理，辦理，交易：All transactions, from banking to shopping, will be performed electronically. 從跑銀行到買東西的所有交易，都可透過電腦來完成。

treat [trit] .... ★★★★★

v. ①對待，處理：They were treated with respect. 他們受到尊重。②醫療，醫治：treat sb. for his illness 為某人治病③款待，招待：He treated me to dinner. 他請我吃飯。

n. 款待，請客：This is my treat. 這次我請客。

treatment [ˈtritmənt] .... ★★★★★

n. 治療：His treatment of the animal was cruel. 他對待這隻動物很殘忍。

urge [ɝdʒ] .... ★★★★★

n. 衝動

v. 推進，催促：Marcus Garvey, who urged a "back to Africa" movement, attempted to establish colonies of Black Americans in Africa. 馬庫斯‧加維提倡「回歸非洲」運動，試圖在非洲建立美洲黑人的聚居地。

08

表揚、批評、責罰、饒恕、仇視相關辭彙

Vocabulary of Praise & Criticism

abuse [əˋbjuz] ....★★★★
v. 濫用，虐待：He abused his privileges in activities outside his official capacity. 他在職務範圍之外任意濫用職權。
n. 濫用

antagonism [ænˋtægə͵nɪzəm] ....★
n. 敵對：We shall have to overcome the antagonism of the natives before our plans for settling in this area can succeed. 我們定居此地的計畫如果想要成功，就必須先克服土著的敵對態度。

antagonist [ænˋtægənɪst] ....★
n. 敵手：a formidable antagonist in the contest 比賽中令人生畏的對手

antagonistic [æn͵tægəˋnɪstɪk] ....★
adj. 敵對的，對抗的：Public elections are sometimes held to settle differences between antagonistic groups in a government body. 全開選舉有時是用來擺平政府機構中對抗團體之間的分歧的。

argue [ˋɑrgjʊ] ....★★★★
v. ①爭論，爭辯（後可接 with sb. about / over sth.）：We argued with the waiter about the price of beverages. 我們與服務員爭論著飲料的價格。②論證，主張：The director argued that they needed a larger room. 主任據理力爭，說他們需要大一點的房間。③說服：They argued me into joining the club. 他們說服我加入了俱樂部。

argument [ˋɑrgjəmənt] ....★★★★★
n. 爭論，論據：They were having an argument about whose turn it was to do the cooking. 他們為該輪到誰做飯而爭吵不休。

asperse [əˋspɝs] ....★
v. 誹謗：asperse somebody's reputation 破壞某人的名譽

aspersion [əˋspɝʒən] ....★
n. 誹謗：cast aspersion on / upon somebody 造謠中傷某人

berate [bɪˋret] ....★
v. 痛罵：He was berated in newspapers. 他在報上受到痛批。

557

bereave [bəˋriv] .... ★

v. 剝奪：Anger bereaves him of words. 憤怒使他說不出話來。

bereavement [bəˋrivmənt] .... ★

n. 喪失：His friends gathered to console him upon his sudden bereavement. 在他為親人的驟逝傷慟時，朋友們都來安慰他。

blame [blem] .... ★★★★

v. 譴責：City residents also blame migrant workers for the sharp rise in the urban crime rate. 城市居民也責怪外勞造成了城市犯罪率大幅度攀升。

n. (不可數) 譴責

castigate [ˋkæstəˏget] .... ★

v. 譴責：His teacher castigated him for his inattentiveness in class. 老師因為他在課堂上不專心聽講而嚴厲地責罵他。

censure [ˋsɛnʃə] .... ★

n. 責難：a review containing unfair censures of a new film 對某一新片大肆抨擊的評論

commend [kəˋmɛnd] .... ★★

v. 讚揚，把…交託給：This TV play does not seem to commend itself to me. 這部電視劇給我的印象似乎不好。

condemn [kənˋdɛm] .... ★★★★

v. 譴責：Most people are willing to condemn violence of any sort as evil. 大多數人都願意把任何暴力行為視作惡行並加以譴責。

controversial [ˏkɑntrəˋvɝʃəl] .... ★★★

n. 爭論：controversial writing 筆戰

controvert [ˋkɑntrəˏvɝt] .... ★★★

v. 反駁，辯論：a point much controverted between A and B 甲和乙之間爭論不休的一點

critic [ˋkrɪtɪk] .... ★★★★

n. 批評家，評論家：sports critic 體育評論家

critical [ˋkrɪtɪkl] .... ★★★★★

adj. 評論的，批評的，危急的，臨界的：This legislation is critical to sustaining the business upturn. 這項法案對於保持商業增長是至關重要的。

criticism [ˋkrɪtəˏsɪzəm] .... ★★★★

n. 批評，評論：These two criticisms provide a good starting point. 這兩種批判提供了良好的開端。

curse [kɝs] .... ★★★★

n. 詛咒，咒語：Our tribe is under a curse. 我們的部族受到詛咒。

decry [dɪˋkraɪ] .... ★

v. 非難，譴責

defame [dɪˋfem] .... ★

v. 誹謗，損毀名譽

denounce [dɪˋnaʊns] .... ★

v. 譴責，聲討，告發：denounce a treaty 通知廢止條約

deprive [dɪˋpraɪv] .... ★★★★

v. 奪去，剝奪，使喪失：Those clubs do not deprive poor children of the opportunity to participate in sports. 那些俱樂部並沒有剝奪窮孩子參加運動的機會。

extol [ɪkˋstol] .... ★

v. 頌揚：Songs of extolling the motherland are ringing far and near. 頌揚祖國的歌聲響徹四方。

haggle [ˋhægl] .... ★

v. 爭論：The farmer haggled over the price of the cattle. 農民為那頭牛的價格爭執。

hostile [ˋhɑstɪl] .... ★★★★

adj. 敵方的，敵意的：Ever since I got better marks than Parker, he has been hostile to me. 自從我得分比派克高以後，他就對我有了敵意。

hostility [hɑsˋtɪlətɪ] .... ★★★★

n. 戰事行動：feelings of hostility 敵意

impute [ɪmˈpjut] .... ★★★★★

v. 歸咎於：They imputed the rocket failure to a faulty gasket. 他們把火箭發射失敗歸咎於故障的墊圈。

indisputable [ˌɪndɪˈspjutəbl] .... ★★★

adj. 無可爭辯的：indisputable evidence 無可爭辯的證據

injurious [ɪnˈdʒʊrɪəs] .... ★★★★

adj. 侮辱的，誹謗的，有害的：Smoking is injurious to health, especially to the lungs. 抽煙對健康有害，尤其對肺有害。

insult [ˈɪnsʌlt] .... ★★★★

n. 侮辱，凌辱：Insults were hurled back and forth between the two writers. 這兩位作家互相辱罵對方。

ironic [aɪˈrɑnɪk] .... ★★★★★

adj. 諷刺的：madness, an ironic fate for such a clear thinker 發瘋，對這樣一個思維清晰的人來說，是一種有嘲弄意味的命運

irreproachable [ˌɪrɪˈprotʃəbl] .... ★★★★★

adj. 無可指責的：irreproachable conduct 無可挑惕的舉止

laud [lɔd] .... ★

v. 讚美：Not until his play *Beyond the Horizon* was produced was Eugene O'Neil lauded as the foremost creative American playwright. 尤金‧歐尼爾直到發表其作品《超越地平線》後，才被譽為美國最富創造力的劇作家。

laudable [ˈlɔdəbl] .... ★

adj. 值得讚美的：laudable feats 可稱頌的功績〔傑出事蹟〕

malign [məˈlaɪn] .... ★

v. 詆毀，誹謗：The politician maligend her opponent as dishonest. 這名政客詆毀她的對手不誠實。

quarrel [ˈkwɔrəl] .... ★★★★

v. 爭吵，爭論：The couple quarreled quite often. 這對夫妻常吵架。

n. 爭吵，口角

辨析 Analyze

argue, debate, dispute, quarrel

1 **argue** vt. & vi. 「爭論，爭吵，爭辯，提出理由證明，（堅決）主張，說服，勸說」，指為自己的意見提供理由或證據，進行爭論，其名詞為 argument（論點，論證）：He argued that the experiment could have been done in another way. 他認為該實驗本來可用別的方式進行的。

2 **debate** vt. & vi. 「辯論，爭論」，指正式地、有條有理地就一個問題進行辯論：The subject was once hotly debated among students. 這個主題曾經在學生中引起熱烈的辯論。

3 **dispute** vt. & vi. 「爭論，爭吵，對⋯表示異議，就⋯發生爭吵」，正式用詞，既可指個人之間的爭論、爭吵，又可指組織、國家間的爭議、爭端：They were disputing whether to start at once or stay. 他們爭論著該馬上出發還是要留下來。

4 **quarrel** vi. 「爭吵，爭論，對⋯表示反對，挑剔，抱怨」，指憤怒地爭吵、吵架：It is no use quarreling about it with him. 和他爭吵這一點是沒有用的。

rebuke [rɪ`bjuk] .... ★

v. 斥責：He was rebuked by his wife. 他被妻
子痛罵一頓。

reproach [rɪ`protʃ] .... ★★

v. 責備：Do not reproach yourself, it was not
your fault. 你不用自責，這不是你的錯。

rumor [`rumɚ] .... ★

n. 傳聞，謠言：The rumor has turned out to
be true. 這謠言已變成真的。

sarcasm [`sɑrkæzm̩] .... ★

n. 諷刺，挖苦：squelch somebody with biting
sarcasm 用尖刻的挖苦壓服人。

sarcastic [sɑr`kæstɪk] .... ★

adj. 諷刺的，挖苦的：He deserves a
reputation of sarcastic, acerbic and
uninhibited polemics. 他的臭名受到尖酸
刻薄的無限制攻詰。

sardonic [sɑr`dɑnɪk] .... ★

adj. 諷刺的，嘲笑的：a sardonic smile 冷笑

satirical [sə`tɪrɪkl̩] .... ★

adj. 諷刺的

scold [skold] .... ★★★

v. 責罵，訓斥：My mother scolded me for
being rude to you. 我母親因為我對你態度粗
魯罵了我一頓。

slander [`slændɚ] .... ★

v. 造謠，誹謗：He slandered me in front of
my friend. 他在我的朋友面前誹謗我。

09

問答、要求、需要、請求相關辭彙

Vocabulary of Demand

beg [bɛg] .... ★★★★★
v. ①乞求，乞討：He was so poor that he begged for his bread. 他窮得討飯度日。②懇求，請求：I begged (of) him not to do it. 我懇求他別這麼做。

beseech [bɪˈsitʃ] .... ★
v. 祈求，懇求：I beseech you to do this before it is too late. 我懇求你這麼做，趁現在還來得及。

clamor [ˈklæmə] .... ★
v. 叫囂：Three blocks away we could hear the protesters clamoring for higher wages and better working conditions. 我們能夠聽見三個街區以外抗議者要求加薪和改善工作環境的叫喊聲。

corroborate [kəˈrɑbəˌret] .... ★
v. 確證：The new theory was corroborated. 新理論得到了證實。

corroborative [kəˈrɑbəˌretɪv] .... ★★★
adj. 確定的，證實的

demand [dɪˈmænd] .... ★★★★★
v. 要求，需要：the high demands of her job 她工作的高度要求

entail [ɪnˈtel] .... ★
v. 惹起，使負擔：Plays that entail direct interaction between actors and audience present no unusual difficulties for actors. 能夠讓演員和觀眾直接交流的戲，對於演員來說不會特別困難。

entreat [ɪnˈtrit] .... ★★
v. 懇求，請求：After his military defeat in 1865, Robert E. Lee entreated the people of the South to work for national harmony. 羅伯特‧李在1865年戰敗以後，請求南方人民為了國家和諧努力。

gainsay [genˈse] .... ★★★★★
v. 否認，反駁（常用於否定句或疑問句）：There is no gainsaying his honesty. 他的誠實是不可否認的。

implore [ɪmˈplor] .... ★★
v. 懇求，乞求：He implored the tribunal to have mercy. 他向法庭懇求寬恕。

invocation [ˌɪnvəˈkeʃən] .... ★
n. 祈禱

invoke [ɪnˈvok] .... ★★★★★
v. 懇求，祈求：I invoked their forgiveness. 我懇求他們原諒。

panhandle [ˈpænˌhændḷ] .... ★
v. 在街上行乞：The beggers panhandled money. 乞丐向陌生人要錢。

petition [pəˈtɪʃən] .... ★★
n. 請願：The villagers all signed a petition asking for a hospital to be built. 村民們都在請願書上簽名要求建一所醫院。
v. 向⋯請願

plea [pli] .... ★★
n. 懇求：a plea for greater tolerance 懇求更大的寬容

plead [plid] .... ★★
v. 抗辯，懇求：Your youth and simplicity plead for you in this instance. 在這種情況下，你的年輕和單純成為有力的辯護論證。

pray [pre] .... ★★★★★
v. ①請求，懇求：He kneeled down and prayed to Allah. 他跪下祈求真主阿拉。②祈禱，祈求

prayer [prɛr] .... ★★★★★
n. ①祈禱，祈求② (pl.) 祈禱文③懇求④祝福

request [rɪˈkwɛst] .... ★★★★★
v. 請求，要求：She requested to go alone. 她要求自己一個人去。

require [rɪˈkwaɪr] .... ★★★★★
v. ①需要：This suggestion requires careful thinking. 這個建議需要仔細考慮。②要求，規定：All passengers are required to show their tickets. 所有的乘客都被要求出示車票。

requirement [rɪˈkwaɪrmənt] .... ★★★★★
n. 需要，要求，條件：If you have any requirements, ask me. 如果你有什麼要求，請向我提出來。

solicit [səˈlɪsɪt] .... ★
v. 懇求，拉客：a candidate who solicited votes among the factory workers 在工廠工人中尋求選票的候選人

solicitation [səˌlɪsəˈteʃən] .... ★
n. 請求，懇求：direct solicitation（在事務所門前貼出通知）直接徵人

solicitous [səˈlɪsɪtəs] .... ★
adj. 渴望的，焦慮的：He made solicitous inquiries about our family. 他對我們一家週到的探問。

人際互動名稱總匯

10

命令、服從、投降、糾正相關辭彙

Vocabulary of Ordering & Obeying

bondage [ˈbɑndɪdʒ] ....★★★★
n. 束縛：He is in bondage to his ambition. 他受他的野心所支配。

compliant [kəmˈplaɪənt] ....★
adj. 依從的

comply [kəmˈplaɪ] ....★★
v. 順從，應允：The chemical company complied with the regulation. 該化學公司遵從了規定。

condescend [ˌkɑndɪˈsɛnd] ....★
v. 屈尊，不擺架子：It is said the general condescended to eat with the soldiers every Sunday. 據說這位將軍每週日都放下身段與士兵們一同進餐。

conform [kənˈfɔrm] ....★★
v. 遵守，順應：Originally, a hallmark was a mark stamped on gold to show that the gold conformed to official standards. 起初，印在金子上的純度標記是用來標示這塊金子符合官方的標準。

correction [kəˈrɛkʃən] ....★★★★
n. ①改正②（不可數）（對罪犯的）懲治

destine [ˈdɛstɪn] ....★★
v. 指定，命運註定：the money destined to pay for their child's education 經指定償付他們孩子教育費用的錢

disobedient [ˌdɪsəˈbidɪənt] ....★★★★★
adj. 不服從的：The mischievous student has been disobedient to his mother since he was a child. 這個搗蛋的學生從小就不聽他母親的話。

enforce [ɪnˈfors] ....★★★★
v. 實行，執行，強制：enforce military discipline 強制實施軍事紀律

fetter [ˈfɛtɚ] ....★
n. 束縛：No man loves his fetters, be they made of gold. 〔諺〕金鑄的腳鐐，沒人喜愛。

imperative [ɪmˈpɛrətɪv] ....★
adj. 急需的，命令的：It is imperative that they arrive on time for the lecture. 他們必須儘快趕到演講現場。

insubordinate [ˌɪnsə`bɔrdn̩ɪt] .... ★★★★★

adj. 不服從的：to have a history of insubordinate behavior 有違抗行為的記錄

leash [liʃ] .... ★

v. 束縛

n. （牽狗的）皮帶：emotions kept in leash 受壓抑的感情

obedience [ə`bidjəns] .... ★★

n. 服從，順從：He acted in obedience to the orders of his superior. 他是遵照他的上級指示行動的。

obediently [ə`bidɪəntlɪ] .... ★

adv. 服從地，順從地：One of the responsibilities of the Coast Guard is to make sure that all ships obediently follow traffic rules in busy harbors. 海岸巡防隊的職責之一，就是確保所有在繁忙的港口的船隻都能遵從交通規則。

obey [ə`be] .... ★★★★★

v. 服從，聽從：Obey the orders or you will be punished. 服從命令，否則你會受到懲罰。

oppress [ə`prɛs] .... ★★

vt . 壓迫，壓制：The tyrant oppressed the conquered peoples. 這位暴君壓迫被征服的民族。

oppressive [ə`prɛsɪv] .... ★★

adj. 難以忍受的，壓迫的：oppressive laws 嚴刑峻法

repudiate [rɪ`pjudɪˌet] .... ★

v. 批判，拒絕：Chaucer not only came to doubt the worth of his extraordinary body of works, but repudiated it. 喬叟不僅懷疑起他那非凡作品體系的價值，而且拒絕接受它。

submission [sʌb`mɪʃən] .... ★★★★★

n. 屈服，服從：Oppression that cannot be overcome does not give rise to revolt but to submission. 不能戰勝的壓迫不會引起反叛，而是會導致歸順。

submissive [sʌb`mɪsɪv] .... ★★★★★

adj. 順從的

submit [səb`mɪt] .... ★★★★★

v. 服從，提交：You know more, so we submit to your decision. 你懂的比較多，所以我們聽從你的決定。

tame [tem] .... ★★★

v. 馴服，制服

adj. 馴服的，易於駕馭的，沉悶的：The reindeer is probably the only deer that people have ever tamed. 馴鹿可能是人類惟一馴服的鹿。

11

領導、承諾相關辭彙

Vocabulary of Leadership & Promising

assuredly [əˈʃʊrɪdlɪ] .... ★★★★★
adv. 無疑地，確信地：The *Social Security Act* must assuredly be termed as a major contribution of President Franklin D. Roosevelt. 《社會安全法案》被明確地稱為富蘭克林‧羅斯福總統的一大德政。

leader [ˈlidə] .... ★★★★★
n. 領袖，領導：a born leader 天生的領導者

leadership [ˈlidəʃɪp] ....★★★★
n. 領導：Under the major's able leadership, the soldiers found safety. 士兵們在少校的英明領導下，找到了安全感。

pledge [plɛdʒ] ....★★★★
n. 誓言
v. 使發誓：pledge loyalty to a nation 向國家宣誓效忠；pledge their cooperation 許諾他們的合作

promise [ˈprɑmɪs] .... ★★★★★
v. ①允許，答應：I promise you I'll be back soon. 我答應你，很快就會回來。②有…可能：Early mist promise a clear day. 早晨有薄霧就很可能是晴天。③允許：I will be back soon, I promised. 我發誓我很快就回來。④有指望，有前途：John promised well as an actor. 約翰當演員是很有前途的。
n. ①承諾，諾言：They fulfilled their promise. 他們實現了自己的諾言。②希望，出息：She showed considerable promise as a tennis player. 她身為網球選手，前途是一片看好。

promising [ˈprɑmɪsɪŋ] ....★★
adj. 有前途的，有希望的：promising crops 長得很好的穀物；a promising iron deposit 有開採價值的鐵礦

superintendent [ˌsupərɪnˈtɛndənt] .... ★
n. 主管，負責人，指揮者

12

陪伴、接吻、擁抱、引導相關辭彙

人際互動類名稱總匯

Relationship

Vocabulary of Companion

accompany [əˋkʌmpənɪ] .... ★★★★★

v. 伴隨：Anne accompanied her husband, the aviator of Charles Lindbergh, on several of his pioneering flights. 安娜陪伴她的飛行員丈夫查理．林德柏格進行了幾次開拓性的飛行。

clasp [klæsp] .... ★★

n. 扣子，鉤子

v. 緊握，緊抱：Some animals, such as rodents, are able to clasp their food with their claws. 有些動物，像是齧齒類動物，能夠用爪子抓住食物。

companion [kəmˋpænjən] .... ★★★★★

adj. 同伴，伴侶：He was my only Chinese companion during my stay in Australia. 他是我在澳洲停留期間惟一的華人夥伴。

companionship [kəmˋpænjənˏʃɪp] .... ★★★★★

n. 伴侶關係

embrace [ɪmˋbres] .... ★★★★

v. 擁抱，包含：Horseback riding embraces both the skill of handling a horse and the mastery of diverse riding styles. 騎馬術包括御馬的技術以及精通各種騎術。

follow [ˋfɑlo] .... ★★★★★

v. ①跟隨，接著（後接賓語）：You go first and I will follow you. 你先走，我就來。②結果是：Because he is good, it does not follow that he is wise. 他人好，並不見得就聰明。③注視，密切注意：His eyes followed her as she went to the door. 她向門走去時，他的眼睛一直注視著她。④沿…行進：Follow this road until you get to the church. 順著這條路一直走到教堂。⑤遵照，採用，仿效：follow sb.'s advice 聽從某人的勸告⑥聽懂，領會：Do you follow me? 你聽懂我的話了嗎？（⑦跟隨，緊接：You go first, and I will follow. 你先走，我就來。）

【片語】as follows 如下

hug [hʌg] .... ★

v. 摟，抱：He still hugs his outmoded beliefs. 他還死守著他那些過時的信條。

kiss [kɪs] .... ★★★★★

v. 吻：He kissed her on the forehead. 他吻了
一下她的前額。

n. 吻：I gave her a kiss on the forehead. 我吻
了一下她的前額。

proximity [prɑk`sɪmətɪ] .... ★★★★★

n. 臨近，親近：The farthest southward
penetration of glaciers on the Pacific Coast
was in the proximity of Puget Sound. 冰河
在太平洋海岸 Puget Sound 最南端的附近消
融。

13

拒絕、接受、證實相關辛彙

Vocabulary of Acceptance & Refusal

acceptance [əkˋsɛptəns] .... ★★★
n. 接受，承認，驗收：My friend was thrilled by his acceptance into the club. 我的朋友獲得同意可加入俱樂部，興奮極了。

admission [ədˋmɪʃən] ....★★★★
n. 准許，允許進入，接納：Few of these books ever found admission to the library. 這些書中只有少數幾部被圖書館收藏。

admit [ədˋmɪt] .... ★★★★★
v. 承認：Peter admitted using threatening behavior. 彼得承認使用了恐嚇手段。

allow [əˋlaʊ] .... ★★★★★
v. ①允許，准許：Passengers are not allowed to smoke. 乘客們不許吸煙。②允許：How much holiday are you allowed? 你可以放多久的假？
【片語】allow for 考慮到

allowance [əˋlaʊəns] .... ★★★
n. 津貼，補助：a housing allowance 住房補貼；an education allowance 教育津貼

approval [əˋpruvl̩] ....★★★★
n. 贊同，批准：The plan is likely to get the approval of the minister. 計畫很可能會得到部長的批准。

approve [əˋpruv] .... ★★★★★
v. 贊成，稱許，批准：I could not approve his conduct. 我不贊成他的所作所為。

ban [bæn] .... ★★★★
v. 禁止：The American Medical Association has called for the sport of boxing to be banned. 美國醫學協會要求禁止拳擊運動。
n. 禁令

certificate [səˋtɪfəkɪt] .... ★★★
n. 證書，證明書，單據：a birth certificate 出生證明

concede [kənˋsid] .... ★★★★★
v. 讓步，承認：The Liberal Democratic Party conceded defeat as soon as the election results were known. 大選結果一揭曉，自由民主黨只好承認敗選。

confirm [kənˈfɝm] .... ★★★★
v. 證實，確認：Results from experiments on invertebrates have confirmed that learning takes place among lower forms of life. 無脊椎動物的實驗結果證明了低級動物在不斷地學習進化。

decline [dɪˈklaɪn] .... ★★★★★
n. 斜坡
v. 衰落，拒絕：In his letter of January 27, Mr. Anderson declined the offer. 安德森先生在1月27日的信中，拒絕了這項提議。

demonstrably [ˈdɛmənstrəblɪ] .... ★★★★
adv. 可論證地

demonstrate [ˈdɛmənˌstret] .... ★★★★
v. 演示，論證：He described the dance step, then took a partner and demonstrated. 他描述舞步，然後帶著舞伴示範。

demonstration [ˌdɛmənˈstreʃən] .... ★★★★
n. 示範，表演，論證：The Faraday effect was the first demonstration of a connection between magnetism and light. 法拉第效應第一次證實了磁和光的關聯。

deny [dɪˈnaɪ] .... ★★★★★
v. 否認，拒絕：The protesters were determined not to be denied. 抗議者決定不達目的決不罷休。

deterrent [dɪˈtɝrənt] .... ★★★★★
n. 制止，威懾：a deterrent to theft 嚇唬竊賊的東西；nuclear deterrent 核威懾

disclaim [dɪsˈklem] .... ★★★★★
v. 拒絕承認，否認：The employer disclaimed all responsibility for the fire accident. 老闆否認對那次火災事故有任何責任。

embargo [ɪmˈbɑrgo] ....★
n. 禁運：an embargo on the sale of computers to unfriendly nations 對不友好國家的電腦禁售令

forbid [fəˈbɪd] .... ★★★★
v. 禁止：Boston's nickname, "Beantown," came from the Puritan tradition of cooking extra beans on Saturday for meals on Sunday, when cooking was forbidden. 波士頓的別名「豆城」，源自於清教徒在星期六為星期天烹煮一些額外豆子的傳統，因為在星期天是禁止開伙的。

辨析
Analyze

ban, forbid, prohibit

1 **ban** vt. 「取締，查禁，禁止」，指依法律或社會壓力禁止，也指輿論上的譴責：Bicycles are banned from the motorway. 高速公路上禁止騎自行車。

2 **forbid** vt. 「不許，禁止」，普通用語；常用句型為 forbid sb. to do sth.，其過去分詞可用作形容詞：the Forbidden City 紫禁城

3 **prohibit** vt. 「禁止」，正式用語，常用句型為 prohibit sb. from doing sth.，其同義句型為 prevent / keep sb. from doing sth.：Smoking is strictly prohibited/banned/forbidden in the hospital according to the law. 醫院裡依法強制禁止吸煙。

inhibit [ɪnˋhɪbɪt] .... ★★★
v. 抑制：Antiseptics inhibit the growth of microorganisms on the surface of the body. 防腐劑能夠抑制肉體表面微生物的生長。

let [lɛt] .... ★★★★★
v. 讓，允許：He did not let himself do anything wrong, but he failed. 他不讓自己做錯事，但他失敗了。

permissible [pəˋmɪsəbl̩] .... ★★★★★
adj. 可容許的：permissible tax deductions 許可的稅賦扣除額

prohibit [prəˋhɪbɪt] .... ★★★★
v. 禁止，阻止：Smoking is strictly prohibited in the process of handling explosive materials. 在處理易爆物時，嚴格禁止吸煙。

proscribe [proˋskraɪb] .... ★★★★★
v. 禁止：Some conductors proscribe sound amplification at their concerts. 有些指揮家不准在他們的音樂會上使用擴音器。

prove [pruv] .... ★★★★★
v. ①證明，證實：He has to prove his innocence. 他不得不證明他的清白。②結果是，原來是：This information proved useful. 這情報最後證明是有用的。

refuse [rɪˋfjuz] .... ★★★★★
v. 拒絕，謝絕：He refused to accept my advice. 他拒絕接受我的勸告。

reject [rɪˋdʒɛkt] .... ★★★★
v. 拋棄，拒收：We rejected his idea for a music club, and decided to have an art club instead. 我們沒有採納他關於成立音樂俱樂部的想法，而是決定成立藝術俱樂部。

tacitly [ˋtæsɪtlɪ] .... ★
adv. 心照不宣的，默許的：Even a novel in which there is no narrator tacitly creates a picture of an author behind the scenes. 即便是在沒有敘述者的小說中，人們也會心照不宣地看到幕後的作者。

verify [ˋvɛrəˌfaɪ] .... ★★★★★
v. 驗證：The representative was asked to verify his earlier statement. 該代表被要求證實他先前的說法。

辨析 Analyze
certify, confirm, prove, testify, verify

1 **certify** *vt.* 「證明，證實」，多指透過文件或書面加以證明，其相應的名詞為 certificate（證書）：I can certify that this is a true copy of the original. 我可以證明這確實是原稿的複本。

2 **confirm** *vt.* 「證實，肯定，確認」，指為以前的看法或觀點提供支持的、肯定的證據，從而使人更相信某事的真實性：The experiment confirmed his theory. 這項實驗證實／肯定了他的理論。

3 **prove** *vt.* 「證明，證實」，指提供證據加以證明，其相應的名詞為 proof（證據）：They proved her innocence, and she was released. 他們證明她是無辜的，於是她便被釋放了。

4 **testify** *vt.* 「作證，證明」，多指在法庭作證，做不及物動詞時後面可接 for、against、to 等介系詞：The witness testified that she had seen the suspect run out of the bank after it had been robbed. 目擊者作證說她看見嫌疑犯在搶銀行之後從銀行裡跑出來。

5 **verify** *vt.* 「證實，核實」，指藉事實證明與實際情況一致：Truth can only be verified through time and practice. 真理只有透過時間和實踐才能檢驗。

14

依靠、協作、面臨、啟發相關辭彙

Vocabulary of Depending & facing

collaborate [kə`læbə͵ret] .... ★
v. 合作：John Witler collaborated on a novel with a friend. 約翰‧惠特勒和朋友合作創作一部小說。

collaboration [kə͵læbə`reʃən] .... ★
n. 合作

confront [kən`frʌnt] .... ★★★★
v. 面對，（使）面臨：Only when the police confronted her with evidence did she admit that she had stolen the money. 警方向她出示證據後，她才承認偷了錢。

depend [dɪ`pɛnd] .... ★★★★★
v. ①依靠，依賴：Children depend on their parents for food and clothes. 孩子們依賴他們的父母提供衣食。②信賴，相信：You may depend upon his coming. 你可以相信他會來的。③決定於，視…而定：It depends on how you tackle the problem. 那要看你如何應付這個問題而定。

dependent [dɪ`pɛndənt] .... ★★★★
adj. 依靠的，依賴的：A water supply in this area is dependent on adequate rainfall. 這個地區的供水依賴充足的降雨。

encounter [ɪn`kaʊntɚ] .... ★★★★
v. 遇到，遭遇，遇見：The young scientists encountered many difficulties during their exploration. 年輕的科學家在探險期間遇到了許多困難。

enlighten [ɪn`laɪtn̩] .... ★★
v. 啟發，開導，啟蒙：Enlightening the people generally, tyranny and oppression of body and mind will vanish like evil spirits at the dawn of day. 「暴君」和「壓迫的身心」在普遍讓人民覺悟後，就會像魔鬼一樣在黎明時分消逝。

incur [ɪn`kɝ] .... ★★★★★
v. 遭遇，招致，承擔：He incurred substantial losses during the stock market crash. 他在股票市場暴跌時蒙受了巨大的損失。

reliance [rɪ`laɪəns] .... ★★★
n. 信賴，依靠：No reliance is to be placed on his words. 他的話靠不住。

rely [rɪ`laɪ] .... ★★★★
v. 依賴，依靠，依仗，信賴：She relies on her parents for tuition. 她的學費靠父母支付。

15

拯救、解除、放逐、放鬆相關辭彙

Vocabulary of Saving & Relieving

degrade [dɪˋgred] .... ★★
v. 使降級，使墮落：You degrade yourself when you tell a lie. 說謊會貶低自己。

discharge [dɪsˋtʃɑrdʒ] .... ★★★★
v. 釋放：After it discharged its cargo of coal, the ship left for Tokyo. 輪船卸了裝載的煤以後就開往東京了。
n. 釋放

efface [ɪˋfes] .... ★
v. 塗抹，消除：It takes many years to efface the unpleasant memories of a war. 許多年後才能沖淡戰爭的不愉快記憶。

eject [ɪˋdʒɛkt] .... ★
v. 噴出，逐出：The patron of the bar was ejected for creating a disturbance. 酒吧的老主顧因為引起騷亂而被請出門。

exempt [ɪgˋzɛmpt] .... ★★★★★
v. 免除：His identity of a foreign official exempted him from the customs duties for these basic necessities. 他是個外交人員，因而這些日用品可免除關稅。
adj. 被免除的

exterminate [ɪkˋstɝmə͵net] .... ★
v. 消滅：exterminate insects with an insecticide 用殺蟲劑滅蟲

liberal [ˋlɪbərəl] .... ★★★★
adj. ①慷慨的，大方的：A liberal person is one who gives away things in large quantity. 一個慷慨的人會大量地施捨東西。②豐富的：The ants put in a liberal supply of food for the winter. 螞蟻儲存了足量的食物過冬。③自由的，思想開朗的：He is a liberal-minded person. 他的思想很開明。

liberate [ˋlɪbə͵ret] .... ★★★
v. ①解放，使獲自由：This area was liberated in 1946. 這個地區在1946年獲得自由。②釋出，放出：The new government has liberated political prisoners. 新政府已經釋放出所有的政治犯。

liberate [ˋlɪbə͵ret] .... ★★★
v. 釋放：Proteins are composed of more than twenty amino acids that are liberated during digestion. 蛋白質是由20多種在消化過程中釋放的氨基酸組成的。

liberation [ˌlɪbəˈreʃən] .... ★★★
n. 釋放：energy liberation 能量釋放

liberty [ˈlɪbətɪ] .... ★★★★★
n. 自由：a historical novel that takes liberties with chronology 一部隨意改變年代順序的歷史小說

purge [pɝdʒ] .... ★
v. 消除，洗刷（罪名等）：He purged his enemies from his party. 他把他的敵人從黨內清出去。

relax [rɪˈlæks] .... ★★★
v. （使）鬆弛，放鬆：Don't worry about it, just try to relax. 不要為這事擔心，放輕鬆。

release [rɪˈlis] .... ★★★★★
v. 解放，釋放，解除，放出：This matter released the principal from his personal responsibility. 這件事免除了校長的個人責任。

relieved [rɪˈlivd] .... ★★★★
adj. 放心的，免除的

rescue [ˈrɛskju] .... ★★★★
v. 拯救：When Washington D.C. was burned in 1814, Dolley Madison rescued many official papers from the White House. 華盛頓特區在1814年被燒時，麥迪遜從白宮中搶救了許多官方的文件。

save [sev] .... ★★★★★
v. 拯救
prep. 除…之外（正式用法）：The enormous size of the sea turtle is a deterrent to all predators save the shark. 除了鯊魚之外，其他所有的捕食者都因為海龜的龐大體積而卻步。

辨析
Analyze

rescue, save

1 **rescue** *vt.*「營救，救援」，指在稍縱即逝的危險時刻搶救人的生命，也可用於引申義指搶救某個古老的文明、瀕臨滅絕的物種或瀕臨倒閉的公司等：He rescued/saved the boy from drowning. 他把那個溺水的男孩救起來了。

2 **save** *vt. & vi.*「救助，搭救，儲蓄，積攢，節省，免去，保存」，指挽救人的生命，也指節約時間、金錢、精力，還指存留起來以後再用：The doctor managed to save his life. 醫生努力把他救活了。

16

人際互動名稱總匯

表示、分派、免除、比較相關辭彙

Vocabulary of Showing, Assignig & Conparing

allocate [ˈæləˌket] .... ★★★
v. 分配，定位置：During the Second World War, all important resources in the United States were allocated by the federal government. 在第二次世界大戰期間，美國國內所有的重要資源都由聯邦政府來分配。

allot [əˈlɑt] .... ★★★
v. 分配，指派：The teacher allotted each boy a role in the play. 教師分配每個男孩飾演戲中的角色。

appear [əˈpɪr] .... ★★★★★
v. 出現，似乎：A car appeared over the hill. 一輛汽車出現在山頭。

appearance [əˈpɪrəns] .... ★★★★★
n. 出現，出場，外表：New banks and post offices all made their appearances in the next two decades. 新開的銀行和郵局都是在那以後的20年間出現的。

appoint [əˈpɔɪnt] .... ★★★★★
vt. ①任命，委派：We must appoint a new teacher at once to the mountain school. 我們必須立即派一名新教師到那山中的小學去。②指定，約定，確定：They appointed a place to exchange stamps. 他們約定一個地方交換郵票。

appointment [əˈpɔɪntmənt] .... ★★★★
n. 約會，任命：He made an appointment to see Prof. White that evening. 他約好那天晚上去見懷特教授。

assign [əˈsaɪn] .... ★★★★★
v. 分配，指派：The police assigned me protection. 警方派人保護我。

comparable [ˈkɑmpərəbl] .... ★★★
adj. 可比的，類似的：The satellite revolution is comparable to Gutenberg's invention of movable type. 衛星的運轉可與古登堡活字印刷的發明相比擬。

comparative [kəmˈpærətɪv] .... ★★★
adj. 比較的，相當的：comparative anatomy 比較解剖學

compare [kəm`pɛr] .... ★★★★★

v. ①比較，對照（後可接with / to）：Compare these two books and take the better one. 比較這兩本書，選出較好的。②比作：Poets have compared sleep to death. 詩人曾把睡眠比作死亡。

【片語】compare to 把⋯比作

comparison [kəm`pærəsn] .... ★★★★

n. 比較，對照，比喻：My shoes are small in comparison with my sister's. 我的鞋子比我妹妹的要小。

contrast [`kɑn,træst] .... ★★★★

n. 對比：There is a great contrast between good and evil. 善與惡有明顯的差別。

v. 對比：Your actions contrast with your principles. 你的行為和道義相比有落差。

denote [dɪ`not] .... ★★

v. 指示，表示：In astronomy, a scale of magnitude from one to six denotes brightness of a star. 在天文學中，一到六個星等的級數是用來表示恒星的亮度。

designate [`dɛzɪg,net] .... ★★

v. 指定，指派：He was designated by the President as the next Secretary of State. 他被總統任命為新國務卿。

discover [dɪs`kʌvɚ] .... ★★★★★

v. ①發現：Harvey discovered the circulation of blood. 哈威發現了血液循環。②暴露，顯示：We soon discovered the truth. 我們很快就發現了真相。

discoverer [dɪs`kʌvərɚ] .... ★★★★★

n. 發現者

discovery [dɪs`kʌvərɪ] .... ★★★★★

n. 發現，發明（物）：His discoveries included 300 uses for peanuts and 200 uses for sweet potatoes. 他的發現包括花生的三百種用途和蕃薯的兩百種用途。

dispatch [dɪ`spætʃ] .... ★★

v. （迅速地）處理：He dispatched the business and left. 他匆匆辦完事後離開了。

distribute [dɪ`strɪbjʊt] .... ★★★★

v. 分發，分送，分佈：180 pounds of muscle were well distributed over his 6-foot frame. 一百八十磅的肌肉均勻長在他六英尺高的身軀上。

distribution [,dɪstrə`bjuʃən] .... ★★★★★

n. 分配，分佈：the distribution of wealth 財富的分配

embodiment [ɪm`bɑdɪmənt] .... ★

n. 體現，化身，具體化：The flag is the embodiment, not of sentiment, but of history. 旗幟不是情感而是歷史的化身。

辨析
Analyze

appointment, date

1 **appointment** n. 「約會，約定，任命，委派」，意為「約會」時多指因公或因私（但非戀愛關係）的約會或約見：The two businessmen had an appointment this afternoon. 這兩個商人今天下午有一場約會。

2 **date** n., vt. & vi. 「約會，約定」，意為「約會」時可指一般關係的約會或約見，但多指未婚男女之間的約會：She gave him a hint that she wouldn't mind being asked for a date. 她給他一道暗示，就是她不會介意與別人約會。

575

embody [ɪmˋbɑdɪ] .... ★

v. 體現，包含：As John Adams embodied the old style, Andrew Jackson embodied the new. 如同約翰‧亞當斯體現了老式風格，安德魯‧傑克遜體現了新風格。

exhibit [ɪgˋzɪbɪt] .... ★★★★★

v. 顯示：Young musicians are eager to exhibit their talent. 年輕的音樂家急於展現他們的才能。

exhibition [͵ɛksəˋbɪʃən] .... ★★★★

*n.*展覽（會）：Have you seen the Picasso's exhibition? 你看過畢卡索的畫展嗎？

hint [hɪnt] .... ★★★★

n. 提示，暗示，主意：Give me a hint about the big news. 給我一點有關那條大新聞的暗示吧。

immune [ɪˋmjun] .... ★★★★★

adj. 免除的，免疫的：The criminal was told he would be immune from punishment if he helped the police. 罪犯被告知如果協助警方，就可以免受刑罰。

implicit [ɪmˋplɪsɪt] .... ★★★★★

adj. 暗示的，含蓄的：an implicit agreement not to raise the touchy subject 不提及敏感話題的默契

辨析
Analyze

appoint, assign, designate, dispatch, install

1　**appoint** *vt.* 「任命，委派，約定，確定，指定（時間、地點）」，指委任或委派職務，常用句型有「appoint sb. to + 職位或任職地點」、「appoint sb. (to be) + 職位」、「appoint sb. (as) + 職位」：He was appointed as ambassador to the United States. 他被任命為駐美大使。

2　**assign** *vt.* 「指派，選派」，指分配或指定到一個地點，還指下達一個大的或小的任務／作業，常用句型有「assign sb. to + 地點」、「assign sb. to do sth.」：I was assigned to Room 210. 我被分到210號房。

3　**designate** *vt.* 「指派，委任」，還指「標出，把…定名為」；意為「委任」時基本可與 appoint 互換，其句型為 designate sb. as + 職位；意為「指派」任務時，多指負擔一定領導責任的重要任務，其句型為 designate sb. to do sth.：She has been designated as the Minister for Education. 她已被任命為教育部長。

4　**dispatch** *vt.* 「派遣，調遣，發送」，也可寫作 despatch，多指派工作人員或下級（尤指軍隊、警方等）到另一個地點去執行或完成任務，其句型為 dispatch sb. (to + 地點) to do sth.：The government dispatched policemen to the island to restore order. 該政府派員警到該島去恢復秩序。

5　**install** *vt.* 「使就職，任命」，強調透過一定的儀式或程序讓某人擔任某一職務，還指「安裝，設置，安置」：We installed the new club president today. 我們今天舉行了俱樂部新任主席的就職儀式。

indicate [ˋɪndəˏket] .... ★★★★★
v. 指示，表示：A signpost indicated the right road for us to follow. 一個路標向我們指出應走的路。

indication [ˏɪndəˋkeʃən] .... ★★★
n. 標誌，象徵，指示，顯示，指標：Did he give you any indication of his feelings? 他向你表露過他的感情嗎？

indicator [ˋɪndəˏketə] .... ★★★
n. 指示者，指示物

manifest [ˋmænəˏfɛst] .... ★★
v. 表明，證明，顯示，表示：The contradiction manifested itself in the employment situation. 在就業問題上矛盾暴露了。
adj. 明白的，明瞭的

profess [prəˋfɛs] .... ★★★★
v. 表示：A modest scholar never professed to have exhausted his subject. 一個謙虛的學者從不自稱已對自己研究的課題作了詳盡無遺的研究。

show [ʃo] .... ★★★★★
v. ①呈現，顯示：Show me where your leg hurts. 讓我看看你的腿哪兒受了傷。②表明，證明：Will you show me how to use this machine? 你能解釋一下怎樣用這部機器嗎？
【片語】show sb. around 帶某人參觀
n. 展覽，展覽會：a flower show 花展

showy [ˋʃoɪ] .... ★★★★★
adj. 顯眼的，耀眼的：a showy violin solo 一段精彩的小提琴獨奏

辨析
Analyze

demonstrate, display, exhibit, illustrate, reveal, show

1 **demonstrate** *vt.*「論證，證明，演示」，指用行動、事實示範或說明，正式用語：The fireman demonstrated / displayed great courage in saving the child. 這個消防員在救這個小孩時表現出極大的勇氣。

2 **display** *vt.*「陳列，展示」，作名詞意為櫥窗陳列，做動詞指陳列、展出、明顯表現出：The ship displayed all its flags when it came into port. 這艘船進港時把船上所有的旗幟都掛起來。

3 **exhibit** *vt.*「陳列，顯示」，指展覽、展出、表現出：Manufacturers are exhibiting their new model cars. 廠商在展示他們的新型式汽車。

4 **illustrate** *vt.*「說明，闡明」，指用實例、實物、圖片等說明、顯示：To illustrate my meaning, let me take the case as an example. 我以此案為例來說明我的意思。

5 **reveal** *vt.*「揭示，洩露」，指顯露出（秘密的東西）、洩露、暴露、透露等：He drew the curtain and revealed the map behind it. 他拉開簾子，露出裡面的地圖。

6 **show** *vt.*「表明，顯示，演出」，指無意或有意顯露出、顯示出，常用語，搭配詞很多，可接子句或不定式：Show me what you have in your bag. 讓我看你的背包裡面裝什麼。

unfold [ʌnˈfold] .... ★★
v. ①將（折疊的東西）展開，打開②（使）顯
　　露，顯示，展示

urgency [ˈɝdʒənsɪ] .... ★★★★★
n. ①緊迫（的事），迫切②強求，催促，堅持

urgent [ˈɝdʒənt] .... ★★★★★
adj. 緊急的，迫切的：I must post this letter;
　　it's urgent. 我必須寄這封信，是急件！

17

扣抵、兌換相關辭彙 Vocabulary of Discount

afford [əˋford] .... ★★★★★
v. 負擔得起，提供：He can hardly afford to miss another day at school. 他幾乎再也不能翹課了。

collateral [kəˋlætərəl] .... ★
n. 抵押品：cash deposit as collateral 保證金，押金； loan against collateral 抵押貸款，擔保貸款

default [dɪˋfɔlt] .... ★★
n. 不履行，缺乏：He won the championship by default. 他由於別人棄權而獲得了冠軍。
v. 不履行：They defaulted in the badminton tournament. 他們沒在羽毛球錦標賽中出場。

discount [ˋdɪskaʊnt] .... ★★★
n. 折扣
v. 打折扣：a discount market 打折商場

exchange [ɪksˋtʃendʒ] .... ★★★★★
v. 兌換，交換：to exchange a position in the private sector for a post in government 為謀公職而放棄私人公司的職位

rebate [ˋribet] .... ★
n. 退款，折扣：Tax rebates can have far-reaching effects on the economy. 可扣抵稅額會對經濟產生深遠的影響。

18

提供、幫助、奉獻相關辭彙

Vocabulary of Devotion

aid [ed] .... ★★★★★
v. 援助，救援：The scientist and agricultural innovator George Washington Carver aided the economy of the South by developing hundreds of crops such as the peanut for commercial uses. 科學家兼農業革新家喬治‧華盛頓‧卡瓦藉由開發上百種像是花生之類的農作物的經濟用途，來援助美國南方經濟。
n. 援助，助手，輔助物

aide [ed] .... ★★★★★
n. 助手，助力：an aide for the former president 前任總統的助理

assist [əˋsɪst] .... ★★★★★
v. 輔助：Eleanor urged legislation to assist the poor and oppressed. 艾琳諾促請立法援助窮人和受壓迫者。

availability [əˏveləˋbɪlətɪ] .... ★★
n. 可用性，可得性：easy availability of jobs 容易找到工作

available [əˋveləbḷ] .... ★★★★★
adj. 可用的，可得到的：While herbs were available in supermarkets year-round, herb vinegar was made in the fall. 雖然一年四季都能在超市買到香草，香醋卻只能在秋季製造。

beget [bɪˋgɛt] .... ★
v. 引起，產生：Hate begets hate. 冤冤相報。

capitalize [ˋkæpətḷˏaɪz] .... ★★★★★
v. 利用，用大寫字母寫，投資：She capitalized on her opponent's mistake and won the game. 她利用她對手的失誤贏得了比賽。

cater [ˋketɚ] .... ★★★★★
v. 投合，迎合：The legislation catered to various special interest groups. 立法兼顧了各種特殊利益團體。

cater [ˋketɚ] .... ★
v. 承辦宴席，迎合

consecrate [ˋkɑnsɪˏkret] .... ★
v. 奉為神聖，奉賢：to consecrate one's life to God 終生奉獻於上帝

contribute [kən'trɪbjut] .... ★★★★★
v. 為…貢獻出，有助於：to contribute food and clothing for the relief of the poor 捐出食品和衣物救濟貧民

contribution [ˌkɑntrə'bjuʃən] .... ★★★★
n. 捐款：public contribution 公眾捐款；restricted contribution 特定用途捐款

dedicate ['dɛdəˌket] .... ★★
v. 奉獻，效力於：He dedicated his life to the service of his country. 他獻身為國服務。

dedicated ['dɛdəˌketɪd] .... ★★
adj. 獻身的，專注的：a dedicated scientist 專心致志的科學家

devote [dɪ'vot] .... ★★★★★
v. 將…奉獻（給），把…專用於，致力：He devoted his whole life to education. 他畢生致力於教育事業。

devoted [dɪ'votɪd] .... ★★★★★
adj. 熱心的：John Adams, one of the American Revolution's most devoted patriots, was the lawyer who successfully defended the British soldiers charged with murder after the Boston Massacre. 約翰·亞當斯是美國獨立戰爭中最忠誠的愛國者之一，他身為律師，成功地控訴英軍在波士頓的大屠殺。

devotion [dɪ'voʃən] .... ★★
n. 獻身，忠誠，專心：The devotion of too much time to sports leaves too little time for study. 把過多的時間用於運動，就使得學習的時間過少了。

donate ['donet] .... ★★★
v. 捐贈：Included in the University of Delaware Gallery's art collection are sixteen photographs of the painter John Sloan, donated by his wife. 在德拉瓦大學藝術館裡的收藏品——畫家約翰·斯羅安的16張攝影作品——是由他太太捐贈的。

donor ['donɚ] .... ★★★
n. 捐助者

endow [ɪn'dau] .... ★★
v. 賦予，具有，授予，資助，捐贈：Nature endowed her with a beautiful singing voice. 大自然賦予她一副美妙的歌喉。

furnish ['fɝnɪʃ] .... ★★★★
v. 供應，提供，陳設，佈置：The story of Orpheus has furnished Pope with an illustration. 奧費斯的傳說為教宗提供了例證。

helper ['hɛlpɚ] .... ★★★★★
n. 幫手，助手

helpful ['hɛlpfəl] .... ★★★
adj. 有幫助的，有用的：It is helpful to think of the process of reflection in the following way. 照以下的方法來想像反射過程是很有幫助的。

helplessly ['hɛlplɪslɪ] .... ★★★★
adv. 無助地：If roundworms are removed from the soil and placed in a liquid, they thrash helplessly around. 當蛔蟲從土壤中被取出來放到液體中時，會無助地來回扭動。

inept [ɪn'ɛpt] .... ★
adj. 不適宜的：If Dr. Smith is inept, he should be removed from his position. 如果史密斯博士不稱職，就應將其調離。

provide [prə'vaɪd] .... ★★★★★
v. 提供：Solar cells have been developed primarily to provide electric power for spacecrafts. 太陽能電池主要是為飛行器提供電能研發的。

provision [prə'vɪʒən] .... ★★★★★
n. 供應，規定，條款：In the United States, the provisions of the constitution of any state may not conflict with those of the federal Constitution. 在美國，各州的法律條款不得與聯邦憲法的條款相牴牾觸。

render [ˈrɛndɚ] .... ★★★★★

v. 表達，提供：An expert in any field may be defined as a person who possesses specialized skills and is capable of rendering very competent services. 任何一個領域的專家，都可被定義為掌握專業技能並能夠提供充分服務的人。

resort [rɪˈzɔrt] .... ★★★★

v. 求助，憑藉，訴諸：The government resorted to censorship of the press. 該政府以新聞審查為手段。

n. 勝地，常去之處，修養地

19

給予、獎賞相關辭彙

Vocabulary of Awarding

attribute [əˋtrɪbjut] .... ★★★★★

v. 歸因於，被認為：David attributed his company's success to the unity of all the staff and their persevering hard work. 大衛說他們公司之所以成功，是由於全體員工團結和堅持不懈努力工作的結果。

benevolent [bəˋnɛvələnt] .... ★

adj. 慈善的：His benevolent nature prevented him from refusing any beggar who accosted him. 他慈善的天性使他無法拒絕任何向他乞討的乞丐。

benign [bɪˋnaɪn] .... ★

adj. 親切的，良好的：The old man was well-liked because of his benign attitude toward friend and stranger alike. 這位老人對待朋友和對待陌生人都一樣的友善，因此得到大家的喜愛。

bequest [bɪˋkwɛst] .... ★

n. 遺產，遺傳：a bequest of a million dollars 一筆一百萬美元的遺產

bestow [bɪˋsto] .... ★★

v. 贈予，利用：I do not deserve all the praises bestowed upon me. 我不配得到這些讚譽。

boon [bun] .... ★★★★★

n. 恩惠：Radio is a boon to the blind. 收音機讓盲人得益無窮。

compensate [ˋkɑmpənˌset] .... ★

v. 補償，賠償：According to the law in some states, parents of minors who damage the property of others must compensate the property owners. 根據有些州的法律，破壞他人財產的未成年人，其父母必須賠償財產擁有者的損失。

compensation [ˌkɑmpənˋseʃən] .... ★★

n. 補償，賠償：to claim compensation for damage 要求賠償損失

complement [ˋkɑmpləmənt] .... ★

n. 補充物

v. 補足：This wine complements the food perfectly. 這頓飯配上這種酒，簡直完美無缺了。

complementary [ˌkɑmpləˋmɛntərɪ] .... ★

adj. 補充的：complementary colors 互補色

entitle [ɪnˈtaɪt!] .... ★★★★

v. 題目為，給⋯稱號，給⋯權利：Arna
Wendell Bontemp's novel *God Sends
Sunday* was adapted for the stage in 1946
as a musical play entitled *St. Louis Woman*.
亞納・威德爾・波特普的小說《上帝賜予禮
拜日》，於1946年被改編為一部名為《聖路
易斯女人》的音樂劇。

entitled [ɪnˈtaɪt!d] .... ★★★★

adj. 有資格的：Mr. Robert was entitled to see
the documents. 羅伯特先生有權看這些
檔。

owe [o] .... ★★★★★

v. ①欠：He owes me 50 dollors. 他欠我50
元。②把⋯歸功於，應感激：He owes his
success to his hardship. 他把他的成功歸於
勤奮。

辨析
Analyze

attribute, owe

1 **attribute** *vt.*「把⋯歸因於，把（過錯、
責任）歸於」，既可用於褒義，也可用於
貶義；做名詞有「屬性、特性」的意思：
He attributed/owed his success to hard
work. 他把他的成功歸因於努力工作。

2 **owe** *vt.*「應該把⋯歸功於」，只用於褒
義，還指「欠下，感激，感恩」：We
owe the theory of relativity to Einstein. 我
們把相對論歸功於愛因斯坦。

20

得失、雇傭、借用、控制相關辭彙

Vocabulary of Gain, Loss & Control

borrow [ˈbɑro] ....★★★★
vt. 借（用）：Some people neither borrow nor lend. 一些人不借也不貸。

bridle [ˈbraɪdl̩] ....★
n. 籠頭，束縛：the bridle of employees 對員工的限制
v. 抑制，約束（表示憤怒或不悅）

circumscribe [ˈsɝkəmˌskraɪb] ....★
v. 劃界限，限制：Their life was extremely circumscribed, with long hours of study and few play. 他們因長時間學習，很少玩耍，所以生活範圍太過局限。

confine [kənˈfaɪn] ....★★★★
v. 限制，局限於，管制，禁閉：Confined to the red cells of the blood, hemoglobin transports oxygen from the lungs to the tissues. 只在紅血球中活動的血紅素，把氧氣從肺運輸到許多組織中。

constrain [kənˈstren] ....★★★★
v. 強迫，限制（動名詞當形容詞）：Novelist and short story writer Willa Cather emphasized the need for artists to be free from the constraining influences of their surroundings. 長篇和短篇小說家威爾．加德，強調了藝術家必須要從其周圍環境的束縛中掙脫出來。

control [kənˈtrol] ....★★★★★
n. ①控制，支配：He has no control over his factory. 他管不住他的工廠。②克制，抑制（感情等）：He lost control of his temper. 他怒不可遏。
【片語】①out of control 失去控制②under control 處於控制之下
v. ①控制，支配：Who controls the factory? 誰管理這家工廠？②克制，抑制（感情等）：Try to control your temper. 克制一下你的脾氣。

controller [kənˈtrolɚ] ....★★★★★
n. 管理員，調節器：a controller, not an observer of events 事件的支配者，而不是旁觀者

curb [kɝb] ....★
v. 控制，抑制：curb one's feelings 控制自己的感情

Relationship

futile [ˈfjutl] .... ★
adj. 無益的，徒勞的：All his attempts to
unlock the car were futile, because he
was using the wrong key. 他多次嘗試打
開車門，但都不得要領，因為他用錯了鑰
匙。

hire [haɪr] .... ★★★★
vt. 租用，雇用：He was hired to kill the
president. 他受雇去殺害總統。

limit [ˈlɪmɪt] .... ★★★★★
n. 界限，限度，範圍
v. 限制，限定：We must limit our expense on
food. 我們必須在飲食上節流。

limitation [ˌlɪməˈteʃən] .... ★★★
n. 限制，制約，局限性，極限，極度：He
knows his limitations. 他自知他的缺陷。

lose [luz] .... ★★★★★
v. ①失去，遺失：I lost my keys. 我把鑰匙丟
了。②迷失，使迷路：He lost his way in
the woods. 他在森林中迷了路。③輸掉：
England lost the match against Italy. 英國隊
輸給了義大利隊。④（鐘錶）走慢
【片語】be lost in sth. 消失在…中，專心於某
事

manipulate [məˈnɪpjəˌlet] .... ★
v. 操作：The treasurer was arrested for trying
to manipulate the company's financial
records. 財務主管由於企圖篡改公司財務帳
目而被逮捕。

manned [mænd] .... ★★
adj. 載人的，人操縱的：a manned spacecraft
載人太空船

mastery [ˈmæstərɪ] .... ★★★★★
n. 掌握，精通：She appealed to his mastery
for help in solving her problem. 她請求他運
用專業能力去解決她的問題。

辨析 Analyze

constrain, control, curb, refrain, restrain

1 **constrain** *vt.*「限制，約束，克制，抑
制」，指限制某人或某物的行為，片語
constrain sb. to do sth. 意為「強迫某人做
某事」：A wheel is constrained to rotate
on its axle. 輪子是限制在輪軸上轉動的。

2 **control** *vt.*「控制，支配，克制，抑
制」，常用語，用法較廣：The pressure
of steam is controlled by this button. 蒸汽
的壓力是由這個按鈕控制的。

3 **curb** *vt.*「控制，約束」，指控制或約束
某種情感或事物，正式用語，語氣較強：
He could no longer curb his anger. 他再
也控制不住憤怒的情緒。

4 **refrain** *vi.*「抑制，克制，戒除」，指抑
制感情或衝動而不做，是這一組詞中唯一
的一個不及物動詞，常用作refrain from
(doing) sth.：For better health you must
refrain from eating too much. 為了更健
康，你必須控制自己不要飲食過量。

5 **restrain** *vt.*「阻止，控制，抑制，遏
制」，指盡力克制感情或抑制行動，比
refrain更正式：She could not restrain her
curiosity to see what was in the box. 她不
禁好奇，想看看盒子裡裝著什麼東西。

obtain [əbˋten] .... ★★★★★

v. 得到：Diving ducks go completely under the surface of the water to obtain their food. 水鴨可以完全潛入水下來獲取食物。

regulate [ˋrɛgjəˏlet] .... ★★★★

v. 調解，調整，控制，對準：In the human body, the liver plays a major role in regulating the concentration of glucose in the blood. 在人體內，肝臟在調節血液的葡萄糖濃度上擔負重任。

repressive [rɪˋprɛsɪv] .... ★★★★★

adj. 鎮壓的，抑制的：a repressive dictatorship 強制性的獨裁政府

restrain [rɪˋstren] .... ★★★★

v. 限制：High interest rates restrain investment. 高利率限制了投資。

restraint [rɪˋstrent] .... ★★★

n. 抑制，制止：You showed great restraint in not crying. 你沒有哭表明你有很強的忍耐力。

restrict [rɪˋstrɪkt] .... ★★★★

v. 限制：By 1900, many municipalities had begun to restrict the use of automobiles in order to ensure pedestrians' safety. 許多自治市到了1900年都開始對汽車進行限制，從而保障行人的安全。

辨析 Analyze

confine, limit, restrict

1 **confine** *vt.* 「限制，使局限，使不外出，禁閉」，多指限制在一個平面或立體的空間內，尤指限制活動範圍，一般含有主觀意願：David was confined to bed for a week with his cold. 大衛由於感冒，有一個星期不能下床活動。

2 **limit** *vt.* 「限制，限定」，強調不得超過預定的某一點或某個數量（如時間、速度、溫度、開支、指標等），如違反或超過可能會有不好的結果或受到懲罰，一般含有主觀意願，表示「（活動）侷限於（範圍內）」時可與 confine 互換：We will limit our living expenses to $50 a day. 我們將把生活開支限定在一天50元。

3 **restrict** *vt.* 「限制，約束，限定」，指限制在確定範圍內，這種限制既可指主觀意願也可指客觀條件：He feels this new law will restrict his freedom. 他覺得新的法律會限制他的自由。

21

習慣、適合相關辭彙

Vocabulary of Custom

accustomed [əˈkʌstəmd] .... ★★
adj. 習慣的：In order to understand the concept of infinity, we must think in much broader terms than we are accustomed to. 為了能夠理解「無窮」的概念，我們的思維必須比我們所習慣的事物更為廣闊。

befit [brˈfɪt] .... ★★★★★
v. 適合：His clothing doesn't befit his position. 他的衣著與他的地位不相稱。

cohabit [koˈhæbɪt] .... ★★
vi. （男女）未婚同居

habit [ˈhæbɪt] .... ★★★★★
n. 習慣：Habit is second nature. 習慣成自然。
【片語】 be in / fall into / get into the habit of 有…習慣；get sb. into the habit of 使某人養成…習慣

habitation [ˌhæbəˈteʃən] .... ★★★★★
n. 居住，住宅
adj. 慣常的，習慣的：When she comes to the office, she gives her habitual greeting to everyone there. 她到辦公室時，總是習慣向辦公室裡的每個人打招呼。

habitually [həˈbɪtʃuəlɪ] .... ★
adv. 習慣地：The upside-down catfish is the only fish that habitually swims on its back. 反轉的鯰魚是惟一一種習慣用背部游泳的魚。

inure [ɪnˈjʊr] .... ★
v. 使習慣：The agreement inures to the benefit of the employees. 這個協定對員工的權益有利。

moderate [ˈmɑdərɪt] .... ★★★★
adj. 溫和的，有節制的：a moderate speed 中速

pertinent [ˈpɝtṇənt] .... ★
adj. 適當的，切題的：The author's reasons for changing his novel are highly pertinent. 這位作家修改其小說的理由是十分適當的。

prerogative [prɪˈrɑgətɪv] .... ★
n. 特權，特性：the principal's prerogative to suspend a student 校長可讓學生休學的權力

人際互動名稱總匯

22

誇張、浮誇、傲慢相關辭彙

Vocabulary of Exaggeration

boast [bost] .... ★★★★

v. 自誇，吹噓：Nashville, Tennessee boasted some of the finest country music performers in the United States. 田納西州納什維村為其擁有一些美國最好的鄉村音樂表演家而自豪。

boastful [ˈbostfəl] .... ★★★★

adj. 自誇的：be boastful of 自誇是…，以…自誇

bombastic [bɑmˈbæstɪk] .... ★★★★

adj. 誇大的：The politician spoke in a bombastic way of all that he would do if elected. 這名政客大肆吹噓他當選後將如何如何。

brag [bræg] .... ★

v. 誇張：Henry brags about his family's wealth. 亨利誇耀他家裡的財富。

exaggeration [ɪgˌzædʒəˈreʃən] .... ★★★

n. 誇大，誇張：In literature, caricatures usually contain verbal exaggeration through which the writer achieves comic and often satiric effects. 在文學上，諷刺文通常包含言語上的誇張，作家透過這種誇張達到喜劇甚至通常是挖苦的效果。

flatter [ˈflætɚ] .... ★★

v. 奉承，阿諛，諂媚：What really flatters a man is that you think him worth flattering. 真正令一個人愉快的是你認為他值得奉承。

impertinent [ɪmˈpɝtn̩ənt] .... ★

adj. 無關的：an impertinent remark 粗魯的言語

pompous [ˈpɑmpəs] .... ★

adj. 自負的，浮誇的：pompous officials who enjoy giving orders 喜歡發號施令的自命不凡的軍官

pretentious [prɪˈtɛnʃəs] .... ★★★★

adj. 裝腔作勢的：a pretentious manner 妄自尊大，盛氣凌人

proud [praʊd] .... ★★★★★

adj. ①驕傲的，妄自尊大的：She was a poor but very proud old woman. 她是一位貧窮但非常高傲的老婦人。②自豪的，得意的：Their country should be proud of them. 他們的國家應該為他們感到驕傲。

23

邀請、出席、缺席、代表、訪問相關辭彙

人際互動類名稱總匯

Vocabulary of Invitation & Attendance

Relationship

absence [ˈæbsn̩s] .... ★★★★
n. ①缺席 ②缺乏，不存在：In the absence of the director, I shall be in charge. 主任不在時，我負責。

absent [ˈæbsn̩t] .... ★★★★
adj. ①缺席，不在（後接 from）：Why was he absent from school yesterday? 昨天他為什麼缺課？②心不在焉的：There's an absent expression on her face. 她露出一副心不在焉的表情。

attend [əˈtɛnd] .... ★★★★★
v. ①出席，參加：They had a simple wedding but quite a few friends attended. 他們的婚禮很簡單，但不少朋友都出席了。②照料：Her aunt attended her in hospital. 她姨媽在醫院照顧她。③專心於，致力於：Attend to your study and stop watching TV. 專心讀書，不要看電視了。

attendant [əˈtɛndənt] .... ★★
n. 侍者，護理人員：ward attendant in hospital 在醫院病房裡的醫務人員

invitation [ˌɪnvəˈteʃən] .... ★★★★
n. 邀請，招待，請帖，請柬：The article was an invitation for public protest against the newspaper. 那篇文章激起大眾抗議該報。

invite [ɪnˈvaɪt] .... ★★★★★
v. 邀請，聘請：Mr. Alexander invited us to dinner. 亞歷山大先生請我們吃晚飯。

inviting [ɪnˈvaɪtɪŋ] .... ★★★★★
adj. 誘人的，引人注目的：an inviting dessert 誘人的甜食

presence [ˈprɛzn̩s] .... ★★★★★
n. 存在，出席，在場：He continues to possess the presence, mental as well as physical, of the young man. 他的身心都繼續保持著年輕人的氣質。

present [ˈprɛzn̩t] .... ★★★★★
adj. 出席的，到場的：It's a pity that you will not be present. 你不能到場真是可惜。
n. ①現在，目前：Your idea is not practical at present. 你的想法現在不適用。②禮品，贈品：On my birthday, I received a toy panda as a present. 我生日那天，收到了一件熊貓玩具的禮物。
【片語】at present 目前，現在

presentation [ˌprizɛnˈteʃən] .... ★★★★
n. 介紹，提出，呈現，給予，展示：The
  presentation of prizes will begin in the town
  hall at nine o'clock. 頒獎儀式將於上午九點
  在鎮公所舉行。

reception [rɪˈsɛpʃən] .... ★★★★
n. 接待，招待會，接受：a warm reception 熱
  情的接待

receptionist [rɪˈsɛpʃənɪst] .... ★★★★
n. 接待員

receptive [rɪˈsɛptɪv] .... ★★★★
adj. 有接受能力的：a mind receptive of new
  ideas 容易接收新思想的頭腦

receptivity [rɪˌsɛpˈtɪvətɪ] .... ★★★★
n. 接受力：electrostatic receptivity 靜電感受性

recipient [rɪˈsɪpɪənt] .... ★★★★★
n. 接受者：The recipients of prizes had their
  names printed in the paper. 獲獎者的名單
  登在報上。

summon [ˈsʌmən] .... ★★
v. ①召集，召喚：The shareholders were
  summoned to a general meeting. 已經召
  集了股東開全體大會。②傳喚：The same
  defendants were summoned to court again.
  同一批被告再度被傳喚到法庭。③鼓起勇
  氣，振作：We summoned (up) our courage
  for the task. 我們鼓起勇氣做這項工作。

visit [ˈvɪzɪt] .... ★★★★★
v. 拜訪，看望（某人），參觀，遊覽：They
  visited the Great Canyon while they were
  on holiday. 他們放假時參觀了大峽谷。
n. 訪問，參觀：He was on a visit to his elder
  sister's home last week. 他上週去大姊家作
  客。
  【片語】①be on a visit to 參觀／訪問②pay
  a visit to（正式）訪問

visitor [ˈvɪzɪtə] .... ★★★★★
n. ①來訪者，客人，參觀者②遊人

24

歡迎、慶祝、祝賀、告別相關辭彙

Vocabulary of Rituals

acclaim [əˋklem] .... ★★★★★
v. 喝彩，歡呼，稱讚：The highly acclaimed dance school founded by Katherine Dunham in New York City was an influential center of Black dance. 由凱瑟琳・鄧亨在紐約創立的的舞蹈學校受到高度讚揚，是一間有影響力的黑人舞蹈中心。

celebrate [ˋsɛləˏbret] .... ★★★★★
v. 慶祝，舉行（儀式）：In his novel *The Old Man and The Sea*, Hemingway celebrates the indomitable courage of an elderly fisherman. 海明威在他的小說《老人與海》中，讚美一位老漁夫不屈不撓的勇氣。

celebration [ˏsɛləˋbreʃən] .... ★★★★★
n. 慶祝：The villagers had a celebration, with a new film to finish up with. 村民們開了場慶祝會，最後放映了一部新電影。

celebrity [sɪˋlɛbrətɪ] .... ★★★★★
n. 名人：a celebrity fundraising dinner 由社會名流募款的晚宴

ceremonial [ˏsɛrəˋmonɪəl] .... ★★★★
adj. 儀式的，禮儀的：ceremonial garb 禮服
n. 禮儀

ceremonious [ˏsɛrəˋmonjəs] .... ★★★★
adj. 隆重的，正式的，恭敬的：Putting on a hat can be a ceremonious act, an elegant gesture in the ritual of dressing. 戴帽子可看作是一種禮貌性的行為，是著裝儀式上一個優雅的舉動。

ceremony [ˋsɛrəˏmonɪ] .... ★★★★
n. 儀式

commemorate [kəˋmɛməˏret] .... ★
vt. 紀念：At last the family, knowing how he felt, have not authorized statues to commemorate F.D.R. 最後，瞭解羅斯福想法的家屬，沒有讓人建造塑像來紀念他。

congratulate [kənˋgrætʃəˏlet] .... ★★★
v. 祝賀，向…道喜：They congratulated him on winning the race. 他們祝賀他賽跑獲勝。

congratulation [kənˏgrætʃəˋleʃən] .... ★★★
n. （常 pl.）祝賀，慶祝：Congratulations to you! 恭禧！

decorum [dɪˈkorəm] .... ★

n. 禮儀：behave with decorum 舉止得體

etiquette [ˈɛtɪkɛt] .... ★

n. 禮節：diplomatic etiquette 外交禮節；
professional etiquette 同行間的禮儀，行規

glorify [ˈglorəˌfaɪ] .... ★

v. 讚美，頌揚：Your descriptions have
glorified an average house into a mansion.
你的描述把一幢普通房子美化成了一棟豪華
公寓。

informal [ɪnˈfɔrml̩] .... ★★★★

adj. 不拘禮節的，隨便的：informal
conversation between the leaders of the
two countries 兩國領導人之間的非正式會
談

informality [ˌɪnfɔrˈmælətɪ] .... ★★★★★

n. 非正式，不拘禮節

salute [səˈlut] .... ★★

v. ①敬禮，鳴禮炮：The soldiers saluted as
the officer past. 當軍官從士兵身邊走過時，
士兵們行敬禮。②迎接，歡迎：salute a
friend with a smile 笑迎朋友

swear [swɛr] .... ★★★★★

v. 宣誓，發誓，詛咒，罵人：I swear I won't
tell anyone your secret. 我發誓不會把你的
秘密告訴任何人。

welcome [ˈwɛlkəm] .... ★★★★★

v. ①歡迎，迎接（某人）：We welcome you to
our home. 我們歡迎你到我們家來。②歡迎
或接受（意見，建議等）：He welcomed my
idea. 他欣然接受我的意見。
int. 歡迎（主人對客人的禮貌用語）：Welcome
to our home! 歡迎到我們家來！
n. 歡迎
adj. 受歡迎的，被允許的
【片語】You are welcome. 不客氣。

25

問候、調解、體諒、虐待相關辛彙

Vocabulary of Greetings & Treatments

apologize [əˋpɑlə͵dʒaɪz] .... ★★★★★
v. 道歉：She apologized to me for not answering promptly. 她因為沒有即時回答我向我道歉。

apology [əˋpɑlədʒɪ] .... ★★★★★
n. 道歉，認錯：I must make an apology for not going to her birthday party. 我沒參加她的生日派對，一定得向她道歉。

compliment [ˋkɑmpləmənt] .... ★★
n. 問候，稱讚
v. 讚美，祝賀：David complimented Mary on her new job. 大衛恭禧瑪麗找到新工作。

complimentary [͵kɑmpləˋmɛntərɪ] .... ★★
adj. 讚美的：a concert that received complimentary reviews 得到輿論好評的音樂會；complimentary tickets 贈票

conciliatory [kənˋsɪlɪə͵torɪ] .... ★
adj. 撫慰的，願意修好的

considerate [kənˋsɪdərɪt] .... ★★★
adj. 考慮周到的

console [kənˋsol] .... ★★
v. 安慰：We tried to console her when her mother died but it was very difficult. 她母親去世時我們設法安慰她，但很難奏效。

enquiry [ɪnˋkwaɪrɪ] .... ★★★★★
n. 調查，詢問：Thank you for your enquiry / enquiries about my health. 謝謝你問候我的健康情況。

excuse [ɪkˋskjuz] .... ★★★★★
n. 藉口
v. 原諒，寬恕，免除：Excuse me for my coming late. 對不起，我來晚了。
【片語】excuse me 對不起，請原諒，勞駕，不好意思

forgive [fəˋgɪv] .... ★★★★
v. 原諒，饒恕，寬恕：forgive sb. for being rude 原諒某人的魯莽

gracious [ˋgreʃəs] .... ★★
adj. 有禮貌的，仁慈的：She welcomed her guests in a gracious manner. 她態度親切地歡迎客人。

grateful [ˈgretfəl] .... ★★
adj. 感謝的：Our grateful thanks are due to you. 我們衷心感謝你。

gratitude [ˈgrætəˌtjud] .... ★★★★
n. 感謝，感激：I am full of gratitude to you for helping me. 我非常感激你幫助我。

greet [grit] .... ★★★★
v. ①問候，招呼：Greet a friend by saying "Good morning." 向友人道早安。②（以特定方式）反應，對⋯作出反應：The news was greeted with dismay. 此消息令人沮喪。③呈現在⋯前：the view that greeted us at the hill top 山頂上呈現在我們面前的景色

greeting [ˈgritɪŋ] .... ★★★
n. 問候，致敬

inquire, enquire [ɪnˈkwaɪr] .... ★★★★★
v. ①詢問，打聽：He inquired of me about our work. 他向我打聽我們的工作情況。②調查，查問：We must inquire whether he really came. 我們必須查問他是否真的來過。

inquiry [ɪnˈkwaɪrɪ] .... ★★★★★
n. 調查研究：The inquiry concerning the accident was handled by the chief of police. 有關這次事故的調查由警察局長著手進行。

inquisitive [ɪnˈkwɪzətɪv] .... ★★★★★
adj. 好奇的：The inquisitive little child bothered his mother. 那個好奇的小孩不停地向他媽媽問這問那。

intercede [ˌɪntɚˈsid] .... ★
v. 調停，求情：to intercede with the governor for a condemned man 替犯人在州長面前說情

investigate [ɪnˈvɛstəˌget] .... ★★★★
v. 調查研究，調查：To investigate a problem is, indeed, to solve it. 調查就是解決問題。

investigation [ɪnˌvɛstəˈgeʃən] .... ★★★★
n. 調查，調查研究：Their investigation report was full of ambiguities. 他們的調查報告模棱兩可。

investigator [ɪnˈvɛstəˌgetɚ] .... ★★★★
n. 調查（研究）人員，投資（額）

maneuver [məˈnuvɚ] .... ★
v. 調查
n. 策略：Logrolling is a sport in which contestants perform various maneuvers while treading on a floating log. 滾原木是一項讓競賽選手站在漂浮的圓木上表演各種動作的運動。

mediate [ˈmidɪet] .... ★★★★★
v. 調停：He mediated a settlement between labor and management. 他在勞資雙方間透過調停達成和解。

obliging [əˈblaɪdʒɪŋ] .... ★★★★★
adj. 好施恩的，願幫忙的：obliging neighbors 樂於助人的鄰居

pardon [ˈpɑrdn̩] .... ★★★★★
n. 原諒，寬恕，對不起：I beg your pardon. 對不起，請再說一遍。
【片語】beg one's pardon 請原諒，對不起

placate [ˈpleket] .... ★
v. 安撫，和解

reconcile [ˈrɛkənsaɪl] .... ★★
v. 和解：He finally reconciled himself to the change in management. 他最後還是接受了管理上的變化。

reconciliation [ˌrɛkənˌsɪlɪˈeʃən] .... ★
n. 和解：reconciliation statement 對帳單

return [rɪˈtɝn] .... ★★★★★
v. ①返回，回來②歸還，送還：You must always return your library book on time. 你必須把書按時還給圖書館。

servant [ˈsɝvənt] .... ★★★★★
n. 僕人

serve [sɝv] .... ★★★★★

v. ①為…服務（或盡責）：I'd like to serve you,
sir. 先生，我願意為您效勞。②招待，端
上：The coffee was served. 咖啡端上來了。
③符合，適用於：a tool that serves many
purposes有多種用途的工具④服務，供職：
They served in the U.S. Congress. 他們在
美國國會服務。⑤有用，起作用：Historical
experience would serve as a most important
source of information. 歷史的經驗會是最重
要的一項資料來源。

service [ˋsɝvɪs] .... ★★★★★

n. 服務，幫助：The restaurant's service is of
first class. 這個飯店的服務是一流的。

settle [ˋsɛtl] .... ★★★★★

v. ①解決，調停：I'll make up my mind and
settle it all. 我要下決心把一切安排妥當。
②支付，結算：settle an account 結帳③
安排，安放：You should settle everything
before you leave. 你走之前應當把一切安
排好。④安家，定居：He is too young to
settle now. 他現在太年輕，成家太早。⑤
（鳥等）飛落，留：A bird settled on the
tree. 一隻鳥停在樹上。
【片語】settle down 安居，過安定的生活，平
靜下來

settlement [ˋsɛtlmənt] .... ★★★★

n. 調停，解決，居留地，住宅區，新居住區，
拓居地：Old Oraibi, dated to 1,100 years
ago is said to be the oldest continuously
occupied settlement in the United States.
「Old Oraibi」據說是美國現今最久遠的人
類聚居地，時間可以追溯回1,100年以前。

thank [θæŋk] .... ★★★★★

v. 感謝，向某人道謝：Thank you for asking
me to your party. 謝謝你邀請我參加聚會。
【片語】thanks to 多虧，由於
n. 謝辭，感恩的話：Many thanks. 多謝

thankful [ˋθæŋkfəl] .... ★★★★

adj. 感謝的，感激的：I expected a bigger
payment, but I suppose one has to be
thankful for small mercies. 我原指望能拿
到更高的報酬，不過我認為，即使只能得
到小小的好處，也應該感謝人家。

人際互動名稱總匯

26

尊敬、愛護、誤會相關辭彙

Vocabulary of Respect & Misunderstanding

cherish [ˈtʃɛrɪʃ] .... ★★
v. 珍愛：We never cherish any unrealistic fancies about those desperate criminals. 我們對那些亡命之徒從來不抱任何不切實際的幻想。

deference [ˈdɛfərəns] .... ★
n. 敬意：People showed great deference to the heroes when they returned in triumph. 人們向凱旋歸來的英雄致以極大敬意。

deferential [ˌdɛfəˈrɛnʃəl] .... ★
adj. 敬意的：deferential bearing 恭順的態度

distort [dɪsˈtɔrt] .... ★
v. 歪曲：That newspaper's accounts on international affairs are sometimes distorted. 那家報紙刊載的國際事件有時是歪曲事實的。

esteem [ɪsˈtim] .... ★★
v. 尊敬：George was esteemed for his contributions in the fields of botany and chemistry. 喬治因其在植物學和化學領域的貢獻受到尊敬。

homage [ˈhɑmɪdʒ] .... ★
n. 敬意：pay homage to somebody 向某人表示敬意

irreverent [ɪˈrɛvərənt] .... ★
adj. 不恭敬的：irreverent humor 挖苦性的幽默

misinterpret [ˈmɪsɪnˈtɝprɪt] .... ★★★★★
v. 曲解，錯譯：The driver misinterpreted the policeman's signal and turned in the wrong direction. 駕駛員錯認了警察的手勢，轉錯了方向。

misunderstand [ˈmɪsʌndɚˈstænd] .... ★★★★★
v. 誤會，錯誤：He misunderstood what I said. 他誤解了我的話。

respect [rɪˈspɛkt] .... ★★★★★
n. ①尊敬，尊重：He is held in the greatest respect by the whole village. 他極度受到全村人的尊敬。②敬意，問候：My mother sends you her respects. 我母親向你問候。
【片語】with respect to 關於，至於
v. 尊敬，尊重：a highly respected professor 一位深受尊敬的教授

revere [rɪˈvɪr] .... ★
v. 尊敬：People revere the general. 人們對那位將軍甚表尊敬。

597

reverence [ˈrɛvərəns] ....★

n. 尊敬：The Liberty Bell is an object of great reverence because it was rung in 1776 to proclaim the signing of the Declaration of Independence. 人們都對自由之鐘懷抱崇敬之情，因為它於1776年（美國）宣佈簽署獨立宣言時被鳴響。

reverend [ˈrɛvərənd] ....★

adj. ①可尊敬的，應受尊敬的，可敬畏的②教士的，聖潔的

n. 教士，牧師

27

欺騙、賄賂、引誘、敲詐相關辭彙

Vocabulary of Cheating

abduct [æbˋdʌkt] .... ★

v. 綁架，誘拐：The bandits abducted the only heir of the millionaire and blackmailed a ransom of 2 million dollars. 那批強盜綁架了那個富翁惟一的繼承人，並且向他勒索兩百萬美元的贖金。

allure [əˋlɪʊr] .... ★

v. 引誘：Promises of quick profits allure the unwary investor. 能快速獲利的承諾吸引了心存僥倖的投資者。

n. 引誘：the allure of the sea 海洋的魅力

bait [bet] .... ★

n. 餌，引誘物：The open purse was a bait for the hungry young man. 這個沒關的錢包，對於那個饑腸轆轆的年輕人是個誘惑。

beguile [bɪˋgaɪl] .... ★

v. 欺騙，消遣：His pleasant ways beguiled me into thinking that he was my good friend. 他友善的樣子欺騙了我，使我以為他是我的好朋友。

cheat [tʃit] .... ★★★

v. ①欺騙，騙取：They cheated him (out) of his money. 他們騙了他的錢。②行騙，作弊：He cheated in the examination. 他考試作弊。

n. ①欺騙，欺騙行為：This is a cheat. 這是一場騙局。②騙子

coax [koks] .... ★

v. 哄，耐心調理：She coaxed him to take the medicine. 她哄他吃藥。

counterfeit [ˋkaʊntɚˌfɪt] .... ★

adj. 偽造的，假冒的：a counterfeit coin 偽幣

n. 贗品

deceit [dɪˋsit] .... ★

n. 欺騙，欺詐：He got the money by deceit. 他靠行騙弄到了錢。

deceitful [dɪˋsitfəl] .... ★

adj. 欺騙的

deceive [dɪˋsiv] .... ★★★★

v. 欺騙，行騙：He deceived her that he could drive a car. 他騙她說他會開車。

deceptive [dɪˋsɛptɪv] .... ★★★★★

adj. 虛偽的，騙人的：Deceptive labeling of certain types of merchandise is not allowed under the *Pure Food* and *Drug Act* of 1906. 1906年頒佈的《純淨食品法》和《藥品法》不允許在某些商品上貼上偽造的標籤。

defraud [dɪˋfrɔd] .... ★

v. 欺詐：Jack is defrauding the commercial law. 傑克在鑽商業法令的漏洞。

delude [dɪˋlud] .... ★

v. 欺騙，迷惑：This is a fraudulent ad that deludes consumers into sending in money. 這是一則騙消費者花錢的假廣告。

entice [ɪnˋtaɪs] .... ★

v. 誘惑：The promise of higher pay enticed me into the new job. 高薪誘使我從事了這項新工作。

enticing [ɪnˋtaɪsɪŋ] .... ★★

adj. 引誘的，迷人的

entrap [ɪnˋtræp] .... ★

v. 以網或陷阱捕捉：His boss entrapped him into making a very damaging admission. 他的老闆誘使他做出十分有害的承諾。

entrapment [ɪnˋtræpmənt] .... ★

n. 誘捕的行動／過程

extort [ɪkˋstɔrt] .... ★

v. 勒索，強索：The police used torture to extort a confession from him. 警方對他用刑逼供。

folly [ˋfɑlɪ] .... ★★★

n. 愚笨，愚蠢

fool [ful] .... ★★★★★

n. 蠢人：What a fool! 好一個傻瓜！

v. 欺騙，愚弄：He had me fooled. 他騙了我。

foolish [ˋfulɪʃ] .... ★★★★

adj. 愚蠢的，傻的：It was foolish of you to believe in such a person. 你會相信這樣的人真傻。

forge [fɔrdʒ] .... ★★

v. & n. 鑄造，偽造：Everything new comes from the forge of hard and bitter struggle. 一切新的東西都是從艱苦奮鬥中誕生的。

fraud [frɔd] .... ★

n. 欺騙

fraudulent [ˋfrɔdʒələnt] .... ★

adj. 欺詐的，不誠實的：He got the job of science teacher by fraudulent means. 他用欺騙手法當上了科學教師位。

hoax [hoks] .... ★

n. 愚弄：A telephone caller said there was a bomb in the hotel but it was just a hoax. 打電話的人聲稱旅館裡有一顆炸彈，但這不過是一場惡作劇而已。

induce [ɪnˋdjus] .... ★★

v. 導致，誘使：The use of penicillin is limited by its tendency to induce allergic reactions. 由於盤尼西林容易引起過敏，因此在使用上受到限制。

kidnap [ˋkɪdnæp] .... ★

v. 綁架：The kidnapping of pets has become a national problem. 綁架寵物已經成為全國性的問題。

lull [lʌl] .... ★

n. 歇息

v. 使平靜：The monotonous voice of the movement of the train lulled me to sleep. 火車移動的單調聲音使我昏昏欲睡。

lure [lur] .... ★

v. 引誘：Niagara Falls is a great tourist attraction, luring millions of visitors each year. 尼加拉瓜大瀑布是一個著名的觀光景點，每年都吸引數百萬的遊客。

n. 誘惑

misleading [mɪsˋlidɪŋ] .... ★★★

adj. 騙人的：a misleading similarity 誤導人的相似之處

misuse [mɪsˈjuz] .... ★★★

vt. ①誤用，濫用：I noticed you misused the word "rurban" in your letter. 我在你的信中發現你把rurban這個字用錯了。②虐待：Misusing animals in our country is forbidden. 在我們國家不允許虐待動物。

outwit [aʊtˈwɪt] .... ★

v. 哄騙：The thief outwitted the police and escaped. 小偷耍花招瞞過警方跑掉了。

suffer [ˈsʌfɚ] .... ★★★★★

v. ①遭受，蒙受：They suffered ill treatment. 他們受到虐待。②忍受，承受：Nobody can suffer such insults. 沒有人能忍受這樣的侮辱。③受痛苦，患病：suffer from headache 頭痛④受損失：His investment suffered while he was away from there. 當他離開那兒，他的投資就損失了。

tempt [tɛmpt] .... ★★★★

v. 誘使：tempt providence 冒大險，作不必要的冒險

temptation [tɛmpˈteʃən] .... ★★★★

n. 誘惑，引誘：The temptation to steal is greater than ever before, especially in large shops. 偷竊的誘惑力比以往更強烈了，在大商店裡尤其如此。

trap [træp] .... ★★★★

n. 陷阱

v. 誘捕，陷害，阻止：Smoke particles and other air pollutants are often trapped in the atmosphere, thus forming smog. 煙的顆粒和其他的空氣污染物，經常會停留在大氣層中，從而形成了煙霧。

trick [trɪk] .... ★★★★

v. 欺詐，哄騙：trick sb. out of office 騙某人離職

n. ①戲法，把戲：amazing tricks 令人驚歎的戲法②技巧，竅門：a rhetorical trick 修辭技巧③詭計，花招：a dirty trick 卑鄙的花招

tricky [ˈtrɪkɪ] .... ★★★★

adj. 難處理的，狡猾的：a tricky recipe 難以處理的配方

wheedle [ˈhwidl̩] .... ★

v. 勸誘，哄騙：The child wheedled seven dollars out of his father. 那孩子向爸爸撒嬌要到7塊美元。

辨析 Analyze

cheat, deceive, trick

1 **cheat** *vt. & vi.*「欺騙，騙取，作弊」，指為達到目的而採取不誠實的手段，如：An honest student should never cheat in his / her examinations. 一個誠實的學生應該永不作弊。

2 **deceive** *vt.*「欺騙，蒙蔽」，指以假亂真，以次充好，以達到不可告人的目的：The old couple was deceived into buying that fake diamond ring. 這對老夫婦受騙買下那顆假鑽石戒指。

3 **trick** *vt.*「欺詐，哄騙」，指以虛假的資訊哄騙某人做某事，常用句型有 trick sb. into doing sth.（騙某人做某事）和 trick sb. out of sth.（騙取某人的某物）：He tricked her into marrying him by pretending that he was rich. 他假裝很有錢，騙她與他結了婚。

28

告知、勸告、宣佈、預告相關辭彙

Vocabulary of Ingorming & Claiming

Relationship

announce [əˋnaʊns] .... ★★★★★
v. 宣佈，通告：His stockbroker announced his portfolios as being valueless. 他的證券經紀人宣稱他的有價證券毫無價值。

announcement [əˋnaʊnsmənt] .... ★★★★★
n. 通告，（廣播等）通知：The announcement of their engagement surprised every one. 他們倆宣佈訂婚，讓大家驚訝不已。

announcer [əˋnaʊnsɚ] .... ★
n. （電臺）播音員，宣告者

auspice [ˋɔspɪs] .... ★
n. 前兆

auspicious [ɔˋspɪʃəs] .... ★
n. 吉兆的，幸運的：With favorable weather conditions, it was an auspicious moment to set sail. 天氣狀況良好，正是揚帆出航的好時機。

counsel [ˋkaʊnsl] .... ★★★★★
v. 勸告
n. 商議，忠告，律師：Listen to an old man's counsel. 要聽老人言。

counselor [ˋkaʊnslɚ] .... ★★★★★
n. 顧問

declaration [ˌdɛkləˋreʃən] .... ★★★★
n. 宣告，宣佈，宣言：Declaration of Independence （美國）獨立宣言

declare [dɪˋklɛr] .... ★★★★★
v. ①斷言，宣稱：The accused man declared that he was not guilty. 被告人聲稱他無罪。②聲明，宣告：declare the result of an election 宣佈選舉結果
【片語】①declare off 宣佈作罷，取消（約定）②declare oneself 發表意見，表明態度

dislike [dɪsˋlaɪk] .... ★★★★★
v. 不喜歡，厭惡：If you behave like that, you will get yourself disliked. 如果你那樣做，會討人厭的。
n. 不喜歡，厭惡

forecast [ˋforˌkæst] .... ★★★
v. 預報，預測：Large passenger planes usually carry weather instruments with which to forecast storms. 大型客機通常備有氣象設備來預測暴風雨。

forecaster [for`kæstɚ] .... ★★★
n. 預報者，預測者

forefinger [`for͵fɪŋgɚ] .... ★★★
n. 食指

foresee [for`si] .... ★★
v. 預知：Those who can foresee difficulties on their way to success may keep calm when they really appear. 在成功之路上能夠預見困難的人，在困難真正出現的時候，能保持冷靜的態度。

foresight [`for͵saɪt] .... ★★★★★
n. 預見，遠見

forestall [for`stɔl] .... ★★★★★
v. 預先阻止：Strict sanitary procedures help to forestall outbreaks of disease. 嚴格的衛生清潔程序能夠防止疾病的爆發。

foretell [for`tɛl] .... ★★★★★
v. 預言：foretell the future 預示未來

impart [ɪm`part] .... ★★
v. 給予，傳遞，告訴：A good teacher imparts wisdom to his pupils. 好的教師把智慧傳給學生。

inform [ɪn`fɔrm] .... ★★★★
v. 通知，告訴：Keep me informed of fresh developments. 隨時告訴我新的發展狀況。

precursor [prɪ`kɝsɚ] .... ★
n. 先兆，先驅：Opposition by colonists to unfair taxation by the British was a precursor of the Revolution. 殖民地居民對英國不公正稅收的反抗，預示著革命的到來。

predict [prɪ`dɪkt] .... ★★★
v. 預言，預告，預測：We cannot accurately predict how much of the carbon dioxide released by factories as waste will remain permanently in the atmosphere. 我們無法精確地預測工廠排出的二氧化碳廢氣，有多少會永久地停留在大氣之中。

predictable [prɪ`dɪktəbḷ] .... ★★★
adj. 可預言的

proclaim [prə`klem] .... ★★
v. 宣佈，聲明：I wear a button that proclaims my choice for president. 我別一枚表明我選誰當主席的圓形小徽章。

proclamation [͵prɑklə`meʃən] .... ★★
n. 宣佈，公佈

辨析
Analyze

forecast, foresee, predict

1 **forecast** *vt.* 「預測，預報」，多用來指對大眾發佈的預報：The radio station forecasts a change in the weather. 廣播電臺預報天氣的變化。

2 **foresee** *vt.* 「預見，預知」，指對未來事件推測和判斷，但不強調對外宣佈或公佈：He foresaw that his journey would be delayed by bad weather. 他預見到他的旅程會因天氣不好而延誤。

3 **predict** *vt.* 「預言」，通常指根據事實推斷：An astronomer predicts the return of a comet. 天文學家預言彗星會再現。

profane [prəˈfen] .... ★

v. 褻瀆

adj. 褻瀆的：sacred and profane music 聖樂
和俗樂；To smoke in a church or mosque
would be a profane act. 在教堂或清真寺
內吸煙會是一種褻瀆神靈的行為。

pronounce [prəˈnaʊns] .... ★★★★

v. ①發音：I can't pronounce Japanese
names. 我不會唸日本名字。②宣佈，宣
讀：The doctor pronounced the man dead.
醫生宣佈那名男子已死亡。

prophecy [ˈprɑfəsɪ] .... ★★

n. 預言：have the gift of prophecy 有預言的天
賦

warn [wɔrn] .... ★★★★

v. 警告：She warned me about the dangerous
road, so I crossed it carefully. 她提醒我這條
路很危險，因此我過馬路時很小心。

warning [ˈwɔrnɪŋ] .... ★★

n. ①警告，告誡：The sirens sounded an air-
raid warning. 汽笛響起了空襲警報。②預先
通知

adj. 警告的，告誡的

辨析
Analyze

announce, declare, proclaim

1 **announce** *vt.*「宣佈，宣告」，指向人
們公開宣告諸如國家事務、商品資訊、
新聞或消息等，其名詞為 announcement
（通知）：The premier announced his
cabinet appointments yesterday. 昨天首
相宣佈了他的多位內閣成員任命案。

2 **declare** *vt.*「宣佈，宣告，聲明，斷言，
宣稱」，指在正式場合宣佈官方的立場和
態度，或公開表示自己的意見，其名詞為
declaration（宣言，聲明）；還指「（在
海關）申報（納稅商品）」：Bulgaria
declared its independence in 1908. 保加
利亞於1908年宣佈獨立。

3 **proclaim** *vt.*「宣告，宣佈，聲明」，一
般指官方在正式場合向大眾公佈一些國家
重要的事情，也可用於個人或一般場合，
較為正式，其名詞為 proclamation（文
告）：In 1912 Dr. Sun Yat-sen proclaimed
the founding of the Republic of China.
1912年孫中山宣告了中華民國成立。

29

嘲笑、譏諷相關辭彙

Vocabulary of Scorn

absurd [əb'sɝd] .... ★★

adj. 荒謬的：The idea that the number 13 brings bad luck is absurd. 認為13這個數字會帶來不吉利的想法是荒謬的。

acrimony ['ækrə,monɪ] .... ★

n. 刻薄：The dispute was renewed with increasing acrimony. 爭論重新開始時，充斥著更多刻薄的言語。

deride [dɪ'raɪd] .... ★

v. 嘲笑，愚弄：They deride him for his fear of the dark. 他害怕黑暗，他們因此嘲笑他。

flout [flaʊt] .... ★

v. 嘲弄，藐視：They flouted all our offers of help and friendship. 他們對我們提供的所有幫助和友好行為表示不屑。

funny ['fʌnɪ] .... ★★★★

adj. ①古怪的，反常的：There is some thing funny about the affair. 這件事有點奇怪。②滑稽的，逗人發笑的：funny stories 滑稽的故事

gibe [dʒaɪb] .... ★

n. 譏笑：Don't make gibes about her behavior. 別嘲笑她的行為。

jeer [dʒɪr] .... ★

v. 揶揄，嘲笑：Don't jeer at the person who came last in the race—it's very unkind. 不要嘲笑賽跑中跑在最後的人，這是很不友善的。The crowd jeered at the politicians who had failed in the election. 那群人嘲笑落選的政客。

mock [mɑk] .... ★★

n. 嘲弄

v. 挖苦：Political cartoons often convey messages by mocking a particular type of personality or institution. 政治漫畫通常有諷刺某種特定人物或機構的意味。

ridicule ['rɪdɪkjul] .... ★

v. 嘲弄，挖苦，奚落：The song "Yankee Doodle" was originally sung by British troops to ridicule the American colonists. 「洋基歌」這首歌最早是由英國軍隊所唱的，用來嘲笑美國的殖民者。

ridiculous [rɪˋdɪkjələs] .... ★★★★

adj. 荒謬的：a ridiculous suggestion／figure 可
笑的建議／人；ridiculous in dress／shape
衣服／形狀好笑的

scoff [skɔf] .... ★

v. 嘲笑，嘲弄

n. 嘲笑，嘲弄，笑柄：be the scoff of the town
成為全城鎮的笑柄

scorn [skɔrn] .... ★★★★

n. ①輕蔑，藐視②嘲笑

vt. ①輕蔑，藐視：She scorned all our offers
of help. 她對我們所提供的援助表示不屑。
②不屑做

scornful [ˋskɔrnfəl] .... ★★★★

adj. 輕蔑的：He was scornful of the dress she
was wearing. 他對她穿的洋裝不屑一顧。

sneer [snɪr] .... ★★

v. 嘲笑：James sneered at my old bicycle. He
has a new one. 詹姆斯嘲笑我的舊自行車；
他有一輛新的。

taunt [tɔnt] .... ★

n. 嘲笑：They endure the taunts of their
neighbors. 他們忍受鄰人的笑罵。

tease [tiz] .... ★

v. 逗樂，戲弄，強求：If you always tease
others like that, you'll forfeit the good
opinion of your friends. 你如果老是那樣捉弄
別人，你就會喪失朋友們的好感。

辨析
Analyze

absurd, funny, ridiculous

1 **absurd** *a.*「荒謬的，荒唐的」，指在理
性上不合情理或違反真實情況，使人感到
荒唐：Today it is absurd to believe that
the earth is flat. 今天若相信地球是扁平
的，就真的荒唐可笑了。

2 **funny** *a.*「滑稽的，有趣的，可笑的，
稀奇的，古怪的」，指因幽默而引人發笑
的，中性詞：What a funny story／joke／
man! 真是個可笑的故事／有趣的笑話／
滑稽的人！

3 **ridiculous** *a.*「可笑的，荒謬的」，
指某事物不合常理、令人發笑，常含貶
義：It is ridiculous to dispute about such
thing. 爭論這樣的事很可笑。

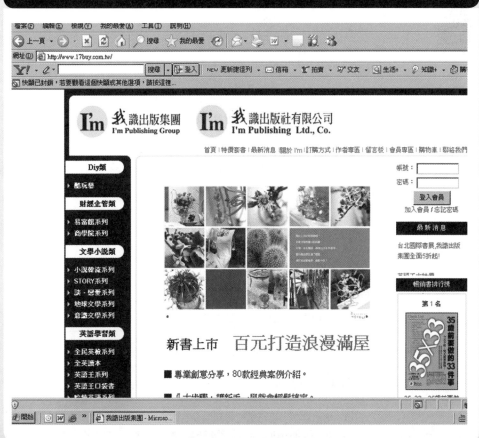

國家圖書館出版品預行編目（CIP）資料

完全命中托福單字 ／ 蔣志榆・馬亭奇 著 -- 初版. --
　臺北市：我識, 2007〔民96〕
　面： 公分
　ISBN 978-986-7346-88-9 （平裝）

1. 英國語言 - 詞彙

805.1894　　　　　　　　　　　　96004360

書名 / 完全命中托福單字
作者 / 蔣志榆・馬亭奇
發行人 / 蔣敬祖
編輯顧問 / 常祈天
主編 / 戴嫩凌
執行編輯 / 曾羽辰・謝昀蓁・楊堡方
視覺指導 / 黃馨儀
美術編輯 / 麵包
法律顧問 / 北辰著作權事務所蕭雄淋律師
印製 / 金讚印刷事業有限公司
初版 / 2007年4月
再版二十刷 / 2012年04月
出版單位 / 我識出版集團－我識出版社有限公司
電話 / (02) 2345-7222
傳真 / (02) 2345-5758
地址 / 台北市忠孝東路五段372巷27弄78之1號1樓
郵政劃撥 / 19793190
戶名 / 我識出版社
網址 / www.17buy.com.tw
E-mail / iam.group@17buy.com.tw
facebook網址 / www.facebook.com/ImPublishing
定價 / 新台幣 349 元 / 港幣 116 元

總經銷 / 我識出版社有限公司業務部
地址 / 新北市汐止區新台五路一段114號12樓
電話 / (02) 2696-1357　傳真 / (02) 2696-1359

地區經銷 / 易可數位行銷股份有限公司
地址 / 新北市新店區寶橋路235巷6弄3號5樓

港澳總經銷 / 和平圖書有限公司
地址 / 香港柴灣嘉業街12號百樂門大廈17樓
電話 / (852) 2804-6687　傳真 / (852) 2804-6409

I'm

我識出版社
17buy.com.tw

I'm

我識出版社
17buy.com.tw